INFINITY
— and the Empire of His Dreams —

INFINITY
— and the Empire of His Dreams —

Light Tracey

CrazedNovelist Books
Atlanta, Georgia

Copyright © 2026 by Light Tracey
Cover design by MizuShiba
Cover illustration by MizuShiba
Map illustration by Ian Durneen
Cover copyright © 2026 by CrazedNovelist Publishing, LLC
Interior copyright © 2026 by A.E. Williams Editorial

CrazedNovelist Books
CrazedNovelist Publishing, LLC
4371 Winters Chapel Rd.
Atlanta, GA 30360
crazednovelistbooks.com

First Edition: December 23, 2025

Published by CrazedNovelist Books, an imprint of CrazedNovelist Publishing, LLC.

Library of Congress Control Number: 2026934177
ISBNs: 979-8-9941096-0-1 (trade paperback), 979-8-9941096-1-8 (ebook)

Printed in the United States of America

11 10 9 8 7 6 5 4 3 2

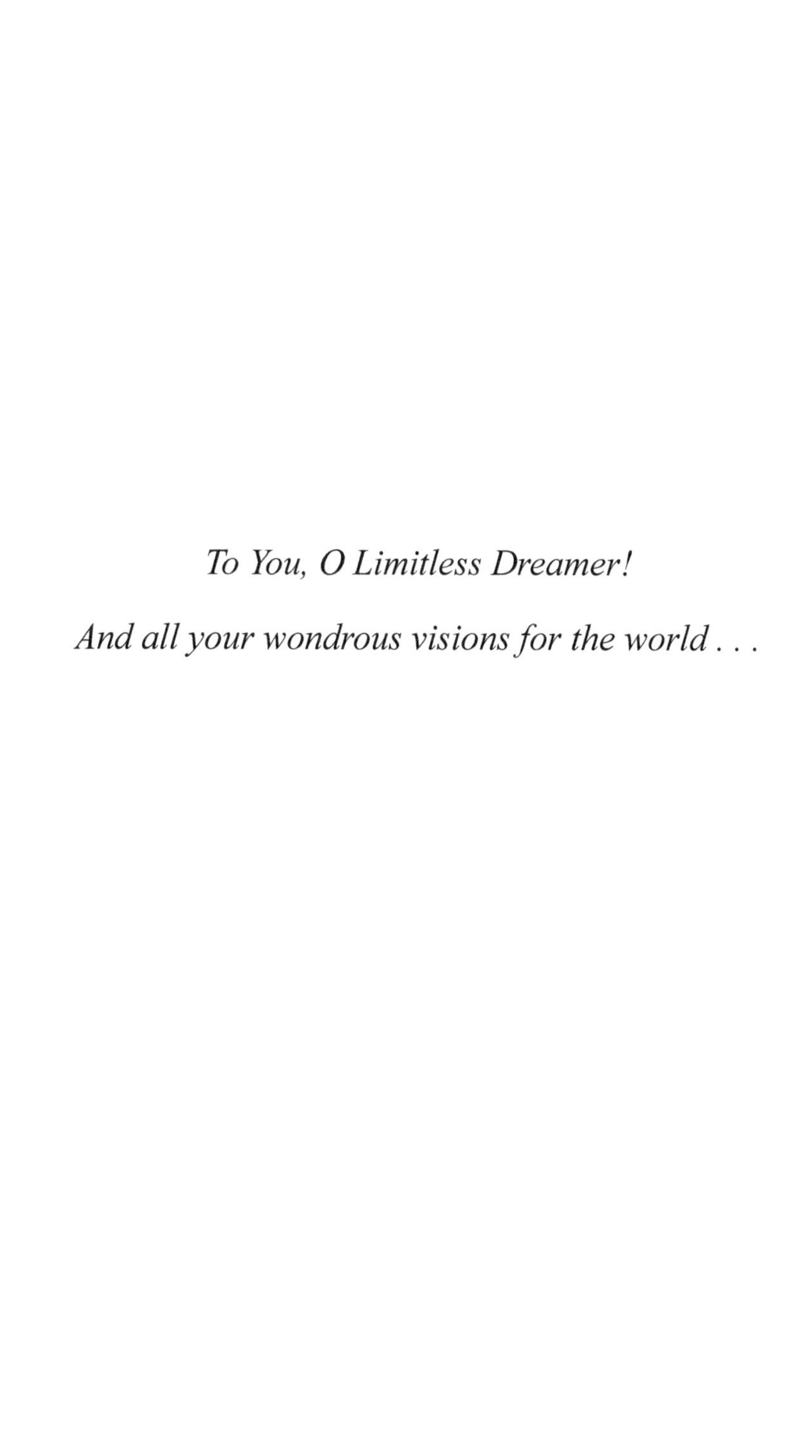

To You, O Limitless Dreamer!

And all your wondrous visions for the world . . .

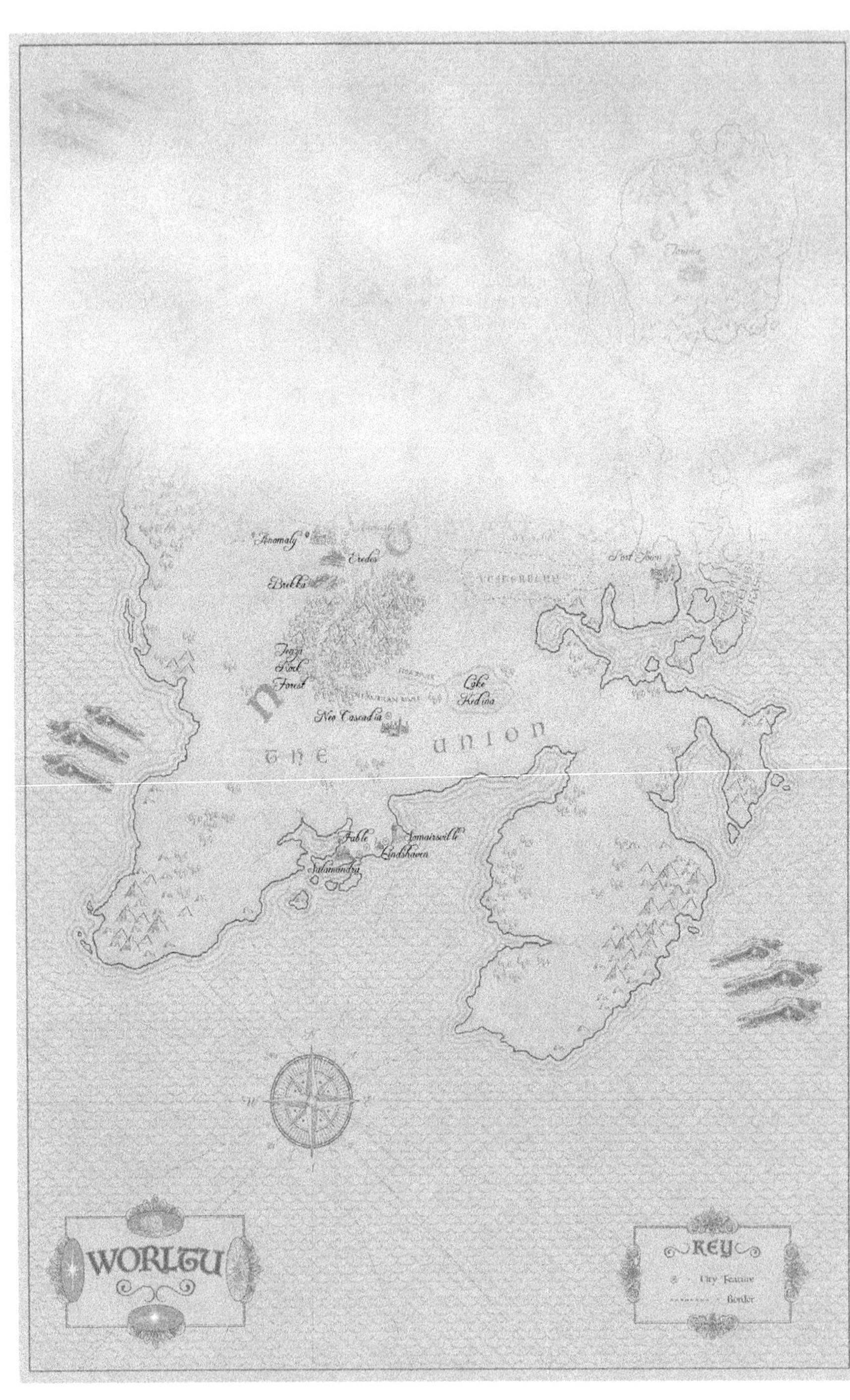

Anomaly
Eredos
Brekka
Fraya
Red
Forest
Neo Cascadia
Coke
Medina
the union
Port Joon
Fable
Lomairseille
Lindshaven
Salamandra
WORLTU
KEY
City Feature
Border

The Adventures of Little Eddie Bowitz and Jamal Vans

If you've ever seen the sparking moon, you'll know . . .

There's magic that lurks far beyond the stars above, a rare midnight's gleaming. This celestial presence offers solace that someday our dreams may be married with supreme truth.

The sparking moon, like the wishing star, doesn't happen upon just anyone. Like truest love, it graces those who offer their trust with reverence in their sacred heart.

That is what Little Eddie Bowitz and his friend Jamal Vans believed to be of purest truth.

There was magic out there. The mystic lay just beyond the veil, and the greatest journeys merely waited to be seized by the brave.

So, they would rise early to meet in the gardens to make their plans from the craftwork of dirt and rock.

More often than not, one was always waiting for the other. The rickety squeal of the hinges served as the bell for their assembly; the distant dog's cry, a rally for the brave.

Though the humble roots of their adventure often lay just beyond the doors of home, their grandiose ambitions lay upon a summit. It was a place of grandeur, a stark contrast from their suburban town of Somairsville, a humble community of single-story brick houses.

It wasn't far. The boys knew that if you made it past the backyard gate and rushed through Mellow Park, the mythic ascent lay only across two quiet streets.

The Golden Peak could be seen from virtually anywhere. The hillside was not simply the pinnacle of town but, moreover, the heart of its charm and concentration of the daily concert of life. Every morning, the sun rose over the tree-covered slope to bring birth to a new day.

By tradition, the people celebrated seasonal festivals upon the Great Flat, which oversaw a grand valley, a rolling green that bounded on for over a mile. It was abundant with verdant resplendence, and existed as an ever-still ocean of land until it reached the distant Farside Hill.

Every season was an exhibit of nature's incomparable craftsmanship, a fertile ground for the most distinctive and cherished memories. In spring, tranquil showers reinvigorated the soil and resurrected the summit gardens with breathtaking flora, while in the summertime, hot air balloons drifted lazily above the emerald sea. By fall, the winds became busy with flurries of amber leaves, and come winter, the fallen would be erased beneath a dense sheet of crystalline snow. It was a timeless grace. A splendid enactment of the sacred cycle of life.

Most important to Little Eddie and Jamal, however, was that its vastness served as evidence that something much greater awaited them, that, perhaps, the incredible lay just beyond that distant crest, somewhere out in the forbidden lands. It was where mysterious creatures surely roamed when no one was looking. The ones that left footprints down on the slope. Those which privy parents would explain away as being little more than natural formations.

It was there in the mile-long dive, that thousand-year-old runes lay hidden among the stones, still imbued with cryptic boons to bless those who found them. Adventure awaited as long as they were willing to seek it out, and according to Eddie's grandfather, the valley was their town's most well-kept secret. So carefully protected that few were willing to recognize it as the truth, and all denial was simply a part of the dynamic shroud.

The old man's words gave fire to their ambitions, however, strict rules from home permitted the arrest of their blossoming spirit. But the invigorated spirit will always long to be unleashed, and so, someday it shall.

. . . And what a beautiful day that would be.

It was Saturday morning, and Mrs. Vans, in her usual lavender nightgown, had already taken up her post out on the driveway, with hands planted into her waist, as she basked in the light of dawn. Then, as per routine, she went back to a white swing in front of the house and sat there as her son went from here to there, upturning stones, digging, then scurrying away each time an exposed insect zipped across the dirt.

"Don't come crying to me when one of them bites you, Jamal," she warned.

***

In the house next door, Little Eddie Bowitz peeked through the window of his room, excited for the day ahead. There was no plan, yet his ideas were so overabundant that they lifted a thousand possibilities.

Eddie leapt down from his bed and hopscotched through a scattered assortment of toys, namely a toy robot, a few action figures, and a toy telephone equipped with a rotary dial. Out through the doorway, he flew past the bathroom, where his mother was down on both knees, hard at work scrubbing away at the toilet.

"Hey, Eddie, what did I tell you about six-year-old boy responsibilities?" she called out to him as he passed her without a thought.

He came running back and slid to a stop on socks adorned with the image of various superheroes.

"Clean the bathroom after I'm done, but I was gonna—"

"Ah," she interrupted. "You know that means right after. Not in the morning."

The boy pushed himself dramatically against the wall.

"But it's dark. I can't see it," he complained.

"Then turn on the lights, Eddie, and maybe we wouldn't have to clean the floor every single day."

They stared each other down in a brief contest of wills.

"Next time?" she negotiated.

"Okay, promise!" he boomed, then popped out of the doorway and shot down the hall.

He cut the corner at the hall's end, which branched between the living room, and a separate hall to the front door. The portal to freedom lay open, guarded by only the teasing screen. The boy skated across the wood floors, reached out, and slammed his palms against the flimsy frame.

Curious eyes searched the front yard. All was still, aside from the subtle twitch of a squirrel in the tree, which was undoubtedly startled by his thunderous impact.

Eddie turned to the kitchen just beside the door, where his father stood at the sink, drying off dishes with solemn calm baked into his face. It was a look, far too familiar to be recognized as anything other than normal.

"Dad, can I go outside with JJ?" he pleaded.

"Did you ask your mom if she needs help with anything?"

The boy released a quick sigh of frustration.

"No, but I can do it tonight. It's only Saturday," he negotiated. "Anything, I promise!"

"But you're a big boy now, and Saturday is cleaning day. You know that."

Eddie lingered as he assessed a plan of action. He spun around and flew back down the hallway, cut back toward the bathroom, and slid to the door.

He repeated his plea to his mother with double the speed and intensity, with the hope it would amplify his chances of success.

His mother reluctantly accepted, but not without voicing her protest that he should accomplish work before going out to play. But as he was just a boy, she figured there would be plenty of time to teach him.

And so, with the terms of the agreement being a bath, a change of clothes, and a quick breakfast, he would soon be freed from the bonds of restraint.

A sandwich and eight apple slices were prepared at the counter, then brought to a dining area at the end of the kitchen. It was a modest and intimate space with just enough room to accommodate a table and a box television which sat atop the back of a glossy ceramic elephant.

At the table's end, sat Eddie's grandfather. His eyes perused the newspaper's front page, which was headlined "Golden Sun Festival, Rain or Shine!"

As he read, he hummed a tune, of which a few lyrics slipped out.

"There's a festival around the corner . . .
And don't you know it? . . . A golden sun for you and me . . .
A new day for us!"

Eddie's mother laid a bowl on the table, then whisked away to retrieve him. It wasn't long after that the boy raced through the kitchen and leapt into the seat across from the old man.

"Hey, Grandpa!" he greeted with a mouth already stuffed with apple.

"Well, slow down, boy! Slow down. What's the hurry?"

Eddie looked to his grandfather with the next slice, prepared in hand.

"Going to see JJ! Yesterday, you know he said he found something super special. So special that he wouldn't tell me what it was!"

The boy's grandfather beamed.

"That right? Now, that must be something truly special, then. No doubt about it. Isn't that right, Douglas?" the old man asked in a glance to Eddie's father, who was still occupied with dishes in the sink.

"Hm? Oh, that's right. Surely is."

The old man laughed.

"As stiff as a Beilkan, aren't ya? Or maybe that's just the engineer in him," he said with a playful slap to Eddie's shoulder.

"Say, maybe you and Jamal can cook something up for him before he has to go work another double on the festival day, again. Third year in a row! That's bad luck, I tell ya," his grandfather advised.

Eddie reserved a moment from his gorge.

"Like what?" the boy asked.

"Oh, I don't know. A spell or something! I'm sure you two will figure it out. You always do, right?"

Inspired, the boy nodded with a grin ballooned by an ambitious last bite of sandwich.

"Otherwise, he'll be dancing bones before he has any fun in his life," his grandfather exclaimed in a comical demonstration with his arms.

With the plate cleared, Eddie pushed the chair out and dropped to the ground.

"Don't worry, dad! Me and JJ will save you from becoming dancing bones!" he cheered with a pledge in his heart as he took flight for the door.

"Thank you, son," the boy's father replied with an annoyed glance to the old man.

The boy burst through the screen door, and it crashed against the brick wall. The ruckus prompted a yelp of anger from his mother. She stepped out into the doorway of the kitchen with a duster in hand.

"What was all that about?" she asked as she twirled the handle between her fingers.

"Just my father doing what he does best: building a hero out of our son, and a villain out of me."

"Trust me. If I didn't care, I wouldn't say anything."

The boy's father sighed as he dropped the rag on the sink, his task completed.

"Sometimes I wish you wouldn't. I can't just take off work and make time whenever I like. It's just not possible."

The old man stared at him with an inquisitive eye. He was the keeper of some secret, long lost to his son, though one he could surely remember, if only he tried.

"Well . . . the things we choose to believe in . . . are the most powerful of all, or all-powerful, they will surely become."

Outside, Eddie fled past the big tree at the center of the yard, which doused the area in shade. He cut right across into the Vans's driveway where Mrs. Vans still sat upon her swing, with a solemn gaze set upon oblivion. Eddie turned to her as soon as she came into his view and stumbled to a halt.

"Good morning, Mrs. Vans!" he greeted.

"Good morning, Eddie."

Her eyes remained fixed. Emotionless and bleak. Eddie had taken notice of her gaze but knew it wouldn't be polite to trouble her with his curiosity.

"Eddie, come here!" shouted Jamal, who knelt, half exposed between the shrubs in the garden, beyond the driveway.

The boy dashed over and took his friend's side. Jamal, who had awaited his arrival, took hold of a lumpy-edged rock with both hands. With a summoning of full strength, he pulled it right over.

A streak of bright red seized them. They froze up in a bolt of excitement as an elusive crimson centipede bolted across the black dirt. Eddie whisked away from his habitual spot of excavation, back to the center of the Vans's driveway, while Jamal remained frozen with a shriek.

"Uh-oh, JJ. Don't go getting your friend bit up by bugs. Just because you want to, doesn't mean everyone else does," his mother scorned.

To the beckon of laughter, Eddie returned to his side at the bush. Jamal took the rock once more and dragged it back through the loosened earth. Revealed beneath was a plastic pencil box with a bubble-textured top, still half buried under mulch and dirt.

"This is it," whispered Jamal.

Captivated by its mystique, Eddie experienced a rush of excitement. Jamal wiped off the last of the dirt and pulled the latched lip which separated the top from bottom. He only caught a glimpse of it before the sound of footsteps stole his glow. Eddie popped away from the box, overcome by instinctual guilt.

"No. Get out, now. If you're not going to listen, you're going back in the house, JJ."

Jamal crawled out from under the bush and slammed his hands against the ground.

"But I just came out," he protested.

"You been out here for an hour, and you're already starting to catch an attitude."

"No, I'm not. I was just getting my treasure chest," he said as he revealed to her the dinged-up plastic case.

Eddie remained locked in silence, with his hand wrapped around his pointer finger, discomforted by their discourse. Mrs. Vans grimaced at the very sight of the filthy, fictitious artifact.

"Where did you get that nasty thing from? Did you get that out of the garbage can?" she snapped.

"It's my old pencil box from school."

"You either wash it off and put it in the house or throw it in the trash. Which one are you going to do?" she asked with a hand placed firmly upon her hip.

Jamal grabbed the box, planted one foot, rose up, and planted the other. He scowled at the ground as he marched over toward the yellow hose, which was wrapped tight beside the front door.

"And you can stop acting like that right now."

Jamal groaned.

"Hey!" his mother snapped. "What did I just get done telling you!?"

Eddie knew their butting of heads was a sure sign it was only a matter of time before he was sent in for good. Hoping to avoid such an outcome, he decided to make a proposal.

Eddie met Jamal at the hose as he doused the box with water, occasionally creating a jet when he pressed his thumb down into the stream. Mrs. Vans loomed over them for a moment, which stalled Eddie from speaking outright. After a moment of hawkish supervision, she stepped off to the driveway where their burgundy sedan was parked and disappeared around the corner of the house.

"J! Wanna go to Miles's house and play games? You know! I bet he's got a new one," Eddie proposed as Jamal blasted the last of the dirt away.

Lucas Miles Dominik, who, by steadfast request, went strictly by Miles, was a ten-year-old boy who lived right down the street at a house where the forest line met severed concrete.

The boys had long discovered that Mrs. Dominik was far more lenient with the content of the games that she allowed her son to play. Thus, a trip to their house was guaranteed to provide exhilarating thrills.

He was a guru of a sort, who lived hidden among the tangled forest of cords, always with a new hidden knowledge he'd be willing to share if only they pestered him enough. He was a collector of oddities and had a deeper understanding of the land beyond the peak, which meant their interest was forever helpless in the grasp of his tales. They didn't go often, but those lulls between whimsical congregations only made each visit more exciting.

Jamal scratched his chin as he mulled over his suggestion.

"Momma's in a bad mood. Let me ask Dad," Jamal whispered with such intentional force that it made Eddie cringe in fear of being overheard.

With the job complete, Jamal retrieved the box from the ground. He took his shirt and wiped it down until most of the water had been soaked up.

Eddie's eyes lingered on the shabby treasured chest, its contents still a mystery.

"Good enough! Let's go, Eddie!"

His cry snapped Eddie from his starry-eyed departure.

Jamal moved to the door and yanked it open. Eddie tailed him up the step, into the house. Inside, they faced down a grandfather clock, which stood in an alcove at the hallway's end, its face shrouded by deep shadow.

The boy froze, then turned to Eddie.

"Be right back. Hold on a second, okay?"

Eddie agreed with a nod.

Jamal hurried through the hall, then cut to the right and disappeared around the corner. Eddie stepped forward but faltered as he sought to keep near the door, far out of sight and out of mind.

The hallway was dark and quiet. Its walls were lined with family photos encased in wooden frames. They, too, were shrouded in a darkness that left him unsettled. It was an undercurrent that he had only recently detected, the kind of eeriness that steered him toward a particular truth. With the darkness came distance between their families, an unspoken severance of regular interaction. From faint memory, he could recall a time of better days, light through the windows and open doors to the back patio where Jamal's father would cook upon his cherished grill. These were different days. Gone, but neither unsung nor forgotten.

He heard the sound of voices from the far end, then hacking. Eddie rolled back and forth from toe to heel.

The coughing continued, intensified, then settled.

Stirring, the boy peered up at the clock. The hour hand struck forth, then returned to perfect stillness, as the seconds chipped away at time with their monotonous tick. The sound of voices caught his attention once more. They were just beyond the corner. Enchanted by his curiosity, he crept forward.

The corner of the wall pulled away, and the living room was revealed to peeping eyes.

Jamal's father sat in his brown leather armchair situated in front of the TV. The broadcast featured coverage of a conflict far from home. There was a newswoman who stood in front of a charred car, yet no words came from her mouth as she spoke.

The determined petitioner stood at his father's side, his palms dug into the leather armrest as he bounced beside it. Eddie noticed something quite unusual, twiddled between the man's rough-skinned fingers.

It was a gray shard with five distinct points, a star of solid stone. In the magic of coincidence, a soft glimmering ray infiltrated the darkness of the room through a splinter in the long blinds which covered the sliding door to the backyard. They shifted in a gentle gust from an air conditioner vent along the floor and caused the light to split, vanish, and reappear again.

Bewitched, Eddie leaned in to get a better look, and as he did, he saw Jamal's box opened upon a wooden side table next to a small variety of pill bottles.

"You find this outside?" his father asked in such a grating rasp that Eddie couldn't quite decipher the precise emotion behind his words.

Jamal nodded half-heartedly.

His father tried to laugh but choked.

"Alright, alright. A wishing star, huh?"

Eddie's eyes grew in astonishment at the words that he had heard. His father offered no contest to the claim, and as he handled that special stone, he seemed to do so with a distinct reverence. It was the kind of care that offered validation to its declared mystic heritage.

Jamal's father reached over to the box, took it off the table, then returned the rock to the plastic belly, and closed it. He then handed it over to his son, struggling to lift his forearm from the cushion.

"Go on, J. Go on and play until I get up from my nap. We'll do something then, okay?"

His father bid him farewell with a wave of two half-lifted fingers. Eddie slipped away from the corner and crept back through the hall to the door once more. Almost immediately, his mind became swept in enchantment by the star-shaped rock that he had seen.

Why was it so special? What power could it hold? He mulled over the possibilities, as surely his friend wouldn't have put something without value within that buried box. And surely, no object void of value would ever need to be hidden.

The wonderer flinched at the sound of frantic steps. Jamal reappeared with a triumphant punch to the skies.

"Yes! He said we can go play until he gets up," Jamal reported.

Eddie turned to find he no longer had possession of the box yet resisted the urge to badger him.

"Does your dad need some veggie juice? That's what mom gives me when I get really sick."

Jamal shrugged.

"I don't know. Mom says that he just needs rest."

Eddie nodded, unwilling to push the discussion any further.

It had been some time since he had seen Mr. Vans out working in his big vegetable garden out back. Every year, at the cusp of summer, he would come over with his basket of crops to share his modest yield. A work of love and patience, the fruits of his labor were revered among the neighbors. Since then, the few times he was able to see the backyard, it had fallen further and further into dilapidation. Alongside its decay, so came the darkness which inhabited their house.

Freed from parental grasp, the boys broke for the door. Jamal burst through, while his friend slipped out behind him. Eddie turned to pull the door shut, and as he did, stole a parting glimpse of the grandfather clock's face.

Outside, Mrs. Vans was busy with the removal of weeds from the little garden along the side of the house. In aged yellow yard gloves, she pulled the razor-leafed sprouts from the ground and cast them into a black trash bag. Jamal cut through the bushes to expedite the delivery of his father's permission. Eddie trailed him through the mulch.

Mrs. Vans's brow lifted as her little boy arrived beside her and made his breathless claim.

"He said that?" she said.

In those words alone, Eddie expected nothing less than a complete overturn of his father's decision. In the days of late, she seemed apt to jump right to her son's containment within the walls of her home. He lacked a reason to expect today to be any different.

Her shoulders fell with a breath of surrender, however, the sound of triumph to the ears of children.

"Okay, go on then. But you better be home before two. We're going to have lunch together."

"Okay, thank you, love you, bye!" Jamal replied in a bolt across the yard, which left Eddie to give chase.

"And you make sure to look both ways before crossing the road," she hollered after him.

"The road ends here anyway," Jamal said, emboldened by his distance from her.

One after the other, they rounded onto the sidewalk. Frantic steps fell upon cement riddled to the far end with marks of age, missing shards and cracks and overrun by weeds.

Hurried steps soon brought them before the road's brink, the place where the suburb ended and the dense forest began.

There was no cul-de-sac or roundabout. Instead, there was but a lonely strip of bulky guardrail fitted with three vermillion diamonds to ward off wanderers, those lost, and those misguided from civilization's imminent end.

Alone, the barrier held back the forest from endless expansion and left the trees at the outskirts to loom over with an eerie bend, the spirit of nature eager to lay claim to that which lay out of its reach.

Beyond that thoughtless, jagged brink, neither boy had ever dared to cross. Whatever contents lay within, however, captivated their imaginations every time they drew near. Like a siren perched at the world's end, it called out to their adventurous hearts and begged them to venture forth. Unlike the valley, however, the forest offered no coward a glimpse of its secrets. Beyond the severed pavement, there was nothing but thicket and through that only shadows, which seemed to twitch in the darkest of nights.

Jamal had stopped just before the end of the sidewalk, which vanished a mere twenty feet behind the road. He gazed a moment into that strange portal as its uncanny mystique stole him away.

Eddie slid to a stop beside him.

In a moment, they were both looking in. There came a revitalizing waft and then, a serene hush as the branches faded back to stillness. Their eyes followed the tree trunks up into the canopy, which arched over the shadowy breach as somnolent whispers escaped from the passage into the forbidden realm.

Frightened, they cut left and made for a small white house, separated from the tree line by a single neighbor.

The unkempt yard was littered with toys made indistinguishable from junk due to neglect. Forgotten and fragmented, they were left in a state that would hardly garner the interest of a child, nor burden the eye of any ne'er-do-well bargain hunter.

And so, a vivid glimpse into the discord that lay within was all the mess offered. A welcome sight of familiarity to the neighborhood boys.

They raced up the shattered driveway and were forced alongside a rust-plagued minivan, whose decay was covered in washed-out bumper stickers.

The van had been slung into the driveway and left at a slant, a sure sign to the boys that Mrs. Dominik had reached her limit at one point during the day. They could only hope that the frustration had dissipated.

The squeeze nearly put them into the grass before it gave way beyond the van's front end. They cut the corner before the garage door and followed the sidewalk to the tattered screen door.

They stumbled to a halt in an immediate pivot from full speed. When he had found stability on his feet, Jamal pressed his face into the mesh. The door beyond lay slightly ajar and left little exposed to his peeping eyes.

He pulled away, leapt to strike the doorbell, then waited beside Eddie for someone to answer.

"Hold on!" bleated the hoarse crow from within. They had long come to relish that cry of frustration as a harbinger of haphazard entertainment, and though harsh, only made them giddy with anticipation.

From within, weighted barefoot steps thundered across tile floors. The door was pulled beyond the screen. Mrs. Dominik, comfortable in a pair of green running shorts and a pink tee, adorned with a vectorized crown, examined her unexpected guests with sugared disgust.

"Oh, great, you guys again?" she said but pulled open the screen to accommodate their entry.

"Come on," she said with an invitational swoop of the arm. The boys filed in and then zipped past her.

"Miles, your little friends are here to see you," the suburban empress announced as she thundered back down the hall.

"Get your ass out here and say hello. Entertain. Be cordial!" she bellowed.

Eddie and Jamal lacked patience. They bolted through the living room, a site of the vicious hurricane of complacency. There was an open buffet of unkempt blankets thrown over the backrest of the sofa, and upon them lounged two feline defenders, who scolded the unwelcome visitors from a loaf as they maneuvered a minefield of clutter. The hoarded mass consisted of anything and everything and laid siege to every inch of the area beyond the sofa, which lay hidden, eternal, behind blackout curtains.

It was a place that would make the collected mind tremble in distress, but for the boys, it was where rules came crashing down and expression became boundless. Here, their young minds were subject to chaotic stimulation. Endless possibility, without repercussion. Impunity, so long as their respite remained just that, and nothing more.

The far-side cat swiped at Eddie with a hiss as they bounded over an avalanche of laundry that made the passage between the couch and back wall otherwise impassible.

Eddie chuckled as the cat's strike came up a miss. Only a small assortment of clutter parted them from the hallway that held their destination. There was a tipped dollhouse with its half-foot tall, frizzy-haired inhabitants spewed all about. In the middle of the bunch was a hairdryer, still plugged into the wall, and a toy replica thoughtlessly tossed aside to the corner of the room.

"Miles, get your ass out here, and get these boys to quit pissing off my cats," Mrs. Dominik bellowed once more.

"Alright, Mom. Just give me a second, damn."

From a door down the hallway, the young sage of Emerald Street emerged. He was a boy much bigger than them, who had inherited the same largeness of his mother, as well as the same careless attitude.

In his hands was a clear-cased handheld gaming device, from which all sorts of catchy sounds zipped and zapped. Whatever madness engaged his adolescent mind upon its humble, boxy screen rendered him effectively spellbound by the charm of frantic eight-bit brilliance.

"Alright, what do you guys want?" he asked as he wiped chip crumbs from the gruesome image of a monster truck flattening a hearse on his shirt.

To the boys, it was part of his charm. His disposition had long captivated them, as it was something they'd dare not bring home with them. Miles, being their elder, had little trouble assuming the role of leadership during any of their invasions of his house, and they believed perhaps someday, his confidence and freedoms would be theirs too.

"Miles, do you care if we stay a bit?" asked Jamal with his head cocked with innocence.

"Yeah. We wanna see you play the scary one again," Eddie said.

"Ooo, the game with the dinos? Yeah, beat that one last month, and we finally had to return it. Rental store was pissed."

"I thought you were gonna burn it for us," Jamal complained.

Miles dropped his zombielike gaze from the illuminated screen as he was rescued by sheer disbelief.

"Dude, you think your dad would actually let you play that game? He wouldn't even let you play a racing game where the driver could *sometimes* fly out the windshield."

"He lets me do way more stuff than Mom, now. I don't think he cares anymore. Maybe he likes games, too," Jamal guessed with a shrug.

Mrs. Dominik, who had lingered in the entry hall, quietly returned to the door. She grabbed a pair of sunglasses, which dangled from a hook on the wall, slipped into a pair of green flip-flops beside the door, then stepped outside into the morning light with a sigh.

In that retreat, her eyes searched the hillside, where the sun rose above the land. She lowered her head to find Mrs. Vans at the edge of her property down the street. With a neighborly wave, she stepped away from the door, and the two women started on a course to each other.

Inside, the boys overheard their morning exchange.

Jamal's face lit up to the sound of his mother's voice and took off for the room from which Miles had emerged. Eddie raced behind him, both in fear that their time was already up.

"Okay, go right in and make yourselves at home, I guess?" said Miles before he turned around and marched after them.

The cyclone-stricken room provided little space to accommodate them, but among the clutter were the things of legend. Some of the most special being the ancient sword and helm which hung above the closet, whose door sat derailed in the carpet beside the track.

They were no mere movie props. Miles would weave tales of grand sensations upon his adornment of these old relics before journeys outside of town, and that he would not go without them, due to the unfathomable evil which lay beyond the peaceful simplicity of home.

He would tell them of an ancient story of a great hero who stood bravely against the Beilkan army and marched his soldiers all the way north to the shores of their empire.

In one iteration, the hero was the same champion who slayed the feared Gray Wolf of Beilka, a knight so cunning that his enemies sought to wait out his death. The tale went that upon catching wind of their plan, the Beilkan King struck a deal with a mage from the otherworld, who crafted runes to be placed upon his knight's armor. Those runes were so powerful that they allowed him to live 138 years, until the day of his defeat.

Though the story and hero's name always changed, their faith in his words never swayed, as when he adorned the helm and sword before them, he would transform before their very eyes.

The spirit of the hero would take hold of him and manifest through his voice, deep and unafraid, ready for the winds of adventure. He would promise to guide them to the north someday, so that they, too, could face the Beilkans alongside him and claim a decisive victory over the enraged specter of the revenant Gray Wolf. Though a daunting invitation, the spectacular performance of the hero never failed to kindle their spirits with an invincible flame of valor.

Along the wall beside the closet was a dusty dresser which, as long as memory served, had lacked a knob on both the fourth and second drawer. Upon it were notebooks full of only the rarest collectible cards, flung open for the sage's eyes to bear or utilize for his game. Though neither boy knew the rules of this competition of monsters and magics, they were often used as training dummies to spar against Miles's wittiest compositions.

This would strictly involve them drawing cards and playing them as instructed, which left them to simply admire the illustrations of dragons, magicians, and beasts.

Other decks were stacked against the wall next to a small, chipped entertainment stand at the corner of the room, which held a bulky television at dead center.

Jamal leapt over a cord that connected a slim gray console on the entertainment stand to a controller, which lay on the lower mattress of a red double bunk. He dropped down, then crawled beneath as if there was war outside.

Eddie entered just in time to see his shoes vanish underneath. The boy plopped down right in front of the television, eager for the show to begin. Miles stomped in behind them and tossed himself onto the mattress, his face maintaining two inches from the game screen, throughout.

"Better watch out. Lacy's under there," Miles warned his imperiled guest.

A hiss of a disturbed feline sharply followed a yelp from Jamal, who scurried out as a gray blur bolted from the room on razor claws.

"You got any new games, Miles?" Jamal asked as he pulled himself beside Eddie.

A strident stumble of horns caused Miles to sigh. He turned off the handheld and tossed it aside, lost to the sea of unmade sheets.

"Sure, hold on. I've been meaning to test something on one I snagged a couple weeks ago."

Miles carefully tiptoed his way to the entertainment center with his fingers pressed together like a wise guru. He purposefully took his seat between the clutter of the room. He then raised his hand to a row of glossy cases lined up in a cubby beneath the stand's upper shelf. His fingers wiggled as he searched out the case of his desire.

"Here we go."

He flicked the case forth with the tip of his finger, then slid it out from the row. The boys gazed down upon it. The artwork on the included booklet was that of a battle-hardened fighter with red gloves and a vicious glare. A ruinous inferno swept around the warrior, and in small boxes were fierce competitors, which included the likes of a beast man, a boxer, and a black-cloaked assassin among others.

"Don't tell your parents you played this game, alright?" he asked as he opened the case and popped the disk out.

"We won't say nothin', right Eddie?" Jamal asked, with genuine faith in their commitment to silence.

Eddie turned stone-faced as he placed his fingers at the corner of his mouth and mimicked the closing of a zipper.

Miles opened the console's disk door, then, with extreme care—the likes of which never extended to anything beyond his treasures—eased the disk into the spindle. He then took a second controller from the TV stand and began the process of unraveling the cord which was neatly wrapped around the silver shell. When the task was done, he jacked the cable in and powered up the console via a large circular button.

Miles held up the controller with a smug grin.

Jamal's hand shot up before Eddie could even think to contest him.

"Come on, let me play. We're gonna play teams, right?" the boy asked.

Miles laughed like a menace, which would have made his intentions obvious to anyone but the boys.

Miles zipped over to his character of choice, the same character featured on the cover, while Jamal browsed his choices. Miles awaited his selection with his chin dug into his palm as the timer at the top ticked down. It successfully evaded the boys' attention until the timer struck zero, and the game auto-locked him into an enormously overgrown turkey.

"What the heck!? I didn't mean to pick the freakin' turkey!"

Eddie curled over in laughter at the very sight of the comical addition to the roster.

"Turk is super good, dude," Miles replied as he stretched himself up in preparation for his bout.

Jamal and Miles faced off in a power plant just beyond a row of supercharged generators, which were periodically overwhelmed with raw energy. Jamal's turkey was subjected to a brutal punishment, with its only saving grace being a static low peck, in which the reach of its neck repeatedly prevented Miles's ruthless retaliatory flurry.

Eddie wailed in laughter as the cartoonish beast was chased about the map, then, in a grand finale to their fight, was launched into the generators and fried to a cooked masterpiece.

"What the heck was that?" Jamal complained.

"Loser passes their controller. You know the rules," Miles directed.

Jamal surrendered the controller to Eddie. They reentered the character selection screen, to which Miles immediately returned to the same character. Eddie browsed aimlessly until he made a sudden dash for the dinner bird.

The boys let out a shriek of laughter as the bobble-eyed turkey appeared back on screen with a dopey gobble.

Eddie suffered the same punishment as his companion, only more ruthless in execution, as Miles punished the predicted use of the bird's peck.

He tried to resist the inevitable defeat and his desperate mash somehow managed to get the bird to open its wings in a mad flutter of anger, which caused both boys to shriek in laughter.

Both boys were subjected to repeated defeat until they were each sprawled out on the ground as they took turns mashing buttons in throwaway attempts at victory.

"You guys have no idea what you're doing," Miles declared.

Jamal sighed, then looked to Eddie, who sat quietly with his legs folded.

"You wanna try again?" he asked, offering out the controller, at which Eddie stared, not wanting to face embarrassment yet again without the cushion of humor.

"How about I show you guys the treasure chest?" Miles suggested. "Don't be sad because you're bad. It's really a game for adults, anyway," he assured them.

"Yeah, show us some stuff from the valley!" Eddie bloomed.

"Did you find anything cool out there?" asked Jamal as he dropped the controller to the floor.

Miles raised his finger as he scanned for memories of obtaining such treasures. The ten-year-old and his friends were permitted much more access to the valley by their families, especially on holidays when the adults would stand watch from the hilltop. Both Eddie and Jamal were often left to watch with envy as they scoured the land both far and wide throughout the day, and laid claim to the most unique of things.

Miles nodded in a return from his pensive departure, then rose from the ground and made for the closet. The boys followed him with starry eyes. He rubbed his hands together before he took the closet door and lifted it off the ground, then laid it against the wall. He entered within and drew from the darkness a brown leather case.

"As a matter of fact, me and Bret were out there last week," he said as he returned to the bed.

He laid down the case, then found himself swarmed by both boys, to which he held out his arms to stave them off. Though tempted, they knew Miles was very sensitive about anyone laying a finger on his personal belongings, and so they resisted further excitement.

When he was sure that the boys were calm, he pulled down the latches and opened the case. Inside was a stack of pocketed binder pages, labeled with ripped papers with indecipherable symbols drawn in permanent marker. Behind the paper labels were stones of various shapes and sizes, matched with the symbol of their respective category.

"So, the ones you haven't seen before are over here," he said as he brought his finger down on the pocket at the top right corner.

The symbol on the label was comprised of a spiral and centralized dot.

"What are those ones?" Jamal asked as he leaned in close.

"These are hero runes. They give you bravery. You both know about the skill runes," he said as he moved his finger over to another pocket near the center of the page.

"The ones I said you were both direly in need of. Well, you can carry these together when you're trying something new for an added benefit. Additionally, the hero runes invite adventure into your life. So yeah, they're pretty cool," he said.

Eddie cocked his head as he looked down at the rocks.

"How do you tell which ones are the hero runes?" he asked.

Miles carefully went to the pocket and slipped out one of the rocks. He then flipped it on its backside and ran his finger over the three layers on the side of it. Each one was a different color.

"They've been super valuable to me so far. Nearly won a tournament down at GB Games for a launch party, like right after we found it. Unfortunately for you two, you can't find them in the shallow parts of the valley."

Jamal's eyes bulged as he gripped his head with both hands.

"What!? Then how are we gonna become heroes!?"

"Miles! We're getting ready to have lunch. Hot dogs and mac and cheese. Ask your friends if they're hungry, please. Don't be rude in my house."

Miles's mother then appeared at the doorway, then pressed her foot against the knee of her other leg as she leaned upon the frame.

Miles let out a loud sigh.

"I mean—I was about to ask, like, after we were done talking about other stuff," he explained with eyes narrowed in annoyance with her abrupt demands.

"Ask," she commanded. "And if they do, you can make their plates for them . . . and do the dishes. Thanks, dear, love ya, bye," she said with a wide grin as she stepped away down the hall.

Miles put his fingers against his forehead with the headache of a businessman.

Just then, a young girl with a curly ponytail popped into the doorway.

"Hi, boys!" she said with overwhelming enthusiasm and a toothy grin to follow it up.

"Hi, Jamie," both boys replied with a wave.

"Jamie, go away. Thank you for understanding, bye," her brother droned.

Her face coiled up in disgust with him. With a quick flash of her tongue to the side of his head, she leapt out of the doorway and frolicked back into the living room.

"Boys, never allow your parents to produce little sisters. At first, it's like the big things. You know, don't go in my room, don't touch my stuff, or hang around while my friends are here, but now I just feel annoyed anytime she's around," he confessed.

Jamal fidgeted, as curiosity pestered him.

"Hey, Miles," he called, in a swift cave to its influence.

The nettled sage, who had buried his face into his palms, lifted in a glazed stare. Jamal drew from his pocket the wishing star and presented it to the connoisseur of stones.

"Can you tell us what this one does?" he asked.

Miles leaned in close with an analytical gaze set upon the star-shaped rock. He reached out, carefully received it with steady hands, then proceeded into superficial inspection.

Eddie glowed as he became enthralled once more by the mere sight of that stellate trinket.

"Where in the actual fuck did you guys find this?"

Miles snapped away to a desk that sat beside the closet and flipped on a gray swing-arm lamp. The boys ran over behind him as he plopped down in his rickety office chair and began to inspect their treasure with more spiritual thoroughness.

"For real. Where'd you find this, dude?" he asked once more.

"The valley," Jamal said.

"On the summit?" Miles investigated with a glance.

"Yeah," replied Jamal with a half-hearted nod.

Miles turned back to the rock and lifted it with his fingertips.

"That's nuts. We've never seen anything like this on the summit."

"Wow. Is it a real wishing star?" Eddie asked.

Jamal yet fidgeted, something still heavy on his mind.

"Hey, Miles."

The boy turned in his chair to hear him out.

"You've been down in the valley lots of times. Have you ever seen someone out there?"

The seasoned adventurer's brow rose to the uncanny sincerity in those eyes.

"Uhh no? Have you?"

Jamal's eyes widened as he felt the bewildered stares of both Eddie and Miles dig into him. He shook his head to ward off suspicion.

"Nope. I just heard stories, you know?"

"Uh, nope. Can't say I have."

Miles turned back to the star and inspected it closely once more.

"What'd you call this thing? A wishing star?" asked Miles.

Jamal nodded. "Yeah, the wishing star," he confirmed.

"Not gonna lie. It's a pretty nice find."

He traced the jagged edges with his finger, then stopped as a divine sensation informed him more deeply of its mystic origins.

"Oh, yeah, there's a lot within this. Tons of energy."

"What can it do!?" Jamal erupted.

Miles concentrated further. "Incredible things with this. I mean, do you honestly think you can just go out and find star-shaped rocks anywhere?" He shook his head to answer for them. "Nah. You can't."

The boys' blood boiled in excitement. He was right. This rock was unlike any other. No simple fragment, nor a throwaway piece of nature. It was unique, whole, designed for something incredible.

"He's right! You can't just find a freakin' *star rock* anywhere," Jamal said to Eddie, who beamed back.

"You found a real wishing star!" he cheered.

Miles kicked off the ground and whipped back around to them with his fingertips pressed together. He nodded with a grin, amused by their enthusiasm for otherworldly trinkets.

"Guess what, boys? I'm gonna make you two honorary members of the Adventure Corps."

Their faces lit up in joy.

"For real?" Jamal boomed.

"I'm going to start middle school soon. So, I need to find the next generation. For the two of you, I'm willing to part with a hero rune, each."

Miles turned over the wishing star to Jamal, cusped respectfully in both hands. "First, I'll give that back."

Jamal clutched the sacred star in his grip. Miles rose from the chair, and the boys tailed him as he returned to the box and took from the pockets two of his valued stones. He bestowed them to both of the boys, who gleefully received them.

"The Golden Sun Festival is only four days away. Now that you're a part of our group, I'll do you guys a favor. I'm going to see if you can't come out on an adventure with me and the other guys. Everyone's parents will be there. It should be cool." Miles shrugged.

"Wow! Really? You'll ask!?" Eddie said, beaming.

The young sage of the stones nodded.

"We might not find a rock just like this, but I bet we can cover a lot of ground before sunset and snag some crazy good stuff."

Jamal leapt with a pump of his fist in an outburst of joy.

"Yes! I know just where to go," he promised.

There came three knocks on the doorframe. Miles's mother stepped through and leaned her shoulder into the frame.

"Boys, JJ's momma wants him back at home for a second. Right now, okay? Eddie, you're free to stay or go. We're almost finished with lunch."

Jamal let out a long sigh as he reached for the heavens in plea of rescue.

"I'll go with you, JJ," said Eddie.

"Okay. Come on, let's go!"

"Yo! Meeting's going to be at 8:00 a.m. sharp on the festival day. My place. Don't be late, rookies," Miles announced.

Jamal, followed by Eddie, gave their new commander a salute, then reversed course and took flight past Mrs. Dominik through the hallway.

"Bye, boys!" called Jamie from the couch, to whom they cast a wave farewell from sprint.

Miles listened for the front door to crash shut, then returned to his throne, plopped down, and spun back to his mother like a deviant overlord.

"Laziness wins again."

"I think the grass needs a mowin', dear. I'll double-check for you."

Proving Grounds of Fate

With that promise of adventure fresh in their minds, they retreated from the house and stormed back across the street without a care in the world.

They raced up to the front door and stumbled to a halt before the long glass.

"Eddie," said Jamal as he tapped the gifted stone in his hand.

"Oh, yeah," Eddie replied.

The boys concealed the runes within their pockets before Jamal opened the door and led their entry into the shadows. The zesty aroma of seared, seasoned meat on the stovetop greeted them at the door. Jamal's mother stepped out from the kitchen and set upon her little boy a telling, somber gaze.

"JJ, your daddy wants to talk to you," she informed.

He blew past her without reply and made straight for the living room, where he knew his father would be. Eddie slowed as he trailed to the end of the hall once more.

"Hey there, little man! Eddie still with you?"

"Yep, he's right back there. Eddie come out!" his friend called.

He obliged with two steps out into the open.

"You hiding back there, Eddie? Come on over and say hello," the gaunt-faced patriarch requested.

Eddie ran over and stood beside Jamal. "Sorry, Mom said don't bother you while you're sick."

But the man waved off his concern. "Oh, you're not bothering anybody. Y'know, I've been itching to get together with your granddad again and make some of those birdhouses," he declared just before he came under siege by the oppressive fits of cough that had come to plague him.

The birdhouses crafted by Eddie's grandfather and Mr. Vans were beautiful. They were talks of the town. Icons one could find at almost any gathering place, even the parking lot of the extravagant Oasis Mall. Known for their intricate detail and breathtaking design, their works offered hospitality to the annual migration of various species. From sleepy townhouses to wondrous temples of a foreign land, and even fantastic castles, each offered visions of a distant world from the comforts of their little town.

There came footsteps from the kitchen. Behind them, Jamal's mother stepped out into the doorway and crossed her arms as she leaned against the wall.

"You going to talk to him?" she asked.

Jamal's father grumbled. "Let them go out and play. I got all day to do it." He took in a breath to stabilize himself. "And they don't need to be sitting around in the house on such a beautiful day, either. Go on," he concluded as he waved them off with his hand.

Jamal leapt into the air. "*Yes!* Thanks, Dad. Mom really needs to learn a thing or two from you."

Eddie, for the first time since they entered the room, looked up to truly see the man's face, which was pleasantly aglow with a smile. His face was sunken, his eyes tired, strained merely by the effort put forth to look alive.

A flash from the television stole Eddie's attention. Depicted through the subtle flow of the scan lines was a helicopter in takeoff, a ragtag troop marching through a burning town, and the flag of Beilka, aloft against the clouds. Then came footage of a sweaty-faced young soldier with eyes full of horrors and a finger thrown to a blurred mass grave. The title, "Hero General," was emblazoned along the news ticker below the edited playback.

"You see that, down there? Those are kids—rounded up and shot. This is what we deal with every day, and none of you seem to give a . . ."

The recording went silent to safeguard the viewership from his vulgar fury, then returned to the newscaster for proper dissemination of the situation. On split screen was a younger woman in an office, whose navy-uniform exhibited numerous insignias that reflected an impressive service record.

". . . More on this story with someone close to the helm of command. Second Lieutenant Cheryl Rhodes, we understand you've been assigned to the task force involved with managing the crisis. What are your thoughts on the situation as it continues to deteriorate?"

"I believe, as do many of our nation's representatives, that we could be doing a lot more," the lieutenant assessed with tame enthusiasm.

Unbeknownst to Eddie, Jamal, too, had begun to stare at the coverage of the distant conflict. His father noticed the boys' distraction with the horrors on the screen. He shooed them off with his hands.

"Alright, go on. That's enough of that TV."

The boys snapped from their gaze.

"Good to see you again, Eddie. I haven't been able to make any adjustments to the jungle gym, but I'll ask your granddaddy to come help me with it sometime."

Eddie nodded with a smile. And with that, Jamal's father rested his back and closed his eyes.

"Go on," said Jamal's mother. "I'll let you know when it's time to come back in."

Outside, the boys raced for the playset, which was composed of two independent structures, bridged by twin zip lines. There were a pair of stairs on one end, and a pair of slides on the other.

Wood chips made up a soft bed beneath the play area, and upon a small mound underneath one of the slides was the secret box. Jamal led Eddie right to it and dropped into a short skid upon arrival. Eddie took a seat beside him, and the hush of the wind joined them in silence.

His surprise already revealed, Jamal pulled the star from his pocket for Eddie to see in plain sight and blew air into his cheeks, knowing the reaction wouldn't be nearly as exciting. Eddie, nonetheless, grew electrified.

"Where did you find this?" he asked with a glow.

"I found it in the valley one day. I went way out there! Way farther than ever before," he said emphasizing with both hands the great distance he had gone. "I went so far that I should have brought a sword—or like seven of Miles's hero runes!"

Eddie became rapt by his daring tale. He knew just as well as his friend that going far beyond the summit was dangerous. And yet, he had made it back alive. Questions swarmed his head. Why did he decide to go? Was his family worried? Did he go at night? Certainly, not.

However, Eddie knew more than anything that if Jamal had found this out there, then there was no doubt that it was very special indeed.

He took the star in gentle fingers and turned it.

"Wow, it's a real star—like it came down from the sky."

"I know, that's why I wanted to show you," Jamal explained.

They both exchanged glances.

"You think it's real, like really real?" Eddie asked.

Jamal shrugged. "I dunno. I just found it, man. I mean—Miles says it's pretty special, so that's gotta be something, right?"

And he saw the way his friend marveled over the little object, and it gave him a clever idea. "Hey, you can keep it if you want."

Eddie's eyes widened. "Really? I can have it?"

Jamal put his finger on his chin and thought about it to Eddie's suspense. "No! But you can win it in a race if you want it that bad!" Jamal declared.

Eddie leapt up into the air. "Let's race!"

Jamal grabbed the box and stood. "Fork over the star."

Eddie handed it over without hesitation, eager to kick off the competition. Jamal placed the stone back into his pocket.

"Come on, let's get to the start," he ordered.

Together, they took flight past the far end of the playset, then shot between two mounds of mulch from which withered vegetables lingered in the middle. They then arrived before a shed at the end of the yard with chipped green paint.

Just outside of the double doors was a small patch of trampled earth. Eddie sprang around then dropped into a clumsy four-point stance, ready to give it his all. Jamal went right to the shed, pushed off the rickety door, then spun around and walked away.

"Now, listen up. This is an important race, so this time, we're going *through* the pool," he announced as he marched back and forth through the grass like a sergeant.

He stomped over to Eddie, who was still frozen at the ready position.

"Even if we get in trouble."

Eddie nodded in determination. Though he had never defeated his friend in a race, he would never be found disheartened by their friendly competitions.

The first obstacle was the playset that had been built by the dedicated hammer of Jamal's father and Eddie's grandfather over the course of the last two years. Both islands and the zip line would need to be conquered with mastery. There were two slides up the front, and two stairs down the back. Everything that could be enjoyed, could be enjoyed with a friend, which made it the perfect starting point of any of their races.

"Up the slide, over the line, around the rocks, out the gate, past the big tree, through the pool, under the fence, around the red top twice, up the ramp, through the back way, and out to the sidewalk to finish," said Jamal, counting them off with his fingers and finishing with an X shape slash with his arms.

"I know, I know," Eddie insisted.

Jamal stepped next to his opponent and lifted the star high into the air. "For the wishing star, the ultimate *race!*"

He set the star into his pocket, then sank down into a clumsy but fierce split stance.

"Ready."

They both got lower.

"Set. Go!" shouted Jamal.

The boys launched onto the tips of their toes down the middle of the garden. Their shoes shook the slides as they made an impact and ascended to the very top.

Nearly neck and neck, they raced to the handles of the zip line, seized hold, then leapt out.

Jamal slung his weight with the swoop of his legs. The maneuver shot him out in front of Eddie, who stumbled to find his balance at first. The mismanaged weight caused a grind upon his launch which ate away at his gathered momentum. The underdog's grasp on the iron bar began to weaken as his fingers were subjected to a burn. The slight discomfort caused him to release the bar, and he landed among the wood chips. Jamal meanwhile landed out in front, went to the very end, and leapt across the steps at full speed.

"Come on and keep up, slowpoke," Jamal shouted to Eddie as he crossed under the rest of the playset to catch back up.

He passed the steps to the bottom just as Jamal had started around the tree which sat in the middle of a rock garden skirt. A few irregular stones moved beneath his weight, but he managed to strike with balance each time.

Just behind him, Eddie started over the rock bed with graceless footing. He felt a jolt as his foot collapsed into gaps between the stones. Without much wasted time, he freed his foot and pushed on ahead. Now, a little further behind.

Both boys wrapped the tree, with Jamal in the lead and Eddie right behind. They left the rocky terrain for the grassy yard, which ended at the gates to the front driveway.

Jamal threw out his arms and delivered a mighty shove to the doors, which sent them flying out on each side. Eddie felt a rush of anxiety as the right-hand door slammed against the side of the house with a mighty crash followed by raucous vibrations. But with no immediate authority to slow them, he chased the flapping shirt of his friend, not too far out in front of him.

Jamal cut into Eddie's yard as soon as he was about halfway down the driveway. Eddie followed in his tracks.

The favored attacked each root of the big tree, using them like springs to edge himself farther out in front, while Eddie tried to emulate the same movement.

Upon reaching the driveway of Eddie's house, they were greeted by an open gate. The pool lay smack at the center of the yard, and though its circumference would be easily manageable, the only way to win was through it.

The staircase to the top deck lay further left. Jamal stayed his path, however, and went right for the newly installed solar panels of which the far edges were aligned with the top of the pool. Eddie knew without question that it was there he had taken aim. Free of hesitation, he focused and readied himself to jump.

They were past the gate. Jamal went right for the panels as anticipated, Eddie right behind him.

"Hope you practiced your doggie paddle, slowpoke!" Jamal taunted.

Eddie's mind didn't wander, however. He remained dialed in, letting his subconscious remember the motions. One after the other they rose up the glimmering plane, shot off the top, then plunged into the icy water.

The surface became rapids as both boys threw their arms forward in an explosive crawl to the other side. The only ladder from the pool lay right between them. Eddie took aim for it while Jamal went for the edge, grabbed ahold of it, and pulled himself atop the narrow wall.

Eddie seized hold of the silver arm just in time to see Jamal wave goodbye. His agile friend pushed from the ledge, landed upon the ground, and took off for the fence.

Desperate to catch up, Eddie leapt up, skipping a few steps to the top in one jump. Against the fear in his heart, he pushed from the top and plummeted to the ground.

His bravery paid off as he struck with feet in good form and sprung off toward Jamal, who had gone right for a panel marked by chalk scribbles. He went low, put his hands out, and popped back the entire thing, then squeezed through.

Eddie took off after him, dropped into a slide, and pushed through the panel. They had arrived together, in the little park behind Emerald Street. He recaptured Jamal in his sights and lifted back into full speed as his opponent neared the roundabout at the heart of the park. At a tree on the outskirts of the grassy flat, a lone white dog with pointed ears became roused by the commotion.

Jamal latched his arm onto the red playground spinner, and it began to whirl. He laughed as Eddie pushed through fatigue with long gasps of breath. Upon arrival, he grabbed ahold of the bar just across from Jamal, and together they whipped around and around, nearly forgetting the rules of their race.

The boys both released their grip and tumbled back across the ground. They rose with victory still in their hearts but balance lost from their feet. They stumbled here and there before their equilibrium was reset and the race could continue in earnest.

They were off for the final leg of the course, a rock-congested dirt corridor between Eddie's fence and the neighbor's.

The white dog let out a flurry of yelps, then cut after them through the grass.

"Oh, crap, it's Sid!" Jamal warned, as he peered back over his shoulder.

Eddie peeked over his shoulder and gasped at the impassioned mutt.

They flew with the assistance of newborn adrenaline as the dog made incredible gains on them. Before they could reach the first stone, their furry pursuer was running alongside them with its tongue out in the wind.

Jamal entered the corridor, followed by the energetic canine, Eddie right behind them. The path dipped down into a gulch between the wooden fences. The rocky terrain beneath their feet made for a challenge of balance as a glimpse of the finish line appeared right beyond the big rock, which was laid against the Bowitz's fence.

At the bottom, Jamal's rapid advance was brought to a halt as he was forced to squeeze his body through the tight quarters, with toes pointed out to each side. The dog meanwhile hopped and buried its nose between the rock and his leg, hurrying him through for its own passage.

In the few moments after he passed it, the dog rushed through. Eddie maneuvered carefully through the rocks under foot, slowed by instinct developed from past injury through the pass, eventually making it to the rock and slipping easily through.

Jamal crossed into the front yard of Eddie's house, the dog still running closely at his side. As he slowed into a sloppy hustle, he misplaced his step. He caught the dog's hind leg and found himself launched forward with both hands out to rescue himself.

The dog skimped along as Eddie slowed, then collapsed to the ground in exaggerated exhaustion. He had lost.

"Get off me, Sid!" ordered Jamal as he waved away the dog which had sat right next to his head.

Eddie turned on his back and looked up just in time to receive a lick across the face from the dog, who had begun to whine in distress from their actions.

He shook his head and covered his face with his hands until the furry runner-up went and lay down in the grass, panting in the summer sun.

Jamal had risen and approached him, the exhilaration of a victor on his face.

"Got you again! But you did pretty good," Jamal encouraged.

"Yeah, walking on the rocks isn't easy."

"You would have done better if Sid didn't get in the way," he said with a turn to the dog, which lay panting, looking around as if ignorant of any wrongdoing.

He sighed, somewhat glad to hear such nice words from his friend, yet drained nonetheless from his inability to claim victory.

Jamal dug around in his pocket until he produced in his hand the star-shaped treasure. Without hesitation, he presented it to his defeated friend.

"Here. Even though you didn't win, go ahead and take it."

Eddie turned almost immediately and lifted himself off the ground. "Really? Why?"

Jamal shrugged. "You really like it, don't you? It's a friend deal. We can race for it again later."

Eddie hesitated for a moment but didn't know why, then took that precious trinket for the first time in his own hands and felt an overwhelming joy.

"Wow . . . thanks. Yeah! We'll race again for it next time."

Jamal nodded in agreement.

"So, make a wish with it tonight and see if it works," Jamal suggested.

Eddie nodded. "Okay, but I don't know what to wish for."

"Oh, I know! Wish for—"

"Jamal! What the hell are you doing out here? And why are you wet?"

A cold shiver ran through the boys' spine at once.

"Mom, it was Sid—"

"Don't even try to blame it on the dog again, JJ. It won't work."

Jamal's mother had come over with great speed, and her son retreated a step back as she came to a stop in front of them.

"Say goodbye. You're going inside now," she said.

Jamal threw his head up in the air as his shoulders sank.

"Bye, Eddie. Let me know how your wish goes. I know what I would wish for, right now," he said angrily, then marched over to his mother who greeted him by grabbing his arm.

"And I'll tell you what I would wish for. A boy who doesn't run out the backdoor every other Thursday. Now, come on."

Eddie watched them until they disappeared beyond the corner. In the distance, a man bellowed out the dog's name. It rose and departed with haste back through the corridor to the park, and Eddie was left alone.

He peered down on the star in his hands, then up into the sky.

What would come of a wish to the stars?

The Road to Nowhere

In the early morning of the next day, the golden rays brought the vibrance of the summertime across the little town. The green grass glowed, the dew of dawn gleamed like dreamy stars in daylight, and a gentle wind from the valley set the trees into sway.

The rumble of the lawnmower in the backyard brought Eddie from sleep. His eyes opened, and his consciousness was taken at once by the allure of the wishing star. He rose, pushed off the bed, and planted with a thud. The star lay upon the wooden desk, whose burgundy wood was made rich by the light of the sun.

The boy inspected the star for a moment and then peered out of the window. His mind was still. Neither fantasy nor wonder flourished as he watched the glow of sunrise, something of magic in itself. It filled him with enthusiasm for the day ahead. He would make this one unlike any before or any after.

The boy took the white plastic handle of the window and slid it open. Through the screen, the grace of the winds swept across his cheek and the fragrance of the cut grass filled him. Near the tree, his father pushed the red mower across the next line of grass. The long strands had nearly been tamed, but he came to a stop and released the handle. With a wipe across his brow, he stepped away toward the house and left the yard to the tranquil sounds of morning.

The boy laid his arms across the windowsill and buried his chin into his slender forearm. He took a moment to relish in the rustle of leaves and the song of birds. A congregation of rosy-cheeked singers were perched upon the back fence, along which were four birdhouses.

Each one was a product of the collaboration. Mr. Vans would meet at Victor Bowitz's workshop, which lay hidden away at the end of a hallway beneath the attic steps. It was once a yearly project for them. Jamal and Eddie, though entirely disengaged with each production, often sat beyond the door and watched them work their craft until their interest was exhausted.

Among those creations along the fence was a golden craftwork that had watched over the backyard for as long as he could remember. It was a brilliant ring perch, with four dangling keys frozen in a timeless wind. Secured on two inhibitor rods was an extended wood branch, which offered a simple respite to winged travelers. Welded at the center of the ring was a bird crafted from gilded metal sheet, its wings outstretched and eyes closed as it lifted an impassioned serenade to the morning.

It had always been his favorite. For in that bird, he felt something of a connection. It was an unexplainable bond. Perhaps, simply curiosity for another who had a message, a message seemingly lost to the ears of the contemporary, yet with an answer surely out there. It just had to be sought out. He was quite certain of that.

There came a knock. The boy turned over his shoulder and found his grandfather in the doorway. He stood in a light brown jacket and his favorite wool newsboy hat as if he had already been out.

"Hey, kiddo. Glad to see you're up and at 'em," he said.

The boy nodded, then turned back to the window.

"The other birds are on the gold one."

"The gold one? The perch?" his grandfather asked.

He approached the window and stood next to the boy with his hands dug into his pockets.

"Well, look at that. You know, I made that perch years ago when your father was only a little older than you. It was made in memory of a special bird, who sang a special song. It would come in the morning, as the honey doves do, and sing to the sunrise, and come back again at night to coo to the moon."

The old man smiled as he looked back on those fond memories. "Yeah, it would come to sing on my old wooden perch that's long gone now."

"Why was he special, though?" the boy asked.

"In the summertime, year after year, the same honey dove would return to my old perch, the first one I ever made. It would reach out its wings and sing with all its heart—every single day. And his songs were quite a performance!"

"Why did he do that?"

"I'm not sure. Perhaps, that's what made it happy. The same way it might for any one of us."

"What happened to him? Did you keep him?"

The old man sighed in a calm remorse. A truth well hidden from the boy's perception.

"Well, that's him. He's made of gold, now, and he sings that beautiful and unique song forever in memories, Eddie."

Those words made the boy ponder. Though he had never heard the bird's song, he conjured up a melody in his head to reflect what it might have sounded like. That would have to do, at least for now.

"Tell you what, how about I take you on an adventure today?" the old man asked with a grin, sure that it would spark the boy's interest.

Little Eddie blossomed with excitement.

"Really!? Where?"

"If you hurry up and get ready, I'll tell you," his grandfather teased as he stepped away from the window and departed the room.

As Eddie rushed to make ready for the sudden excursion, his grandfather returned to the kitchen, maneuvered around a few paint trays filled with murky water, and sat at the table. Mr. Bowitz lie crouched under the sink while his visibly frustrated wife stood above with one hand pressed onto the counter.

"I'm telling you, it's probably just clogged," she asserted.

"It's not clogged. The whole piece is rusted out. I'll just have to run to the store and pick up a replacement," his father grumbled.

"I'm gonna take the boy out to the park," the old man said.

There was a bang from under the sink. Mr. Bowitz pulled himself out, his face red with contained fury.

"Weren't you going to help me replace the bad shingles on the roof today?" he pressed.

"We're not going to be gone the entire day. It's just something to keep him active. Maybe meet some new friends."

"Today was about getting things ready around the house," Mr. Bowitz interrupted. "The festival is three days away. There's plenty of opportunity to have fun when the work is done."

"Alright, honey. Calm down. I will help you with the housework if you need to leave for the store."

"Fine!" Eddie's father snapped. "You're going to the park? Go on, then. We'll take care of everything."

Mr. Bowitz returned beneath the sink to continue the removal of the pipe.

"Just remember, son. The iron's always hot. If you know that's true, then all you need is the strength."

The old man turned without a word more to say. With a deep grimace, he stepped through the kitchen and went out the front door. Mrs. Bowitz looked down at the man hidden beneath the sink and shook her head.

"Why are you so testy with your dad lately? He just wants to be a part of your son's life."

"It's just not the same man who raised me, Rachael. No matter what he says," Mr. Bowitz strained as he worked to remove the piece.

It wasn't long after that the boy emerged from the house. He found his grandfather by the big tree, peering out at something deep within the forest at the road's end.

As Eddie made his way over on a spirited run, his father looked out at him through the window of the kitchen. In his eyes was the longing of a boy, buried beneath the build of a man. Opportunity lay there in the moment, and it wouldn't wait for him or anyone else for long.

He offered a nod in silent acknowledgment of that truth. One often lay before him. With much work ahead, he stepped away and left them on their adventure.

"Are you ready for some real adventure, kiddo?" his grandpa asked with a glow.

The boy swelled with excitement. "Yeah! Where are we going?" he asked.

"We're going to the park, of course!"

The boy cocked his head, the excitement sapped from his heart. "The park? That's not that far away!" the boy declared.

The old man knelt on the last legs of his faux youth. "But we're going to the park on the far side," he clarified.

Awe filled the void left behind. He had only been to the park across town once before. Even with his mighty adventurous heart, he had never dared to venture there alone. It lay beyond a bridge over the freeway, in an area of open, undeveloped grassland.

The boy's expression was the only answer his grandfather needed. He began across the yard to the sidewalk.

The boy gave chase.

"It's gonna take us forever to get there," the boy cried as he bounced along.

"About thirty to thirty-five minutes if you keep up," his grandfather teased.

"I can keep up," he assured. "I've been there before."

"Well, tell me, boy. What do you know of the Far Side Road?"

"The Nowhere's Road?"

"No, the Far Side Road. They are not the same," his grandfather assured.

The boy pondered.

"Well . . . it was once the only road into town, a road many adventurers like yourself would take to the hillside of Somairsville. They called this place paradise; it's a land bathed in the sanctity of the sun," the old man explained.

They came upon a stick on the lawn beside the road. Inspired by the legend, the boy took up the crisp twig and held it like a sword.

"Adventurers like me?" he asked as he took swipes at the air, which caused the old man chuckle at his harmless valor.

"That's right! I reckon nobody's traveled that particular old road for hundreds and hundreds of years. Nowadays, the freeway can take you anywhere your heart desires, and the old road is immortalized by the Road to Nowhere."

He chuckled. "More young people these days leave Somairsville to find a new life, especially in big Salamandra City. So, guess you could say things have changed around here. Not so much paradise to many people anymore."

"So, is there any real adventure here, grandpa?" the boy investigated, his trust invested in the old man's answer.

"Maybe it's here. Maybe it's there. That's for us to figure out. The spirit of the adventurer is our guide today!" he stressed.

The boy needed no further motivation to heed the call. Like the missing ingredient in the magic brew, his inner sense became an explosion of vibrant visions of the hidden beyond.

Knee-high stone barriers rose and fell alongside the path. The boy leapt onto them and traced his steps alongside his grandfather as he continued his stories of the times before his service to the Union.

Before long, the sidewalk led them to the main artery of the town, Sol Road. It was lined end to end with two-story brick homes with modest yards; lush green was protected by code enforcement. The streetlights there stood draped with flags that depicted a vector sun, a telltale sign that the summer festival was just around the corner.

The road dove through a residential valley then reached back up to the distant shopping district on the other side of town. There stood a galleria unlike any other for miles, a hallmark of the town of Somairsville. A central hub, whose sheer magnificence was only matched by the grace of the hills.

Its smooth, sandy walls towered high and boasted lush, regal splendor in broad daylight and a distinctive elegance by evening, as its lavish hanging gardens came to life in the glow of spotlights. Though relatively small, the entire structure was mirrored to architectural perfection across the freeway.

Those lavish bastions were bonded by both a suspended black-glass breezeway and a gold-tinted observation deck above it, the latter of which could only be accessed from two elevator towers. That golden crown hosted a coffee house by day and a steakhouse by night, along with a posh lounge with a panoramic view, each amenity available for those who could afford the extravagant membership fee.

To long-distance travelers on the highway, it was but a mysterious abstract shrine; the remote luxuriousness of The Oasis had become a fascination to those who passed through and popularized journeys to that obscure temple of capitalism. Although daunting, the towering doors into that utopian bazaar stood open to the masses, yet exclusive.

On the way down, the boy trotted along with the push of gravity as his grandfather paced behind. The morning sunbeams offered a reinvigorating warmth against the occasional brisk gale, which made the boy hug himself each time to ward off its icy embrace.

They soon rounded through the bottom of the bell, whose bumpy lands offered space for a few small shops and a tall cathedral, which lay nestled in green across the street. They passed the old floral shoppe first, whose front entrance lay congested with hanging black pots, overflowed with the blossoms of imminent summer. Beneath them was a table lined with long-stemmed beauties lovingly organized in a variety of stylish pots.

Though it tempted the eyes of children with kites on each corner, Eddie knew better than to enter. For Miles had warned them only a short while ago that if you entered upon the pink and black tiles of the floral shoppe, you may never return. A warning delivered straight from the mouth of the sage's wise father, a jovial man who was known as a master of the sleight of hand when it came to whoopee cushions, fake spiders, and rubber snakes.

Next, they passed the town bike shop. The sectional garage door was pulled halfway up, though neither the shopkeeper nor his careless teenage son were anywhere to be seen. Eddie peered beneath and got a glimpse of the bottom half of a few red bikes in the penumbra. The old man refocused his curious grandson on the path forward, and it wasn't long before they had reached the top and arrived before the mirage.

Centralized upon a triangular median across the road was a sun-shaped slab, which accommodated a sundial forged from the same sandy stone as The Oasis. Though it was but a walk away, the galleria was beyond financial reach for the Bowitz family. It was a trip taken only on a rare occasion, when such spending could be justified for an anniversary or an extra-special New Year's celebration gift. For their season-to-season necessities, Big Ted's Supercenter offered alternatives at fractional prices.

Eddie squinted across the street to distant shimmers as the sunny rays gave birth to a riverlike mirage along the black concrete. The melt of easy jazz wafted in the distance from speakers in the sparsely filled parking lot, which provided an eerie ambience to their journey across town. It was a fuzzy drift that Eddie found a little too uncanny to be fascinated with.

"Almost there now, kiddo. Just a walk past the mall." The old man pointed to the distant end of the sidewalk. "Look there. You see it?"

The boy nodded as he caught a glimpse of the bridge which connected the town to the verdant outskirts across the freeway. As they reached the end of that final stretch, the old man took his giddy companion's hand.

A splendid fountain, built into the corner of the intersection, had come into view on their right. An entryway flair for the side entrance of the mall, the ground rose to a point over a glittery pool. Both sides of that sharp rise were padded up by wooden planks, which gave it the appearance of the bow of a ship. Affixed near the top was a marvelous figurehead of three golden swordfish in breach; the heavenly bodies attributed to that gilded sparkle in the water.

They began their journey over the white-striped crosswalk to the far side, then began over the bridge.

Beyond two stone guardians on the other side of the bridge, the road cut into the plains, then swung up into the sky. Beyond that lonely peak between the hills, however, it was left incomplete after the first of two supports and lay guarded by two concrete roadblocks.

"There it is. The Road to Nowhere. That wasn't too bad a trip, now was it? We get to see it one last time before Mayor Hillenburg comes in with his big ol' bulldozer and tears it down."

"Why are they gonna tear it down, Grandpa?" the boy asked as he swung out against the old man's grasp.

"Well, they're going to build a great big hotel for the mall and a lot of other fun stuff. Maybe they'll build an amusement park with a buncha big, superfast roller coasters, too!" he said with a fierce whoosh and dive of his hand.

"Really!? You think so?"

"Nothing wrong with dreaming!" his grandfather said, with which the electrified boy nodded in agreement.

The adventurous duo passed between the two pedestals that guarded the road into Somairsville. Upon them were two fair maidens of stone, who, from a kneel, peeked with innocent smiles behind propped colossal suns, whose surfaces lay carved with intricate tribal zigzags. Twin radiance which, in legend, blinded foreigners with the sheer magnificence of the land of the golden sun.

The newly finished Far Side Park was just before that forgotten route. There were two stone-pillared picnic shelters near the foot of the rubber land, upon which an impressive playground was situated.

It was well equipped, packed to the far edge with every sort of bridge, bar, swing, and slide. They wound and twisted in such a dynamic flow that it was difficult to see through to the other side, the perfect kind of chaos that spurred excitement in the heart of every child.

But on that breezy day, it was empty, and an aura of melancholy was left in the absence of the raucous of youth. The boy, nonetheless, raced off to it with the permission of his grandfather. The old man, temporarily relieved of entertaining duties, went over to a nearby plastic-coated bench and took a seat.

The boy played there until the sun had reached into the other side of the sky, and the rays began to wane through passing clouds.

Eddie went to the helm of a pirate ship, which was on an eternal course to sail directly upon the bench on which his grandfather sat. He pulled himself to the guarded edge and peered off below. Down in the rubber sea, the hull was circled by two blue sharks.

The boy fled to the wheel and seized it with both hands, then flung it into a chaotic whirl. He let out a shriek of excitement as it wobbled on the spindle. In his imagination, a little more force might have broken it right off.

As the wheel relaxed into a smooth spin, the distant infrastructural brink stole his attention. From there he could see the edge, the pavement, and the very first pilaster of many that would never be.

It wouldn't take him long to reach it, he thought. Though it was haunting, the feeling of standing up there would surely be incredible, that strange gateway to another world. He became mesmerized by fantasies of where it might take him, a plane of light extending far off into the distance.

That which lay beyond the reality, close yet very far away.

His eyes fell upon his grandfather, who sat with silent tranquility. He waved in frantic jubilance, but the old man remained fixed upon the sky. Eddie raised his eyes too but saw nothing but clouds and endless blue. He searched all around the heavens but found nothing at all.

Taken by intrigue, the boy spirited back across a string of bridges that connected the colorful playsets toward a yellow slide at the end. He jumped, dropped through the spiral tube, and crawled to a halt at the lip. Exhausted, he made his return over the hot rubber mound, which emitted breaths of heat under foot.

Upon arrival, he pulled himself onto the bench and took a seat beside his grandfather, who still gazed up at something high above in the great blue.

"Well, look there. Did you see the light flicker right over there beyond the edge of the moon?" asked his grandfather as he raised his finger.

Eddie peered up in hopes of catching a glimpse, but he saw no such shining beyond the moon or anywhere near it. The old man chuckled at the boy's dedicated eyes.

"Aw, don't worry, kiddo," the old man encouraged as the boy's eyes fell upon the world. "If you've ever seen the sparking moon, then you know . . . the magic lies in the eyes of the beholder. Matter of fact, let me tell you about something rather mythical, boy," his grandfather said as he got shoulder to shoulder with him.

The boy looked to him and perked up his ears, never failing to be spurred to the heart by myth and legend.

"Back a long, long time ago, when I was about your size, I used to go hunting for things all over the place. Why, I'd go hunting for relics and treasures buried under the land of Great Granddad's farm."

"Just like me?"

"Just like you," the man confirmed. "But because I had to work all day, I had to do my treasure hunting at night," the old man stressed.

The boy gritted his teeth and froze up in an overdramatic display of fear.

"That's right. And one night, when I was out looking for things, I looked up to the sky, and do you know what I saw?"

"Stars, right?"

"Not just any star. A star brighter than any other. Shining so brilliantly that I couldn't take my eyes off it."

"It was special?" the boy said, gawking, his mind enchanted by the mystique of their precious star of stone.

"As I watched, it fell from the sky so beautifully that I never wanted to take my eyes off it. If I could, I would have watched until it hit the ground, then maybe I would go adventuring for years just to find it again."

"Did you go get it!?" the boy asked as the combustive foundations of his imagination were sparked, and he erupted into a bonfire of excitement.

But his grandfather cocked his head in wordless acknowledgment that it hadn't been the case.

"Well, I had to go to sleep, eventually. So, I went home. Then, I got up and worked all day, had dinner—but before I went to bed that night, I went out in hopes that I would see it again."

The old man seemed to stare as if he gazed right into the memory itself.

"I snuck out. Went out right into the middle of the field, and when I looked up, it was gone."

"Don't stars all look the same, though? Maybe it was there and you just didn't notice."

The old man shook his head. "No, I don't think so. But I wanted to tell you that story. Who knows! Maybe you'll find it someday!" the old man joked.

"Didn't you tell Great Granddad about it?"

The old man shook his head again. "No, he wasn't interested in such things. Maybe, he was at some point. But I'll never know."

The boy mulled something over in his head. "That thing you saw, did it look like this?" Eddie asked as he produced the wishing star from his pocket.

And the old man looked down upon it with a determined squint. The boy lifted it up to his grandfather, who received it with care and respect deserving of such a treasure.

"My! Would ya look at that?"

"JJ gave it to me. It's his special star. I didn't find it," he said.

The old man's smile bloomed upon hearing of the act of friendship between them. "Well, that's no ordinary gift, now, is it?"

He saw the way the boy looked up at the star and knew from his gaze alone that he sought deeper meaning in it.

"If you could put one wish out into the stars right now, do you know what it would be, Eddie?"

There had to be a million things he would wish for, but the idea of choosing just one was too overwhelming.

"I don't know! What would you wish for, Grandpa?" he asked, in search of guidance.

The old man chuckled as he shook his head. "You have to figure that out for yourself. Nobody else can do it for you. Don't you know the rules of the wishing star!?" he asked with a raised brow in hopes to stir the boy's imagination.

"Okay!"

The old man returned the stone to Eddie, who then leapt from the bench and walked over to the roadside. His mind spiraled, lost without direction. Like the monument to adventure before him, the answer lay far beyond his reach.

Yet, a journey to find an answer to his questions tempted him. Though how long he would have to go to find that answer, he was unsure. They lay beyond the valley, through the forest, and at the road's end, all beyond a boy's reach.

But he closed his eyes, and his mind took him there, beyond the obstacles which parted him from the world waiting on the other side of time. The veteran adventurer stepped to his side and looked upon the same road with a stern glimmer of wisdom in his eye.

"Remember: nowhere is anywhere. Nowhere is everywhere."

The boy turned to him. "What's that mean?"

"Go find out someday, kid," his grandfather said with a grin.

Eddie stared, burdened by the task.

"Would ya?" the old man pressed.

The boy nodded with fierce resolve.

"I can do it. I want to see all kinds of stuff, someday," he declared.

"Good. Then, give me your star for the day. I'll take it to my shop and make it last forever."

"What!? Forever? Really?" said the boy, taken aback.

"That's right, forever. So you and your friend can have it wherever you go, for as long as you live. And just like my special bird, you never stop doing your best in everything you do, alright?"

The boy nodded.

"You promise?"

Little Eddie's eyes fell upon the wishing star in his hand. "I promise," the boy assured.

"And remember, boy: What we choose to believe in is most powerful of all. Don't, in a day in your long life, ever forget that."

"Yes sir, Captain!" the boy said with a salute.

A Whisper Through the Winds of Somairsville

Almost as soon as they had returned, Eddie's grandfather committed himself to the workshop to forge the promised guard. It was a humble nook with the remnant trim of cheap carpet and foam padding along the perimeter of the bare concrete. A workshop made right from the craftsman's bench, there were silvery shelves which spanned the wall and hosted holders forged from scrap metal, cables, and several sheet metal trays with a broad assortment of cable lugs, nozzles, and plugs, among other utilities for his work.

The workspace was neatly kept, organized by the master's keen mind and dedicated hand. On a shelf just beside the bench was a metal-cutting band saw, the welding machine, and ten pristine steel prisms with a diamond on each end.

At the far end of the shop was the last wooden object left from the neighborhood duo's collaborations: an unassuming broom stick, shaved neatly down, and a brush head fastened by screw. It lay against the brick wall just beneath a window with corners sown with cobwebs, easily detectable from the light of noon that pierced the big tree's canopy.

The boy would meander down the corridor just beside the front door to the bolted access, where the sound of sparks entertained. He would inevitably grow bored again and rise from the single step and retreat back to his room in search of a way to burn away the time.

His father, who had finished with his tasks in the yard before work, stepped back into the living room and took notice of the boy's ins and outs. He stood there as he wiped the sweat from his brow with a rag, the time for his departure growing ever closer. Something caused him to linger, however. Whether it was due to the mounting weight of criticism or the burden of fatherhood, he knew only that he wished to understand, and today, if only for the mere sake of the festival around the bend, he wouldn't let himself get in the way.

As the boy raced around toward his room once more, he called out to inquire about the source of his anxiousness.

"What's got you all wound-up today, Ed?"

The boy slid on his white socks across the carpet to bring himself to a halt.

"Grandpa is making a super special wishing star for me and JJ," he exclaimed as he rushed back over.

"Is he? Sounds pretty neat!" he replied as the boy made a pass around him, then sped back for his room, and cut back into the doorway.

Left alone, Eddie's father passed a glance at the clock on the wall above the sofa. Time rushed him forward. He knew an unsatisfactory future awaited him if he failed to take action, and so, with that harsh fate in mind, the mindful engineer went to the workshop to investigate.

Mr. Bowitz struck the door twice, and the sound of sparks fell to silence. After a slam and a shuffle, the bolt was pulled, and the door swung open. He came face-to-face with the red-faced craftsman in his black apron and gloves who was visibly bothered to be interrupted during his work.

"Yeah, what is it?"

"Hey! The boy mentioned you were making something with his stone."

"Oh, you found out about that? Yeah, I'm putting a little edge guard on it. It's just a rock, so I figure it would make it a bit nicer . . . and I'll throw on a string hoop to make it easy to keep up with."

Eddie's father nodded, although he struggled to express the motive behind his visit to the workshop.

"Well, you probably have to get to work. I don't want to keep you up," the old man said with a turn and nonchalant wave.

"No—Dad, it's fine. I'd like to help if you wouldn't mind."

And the craftsman turned over his shoulder, flabbergasted by this unusual gesture, though it was nothing but welcome.

"Well, alright, then. Grab a helmet, apron, and gloves and let's get to it."

And so, both father and son set about the task of crafting a worthy barrier to safeguard that precious stone. Hours later, their work would be complete, and the gem of their labor was ready to be bestowed. They assembled with the boy in the living room and handed over childhood's reborn crown jewel. With the forerunner stone fixed at the center, the relic was well guarded for their harshest adventures to come. As Eddie's father put his little hand through the blue ribbon, the boy felt ready to take on the world beyond the most distant valley.

"Wow! Wait until *JJ* sees this!"

With spirit electrified by the gift of their cooperation, the boy departed the house into the backyard to cast it up to the skies in celebration. The two engineers of his elation watched with muted pride as he took flight across the grass, living the life a boy should.

"Well, I better go endure the wrath of Mr. Duwall. I know he's not going to be happy with me."

His father snickered and shook his head but complimented him with a pat on the shoulder.

"You did good. Don't let anything take that away from you, son."

The rest of the day, Eddie was captivated by its glory. He tasked himself for the remainder of the afternoon in assorting rock from the flowerbed at the corner of the fence to raise a monument to the wishing star's grace. His grandfather had meanwhile kicked up his feet in front of the TV in the living room, resting off the busy day.

Tucked into the thick cushions of a small couch along the back wall of the room was Uncle Andy, the frail brother of Eddie's grandfather. Never married and forever scowling beneath a bushy mustache, he was an expected visitor around the festival season, though he was often keen to voice his discontent with the jubilation. With a skeptical glare, fierce upon the newscaster on the television, he quietly sipped from his coffee mug.

Mrs. Bowitz emerged from down the hallway and stopped in the living room. She too, became fixated on the television.

"Once more, the Union Space Administration is verifying recent reports of bizarre cosmic events. Similar reports coming to us not only from Union institutions, but also from Beilka, several Beilkan satellite states, along with officials involved in JSEP, the Joint Space Exploration Program, which heads the Maris Mons test facility. All of the officials we've talked to are telling us there's no need for any alarm, however, as these events are a few hundred million lightyears from home."

The door to the backyard burst open, and little Eddie came stumbling in.

"It's almost done!" he shouted in glee.

"Shh. Quiet, Eddie. We're trying to listen to the news," said Uncle Andy as he threw his arm out to shoo him.

"Concern was originally raised two years ago when the phenomenon of a 'moving star' began frequenting the night sky, but only now are we witnessing an apparent galactic collapse in a system that had no observed supergiants within age to achieve supernova capability."

"Whoa. Did you hear that, Grandpa?"

"Eddie, go outside and play," his mother ordered.

The boy spun around and burst back through the door.

"And what did I tell you about the door, Ed?" she yelled after him, then returned her attention to the television.

"Scientists believe there has been some sort of unprecedented gravitational event but are still unsure of the exact cause. We'll be keeping you posted as new information is released. They're assuring us they have a close eye on the night sky. Back to you, Chris."

"The universe continues to be an extraordinary place where extraordinary things happen, folks."

"Bah. A buncha straight malarkey. Telescopes probably malfunctioned," Uncle Andy mocked.

"It's no lie," his bone-tired brother replied.

"Come on, Al. Give me break."

"I know because I've seen it, Andy," said Eddie's grandfather as his eyes cracked just enough to see his brother's concern.

Uncle Andy spread in a wide grin, and he leaned in toward him.

"You're saying you've seen an entire universe disappear into *thin air?*" he asked, then threw his arms up to spur a semblance of common sense.

The old man didn't budge.

"We were on the central front. Three hundred and forty miles outside of the City of Fortune—nothing but rock, dust, and venomous snakes. Just beyond the Fehrerbanti. Their turf. They had hit us early in the morning, sent trucks loaded with explosives right through the camp. I was ordered night watch later that same day. After about a few hours of milling around, waiting maybe to die, I looked up, and I saw a glimmer at the edge of the moon."

"It was the shockwave," his brother interrupted.

"And I don't know how long I looked at it, but it wasn't like the light of a star, that constant beam, or the streak from a meteorite."

The old man lifted his hands and began an odd pattern of opening and closing them.

"It flashed just like this."

Both Uncle Andy and Rachael Bowitz looked at the old man in his trance with great unease.

"Then it was gone, Andy."

"It was the damn shockwave."

"But that wasn't the first time I had seen it. No. The first time was right up there," the old soldier enlightened, his finger pointed in the direction of the hillside. "When we were just boys. You didn't do your homework, so you stayed in the house with Ma."

Uncle Andy shuffled in his worn nylon construction company jacket as great unease swept over him.

"That time, *I* saw it," Victor said, putting his old finger into his chest. "And Dad saw it."

He redirected that finger to a colorless photograph over the fireplace of an aged man in Union military uniform. The lieutenant's smile, so faint that, at a glance, it might come off as an emotionless stare.

"And you know just as I do what kind of man Dad was," Victor Bowitz said. Uncle Andy shook from the mental haze that had begun to cloud him. "They said it was a *moving star*. So, you're not talking about the same thing anyway," Uncle Andy replied.

"Andy . . ." Victor said.

Before he could speak further, Uncle Andy threw out a hand to silence him. "No, I've heard enough about it," Andy said. "I'm telling you, the older you get, the more that war has weighed down on your head. You've got to drop all the mumbo jumbo you spew around people, especially Eddie."

"Oh, he's just a boy," Rachael Bowitz said.

"But Rachael, don't you see him with that rock he's got? Who do you think he got it from?" asked Uncle Andy.

"He got it from little JJ next door just a few days ago," she corrected.

Uncle Andy leaned back and shook his head at his brother, who simply looked back with tired eyes.

"But who threw on a metal frame and attached a ribbon for him? He's trying to add value to complete rubble," he strained.

"He's just a boy, Andy. He'll grow out of it, for heaven's sake."

Rachael Bowitz went to the screen door and passed through to the backyard, leaving the two brothers behind. Silence set in between them, and Eddie's grandfather's eyes slowly closed shut once more as he slipped into a deep slumber.

A mother's hawkish eye caught her son at the corner of the fence with his odd rock formation. The boy turned and saw her. Then, in a panic, lifted a final hefty rock to the top of a stack to complete his third pillar, symmetrically situated around the wishing star, which lay upon a centered slab. His mother passed around the pool and panel to get a better look, not quite sure what she was looking at.

"Eddie, what is all this? Dear, you need to clean this all up. You know your father hates it when you move all the garden stones around."

"But mom, this is the *temple*. I can't just tear it down," the boy insisted.

"The what?" his mother asked, perplexed. She stood there, pondering what to do. "Well, as long as you explain what you're doing to your father, I'm sure he'll be fine."

The boy pumped his arm in celebration and carried on with perfecting the layout of his makeshift structure. His mother folded her arms as her mind began to drift back to the words of her father-in-law. And the longer her mind lingered there, the more her head began to tip back until she gazed up into the sky.

The sun had nearly fallen over the western hills, which left the sky blanketed in a deepened blue veil. A hundred thousand twinkling eyes gazed back at her, and her eyes began to jump around in search of a sign. And although they were all but stars, she became overwhelmed by a feeling that couldn't be shaken off. The feeling that she and her son were sharing their company with a foreign presence. One that was neither good nor evil, yet lurked, emotionlessly at the far corner of oblivion.

So very far away, yet eerily close.

She was rattled by the slip of a shoe on rock.

It was Eddie, who had stumbled once in his climb to the peak of a large, mountain-shaped boulder, which protruded from the earth along the fence. Upon reaching the three-foot summit, he gazed, too, upon the starry abyss, his reinforced trinket in hand.

Disengaged from her trance, Rachael Bowitz returned to the house as to put distance between herself and the feelings that remained in the yard. In the doorway stood Uncle Andy, who watched on with deepened concern. He held the door open and let the boy's mildly disoriented mother pass him by.

He remained there, even after she had gone, with a careful eye on Eddie as he raised the wishing star to the darkening sky. He took a step onto the concrete landing, prepared to attempt an intervention.

"Eddie!" he called.

The boy turned in heed of him.

"Why doncha give me that rock you got there."

Eddie pulled the trinket to his chest, his eyes aglow in distress.

"Surely there's something more fun you'd rather have. Maybe an instrument or a toy car or even one of those game boxes!"

Though tempting, the boy restrained his imagination from swaying him and shook his head.

"No! JJ found it in the valley. It's a special one."

Uncle Andy put his hands in his pocket and walked closer. "Oh, Eddie, that's just a rock . . . I mean, it doesn't even look all that much like a star. You got missing pieces here and here," he said as he drew a finger and pointed out the imperfections.

Eddie shook his head, unfazed by his criticism. Uncle Andy stuck out his hand, undeterred by his refusal.

"Just give it to me, and your mom can take you to the store tomorrow. I'll pay for whatever it is."

But Eddie wouldn't let it be. With the star pulled tight to his chest, he descended the mountain rock and sped off to the gate to the front yard. With a pull of the latch, he slipped through the space and was gone.

Uncle Andy, unprepared for such ardent resistance, remained. Defeated, he returned to the door, and as he reentered the house, he was almost immediately caught by the eyes of his brother.

"Guess he won't part with it. Especially now, seeing what you went and did to it."

Eddie's grandfather remained quiet for a moment as if he were not going to respond. "Why don't you go out to see the sunrise, nowadays? Don't ya care anymore?"

"Nobody cares anymore, Victor. A fair amount of folks who live here *nowadays* don't even attend the festival at all, and I don't bother putting my bad knees through it."

"That right?" The old man closed his eyes again without another word. Uncle Andy sighed, seeing the age in both of them.

"But I *suppose* I'll go up one more time with ya, if you really want."

His brother nodded in his nap. "I would," he confirmed. "I would really enjoy that."

In the front yard, Eddie hid with his back against the big tree. A draft of wind swept through the yard and picked up a wave of loose yellow leaves. The rustle faded, and he heard the gate slam shut.

The boy stifled his breath, unsure if Uncle Andy had pursued him.

"Eddie!"

Spooked by the urgent call, the boy stumbled over his own feet, struck an exposed root, then toppled over. The wishing star was thrown from his grasp and flipped across the yard from tip to tip until it came to rest in the grass.

"Eddie," the voice called again, this time in a corrected hush.

Little Eddie looked up and saw Jamal atop the much smaller tree in the Vans family's yard. He sat in a ridge between a fan of its branches with arms crossed as he glared down at his fallen friend.

"I heard you were going to trade away my wishing star."

Eddie shook his head with ferocious energy. "No, I told him I wouldn't do it."

Jamal's eyes narrowed. Then he burst out with laughter. His friend leapt to the ground and planted with both hands into the grass.

Eddie scrambled to his feet as Jamal approached.

"It was just a joke, Eddie. Relax."

The boys met at the fallen star.

"Whoa, what happened to it?" Jamal asked as he bent down and retrieved it from the grass.

"Grandpa. He added the metal stuff and the ribbon so you can't lose it," Eddie said.

"Wow!" said Jamal as he held it up and examined the glimmering guard. He then grew quiet as a dark cloud swirled in his mind.

"Eddie, listen. I need to take this back."

The boy's eyes grew wide, but he nodded in prompt agreement.

"Just for a few days, okay?" his friend assured him.

"Okay. What's wrong?" Eddie asked while Jamal peered down with sad eyes at the star rock.

"Don't worry." Jamal's head snapped up with confidence. "When it's done, you won't even believe it!"

The glow in Eddie's eyes was reborn in a resurgence of faith. Jamal took his dear friend's shoulder and peered into his eyes.

"The festival is only two days away. By the time it comes, we'll know if this thing has any power at all."

"You mean real power?"

Jamal stalled, as if a thought had caused him to second guess himself, and his hand fell from Eddie's shoulder. The wishing star plopped down and dangled by the ribbon.

"I hope so."

A gale struck through the yard and sent a cascade of leaves fluttering from the small tree Jamal had climbed.

"Whoa, why is this tree losing all its leaves. Summer just started!" said Eddie.

He held out his hands and gazed up in awe as the sudden downpour of leaves engulfed them.

"I think because it's dying, Eddie."

And to his surprise, he saw tears fall from his friend's eyes as he fought them with his sleeve.

"JJ, are you okay? What's wrong?"

"Yeah, I'm okay. This is going to make everything right."

Eddie nodded.

"Don't worry. It'll be okay. You have the wishing star now, and if you ever need any help, just ask. I'll be there." *Your oath is a shining star to me.*

"You know," Eddie continued, "my grandpa told me that when you believe in something, it becomes super powerful. So, if we both believe together . . ."

Jamal punched into his open palm, inspired by the trust between them.

"Then there's no way it won't work. This is our last chance before the festival. Eddie, let's bring a real miracle to this one. Big. Like the brightest sun they've ever seen."

His words transfixed Eddie's mind in a marvelous flow of all that could be. He blinked and nodded, unable to speak.

"Magic! It's the only thing that hasn't given up. Everyone else did."

"And neither will we!" Eddie rallied, with his fists clenched in the bliss of faith.

His words reinvigorated Jamal once more, whose eyes became bold and impassioned.

"Right. Okay, okay," Jamal said to calm himself. "I'll come find you. Remember, okay?"

"How could I ever forget?"

Missing Star

There was a festival around the corner, and there would be a million lights. Every moment would serve as fertile ground to lay the seeds of deep memories, and it would be those portals to which one would return when time had stretched the spirit thin and the road ahead had grown narrow and short.

There's a festival tomorrow, and everyone knows it.

When the golden sun rises, so sets the misery of the past.

The streets bustled with families who journeyed to the summit to add finishing touches to the community effort to prepare picnic sites and open grills for the annual embrace of summer.

Little Eddie Bowitz had taken the morning to prod the ground around the house in search of all that was wondrous, mostly in an effort to burn the day away. His mind lay burdened, and his lack of patience trapped him in perpetual restlessness.

Uncle Andy and his grandfather had gone for the summit as agreed, and his father had departed for work as expected. That left Rachael Bowitz alone to tend to the work before the imminent festivities.

Under the loose supervision of his mother, who worked the garden under the shade of a straw hat, Eddie snuck peeks of the Vans's house and their empty driveway between excavations. He returned to the big tree and traced the roots with careful steps as his mother planted fresh flowers in the newly laid soil of their little garden strip.

His enthusiasm for the yard soon faded, as so did the sunlight wane due to a fleet of sailing clouds. He sat in the emerald grass and looked out across the yard as the grand beams reemerged, swept the shadows away, and brought a waft of warmth only to be overshadowed again as the next cloud passed.

With sunlight held captive behind the gray curtain, he fled the chilly shade to the cerulean porch swing, which was situated at the center of the strip garden upon a sea of gray pebbles. The boy jumped into the seat, stabilized, then rocked back and forth until it was set into a delightful swing.

"Eddie, can you help me put the weeds in the garbage bin?" his mother called from around the side of the house.

Her little boy offered no response, however, which prompted her to appear from the corner and set her sights on him. Eddie sank into the chair in cartoonish fashion and began to pick away at the chipped paint of the swing.

"Honey, you need to learn how to help out, especially around this time. It's festival season. This is when everyone comes together to help, including little boys and girls."

Eddie remained paralyzed as he gauged whether he had the energy to respond in lieu of such a draining task. In an opt for silent obedience, he straightened up and pushed himself off the swing. The weeds lay strewn across the garden beds. Without patience for it, he zoomed off and began to snatch up every weed, dead flower, and fallen petal.

"Okay, a little less enthusiasm, dear, but thank you."

Oblivious to her complaint, the boy cut back to the driveway with his hands cusped full of forsaken greenery. It led him to the side of the house where a green bin was positioned just beyond reach of the backyard gate.

He ran over, pushed open the lid, and released the cascade of debris before the lid slammed shut. With the job done, he turned back to the driveway and made the unfortunate discovery of a long trail of scrap that had escaped his grasp.

"Hey, Sheri, good to see ya," Eddie heard his mother call beyond the red brick wall.

After a brief tidy up, Eddie reemerged out front. He caught sight of Mrs. Dominik standing beyond the yard in a plain white T-shirt and pink shorts. Her eyes were veiled by her signature black sunglasses, which were pushed all the way to the top of her nose. She stood with her hands on her hips as she smacked on a piece of gum.

"Me and Trouble, Jr. just floated out to see if they were home yet."

Miles passed behind her on his bike, headed for the dead end.

"Sup, Eddie," he said with a bump of his head.

Eddie waved as the sage split away, rode off into the street, then lifted completely from his seat to gain momentum.

"Yeah." Mrs. Bowitz choked as she stumbled to reply in earnest in the company of her son.

"Ed, why don't you get your game and head to the hilltop to check on Grandpa and Uncle Andy? Can you do that for me, honey?"

Eddie cocked his head.

"I thought you needed help," Eddie replied.

"I do need help. I'm going to be making lunch soon, so I need you to go get everyone together, okay?"

Convinced by the noticeable emptiness in his stomach, he dashed for the door to retrieve the handheld device. Hushed words fell upon his ears, but he paid them no heed. The handheld sat on the passthrough counter between the living room and kitchen. A ripped-open pack of batteries sat nearby. He took the device along with two batteries, which he slid into his pocket.

Ready for the journey, he turned back and bolted for the front door.

Outside, he found his mother waiting. Mrs. Dominik stood with the exact same expression and posture as if she had been frozen in time.

"Alright, honey, don't go anywhere other than the path, okay?"

Eddie nodded in compliance with the age-old rule.

"Okay, okay. I never do anyway," he cried as he took off down the driveway.

"And don't run! Walk. It's not a race, honey," she called after him.

At the bottom, he took a sharp left onto the sidewalk, then skipped lines in the concrete with long strides. He passed a row of unkept bushes at the edge of the neighbor's yard. Eddie had never known much about them, but there were two kids that lived there whom he and Jamal shared occasional conversation with through the fence.

The rough foliage of the bushes in their yard had long fended off his curiosity; however, it didn't stop him from taking a swipe through them as he passed.

With a sting from that curiosity still resonant in his hand, he reached the intersection with the road that led to the hillside. There, risen to the skies on a flagpole at the corner house beside him, was the glorious flag of Beilka. A symbol that Uncle Andy and even his late grandmother had warned him to fear, for those who raised it were the enemies of the people. Though he had never seen the man, those warnings made on late-night walks were enough to keep the boy from any part of his yard.

At the very far end of the street, he spotted groups of people descending the stairs, though none went up. Beyond the line drawn by the summit, dense clouds had gathered. He could only see beauty in it, even as fierce winds drove in from the emerald crest.

As he ran along the perimeter of the park, he caught a glimpse of the food trucks that had arrived and mooned out near the back of the field. The carnival, being the absolute favorite for any child in Somairsville, was still nowhere to be seen. His mind lingered once more on thoughts of his missing friend. The festival grew ever closer in his absence, but faith was yet inextinguishable.

A powerful gale struck him and caused him to stop to retain his balance. A second of even greater force put him back a step. He drove through, then fought his way across the roundabout to the single step rise, which marked the bottom of the old staircase to the summit.

He keeled over to catch his breath as a family of four descended the last step and passed him by. They were engaged in intense jovial discourse in regard to the morrow's string of activities.

Eddie looked upon the symmetric lines cut through the old stone circle, which depicted a sunrise and, equally, the coming of summer. Age, however, had put cracks through the beams, and its image was nearly lost in the noise in some places.

Like the dead returned to life, he overexaggerated as wind returned to his lungs, then proceeded just as a group of teenage boys came barreling down to the last step and stumbled out across the ground.

They cut across the roundabout in an uproar of laughter and shouting as the winds chased them out.

Eddie ascended on nimble steps. The ruckus soon faded and gave dominance to the rustle of the leaves from the thicket in full blossom on each side of the path.

The boy passed glances through the darkened depths within the trees. Other than general curiosity, he was especially fond of seeking out an anomaly commonly referred to as "the kid in the forest." "The kid" was a small, warped tree, deeper along the slope that could be seen from the steps. Nearly ingrown into another tree beside it, it might appear as someone leaned against the trunk.

The boy played the perspectives from step to step to try and find the illusion.

A story accompanied this odd formation. His grandfather had told him of the tale of a young boy who was too often curious and ventured deep off the path. During an outing, unbeknownst to his parents, a witch found him alone and lured him away.

Unaware of the danger, he tried to charm her. Amused by his performance, she transformed him into a tree, so that she might remember his reckless bravery, forever. Stuck there, he could never adventure again, and stood alone in the darkness of every single night.

Eddie often thought of going over when the daylight was strongest to pay a visit, but fear often stayed reckless steps of his own.

Somairsville held many secrets. That much, the boy was sure of, and he had no reason to doubt their tale.

Eddie jerked as he rose from the depths of his subconscious, then sprang forth toward the summit. He shot off the final step, then cleared through the last of the thicket to find the summit nearly abandoned.

A scan of the area found Uncle Andy and his grandfather way down, near the tall grass that invaded the far reaches of the great flat. They seemed to stand in silence as they peered out to the horizon beyond the valley with the occasional sip from a coffee mug.

Eddie, with no wish to bother them, rummaged through his pocket and retrieved the handheld. He meandered over to a nearby park bench beneath a tree and jumped back into the seat to face the darkening horizon.

He flipped the switch on the device and waited.

A soft tune chimed, then wafted off into silence. He kicked his legs through the air as he waited for the world within to present itself. A gentle, crystal ambience sprinkled from a single speaker. Eddie tapped the buttons with frantic urgency as his head rolled in impatience.

The ambience cut to silence. He navigated the menus to a screen with a list and musical staff, made a selection, and then set the handheld upon the picnic table.

A series of tranquil chords hummed out, one that sounded much like a young woman's voice. A drop into mystic waters echoed, and a star fell from the sky. Then, a graceful and sweeping melody opened up and glided across the soundscape.

Eddie went to the grassy slope that fell into the valley as the music set the scene. Through the dance of sixteen bits, however, an organic distraction from the computerized notes chirped. Though disorganized at first, the rogue soloist became harmonized with the tune in a dynamic fashion that bordered impossibility.

Bewildered, the boy turned over his shoulder to seek out the culprit. Perched upon one of the far-reaching branches of the tree was a lone songbird, a honey dove which seemed to go silent as soon as it was found.

Eddie locked eyes with it and leaned in to get a closer look at its hallmark-blushed cheeks as the bird cocked its head in a curiosity of its own.

Just as the mere thought of the gold-plated memorial crossed his mind, the bird shot off the branch and dove through the valley. Eddie threw himself around and raced for the edge. He cut his foot around and dug the side of his shoe into the bald dirt.

There, at the edge of the descent, he caught a glimpse of that striking avian in its spirited flight for the Farside Summit, the other hand that cupped the valley, a destination he someday wished to conquer.

As that mystic song twinkled behind him, he felt something truly special in what he had seen. Surely, he, too, had found a very special honey dove.

Suddenly, his eyes flicked away to something else. Movement had caught his attention. He leaned in. Someone, far away in the fields below, staggered through the valley.

He lunged forward in a surge of heroism, but the thunderous ringing of a distant bell yanked him back at the brink.

"Eddie! Come on. Didn't you hear that? Storm bell's a ringin'. We better be headed back," his grandfather hollered.

The Djose Bell Tower was a historic structure near old downtown that stood nestled in an earthy cradle in the bottom of the hills farther north. Though its use was primarily reserved to ushering in the turn of the seasons, in the spirit of broader tradition, it was employed as an initial warning for severe weather.

Little Eddie had enough experience with the abrupt peal, its grim resonance causing him to shiver from an embedded terror, one which could only be subdued by the purest courage.

Half petrified, Eddie turned back to find them at the staircase. Uncle Andy was on his first fragile step down while his grandfather waved with a gentle, untroubled beam.

But the boy turned to the valley once more and saw there a second figure approach. It was one he had not seen before.

The sudden entity lingered for a moment, then raised something that gleamed in the light of dawn. It was so bright and intense that the boy could only imagine what it was.

He turned back to his grandfather with the trouble in his eyes. "Grandpa! There's two people down there doing something," he said.

His grandfathered popped up, bewildered by the boy's finding. "You don't say! Let's take a look."

The old man marched over to inspect the situation below. The boy turned and raised his finger to guide his eye. To the boy's surprise, they had become one, so close together and far away that he could no longer distinguish one from the other.

Eddie gasped in innocence, then fled from the brink, back to the bench where his handheld played away its mythic melody. His grandfather inched across a rocky lip until he, too, caught a glimpse of the unified figure deep down in the valley.

"Well, look at that . . . is that two of 'em? A couple of kids out there."

Eddie retrieved the game, then turned back to the puzzled old man. "What are they doing?" the boy asked.

"Just being kids, I think, Eddie."

A towering behemoth from beyond the Farside Summit had manifested and done so at unusual speed. Its thunderous growl quaked throughout the sky and sent a shiver through their hearts.

"Hmm . . . looks like the storm came real early. I hope those two have the sense to get indoors. We better do the same, Eddie."

Eddie nodded as a second strike lashed the skies and left him rattled. Spurred to action, Eddie took flight for the staircase as the crash of the bell further galvanized.

With a draw of breath to his lungs, his grandfather cupped his mouth to send his voice far.

"Hey, you need to take cover. Now! Don't you hear the bell? Get out of the valley," he hollered.

The dark plane reached out over the hill. A spectacular show of golden streaks lit up the sky in swift succession. The old man turned away just as one of the figures lay down into the grass.

Eddie, fixed on his grandfather, stood with one hand on the rail, his mouth agape as he awaited direction.

"Let's just get home. I'm gonna call the sheriff."

They departed the summit together. The boy bolted down the steps as his grandfather inched down behind him. Upon the stone landing, Uncle Andy stood in wait of them with a melancholy stare plastered upon his face, one hand on his coffee mug and the other in his jacket pocket.

"You two done playing up there? There's a storm coming. Can't you hear it?" he asked Eddie as he landed on the shattered sun.

"We already saw it, Uncle Andy. There's two people out in the valley," Eddie reported.

Uncle Andy's expression remained unchanged.

His brother reached the final step with a huff. "I'll let Sheriff Ainsley know when we're back. Probably have to get the trucks moved out on the street, too."

Uncle Andy nodded.

"Hell if the force is going to be able to do anything about it now. They'll just have to tough it out through the night," Andy said.

"Well, that devil came from the northside of nowhere. We weren't supposed to see a drop of rain until ten o'clock tomorrow morning," Victor Bowitz replied.

With his opinion on the matter made up, Uncle Andy turned and crossed to the sidewalk without further investigation of the incident.

Eddie turned to his grandfather.

"So, nobody's going to help them?" The boy worried.

"We'll get it figured out, son. Just leave this one to the adults. You did the right thing by letting me know."

Eddie nodded in obedience with an undefiled trust in his grandfather's word.

 They crossed the street and hurried to make up lost ground as the peal of thunder in the unseen horizon assaulted their ears.

The darkness seemed to give chase as they went. The rays of the afternoon sun had been blocked by the encroaching menace's grim outer ring, and shadows became deep across the land. Fear and excitement captivated the boy in an oddly euphoric enchantment. This concoction of emotion brought energy to his legs and propelled him forward ahead of both his uncle and grandfather.

He raced his anxiety all the way back, in hopes of seeing the car there in the driveway. As he stumbled to a halt just beyond the big tree, he fell still. The car was still missing.

He let out a sigh as the spirit of hope withered within. It remained agleam by the work of faith, however, for there was still tomorrow; as long as tomorrow survived, all was surely not lost.

His eyes shifted across the street and somehow ended up on the dead end not far away. For a moment, he couldn't pull himself away from it. A distinct and disturbing cold coursed to the cradle of the sacred heart. He peered deeper and deeper, through no will of his own. The boy became aware of the ever-so-subtle manipulation, but before he could seize the power to redirect himself, he caught a glimpse of something that lurked within.

Little Eddie Bowitz was sure what he saw was real, the gleam of gold hovering out in the abyss. The intruder in the void was shrouded by a cloak, noticeable in its odd fluctuation as its edges fluttered in the gales. Instead of flapping, it shifted, as if not quite real, or perhaps not properly adjusted.

Eddie found himself frozen and unable to budge, a child caught in the sights of an otherworldly reaper.

In that psychic prison, he noticed that the forest seemed to teem with movement. Reflective hypnotic patterns wrapped the branches and trunks as the beasts of the beyond took hold of the foliage.

"Eddie!"

The boy gasped as he felt his spirit zip back in, just nearly yanked into the abyss.

"Eddie! Come on, sweetheart. You need to come inside."

His entire body trembled as he was shaken from the hex by the sound of his mother's voice. He turned to find her at the front door, the screen held agape by her leg as she leaned forward.

Eddie fled for the door. His mother pushed it open just before he passed beneath her arm.

"Where're Grandpa and Uncle Andy?"

"Coming. Uh. They were right behind me!"

She let out a sigh as he turned the corner back toward his room.

Eddie raced into his room and shut the door. He hid there in shadows more familiar until he heard the door again and banter between his family that settled him.

He crept over to his bed and climbed in. An eeriness permeated the sanctity of his room as he peered over to the bare window. With hawkish precision, he scanned the back fence, which offered him a certain security. If anything were to enter, they would be easily spotted, otherworlder or otherwise.

The storm came fast, and its dark veil had no end. Streaks of heaven's heat ripped the sky and illuminated the yard like instant flashes of pure daylight. The winds dove through the town and rattled the trees outside as a symphony of fear began.

Three knocks on the door relieved him of the horrific performance.

"Eddie? You okay in there?" his grandfather asked.

The boy ran to the door and opened it.

"There ya are! Hey, now, stay away from the windows. No need to be stargazing, now."

The boy nodded.

"Why don't you come to the living room with us? Come say a quick goodbye to your uncle. Then we're all going to watch a movie, and when the power goes out, we're playing board games. How's that sound?"

Alleviated by the charm of their plan and averse to remaining alone any longer, the boy agreed to his grandfather's offer. He jumped down and left the room behind as the deluge was unleashed beyond the window, and he was temporarily distracted from the terrors beyond those walls.

The festival was right around the corner, now, and it would come one way or another.

In the Night of Fate

As per his grandfather's prediction, the storm knocked the power from the house. Night fell upon the little town, and the storm intensified into a howling maelstrom, with strength unlike anything his family had ever seen before.

His grandfather peered out the window from the kitchen as Eddie and his mother remained together in the candlelit living room. The boy tapped a silver game piece from space to space on the floor while his mother awaited a report from the sofa.

"Yep . . . looks like the whole neighborhood is out," his grandfather informed them.

"Geez . . . I just hope Edward gets home safe," said his mother.

"Think I hear him pulling up now," he replied just as a pair of muddied yellow headlights turned up the driveway.

Eddie froze as the house lit up. A clash of lightning roared out, and the boy crawled into the dining room and went under the table.

Not soon after did the door squeal open, and Eddie's father came stumbling through the door, chased in by a violent spray of water.

"Damnit! Can you believe this?" he grumbled as he wiped water from his glasses with his trench coat.

"Come on in and get comfortable. Come on through," urged Eddie's grandfather, ushering his father to safety.

The door wailed as the two men forced it shut against the storm winds, but then, something struck back against them with a tumultuous thud. The horrified cry of a woman caused Eddie to pop his head up and listen in close. His blood ran cold. It was Jamal's mother, and his father and grandfather fought to calm her with their words.

Eddie's mother leapt to her feet and dashed straight for the dining room.

"Honey, go to your room," she ordered.

"But Mom—"

"Go, right now. NOW!" she cried.

Tears swelled in his eyes as he scurried out from beneath the table and ran through the hall, then into the doorway. He remained at the foot of his room to listen in, but his mother swept in and pulled the door shut.

Something had gone terribly wrong. Unwilling to be pushed aside, he put his ear to the door and overheard the tragic news.

"He's gone! He went into the storm! He's gone!"

"Do you know where he went!?" his father asked.

"The forest. He went toward the forest, and I can't find him alone!"

"Holy hell. Just let me get a jacket! Rachael, you two stay put," he heard his grandfather plead.

The boy's eyes grew in dread of the consequences of his friend's bizarre act. What was he thinking? Why would he go? Eddie failed to come up with answers in the moment. He turned to the window where the storm raged. Gale force winds flung tree branches and debris across the yard at terrifying speed.

He went to the desk.

Upon it lay the hero's rune.

He took it tight in his hand, placed it into his pocket, then wiped a tear from his eye.

With courage, he slipped on his shoes, climbed onto his bed, then took the window handle with both hands and pulled it open. A burst of storm wind blew into the room. Dark nature lay beyond, as if accepting his invitation. The boy fought against the terror all around him.

And something within him began to glow.

He placed his hand against the screen and shoved it through to the ground beyond the wall.

And a portal was born between two destinies.

He leapt from safety into the grasp of the superstorm. His shoes plunged into the mud of the drowned yard, his clothes almost entirely drenched even before his first step.

The first squall blew him off his feet and dragged him along the wall. He fought the overwhelming strength of the storm in determined steps, all in an effort to be the hero he said he would. A second terrifying gale ripped through, and the fence which separated their yards gave way and collapsed with a wail. A passage to the front yard was opened, and Little Eddie took to it.

He leapt onto the fallen barrier, raced across, then dropped into the driveway. There, he side-skirted the burgundy sedan, then followed flowing water down into the flooded road.

The land was unveiled by repeated calamitous bolts, which cracked the dark sky with magnificence. Eddie raced down the swamped street toward the foreboding end, with reflections of heaven's wrath in the floodwaters below.

The deluge left the forest dangerous with unseen hazards, but before he could reach them, another tremendous gale took him off his feet. He twisted around as he threw his arms out in a swift maneuver to catch himself. His hands plunged into the storm surge, and his palms bit into the rock and asphalt beneath.

Fear had started to permeate his emboldened heart as he felt pain ripple through his hands. The tears were lost in the merciless storm. Eddie realized the danger was more real than ever, but his friend was out there, and all he needed to do was believe. He drove the power of his faith deep into his core as he trembled at the sight of the tormented canopy as it was torn to pieces and swallowed by the sky.

Eddie pushed off the ground beneath the water and struggled to his feet. The road's end wasn't far now. He slogged through the water, eventually passing by the driveway of the Dominik's house. In a backlit window of the structure, a small shadow stirred from within. As the boy raced for the end of the sidewalk, the nimble figure snapped away.

The audacious rescuer had made it to the road's end. Lightning was all that was left to guide him through. He took his first steps from the wet concrete into the marsh, then forged bravely ahead between the trees.

His footing found stable ground, and the trees shielded him from the intensity of the downpour, though he trembled from the cold. The glow from the sky unveiled the landscape ahead and suddenly revealed a glint from the ground.

He shot forth until he had come upon the mystic wishing star, discarded in the mud. Eddie threw himself to the ground to retrieve it. The sky lit up again as Eddie gazed down upon it. He stood, reinvigorated by the find. With it, he knew his friend had to be close.

He couldn't give up now, not with the wishing star in hand.

The boy drove in deeper, without any idea as to where he was going or where he was. The lights from the sky only revealed a land he found himself lost in. He was surrounded by the trees and their menacing claws that scraped the sky.

Eddie inched forward, then came to a complete stop as his ears perked to the unsettling drone of a distant devil, a great tempest which had touched the world.

"JJ!! Where are you!? I'm here!" the boy cried.

The ferocious crackle of thunder replied to his desperate outcry. The elements of the land rattled, and a gale of remarkable strength threw him into the trunk of a tree.

A distant, yet earsplitting siren screamed through the night. Far from the safety of home and deep within the clutches of calamity, all was unraveling before him. Through the invincibility of youth, he felt his mortality shining.

Eddie pulled his arm from the jagged bark and felt the sting of an injury. His eyes raised to the distant tormented canopies just as they were ripped completely away by a super force.

Something approached, and if he didn't run, he knew it would be his end.

The presence of the entity of death rattled the ground. Yet, he stayed deadlocked between his duty and dread, and their battle stretched his soul to its limits.

He broke.

Against the unmatched power of nature, the boy took flight toward the whirling darkness as it ripped his world to shreds.

The distant wall of debris loomed. Fragments of the forest were lifted in offering and swarmed the sky as they became one with elemental chaos. Ahead, he could make out something. There was a clearing with a large boulder. Someone was there, holding on, he was sure of it.

"JJ! Is that you? Is that YOU?!" he cried out against the howl of calamity.

Vibrations stunned him in place. He could go no farther. His little hand gripped tight the wishing star as judgement approached. Fear swelled within and chased out all hope and bravery. The words were lost. He could make no wish, but in his heart, he begged for mercy.

The figure stood up against the monster, unmoved by its terrible might. It bore down upon him, the titan against the child. The ground was torn asunder, the trees caved and were ripped from the earth by the enraged demon. Eddie's ears went deaf as the clearing disappeared into absolute havoc.

He cried as he took hold of a small tree. The demon's dynamic pull dragged him toward the maw of ends, but just as death had come for him, he was seized.

Someone had taken him by the shoulders, and he found himself yanked off his feet.

"Ed! You crazy!? Come on!"

Miles had swept in and taken him up under his arm. He thrashed through the mud in full retreat from the angry goliath in the darkness. It hurled massive rock and trees through the air and pummeled every corner of the forest. The boy wailed out in terror as the shrapnel cut through the air.

With heart aflame with the will to survive, Miles returned them to the road's end. The menace loomed behind, on approach to bring its misery to all. The young sage raced to his backyard fence. In a calculated maneuver, he slammed one of the planks of the decrepit installation through and fell together with Eddie out into the yard.

Mrs. Dominik appeared out from a hatch in the ground.

"Come on, Miles! Get your fucking ass down here!"

"I'm trying, Mom! Hold on!" he cried back as he took up the boy again, who had cowered on the ground.

The sage raced to sanctuary's gateway as the swarm of the end ripped its way through the tree line. Miles's mother reached out and received the boy from her son, and without a moment left, the daredevil dropped through the hatch, leapt, and pulled the door shut.

Mrs. Dominik held the neighbor boy tight as a ruthless barrage battered the ground above. Miles, his sister, and father huddled tight at the far end of the shelter. Metal was sheered away, and glass burst into a thousand pieces. As a wicked ruin was cast upon the town, the boy held ever more tightly to the star of wishes. The dark winds of cataclysm tore away all that he had, and when it was done, the star would be all that was left.

So, he sowed a wish into time and space with all the energy his heart could relinquish, from the highest peaks of his hopes to the darkest depths of his sorrow. He felt something within but wasn't quite sure if it was real or not, this vibrance that lay deep within his chest. But the inner spark couldn't cause the clouds to part in the way that he wished it would, nor could it summon a mythic brilliance to stave off the hand of death.

Moments of consciousness became sparse as the sound of ruin grew distant. His reckless bravery had worn him and, overwhelmed by terror, the boy remained petrified until he slipped off into deep sleep at some throwaway moment.

High above in the sky, through the towering dark, there came a brilliant flashing, a beacon which gazed through to the world below. Unseen by all beneath the storm, it grew and faded from radiance. The otherworlder winked, then vanished altogether, not to be seen again for years.

When the boy awoke, a new day would dawn, and with it, a new world. The magic his childish heart had placed such faith in had failed him. In wake of the old world's death, however, he would still turn an eye up to the stars. Those faint glimmers would provide a certain comfort, reminiscent of times gone as he searched across glittered heavens for answers in lonely nights.

The day of the tragedy would be driven to the deepest recesses of memory. Though as for the fragments of childhood, he grasped hold of them at the very brink of oblivion and made them sacred. For he could never let them be lost. This was his duty, and thus tragedy made Little Eddie Bowitz eternal.

The Odyssey of the Swordsman

In the days before the great master arrived, his swordsman, Ultra, went to understand the world and all that would someday come to an end. On the first day, he walked the endless coast until he encountered a man in a concealing dark cloak who questioned the meaning of his wanderings.

"For what good is existence without purpose?" he asked in a somber call from nowhere.

But the swordsman remained silent, although curiosity of his own clamored for the answer.

So long as there is only silence, there can be no change. There can be no catharsis to any pondering, grand or small. Silence is stillness, a blade unable to strike.

"Action is the edge that cuts through the impenetrable wall," said the man veiled in shadows. "Death is the only truth. Life will forever be doomed for a dream."

He departed from that familiar dark shadow and went to a place of peace, where the ocean swept away footsteps left in the sand, and the winds sang as the clouds left for nowhere.

In the waters, he gazed upon the indigo cloak from beneath the hood with which he was once blinded. It was frayed, ripped, left in spectacular tatters, the markings of a made champion. Each vicious scar a reason for his enemies to fear a confrontation, for the swordsman had seen many battles in many wars. He knew, though, the next was always inescapable. It had always been so.

The faint cerulean glow from his eyes reflected gently upon the crystal veil below. In frustration, he pulled off that hood and looked closely at the world around him, his luxuriant blue hair exposed to the sun.

But even then, he saw only ghosts in a nightmare.

As he fought to pierce that punishing truth, something truly terrifying reached out in the form of hellish illusion, yet no fear came over him. So, he turned from the water and departed again.

As the sun set on the first day of reformation, he felt nothing and had seen little.

In a lonesome stroll along the beach through the night, the swordsman thought he heard something in the wind. But by the time morning had come, whatever it was had given up and gone.

Forward was the only way left, and so that was the way he would continue.

As the morning sun crept up over the horizon, the man approached a coastal city. He had not stopped to rest as he had tasked himself with making a long journey with no real destination.

As he peered out to that bustling metropolis, memories seeped from the corridors of his tormented mind, but he executed them quickly before they became anything more.

The vision-plagued wanderer walked along the beach throughout the next night and once more heard something in the wind. It was stronger this time, but no less clear. He gave the phantom its time, but as its mumbles were indecipherable, he gave up on it and waited for dawn to come.

The swordsman used the next morning to watch the silver-backed fish in the ocean as they swam together in large schools, swept up through the deep water, and burst out into the ocean spray. A flock of birds high in the blue sky dove toward the lively waters below and seized their morning take in large bills.

To watch this was something that didn't bring him joy but made him feel at one with the world. *This* one. It was a necessity of life. A life that thrived, even with imperfections, with its givings and takings, in cycles of goodwill and sacrifice.

That sense of peace was soon invaded by a sudden hostility. A voice cried out from behind, but he couldn't understand it. The swordsman turned and came to face a white-robed entity of flowing fabric, its hand extended in a plea for mercy.

Great distress haunted its face. Something had slipped his guard. The entity raised its shaken voice and then dashed for him.

There was no time.

He reached for something from under his indigo cloak.

It rang out, then cut!

The entity stumbled over with wide eyes, fell to its knees in the shallow surf, then dissipated, as if it had never been. There came a silence again. Something echoed in the distance. A voice begging for reason.

He looked down upon the flawless blade, the deadly serosura, the edge that refuses all obstruction. The sun's golden rays glowed across the smooth surface of that blessed alloy which fell to a crescent fang.

He felt something this time. It came and it went, but alas, was felt.

As the crash of the waves shook him from the moment, he returned the blade in its sheath, but before it sank to the very bottom, a distorted voice called out.

"Lost star, always remember . . . that in the beginning, there was only death."

The swordsman turned to face that cryptic whisperer, who hid his face beneath a hood of black. With a sinister smirk, he stood a little too close, with heavy ebon boots sunken into the pristine sand and surrounded by a dark looming cloud that manifested wherever he went.

"Erepethiel, why do you stalk me through the shadows like a snake hoping to bite?" he asked the man, who stared back with gold, glimmering eyes.

"Oh, Lord Ultra, you know too well why I've come. Am I wrong to fulfill this task, under order? Especially knowing that I have only the deepest respect for this grandest endeavor of ours."

"Then, what happens now?" the swordsman taunted.

The shadow man lingered, his grin long and wide. "That is not my place. It is yours whose action we await."

"Then be gone. I must go and find a meaning greater than what I have," said Ultra.

"Ah, but there are matters of such critical importance for us to discuss, my lord."

"What matters need my attention?"

The shadow man shook his head, slightly amused with his lack of wit. The answer to his question the likes of which should surely be obvious. "Your sovereign is calling you home. Nebulas awaken in the deep space. He will turn his attention to you. You know this," Erepethiel warned.

"I know," the swordsman replied.

"You have been given much time. So now I must ask, will you return with me?"

The swordsman placed his hand on the hilt of the blade and turned toward a distant pier. Beyond it, a great storm in retreat across the sea.

"There is something more that I must see now that my eyes are open. Neither of us is a fool. We know what he will come to do, and what he will seek to claim. I cannot escape the emptiness, nor can I escape punishment. But while he is not here . . . I will see peace. I wish to know what that looks like, and what it feels like, so I will know and never forget again."

The shadow man chuckled, though he understood those purposes were nothing outlandish. "And which fleeting veil of peace do you hope to gaze through, Lord Ultra? The timeless should be the wiser. There are but two elements you may choose to accept. Chaos . . . or the dream."

The swordsman clung to silence. Erepethiel scoffed.

"I reluctantly depart to relay this defiance. Master will be most disappointed in us." The man from the shadows crept away to make his exit, slow enough that perhaps the swordsman would be given a final opportunity to surrender. "This world . . . Lord Ultra . . . is very malleable. Perhaps, try your hand at creating peace, or you can simply continue to drift meaninglessly alongside the redundant flow of nature.

You know as well as I, these arduous cycles will do nothing to entertain you. You seek purpose, and the time will come to act . . . And how I wonder what it is you will do . . . Farewell, my lord."

When the servant from the shadows had gone, the swordsman lifted his head to the rising sun of dawn.

"Purpose? . . . No. Not anymore."

Eleven Years Ago

"Don't lose your calm demeanor when you start working around politics, son. It's a lot of backtracking . . . a hell of a lot of backtracking when you start messing with anything other than your steak and potatoes."

"I'll keep it in mind, General Myres."

"This'll be your first time joining us as second lieutenant, Schneider. Might want to prepare for some heat. The prime minister and I really fought hard for this."

"Understood, sir. Nothing I can't handle."

"Eleven years it's been since the incident, huh? Time's flown, son."

"Yeah . . . sure has, sir."

The two officers of rank hurried out from a hallway into a splendid dome-roofed lobby with stone carvings of soldiers and triumphant war horses assembled around a main fountain. The ceiling was covered by a mural of several groups of men and women, each wearing very distinct attire, raising a single flag on a ravaged battlefield. The sacred flag bore a white frame wire sphere, centralized on glossy burgundy thread.

The same flag of patriots hung atop a glossy stand, which stood proud beside a grand oak desk where numerous black-suited officials were posted. Behind the reception, a jumbo world map spanned the entirety of the wall. It was primarily dominated by a supercontinent with multiple small islands off the coast. The reach of the World Union of the Emancipated Lands encompassed the entire southern coast, built northward, then spired off as it gave way to smaller independent territories. It was, without question, the largest empire of the modern world, and that map reminded all visitors of that truth.

A bell rang over the clack of footsteps on the pale marble floor.

"All fifth-tier military personnel are to report to the Clemson office," ordered a robotic voice over the loudspeakers.

"That's for us!" barked General Myres as the announcement repeated.

They quickened their pace as they made their way for an elevator across the lobby.

"Do you think it has anything to do with the Vesterbend?"asked Schneider as they boarded the glass-walled lift.

Myres rubbed his chin as he gave it a quick thought.

The doors closed. The general nodded and mashed the button for the second floor. There was a soft chime, and the elevator began to ascend.

"If I were to put money on it, I'd say so. There's been quite a bit of heat in those small farming villages, and some people are a little too eager to cry Beilkan. If you ask me, it sounds like someone dusted off their old playbook." Myres cocked his head as if there were a few cards up his sleeve. "I've got intel figuring out a few things for me, and at least as things are chalked up now, we should be in a good timeframe to sort most of it out before it gets too ugly."

"Pays to stay one step ahead of the game, sir."

"That it does."

The door opened on the second floor. Myres and Schneider emerged out onto the gray-carpeted path, which circled around the outskirts of the main lobby.

They made their way around to a door with two bronze angels hung above the entry, with the word "Clemson" on a plate between them. They steadied their pace as they approached, then Myres blew through the doors in lead of their charge.

The room was lively with the fierce exchanges between five high-ranking officers who sat at a large oval table: four men and one woman. Highly decorated from their elite service, their chests lay covered with silver and gold pins, and their peaked caps bore a silver eagle with a varied number of spears in claw, which identified their rank.

As the presence of the Union supreme commander became recognized, the debate subsided, and silence quickly swept the room.

"Myres, you're right on time to be late!" joked a portly man, who sat in his seat like a grinning king upon a throne.

He had a grandfatherly smile that was known to be warming in the cold of war, and though his eyes went partially hidden behind loosely fit glasses, he bore the appearance of a man of transparency. It was a boon often reinforced by his breezy disposition during times of great stress and hardship. A side only an ally would know from a man once famed by his enemies as "The Desert Savage."

"I have an acute appreciation for dramatic entry, General Henson. Now, let's get down to business," said Myres, with a quick survey of the room to confirm his attendees.

Schneider had gone and taken a seat next to a woman who took no heed of him. Myres, satisfied with the return to order, took a seat at the back of the room. He took off his hat and laid it down on the icy gray table.

"So then, let's get this meeting started. First little order of business . . . Let's give our newest second lieutenant a warm welcome. We're all aware of the history surrounding him, and we're opening up some opportunities to broaden the horizons of some of our personnel. He's shown dedication and a whole helluva lot of courage before and during his service. So, enough of that. Let's have someone get us up to speed and get down to it. Rhodes! Let's hear it," ordered Myres to the almond-haired woman with a single-spear's prestige.

"Yes, sir. We ran through the action plans as you requested, but as some facets of the plan hinge on aid from the Beilkans, we haven't quite been able to get a general consensus," she explained.

"Aid from the Beilkans? That's a little out of the box, don't you think?" Schneider asked.

General Henson breathed a sigh of relief. "I agree. Whenever there's a fire in the Union, Beilka's fanning it—even if they didn't start it."

"I personally wouldn't consider attempted diplomacy out of the box. I think it's worth a shot. The benefit is a very low chance of casualties," she defended.

"What's really out of the box is when we put the lives of our soldiers in the hands of thirty-four-year-olds," said a slender, red-faced man.

Schneider looked up at the man and glared while still retaining a smile that welcomed conflict.

"You can ask the twenty thousand dead at Levinne in the Vesterbend why we have a thirty-four-year-old second lieutenant. That's what happens when old men fail to make hard decisions, General," Schneider said.

"You're talking to a senior member of this military, boy," said the man, failing to suppress his surging fury.

"Alright, knock it off. Schneider, Oswald, that's an order—"

"They just needed someone who had the ability to do what you couldn't," Schneider pressed. "And I'm tired of giving you the same lecture every year."

The old man erupted from his chair and jolted forward, his face red like burning hellfire.

"You don't know what it's like to have lives on the line. You don't know anything about sacrifice, you tight son of a bitch!" he shouted, his voice booming in the room.

Schneider sat back in his chair. The smile had faded into a faint grin. "And if that's your take on reality, then I understand your confusion, general," Schneider replied rather matter-of-factly." You don't know a thing about me, or the struggles my people had to endure. If you need a refresher, read the documents again."

Oswald stared for a moment as he realized what he had said. His eyes sank, and he sat back in his seat in hopes of recovering grace.

"We done yellin' and carryin' on?" asked Myres.

No one said a word.

"Good, then let's recap our possible direction concerning the rebel group, and then I want to hear what we've got accomplished. Rhodes, you've got the floor again. One more time!" barked Myres.

The brigadier general rose. "Yes, sir," she said.

She reached down to a compartment under the table and flipped a switch. An azure beam of light streaked up from the center of the table. The beam hit the boundary of an invisible container near the ceiling and cascaded down into the form of a sphere. The surface soon became populated with various geographical features until it resembled a world with massive oceans, forests, and land masses.

"Coordinating forces from the so-called 'Kingdom' of the Titan King's Renaissance and The Revenant Crown Insurgency have moved eastward toward the Arcadian Sea. If our intel proves correct, they should be trapped, with the insurgency greatly weakened with the recent loss of their leader, Yuvek Chiike of the Round Table. A job well done by the squadrons involved in Operation Ivory Hall. With the Beilkan garrison to the north and Union forces pushing toward the coast, there should be little room for another tactical retreat," she briefed.

As she spoke, the globe turned and zoomed to the relevant areas. Photographic evidence of the bombings appeared alongside a picture of a stern-faced man who wore the hide of wolves upon his shoulders.

Henson let out a jolly bellow as she concluded. "Those Beilkans would rather fry up some mother hen and have themselves a good old time before they would consider helping us," he declared.

"They don't need to do much. Intimidation would be just as valuable as armed intervention. My artillery units will be in range if they stop their retreat for more than nineteen hours. All three hundred and seventy-five guns, right behind the main force. And if they muster the gall for a counter offensive, we'll roll out the red carpet for them. Our aim is to keep them out of the populated city of Wenhelm, and only the Beilkans are in position to do that at this crucial time," she replied sternly.

Henson shook his head. "Asking for anything at all is asking too much," he argued.

As the last word left his mouth, the door to the meeting room swung open. Without word or warning, a titan of a man at a solid seven feet entered with an aggressive stride. He was an aged man whose accomplishments displayed upon his chest revealed a time in service hard fought.

He was accompanied by two officers. As per tradition, the left flank officer bore a goldenrod flag, fierce upon the national Beilkan falcon in flight with the crown of the king to spread the truth of his sovereignty across the land. With a pride undoubtedly excessive, there stood a majestic golden falcon topper upon the pole, complete with golden rays from behind its wings.

The right-flank officer stood with both arms to his side, earlier disarmed of the rifle he was meant to bear.

Near equal height as their leader, each man was an extraordinary giant in the land of the Union but average in their homeland of Beilka.

Myres and the rest watched them with uneasiness. They were dressed in black uniforms with badges depicting the same fierce falcon that appeared upon their flag.

Their spearheaded advance came to a halt at the edge of the table, and the foreign general, with a scan of his foes at the table of his nation's struggle, curled a crude smile, like fire set to paper.

"It all depends on the conditions, my friends," he said in answer to their unsent plea.

His voice, tremendously deep and powerful, projected from wall to wall beat against eardrums like a war drum.

"General Gala, nice of you to show up uninvited . . . on top of the eavesdropping. It's all a Beilkan habit, I swear to high heaven," Myres mocked.

Gala turned to his old nemesis with his chin raised in a brazen manifestation of the deeply sown, haughty idealisms of his homeland.

"General Myres, it seems our peoples are never eager to see each other at the table of war, even when our goals are one in the same. A pity," Gala lamented.

An official in a black suit entered through the door and took immediate surprise with the king's men at the table.

"Ah. And here our guests have arrived," said the man.

Myres took to his feet. "Anyone care to explain why my meeting is being interrupted?" he asked.

"Prime minister's orders, sir. He shared a line with the king and called for the assistance of Beilka personally. They have some—"

"We have some information concerning an insurgent that was captured near our territorial border with the Vesterbend," Gala informed.

His eyes found Schneider at the table, and his gaze lingered as memories reconstructed the identity of the young man in front of his face.

Gala came aglow with a grandfatherly pride. "Ah, we have the great honor to commend the extraordinary bravery that safeguarded his homeland from vile barbarism. It's a shame it's no better today than the day you and your companions fought to rescue it. A tragedy we had wished to remedy with force, though due to the restrictive idiocy of the Treaty of Fortuna, had our hands *justly* tied. You've grown. Though you're still just a child in comparison to most of your peers," he said regarding Rhodes, who sat patiently with her arms folded.

"You've risen far. No doubt attributed to the supreme heritage passed down by your mother. The bloodline which produced men who, in teams of two, could load a half-ton shell into a Zerkka Fortress Buster without the aid of any machinery if need be."

"General Gala, please do not fill his head with tall tales of Beilkan spectacle."

Gala turned to Myres with his lower lip folded out and brow raised, humored by his counterpart's disbelief. "Why do you think we built handles into the shells?" he replied rather naturally.

Myres turned to say something but lost his tongue in thought. Gala, satisfied with that reaction, turned back to Schneider with nationalistic delight. "Greatness surely awaits you, hero general," he concluded.

Schneider offered the Beilkan no response, unwilling to bask in his own holiness.

"And what greatness awaits you, awaits all of great *Beilka*! So, damn any effort by this Union to annex an undeserved inch of the Vesterbend," Gala declared.

Myres waved his hand at Gala to discourage further comments. "Alright, let's drop the arrogance right there," he said.

"We're all entitled to think as we may, General, but let us continue as you wish. After all, this is Salamandra," said Gala as he motioned to his guard.

The guard nodded, produced a small black case from his pocket, opened the top, and handed over a USB drive.

"The kingdom has taken the liberty of preparing a dossier pertaining to recent activities that our intelligence has found disturbing to say the least. Complete theater! Unauthorized display of Beilkan war banners—"

"Hold on. I need to restructure this assembly." Myres's head fell as he lifted his hand to silence the Beilkan general. "General Henson, you're with me. Everyone else, dismissed. We'll reconvene here at noon and go through the relevant details."

His order unleashed bewilderment throughout the congregation, aside from General Henson, who sat in infinite patience behind his shaded glasses.

"Let's begin with haste. I have an appointment with your senate afterwards, and to be frank, I'll be ready to leave for home as soon the tiresome theater concludes," Gala sneered.

Schneider and Rhodes exchanged a subtle glance, then rose together with the rest of those dismissed. With a salute to General Myres, the military leaders filed out one by one with an honorary salute to a flag posted near the door.

When the room had emptied to the specifications of General Myres, the last official pulled the doors shut.

Myres, who had supervised their exit, returned to his seat with a sigh. "So, we have an organized false flag operation all over again."

The Beilkan General nodded with a grim expression, deeply angered by those who would utilize his banner for their misdeeds. "It would seem so, General."

✳✳✳

The elevator doors opened to the first level of the lobby, and out emerged Schneider and Brigadier Rhodes, among others. He kept pace with her as they struck out across the center, past the fountain, upon which three stone warriors raised their swords in victory.

"Vesterbend region is just how we left it years ago, huh?" said Rhodes.

"What do you think is going on now?" asked Schneider as his eye meandered over the passing contractors, government officials, and uniformed personnel from each branch of service.

"Most likely what it sounded like. Someone trying to stir up the region. Can't say I'd place complete trust in the Beilkans knowing they've executed territory grabs before."

"That was over thirty years ago."

"Well, even an amateur strategist would tell you if your opponent can't beat it, why stop doing it?"

After making the journey to the far side of the facility, they exited through a lonely corridor, which connected to a separate five-story tower. The walls of the hallway were adorned with plaque after plaque depicting a simple engraved image along with text that described a moment of great triumph during the struggles of war. They ranged from the individual hero to the heroics of entire battalions in the face of sure annihilation.

"Like I promised, I'll show you the new digs," said Rhodes.

"What floor they put you up on?" he asked.

"Third. I figure if I stick in the game and get a few more wrinkles, they'll put me at the top. Can't complain, though. I'm just down the hall from the skyway to the Stryder Building. Hell of a view. Nice place to step away, even if it's just for five minutes."

"Maybe they'll give you Oswald's office."

"Relax. Nobody's used to you being there. There's a lot of forces that are pushing against this promotion."

"I mean, no offense, but I'm only five years younger than you," Schneider reasoned.

"You can learn a lot of things in five years."

"And you can learn a whole hell of a lot more in thirty. Everyone else in the top brass is at least double your age."

"Don't hate your blessings. I used to be controversial too. Still am to some. We were both young when tragedy yanked us into service, but it provided an opportunity for us to show our mettle and defined who we were, not just to ourselves, but to the world. Think of who you are," Rhodes said as she turned and confronted him with a smile. "You're the hero general. The one who refused to leave the frontlines of home until you and your resistance rescued as many people as possible."

Schneider evaded her eyes as if something didn't quite sit well with him. "Come on. Let's not even humor it. There's plenty of heroes out there that people don't see."

Rhodes's head fell away to safeguard her emotions from his words.

"Never cared for being in the parade that came the first time around. Never did one after. I never wanted to be a hero. I just wanted to do what was right," Schneider insisted.

She smiled, forever taken aback by his humble disposition. "Well, you're special. How about that?"

"Thanks, Mom," he joked with a gentle beam.

"Shut up," she snapped, crippled by an irrepressible smile. She turned away and continued down the hallway to escape him. "There are cameras around here, so don't make any comments like that or I'll have to ban you from being seen with me on base again," she ordered with her finger lifted to the corners of the hall.

Schneider went with a careless swing into his steps. "Yes, ma'am," he complied with casual grace.

At the hall's end, a sliding glass door with a reinforced steel base parted them from the office building. Rhodes reached into her pocket and produced a brown billfold, which she raised to a red eye on a nearby security panel.

There was a soft chirp, and the door glided open, the motion concluded by a satisfying thump.

Inside, the lobby's refined architecture was defined in minimal lighting. That regal ambience was bestowed by a lit rectangular recess on the ceiling, beneath it, a tall floor lamp beside an empty reception counter along with a guide of recessed lights that followed the spiral staircase, which curved alongside a great pillar.

Rhodes struck out across the terrazzo-tiled lobby and swept her hand out to introduce him.

"Shall we?"

They passed by the staircase in favor of an elevator shaft, which lay hidden along a passage not far beyond. Upon ascension to the third floor and some brisk navigation of a few long passages, they arrived at a door which bore the nameplate of one Brigadier General Rhodes.

She led their entry into the dark room, lit only by thin rays of sunlight, which pierced the blinds of a window at the far end.

Schneider flipped a nearby switch. The fluorescent lights flickered on and produced a gentle hum that became nearly inaudible.

It was a tidy office, worked from an executive desk with gold inlay. It sat just beyond the window, through which the sun's beams shined upon rich wood grain, gifting true resplendence.

Halfway through the room, they crossed over a navy area rug with frills along the edge. At the center was a crest depicting two crossed howitzer barrels. Left of the crest was a shield, which blocked the attack of a hostile falcon, a crown knocked from its grasp, while the right was an equally emblematic image of a robe-adorned seraph with the frame-wire world cusped safely in her palms.

They passed a large bookshelf, whose tomes on the top two shelves were obscured by a row of framed photos of family, friends, and comrades, those snapshots in time forever secured from oblivion's creeping grasp.

Beside the bookcase was a pinned-up Union flag, around which hung several awards given for excellence in various fields regarding her military service. Exemplary improvement, outstanding volunteer service, and exemplary achievement were among the certificates on proud display.

On the other end of the bookcase hung a framed college diploma from the University of Beilka for a major in psychology, and beside that was a lone certificate awarded for exemplary achievement in the field of intelligence.

Schneider moseyed over to the desk and sat in her tufted leather chair. Rhodes took a seat casually on the desk and examined his face. He seemed oddly fatigued as he drew in a deep breath and closed his eyes.

"Suitable enough for your liking?" she asked.

"Sorry, just feeling a little bit . . ."

He tried to come up with the right word, but it masterfully eluded him.

". . . I don't know."

She cocked her head. "Is it something you don't want to talk about?"

"It's about the future."

Suddenly, the word began to bounce around in his head, like a sound trapped within a bell.

"I'm listening," he heard her voice call.

It was strangely distant. He reopened his eyes to find her, but the sun's rays pierced her entire figure, and she sat a blur of soft evening colors in the light of morning.

He shook his head, then rubbed his forehead to shake the invasive spirit.

"*Rostal,*" a foreign voice called.

He struggled to ignore it.

"I've been thinking that this engagement will be my last. Vesterbend will have been my first, and Vesterbend will be my last," he said in a tender tone, as if to let her in on a harsh truth.

"—'s dead—Holly sh—"

He struggled to remove himself from the sensations that had grasped his psyche. If he could bring his eyes to hers, then he knew he would be freed. He tried to do so, but failed. His vision had become a blurred collage of colors and shapes, a malleable ground for his sudden torment.

"Don't be so overdramatic like that. Are you trying to scare me or something?" she asked.

The tone of her voice had changed. He could tell she was upset.

"I mean to say that I will remove myself from the service after this is over. I just can't have the life I want like this," he said calmly as he drifted between worlds.

He saw the figure loosen up from its tense state.

"You can't just leave," she said rather casually.

Schneider rubbed his head. He had broken into a sweat. The rays from the window shined deep into the back of his uniform.

"I have a way. The same way we got in," he said.

He kept his eyes locked on an illusion that had appeared in front of him. It warped and fluctuated in the foreign light like a bizarre spirit.

"What about your career? You've come so far in such a short amount of time. Isn't that a waste?" she asked.

"This isn't the life I asked for. It's the one I fell into," he replied, desperate for release. "Stuck between two duties and unable to hold integrity."

"So, was I just a simple pleasure?" she asked him.

"You're far from that," he replied as he tried his best to make eye contact with the thing in front of him.

There was a silence between them. Then he began to hear the sound of shouting. It came from all around as the light kicked into a spiral of raging fury. The burning hurricane was followed by the horrid cacophony of total war.

"I'm happy that you're telling me, but your duty to the Union isn't over yet," she said.

"I'll finish the campaign," he reassured with a tremble.

"We still need you," she said as the sound of falling mortar rounds whistled in the distance.

He looked up in bewilderment.

"It *is* just a dream again—right!?" he swore he said aloud.

"*Cheryl!?*"

He watched as refined memories of the past jumped out from the intense spectacle of hallucination. They spoke.

"You must be great, Rostall!" urged someone familiar.

"Never forget me, will you?" asked a voice of serenity.

"Sir, we're struggling out here," shouted a panicked voice as the manifestation of a soldier erupted from the light then faded.

"I'm right here, waiting for you," the ethereal voice reminded.

"Orders, sir!?" shouted the soldier.

"You don't even understand sacrifice," cried the angry general.

"We're dying out here," said the soldier in an unsettling calm.

A single gunshot rang out.

Then another.

There was nowhere left to run.

He curled away from the manifestations in a fetal position.

The gunshot grew close. He knew it wouldn't stop unless he did something about it, but he felt sick to his stomach. There came a pain that split him like a thousand knives. The overwhelmed hero pressed his face into his arm as the light attempted to force its way through his eyelids.

"I s t i l l n e e d y o u."

Every word was pitched differently, as if the voices of those dependents throughout time and space had been threaded into one.

Schneider raised up as the rifle was brought to his face. To his torment, he found himself in the body of Rhodes, the muzzle pressed to her forehead.

In the next instant, however, he stood at the side of the gunman, the puzzle of torment rearranged again. Her eyes haunted him as she faced the cruel judgement with a face dirtied from war and strife.

He could save her. All he had to do was act. With a bearish lunge of pure instinct, he reached for the gun and seized the wooden stock with barbaric might. As he struggled with the unseen executioner, the light retracted, and the vile cacophony of war ceased.

Schneider grew still as he loosened his grip on the air. Left unsure of what spell had just befallen him, he began to open his eyes. The illusionary rug had been pulled from beneath him, and he was met with dim hues that settled to normality.

Rhodes sat on the desk in silence. She stared at him as if she waited for a reply.

Schneider moved his hands forward, and they slid along the leather arms of the chair. Gone was the intense light, and gone was the haunt.

He straightened up and grimaced in bewilderment.

"What were we just talking about?" he asked.

"I asked you if it's true," she said, wide-eyed and with a quick jolt of the head, clearly annoyed with having to repeat that particular question.

"What's true?" he pressed, determined to acquire a better center on the situation.

She rolled her eyes and sighed.

"You're going to be late if you don't go soon," she said.

He sat in silence for a moment before looking up at the clock on the desk. It was indeed nearly time for him to depart. He got up from her chair and looked around, still somewhat in a daze.

"Are you okay? Why are you acting so strange all of the sudden?" she asked.

"No, everything's fine," he said, escaping from the sensation's remnant grasp.

She stood from the desk. "Well, good luck. And remember—don't be late to the meeting at noon," she reminded him with a look off to the side in disappointed acquiescence.

But as she turned back, she noticed that he still resonated in inner turmoil, and even though she was flustered, she didn't like seeing him that way.

"Hey, what's wrong?" she pressed as she laid her hand on his shoulder.

He fought to find a way to put his experience into words that would be comprehensible, but he could not easily interpret it to another. Fearing the consequences of his honesty, he chose instead to evade discussing it further.

"Now really isn't a good time to get into it," he said.

She smiled with radiant compassion.

"Well, you may just need my remedy for a hard time," she said.

Rhodes went to the window, opened it, then looked up into the sky as a refreshing breeze swept through the screen.

"Simple pleasures! Beautiful, isn't it?" she asked.

Tempted by that treat, he went to the window and sat down on the sill. They gazed at the blue skies together, and for a moment, it seemed like time would not pass. Like all serenity, however, it was fleeting. When time no longer allowed their respite, they left the window and approached the door together.

Schneider turned to face her. "Let's go out somewhere when I've returned from this," he proposed.

She nodded. "Of course. Just call me," she replied.

"When this is finished, my duty to the world will be done. Then, maybe I'll have the time and freedom to enjoy more of those simple pleasures of yours," he said.

All she could do was smile, though she remained visibly conflicted from the evasive zip of her eyes.

He turned out the door and began to make his way down the dim hallway.

"Don't ever forget," Rhodes said.

He turned briefly to his dear companion in the doorway, still aglow.

"How could I ever?"

If It Were the Last Day of My Life

"You know those dreams you have, the ones that are like, so real that you're pissed when you wake up?" asked Lyal Abra who, from a kick-back lounge on a plush couch, stroked long, black locks as he spoke his reverie.

He appeared easygoing, in a tank top which humored with an illustrated raptor in sunglasses. Another young man sat on the arm of the couch as he fingered a silent melody on a well-kept, pearl-colored keytar, with eyes lost behind his medium-length, dark drapes. Though blinded, he kept a steady tempo with the tap of his foot through the air while he moved his fingers to a melody of memory.

The living room was tall, small, and humble. Upon a shelf over a red brick fireplace, several trinkets were on display. Among them was an assortment of small green ceramic jars, an antiquated clock, and remnant segments of a string-drawn toy train. Framed family pictures lined the walls beside it in two perfect parallel diagonals.

The area in front of the television that had been placed in the corner was completely boxed in by two couches and a plump leather armchair while beautiful vases adorned the small end tables that filled the gaps.

There were two hallways that connected to the living room and a staircase right in front of the front door that led to a second-floor loft, visible from the comforts of the first.

Beyond the box was a small opening into the dining room, which lay at the end of the back wall. Aside from the modest, and mostly underutilized, dining room table were two windows which revealed the backyard of the house. A grassy hill, which fell right to the neighbor's fence.

Propped up against the wall were three keytars, each one of them with their own personality of dents, cracks, and worn stickers of urban-themed cartoon characters and graffiti-inspired word art.

"You mean the dreams that may or may not involve Sarah Suggs. Right, Setz?" Mitz Easter said then directed a bold grin to a third teen with matted dreadlocks, who lounged in an office chair beside a computer desk.

Though he was busied with the crafting of a message on his phone, Setz Casture permitted a brief laugh to pass through his distraction. An open book bag sat at the end of the desktop behind him, and within were various audio cords and wires that sprang out like messy hair.

When the message had been sent, he spun around to the computer and shook the mouse. A multicolored cube's bouncing mutation was interrupted as the system woke up to an audio editing program, in full screen. Each segment was covered from end to end with colored bars, bends, and layered effects.

"Nah, Mitz. I mean the ones where you're playing a game or something you've been looking forward to that isn't even out yet. The ones where you believe one hundred percent that what you're seeing is real," said Lyal, using both hands to emphasize an unbearable frustration with the situation.

Setz dragged various parameters on the program's control panel in an earnest effort to transform a vision into reality.

"I hate those dreams," said Setz as he made a few small adjustments to a melody line.

"Well, I've been dreaming lately, boys, and something's been on my mind," Lyal divulged.

"What's it about?" asked Mitz.

"It's really something we should try to do before splitting up and heading off to college or whatever," Lyal replied.

The front door burst open, and Kaiser Riza, a young man in half-hung sunglasses and a loose-fitted cap, stumbled through.

"K-Man, you took that long to pick up some soda?" Setz complained.

Their red-faced companion closed the door as he burst into laughter. "Couldn't even get it. The ex was working the night shift again," he replied.

"And you couldn't just go to another place other than the gas station?" asked Setz.

"She followed me for like five minutes shouting expletives. Then she got her new man to chase me through the neighborhood in his car. He even got out. Like, no joke, I had to jump over seven fences and run from like three dogs."

Kaiser went over to the couch and jumped between Lyal and Mitz, the former being more amused than the latter.

"That's what happens when you screw around with best friends," pitied Mitz as he shook his head.

"That's what happens when best friends hit you with the deepest revelations at the worst possible of times," Kaiser said in defense. "It's actually really nice out if we want to walk up to the store," he continued with bursting optimism as he slicked back his long blond hair.

"I was just about to show you guys what I've been working on for the last two days, you sweaty asshole," Setz protested. He pulled out a pair of large headphones from his bag, along with some unnecessary wires that were strangled on the headband.

"It's not going to kill you," said Lyal as he stood from the couch. "It's only thirty minutes anyway, and we don't want our boy to get his ass whooped."

Setz tossed the headphones on the desk. "We don't? Alright, sure," he said through a sigh.

"I just need to grab the house key. Meet you guys out front," Lyal said.

Setz brought Kaiser up by his shirt and began pushing him until they were out of the house while Mitz went and gently set the keytar against the wall.

"Wow, you don't wanna assault me anymore, Setz? Am I being arrested right now? Oh, please, officer, don't let Momma know," said Kaiser.

Mitz then took out his phone and inspected it as he followed Setz and Kaizer, who were roughhousing in the front yard beyond the window.

"You need to clean out your book bag, dude," said Mitz, his voice barely audible as he joined them in the yard.

Lyal walked to the hallway, which led to a closed door preceded only by the laundry-room corridor on the right-hand side, which also connected to the garage.

He crept forward, then made a gentle turn. On the recessed wall beside the dryer hung a key holder. Only two of the five rings were occupied. One had a set of house and car keys, while the other had a few silver keys, accompanied by a scratched-up plastic keychain with PLASMA ELECTRONIC MUSIC FESTIVAL emblazoned upon it.

He took the appropriate set and stuffed it into his pocket.

The door behind him cracked, which tipped him off that he had been caught. A curvy, middle-aged woman with long, breezy black hair stood in the doorway, comfortable in blue pajama bottoms and a loose pink T-shirt. She put her hand on the doorframe as Lyal turned to face her.

"You going out with the boys?" she asked in a carefree voice.

"Yeah. We'll be back before long," he assured her.

She smiled warmly. "You guys gonna walk?" she inquired.

"Yeah—that's fine. We'll just walk. I just need the house key," he assured with a jingle of the keys in front of her face in mild frustration.

"Okay. Have fun, and don't wear your sunglasses in the dark again. People will think you're a jerk," she advised.

"Well, as you can see, I don't even have them," Lyal said.

Kaiser emerged in the doorway, red-faced and sweating. He stood up straight as Lyal's mother came into his focus.

"Hey, Ms. Abra," he said, beaming. He was posted up on the wall, legs crossed, and devoid of the intention to be taken seriously.

"Hi, Kaiser," she briskly replied. "Be safe, and don't do anything I wouldn't do," she said in return to Lyal. She then paused to ponder her advice. "In my late thirties," she clarified. "Late, late thirties."

"One safe night coming right up, ma'am," Lyal replied as he turned and began walking down the hallway toward the living room.

Setz appeared in the hallway and slammed his hands down onto Kaiser's shoulders.

"Alright. Let's go, playboy," said Setz, forcefully leading Kaiser out of the hallway.

"Don't worry, Ms. Abra. We won't let fanboys in anymore," called Setz from the living room.

This was rewarded with a pleasant chuckle from Lyal's mother, who then returned to the room and shut the door.

Lyal stepped off the porch onto the sidewalk, followed by Kaiser, who was still being pushed along by Setz. Mitz waited in the front lawn, typing on his phone with one hand.

"Damn. I knew she wouldn't let you touch the whip again. Not after what you did to her fender in the parking lot," Kaiser joked.

"Yeah. Whatever, dude. You just better not run if we end up getting jumped."

Mitz plodded over to them. "Guess what? Another galaxy came up missing," he informed.

The boys set aside their bickering and gathered around Mitz. With a swipe, the screen flicked to the top of the page, then rubber-banded to the headline of the news article, which read ELEVEN YEARS LATER, ANOTHER GALAXY GOES DARK.

"What news site is that?" asked Setz.

"Union One," Mitz replied.

"That shit's legit then," said Kaiser in anxious excitement.

"Maybe. But, of course, it could still be bullshit," Mitz insisted.

Lyal looked up into the sky. The others followed suit in silence. Sparsely scattered stars dimly lit the grand expanse.

"Did they say where it's at?" Lyal inquired.

Mitz checked the phone as he sought out the necessary information on the webpage.

"Uh, here's a pic," he said holding the phone up to Lyal.

Setz and Kaiser both peered in from behind. The light of the phone illuminated their faces. A high-resolution picture of a specific cluster of stars was displayed beneath their noses.

"It all looks the same. How are we supposed to know where that is?" asked Kaiser in a surge of frustration.

"Here, I'll find it," said Setz as he pulled out his phone and rapidly punched keys on the screen.

"The stars ain't going anywhere. We can walk while you look for it," said Lyal.

They agreed in silence as they followed him down the shattered concrete sidewalk. The neighborhood was dark. The streetlights alone lit the main road of the suburb. Moderately sized two-story houses lined the sidewalk on both sides of the road, and porch lights revealed the personalities of the townsfolk with the items that adorned their verandas.

The night was quiet, only the infrequent sound of a dog's barking and the occasional passing car overcame the sound of the crickets' incessant chirps.

"So . . . let's talk about those dreams now," said Lyal as he clapped his hands to engage them.

"There's multiples of them?" asked Mitz.

"It's the same one over and over again," Lyal clarified.

"Let's hear it then, buddy," said Kaiser.

"Well, it all starts in a car. It always starts there. We're going somewhere but we don't know where. It looks like highway forty-four right into the city. It's all four of us, but there's a fifth. We don't know her. Not now. But in the dream, we know her."

He exaggerated every statement with body language. The boys watched, trying to make sense out of it.

"What does she look like?" asked Setz, his attention no longer on the sky.

"Is she hot?" asked Kaiser.

"When I see her, there's a bright light outside. It's like a tower of light from the sky—it's huge. Then there's an earthquake or something.

Can't explain it. Everybody looks scared, but not her. She turns to me and says, 'Don't waste time.' Then it's over, but I never wake up after that dream. It's like I remember it in my sleep or it's part of a sequence or something."

Lyal fought to make better sense of the phenomena.

The others remained silent.

"Are we dead? Do we die?" asked Kaiser.

"Of course we're dead. Have you ever seen a pillar of light from the sky?" said Setz with a deadpan stare. He then returned to his search through the heavens.

They continued through an intersection and down a hill that led away from the sleepy suburb. The far side of the road became dominated by forest behind an old iron-wire fence that was either rusted away completely in some places or fallen in the shrubs. The land to their left was cleared, hilly greenery, a distant playground visible from the street side.

At the far end of the descent was a lonely intersection of three streets. A looming green beam from the traffic light glared from afar.

"What do you think it means?" asked Mitz.

"I think it means that now is when the fire of life burns hottest," he theorized. Lyal looked up into the sky at something that wasn't there.

"What's that mean?" asked Setz.

"You know, when we're doing jam sessions on those little five-watt amps, I get to wondering what it would be like to play on a real sound system. The big ones like at Plasma Festival. And I start thinking, right now, we could be searching for spots at small venues and starting to build an identity. We could be working on songs to put into an actual album and put it up online. Right now is when we take chances. Tomorrow is just waiting to see what we'll do," said Lyal in what seemed like a single breath.

"Man, you thought about a lot before we died," said Kaiser.

"You really want to start a band?" asked Mitz.

Lyal chuckled under his breath as his eyes fell from the stars. He shook his head and shrugged. "It's not up to me," he replied.

Setz rubbed the back of his neck and sighed as if he had lost all his energy. "You really think people want to see some dudes playing electronica on keytars?" asked Setz. "I'm not really sure about that market."

Lyal shrugged again. "You'll never know if you don't try."

As they neared the bottom of the hill, a small stream carved through the forest and followed along the right-hand sidewalk. Its waters flowed into a muddy ditch, then through a stone culvert that passed beneath the road.

The steady stream poured over pebbles and rocks and treated their ears to tranquil ambiance behind the song of the night hoppers. Mitz trailed off to the lazy waters, bent down, and scooped up a stone from the mud.

"Yup, there's a lot to consider with that," he said as he threw the stone downstream.

It missed the water and bounced along the ground, until it fell still among a pile of tired gray stones of similar size.

"Nothing happens without persistence," said Lyal as he reached down and snagged a stone from the edge of the path.

Setz eyed his friend carefully, in search of confidence in what he was asking them to do.

"Even if we gave this two hundred percent on the long drive, there's no guarantee we'll make any waves," Setz warned.

Lyal turned to Setz with an untroubled smile and replied, "I know."

Then, he continued onward. The others followed behind.

Kaiser bobbed his head from side to side as he thought over the conversation, then bent down and picked up a rock. He tossed it up, caught it, then threw it in the stream. This time they all watched it fly through the air and plop into the dirt just a few inches from the water.

"You're asking us to put our lives on hold, for what? What makes you think we got a shot at the top?" Setz repeated, still stuck in his skepticism.

Lyal stopped. He started to turn but stopped himself. He tossed the rock behind his back. Kaiser, Setz, and Mitz turned around just in time to see the rock smack down right at the water's edge.

"Maybe, we can get lucky," Lyal teased, then continued walking without inspection of where his stone had landed.

A smile bloomed across Kaiser's face as he rushed to Lyal's side. "Just enjoy the ride then, huh, Lyal?" said Kaiser.

Mitz rushed along and joined at Kaiser's side. "A little optimism can take miles off the journey," he encouraged.

Setz, who lingered in his doubts, looked down to find a pebble beside his foot, one which tempted his faith. But with a dismissive shake of the head, he kicked the stone aside, then moved ahead to catch up with the others.

A subtle green hue crept up their faces as they arrived at the intersection. They made a right turn beneath the stoplights and began along a desolate road that would eventually lead them to the supercenter further up the way.

"Didn't really expect to debate some serious life decisions tonight," said Mitz.

"Life is full of a lot more surprises if you open up to the possibilities," replied Lyal.

"I got one for ya," said Setz.

They turned, one by one, and found that Setz had stopped just a few feet back. As he examined the discovered location with focused eyes, he lifted a finger up to the sky. The others gathered up behind him and guided their eyes up the sleeve of his navy jacket, past his finger, and into space. There, among the vast sparkling ocean, was an undistinguished void of darkness.

Kaiser fell to a knee in a frantic search.

"It was right there, apparently," said Setz.

"Where at? I don't see jack," Kaiser complained.

Lyal reached his arm up alongside Setz's to assist him. "Look for the hole in the stars," said Lyal.

Kaiser squinted his eyes for a moment, but opened them again in surrender.

"Nothing looks any different than anything else. It all looks the same," said Kaiser.

"Well, it's gone now. What did you expect to be there? A clown waving back to you?" replied Setz as he stared down into Kaiser's widened brown eyes, which were almost hidden behind his bangs.

"No, but—wait, what's that?" asked Kaiser.

The others redirected their attention to the sky.

"What's what?" asked Mitz.

"You don't see that . . . flashing?" Kaiser asked.

They each searched for a moment, then became deathly still by what they found.

"I see it," said Mitz.

"Same here," said Lyal.

What appeared to be a simple glimmer flickered in the discovered void.

"Is that thing *moving*?" Setz bellowed in disbelief.

The others tried to catch the movement as well, but the midnight flicker faded to cosmic vacancy and left them with only sheer bewilderment.

"Anyone wanna make a wish?" Kaiser joked.

Suddenly, a deep-space blossom expanded throughout the distant cosmos in a mere instant, which caused the young stargazers to scatter in reflexive astonishment.

"What the f—!" Setz choked.

Just as it had appeared, however, it was gone. Setz, worked into a fluster, struck Kaiser over the head upon their regroup on the sidewalk.

"Whoa! Easy with the head!" Kaiser protested with a chuckle, humored by his animated reaction.

"That's what you've got to say? Make a wish? What the *hell* was *that*?" Setz panicked.

"Chill, it's probably just a satellite that seems like a star or something . . . and somehow it caused a weird reflection," Mitz reasoned.

"That's the explanation everyone wants to hear," said Lyal. He lingered a moment longer on the deceptively still celestial panorama before he stepped away to continue the journey.

"I don't know about that. I'd personally prefer something . . . I don't know . . . a little more interesting," objected Kaiser as he followed behind.

The others joined them, and together they were off again. Setz became locked in a one-handed assault on the keyboard of his phone while he pressed firm against his forehead with his unoccupied fingertips to de-stress.

The bizarre cosmic event seemingly quickened the journey as they each became consumed with internet searches of similar events and relevant breaking news. They didn't find anything to satisfy their curiosity, though surely they hadn't been the only ones to witness it.

As they rose near the top of the ascent, the blue and red display of their destination peeked into view between the trees. With a walk up a short grassy hill, they passed the roadside gas station and arrived in the Russo's Supermarket parking lot. There was a modest number of cars there as the night's last patrons came and went from the two entrances of the large, rectangular building.

They entered the singing entry hall beneath ambient lighting and made straight for the beverage aisle. Kaiser, however, hadn't made it far before he was distracted with a blonde-haired girl at one of the registers. With a cordial wave and approachable reciprocation, he broke away as the rest of the boys continued onward. They secured three bottles of green soda, a few bags of nacho-seasoned chips, then went back to the front, where they knew they'd regroup with their eager romantic.

The boys weaved between the last shoppers' carts until they found themselves back at the front of the store. They scanned the row of checkout aisles but found Kaiser and the girl near the darkened optical department. As they approached, Kaiser caught sight of them and motioned the young woman to return to her register. With short but snappy steps, she crossed back to her post and promptly scanned the bottles and bags.

"He didn't promise to take you out in the convertible, did he?" Setz asked the girl.

She beamed with toothy radiance but shook her head. "No, was he supposed to?" she entertained.

"Well, if he was a gentlemen, shouldn't he?" Setz replied.

Lyal nudged Setz with his elbow and shot him a glare, to which he surrendered with a roll of the eye.

"Come on. Knock it off," said Lyal as the girl finished bagging the items.

Lyal paid the bill, and Mitz collected the bags. They walked over to meet Kaiser, who remained waiting at the door. He frantically dug through his pockets and pulled out two crumpled bills.

"So, uh, who paid?" he asked.

"Me," said Lyal as he snatched both of the bills. "Your cut was only a buck fifty, but you're paying up from last month when you were broke."

Kaiser grinned.

"Yeah, it's cool," he said with two thumbs up.

Kaiser suddenly noticed Lyal staring at something over his shoulder. He turned and saw a familiar black-haired beauty, sharp in bold rimmed glasses. She approached from the entrance with a vivacious bounce in her step, wearing a white lab coat over casual chic. It flapped behind her long legs.

"Well, there's a midnight flower. What's going on, Miyacre?" asked Lyal, rapt by the mere glance she had set upon him through sharpened eyes.

She smiled, but reserved any response until she was right there, in front of him.

"Hey, Ly. Haven't seen you all since the graduation parties. What brings you guys out tonight?" she asked with a neighborly warmth.

"We were just grabbing something to drink," Lyal replied.

"Gotta stay hyped," Setz added.

"Ooh, what'd you guys get? Wine? Beilkan Lager?" she guessed with a dreamy glow.

"Nah, we only got gamer fuel. Not really feeling alcohol tonight, to be honest," said Lyal.

"Did you ask your friends if they were?" Miyacre said with expectation for an immediate response.

Lyal went to speak, but hesitated, then turned to the others.

"Well?" he asked.

"I'm good," said Mitz.

"I'm not going to be the only one drinking," Setz followed.

Lyal turned last to Kaiser and waited with low expectations.

"Beilkan Lager already betrayed me too many times. At least I know soda doesn't hit me over the head with a two-by-four in the mornings," said Kaiser to Lyal's surprise.

"Wow, okay, well, I guess nothing interesting is going on for you guys, huh? Wanna go to a party?" she asked.

Lyal laughed in the face of that assessment. "How about you come to *our* party?" he said.

She tilted her head with a playfully inquisitive gaze. "I don't know. It might be just a bit boring for me," replied Miyacre.

"We didn't even say what we were gonna do, *nyehh*," teased Kaiser, tongue out in a brazen display of childishness.

"So, what are you going to do?" she asked as an immediate follow up.

Kaiser looked up at the ceiling, lost in a brief moment of thought. He puffed up his cheeks and released the air as he set both hands upon his waist. When he had found his simple revelation, he returned his eyes to her. "I honestly didn't even know we were having a party," he admitted rather plainly.

"Lyal!" she cried in counterfeit shock, as she turned to him with a hand pressed against her sternum. "Why are you inviting me to your fake parties?"

Lyal offered up a hearty round of fake laughter, at which she returned to him a look of playful suspicion. "Okay, so it's not a party," he admitted. "But that doesn't mean you shouldn't come. Are you busy?" he asked.

"Uh, I mean, other than that invitation I just extended to you guys, I'm just studying with my dad at the pharmacy," she said, presenting the name tag on a retractable reel, which read "MARK SUREEDY." She released it, and it whipped back against the coat.

"Not doing any real pharmacist work, obviously. He just likes to see me wear it now that we're like, waiting for letters, et cetera. Lucky for you, though, we just finished."

"So, let's get together. You don't need a crowd to have a good time with us," said Lyal.

"Yeah, we are wholesome as fuck," Kaiser said.

Miyacre placed her hands on her hips. "You going to get any good stuff?" she asked once more.

Lyal shook his head but retained his smile. "You also don't need to be tipsy to have a good time with us," he replied in similar fashion to his previous comment.

"I do if I want to have a lot of fun," said Miyacre, laughing. She quickly regained her composure. "Okay, but I'm going to bring a friend."

Kaiser was infused with a silent burst of excitement.

"Yeah!? What about her?" he said trying his best to subtly point out the blond cashier, who had watched them from a distance.

Miyacre turned around and joy lit up her face. The young cashier bloomed to her rosy glow, and at once, they broke for each other in a gleaming scurry.

Within the span of a couple minutes, mostly comprised of casual catching up, they had come to some sort of conclusion. They returned over to the boys, who were now preoccupied with their cell phones.

"So, Ashe says she can go, but her shift ends in about an hour," Miyacre informed.

"Yeah, sorry, and thanks for the random invite," she added.

"That gives you enough time to go home and get dressed," said Lyal as he dropped his phone back into his pocket.

Miyacre laughed and twirled around. "What's wrong with this?" she asked pleasantly. "It's okay. Don't answer that. I'm going now. See you all there," she continued without giving them a chance to reply.

"Come pick me up on your way back," insisted Ashe.

"Okay, no problem," Miyacre replied from over her shoulder. "Just be outside waiting."

Miyacre vanished out into the night. Ashe bade the boys farewell, then returned to her cash register as a large bald man hobbled up to it.

"Let's roll, then," said Lyal.

"Well executed, boys," Kaiser said, congratulating them.

They exited the market together. Setz observed a large smile that had been stuck on Kaiser's face since Miyacre announced Ashe's attendance.

"How long you been talking to her?" he asked with an accusing smugness.

"Who? Me?" asked Kaiser as he turned to Setz to confirm that the question was directed at him.

"We started talking, I don't know, a little over a week ago," he admitted with a shrug. "But I knew she was into me after we rocked it out at the talent show."

"That's not too bad for you, considering your horrible track record," Setz criticized.

"Love is a thing I don't stop chasing. Never had a lot of it where it should have been. Maybe I don't do it right always, but I try my best," Kaiser said.

Setz laughed in an attempt to elicit humor from his revelations, but nothing was earned, and soon, he realized that his friends were looking at him instead.

Regret swept over him.

"I mean, you're right," said Setz. "Sometimes, I think you just move too fast. Nothing wrong with trying to find someone, though. For sure."

"Well, now you're both right. Nothing wrong with love, but ease up on the throttle," said Lyal, laying his arms around both Setz and Kaiser's necks and pulling them close.

The tension evaporated as quickly as it had come.

"Maybe when you take it slow, you'll find more opportunities to learn more about her," said Mitz.

Kaiser remained quiet but nodded. Lyal dropped his arms, and they continued on their way back.

Mitz and Lyal conversed about the various colleges some friends had plans to attend. Setz spent the time once again on his phone, skimming through articles concerning the disappeared galaxy. Kaiser removed himself completely to meditate on his friends' advice, but after only a few minutes, they emerged from isolation and were all talking together about things to do when the two ladies arrived.

It wasn't long before they reached the doorstep of Lyal's house. He unlocked the door, and they entered quietly. Mitz and Setz went right for the couch and plopped down almost simultaneously. Kaiser sat at the computer and shook the mouse. The monitor woke up, and he examined the song on the screen.

Lyal made his way back to the hallway, toward his mother's room. He went up to the door, knocked gently, and then stuffed his hands into his pockets. Within a moment or two, the door opened, and Ms. Abra appeared in the doorway with the same cheerful look that she had left him with.

"What's up, hon?" she asked.

"Just got home. We're going to have some company over. You cool with that?"

"I assume you already made plans before asking?" she asked, though already privy to the answer. "Who's coming?"

"Miyacre and a friend."

"Oh, Miyacre? I haven't seen her in so long!" said Ms. Abra, beaming.

"She still uses the keyboard you gave her," Lyal informed.

"Great, great. So, who's her friend?"

"Don't know her well. She's Kaiser's new girl," he replied.

Ms. Abra chuckled.

"Just a normal teenager, huh?" she joked.

"Well, I'm not like that."

"Everyone has different relationships, hon. You'll find that out real fast." Ms. Abra's face became aglow as an idea struck her. She stepped back into her room. "Here! I want Miyacre to have something," she said.

Lyal followed her in with a nonchalant kick in each step. The room was a sacred temple to the boys. It was decorated with all sorts of pictures and memorabilia from Ms. Abra's youth. On the wall between two windows hung a singular flag crafted from the cut fragments of several others. They were festival flags, brought home from events held all across the world.

Snapshots from those unforgotten stages were framed across the wall beside the door, ones with stories Lyal had come to know by heart.

There was a neat corner turned down on the tall. king-sized bed, which stood before a luxurious black entertainment center at the front of the room.

Hung at the center of its rectangular frame was an eighty-eight-inch flatscreen. Behind glass doors at the center of the left tower were two shelves of illuminated, icy blue glass, which held wine glasses and a few expensive bottles, popped from a recent late-night date. On the right was an elegant, glossy band, which stood crowned above the double doors of a personal refrigerator. One which Lyal and the boys had long come to know as the not-so-secret keeper of beers.

Upon the black shelf beneath the flatscreen was an extensive investment in sound quality, which was enhanced further by the two bed-directed speakers in the corners of the room. Combined, it was an overwhelming boon that had earned his mother countless victories in battles between whose music would play throughout the house.

On a jet-black dresser that hugged the wall beside the door sat a framed photo of a happy and young Ms. Abra in a modest blouse holding her newborn baby. It was a picture Lyal found most embarrassing of all, though it was his mother's favorite. The baby himself had always seemed just a bit too happy for his comfort.

Three small synthesizers were lined up on the back wall, each on its own stand. One was much older looking than the rest, featuring simple cracks and entire pieces chipped away, each lost to time during the hectic blur of touring.

Ms. Abra had gone over to her closet in the far corner of the room. She opened the door and disappeared within.

Lyal meandered further in and scanned over the photos on the wall. Most were taken with friends, both fleeting and steadfast. Others were taken of his mother in her prime, on stages with stacked keyboards on two-tiered stands, her hair slung in mid-performance.

He stopped at one in particular, masterfully shot in black and white. It had always been his favorite. The maven of the keys leaned with coy gleam against a massive stage speaker. The word NEVRSHDE lined the bottom of the shot in an eccentric design that had become unforgettable to those who frequented the scene of yesteryear.

Next to the picture hung a framed electronic music festival poster only mildly creased at the corners. Among the three headline performers, NevrShde was listed in exciting bold lettering. Truly, an old legend among some hopeful dreamers.

"You still going on that date?" asked Lyal as he disengaged from the frozen memories.

His mother emerged from the closet and put her hands on her hips. "Do I look like I'm going on a date?" she asked with an inquisitive glare.

"I mean, it's only eleven o'clock. You could get ready in an hour," he said, encouraging her.

"Uh, no," she replied as she returned to the closet.

The slide of boxes on the carpet floor and the rattle of clothes hangers rang out from within.

"Is the new guy a keeper?" he asked as he spotted a red rose on the entertainment center.

"He may not be the best with promises, but he's a relatively nice guy," she replied.

"Sounds . . . encouraging," he commented with faint enthusiasm as he leaned against the wall.

She reemerged from the closet. In her hand was a black hard drive, overabundant with marks and scratches.

"I want to give her some of my old custom plugins and some other stuff, you know," said Ms. Abra.

"She really just plays on the keyboard, and isn't really tech savvy when it comes to making stuff on programs," said Lyal.

"That gives you something to do with her. Nudge, nudge, hint, hint. I've taught you a bunch, now you teach. Go on. I got a feeling she might enjoy it," said Ms. Abra, privy with the raise of her brow.

He thought over her idea, still not entirely sure of his own feelings for Miyacre, yet enticed to entertain if it were in his power.

Lyal took the hard drive. As he examined it, a sensation struck him. The excitement of his mother's life raced through his head in brief fantasies of roaring speakers, thousands of raised hands, and a deep bass that made the crowd's hearts tremble as they lit up the night with their neon lights. But when the fantasies evaporated, he realized that he was merely home.

Their high school days had passed them by, without a real shot taken for the stars. Though he knew the time would come. If they were going to do it, now was the time to commit to something greater.

"Don't worry. That's not my main drive, the one that has everything," she assured him, afraid she had caused offense.

"Do you ever wish you were back there?" asked Lyal, still partly captivated by his fantasies.

"Back on stage? In the crazy days? I've been fortunate at many times in my life, and all in different ways. But I think, most importantly, I learned at a young age not to live in the past, and just take life as it comes," she said, looking deeply into her son's eyes.

"Nah, that's easy to say from the top, but I know it took a helluva lot of drive to get to where you did."

"And living in the past did nothing of that for me. It's a movement of life. Listen, whatever you're going to do with this music thing, just make sure you're having fun every step of the way."

And Lyal pushed off the wall as that advice rang true in his heart. "Yeah, you're right. Can't find all of our blessings at once, I guess."

She smiled widely, wrapped temporarily in memories of her own. "I'm fortunate that my son's been my biggest fan since he was eleven. Remember when you only liked jazz and you would literally hold your ears if I played you anything I ever made?"

He nodded as he recalled several occasions when he outright rejected listening to any of her music. The first incident of which had caused her to weep alone until he thoughtfully intervened to soothe her distraught heart. "Things change, you know," he said.

"Yes, so make sure you let change in. When life moves forward, so must we."

Lyal had always appreciated his mother's words. They were full of wisdom, and she was no doubt a woman who had made many mistakes in order to gain that knowledge. She was more than a mother to him; she was an icon. Someone out of a legend, a champion from the foreign world he wished to someday be a part of.

"I'm not always sure which way is forward. I just know, right now, I'm nowhere," he said.

"When you're ambitious—or when you make a lot of mistakes—sometimes home feels like nowhere. Even if you reach the stars someday, remember that you can always come back here. This will always be home," she replied as she reached over and shuffled his hair between her slender fingers.

"Now, go on and get back to your friends. They're probably wondering where you're at," she said as she returned to the bed. She took the remote control off the top of the cream-colored comforter.

"Yep, doin' it," he replied. Lyal turned and walked through the door.

Just as he was about to leave, she called out to him.

"Remember that this is the most precious time of my life, son. Nothing else I've done is more important than being your mom."

He turned in heed of that solemn reiteration. "I know, Mom," he replied, then turned and exited out into the hallway.

Lyal reentered the living room to the frantic stumble of footsteps.

He swept the room in a quick scan.

Setz sat at the computer chair. Kaiser and Mitz lounged on the sofas.

"Yeah, man. The bagels at Cornell's are amazing," said Kaiser in an overly enthusiastic tone.

Setz turned his head to him and stared blankly. Lyal watched his friends with patient eyes and didn't budge. They turned and looked at him one by one.

"How long were you guys listening?" he asked.

"About three minutes or something along those lines," Mitz admitted rather casually.

"You guys can't actually mind your own business," said Lyal as he walked over to join them.

"Can't be helped. Your mom's mythic status—to us anyway," said Kaiser.

"Yeah, the pretend bagel conversation is such a classic, isn't it? Really sells the bullshit," said Setz, his words drenched in sarcasm.

"I mean, you didn't help," Kaiser replied.

"Dudes, we didn't decide what we're going to do when the gals get here," Mitz said.

Lyal walked over and took a knee next to the computer. He peered at the program on the screen to where a thin yellow line was drawn down at 00:00. The beginning of all magic.

"Don't worry about it. We'll figure it out when they get here," said Lyal.

"In the meantime, I want all of us to hear the latest version Setz and I cranked out before they get here. It's been months of work on the computer, but this is what we'd have to translate to keyboard," said Lyal.

Silence caused him to turn back, and he could see the doubt in their eyes yet hoped that his faith would become infectious.

They gathered at the computer. Lyal moved the book bag to the ground and then set the hard drive on the desk, which immediately caught the attention of his friends.

Its personality imbued an undeniable allure. Every scratch, chip, and faded sticker of half-ripped smiley faces all lending to the mystique of that lost artifact of a storied era.

"Whoa, what's that?" asked Mitz.

"An ancient relic?" Kaiser added.

"They're just plugs," said Lyal. He pulled out a USB cord from the tangled mess beneath the computer desk and stuck the metal tip into the port of the hard drive. "I'll install them real quick," he said as he rose back up.

A box opened on the screen, and the promised files were revealed. However, there were two other folders.

One named PLUGS and the other named RAW FILES.

Their eyes grew wide as the mysticism captivated them all at once.

"Oh, sh—" said Kaiser, nearly salivating. "She gave you the raw files."

"Man, I would never trust my son or daughter with that," said Setz.

Lyal scrolled over the raw files folder and opened it. Revealed was the list of files, which included both finished and unfinished projects, original tracks, albums, and remixes. Though that collection of files was but a mere fragment of her work, it still managed to completely tower over them.

He hovered on the first one, entitled SOME FREE TRIAL BULLSHIT</3.

The others leapt forward with impassioned cries of protest.

"Don't open that! The metadata, man. Nobody's opened that in like, twenty-five to thirty years. Who knows what kind of spirits you'll awaken," Kaiser warned while down on his knees like a servant.

Lyal shook his head in frustration. "Yo. Alright, let's get a grip. We'll download the plugs later. Let's close this."

Lyal closed out of the window and opened another folder, which sat at the corner of the desktop and was entitled ELECTROENERGEN. Within lay a single raw file, a stark comparison to the legend's. A reality that continued to marinate in Lyal's psyche as the file opened.

But when he saw all the notes, effects, and lyrics that composed their three-and-a-half-minute song, he rediscovered his determination.

He eyed the play button, and with a heart of faith and friends at his side, he turned to Setz and asked, "How about it?"

"Hit it," Setz replied.

A Messenger from the Wasteland

A sleek black sedan rushed down the busy highway in pursuit of a small escort of goliath military trucks. The skyline of Salamandra City had blazed to life after the setting of the evening sun, and throughout her streets swept a neon afterlife.

In the back of the car sat both Schneider and Myres. The gloomy darkness inside was every so often lit by eruptions of light from the passing streetlights outside. Schneider quietly flipped through the pages of a book entitled *Oh Well! A Retrospective on the Political Failures That Heralded the Titan War.* Myres sat with his eyes closed and hands clasped together in a brief slumber to recharge himself.

A muffled voice could be heard speaking over a radio beyond a window that separated the front of the car from the back. Schneider paid it no heed until the driver rolled down the window and relayed news of their imminent arrival.

Schneider acknowledged him in a soft voice, then placed a bookmark down on his page and closed the book.

"Thanks for coming along for the ride," said Myres as the window rolled back to the top.

Schneider looked to him, though the general's eyes remained shut.

"Happy to be of service, sir," Schneider replied.

Myres's eyes opened, and he greeted Schneider with a grin.

"I told you about a hundred times to call me Jim in private," said Myres.

Schneider sat in silence for a moment. "You don't request many of the other higher-ranking officials to do it, so it's a bit jarring," Schneider admitted.

"Rank doesn't always determine what a man might prefer you to call him by. My rules are simple. In the company of others, on duty or during operations, do it by the books. In private . . . just call me Jim. That's not too hard, is it?"

"So, what *does* determine what a man can call you?" Schneider pressed with genuine interest.

"Well, if I think you're a son of a bitch, you can't call me Jim. Or maybe, if I don't know if you're a son of a bitch or not, you can't call me Jim. It's more simple than it sounds."

Schneider laughed.

He didn't quite understand but was amused by the logic. Myres's laid back disposition in this matter was unusual for Schneider, but he accepted it. Nevertheless, he had little faith in his ability to adhere to this sudden departure from standard decorum.

"Can I ask you, what exactly does General Gala believe he's captured? You've made it out to seem like more than a simple fugitive of the law."

Myres gave a slow nod. "He did indeed make a point about something being very peculiar about him. Unlike Gala, I am not a man who believes in any kind of nonsense," said Myres.

"What do you believe in, General?" asked Schneider, curious of his ideological divide with the titan general.

Myres took a deep breath and exhaled slowly as he rounded up some examples.

"Well, I believe in what's right in front of me. The steak that's sitting on the table, the papers on the desk, and the problems that our nation faces," he explained.

Schneider rubbed his chin. "Realistic enough."

"And what about you, Schneider. What do you believe in?" asked Myres.

The lieutenant sat in silence for a moment before he found his answer. "I believe in what I think is possible, sir," he replied.

"And what do you think is possible?"

"It's a hard question to answer. What's possible and what's impossible never seem to remain static," replied Schneider.

Myres tapped his finger on the leather armrest of the door, impatient in his wait for rationalism. "But some things will always remain impossible," Myres insisted.

Schneider hesitated, now conscious of their artful confrontation. "It depends on how one thinks," he reasoned. "Perhaps one might think a ragtag resistance fending off well-armed terrorists to be quite impossible."

Schneider rubbed his eyes, suddenly under siege by the bizarre sensation that had come to plague him. It overwhelmed him quick. The lieutenant covered his face and slowly stooped over.

"Is everything okay?" asked Myres, bewildered by his odd behavior.

"It's just a little bright in here," Schneider insisted.

Myres looked around the shadow-flooded car in confusion. He then smacked Schneider's knee with the back of his hand.

"You alright in there, son?" he asked.

The general became worried by his worsening condition. It was clear that they lacked the facilities for an emergency, so Myres silently decided it was time to act. Just as he went to tap the partition glass, however, the vision-plagued lieutenant rose back to life and latched onto his arm.

"Everything's fine," Schneider insisted. "Let's just finish this business."

Myres yanked his arm away. "Well, is that right? Then look alive. You're on duty."

"Yes, sir," Schneider replied, yet unsure whether he could keep his condition under control.

The convoy pulled off the road and approached the gates of a dreary gray compound, surrounded by a tall metal fence. Above the front entryway was the great golden seal of the Beilkan Falcon, which radiated from the beams of twin spotlights.

"Looks like we're here," said Schneider as he scanned the facility.

"Wonder why they decided to bring him here instead of right on home to Beilka," said Myres.

"I assume whatever inclined them to invite us here happened at the time of his capture," Schneider surmised.

"Seems like a logical assessment," said Myres in a drifting tone.

The convoy advanced until they were halted by two armed sentries from a concrete guardhouse. Following a brief exchange and an affirmative nod from one of the guards, the lead truck started down the road into the compound, followed closely by the rest.

The guards glared, deeply rooted in their suspicions as those officials of rank passed behind tinted windows.

"Well, I was wondering when we'd get to the friendly side of town," Myres joked.

He looked over to Schneider, who was once again bent over with his hand over his eyes.

"You going to tell me what's wrong yet, or are we not well-off enough to exchange this kind of information?" asked Myres.

"It's just a headache I've been getting lately," Schneider admitted at last.

They felt the car brake to a stop. They had arrived before the front entrance, and the guards motioned them to exit the vehicle. Schneider immediately reached for the handle and opened the door to make his escape, embarrassed by his indisputable state of weakness.

"It'll pass. There's no need to waste any more time with it," said Schneider as he laid the book on the seat and stepped out of the car.

Myres shook his head and followed suit. A Beilkan guard greeted them with a silent invitation to pass through the opened glass doors.

They were escorted in through a short hallway, which ended at a pair of bulky, reinforced steel doors. They approached and waited. The subtle whine of mechanical movement invaded the silence. They both searched for the source and found a small security camera in the corner of the room with its sights set on them.

"Please, come in. Welcome to the Beilkan Treaty Command Center," greeted a gentle feminine voice.

The door parted in a slide, revealing a lobby area where General Gala already stood in wait of them. Behind him was an unusual tower-like desk where a woman in an elegant imperial uniform worked on high.

She kept her focus on a computer screen, which set a soft glow on her face as her fingers clacked away on the keys without pause. Next to the desk was a glass door with a thin metal lining. On the wall beside it was a posted warning: UNAUTHORIZED ENTRY FORBIDDEN UNDER PENALTY OF BEILKAN LAW.

The summoned Union officials approached Gala. Their boots soon found burgundy carpet, and they were surrounded by paintings on every wall. Those donated works depicted various Beilkan landmarks and leaders, ranging from Surgaradon Castle, the home of the Beilkan royal family, to the Great Jaddgen Shipyard, to King Leonarber, who led the Beilkans during the Second Beilkan War until his famed demise upon the battlefield.

"Welcome. Please, don't take time to make yourselves at home. We're on a tight schedule," said Gala as he turned and made right for the door behind him.

Schneider and Myres followed him on his instant warpath. The judge hit a button on her desk, in heed of her general's urgency. With a loud buzz, the door slid open, and they entered together into the restricted passage, a barren hall of conservative efficiency, stripped of all majesty introduced in the lobby.

"You added a couple new paintings since I was here years ago," said Myres.

"Never mind the décor. There are more important things at hand," replied Gala.

The hallway broke off into several paths as it stretched deeper into the facility. It was bare, primarily composed of walls, doors, the occasional air conditioner vents, and message boards with pinned postings. They passed by two hallways and came to a third, which Gala led them into.

Not far from the main hall was an imposing security door. AUTHORIZED PERSONNEL ONLY was written above it, accompanied by a large red crown of intricate design emblazoned on the door itself.

Next to the door was a security pad. General Gala drew a card key from his pocket, swiped it through the pad, then proceeded to enter a twenty-digit code in a matter of seconds.

The door opened, but Gala did not proceed. Instead, he turned and passed a glance to his trusted company.

"Well, let's see this magic man of yours," said Myres.

Gala's stern expression remained unaltered. "When you enter the containment zone, you are not to speak to the prisoner until I give you the order. Are we understood?" asked Gala, unable to accept any form of objection. "This is a Beilkan prisoner, and I intend to bring him before the king's court in good health. His mind is not well, however, so you will follow our lead."

"Understood," replied Schneider, committed to composure, as opposed to his bewildered superior.

"Is there a *catch* I didn't quite pick up on at the briefing, or are we actually just checking out a POW?" Myres investigated.

Gala offered no response and then turned for the door and proceeded down the steps.

"Alright, then," grumbled Myres.

Schneider and Myres followed suit and were soon met with an icy wall of air. The aged general rubbed his arms and let out a long-condensed breath.

"You taking us back to the ice age, General?" Myres complained.

"It's necessary to keep the servers cool," said Gala.

"You keep prisoners in the same room as your *servers?*" stressed Myres, in disbelief.

"In the storage beneath it, yes. It is a temporary prison," Gala assured.

The descent into the lower levels was arduous. The metal stairwells were steep and the environment dark and narrow. After a descent of two levels, they arrived at a short hallway with several rows of servers guarded behind steel cages. As they went, Schneider noticed a recurring warning upon each wall of the underground. Grisly white skulls were illustrated at the center of the postings, accompanied only by an inscription which read A SPY STUMBLES TO THE NOOSE in Beilkan.

They proceeded through the center aisle between the humming infrastructure toward a door at the far end of the chamber. Schneider glanced over to the LED screens and inspected the statuses of the servers. They changed at irregular intervals from online to unknown.

"Something's interfering with the servers," Schneider said.

As Gala reached the end of the hallway, he shoved open the door, which whined on its hinges.

"That's correct. It's a transmission that's been coming in since this morning. Right here and nowhere else," General Gala replied.

"Is it one of his buddies trying to reach him?" Myres inquired.

"It's just been unintelligible interference. Come now, and I will show you," replied Gala.

Schneider and Myres followed Gala through the door, descended a short flight of stairs, and entered a shadowy outpost with various sophisticated electronic equipment at work. An operations team of Beilkan officials rushed around the room as they performed unknown tasks, either on the computers or on the towering mainframes of their systems.

Gala led the way to a centralized control console, where a man in a decorated imperial uniform jittered in his frantic assessment of the generated statistics on the monitor.

"Officer Jinzal, how goes it?" Gala barked, to which the engineer snapped up from his seat and saluted the resolute commander.

Schneider and Myres took quick notice of profuse sweat dripping down the subordinate's boiled countenance. Something rather exceptional was clearly amiss.

"The interference, sir—"

"Let our guests hear the transmission," Gala ordered without heed of his urgent cry.

The officer acknowledged his command with a brisk salute and went to work on the keyboard with necessary haste.

No sooner did the live feed from the intercepted broadcast appear on-screen within a narrow window. The program revealed sound waves so intense that they resembled a thick, singular bar all the way across.

The officer hit a button on the keyboard, and their ears were subjected to an instantaneous wall of sound. The hellish burst of static caused the busy team to leap in surprise. As the ocean of static settled, they came to linger in cursed serenity. At first, it was nothing but noise, but soon, they all became aware of something of a whisper in the electronic storm.

"Shh . . ."

"Alss . . ."

"Th . . . World . . ."

"All . . ."

"Ri—Right."

The lights of the facility failed were reborn, failed, then came to life once more. The roar of the backup generators cried out as they sustained the power to the equipment. Some of the units turned up damaged from the surge, which was made evident by the frantic shouts of engineers, who were quick to leap to their repair.

General Gala gazed up at the speaker above the monitor as if he awaited something more. A distinct dread had swept over the Beilkan staff at the control console. Gala's eyes darted back to his officer at the helm.

"It's never done that," Gala whispered, fierce in his madness.

"I know, sir. I'm attempting to trace the source now," he panicked.

Gala rushed to his side and looked upon the personal monitor built into the console frame. A red dot had appeared on a booted-up digital map, which indicated a broadcast from far above the planet's surface. It suddenly split, and the dots flooded across the map until the screen stuttered in a glitchy flicker. Only one remained again.

"Where is it coming from!?" Gala asked.

"It's still originating from beyond the atmosphere," the officer replied.

"You care to explain what's going on? I'm feeling luckier this time that you're going to actually start talking," said Myres as he crossed his arms, exhausted with being kept in the dark.

Gala redirected his eyes to the Union general. "General Myres, this transmission . . . it comes from nowhere. Tell me the nature of that which comes from nowhere?"

"Sounds like a mistake," replied Myres with the mere shrug of his shoulders.

General Gala shook his head in rejection of that easy assessment. "There is no mistake. Science has forsaken us!" Gala cried.

"What about the transmission was different?" Schneider probed.

Gala turned to him with a face so deeply perplexed that it was something of haunting uncanniness. "Didn't you hear it?" he pleaded.

Another door at the end of the room slid open, and a second Beilkan officer emerged. He darted right for Gala and saluted him upon arrival, his face vibrant in an anxiety, which further unsettled the officers.

"What is it, officer?" Gala inquired.

"The situation in the holding cell has intensified after that last surge. Perhaps the general would like to proceed immediately, before the next test occurs," the officer advised.

"In that case, yes. I suppose I would. Gentlemen, if you would be so kind as to follow me," said Gala.

The steadied general stepped out in front of the pack and led the way toward the door from which his anxious officer had emerged. Schneider and Myres followed behind the Beilkans, eager to come face-to-face with Gala's most peculiar prisoner. As their resolved guide reached the gateway into the beneath, the door slid open, and they passed through, one by one.

They began down a ramp into the dark abyss, a storage of decrepit servers and outdated support systems, organized within walled lots, each labeled by letter on a posted plate. A flight of stairs greeted them at the end of the chamber, and they descended on a sweep.

On the lower level, they became surrounded by caged diesel generators. Archaic behemoths, clinging to life on taped wire and dingy pipes. Their dusty bulbs were merely able to decorate the darkness, not chase it away. They produced a dreadful symphony from unsteadied whining, which left one's mind unable to be at peace.

The cold wrapped them in its icy embrace as they reached the last stretch into the Beilkan's abyss. They entered through a doorless metal frame at the chamber's end and passed into the old storage. A graveyard of outdated experimental comm towers lay like iron skeletons in an industrial orchard of science fiction.

The door at the end of the room lay cracked and, as they approached, a soldier stationed on the other side pushed it open to accommodate their fierce advance. The general and Union delegation had arrived at last at the deepest storage cell. Most of its contents had been emptied, aside from the boiler system and a handful of bolts and washers that lay strewn across the concrete floor.

There, at the center of the room, was a man with an unkept gray beard slouched beneath the light of fluorescent strips upon the ceiling. Two Beilkan guards stood on each side of him, with rifles aimed at the back of his head. His gaunt malnourishment was visible in the tears of his war-torn earthy fatigues.

As General Gala approached with his company, the guards directed their attention to him.

"Is he ready to talk again?" asked Gala.

"If he isn't, we can arrange motivation," assured one of the guards as he jolted forth the barrel of his rifle.

Even in light of that impassioned threat, he remained motionless. Undeterred, General Gala approached his disheveled prisoner and knelt.

"Soon, we will be departing for the land of *iron and impatience*. I assure you, the king of the giants will be far less forgiving to defiance. So, tell us what you know, and I will ensure your safety," said Gala with solemn intent.

"What safety will you bring to me? You are but a man, as is your king . . . and mankind cannot save itself from salvation. Not any longer," said the man, his voice barely louder than a whisper.

Myres dragged his hand down his face. "See, what you have here is a lunatic, Gala," he reluctantly enlightened.

Gala threw up his hand and shushed his counterpart before he was given a chance to continue. "Be patient, Myres!" ordered Gala in a suppressed bark.

The fiery Beilkan had kept his focus on the captive. "What is the objective of your insurgency?"

As Gala began to question the man, Schneider, who had been keen to pay attention to any minute detail of the man's behavior, was overcome by the obscure sensation. He pressed his hand against his eyes to safeguard himself, though he did so in vain. The prisoner's head rose. He looked right past General Gala to Schneider with vacant blue eyes.

"Do you see what lies in the beyond? Beyond what we see with our eyes? Time breaks, memories rise up like the living dead, and the elements of life lash out like a raging beast," the captive preached.

Myres looked to Schneider with a raised brow. "I knew we shoulda taken you back. Now you got this looney putting his irons on you with this mumbo jumbo."

"Don't be afraid. I have seen incredible things," the prisoner proclaimed with unnerving composure. "You will, too."

Gala snapped his fingers to try to wrangle away the prisoner's attention from Schneider. The wrinkles in his face grew deep as his frown sank. "What things do you speak of?" asked Gala.

The man brought his eyes to the angry bull. "The indigo sun rises over a land of ignorance. A world ruled by survival, instinct, and social order. Its great light expels the disillusions. Takes that which is uncontrollable and controls it. Makes things that are incomprehensible, there, before our eyes," said the man, growing more excited with each bizarre declaration.

Under the strain of tension, one of the guards threw his foot forward and struck the man in the back. The captive yelped in pain as he flung forward from the strength of the Beilkan's cruel wallop. General Gala raised his hand in disapproval, and the guard stepped away.

"Haven't you given us enough of the scenic route? Give us the frank answer, and maybe you can go back to living a normal life someday, son," Myres pleaded.

Gala erupted and charged toward Myres. "I asked you not to speak directly to him for good reason! And you have no authority to promise this man anything as long as he is in *my* custody," snarled the Beilkan, with a face cooked in red fury.

"In the meadows—in the meadows of peacetime, you will find me. Your wars—have left us tired. But soon, there will be no more. We have served a better tomorrow . . . One you could never even dream of."

Myres looked with casual innocence at his raging counterpart. "Care to translate? The communication level between you, him, and myself are about on par," Myres informed.

Gala stepped away and reined in his anger. "He spoke of something similar when we picked him up off the black asphalt in the Northern reaches. We suspect it to be some kind of weapon they seek to build," said Gala.

"No, no, you've just misunderstood," said the man in a whisper.

"What was that? Say it again," ordered Gala as he redirected on the vacant prisoner.

"There's something much bigger than us—that crude, corrupted insurgency. Something that pulls the strings from oblivion. Watches us with eyes that never blink," the man trembled. "Endless eyes— everywhere!"

"Who is it!?" Gala shouted.

It was then that the man lifted his head and looked upon his bewildered audience as tears swept the dirt from his face.

"Who is it!?" Gala barked again, becoming further enraged.

The man, however, remained silent in the face of the titan's verbal wrath.

"You find anything on him when he was captured?" Myres inquired as he scratched his chin.

Gala turned to Myres and swallowed his anger as sweat ran down his brow. He motioned to one of the guards, who drew a golden pocket watch from his coat and handed it over to his general. The delusional prisoner laid vigilant eyes on the watch as it passed from one unworthy hand to another.

"Just this useless watch. It doesn't seem too good at keeping time. Perhaps he intended to sell it? Useless," Gala concluded as he threw the broken antique to the man's feet.

At first, he remained frozen, but then he inched forward and picked it up into his trembling hands. He examined the watch and ran his fingers along the numerous dents, scratches, and small blossoming reflections that came and went on the gilded surface. He clenched it tightly and took to his feet.

The guards took aim as he lifted that relic in a surge of fury.

"You call this useless? Do you not know? This is happiness, sadness, success, and failure. All things that never were, and all that has ever been. It is both absolute and variable," he declared in empowered crescendo. "It is the whole reason why we—why we . . ."

Schneider, who had once felt no desire to betray Gala's request of silence, suddenly found himself unable to remain unheard. The incessant yelling from the man had caused his head to pound, and he couldn't fight it any longer.

"What does *time* have to do with the insurgency!?" Schneider shouted.

"The insurgency . . . ? No . . . Once I left them . . . This was the only promise I had left. A chance to reclaim something that had remained forever out of my reach," the man lamented.

"Who made these promises?" asked Schneider.

The prisoner's eyes darted away in a sudden anxiousness. "He is the darkness on the walls, and I know he is with me now," the man uttered.

"What was that?" Gala investigated, shaken by what he had heard.

The stalked captive sealed his eyes tightly and took a deep breath. "Do you know of the abyss? Have you looked deep into it? It does not simply gaze back. It marches and comes to claim us as its own."

"Gala, you going to explain any of this?" asked Myres, still unable to make sense of him, his previous synopsis of the prisoner unchallenged.

General Gala, quickly overrun with rage, darted his eyes between prisoner and guest before he rested his fury solely upon the insurgent.

"No more nonsense. I want you to make clear what you're trying to say, this instant," Gala ordered.

". . . The stars are falling," replied the man as the lights in the room began to flicker.

"Another transmission?" asked one of the guards. He looked over to his armed comrade and noticed his legs rattling. "Are you alright? Your legs!"

He went silent as he felt the vibration crawl up his body. The power built in intensity until the entire room was taken by the quake.

"Earthquake, sir!" the guard shouted to Gala, who struggled to keep his balance.

"And now, time is running out," the man concluded as he peered up to the ceiling.

The lights trembled, and the walls began to crack. The facility's alarms blared as it was subjected to an unexpected catastrophe, one of which it was not designed to handle.

"A quake in Salamandra? Unheard of! It's in the court's hands now. We must evacuate at once," ordered General Gala.

He motioned to each of the guards, who had dropped low to the ground in order to secure the captive with a semblance of stability.

"You two! We're moving him to the airship immediately."

"Yes, sir," they replied at once.

He turned to the last soldier, who had clung to a steam pipe near the door, which, to his fortune, was wrapped by thick insulation. "And you! Go and send word to prepare the ship as soon as possible."

With a frantic nod, the soldier departed through the door on clumsy steps. Myres went over to Schneider, who fought to recover from being thrown off his feet.

"Up and at 'em, Schneider! Last place we want to be is underground during an earthquake. Forget about dying though. We might get entombed down here with these guys and their damn shaman," joked Myres as he pulled Schneider up and began to lead him to the door.

The soldiers pulled up the prisoner and forcefully led him to the exit.

The steam pipe near the door gave off a long moan. None gave it attention, however, as that imperiled coalition struggled to reach the exit upon thundering earth.

Schneider, Myres, and Gala stumbled through the exit with the others just behind them.

Just as the soldiers and the Beilkan prisoner reached the door, however, the pipe gave one last moan, then burst. The breach emitted a thick smokescreen throughout the room and sent the soldiers to the floor, who screamed from the burning intensity of the scalding shroud.

"Damn it all!" said Gala as he turned back to assist his soldiers.

"Hold on," said Myres, as he dropped Schneider's arm and ran after Gala.

Schneider turned and tried to follow but collapsed to his knees in a bizarre fatigue. He watched Gala and Myres in a starry daze as they pulled the two squirming guards from the vicious jet stream.

Once dragged clear of the hazard, Myres took a knee and attempted to calm the writhing guard with reassurances over the blare of the broken pipe. Schneider pulled himself up and made his approach to the scene of chaos on a limp. Gala made several attempts to enter the white screen but was forced back by lashes of pain each time.

"I can't get through. It's hopeless," shouted Gala to Myres over the wailing breach.

"You can't just leave him for dead," asserted Schneider as he finally got to his feet.

"If he isn't already dead, we'll all die trying to save him," Gala replied.

Schneider took thoughtless steps forward. His heart began to thump as his pace hastened, and before anyone could realize it, he was in full sprint.

The sound of his footsteps sold him out.

"Hey! Stop him," Myres shouted to Gala, only now privy to the reckless lieutenant's intent.

The old Union general rose and took a desperate swipe. His grasp came up short of Schneider's arm, however, just before he was swallowed in the white wall of steam.

"What have you done, boy?" asked Myres.

Without further hesitation, he rushed back over to assist Gala, who desperately searched the cloud for any sign of movement.

"Lieutenant! Are you alright in there!?" Gala hollered.

The earth roared, and the ground was subject to another sharp quake, which toppled the two aged generals in the force of its rage. Myres recovered first to his feet as the intensity subsided, then raced over to Gala and seized him by the shoulder in the desperation of the moment.

"Where do you turn off this line? We need it off now," shouted Myres.

"Upstairs, further along the main hall! It'll be too late—"

"Then call it in," Myres interrupted.

Gala pulled out his phone and frantically dialed the line to the service desk. He fled the screech as he drove the phone into his ear. Then erupted in frustration as he was met with immediate failure.

"I can't get a signal. We're too deep inside," Gala reported.

"Then, I'm going in," said Myres as he turned for the vaporous jet stream.

No sooner had he declared his reckless intent did he encounter fierce resistance, as General Gala snatched his arm. The determined general attempted to pull away, but Gala seized him with both hands and ripped him away with enormous force.

"Don't be reckless like the boy," Gala urged as he threw his counterpart away from the hazard.

Myres stormed up to Gala's face with veins bulged across his temple.

"Then get upstairs and turn off that goddamn pipeline," Myres threatened.

Gala nodded with respect in Myres's cast-iron dedication to his comrade and, with a dedication of his own, turned from his old nemesis in a spirited flight to rescue his lieutenant.

Left alone, Myres turned back to the treacherous veil, unsure if either of them were alive or dead.

Beyond the dense screen lay Schneider, thrown to the brink of consciousness but somehow unscathed. Not far away, the troubled prisoner lay face down in deathly stillness.

Neither inched until a tremor stirred them.

Schneider lifted his head, then began to rise on fragile strength. He searched the area with conviction until his eyes found the target.

"Get up—you still have a duty to the Union . . . and an unimaginable debt to my homeland," he commanded.

The man remained unresponsive, however.

"These questions won't go unanswered. Get up," Schneider ordered again.

He seized the Beilkan's prisoner by the shoulder and rolled him onto his back. The fanatic had suffered a severe scalding, with blistered, red patches of skin pervasive across the side of his face, neck, and arm. After a brief delay, however, his eyes opened, which sent a wave of relief through the reckless upstart. His efforts had not been in vain.

"Some questions are meant to be just that. When the miracle comes, there will be no mysteries left to ponder. The grand essence of our world shall depart for oblivion . . . all of us as one. And what will matter to you then?" asked the man with genuine interest in his answer.

Schneider's relief vanished and his gaze became empty. "What do you believe is going to happen?" Schneider asked, calm and resolute.

The man quietly drew up his hand and peered up at something cusped in his fingers. It was the worthless watch.

The fanatic looked upon it with a glint of disappointment.

"For me—the story is over, my friend. Perhaps this dream of mine was not meant to be in this life. But, in paradise, it will hardly matter," the man lamented in his ill-sown faith.

"You're not—answering me," Schneider warned as his patience teetered.

"What is there left to answer!?" cried the man in a spit of frustration. "The faithful have been swallowed by their dreams, and the—"

Schneider released a sigh as something within him gave way. With the vivid manifestation of the executioner, he drew back a clenched fist and unleashed dark, pent-up rage against the prisoner's cheek. He felt each knuckle put the blistered epidermis right against the bone. A strike that surely offered temporary suspension of the fanatic's fascinations.

Schneider steadied himself without a gleam of remorse. The unjust wallop had relieved the man of the watch. It tumbled across the ground as he wailed, his body curled in pain from the sudden assault. The cold air spread Schneider's nostrils like that of an enraged bull.

"So . . . I'm going to ask you one more time . . . What do you believe is about to happen?" Schneider asked in a cold whisper, his conscience and fist ready to strike again. "You said it yourself . . . Your story is over . . . " Schneider continued as he seized the man by the collar and hoisted him up.

"You murderers all deserve something far worse than this—I enlisted in the service a long time ago, so one day . . . I could lead an entire battalion of heavy armor just to run your pathetic, frail bones into the dust of the wasteland—a fantasy I was eager to lay aside. Then—you barbarians decided to return . . . but for what? What dreams did you think you were owed? Or were you simply not content unless farmers suffered? People who didn't give a fuck about you or what you stood for. Well!? Answer the question."

The man trembled in newfound fear as blood poured from his nose. Schneider waited in anticipation for an answer.

"I—have served the puppet masters since the very beginning, when the work of the first visionaries amassed Beilkans at the border and any one of your countrymen would have ripped the Treaty of Fortuna to pieces. Years ago—I was favored for my knowledge of the Vesterbend . . . but for eleven years after, I waited for my prize, and it was never— delivered. I came to the conclusion the second time around that things might end up the same," he spat in anger.

Schneider released the man, satisfied with his compliance. The insurgent raised up on his elbows, his face twisted in disgust of his inauspicious fate. "So, I stole from the camp and set out on my own, and not without a little bloodshed along the way," he admitted. "I left a hollow man, devoid of purpose, walking the miserable brink of nihilism . . . as some do, when they reach the middle of their life, empty-handed."

However, the man lifted a trembling finger in indication of a particular occurrence, which had certainly altered his course of mind.

"But I met a man—I met a man deep in the wasteland! Who transformed the things I believed! And he left me with that gift," he said, quivering as he pointed to the pocket watch.

"He told me to journey near the Beilkan base. He said destiny— destiny would guide me the rest of the way . . . But I was taken captive, and now I am here."

Schneider smirked. "So, you were made a fool of."

The man shook his head in ardent defiance of that claim. "No! No, I am no fool. You have not seen what I have seen . . . H-have you seen the moving star!? It is upon us, you blinded Union slave. Tomorrow! Tomorrow is upon us. Unstoppable, like a ravenous storm, and not one of us is ready for it! So, beware the answers you seek. I have none left for you," the man said as the eruption from the burst pipe began to subside.

"Who was the man that gave you the watch?" Schneider pressed, unfinished with him.

The insurgent lowered to the ground as his breaths became unsteady and sharp.

"We're swallowed up in a dream . . ."

His head hit the concrete as the last glow faded from his eyes.

"But soon—our dream—will be one," he proclaimed with a grim vacancy.

Schneider checked the pulse in his neck. The fanatic insurgent had passed.

He felt the sudden weight of his actions. Though he was unsure if he had a direct hand in his passing.

The lieutenant sauntered over to the forcefully relinquished watch the man had instilled such bizarre faith and retrieved it from the ground. It was cold to the touch, somehow more icy than imaginable; it was a coldness that had the attribute of unfathomable depth.

A sensation that was impossible yet unshakable.

He felt, too, the faint existence of an unseen realm of infinite chambers, where choices branched so vastly that it left him overwhelmed. Schneider yanked his consciousness from that dream plaza and refocused himself in the moment. Without a doubt, there was something unusual about this orphaned trinket, but why had its sensations gone undetected by the Beilkans? The questions of which the insurgent warned him to abandon only grew louder as he stood there, alone yet under surveillance from something that surely wasn't there.

A quake rippled through the room and shook the lieutenant from his deepening contemplation.

The crisis had not yet subsided.

Two shadowy figures emerged from the lingering cloud of steam, and Schneider slipped the watch into his jacket's inner pocket.

"What the hell has gotten into that head of yours, son?" asked Myres as he emerged.

A dispatched medic hurried past them, dropped down, and searched for a pulse on their ill-fated prisoner. Myres searched Schneider's face for an answer as his lieutenant took a deep breath to feign his remorse.

"It's too late," the medic announced as he checked over the body once more to secure confidence for when he would have to face his commander with the news.

"I tried," Schneider lied. "Thankfully, he did shed some clarity on the insurgency's objectives, which I think might aid us in moving forward."

"That right?" asked Myres, taken by surprise. "Looks like you're in good shape, too—but how is your face not redder than a chili pepper?"

And that observation caused the lieutenant to linger in shared bewilderment.

"I'm not sure," replied Schneider as he glided his fingers across the unscathed skin of his cheek.

Upon deeper recollection, however, a rather striking image stood out from that vulnerable moment in which he had tested death.

"Actually—as I entered through the steam, I do remember passing by some kind of dark pillar, or a form, or something." He shook his head, discomforted by what his mind had excavated.

"I don't know why I remember that," said Schneider in an attempt to discard it.

The ground was subjected to a terrifying quake that sent the antique comm towers crashing down in the other room.

"Forget it. Let's move, son—and stay sharp. We've got the whole damn warehouse falling apart behind us," Myres informed as he stabilized from the jolt.

The general looked over Schneider's shoulder to the medic, who came up from a last-ditch attempt at resuscitation by way of the breath of life.

"If you're thinking about leaving, now is a good time to do it," he shouted.

"Nothing more we can do," the medic concluded as he abandoned his rescue and made for the exit.

The Union commanders raced through the door and began to make the journey back to the main hall as sudden quakes from the depths tested their balance. They maneuvered through the downed towers, climbed each of the staircases toward salvation, and edged around high-voltage hazards before they finally arrived above ground.

Once there, they were hailed by the Beilkan medic and a few soldiers who, together, escorted them with urgency through the main hall. When they emerged back into the lobby, they were greeted by General Gala, who was doused in a sweat.

Myres went to speak but was immediately cut off.

"There's been a report that we've lost contact with the Union Mephelis base outside of the Vesterbend. A distress call from our Gaillega base across the border seems to indicate some sort of—broader attack," Gala reported with unease.

Schneider's eyes widened in sheer disbelief. "An attack? There were no reports of insurgent activity anywhere near those areas. How could an army capable enough to take on those installations slip under the radar?" the lieutenant pondered in dismay.

The assembled Beilkan officials and staffers fell into silence in light of that grave news, then looked to the Union's supreme commander. To those who didn't know him, Myres showed little reaction to the news as if he hadn't the mettle to lead. General Gala, however, could see that his old nemesis looked right through them all to the options on his table.

The fragile silence in the room was chipped away by small chatter among the Beilkans. Myres took a deep breath as he reached a conclusion from his silent assessment.

"That means attacks on other targets might not be far behind," the pensive Union general speculated.

Gala nodded.

"Nobody is ready," Schneider thoughtlessly echoed, with an ounce more credence in the warnings left by the misled insurgent.

That peculiar line drew the attention of both generals, who turned on him in bewilderment. Realizing the focus he had attracted, Schneider moved quickly to explain his words.

"That was his last warning," Schneider relayed.

Gala eyed him closely. "You mean the dissident?" he asked.

"He had a talk with him," Myres explained.

"I think this attack must be what he was referring to," replied Schneider.

"Where is the king's captive?" asked Gala as he turned to his Beilkan staff.

"Deceased, sir. The earthquake made the body's evacuation from the lower levels too hazardous," the medic informed.

"The insurgency shouldn't have the firepower to overcome such a large Union base," said Gala in turn to Myres, in full expectation of validation.

"Well, if a fallen base isn't proof enough that they can, you won't get much better. If what he says is true, then the insurgency may be stronger than we ever imagined. We spent a good deal of time with politics and ethics instead of action, and perhaps this is the consequence," Myres lamented.

Gala scoffed. "Then eleven years has changed nothing."

"What matters now is that we get back to command to begin preparations for an organized and effective Union response," said Myres.

"Then Godspeed. The city seems to have been spared from the worst, but there's reportedly major damage to the infrastructural integrity of the roads and highway," Gala relayed.

"Then we aren't getting back as quickly as we came. I need to make some private calls," said Myres.

Gala turned promptly to the judge upon the towering bench. "Have the gate cleared for them," he ordered.

"Yes, sir," the keeper replied.

Gala then turned to two soldiers, who waited at attention. "These two gentlemen are leaving. Escort them off the premises safely," he commanded with a slice through the air with his finger.

Beyond the doors of the Beilkan facility was mild devastation. The road lay shattered before them, and the parking lot was split by shallow fissures. The skies were alive with the shrill of sirens and wail of horns, horrid evidence that the city of Salamandra had been thrown into chaos.

To clear the path, a small team of staff and soldiers had been assembled. Adrenaline-fueled, they hauled pieces of road off to the corner of the security wall, where a small pile of rubble had been amassed.

Their car eased up to the porte cochere with the crunch and pop of small debris beneath the wheels. The Union envoys entered the car with haste, then buckled in for the journey back.

"Get us back to Homestead. Double-time," Myres ordered.

"Road back through downtown's a mess, but emergency services are getting a route cleared," replied the driver as he shifted gears.

"Let's roll," Myres replied.

"Understood, sir," said the driver as the car pulled through the front gate and turned onto the main road behind the escort trucks.

The convoy roared through dynamic scenes of chaos that had engulfed each and every street. All were overrun by the masses that had gathered to witness the damage inflicted upon their community by the implausible quake. Salamandra City was a place that lay far from any active fault lines.

Faced with assault on two fronts and upon the very framework of possibility, the words of the insurgent sank ever deeper into Schneider's conscious. Something was amiss, and they needed no better demonstration. What was coming? Perhaps it was truly already there.

"What's the Union's response, sir?" asked Schneider as he peered out to the roots of nightmare on display beyond the window.

"We hit them like lightning," Myres declared just before there came a ring from his pocket. He pulled out the phone and lifted it to his ear. "Yes, go ahead, Prime Minister."

Tomorrow

The living room TV flashed to life with a high-pitched whine, and its image settled from white intensity to colorful vibrance. This was followed by the clack of the remote control on the glass side table and footsteps that faded into the kitchen.

The long rays of dawn reached through the windows and laid warm, rectangular sanctuaries across the beige carpet as well as a soft glare upon the television screen. A messy-haired troupe of sleeping youth, the four friends, and their haphazard company lay across the two couches, aside from Setz, who solely occupied the office chair.

Miyacre and Lyal lay together in the corner of the couch, her head rested upon his shoulder, and the waterfalls of her luxuriant almond hair were strewn across his sleeveless shirt.

She began to stir as a chiming cadence from the television grew in crescendo. She rose, and her squinted eyes passed from the rising sun beyond the window to the television screen before them.

Upon the glass, that same sun of morning crept over the Union Capital Building in the distant Salamandra City. Soldiers stood at attention in dramatic quarter-mile phalanxes, all faced toward a stage at the head of Union Park, decorated across the bend with the patriotic flags, which represented each branch of their military. At center stage was a single podium, emblazoned on the front, the gilded seal of the prime minister.

The camera panned across that scene of solemn quietude in the hopes of evoking some deep reverence from the compatriot viewership. Between each awesome phalanx stood a group of soldiers who bore enormous Union flags, which waved gently in the breeze of the new dawn.

The pan ended with a jump to a static shot of the stage. There stood multiple members of the Union High Command. Generals Myres and Henson flanked the podium while Schneider, Rhodes, and the rest, were lined up outside of them with an aesthetic five-yard gap. Behind them, in seats along the back wall, sat the elected representatives of the Union Senate. As the sun peeked over the capital building, the shadows of hoisted flags along the wall draped over the stage.

Miyacre shook Lyal's shoulder, but he rolled away in response.

She punched him. "Something's going down," she droned on in morning fatigue.

Lyal rolled back to her and leaned up. "What's up?" he asked, disoriented from the sudden awakening.

She directed his attention with the jerk of her thumb, which he followed to the television in a sleepy glaze. An official in a black suit had approached the podium and, upon his arrival, leaned down to the microphone.

"Good morning, my fellow patriots of our sacred Union. It is with great honor, that I invite Prime Minister Roland to stand before us all. Let us begin today's agenda with our national anthem, The Millennium Resistance. Thank you."

He turned and departed on dignified stride, and the shot cut to a stately orchestra located offstage, which began to perform the sovereign march on cue. Ms. Abra reentered the room, took hold of the backrest, and leaned over the couch.

"Wonder what's going on in both my house and on the TV," she asked with a glance down at Mitz, who had awoken behind a personal curtain of hair.

He shuffled over to Setz, reached out over the couch, and slapped him across the cheek. Mitz yanked back his arm as the startled sleeper barreled over to the ground in alarm. The disturbance caused Kaiser and Ashe to spring up from their peaceful repose.

"Yo! What have I told you about doing that?" Setz fumed as he lifted himself from the ground toward Mitz in a blind rage, which was quickly extinguished by the sight of Ms. Abra.

"Wouldn't have been any different if I had done it any other way. I've tried them all," Mitz assured him.

Kaiser stretched out as he crowed in delight at Setz's inordinate reaction to the rousing strike.

"Whatever, man," Setz dismissed as he fell back into the chair.

Mitz turned to Lyal. "What's going down, anyway?" he inquired.

Lyal shrugged. "Just woke up."

Ashe, too, crept out into a deep stretch as she eyed the masterful musicians, each focused on their impassioned performance for the nation.

"Are they really doing election stuff already?" she ridiculed.

"Man, you're really watching this?" Kaiser hassled as he rubbed his eyes.

". . . *Just* woke up," Lyal repeated.

"Elections aren't for another three years, hon. I'm sure it has something to do with all the fighting up north," Ms. Abra speculated.

"Please, don't call a draft or anything stupid. We literally just made it to eighteen," Setz pleaded with folded hands.

Ms. Abra chuckled at his spectacular conjecture. "I'm sure we won't need anything like that. It's not a country we're fighting. Just a bunch of very sad people," Ms. Abra assured him.

"Look at this," said Lyal, with a nod to the television.

On screen was a static frontal view of the podium. The anthem had concluded. A husky man in a black overcoat and cane in hand approached. He reached up to adjust a pair of thin metal glasses, then swept his hand down his bushy white mustache.

As he made his arrival at the podium, he slammed the bottom of the cane into the ground. He looked to the crowds with reverence in the silence he now commanded.

"Tyranny has many faces. It intimidates with a thousand wicked heads and wields endless devices to bring ruin to the just world. Tyranny is merciless and it employs many injustices. Tyranny feeds on its own truth and hides its lies behind a guise. Tyranny seizes on the spoils of the free and threatens a barrel to their heads. But today, the Union of the Resistance will demonstrate to tyranny, that the will of the free people shall not be intimidated. Our setbacks will only make us wiser foes, a truth made undeniably evident by the brave generations who drove out relentless Beilkan conquerors from these lands we call home. A truth crude provokers should have learned to fear.

"Yesterday . . . in the dark of night, a ruthless attack was launched against a Union base, which was established nine years ago to assist with maintaining peace in a land, defiled by inhuman oppression. Last week . . . a barbaric assault nearly decimated a small town, which was little more than a farming community. Two years ago, an insurgency against decency reemerged to wreak havoc among good people for the repugnant glory of the bloodthirsty. But tomorrow! Tomorrow, there will be no bloodshed for the sake of cowards. Tomorrow, the people of the Vesterbend may be able to rest in their homes without fear of waking to ashes.

"Tomorrow, maybe the world will stand for a truer peace, and seek reasons to cooperate, rather than reasons to fly the banners of war. Tomorrow, there will be peace, because tomorrow is ours. We will not surrender it to those who have no respect for the innocent. So, it is with great enthusiasm for the future that I announce we will secure tomorrow from tyranny, and we will reinstall peace with a full commitment from the World Union of these Emancipated Lands."

Waves of distortion and static broke through the picture in the onset of an unusual phenomena.

Ms. Abra cocked her head in bewilderment as the disturbance intensified. "What in the heck . . ."

An incomprehensible noise blared, cut away, then returned. The stream of video persisted through the arcane interference.

"Tomorrow, there's nothing to fear," declared the prime minister as his face came and went upon the screen.

Bewilderment had soon shaped every face there in the living room, just as the entity made its final decree.

". . . For . . . tomorrow . . . is ours . . ."

". . . Tomo . . . rrow . . . is . . ."

The Prime Minister's face vanished as all became lost in a sea of static.

Nonplussed by the anomaly, they lingered together in silence. An oppressive denseness lay upon them as they were left to ponder what had just occurred before their eyes.

"What's up with that? It's not like you're using a dish," said Kaiser.

Ms. Abra took the remote and turned off the TV. A tranquilizing silence returned to the room.

"Well, that was strange. In any case, who wants pancakes!?" asked Ms. Abra, eager to lighten the mood.

Mitz flung his hand up in a sudden burst of excitement. "Mitz does," he declared.

"Setz . . . also does," Setz added rather naturally.

"Mmm, pancakes? You're going to ruin me, Ms. Abra," Miyacre resisted as she draped over the back of the couch.

The reformed hedonist protested her reservations with vivid astonishment.

"You're already down to the bone, girl. Have a little sweet stuff in your life while you're young," Ms. Abra advised with playful sass.

"You don't have to tell me twice," Miyacre assured in an unconcealed glow.

The young teens pried themselves up from body-heated comfort and moved into the kitchen. Works from the mother's brush, the walls were decorated with paintings, which depicted petal flurries of lavender, rouge, and cyan blue. From two windows, the dawn's light spilled across pristine-white marble countertops. A pleasant luxury which was found, too, across a center island, where the ingredients for the promised pancakes, neatly organized, sat beside an open laptop.

Ms. Abra, Miyacre, and Lyal went to work in preparation of breakfast while the rest opened the door to the backyard and stepped outside to converse on the back patio.

Lyal took a whisk from the counter, as Miyacre added the milk and egg to the powder. She slid over the prepared bowl to Lyal, and he began to mix the ingredients into a batter. Ms. Abra tapped away on the laptop's touchpad until an energetic melody of electronic chords burst from the speaker. The rhythm had been birthed in excitement but soon calmed into something more tranquil. Then, it glided, stopped in oblivion, dove down, and ascended into light speed.

Miyacre rocked to the beat as the energy took them to outer space and inspired her movements to become rather reckless. The risqué performance commanded the attention of both Lyal and his mother, the latter of whom echoed her brazen shimmy, though refused to indulge with rampancy.

"Watch out, girl," Lyal flirted with a raised brow.

The build exploded into an all-out blitz of thick bass and sharp synths, which roused the frolicsome teens into a playful bounce of the shoulder.

"It's really been over twenty years—wow," said Ms. Abra, lost in a moment of pleasant nostalgia. "I'm sorry I'm putting you guys through this."

"I can get down to some of this," said Miyacre.

"Clearly," Ms. Abra joked, at which they shared a laugh.

"Must have been wild to chop it up against Lucky Number Eight, huh? Can't believe he dropped snippets of this track on you as part of the album prerelease," Lyal fantasized.

Ms. Abra nodded.

"Almost lucky," she confirmed.

"It was a really transformative loss, in a way that people really got to see who he was and what he was about. It was just a track that, you know . . . you could tell right from the start, that there was so much heart and soul in it, that you didn't stand a chance, unless you brought the same level of intensity. That was when only a very few number of producers would even do a duel. Because they were like . . . whatever," she said with the roll of her eyes.

"Great for selling tickets, but they took a lot of work and collaboration. I think at the start of the night, he didn't even want to do it."

"Must have been disappointing to lose. I mean, I hate losing, personally. Like, at anything," said Miyacre, still locked in the sway of rhythmic hypnosis.

"It wasn't all about the winning, so much as it was about offering a really . . . unique and organic live experience. I mean—I screwed up . . . so much stuff during those duels . . . but people liked them when they happened. And that night with LN8, even I was having a good time getting my ass kicked," she admitted as the back door opened. "I usually do."

That rehabilitated reminiscer's eyes widened as her thoughtless remark revealed intrinsic carnal truth.

Miyacre's jaw dropped.

"Whoa, whoa, whoa, watch out. The rating has just increased. Adult swim! Adult swim! All kids out of the water!" Kaiser thundered as he led their reentry from the porch.

"Mom, *chill*," Lyal complained.

A jovial ruckus ensued as that authentic revelation passed through their systems, and when they were settled, the others took a seat at a round dining table, which was nestled along the kitchen's bay window.

"You know, I bet those are some incredible memories to share with people. I wish I had that kind of stuff to talk about in my life right now. Really eager to start building up experiences, you know?" said Miyacre as she clicked away at the touchpad in a mellow hunt.

"The future is what it's all about. I can't wait to do something super unique, and really make the best out of this life . . . And I think we've got it; me and these guys. All we need to do is put in the hard work," Lyal encouraged.

"My best advice to *all* of you is to remember where you are, where you want to go, and the small steps you're gonna take to get there. Not everybody can leap a staircase, but almost anyone can climb it step-by-step. Now is where you lay the foundations of everything else to come. And life . . . it's a marathon, not a race," said Ms. Abra.

"And honestly, you're all just eighteen," she added.

"Weren't you, like, eighteen when you played your first show?" Lyal pressed.

"Yeah—in some dude's basement."

There came a ring from Ms. Abra's bedroom, which she took urgent notice of.

"Oh, that must be him. Hey, Miyacre, watch all this for me, would you? My son has a really short attention span, and I can't trust him."

Lyal scoffed with the raise of his eyebrow. "It is when you talk to your boyfriends for, like, two hours."

"That's only on Saturdays."

But her son shook his head in rejection of that bold claim. "Not the case, at all," he contested rather naturally.

She shot him a glare, then stepped off into the hallway. "Whatever, I know what I'm doing," his mother assured from around the corner.

"Don't worry. Handle that," Miyacre encouraged, still fixated on the computer as she browsed through downloaded music.

To pass the time, Lyal produced a red rubber ball, which he bounced upon the tall kitchen wall over the countertop. He remained in a groove of throwing and catching until he became bored with easy success.

"Miyacre—catch," he said as he shot at a wide angle.

"Hm? Whoa, what!" she cried as the ball zoomed for her face.

Miyacre dove below the counter. The ball struck the top, hit the wall, then soared over to the table, where Kaiser scooped it from a vicious ricochet in the corner between the wall and the backyard door.

"Nice catch, Miyacre," Kaiser razzed.

"Try not to aim at my face when I'm not even paying attention."

Kaiser returned the ball to Lyal, who continued in his solitary game of catch. She watched him in refusal of being caught off guard again.

"What?" he asked in feigned innocence.

"Uh-uh, I know what you're trying to do. Give it," she demanded.

Lyal wound up, as if he were about to pitch it to the wall. Miyacre fled the room with a shriek. Laughter from the lighthearted scoundrel welcomed her back, however.

"You're an ass, you know that?" She held out her hand as he continued to bounce the ball. "Give it," she demanded again.

In surrender, he tossed the ball over to her, which she placed into a drawer without hesitation.

"Hey, what!?" he protested in a dumbfounded laugh.

"You're done being five, sir," she declared with the fling of her fingers and roll of the eyes as she returned to the computer to continue her search.

Ms. Abra reentered the room and placed her hands on her hips.

"Are you scuffing up my freakin' walls again, Lyal? Damnit," she razzed.

Lyal shrugged.

"I mean, I didn't know a rubber ball—whatever. I'm done with it now, anyway," Lyal said in abandonment of his defense.

"When you move out into your own place, you can scuff up your own walls," she said with the slap of her hand upon the counter in playful exaggeration of her grievance.

"Hey! Found it!" Miyacre beamed as she pulled back from the screen with a celebratory pump of clenched fist.

Lyal and Ms. Abra set aside their playful spat and leaned in to see what had energized her spirit. The fierce thunder from the speakers, however, told them before their eyes could find the words.

An expressive wind cleared like mist from a path, opened by the ring of bells. A tranquil scene, it was crept upon by a punchy, yet distant synth, like some journeying visitor on approach to sacred grounds. Then, with the strike of bass, the melody fell away and became a mere resonant haunt in the vastness left behind.

A wanderer, left in his awe.

Through the cosmos, a lonely star beamed as the wind chime rattled, and the pedals of her otherworld fluttered through the aural forest. Lyal, in that moment, felt himself tumble through her alternate dimension and touch down upon the sparkling emerald grasses. A land of radiant bloom and crystal caverns. He was left to the temple grounds, the wanderer's journey and his own, now one in the same.

"Oh, hey! It's me," said Ms. Abra as she looked down upon the glamorized immortalization of herself on the screen.

With NEVRSHIDE emblazoned across the bottom of the image, the once sparkle-skinned diva of the night stood with a shining beam atop a DJ booth, crafted from a chaotic puzzle of triangular blush-tinted glass.

She stood with legs split wide, heels dug into the crystalline top, and turned at the waist to her invisible audience. With clenched fists set upon slanted hips, she was bold and confident at her peak. Forever preserved in that distinctive era, she donned a short-cut neon tee and high-waisted silk pants with slits, which permitted playful peeking.

The song intensified alongside a pressurized sweep. The airy blast sharpened until it had all but consumed the lingering haunt, then released as the melody line resurged to full strength and kicked into racing speed.

Lyal examined the album cover, which served as the static image for the video playback. It had been uploaded five years ago by a nameless fan and had garnered nearly two and a half million views. Though relatively young upon the video sharing platform, it was an experience known throughout the decades, part of a legacy he could only hope to accomplish himself.

"Damn, you looked good," said Miyacre as she performed an expressive fangirl ogle.

Ms. Abra hummed the old chorus as she continued the motherly preparations of breakfast, an odd juxtaposition of times in her life. "Yeah, don't remind me. It's been awhile since I've looked at that cover," she said in a break from her nostalgia-induced performance.

"I totally forgot that your mom was the around-the-block celebrity," Ashe recalled as she fought the butterflies' tickle with a toothy glow.

"Oh, hon, please don't look at it like that. That's never been the way I've wanted it to come off," she insisted.

"Yeah, no, I understand. It's just like, hey, whoa, *accolades*," Ashe explained with an expressive pop of her eyes.

A rumble from the cheery admirer's phone invoked a reflexive retrieval. She twisted in the seat and slid the flat, silver-backed smartphone from the pocket of her snug-fit jeans.

It was a striking new device that drew the immediate attention of Mitz.

"Oh, nice. You got one already?" he remarked.

"Uh-huh. Dad just *had* to go out and get us all one. World changing. His words, not mine. Not that I'm complaining," she admitted.

"Isn't your dad involved in, like, top secret rocket scientist stuff?" Kaiser recalled as Ashe read through the message from the application.

"He's assigned to the Joint Space Exploration Program. An engineer," she corrected. She lingered with a cynical grin, amused by the promise that had been delivered to her. "They do a lot of work up at Maris Mons." She tossed the phone aside on the table and offered her full attention.

"Maris what?" Kaiser probed.

"Maris Mons? The rocket testing site? He's actually flying out there tomorrow because the government wants to test—whatever part they've been working on, all next week."

She grabbed her phone and wagged it in front of them, aglow in facetious amusement. "Just got the text. Happy birthday to me."

"Really? Well, that's pretty cool that he does that," Ms. Abra complimented, though under no illusions in regard to the girl's obvious struggle.

Ashe shook her head with a roll of the eyes, then returned to frantic meandering on her phone.

"We never get to see him. He's always on base or . . . doing other stupid stuff for work." She sighed as she fought to suppress a deeper frustration. "I just kind of, look at his face in the glow of a laptop. He just—stares at it," she ridiculed with a sharp grimace.

"Hey . . . at least he's not a deadbeat," said Kaiser.

"Absolutely got a point there," Lyal added.

But Ashe shook her head again, in total rejection of their defenses. "Whatever. I just hope he regrets it someday."

Ms. Abra's natural glow escaped her as she found herself looking in something of a mirror, one she felt she couldn't turn away from at this stage in her own life. "Well, let's all get to the table. The pancakes should be done soon," she said.

"Yes, ma'am," said Miyacre.

"Ashe—" Ms. Abra called.

"Yes!?" she replied in a rather chipper tune.

"Would it be okay if I talked to you about something later on? It doesn't have to be now," she clarified.

The girl straightened in her chair, taken aback by her request, but unintimidated. "Oh—sure, of course. Just—anytime you want to, just let me know."

"Okay!" Ms. Abra beamed.

"Okay!" Ashe matched.

The energy in the room settled. Lyal laid his elbows on the counter as he listened to the decades-old track. He did his best to dissect it into its basic elements in an effort to understand both why it worked and how it worked.

His mother turned from the stove and caught him in the trance. "Don't think too much about it, honey."

Lyal slapped the counter in mild frustration. "You were my age when you were doing it. That *kills* me."

She smirked, went over to him, and leaned in to make their exchange a little more personal.

"Listen, there's no need to rush into anything just yet. You know I'm going to help you get to where you want to be—but you just gotta be ready. You make those songs with your friends, and we'll get the ball rolling together."

Lyal nodded as a deep breath lightened the weight from his shoulders and allowed his confidence to return.

She leaned back up, satisfied with that release.

"I wasn't ready when I went in . . . and, I want you to avoid some of the mistakes I made."

"But maybe it's better when you go in unprepared," he contended.

"You're a very wise young man, and I'm not going to disagree. But let your mom do this for you, please? Going home without pay checks isn't something I want you to have to maneuver. Or living in your car for any set amount of time—learn that lesson from me."

Lyal nodded and let a grin slip through his renewed composure. "Yeah, you're—probably right about that."

"*Probably?*" said Ms. Abra with a smirk. "I think I probably am, too."

Ms. Abra returned to the finalizations of her labor and left Lyal to dally in his fantasies.

Not long after, the graduates were gathered at the table, each with a hearty golden stack. Ms. Abra stood at the counter as she clicked through pages of a news site on the laptop while her son and their guests lent reluctant ears to Kaiser, who had agreed to try his hand at a freestyle.

Setz and Mitz struck the edge of the table to give him a beat.

"Hey, baby girl, don't like my dentals? What you got there? Is that a rental? A little crazy, don't check my mentals. I mean—mental records, shit!"

Kaiser dove beneath the table as he cackled in laughter.

Ashe, who had agreed to harmonize alongside him, abruptly cut her accompaniment, and released a wind of disbelief as her head fell upon the table.

"Never going to help you guys with vocals if this is who I'm dealing with," she declared as she looked up to Miyacre, who had one side of her lip lifted in shared disgust with his performance.

"Don't lose your vocal talent already, Kaiser," said Ms. Abra without looking up from the screen.

"Yeah, that was seven steps beyond ridiculous," said Setz as he took out his phone.

"I see how it is. I'll just roll out solo, it's alright," Kaiser joked as he raised back up with arms out in faux confidence.

"Rest in respect," Ashe cheered.

"Yo, Lyal, check this out," said Mitz, his phone extended out with a faint song playing from the speakers.

Lyal took it. It was a video with a humble 134 views, which featured a static image of loose-leaf papers emblazoned with vectorized question marks.

"What's up?" he asked Mitz, who leaned back with a satiated glaze.

He put the phone to his ear and became immersed in the dance of synthesized delight. It was a trance-inducing, chip-tune track, a style he knew Mitz to be quite fond of. It enchanted with dreamy, plucked chords, which soothed as they brought to mind carefree steps on simplistic, sunny days. A happy-go-lucky composition was tied together by solemn hooks, which hinted of some grander journey ahead.

"Look at the comments," Mitz redirected.

Lyal pulled the phone away from his cheek and looked.

Below was a solitary comment and a single reply.

Who are you talking to?

The only reply was written by the same poster.

Never mind, I don't want to know.

Lyal and Mitz exchanged a glance.

"Deeper meanings?" Mitz entertained.

"I don't know, man. Maybe it's just someone being weird," Lyal replied.

Mitz shrugged. "I found it interesting."

Lyal returned the phone, then closed his eyes to bask in the glow of morning. Something about that moment captivated him. In many ways, it was like any other, another lazy spring day, on another year. This year, however, was rather exceptional. A time to be cherished while it was there. Their days without responsibility had reached their end. High school was over, and here they were, on the last lingering days of the normality they had known most of their lives.

For the remainder of the moment, he listened only to an unintelligible melody of life around him as he felt the time slip away. Kaiser leaned back in the ladder-back chair as he munched on his pancakes, so loudly that it caused Miyacre to freeze and glare at him with her fork left in suspension.

"Dude, put the chair down. You're going to break the legs," Setz scolded.

Impatient for compliance, Setz reached forth and yanked the chair down from the top. The tipped legs fell flat upon polished porcelain with a thud.

"Chill—I would never break any of Ms. Abra's nice stuff. Honestly, I don't even know why you live here in Lindshaven. I mean—you got money."

Ms. Abra chuckled to that narrow-minded, but understandably juvenile, pondering. "I knew where I wanted to raise my son. And look—he didn't turn out too bad," she joked.

"It's not like your house is small, Kaiser. It's just a mess," said Mitz.

"My mom is a *fucking* slob," Kaiser replied, his eyes widened to instill faith in his bold declaration.

"Apples and trees, Kaiser. Apples and trees," said Setz as he chewed aggressively on the last scraps.

Setz leaned up and pulled out his phone and typed out a message with his thumb.

Kaiser took a bite out of his pancake and leaned back, eyeing his critic with malicious intent. From a concealed position in his lap, he prepared a device from his pocket. With the draw of a line from pinched fingers, he took aim with a sealed eye, and then, with his target locked, released.

A magnet on a retractable line sprung out and slapped the back of Setz's phone. Kaiser yanked it, but Setz lunged out and snatched it back before the sudden rogue could secure it. The experienced victim latched onto the string and ripped it away from Kaiser's grasp.

"Give me that stupid thing, you damn clown. Hey—I thought you promised to get rid of this."

"Okay, guys, can we really not do this at the table," Miyacre pleaded.

Kaiser laughed heartily, with a load of pancakes still stuffed in his cheeks. Setz stuffed the string messily into his pocket, leaving the Velcro handle exposed.

"Hey—if you admit it's useful, I'll never do it again," Kaiser swore as he jabbed his finger at Setz to emphasize his words.

"Useful at pissing people off? Yeah, okay," Setz mocked. "And when you get arrested for messing with the wrong one, maybe you can show the security guards how you can latch hold of the steel bars and walk yourself into the cell."

Lyal, though still in his mental retreat, had become conscious of their struggle and smirked as they bickered. He could find no better friends if he tried. He was fortunate to have forged such a family. One that would, without a doubt in his mind, hold up in the longest tests of time. He felt the light intensify, as did its warmth.

Something shook him from his reverie, however, the talk of distant a ruin.

"Did you see the news about the earthquake in Salamandra? They said that it shouldn't even have been possible," Miyacre said.

"And fourteen people died too. Sad, isn't it?" Ashe remarked.

"Thankfully, it didn't affect us over here," Ms. Abra said.

His smile sank as unease set in, and he became subjected to the surreal haunt of an indigo tinted invasion from beyond the windows. The nether's shade engulfed the faces of all of them, both friends and mother alike, while Lyal listened on, dragged from sanctity and awoken to some obscure reality.

"I heard them saying there's a war on the horizon," someone remarked.

"So, if we can't keep chasing dreams, what will you do then…?" The phantom voice asked.

Those muddled voices from nowhere settled in his subconscious and caused his spirit to sink. His eyes crept up. Above the door to the backyard, on high, hung an unassuming clock. It ticked and tocked, the rhythm of their time in perfect control, constant, focused, and unrelenting. Forward it went, the moment in race, a future approaching, refusing to turn back. Refusing to cease.

A visionless reverie turned uncanny nightmare, the unknown entity seeped through the fabric of imagination.

And he felt it coming through.

It raced throughout the nether-touched lands beyond the glass with such speed that when it reached out and touched the center of his mind's eye, it was virtually invisible.

And as that ethereal intruder coursed through a mind burdened by the onset of a harsh new reality, it witnessed him secure faith in the shining spirit of his dream. No matter what he and his friends might face in the realm of tomorrow, Lyal swore to never let faith in the dream go.

As that solemn exchange concluded, he was urged to reemerge.

Lyal peeked right into a familiar pair of alluring green eyes. Miyacre leaned toward him in her chair, as if in wait of a response. He shot her a look of bewilderment, to which she responded with a startled laugh.

"You tired or something?" she asked.

"Nah, it's just—early, man," he replied with a long stretch.

They were the only ones left at the table, joined in company by Ms. Abra and Kaiser, who had offered assistance with the dishes.

Banter from the others could be heard in the living room.

"Well, get your eyes open. We're taking a road trip," she smirked in mellow glee.

"Road trip? Where?" he asked, taken aback with how much he had missed.

Miyacre's eyes shifted from side to side as she pondered a distinct destination. "Anywhere. Adventure doesn't need a road map," she replied in a casual lounge, her elbow dug into the table and fist pressed into cheek.

"In other words, we have no idea where we're going, and are about to go waste gas," Kaiser clarified.

Ms. Abra beamed as she filed the last plate onto a rack beside the sink. "That's why I love you, Miyacre! Such a good spirit," she admired.

"I try, but being free-spirited doesn't get you far with these boys, Ms. Abra," she replied, with a secretive wink to Lyal, who was preoccupied by typing on his cellphone.

"Isn't it a shame?" Ms. Abra replied, in jest to her oblivious son.

"Alright, let's go then," said Lyal as he return the phone to his pocket.

"No excuses?" Miyacre asked with playful scrutiny.

"Do you want an excuse?" he replied.

Pleased by his acquiescence, she lifted from the table with a smile, then went to aid in the last cleaning efforts.

It wasn't long before they had finished the task in the kitchen. The boys convened upstairs in Lyal's bathroom and squeezed around each other in a scramble to utilize what expedients were available to recondition for the journey. Meanwhile, the two girls put themselves together in Ms. Abra's bathroom, to which they had been given exclusive permission.

As his friends made their way back down, Lyal changed from the tank top in favor of a plain white tee, with a burgundy bomber to top it off.

In due time, they had all reconvened at the door and slipped quickly into their shoes, eager for the promised roads of freedom to be theirs.

Ms. Abra had stepped out into the living room to see them off on that familiar journey.

"Lyal! Come here a second," she called.

He rose from the last squeeze into new white sneakers and found her beckoning with a finger.

"Meet you guys outside," he informed the others as they filed out the door.

He leapt down from the step and went to her.

"You know mom's only rules," Ms. Abra said.

"Be safe, have fun, and check in," Lyal named off with the count of his fingers.

She glowed in a maternal fulfillment in that, perhaps, her old teachings had found a place in the foundations of her boy. "Take care of each other, okay?"

"We will, mom," Lyal said, amused with her concern. "We'll be gone a few days, tops."

Her eyes lingered on him as she stole a moment. She offered a smile through the anxiety stirred up from the sudden chaos in the world. Once a fleer of domestic oppression, she wouldn't let him see her struggle to let go. It wasn't the kind of mother she had promised to become. That hesitancy, no matter its rationale, had the capacity for intrusion and thus could never sit right with her.

And so, she set herself aside, and let him go to the world.

"Okay," she whispered, then settled into a gentle beam.

He turned from her, but a strange sensation nagged him. He passed a glance over his shoulder from the open door. From his pocket, he raised a pair of sunglasses. He snapped open the temples with a flick of his wrist, laid the veil across his eyes, then left her in that reticent gleam as he pulled the door shut.

Lyal reassembled with the others, then together, they made for an old, round-bodied SUV, which sat crooked in the driveway. Kaiser shadowed Setz and then, in a crafty maneuver, he slipped out in front of him and swiped the magnet sling from his pocket.

"Still swinging it in, huh?" asked Setz as he popped open the door and jumped into the backseat.

"Not hearing it from the guy who wrecked his dad's truck just last month. Although, I realize you're really adamant that it wasn't your fault," Miyacre retaliated.

"Don't believe me, look at the police report. When you're going fifteen in a fifty on a winding backroad, and I come around in a pickup truck, best believe there will be nothing left of your smart car," he said with forceful indignation.

"Only memories," Mitz lamented.

"You're lucky you didn't kill anybody," Miyacre stressed.

Lyal hopped into the passenger seat and laid his head back against the headrest. Kaiser stumbled his way between the seats and threw himself back into the third row.

Ashe stepped in behind Mitz with her face down in her phone. As she sat down beside him, she let out a soft snicker.

"Guess I'm supposed to come home today before three o'clock. They must have forgot about the graduation . . . Let's go," she said as she locked the phone and let those messages go ignored.

"Hearing you, girl," Miyacre rejoiced.

When everyone was secured inside, Miyacre put on a pair of sunglasses and ignited the engine with a theatric twist.

She threw the handle into reverse, then stomped the gas into a thoughtless, full speed reverse back onto the main road. Before the car came to a complete stop, she whipped back into drive and gunned the engine, which caused the rear tires to screech in a brief spinout.

She scanned her mirrors as her captive passengers reoriented themselves in wake of the wild maneuver.

"Yo! Yo! You have no room to talk about my driving," said Setz, with arms still glued to the top of the roof.

"While I have a car, I can talk all I want," she argued.

"Oh! That makes sense," Setz replied with cheeriness, as if her claim was rooted in some pragmatic truth.

Miyacre and Setz continued their back-and-forth bickering until infiltration by the others managed to steer them from their discourse. Soon, they had reached the ends of familiarity on the outskirts of town. With home in the rearview, their adventure had begun.

The SUV bumped along the old road. Though it shared the name of their town's main conduit, this far down, the surroundings shared little similarities with home. Where in Lindshaven there was liveliness, here was dereliction of such scale that to some, it transcended mere destitution and could be realized as something rather spectacular.

Rampant negligence lay evident throughout that forgotten passage to the contemporary ruins, from the trash built up along the crumbled curbside to the vacant structures that passed by, one after the other.

They approached the heart of that lost consumerist plaza, a place which bore the most recognizable landmark of the old suburb of Fable. Beyond the endless cracked pavement of the parking lots, which served only as urban gardens of untamed weeds, were old shopping strips. An unmaintained museum of yesteryear's architectural trends, they were topped with turquoise roofing, which had become washed out from fifty years beneath the sun.

Although many saw Fable as a regional stain of urban ruin, it had once thrived as a pleasant suburbia. The town had been whittled to the infrastructural bone in a prolonged decline as gentrification in neighboring cities drew wealth out of the area, and with little change made to contest the shift, stagnation resulted in a remarkable decade-long exodus.

That corrosive event saw a once-bustling communal hub become nothing more than a hollowed commercial graveyard. However, the land of uncanny vacancy soon attracted the interest of local artists, who found a distinct majesty in its vast emptiness. The kind of which an archeologist finds in old bones.

Thus, it became something of a gathering ground on which small festivals would pop up as a newborn community peddled their intimate creations to privy guests.

They were familiar grounds to everyone aside from Ashe, who had taken an immediate fascination with all of it. Her face didn't leave the window as they passed deep into the barren-faced shopping district, which had become expansive as they approached the lots of the forgotten mall.

To that liberated adventurer, it was a pleasant escape from the often-stale, middle-class luxury of Lindshaven. So, Ashe drew her phone and took aim at the bizarre wonders that passed in the distance.

"Spooky place," she remarked as she snapped pictures of the abandon strip and its oversized lot that harkened back to better days.

At the center of the strip was a large, square-shaped slab that stood above the storefront. Though the grocer's signage had long been removed, the outline of its name remained in a ghostly shadow, a peculiar message spray painted across it.

It read Welcome to the Void in bold black lettering, an oddity Ashe made sure to catch a snapshot of.

"Let me show you something really cool," said Miyacre.

Each of the boys were privy to the outlandish marvel that she wished their uninitiated friend to discover. Though infrequent, they had made several outings throughout the years to see it themselves, whether it was alongside friends with skateboards or simply among each other on Sunday evenings. They would meander in sun-drenched timelessness until the pale moon shined, and Monday's inevitable arrival pulled them back home.

"Summer's End?" asked Lyal.

"No doubt about it," Mitz replied.

It was but a short drive to reach that landmark destination. In the distance appeared the fallen white fortress, a citadel of consumerism whose towering walls cut through the pristine blue skies.

Miyacre raced the SUV down the central drive, but slowed, however, as they arrived upon a roundabout, which hugged a bone-dry fountain. Upon a centralized podium, which stood encircled by rust-tainted water nozzles and hollowed illumination lamps, were twin seraphs, who lifted a stone clock in graceful presentation of the time to passing visitors. SUMMER'S END MALL was declared in bold stone-carved letters, which rested front and center upon the fountain's perimeter wall.

It was a picturesque entry to the mall grounds, which had laid petrified in the grace of stasis ever since the day capitalism's citadel fell exhausted. A monstrous void left behind, its failure ignited a ruinous vacuum, which time proved a decisive death knell for even the most resilient businesses, who were eventually reaped by inherited financial woes. That crippling plague ultimately left the development contaminated and dissuaded savvy startups and lucrative chains from ever taking root anywhere near the hulking corpse.

"I've actually seen this place from the interstate going to Salamandra," Ashe recalled, snapping pictures of the folded forum as they left the roundabout behind for a road that traced the outskirts of the parking lot.

"Yup . . . This is where they used to break in and do some crazy live shows," Lyal fantasized. "Not that I know firsthand. Just heard the stories, as usual."

"Who's they?" Ashe investigated.

"The Electropocolypse Movement. It was based right out of Salamandra," he replied.

"Is that something your mom was involved in?" Ashe explored as she inspected her shots.

"It was post-me, so nah, not really. But she knew about them. These guys were all about staying off the grid and away from the cameras. Valued a tight-knit community and exclusive lives shows over the lucrative reach of the internet," Lyal enlightened as he looked to the hollowed temple in a daydream of big bass thunder from the underground resistance.

"Whew! Anti-internet? That was doomed to fail," said Mitz.

Lyal shrugged, heartened by the romance of the faithful.

"No bubbled dream lasts forever, but I bet you it was really cool to have been there. Even if one day everyone had to move on . . . and face tomorrow. Kinda wish it stuck around a little bit longer," he lamented.

"I heard it was all party until the break of dawn," Kaiser hyped.

"I heard it was like a cult or something," said Mitz.

"Who told you that?" asked Kaiser.

"Jared Robbles. He was always talking about this kind of stuff in my biology class," replied Mitz, but Kaiser had already retreated away in disinterest.

"Dude, Jared doesn't know what he's talking about. He told me he belonged to a gang, but the name changed five times in one week. I made a concerted effort to ask every day," said Kaiser.

"Jared Robbles is the most honorable man in the universe. It's not mentally possible for him to a lie, about anything," Mitz stressed with a phony yet forceful confidence.

"Jared Robbles? Oh, wow, let's talk about that supersized nose," joked Ashe.

"Or that electrifying breath," Setz added with the roll of his eyes.

"Man, what do you guys know about the god that is J Rob? Please, disembark the poser train. Like, honestly," Lyal razzed.

"Holy shit, can we stop saying that name . . . for five seconds? We are almost there," Miyacre complained as she cut the air with an open palm.

"Ooh, the mom coming out in you already," joked Mitz.

"Shut up," she snapped back, visibly flustered.

"Jared Robbles," Kaiser added with a shrug.

Miyacre released a long sigh, then chuckled. "Why did we agree to do this?"

"Why *did* we agree to do this?" Kaiser said in return of ball to her court.

"I don't know," she whispered through a light beam as her head shook. "Anyway, there it is."

They had arrived at the opposite end of the mall. Miyacre made a sharp turn into a desolate lot, then cut right through the middle. Ashe lowered her phone as her eyes rose to the freakish anomaly upon the colossus's wall.

A hazy neon cascade melted down the side of the urban canvas, and from precise strokes, an unusual figure was carved from the chaos of color. The indigo-hooded man looked upon the world with his hand reached out, as if to allow one to grab hold. In both eyes, he held the world, faintly painted as a reflection, and on high was a melted clock frozen on midnight.

The vibrant mural expelled the dullness from the dead mall's wall, transforming it into an overwhelming beacon of stimulation.

"Wow, that's surreal," Ashe gawked as Miyacre pulled the car across a few parking spaces, which lay beneath the gaze of the interstellar visitor.

"An invitation to an intergalactic journey," Setz mused as he peered out from over her shoulder.

"That's a pleasant thought," said Miyacre as she threw the gear stick into park.

"Isn't it?" Lyal tacked on.

Miyacre slapped the top of her legs with both hands. "Well, what are we waiting for?"

She turned off the car and yanked the key out of the starter. Together, they exited the air-conditioned cabin and stepped into the sun-scorched wasteland. They were greeted by the radiant warmth of baked pavement beneath their feet, and then, in an unhurried amble, made their way to the mural that towered high above their heads.

They stood at about the height of the man's fingertips, and as they gathered beneath, each of them looked up into the world-bearing eyes of the outlander. For a moment, each believed that his wordless invitation extended to them explicitly, and that perhaps, something truly remarkable lay just beyond indulgent suspension.

"What's the story behind this guy?" Ashe investigated.

"The guys who painted it call it *The Cosmos Cycler*," Lyal enlightened.

"Some say they got the inspiration from a super trippy dream that, like, all three of them had in the same night," said Kaiser.

"Mom has always been pretty adamant that they legitimately met this guy . . . And he was so bizarre that they *thought* it had to be a dream," said Lyal. "*Though*, I never got an explanation of why they might have believed that. Definitely gonna ask for some clarity when we get back."

"That's so cool. I love the eyes," Ashe complimented as she moved closer. "You know what? How about a picture?" she suggested as she waved the new phone in the air.

Without giving it much thought, they stepped up to the curb and grouped together on the sidewalk. Ashe held up the phone and positioned her shot, but hesitated.

"How about everyone touch the hand?" she called.

"Yeah, let's go to the otherworld, baby!" cheered Kaiser as he eagerly reached out and slapped his hand upon the mural.

"Here's to being young and freaky!" said Miyacre as she joined Kaiser by setting her hand upon the wall's cool surface.

"Here's to a tomorrow for us," said Lyal as he joined them with dream secured in his mind.

Time seemed to slow as each of his friends placed a hand on the mural behind them. It was but a subconscious manipulation derived from their eager acceptance of the cyclist's beckon.

Lyal had become anxious. He was eager to forge a path of brilliance but could do nothing from here. His mind cut to a familiar darkness in which the light of a computer screen burned into desperate eyes as sunlight peeked through the windows. He heard the sound of cheering, then—music. He wanted to be happy, there among his friends, but ambition threatened to drown him in nervousness. The boy pulled his hand off the wall and rubbed his forehead as he fought to put distance between his overburdened conscience and those feelings.

He knew what would await him when the visions faded. An empty parking lot, in an empty place, and an even greater emptiness expanding within.

"Lyal! You okay?" Ashe called.

Lyal flinched as her voice snatched him from the mental prison. "Yeah! I'm . . . zoning out, sorry," he replied, liberated from the dream state.

He returned his hand to the mural, alongside the others.

Ashe lifted the camera back into position. She snapped a few more pictures from a few different angles, then rose with a nod of satisfaction.

Miyacre departed with haste to aid in vetting the shots as the boys moseyed over behind her. In light of their diligent investigation, two shots were promptly deleted after the inspection revealed a shut-eyed Kaiser in one and a distracted Lyal in the other.

From the final three, they chose the one they fancied most. With a small touchup to bring out the glow of the skin and add a hint of vividness to the eyes, the girls deemed it complete.

It was saved and agreed to be delivered as keepsake, a quaint first step to their spontaneous outing. Ashe, however, quietly became consumed with small edits, and the delivery was delayed. In the meantime, they set off to return to the car.

Lyal turned and experienced faint captivation by the resonance of grandeur as they left the cycler behind.

"What are our chances of being tossed into this war?" he asked as he turned from the mural.

"Zero," Setz replied rather plainly.

"Well, the way I see it, even if they do draft us, we'll have to go to training, which could take months, and by that time, the whole thing will be over," Mitz explained as he dragged his feet over the gravel, kicking up a dust cloud in the process.

"We're obviously not the warrior type anyway. They'll take one look at us and send us right back through the front door," Kaiser insisted.

"Yeah—they'll do that to *you*. A dude on cognitive life support," Setz clarified.

"And to this day, your mom continues to be a pillar in my life."

"Shut the hell up," Setz replied with genuine disgust.

Ashe, who was skimming through unread messages, stepped abruptly out of the way of the flying debris that smacked against the back of her phone. "Yo, watch out, you're banging up my phone," she complained.

"Huh? Oh—sorry," mumbled Mitz, seemingly oblivious to his careless stride.

Miyacre hovered over Ashe's phone in curiosity. "You about to send them out?" she pestered.

"Yeah! Everyone is on UME and Friends, right?" Ashe probed.

"Nope, I'm still using Friend Space," said Lyal.

"Same here," said Setz.

"Screw it, I'll just text it to you, Miyacre," she resolved.

"Handling it," she replied.

"I know it's not super popular, but is anyone using Mumbler?" asked Kaiser.

"Mumbler? Doesn't sound like the best chat app, does it?" Lyal razzed.

"Actually, you would be surprised. If more people used it, I would use it way more often," replied Kaiser.

"And that is the most logical thing you've ever said," Setz complimented.

"Well then, take a picture and write it in your blog, chump," said Kaiser as he swung his arms out in theatric invitation.

Everyone arrived at the car, aside from Ashe, who lagged behind as she completed the task.

". . . Alright, done!" Ashe notified. "I might as well post these up, too . . ." Her voice sank into silence. "What the hell is that?"

The group of friends froze over as the dread in her voice shook them to the bone. Ashe had locked up in an inquisitive squint at whatever anomaly lay on the screen.

"Okay, I'm bugging out. Did you guys see a guy out here?" she said, panicking.

Mitz, Lyal, and Miyacre were spurred into a hurry. Setz and Kaiser, who had leaned against the car, pushed themselves up and followed behind. Ashe remained fixed in place as they gathered around her. Each of them laid their eyes upon the screen of the phone. The picture was overexposed, and everything glowed as if it were a photo taken of a dream.

Had it been the only odd detail, it wouldn't have caused such a stir. But there was something else amiss. Out in the middle of the empty parking lot stood something that surely didn't belong. It was a dark figure with both hands sunken deep into the pockets of an unnecessary overcoat. The details of his attire were difficult to distinguish due to the dark graininess that composed him, though it appeared his face was hidden beneath a hat.

Not one of them had any memory of such a figure at all.

Simply put, nobody had been there.

"So—he was definitely not standing there when I took this picture," Ashe swore.

Setz laid on eyes of heavy disbelief. Feeling his gaze on the back of her neck, she turned to him in ardent defense. "You weren't even paying attention, so don't even say a word," she snapped, an outburst that drove him back with hands raised in insistence of his innocence.

"Relax, I just don't believe it's anything . . . spiritual. That alright?" Setz clarified.

"None of us saw anything there, right?" Ashe pressed.

They collectively shook their heads while Kaiser nodded at Setz with a teasing smirk.

Setz repositioned himself to stand face-to-face with Kaiser. "Bullshit," he declared.

"Hey, I can't prove it. I'm just sayin'," Kaiser defended. "On my word, man. I didn't see nobody."

Setz looked down at the picture again, half expecting the man to have simply disappeared. But there he stood, frozen in time, looking out at them as they adventured across the land of the bizarre.

"If there was ever a place for some weird shit to happen, this would be it," said Mitz.

Then, silence fell upon them, not a one of them knowing what to say next, which in turn caused Ashe to fall further into frustration.

"So, that's all we're going to say about it?" she fumed.

They each passed a glance from one to the other, but none came up with anything to put forward.

"Where we going next?" asked Lyal, deciding it best to push the conversation to something else.

Miyacre sighed and gave a casual shrug. "I don't know. Feels like we're at the end of the world. Where else is there to go?"

"Anyone feel like going home?" Lyal probed.

They each pondered it over in silence. His question had made them privy to the fear inflicted by the grasp of the unknown, a fear that could threaten to guide their young spirits, if they so allowed. Hesitant to succumb to it while so much of the world lay before them, they decided it more compelling to stay the course of adventure and leave this land of tombs behind.

And so, they reentered the car, and Miyacre ignited the engine once more. As they departed, their eyes scoured the emptiness for signs of evidence. Its allure even tempted the mind of the skeptic as he suspended incredulity in occasional glances to the lots.

They charted a course for the highway, without a plan or destination to guide them. Forward, unto the horizon, they would go, rattled, but yet unafraid of tomorrow. For it was their time to be alive, and they wouldn't let war, nor a specter, turn them away.

Freed from the world, all that lay ahead of them was tomorrow.

And tomorrow, would surely be theirs.

So, they left the hand to the otherworld behind them, along with the ghosts of Fable. As the forgotten mall sank into the distance, it slipped completely into memory.

Blinker in the Night

A drip of sweat rolled down Schneider's brow as he sat in the darkness of his office. Three chairs had been assembled in a small arc beyond the front of his desk. He pulled the collar of his uniform and relaxed his shoulders as it loosened, then scanned across the various honors framed upon the wall from his relatively short period of service.

Among them was The Order of the Ten Stars, an achievement only given to thirty-three others in the history of its existence. The very sight of it brought great stress upon him, that medal of heroism bestowed upon those who changed the outcome of history. The sensation grew stronger as the door to his office opened without a sound, and three men sauntered in and quietly shut the door behind them.

Schneider flipped the switch on his desk lamp, and the light illuminated their faces.

Two of them were Union soldiers, a corporal and a sergeant, each well-built and of Beilkan height, complete with the repulsive smirking arrogance. The one who had led them in, however, wore a flawless black suit. He was wide bodied and stood a whole foot shorter than his guard, with white locks brushed back behind his ears. His face had sharply defined features despite his size, and his skin was carved by deep wrinkles. With a solemn scowl, his countenance, in and of itself, was oppressive.

Schneider's grim company took a seat in the prepared arrangement with the shadow-fallen official at the center, face-to-face with the second lieutenant. The dapper authority huffed as he leaned forward in his seat, a man who never rested, one who was always busied with his next step.

Schneider spoke not a word as he fixated upon them in icy patience.

"Before all the trouble, I received word that we had acquired some new allies in the Beilkan Grand Council. Three new ones . . . which would bring us up to twenty-four out of a hundred and twenty-two," the shadowy schemer informed.

"Well, given those recent events, I doubt your little coalition will hold together," Schneider scoffed.

"And why's that? Because some planes went out to investigate and none of them returned? I've got every bit of intel you have Schneider . . . And regardless of who's behind this—Beilkan or otherwise—you can be sure I'll end up ahead of it," he sneered. "But before we continue, I'd like to acquaint you with two of my longtime subordinates. This here is Vekner," he introduced, with a lift of his hand to the corporal on his left. "And this sergeant on my right is Lakker."

Both offered a silent nod, their brows raised to inform him of their brazen lack of respect. Schneider maintained his hawkish glare, disinterested with their groundless elevation.

"What is it you've really come to discuss? We don't have much time, Gruman," replied Schneider.

The man looked to both of his subordinates, who returned brief glances but remained quiet. Gruman returned to Schneider with a nod in respect to his plea.

"Let's not play naïve. It has everything to do with your desire to resign from the armed forces. A task that we both know wouldn't be easy to accomplish without great sacrifice to your reputation . . . Though, I know a desperate man will always find a way, one way or another. And you, my friend, are a very desperate man, indeed," Gruman acknowledged.

"So, she told you, huh . . . ? You know, after the Vesterbend was liberated, there was nothing more I needed from the organization. You made your sacrifices to get me in, and for years I've risked everything to repay it . . . but now I'm done with it. I have no interest in the absurd goals that lie far beyond our reach."

"What makes you think anything is beyond our reach, Schneider?" asked Gruman through a sharp smirk.

"You want to raise some kind of *utopia*. How many have tried and failed that? I've been on the side of the resistors, and I know a political maneuver and a heavy hand can't change every society. It's just failure echoing through the pages of history and into the future. That's not my struggle," Schneider asserted.

Gruman's head fell as he broke into laughter, a pleasure which was shared by his two accomplices.

"Sheeba will have her peace," the ambitious revolutionary muttered, much to Schneider's bewilderment.

He rose with a deep breath, determined to prove that faithless claim otherwise.

"Now, all across the world—I hear the people calling out for better justice. The cheated, the beaten, and the brave. Good justice is the social business that makes people want justice. Full circle. It's the service that gives society stability, and good social business is the lifeline that maintains the righteous heart," Gruman decreed.

He then leaned forward with a suspicious glare.

"How's your righteous heart doin', Schneider?" asked Gruman through a smirk.

Schneider relaxed in his seat and turned his head from them in an offhanded attempt to conceal a grin that had swept across his face. His guests remained unmoved.

"Social business, huh? What kind of game are you playing?" asked Schneider as he turned back to them. His levity appropriately faded.

"You don't completely understand, *yet,*" replied Gruman. "When you do, however, you'll become twice the leader you are today. Mark my words."

Schneider hunted Gruman's stone countenance for uncertainty but found only troubling resolve. The compromised serviceman and the puppeteer held firm under the intensity of each other's glare.

"Tempting, but I'll have to pass," Schneider resolved.

Gruman crept into laughter once more. "I'm sorry—forgive me, but . . . I remember a time . . . eleven years ago, when I met a young fighter in burned-out ruins of a barn, who told me . . ." He raised his narrowed eyes to Schneider, whose attention had been seized by that unmistakable tale. "That he would do anything for . . . good social business. A kind of business that didn't quite exist in proper strength while worthless scum razed your home."

"Enough—"

"We helped you, when nobody else would . . . Do you understand me?"

"Yes, Lord Dominus . . ." he replied with newfound respect in his tone.

"Very good . . . Do not give up on me before your debt is repaid. You are a cherished instrument in my network, and though much of that web is invisible to your eyes, you must be willing to believe in its good works."

"What do you need me to do?"

Gruman readjusted in his seat, comfortable in his new control of the situation. "Schneider . . . How long have they just been tolerant while the depraved have run wild across the world? When the radicals defiled the Vesterbend—I ask you, who were the ones who called themselves good people but chose easily to stand idle while towns burned? For what end? Because it was political convenience? No . . . because their crimes went *unpunished*. There was a lack of consequence for their actions. The Second Authority . . . we dirty our hands so that the seeds of the righteous new world can come to bloom . . . and if the blood of the complacent must nourish the ground, then . . . so be it."

Schneider listened carefully. Though he was troubled by these remarks, he resisted any sign of a damning reaction. Gruman, as long as he had known him, had been a man often enkindled by the idealisms of the righteous. Though, in recent years, the words shared between them had been ever more laced by blatant radical fervor as his obscure organization continued to gain influence across the world.

Gruman leaned back and pulled a small white box from his jacket pocket. He threw it to Schneider, who snatched it from the air with due surprise.

The shadowy coordinator stood, and his two subordinates followed suit. Schneider examined the box, then opened the top. They were cigarettes, almost completely white, save for a single black X, whose ends were designed in the shape of pendulum knives.

On the inside of the box flap was the phrase "On Wings of Righteousness, May I Never Fall."

"This is just the beginning of something much greater. For you, for me, for all of us," droned Gruman as they turned for the door.

"Sorry, I don't smoke," said Schneider as he tossed the box on the table.

Gruman turned his head to address that protest. "If you find yourself in a situation you can't handle or see things you wished you never saw, you just might try things you wouldn't have ever considered," Gruman enlightened.

"Is that right?" said Schneider, confident he would never need them.

A conservative chime rang throughout the room. Gruman froze, reached into his pocket, and drew from it a jet-black cellphone. He held it up to his ear and remained silent as someone began to speak. Schneider looked to Gruman's men, who waited in anticipation for what would need to be done.

The shadowy orchestrator lowered his hand and became hauntingly still. "And from the gates of obscurity . . . comes absurdity." Gruman shuddered.

He returned the phone to his pocket, then ordered his men out of the room with a silent nod to the door.

"Code eleven. Seventy-Seventh Street. Total," he directed.

With their orders, they departed in silence into a frantic all-out sprint. Schneider perked up, stirred by their sudden urgency.

"What's the situation?" he inquired.

Gruman, however, remained silent as if he didn't hear him. He turned and walked back toward the desk.

"Gruman, answer the question," Schneider ordered, his voice raised in the pinch of anxiety.

The steady dominus continued past his troubled subordinate to the window behind the desk. He stood there a moment to prepare himself, then pulled down a single blind so that he could peer out at what lay beyond.

"Gruman, have we been discovered!?"

The sovereign judge-man scratched at his chin as he took in deep breaths through his nostrils.

"You know, when I was a kid," he finally broke, "I would go riding with my grandfather in his truck to the hills, to fly the kites that he made for us grandkids. He was a true inspiration, with over fifty years of service to the organization. He used to tell me all about it: the old ways, their successes, and their failures. In hindsight, a great deal of trust was placed in me. Though, as a boy, after I had heard these stories so often, they got a little dull, so I would spend the ride looking at the clouds."

"What's that got to do with anything?" Schneider inquired.

"On one particular day, as he was telling me about the battle against who and who, because of this and that . . . in the sky, I thought I saw something unbelievable. Something so unbelievably real that I thought we ought to stop the truck to get a better look. But my grandad, grounded in reality as he was, told me to forget whatever it was I saw. He told me my imagination had gotten into my eyes. Because things that were unbelievable were the stuff of a child's mind, and I was a big eight-year-old, and he had no time for foolishness," said Gruman.

"What's happened, Gruman?" pressed Schneider as he became iced over by the sound of air sirens, which roared throughout the distance.

The tense lieutenant heard a buzz from the table. He saw that his phone had begun to rumble across the surface as the ringtone chimed over and over again. A faint cerulean light bled between the blinds and illuminated Gruman's rugged face. Although the sight was truly bizarre, Gruman's disposition remained lax, his iron spirit unwavering.

"Thought you might like that story," said Gruman as he rubbed a drop of sweat from his cheek.

"I need you—to calmly tell me what's going on," Schneider warned as the eerie glow from beyond pulsated.

"Come and see—see for yourself," Gruman summoned as he stood attentively with his arms crossed behind his back, collected, even as the sounds of commotion grew louder.

Beyond the door of the academy were the sounds of hurried footsteps and shouting. The lieutenant and shadow official's phones rumbled with incessant urgency while the lights from the fire alarm bathed the hall in red.

"I want you to make me a promise, right now. That no matter what happens after this moment, you won't lose sight of reality. And by that, I mean specifically—what it means to live and what it means to die," said Gruman.

Schneider, shaken, stood from the chair and went there, to the window, with indigo aglow in his terrified eyes. He took a place next to Gruman and, full of uncertainty of what he was about to see, pulled down the blinds.

He did not speak. The air in his lungs froze. And in his mind, there was such a deep emptiness that a single thought could echo forever and never return to silence again.

"Can you do that, Rostal?"

Who Are You?

But even if all the stars fall tonight, do not be afraid

For I am here for you, and you are here for me

Face down the treacherous corridor without a fear in your eternal soul

For at its end lies Infinity Paradise

And if you should fall along the way

I will take you up and carry you there

Starfall

It was a night like no other. The milky heavens glimmered above the luminous city. The night birds did not sing, the city did not bustle. All the world was still in a petrifying and ominous silence. It was paralyzed in time by something that brought people from all over the city to the streets and balconies to bask in the glow of the transcendent.

Above, high in the sky, loomed an anomaly of flashing lights. They outlined the flowing shape of an enormous starship, armed with a thousand guns. The starlight cruiser reached across the city that it besieged with sheer majesty. The colossal traveler, nearly twice the capitol's size.

It lingered over Salamandra City with a glorious silver emblem upon its bridge, which reached out like a pair of narrow wings. Beneath its hull fell pulsing cosmic teardrops, which streamed through the skies until they became hot crimson streaks, those shards of intergalactic debris brought along from its journey.

At oblivion's doorstep were twenty others, some of even more monstrous size than the ship that had descended. The behemoth's exterior shimmered as if coated by mystic waters that reflected an unseen sun. It was a beauty that captivated more deeply than fear, if only one had the courage to watch.

The sound of hydraulics ripped through the city as a set of massive doors on the underbelly of the ship began to spread.

On the beach beyond the city, the swordsman watched carefully. A familiar feeling began to swell within, and this time, there could be no defense. He looked up to the stars above, and they looked back unto him.

The event in space lasted for minutes until the doors reached their limit and came to a screeching halt. A cushioned boom from within the ship was heard throughout the city. From a luminous portal below erupted a dizzying array of spectral orbs, which descended upon the city.

Like something out of a dream, thousands became transfixed upon the spectacle in the sky as that cosmic performance tempted spectators from every home out onto every street. The denizens of that targeted world became unified by an unprecedented wallop of awe. From citizen to public servant, they offered the deep-space wonder unblinking eyes as the universe unleashed its tears of anguish upon them. To some, it brought sensations of lightness and ease, as if utopia had finally come to the world.

The orbs descended until they came in close proximity to the ground, then bobbed above the surface. They glided in the air and left wavy trails of light in their wake.

Police teams were scrambled to secure areas where the first orbs had fallen, desperate to clear away crowds of spectators from the whimsical cosmic spirits. However, as time passed without incident, even they began to grow lax, with only the constant shout of their offsite commanders through the earpiece to keep them loosely focused on the task.

In other parts of the city, however, there were no such barriers. People, both young and old, indulged in interaction with the cosmic gifts, like fairies in the night. Children gave chase in clustered groups, laughing, jumping, and shouting as they admired the grace of their movements. Soon after, the streets had become so overwhelmed by the dancing bulbs that nothing short of a total lockdown could keep the populace separated from those arcane entities.

Couples held each other close, sharing the light with gentle hands. Others offered up their dreams and wishes to the sky. And for a moment, time was truly still, and all the things that had once mattered had seemed to lose relevance. The lonely and forgotten, the happy and satisfied, all unified as one beneath the gaze of High Fantasy. Inconveniences, pains, and troubles had been swept away by the mighty force of the beyond the reality.

Ultra stumbled back and threw his hand over a throbbing eye.

From between his fingers, cerulean light pierced.

There was a roar from the ocean. A gale struck the beach and kicked up a wall of sand and spray. The afflicted swordsman struggled against nature's might as his tattered cloak flung and wrapped in the force of the winds. A cannonade of unintelligible whispers split into his head. Like fine needles, they sent gruesome shockwaves of pain throughout his entire body.

He turned from the disturbed waters and caught first sight of the seraphic white robes of an entity, which had appeared behind him; a young cleric, lost in her prayers.

In the city, the orbs had nearly fallen to every nook and insignificant cranny. The dreamy cerulean glow bathed the city streets, lit every dark alley, and shined through the windows of every building. When they had left nothing to the darkness of night, the orbs' light began to grow intense.

The gale at the beach began to waver until it had become nothing but a humble breeze. Then, in the calm aftermath came an ethereal voice, soft and gentle.

"What will you do if our dream ends? Lord Ultra? What will you draw for now?"

The robed woman turned up to the stars, her eyes still pressed shut in her endless dreaming. Ultra watched as she lifted her finger, and a starlike glow began to pulse beyond her forehead. The swordsman turned to the city, and in his eyes shined the hundred thousand orbs of light.

"For glory or for grace?" the unseen other asked.

He came to the grim realization that there was nothing he could do.

In the city, the gleam of cosmic sprites grew intense. The once-calm orbs reddened in a mere moment and erupted with ruinous crimson light. Red waves rippled through the city in that last moment of peace. Children leapt, people embraced, and dreamers cast a final wish.

It was a moment that would never return again. A grand divide between two very distinct realities.

The whole city lit up as the angry stars exploded at once. It unleashed a terrible wave of unprecedented destruction throughout the entire city.

In a mere moment, the great Union capital was decimated.

A deafening draconic roar chased hellfire as a massive fireball rolled into the night like a crimson bloom, which then curled into ebon death. The explosions raged in Ultra's eyes as the city skyline began to cave under the sheer power of the attack. The seraphic entity, which had come before him to challenge his will, fell to her knees in anguish and faded away.

"Our time is running out." That serene voice trembled.

From the sky, the cruiser launched hundreds of armored pods, which came plummeting down upon the enflamed ruins. The sound of sirens blared throughout the city as surviving missile defense systems took aim and opened fire with rockets that painted the sky with smoke.

Two pods struck the beach and pulverized a small tower of rock as they made an impact. A cone of debris erupted up from the impact zone and showered across the sand.

The swordsman turned his head and eyed them carefully. The first pod's door ejected and came down upon the sand, followed closely by the second. A dense pall of steam poured from the dark chamber, nearly cloaking the beaming, cerulean-eyed colossus within.

A heavily armored boot slammed down onto the rock and sent a cascade of shattered stone down into the sand. A reinforced gauntlet latched onto the side of the hulking frame, and a fully armored ten-foot-tall soldier pulled itself from the shroud.

It hauled up an enormous gun from within as a second trooper rose up from the other pod. They froze on the rocks, their sights set on Ultra, who, too, remained motionless.

The swordsman looked at the soldiers as waves of confusion swept over him. He wallowed in it for only a moment more before he drew his shining blade and dashed toward the invaders in a resolute assault.

The first blow pierced clean through the first trooper. A jet of compressed air whistled out from a ruptured hose to its mask. The invader began to topple over as Ultra retracted the blade and, in a split second, cut through the second trooper.

Both soldiers crashed upon the ground with a thunderous quake, which pulverized the earth beneath their immense weight.

Seeing that it was done, Ultra sheathed the blade. With the words of the seraph etched deep in his conscience, he dashed toward the city with one true destiny left to pursue.

Invasion Night: LIVE30XX!!

The once-undefiled Union capital lay engulfed in ravenous fire, which bestowed upon its streets endless glow beneath the cloak of night. The cosmic eruption left her old architecture blasted and mutilated, a dizzying and inescapable ruin, which trapped fortune-favored survivors in a realm of nightmare.

The north area of the military headquarters, Homestead, had been nearly reduced to rubble. The facility there lay blasted open, its ceiling caved and resultantly gutted from the collapse.

Two stories up, a door in the severed barracks swung open and out fell Eddie Bowitz, who plummeted into the ember-lit gloom of the ruins below.

A crater of debris had consumed the once-grandiose lobby, pulverized by a massive slab of roofing. His foot caught the slanted ground below, and he dropped into a vicious tumble across rock and rubble.

The ground was subject to a heavy quake as Eddie came to a rest at the bottom of the crevice. The boy looked up with frantic eyes as he awoke on the stage of apocalypse. Just ahead, among the rubble, lay the gold-trim star taken from his pocket in the fall.

Resonant vibrations rattled unstable structural precipices above, all along the perimeter of the exposed second and third floors. With the alarming din of stressed steel and the earsplitting crack of stone, the precipices drooped and released a hail of shards through the air.

Imperiled, yet unwilling to leave without his precious trinket, he fled over and scooped it up off the ground. The boy dropped down and threw his arms over his head as the rocks pummeled the ground and didn't move an inch until it had stopped.

He opened his eyes and lifted to his feet. Safely recovered, he returned the star to his military jacket's inner pocket, then inspected the area for a means of escape.

Then, a peculiar sound caught his ear. It was like a horn that transformed into an airy, ethereal breath, which eerily lingered until it faded to silence. He peered up to the sky, and his breath was taken by what he saw. The indigo-plated starship droned through the dark void above, its perimeter lights dancing like a festival in the night. It was from that colossus that the sound had surely come.

The ground quaked again and threw Eddie into a sideway stumble. The cadet struck his balance, however, as the ruinous pit settled fast to stillness. Quiet again, with only the ambience of intense but distant gunfights.

The fragile tranquility was short lived as a dread chorus of steel wailed out from behind him. Eddie turned as the severed structure slouched over, then gave a few more feet. It jolted to a halt and released a shower of bricks into the air. Wide-eyed, Eddie fled the titanic shadow as the projectiles pummeled the ground around him and split into dangerous shrapnel. The rock pelted his body though his well-crafted military garb and helmet aided in his protection.

Just as he had cleared the shadow, he felt his foot slip. His leg shot up as his view turned toward the heavens. His back slammed into the rocky debris and left him breathless as a sharp pain coursed through his body.

Eddie knew he had to stand if he had any desire to escape. So, against the oppressive pain, he lifted from the rubble as dreaded raid sirens roared all across the city. Isolated by his misplaced step, it was of utmost urgency that he regroup with the armed forces as soon as possible. If he remained alone for too long, he knew he would be dead.

The cadet raced through the ruined lobby riddled with crushed and humiliated grandeur, then caught sight of a promising means of escape. Ahead lay the fallen skyway, whose collapse had cleared a way through the building's wall foundation and over an impassable chasm. The main road had collapsed into the old sewer system, and hellfire had been born within.

Somewhere, out in the burning nightmare, there came the terrifying sheer of steel beams and the din of architectural failure. No sooner had the hellish sound threatened did the liberated mass set off a ruinous cacophony of cascading annihilation, one that sent a jolt through the boy's heart and fixed him in place.

A grand quake stole the balance from his legs as the kinetic wave ripped past.

The resonant growl informed him that the immense structural collapse was of a building much farther away. He was sure of it. With urgency nonetheless, he broke for the collapsed bridge and raced over with conscious leaps across cracked stone and crevice.

His feet soon found the shattered concrete of the sidewalk, and against better judgement, he succumbed to his curiosity and turned to catch a last glimpse of the decimated barracks.

Tarnished Union flags lay strewn across the rubble of the once-proud institution, draped over crumbled pedestals and tossed helplessly in the winds of end. A sharp glimmer pulled his eye from that unimaginable yet actualized vision of calamity. Above the bowl in the barracks, he caught a glimpse of a bizarre floating mass, whose cerulean gleam pierced the gray veil of dust.

His chest began to rumble as it neared. It crept out from the dark as it descended upon the decimated lobby, but Eddie turned away before fear could seize him any further. Eager to clear the roadside, he made a dash for a burning alleyway, which was dense with smoke but marked with two red flares.

They had to be close, Eddie assured himself.

The junior soldier dropped out from full sprint as he put the road and the anomaly behind him. It had been a reckless move. He keeled over as he choked on the smog, yet remained desperate to push through. Watery-eyed, he tried to wipe the sweat from his face, but his hand only displaced the dirt and moisture.

He closed his eyes a brief moment to subdue the sting, and from the darkness behind his eyes, he heard the footsteps of armored giants and the cry of manipulated metal.

There was no time to rest.

The road ahead, however, was claustrophobic treachery. He tried to blink as he pushed forward but could grasp no clear vision through the stubborn screen. In his persistent peek, a rogue billow from ignited wreckage blew into his face. The boy shielded his eyes with both arms and drove right through. In a stumble across rocky debris, he emerged from havoc's black screen with lungs tormented from the short journey through unrelenting devastation.

Not far ahead was the vertical smoking car whose wheels lay pressed against the alley wall. The hood was smashed into the ground, and all around was glass. The way forward would be a narrow squeeze, as a collapsed wall from the other side offered little room to pass beyond the inferno.

Eddie peered up. Through the smoke, he caught sight of the entire corner pillar of the parking garage, suspended across the alleyway. The concrete tower lay in the buildings, like a knife half-cut into cake. Throughout the road was a dense pileup. Tipped, turned, and stacked cars caused him to become unsure if the way forward could be safely negotiated.

But there was no way back, and he knew it. So, pushed by the hand of the will to survive, he inched past the smoking engine bay.

With all his strength, he fought to avoid eye contact with the driver's seat, afraid of what he might see there. But in a subtle slip of his eye, he wandered to a peculiar something that hung on the rearview mirror.

Crafted from colorful paperboard and assembled with glue, a little paper butterfly dangled above the ravenous flames of war. His face fell in horror as hellfire from the dash fondled the edges of childhood's creation. From a tiny ember was born a new fire. It laid claim to the innocent in sweeping ruthlessness and razed the pipe cleaner loop until it was too weak to hold on.

Eddie stumbled back at the other end of the passage as the cherished gift was swallowed into the engulfed dashboard, surely reduced to nothing but disgusting ashes.

Beyond, he found no salvation. Free of the last car of the mangled pileup, the road was gone after a distant curve. A fallen tower, that had been effectively shrouded by smog, lay like a guillotine across the portal out and left him trapped with his torment.

Over the ambience of chaos, Eddie's ears piqued to an unusual screech that left him unsettled. He became still as he tracked the noise across the sky, but that stagnancy had unknowingly put him in peril.

An armored airship cut down over the alley at the far end and whipped away the smog beneath its thrusters. Eddie froze as it settled into a hover, a creation of the like he had never seen before. Unsure if it had seen him through the shroud, he remained still, confident that a sudden dash to nowhere would only aid in the revelation of his vulnerable position.

Twin high beams from the mechanical menace struck through him, and his blood went cold.

"What are you waiting for? Time to strike you through the back? Go!" cried an angry voice from annihilation.

The airship let out a horrific screech, then tipped forward into full throttle. Its enraged flight unleashed a monstrous cloud of debris in its wake and drove a jet stream of smoke out through the other end of the alleyway.

Eddie, wide-eyed and galvanized to action, twisted around and took flight toward the other end. He was off on the tips of his toes as the ship closed the gap with breathtaking speed. In a throwaway glance to the left, he noticed the walls of a passage, though one that was nearly sealed off due to a major collapse of a brick low-rise that had stood at the corner.

With the way forward surely death, Eddie changed course with the intent to either scale the rubble or find a way through.

He was upon the crumbled slide when he caught a glimpse of a tiny portal between the concrete mess. Driven to desperation by the angry screech of invader engines, the boy dove and slid along the shards of ruin. His foot struck crumbled rubble within. Endangered yet, he hoisted himself up on some exposed pipe and shimmied through the portal in a desperate squeeze to the other end.

He hadn't gone far when the portal gave way to an open cavity. Eddie released the pipe, pulled himself through a hole in the wall, then fell to the road in exhaustion. It was only then that he noticed the eerie silence that had taken hold. Bewildered, he listened for the drone of the airship but heard only a faint electric hum as if it waited for him just around the corner.

From concentration, he could hear the faint sound of rocks as they rolled and tapped across the alley. Eddie lifted from the ground, and in a peek through the portal, he caught a glimpse of a cerulean glow, which had swelled across the ground. The sky scourge's engines rumbled just beyond the wall, and the fear of its demonstrated capability kept its prey fixed in place, like something of a hiding child. The menace simply lingered there, however, and when a minute passed, nothing more had occurred.

Bewildered, Eddie rose, then took a step back toward the end of the alley, yet unable to turn from the danger right there in front of him. The sharp yelp of a young woman startled him, and he turned from the danger to the blasted avenue, where the pitter-patter of frantic steps faded.

The boy whipped back to the corner beyond the narrow portal, the area still draped in blue. With decisive strength, he fled the alley, and the machine remained.

He slipped out onto the desolate road, which cut through indistinguishable ruin. On either side, however, the girl was nowhere to be found. The cadet performed a quick scan of the fine rubble for signs of her steps but discovered nothing that could offer him guidance.

Alone, he wandered into the street in search of the way forward.

The left-hand way intersected with a diagonal road, which lay haunted by the distant collapse of a twelve-story skyscraper that had toppled over yet remained mostly intact due to a collision with a sturdy low-rise across the street. The tower's mid-stories had been blasted open and lay exposed as the structure arched over the intersection. In a lingering gaze, he could see tiny fragments pouring out from within.

To pass beneath or anywhere near the arch would surely tempt the devil's hand, and someone overcome by fear would certainly never take such a path. So, he turned right and maneuvered around a slew of abandoned cars. As he proceeded, structural collapse and automotive pileups caused the road to narrow into a passage. He squeezed through slabs of concrete and climbed over the tops of abandoned cars, trucks, and SUVs. Deeper within, he was forced to maneuver around rebar that protruded from the concrete mass, along with sharpened floorboards, crafted from violent splits.

He wound tight corners within the squeeze until he came across a horrid sight that repulsed him to the wall of rubble on the opposite end of the passage.

Innocent eyes beheld a corpse, which lay slumped over against a crushed car; a young man, who bore the same helmet and uniform as he. From the insignias along his sleeve, it was evident that this was the body of an ill-starred cadet, who had likely escaped to the ravine after suffering a wound from gunfire, evident in the seared hole in his uniform. Below which, his lifeless hand had fallen. That gruesome discovery offered an unwelcome glimpse into fragile mortality, a reality the boy had never come to cope with.

He fled the charred remains and hurried with reckless abandon until he arrived at a crumbled wall. It had been penetrated by some high-speed projectile, likely from debris rather than any weapon. As fate provided no other course, he inched close, then stepped through into the dark chamber.

Within, the incessant flow of water charmed the brick ridden room with a subtle tranquility, a modest respite from the cacophony of war that had yet haunted the safe house. Fortune had delivered him to a small janitorial room that remained relatively preserved, save a wall on the far side that had partially fallen forward. Beyond the jagged portal was a darkened restaurant and bar, which lay flooded due to a breached pipe that hung from the struggling ceiling.

There was a door on his left that had been left ajar. With the need to keep his momentum so that he might find someone or anyone at all, he stepped off with haste to leave the respite behind.

As he approached the door, he heard the sounds of struggling. His eyes widened as his heart rate elevated in anticipation of finding another. He pushed through the door and shot past the open, barred gate meant to guard the receded entryway.

Desperate to lend his aid, he emerged into a gray corridor that once offered passage through the civic center. The left end had been sealed by collapse; the other end, however, bore the source of the frantic commotion.

There, at the very end of the passage, he caught sight of her, at last. It was a civilian girl, wedged in a prison of bars and planks from a fallen scaffold. In her eyes shone a deepened fear from something that she saw in the streets.

"Hey! Stop," Eddie called to her. "Let me help you!"

She remained focused on her struggle to liberate herself from the dangerous snare and threw her weight into the bars to make a gap in the cage. The steel ends scraped across the ground as her efforts bought progress.

With just enough room to squeeze her waist through, she pressed the opportunity and attempted to shove forward. She had almost succeeded when a slip of fortune resulted in a jolt that robbed her momentum. A sharp board had slipped across the side of her neck and latched hold of a necklace, which glittered in hellfire's light.

Startled, she drove forward until the wooden edge had made its pass. Freed, she let out a gasp in terror of whatever had awaited her, then fled in a renewed break for salvation. Eddie had taken off down the path to lend his aid, but he arrived at the scaffolds only in time to see her in desperate flight through the alley across the street.

She was surely in search of those she loved, the boy reasoned. No one should have to stand alone in a nightmare, surely not now, when the hand of tragedy had fallen so hard, and the greatest pain lay hidden behind the fires of ruthless transgressions.

Something caught his eye there in ruin's prison, a glimmer from the lost treasure, which lay draped over a rod near the ground. The boy knelt and retrieved it. With the careful pinch of its severed spring ring clasp, he stole a moment to inspect it. The necklace sported a spectacular avian pendent with familiar rosy golden cheeks and an impressive sapphire centered upon its chest.

Eddie lingered a moment, as a particular feeling captivated his heart. He turned the necklace over and found upon the pendant a finely carved heart.

Eleven years had changed nothing in him. With that precious treasure in hand, Little Eddie Bowitz vowed to return it. He would rip fate from the hand of tragedy if he had to, and with that solemn oath, into his jacket pocket he placed her cherished item, alongside his own.

Infused with an old passion, he assaulted the bars with both hands, to which they screeched as he cleared his way. As the gap opened before him, he sank down, then exploded forward like a wild cat. The boy tumbled across the ground as the scaffolds came down behind him with earsplitting tumult.

He peered at the sealed path behind him. The way back was gone. Only forward remained.

The promise-bound soldier stood, then searched along the cobblestone road for signs of the terror that the girl had witnessed there. Upon quick inspection, however, he found that there was no one, nor thing, anywhere at all. All that lived upon that road was the fire, in and around the blasted storefronts. Faintly disquieted by this conclusion, he pushed on ahead into the alley across the street.

He picked up speed. The boy knew he could catch up if he put all of his heart into his steps. The winding path had several gaps through which one could escape the alley. He inspected each one as they passed, and though she could have disappeared down any one of them, the path forward seemed invitingly clear.

"Hey! Are you out here? I'm a soldier! I can help you!" Eddie shouted as he drove further in.

The fires had faded there, and only smoldering rubble lined the streets beside the antiquated buildings of the old neighborhood. He was coming up to an end. The final complex wrapped the path with two cream-bricked wings and cradled those in between in a close intimacy. Further ahead, however, the wings had collapsed in from detonations from the street and transformed the passage into a narrow ravine of ruin.

The path split just before it began: a passage to the left and another on the right. Straight ahead, however, at the back of the ravine, was a heavy black door, and it stood ajar.

The boy crept forward, lured by its promising mystique. He began through the treacherous ravine with careful steps. As the squeeze tightened, he was challenged to maneuver around sharp concrete, rebar, and pipe jutting out here and there through the discomforting mangle.

The door came just beyond his reach, a foreboding darkness awaiting him within. He laid a resolute hand upon its cold surface and drove into the dark.

Light flooded the room, and he found her. At last, she did not run, nor hurry. She lay sprawled upon the concrete floor, one arm reaching for a salvation that would never come. It was a miserable end. Eleven years had changed nothing in him, nor in the world.

He fell back against the doorframe as a familiar sadness infected him. He detested the way she lay half-swallowed in darkness, completely unseen from the shoulders up. An innocent existence, taken by the cruel hand of chance. The pile of rubble that engorged the doorway beyond her had surely been the culprit.

The boy laid a hand upon the pocket where the necklace sat and, in a moment, saw himself place it there on the floor beside her.

But no—he couldn't let it be. He couldn't allow it to go forgotten.

A muffled thud answered his sadness from beyond the rubble. Eddie snapped from his darkened spiral.

The rubble shook, shifted, then bulged, as a horrific monstrosity of armor and plate pulled itself through a newly formed gap. The titan's mighty arm hoisted up a fallen steel beam in defiance of its impressive weight.

There, in the dark tomb, Little Eddie Bowitz caught his first glimpse of Eternia's armed force and their beaming cerulean gaze. The colossal husk drove its way through with scrapes and screeches, its armor too formidable to be pierced, the entity too powerful to be hindered.

Its boots struck forward, and the deathly thunder shook the boy from paralysis and galvanized him to make his overdue exit. He turned to escape the gazing giant but came face-to-face with another who wielded an enormous gun that nearly paralleled Eddie in size.

The behemoth took in a breath that stole the wind from Eddie's chest and cast him to the mercy of pure instinct. Without a thought or plan, the boy threw himself between the giant's leg and the doorframe. He squeezed and flailed like a rat until he was free on the other side.

The boy suffered no pain from the scrapes across his waist and arms, which had been inflicted by the desperate maneuver. In a break for his own salvation, Little Eddie fled for the end of the disaster ravine with no heed for the wreckage that ripped through his uniform and dug into his tender flesh.

Though the flight had been reckless, the boy arrived back at the intersection with his life. Hounded yet by terror, he cut down the path on his right, then raced forward without a destination or a cause. As his fear sank deeper into his consciousness, stronger was the sensation that he was being followed. Though he was undoubtedly alone, he felt them everywhere: in every building, in every window, around every corner, and behind any fathomable curtain claimed by the unknown.

The way dipped down on a rubble-ridden slope, and Eddie flung himself forward as his steps found loose rock beneath his boots. He had nearly lain his cheek into the red brick below, but managed to catch himself on palm, knee, and knuckle. With pain numbed by the flow of adrenaline, he lifted back to his feet and continued onward again.

The way forward split ahead. He rushed into the second intersection and cut to the left to vary his trail, but he froze as he found the gaze of one hundred beaming eyes around that corner upon a hill of rubble. His heart skipped a beat as he was assaulted by the psychic screams of the invisible dead, which were then absorbed by the cavernous breath of the cerulean-eyed titans.

Nauseated, he turned back before any of the soldiers had drawn their guns on him and made straight once more, but not without checking over his shoulder to see if any had followed.

They had stared right into the tormented hollow that he had worked for years to bury. A sacred crypt, uncovered in a mere glimpse by those invaders who seemed to appear from nowhere at all.

At the alley's end was a head-on view of the once flawless porte cocheres of the Salamandran Grand Sky Hotel, which was surprisingly intact, just beyond the avenue. With a fond memory of its breathtaking majesty upon first moving to the city, he raced toward it in hopes it might offer sanctuary and perhaps give him a vantage to seek out the resistance.

It had been one of many architectural monuments that helped to numb him as he began a new life in the capital long ago. He often indulged in simple dreams in which he, too, would aid in the construction of such marvels, though he was never the greatest achiever in the subject of mathematics. He was forever full of dreams nonetheless, his existence intrinsically sustained by them.

Eddie rounded the Seraph's Fountain, which introduced the structure: an ornamental extravagance in which the winged people bathed in the elegance of mood lighting.

Upon his arrival at the half-collapsed porte cocheres, he found the sliding glass doors opened. Beyond was an enormous lobby with twin escalators that rose to a wondrous balcony, which he knew to be equipped with bars and wicker chairs. He had knowledge of its amenities only as he had snuck off on the rare occasion when days were hard and there was no one to listen. The winds from the top were refreshing in the summertime, and the altitude often reminded him of home.

Two statues of winged men flanked each side of the escalators, which were mere stairs due to the lack of power to the facility. The boy ascended step-by-step to the very top, offering occasional glances to the solemn-faced angels below who pleaded to the heavens with raised arms.

At the last step, Eddie turned from those guardians of the sky and stepped out onto a wide berth, which led to the balcony. Above, he caught a glimpse of the indigo-plated starship that had eclipsed the heavens and gazed upon that invader majesty with indefensible wonder.

The boy felt something as he looked upon the watery melt, a feeling he had not had in so long, and he soon experienced a peculiar separation there upon the hotel, which had lifted him closer to that unusual craft. It was a feeling that, perhaps, should not go long unchecked.

From the sky fell beaming particles to every corner of the city. They streamed down for what seemed like minutes until ruinous fire blossomed upon the city, marking their journey's end.

A wondrous painting brought to life, the cadet became fixated upon the spectacle, completely oblivious to what it meant for all those others who surely suffered the strike. Something about being there brought uncontested comfort to him. Like the late blossoming of some wilted bulb that had long been given up on, the young guardian of dreams couldn't help but bask in the lights of the arcane extravaganza.

As he lingered there, the sudden blare of distant gunfire snapped him from his prolonged reverie. His eyes fell from the cosmic voyager, caught the sharp line of the unguarded ledge, then followed it across to the far end.

His curious sweep suddenly arrived upon a figure who accompanied him there upon the balcony. Eddie froze up, as this man was of no origin of his world. Beneath a hood, the swordsman stood in heavy, torn boots and a tattered indigo cloak, reinforced underneath by something that looked of leather plate.

Eddie inched closer to get a better look. The color of his garb was distinctly similar to that of the invader troopers. There was no doubt he was one of them, too.

In gauntlet-guarded grasp was the blade, which shimmered with flashes of white in the darkness. Without a word, the swordsman leapt from the balcony with the finesse and confidence of a wild hunter. Subconscious steps in pursuit of the hooded soldier nearly put his foot right over the darkened ruins below. He flinched, then yanked his foot away from the abyssal grave, planting it on the ground.

The boy enjoyed a deep breath, having nearly thrown away his life. Beyond the free fall, he rediscovered the invader swordsman as he bolted across the crumbling rooftops. He had never seen anyone move so fast.

Left there alone to gawk at what he had seen, the boy soon realized that he, too, would need to continue on his way. There was nowhere else to go but back down, but Eddie scanned the horizon once more on a whim and noticed a group of soldiers fighting upon a distant road. *At last*, he thought. At last, he had found others.

He nearly collapsed to the ground in relief, in stark realization of just how terrified he had been. He knew he couldn't rest long, however, as it was his duty to assist. Their struggle seemed tense with guns ablaze against the invader force, though, here, he could do nothing. So, he stepped off in search of an optimal route to regroup with them in hopes of lending his aid.

Before he could lay eyes on the street again, however, there came a thunder from behind him. Startled by the sudden intruder, he turned back to the escalators and stared until a second thud confirmed his enemy's approach. They had found him, just as he knew they would.

Imperiled once again, the boy rushed to the ledge, peered down, and caught sight of a smaller balcony, not far below. It didn't hang out much further than the grand balcony, and so he sat down on the ledge and let his feet dangle off. Confident that he had enough clearance, Eddie bravely pushed off from the ledge and fell to the balcony below.

As he rose, a squadron of Union jet fighters split through the sky, then roared toward the idle cruiser. He resumed his search for the soldiers who fought through the city, but before he could relocate them, a glimmer from above stole his attention.

It dove straight down from the underbelly of the starship, a shining beacon in the darkest night. Suddenly, however, the deployed starlight's movement appeared to cease. No longer did it fall, but instead, its luminosity grew to striking intensity. Eddie's eyes grew wide as he realized the meteoric approach of the ferocious shooting star. He hunted around for a possible objective, for something important, but it soon became clear to him that the hotel was indeed its recipient.

The boy sprang into a panicked search for an escape but froze at the shatter of glass. He turned and discovered a hulking invader soldier, who had driven its armored shoulder into the balcony door; the fearsome impact left even the steel frame deformed.

Trapped, and with few options left, Eddie looked once more over the brink for an escape. Just off to the left was a downed radio tower, which had pierced into the glass exterior of the hotel and created a perilous opportunity to reach the low-rise across the boulevard.

Behind him, the invader pushed the hinges of the balcony door right off the frame and carried the door in its hand a few steps before discarding it to the ground.

Eddie rushed along the guardrail and arrived at the optimal drop-off point. He lifted up onto the bar and dangled his legs over the cross-iron tower below. In perked ears, there upon the perilous brink, he caught the swing and snatch of the invader cannon as it was hoisted up behind him. Without complete reassurance, the boy shoved off of the defied sanctuary to the tower below, which he now realized was a much farther drop than he had anticipated.

He slammed down onto the flat outer bar of the radio tower with a hair-raising wobble. Fortunately, it had been wide enough to accommodate him, though his right knee suffered the blunt of the fall at the edge of the metal plane. The cadet lifted himself up and experienced a sharp pain the very moment he tried to put weight onto that shattered knee. It pierced so deeply that he cried out as the gruesome sensation ripped through his entire body.

Effectively crippled, the soldier rolled onto his back. Unable to straighten his leg, he lay there, surely as both invader and blazing star neared to lay their pitiful claim.

As he lingered in decisive helplessness, the boy became overwhelmed by a truly bizarre sensation. It was a soothing boon, which strengthened in each passing moment; a good feeling, one of painless awakenings to the golden sun in the morning, without a worry in the world. That cleansing sweep expelled the injuries of his innocent mistakes and made him new again.

The boy relaxed his limbs and experienced a sudden dizziness as he stretched out wide. With closed eyes, he relished in that healing boon that coursed through his blood until it faded away.

His eyes flashed open, lively and alert, as he snapped from arcane disorientation and flipped back onto his knees. There was no pain at all. It was impossible, he thought. It couldn't be.

He got up and moved his body, feeling nothing but total renewal. Even through the bloodied tears across his uniform, he found only forgiven skin. At the brink of death, he had lain rather thoughtlessly, but now his mind was full of questions.

But the harsh whistle of disturbed air shook him from astonishment, and in renewed urgency, he shot across the steel support as fast as he could. Just as the cadet had passed halfway across the comm tower, another jet blew past overhead and knocked him from his balance.

With renewed vigor, he steadied himself with the swing of his arms, then finished the crossing to the concrete base on the other side. Upon arrival at the support beam's severed end, he leapt down to the blasted concrete of the rooftop, his treacherous passage successful.

The wind began to howl as the projectile drew near. Eddie dashed for the nearby stairwell, threw open the door, then turned to pull it shut. In that last moment, he caught a glimpse of a group of invader soldiers that had gathered at the balcony high above. His gaze on them held until a flash prompted him to slap the door shut.

His ears were subjected to an instantaneous deafening. Brilliance cut around the perimeter of the door, and in a split second, the light breached the room. An empyrean glow enveloped the boy as he attained the sensation of flight.

In the silent aftermath, he went slowly. Like a liberated leaf blown by a gale, the boy had come to glide through alternative time and space, and his mind wandered nowhere as all his fears dissipated.

A Realm Beyond the End

Soothing bands of white luminescence passed over Eddie, one after the other, in a tranquilizing crawl, his first distinctive experience from beyond the veil. When the last of the waves had vanished beyond sight, he found himself taken from his flight and left in stillness.

Upon conclusion of that transmutative event, there came a soft flash. A gleam had pierced the darkness, so small he could block it with the tip of his finger. It was then that he became conscious of his body, and no sooner did he suffer a deep coldness that sank down into his skin's tender dermis. The arcane touch caused him to grow still, as if wrapped by the blanket of death, with only the gift of the oppressive embrace of loneliness.

His eyes focused as they began to capture the faint reflected light on metallic indigo architecture. From those silvery bands, he was able to make out a hallway and its basic structural elements. Angled steel supports stood mirrored on both sides, repeating unto the unseen end—a microscopic glint of white radiance. Overhead were black domes that appeared every fifty feet, and on each side of him were gutters, crisscrossed to eternity by radiant conduits.

A movement of light stole spellbound eyes. An emerald gleam beamed through the hall via the cybernetic trace in the floor. It was a whimsical journey that left a resonant glow in its wake. No sooner had he noticed it did the freeze thaw, and control returned to the captive soldier's legs. His eyes hunted all around the dark hall for clues of his location until the neon bolt recaptured his attention with an identical soundless gesture, urging him to following.

The inter-dimensional prisoner took his first steps forward into the otherworld. The bolt took a sudden sharp turn to the right, but he was sure the second hall hadn't been there before. With only Eternia's uncanny beckon, both behind and ahead of him, he conceded to the vector's guidance without protest.

The plane-snatched soldier ambled for the designated destination, and as he went, he felt a droning sink into his ears, one which was resonant and constant. Upon arrival at the authorized intersection, he discovered an identical hallway with similar seamless architecture. Emerald starlight yet beckoned him forth, however, and so he went like a puppet pulled by strings.

Suddenly, a familiar artifact lay clutched in his hand; each finger was wedged between narrowed cold steel. This time, he was absolutely sure it hadn't been there before and was challenged not to doubt himself as reality bent and twisted in the mere pass of a moment.

The boy lifted that transmitted gift to bewildered eyes, though he had known exactly what it was. How could he not?

The wishing star lay there in hand, its washed out ribbon slung over and hauntingly still in the windless chamber.

There came the eerie resonance of restless footsteps. Something else lay trapped within Eternia's halls, and though he momentarily gave the commotion due attention, he made no effort to further investigate the rogue presence. The reckless steps of the unhinged hunter grew louder but settled in a prolonged fade, and when silence had returned, the boy naïvely proceeded with his pursuit of the neon snake.

His persistent guide soon delivered him before a doorway and, with its mission complete, ceased to appear again. The way forward lay clear, the sliding door rested in the slot, and a joyous spiral of dazzling lights chased the perimeter of the frame as if his arrival had been all but expected.

Beyond the shining frame, he caught sight of a long desk for the assembly of the servants of Eternia. It had a smooth and glossy surface, flawless, unlike the matte steel material that composed the ground and walls.

At the opposite end of the room was a panoramic window, encased by an elegant frame of reinforced indigo alloy, which was carved from end to end with unintelligible glyph work. Eddie, captivated by what his eyes beheld, moved across the room until he had arrived right before the glass, which parted him from the unprecedented majesty of endless stars.

The innocent hand of the mortal fell upon the gleaming glyphs of the otherworlders. The pass of his fingers cut away the silvery light of their bizarre resplendence, whose grace sanctified darkness and gave purpose to absolute emptiness.

Faced with no evident means of escape from Eternia's halls, his heart answered only with adamantine fascination. Confronted with endless abyss through an unknown world, he discovered in himself only enthusiasm for what might await devoted curiosity.

He could only dream of sharing this vision with the world. His fantasies of what lay within became unleashed, and unforgotten dreams lay siege to the unknown like a ravenous wildfire. Upon that fateful exhibition of most sincere disposition, what had held him hostage certified a faint glimmer. A drone from the mega depths shook him to his vulnerable soul, and he fought to stave it off with a hand clutched to his heart.

The otherworld reacted to him. He had been found, targeted by the telepath, who lurked somewhere within the breach in reality, deep within the dream.

The vibrations dug deeper and caused him to stumble. An aimless glimpse to the glass revealed a woman under a pristine white hood just behind him, lost in prayer with her hands clasped.

The drone turned into a violent quake that forced his eyes shut as the arcane world was transformed in a nauseating blur. The boy threw his arm forward, and it met the icy glass as his head pounded. Visions behind his eyes, however, motivated him to quickly reawaken, as they had sought to piece together the gruesome reality of a stranger's tragedy.

Shaken from the ephemeral nightmare, he was brought to perfect stillness. His eyes were not his own now, however. Eddie looked over his shoulder in expectation to see that flawless robed maiden, but he had been left virtually alone.

His heart pounded in both true and foreign fear.

There came the sound of running. It was closer than before—nearly upon him. He gripped the wishing star tight as ethereal flowers of strange familiarity sprouted from the floor, the chairs, and all across the table. His eyes darted from one to the other, bewildered by the magics of the otherworld.

Then, something stole his attention in the doorway. To his horror, a raging demon had cut the corner—a hooded swordsman in a hypnosis of rampant fury and blade flurries out to strike.

Eddie stepped back from moonlike eyes that were etched deep with bloodthirsty insanity—an entity on a plummet straight to the pits of hell. The hostile swordsman gritted his teeth as Eddie felt his back hit the glass. The innocent recipient of needless wrath held out his hand, then let out a terrified yelp, though that voice was not his own.

The swordsman stumbled forth as he shot into a merciless assault.

Eddie shut his eyes. It was all he could do.

But through fear, and in defiance of inevitable death, he reopened his eyes.

He found himself there, beneath the frozen blade, and just before the darkness took him, he gazed into eyes relinquished of hate, now filled with remorse, regret, and sadness.

And the blade never fell.

***

Eddie's eyes shot open as his spirit was returned from the otherworld. His chest rose and fell in frantic breaths as he lay upon the ground, covered in dust from the explosion that decimated the Grand Sky Hotel. As the moments passed, he realized he had returned to the war zone. The odd phenomena, whatever it had been, was no more.

On shaking legs, he trembled to his feet, using the wall to stabilize himself. An eerie creak dinned throughout the corridor. He peered up the flight of stairs he had been thrown down. There, the door swung on damaged hinges, the top mechanism broken clean off. Beyond the door was a sea of dancing crimson around a gouged heart of ruin.

The structure was subjected to a severe quake, and far away, a siren roared. He knew he had to escape. The damage done remained unknown, and he had little desire to be alone here any longer. Eddie descended the steps with a hobble. Sweat fell from his brow as he wrapped the staircase over and over again.

An intense heat swelled throughout the stairwell as he neared the mid-level. It became so fierce that he had to keep his distance from each door he passed, though to his fortune, it dissipated as he raced down the staircase to the fourth floor.

The lone soldier had finally reached a landing. Upon the wall was a gold-plated four. Beside it were opened double doors and a short run of carpet into a sumptuous lobby. The walls wrapped around a centralized marble statue and met again at the distant exit—a glass door, reinforced with a recessed steel mount.

The work of stone depicted a young woman in a ceremonial robe, back bent in dramatic fashion, and her endless gaze and a sole finger set upon the domed ceiling. Eddie crept forward until he neared the statue, then peered up to find a wondrous display of constellations, at which he had no time to gawk.

A glow caught his eye in the connection of stars, however, along with cracks of red-hot ember. He froze as ash and flame seeped through the ceiling. The cracks spread into a web throughout the cosmic mosaic, and the structure let out a groan as it was eaten away beyond the cosmic veil.

He dashed for the glass doors on the other side just as the ceiling split open behind him. Eddie dove forward as the artist's vision of heaven was laid to ruin with a thunderous crash. The floor caved under the fierce cascade of superheated rubble, and the statue tipped back into the clutches of ruin.

The rest of the ceiling broke away as Eddie bolted for the doors. He stumbled, dropped to the ground, and slid across the glossy floor. The structure quaked as it was gutted by the collapse. With no way out, the boy threw his arms over his head and curled himself up in a last line of defense against death's dynamic grasp.

Soon, however, the quake became a mere resonant rumble, and as the ground became still again, Eddie popped his head up and fumbled to his feet.

Shaken, he turned back to the hellish descent and peered over from the safety of the remnant marble shard, down three rings of fire into the inferno. With his reckless curiosity satiated, Eddie backed away as he realized the danger, then turned for the door.

He reached through darkness for the handle, but his fingers met a stone chunk, which had punched through the silver plates and become lodged in the surrounding security frame. Determined to escape, he seized the marble missile with both hands and wiggled it loose from its cradle of metal bars. No sooner had he relieved the pulverized structure of the launched rubble than did the doors drift open. With his path cleared, he tossed the rock to the ground, then drove through the door with his shoulder, back out into the embrace of the nightmare.

A cobblestone road split a ravaged multileveled market, which bridged the gap between the gutted hotel and its surviving sister structure. Debris had lain waste to the square glass walls of the blazing outlets, and the widespread furnace within raised a raging curtain of black into the night.

As Eddie pressed through the scorched channel for the double doors at the far end, he became aware of gleaming gazes set upon him from the smoldering hollows further along. There came movement beyond the breached storefront, and he caught sight of the blue glimmers in the darkness.

The cadet quickened his pace as danger closed in all around. The walls of the market soon narrowed on the path, and it became the sole passage to the neighboring square.

A flash came from the right. A giant pushed through the store racks. Then came another on the left. A massive gun roared to life with shining cerulean vibrance. Eddie's eyes darted from one side to the other as he neared the end of the squeeze. There was a disturbance through the chaos of the moment. A blur swept through the shadows, and the giants fell one after another. It leapt overhead to the other side at such speed that the boy could only catch the flutter of fabric left behind in his ear.

The titans crashed upon the tiled floor, felled by the flash-blade assassin. The dimensional traveler grew anxious as those rapid steps touched on memories that neared the edge of oblivion.

He refocused in hopes of finding the door within reach but instead was brought to the backs of his heels. There, at the end of the passage, was a cerulean-eyed invader trooper who impeded the way forward with its enormous size. Eddie fell to his backside and skimmed across the ground until he came to a gentle halt before the monstrosity.

It gazed down at him, that entity that championed the reverence held by death, then raised its weapon to do the work. The boy remained frozen, however, unable to rescue himself from arresting fixation. Like he would to the vast night sky, he found himself gazing into the soldier's glimmer.

The invader aligned its gun with the cadet. With a deep groan, the back of the barrel roared to life with cerulean brilliance, ready to fire.

The boy's eyes widened as he faced down the glimmer of end. Then came a second disturbance. Something kicked from the ground. Eddie turned over his shoulder. An indigo blur snapped from wall to wall through the squeeze, then shot forth as it passed over the targeted soldier, who sat dumbstruck.

The midnight phantom bolted over the soldier's head and graced its reinforced helmet with an effortless pass of flawless, shining edge. Eddie turned back as the breakneck blur hit the ground behind the titan, planted with one hand upon the concrete and the blade out to his side. The invader grew still as a thin line glimmered through the immaculate cut in its astral armor.

The giant tipped back and struck the ground with a conclusive tremor throughout the stone. Eddie Bowitz remained stupefied as the swordsman rose. His eyes fell upon the boy, who scuffled back in retreat at first but fell still when he saw the swordsman's brow raise. There shined the gleam of cerulean in one of his eyes, though it soon vanished rather unceremoniously. His reticent savior was much like them, yet somehow different.

"Wh-who are you?" the boy stuttered.

The soft crackle of fire and a distant firefight swallowed the time between question and answer.

"You shouldn't be here," the swordsman replied in a cold drag, devoid of emotion or urgency.

Eddie cringed as a faint memory begged him to heed its dire warning. "Wait. What? What are you talking about?"

"You shouldn't be here," the swordsman repeated. "This city is doomed. Escape, if you have something to stand for . . ."

The boy rose in frantic credence of his warning. "What's happening here? What are these things?" he asked of the invader giants.

"It doesn't matter anymore. It's time to fight or die. Can you understand that?"

Eddie swallowed his fear and nodded in compliance. "The way forward is blocked—"

The swordsman gripped his head, overwhelmed by a sudden pain, which caused his eyes to shine through his curled fingers.

"Forward is the only way! Go! Get out!" the swordsman cried as his eyes burst to life in cerulean light.

He raised his radiant blade, imbued with arcane magics. Eddie inched back, then leapt away as the swordsman unleashed the gathered force with a vicious swipe to the bar-guarded doors. A white slash whooshed forth from the blade's edge and cut through glass, bar, and frame at once. Beyond the slit, a purply fissure roared open in midair and ripped away the entire entrance with its fierce gravitational well. The rupture closed, and the remnant debris spilled across the marble floors. The gateway had been breached, and the way forward appeared.

"Do not linger. Be wary of what's familiar. Nothing but horrors will come looking for you here," the swordsman warned as he lifted from the strike.

With no gift left for his journey, the swordsman took off at blinding speed for the edge, leapt upon the stone parapet, then shot off into the fiery war zone. Eddie gave chase to the end and grabbed hold of the railing, which traced the center of the blasted boundary. Wonderstruck eyes scanned absolute desolation, but he found no sign of his savior. The swordsman had gone, but his mystique lingered, leaving Eddie captivated in the most profound of ways.

He placed his hand upon his head. The memories of the otherworld had all but faded, though something had been undoubtedly familiar about the swordsman. The further he pursued that familiarity, however, the more distant it became, until at last he had to question if the feeling was genuine at all.

The swordsman's warning soon took prominence over his searching for him, and the boy turned to the portal that had replaced fortified doors.

"Forward . . . I wonder who that guy is," he pondered aloud.

But he shook himself from deeper explorations and refocused on his escape. He made for the blasted gate and crunched over spilt glass as he crossed to the far end. There, the staircase wound down to the ground floor, which he took with spirited steps.

As he neared the bottom, he overheard the sound of a commotion—the familiar bark of commands from determined officers. The boy leapt down the last flight of the stairs and planted upon a burgundy carpet, then cut left and dashed through a spacious, abandoned lobby.

A stone arch over the front entrance had collapsed and left the exit half choked. It didn't slow the boy's pace, however, as the voices had grown distant, and he couldn't afford to be left alone again.

He accelerated and bounded over the rubble.

As he crossed over the triangular stone peak, his eyes beheld a pile of jagged edges on the other side. His arms flailed as his boot dove between the stones. He became snared, and the sudden halt snatched him from the air. Both hands went out and, by fortune alone, struck bare cement.

Eerily, he felt nothing from the fall, though as he stood and yanked his boot from between the rocks, he cringed at the thought of what could have been. Without the time to dwell on it, he dusted off his hands as he turned to the desolate street.

Just across the road, there was an alleyway in which he could still hear the faint cry of dire orders through warfare's horrid cacophony. He blitzed across the street, blockaded on each side by abandoned traffic, and wound down a passage of crimson bricks. As he raced ahead toward a distant fire, he found those he had been searching for. The boot of the last soldier turned the bank at the top of a thousand fallen bricks.

Though the road had been treacherous, he had made it. It was in no small part due to the swordsman's incredible charity. Perhaps there were heroes from beyond which had come to their aid. In that mere possibility, he retained solace.

But who were these invaders from beyond the stars, and why had they come? What connection might the swordsman have to all of this? Most importantly of all to Eddie, why did answers not matter to him? The boy took on an acute fascination with this hero and their sole encounter. It electrified him with the inspiration to forge ahead and cast out his fear all at once. So, with a heart imbued with courage, the cadet gave chase to the shadows of his comrades that had been cast along the ruined wall.

The Battle of Salamandra

A shower of drop pods streaked through the stars, the second wave of mechanical menace now supported by heavy transport crafts. Military jets engaged the transports at breakneck speeds as the neglected drop pods pulverized streets, shops, and squares. From each one emerged another soldier who, after priming its weapon, hunted down fortunate survivors of the initial ruthless attack.

At the Union State Building, a defensive had been formed against the attackers who closed in from all sides of the decimated city. The resistance took cover behind fluted columns and grand statues whose pristine forms were defiled by the weapons of war.

Ripples of gunfire drowned each other out as the invaders made their advance through the ruins and into the blasted courtyard. Although their lethargic movements and the glow in their eyes made them easy targets, the troopers were formidable even in the face of the most ruthless barrage from the Union's gold-standard assault rifles.

Determined soldiers took aim at the titans' reinforced helmets, which encased the nether's glow. Not a single bullet, however, seemed capable of penetration at any point of perceived weakness.

Faced with mounting attackers, individual assessments of the situation grew grim.

They fired at leg joints, beneath shoulder pads, and any other point where heavy plate was minimized in favor of improved mobility. It wasn't long before the defenders found the entire building surrounded by scores of enormous invader husks.

Out from the state building's colossal doors emerged a squad of four soldiers with rifles drawn. Ill-equipped in simple battledress, the fresh defenders came under immediate assault from the indigo strike force in that desperate bolt for the portico's ample stone parapet. As they approached, the squad split between the grand staircase and dropped behind the wall's safety.

"Going loud," shouted Corporal Jedd as he mounted his heavy machine gun upon the flat top.

"Let 'em have it, madman," ordered Sergeant Sky.

"With pleasure," Jedd acknowledged between his teeth.

The high caliber weapon lit the night as it unleashed a bullet storm upon the invader force. The barrage attracted the attention of several approaching troopers, and soon, all of them had set the madman in their crosshairs. A vicious counterattack of sapphire fury forced Jedd back down for cover.

"Now," ordered Sky.

The rest of the squad emerged from the battered line and opened fire on the distracted advance. An inferno erupted among the invaders as prepared explosive rounds bathed the courtyard in fire.

The fiery barrage sent the troopers stumbling back with each hit, and though the result appeared promising, their desperate attack ceased as the special munitions ran dry.

The delayed invaders steadied, then reassessed the squad in perfect stillness before they emerged from the settling pall in a renewed advance.

It was as if they had done nothing at all. Though the rounds had caused superficial damage, not one of their foes had come out on even a faint limp. The invaders hoisted up their weapons and unleashed retaliatory hellfire upon the defenders.

"They're not stoppin'," shouted Corporal Garfield from the parapet beyond the grand staircase as he made a frantic effort to reload his gun.

"Can't blow 'em up. What the hell do you do with 'em?" shouted Corporal Mac, just a pillar down.

From the door to the capitol building, a soldier kicked a rocket launcher across the ground. Sergeant Sky reached out and caught it from the slide.

"Use a bigger boom," he enlightened as he mounted it on his shoulder. "Cover fire!" the able sergeant commanded.

His determined squad emerged as directed and unleashed a fierce counterattack to draw the enemy's fire. As the invaders engaged the imminent threat, Sky lifted up, took aim, and fired the rocket from the chamber.

The hiss of the explosive was silenced by a thunderous peal as the rocket found its mark on the chest plate of a caped trooper, near the center of the pack. A shockwave ripped through the courtyard as the blazing fireball roared into a curling plume of smoke.

The squad lingered behind deteriorated ruin as a distant gunfight settled in the quiet aftermath.

"How's that?" called Jedd from the other side of the column that separated him from Sky.

Unsure, the sergeant peered over the wall. The cloud of smoke and dust had settled, but despite the conditions, it was clear to see that at least one was down, but many more were coming.

"Got one, but there's still plenty," Sky reported.

"Shit—how many rockets you got left!?" Jedd inquired, flustered with anxiety.

Sky tossed the smoking launcher to the floor and readied his assault rifle.

"None. The capitol wasn't exactly prepared ahead of time with a weapons cache. We're holding this position until all government officials clear the building," Sky asserted.

Suddenly, the wall next to Jedd was breached by gunfire. Stones sliced into his cheek as he threw himself away from the sudden rupture.

"Son of a bitch," he growled.

Mac sprang up and fired off a wave of bullets, but he fell fast as return fire flew overhead and ripped through the wall of the Union Capitol Building.

"We aren't gonna last long out here!" Mac shouted.

In recognition of their dire predicament, Sky drew an oval shaped comm device from his jacket.

"Link—Sal Command, battle box zero. C-840, Saber Squad. Red," Sky recited into the device.

He waited as the thunderous steps drew closer. Jedd replanted the machine gun on the wall and fired off a focused barrage at the nearest invader. The bullets found a miracle mark. The soldier careened to the side, then collapsed just in front of another. The unscathed trooper trudged past its fallen ally and opened fire on Jedd with its colossal, rapid-fire gun. The madman, with a small vengeance exacted, dropped back to the ground as the cerulean bolts stormed overhead and punched through one of the capitol's grand imperial windows.

"How's the conversation coming!? These guys are just walking up on a fortified position like they don't give a damn," Jedd spat.

"Thank sweet heaven they're taking their time, though," said Garfield.

A wild hail of gunfire blasted through the battered wall and ripped through the capitol behind them. Sky threw down the comm device as fragments of the Union's glory crumbled around his pressed defensive.

"There's nothing but interference! They've got to be jamming the signal!" Sky shouted.

"What do we do, then!? They're about to turn us into the capitol's welcome mat," cried Jedd.

"Hold it! Looks like they've halted their advance . . . but we got another problem on our hands," Garfield warned as he peered over the jagged rock, then sank back down behind it.

"What? What is it?" cried Jedd.

The rest of the squad peered over the jagged line. From the fringes of the blasted courtyard approached a hooded invader. Dressed in a flawless indigo cloak, he had no gun to fight his battle, but a blade lay sheathed at his side.

The invader elite stepped through the horde of lesser troopers, who had come to a collective halt with barrels rested in hand. The winds of havoc rippled through his uniform as he stopped in front of the pack, then waited in offer to the squad—a chance to meditate on their next move.

"Fool's just got a sword. Let's mow him down quick," said Jedd, gripping his gun in thirst for another kill.

"I got a bad feeling about this, Jedd," Sky warned.

The doors behind them swung open, and out from within emerged an elite squad of five heavily armed soldiers in jet-black, full-body armor. Supreme, in the highest tech available to the state, they rushed out to cover alongside the beleaguered sergeant, ready to lend much needed aid.

"Sergeant Sky, what's the situation?" the squad leader asked, his voice muffled behind his digital helmet and concerned eyes hidden behind its reflective visor.

"We stumbled out, surrounded. Four guns looking out to a hundred, and nothing short of a rocket could put a stone under their foot. Hostiles are formidable and seem to act independently. Possibly some kind of . . . combat androids," Sky relayed.

"Well, don't forget to mention their rather average-sized sword clown," Jedd reminded. "That would be rather insulting!"

"And who would that be?" the armored commander inquired.

"Right over the wall. Front and center. Appears to be an officer of some kind," Sky explained.

The squad leader gave a signal for his team to investigate. They inched up over the wall just enough so they could set their sights on the idle swordsman. The invader troopers maintained order through stillness, unmoved by the cautious peeks of their foes along the battered parapet.

"Saber Squad, hold the line here. Evac route for top suit has almost been established, but we won't have much time before that line gets pressed. Once the prime minister and senators reunite with high command, we'll take our first swing to push them out of the city. Twenty minutes . . . and then we abandon the capitol . . . take the west exit, understood?"

Nonplussed, Sergeant Sky nodded with mouth agape as he acknowledged that weighty order.

"Lotus Squad," the resolute commander announced. "We're addressing the enemy at the doorstep. Corporal Kaufman, you and I are on the leader. Rest of you cover those troopers. Let's move."

The ebon task force moved out from cover with their weapons drawn on the hooded invader. The enemy remained unflinching throughout that daring advance down the grand staircase.

"Weapons down! Down! I want them down," the squad leader ordered the sapphire-eyed legion.

The rest of Lotus Squad echoed the same order as they closed the distance between themselves and the lone swordsman.

"Hands up or we shoot," he warned with the upward snap of his barrel.

The armored enforcer pointed the gun at the nearby troopers, then fired a warning shot at the ground. The blade's master remained in motionless defiance, however, as its eyes pierced those enemies who stood against them and looked right into a promised destiny—the likes of which none of the besieged could ever imagine.

An eeriness lingered on the battlefield and grew heavy on the consciences of the members of the Saber Squad.

"Just shoot him. Just shoot him," Jedd murmured.

The squad leader set crosshairs between the eyes of the hooded invader. His breaths became long and heavy as the enemy refused to budge.

"Have you come to negotiate!?" the squad leader asked.

There came a subtle shift of the radiant pierce, and the resolute soldier became unsettled as a nauseating chill swept through him. He had found himself in the face of High Fantasy's sovereign will, and though he knew not what was coming, nor the nature of the gazing-deep cosmic entity, he enjoyed absolute confidence in knowing that he would not budge from the line it had struck upon him. The fate imposed by an enemy who would defile their hallowed city could never be allowed to prevail.

"If you do not comply, then by the order of—" the squad leader started, but never finished.

Tomorrow could wait no longer. The invader snapped forth in an arc flash assault, and the words from the patriot's mouth were silenced as its sword sank into the top of his helmet. The death-struck defender's knees buckled. He dropped to the ground but was seized by the neck before he could fall away.

The rest of the squad stumbled away in horror of the flash-assassin's miracle, left completely unaware that all those beaming gazes had turned unto them. With destiny to claim, the troopers raised their weapons and fired on the dazed resistance.

"What the hell!?" shouted Jedd as he leapt to the offensive.

He raised his weapon and gunned directly for the blade's master, who pulled the sword from the reinforced helm, then tossed the limp carcass aside.

The swordsman turned toward Jedd as his spray of bullets veered off course under the influence of an invisible barrier. Unthreatened, it drew a metallic sphere from behind its unscathed cloak, pulled back, and hooked it through the air on a course for Jedd and Sky's position.

"Get down, get down!" shouted Sky as he dove for the ground.

The device let out an ear-piercing screech, then ignited the balcony with a grand eruption, which sent a wave of fine shards of shrapnel out behind the defensive line. Anchored by wrathful passion, Jedd was swept by the blast and struck the ground with tremendous force.

The walls crumbled across the elevated portico as a shockwave rang throughout the sky. The sergeant lay motionless in a shroud of smoke, and after a moment, his eyes reopened to the settling shroud. His vision blurred as he lifted himself up to the sound of gunfire, which silenced heart-rending screams. From hand and knee, he shuffled through the veil, then rose as he failed to find his way out.

"Jedd, what's your status?" Sky cried, as he limped through the smoke that ebbed and flowed under his footsteps.

"Is anyone still with me?" he called out to the gray abyss.

There was no response.

He went with careful steps and came upon the staircase that led down to the battle-stricken courtyard. There, at obscurity's brink, lay one of the fallen Lotus Squad troopers, who crawled up, inch by inch.

Sky, still in a daze, descended to assist. He knelt down and inspected the gruesome wounds across the soldier's waist, each framed by seared armor.

"I'm going to get you to help, okay?" the sergeant assured, although he knew the odds weren't well in their favor.

The soldier gave no reply, however, and turned over to face the dark sky. The sergeant moved to take her but was seized by the arm.

"Do you see what I see?" she asked with a deathly tremble.

"What is it?" Sky replied.

"So many things—wonderful things, hidden from us."

Those peculiar words befuddled the sergeant, but he saw a rational cause for the delusions beyond the works of imminent death. He reached for the mask.

"Here, let me get this off you."

Faintly familiar with the suit of the armored corps, he pressed deeply on a button beneath the chin, which released the lock. As he pulled the mask off, freed locks of hair flowed out onto the ground— shining rivers of blond. With a bloodied nose and tired eyes, she did not turn, nor acknowledge him with a glance.

"Don't you see it, too?" she asked again.

She raised her trembling finger to the sky. The sergeant placed the helmet to the side, then peered up, but found only the stars and cosmic cruisers through the fading gray veil.

"I can hear them calling me from there. It says I'll be home!"

Her body shook as death quietly passed its hand.

"Soon—I'll be—" She drew in a last quivering breath as her arm fell to the ground.

Sky's head fell in the wake of her passing. He was left in sheer astonishment of how much had been lost in so little time, with mere moments the sole divide between normality and the absolute decimation of their proud capital.

But the sergeant seized strength in his sworn duty to the Union and his brothers and sisters in arms. That alone was all that was needed to make sense for now. He rose up with intent to fall back, but the air from his lungs was taken by the sight of the invader blade's master on approach to the bottom of the staircase.

The reaper's radiant sapphire gaze had been set upon him, and it left him in complete petrification—mind, body, and spirit—as the cruel assailant drew up his blade to cast its judgment.

He heard something, however—a swift displacement of wind. The blade's master cut through the air; the rogue indigo shadow leapt from the darkness and brought a shining blade down against the invader's attack. Sky shuddered at the piercing clash, the likes of which he had not beheld since the adventures of his boyhood's benign imagination.

There, against the menace, stood Ultra, locked blade to blade with one who seemed more a brother.

"Not yet," the rugged rescuer uttered.

He overpowered the invader allegiant, and they reengaged in a blinding flurry of strikes. From the staircase to the portico, they clashed, dodged, and miscalculated blows, which shattered the blasted parapet, carved divots into columns, and cut immaculate lines through the ground.

Sky remained motionless, held in awe, a mere spectator of the duel between two combatants of incredible ability. He shook from his trance as their flash maneuvers returned his eye to the gazing troopers. Under pressure of the invader's renewed advance, Sky turned and raced back up the grand staircase in search of cover.

The celestial combatants emerged from divine lightning, back upon the capitol's trampled courtyard. Seemingly matched, they each hunted for an opening—one strike was all that was needed to conclude their bout.

Ultra, in a change of strategy, flipped his blade and took it in a reverse grip to invite an attack.

The invader, in reciprocation of his bait, raised the blade with both hands.

The opportunity had been presented. Ultra shot forward in a low sweep, then raised the blade until the bottom of the grip connected with the bottom of his opponent's. The invader's arms stretched forth as Ultra rose up from beneath.

By his lightning charge, their bout was done. The razor-sharp tip of Ultra's blade pointed down between the eyes of his opponent, like a vicious fang.

Spellbound by duty and unable to release its weapon, the invader blade's master found itself outmaneuvered. Ultra bit down into the inhibited foe, who then collapsed to its knees in a lifeless departure. In solemn triumph, Ultra retracted the blade, sidestepped the fallen body, then slashed the air with the immaculate silver liberator in a snappy gesture to victory.

The awestruck sergeant rose over the blasted line atop the portico and peered down at the result of the invader's fantastic bout. Ultra remained planted at the head of the stairs as he stared the troopers down like a hawk to helpless prey.

"Hey—Sky . . . Who—the hell is that?" panted Jedd, who lay on the ground behind the wall's rubble.

"Hold on, Jedd, I'm going to get you help," Sky assured, relieved to hear his voice.

"Damnit, I'm alright! Just a little ringing in the ears and a splitting headache," he replied.

Sky scanned the area for the rest of his squad. He attempted multiple times to contact them with shouts to the eerie silence, but there came no reply. He reined in his emotions, almost certain of a pitiful outcome, then lifted into a breach in the ravaged parapet to project his voice.

"You there! I don't know who you are, but we could really use a hand here," Sky uttered.

"You should be running now," Ultra responded without severing his gaze.

"We can't fall back until the capitol is evacuated."

"Then you will die," the swordsman replied rather naturally.

Sky, angered by his grim assessment, grabbed his rifle from the ground and readied it. "I'll die trying," he declared.

"I know," replied Ultra.

Sky held in defiant silence. There was a distinct rumble over the sound of distant chaos. A second, more violent rumble occurred, which left the debris rattling on the ground.

Something was approaching.

From among the bouncing rock, he caught sight of the discarded communicator. Galvanized to action, he scrambled over, seized it from the ground, and hurried to hook it back around his ear.

"Link—Sal Command, battle box zero. C-840, Saber Squad. Red. Please respond. Enemy assault on the south entrance is overwhelming. Two members of Saber Squad are MIA. Lotus Squad has been wiped out. Escort team will need assistance. Repeat. Escort team will need assistance."

"It comes," Ultra uttered.

A subterranean colossus struck the ground at the center of the plaza and unleashed a web of shattered stone. What lay beneath released a cavernous breath of steam, which lingered in the form of an ethereal echo. Shards of the patriots' defiled promenade rolled off a spired top as the monstrosity's two enormous apertures peeked out from the depths.

"You seeing this, sergeant? What in the *hell* is that?" Jedd shouted, staring out from behind cover.

The observation deck forced its way through to the hellish accompaniment of hydraulics, a wire-infested shaft in its wake. With armored plate shrouded by a sea of tiny bulbs, the tower's neck glowed with all the brilliance of the stars. The plates screeched into rotation, and the stars were spun into a dizzying cosmic cyclone.

The ground cracked and popped as it made its eerily majestic ascent, soon to be revealed to them in whole, a gazing tower from the brink of imagination.

Sky sat with all his thoughts stolen from him. He could not choose whether to run or fight; the terror in his heart equaled the wonder in his conscious, which together left him in unprecedented paralysis.

His formidable will had crumbled to sovereign's tyrant, and all he could do was be a helpless witness, as two yellow spotlights gazed out at him.

"Are you close with madness? You'll need it in order to fight back," said Ultra.

"What in the hell is *that?*" the madman roared.

"Start making sense. I need you to start making sense," Sky said, trembling.

As the monstrosity reached its limit high above the capitol building, it let out a piercing, mechanical whine that ramped into a deafening roar—an oppressive siren serving as the ominous harbinger of the end of worlds.

"Very soon, it will," Ultra mumbled, prepared to go head-to-head with the titan from oblivion.

Sky gripped his rifle, his determination reignited by frustration.

"Enough of the poetry," he erupted against the swordsman's perceived silence.

Jedd held his gun close to his chest and, in his head, ran through the next few seconds of his life like a videoclip as the machine's roar settled into a gut-wrenching echo.

"Don't be afraid," the swordsman uttered as he gazed up into the eyes of the machine, a child before a monster.

"Just shoot at it, right? That's all you have to do," Jedd assured himself.

With secured commitment, the madman leapt from cover and unleashed a torrent of gunfire all along the neck of the tower. The glassy exterior shattered and broke under the spray of bullets. Under assault, the observation deck rotated until its uncanny gaze was set upon the assailant.

Sky rose up alongside his comrade from the other side of the column and opened fire upon the exposed machinery within the shaft. The clip emptied fast, however, and he found himself frozen again as his subconscious became fixated in a struggle to assess the exact nature of what had just turned to him. With a mind subdued by wonder, he began to take notice of strange whispers each moment that he lingered in its piercing gaze.

e t e r n i a   b e c k o n s

In an intervention of fate, the spellbound sergeant was flung to the floor by an unseen force just as the earth exploded beneath him. He struck the ground, and as he slid through dust and light debris, he looked on in astonishment at an obsidian spike that had punched through the ground upon which he had just stood with Ultra right beside it.

"It's coming for you. Run," the unfazed savior ordered.

Sky nodded with a tremble, stunned that death had nearly stolen him. In heed of the swordsman's warning, he lifted to his feet and took off toward the far end of the south portico.

Spike after spike shot up from beneath, each nearly claiming his life. He had never felt such terror, as he struggled to stay ahead of the subterranean assault. The tower opened fire with twin gatling turrets, mounted beneath its deck. The superheated rounds put holes through the capitol's wall, evaporated chunks of statues, and tore the ground asunder. Miraculously, its target remained unscathed thanks to safeguarding from that ill-fated architecture.

Jedd had taken to his feet and snuck down the steps in pursuit of something in the rubble below, his face flushed and eyes bulged in battle-born rage.

Meanwhile, Ultra confronted the invader troopers below. They attempted to engage him, but his lightning maneuvers made him an impossible target to keep in their sights. One by one they succumbed to the ruthless cut of his blade until the courtyard had been cleared of their presence.

With the troopers dispatched, Ultra raced to the colossus, who was seemingly unaware of his presence. He jammed his blade into the rotating neck, causing it to lock up with a spectacular shriek of electric arcs.

With the tower stunned, he sheathed the blade and leapt into a frantic ascent. Against the clock, he utilized the jutted planes of the metal plates to sling himself up to the vulnerable observation deck.

Jedd had entered the battle-torn arena and crept to the nearest slain invader. His eyes glowed in vengeance-fueled excitement as he reached for the gun on the ground.

"I'll make good use of this." Jedd strained as he lugged up the invader's incredible weapon.

His body trembled as he struggled to bring the tip of the barrel off the ground. In a frustrated release, he let the rifle crash to the shattered stone, then laid down beside it. Like a sniper in the brush, he aligned the sights with the bottom of the tower's neck. No matter how many times he pulled the trigger, however, the gun would not discharge.

"Piece of junk," he seethed as he lifted from the ground.

The madman returned up the staircase, drew his pistol, then put every round into the tower in front of him.

Sky slowed his pace as he came upon the end of the portico. The spikes behind him had ceased to chase, and so he looked to the machine and found Ultra atop the observation deck, his blade drawn to strike.

The blade grew radiant as he held it back behind his head. With necessary potency, he unleashed the gathered strength with a vicious slash against the armored exterior, ripping a gap through it.

With an exploitable opening created, Ultra leapt high into the air. In a twist to gather strength, he ripped his arm across and fired the blade like a boomerang into the gash.

Snaps, zaps, and bangs rippled right down to the bottom, accompanied by two explosions at the heart of the beast near the base. The decisive strike had ended its every function at once. The machine swayed in its final moment, and like the breath of steam that had proceeded its emergence, the electronic failure of its systems echoed out with a cavernous depth that rang out for miles.

Ultra leapt from the top as the neck snapped at the ruptured power core and hit the ground just before the observation deck crashed upon the roof, door, and grand staircase of the south portico.

The dust settled in the wake of the breathtaking collapse. Sky, a man relatively grounded when it came to that of sheer fantasy, was shell-shocked, unable to believe what he had seen. The things of dreams had threatened his life and saved it, all the same.

From the dust cloud emerged Ultra, blade in hand. He ascended the staircase and found Jedd on his back not far from the fallen shaft, with eyes widened in the vivid madness of one who had looked upon the grisly face of death.

"Well, that was a heart attack," he joked upon the invader's arrival at the top.

Exhausted from his flight, Sky staggered back toward the top of the pulverized staircase where the two had convened. As Ultra drew closer, Jedd greeted him with the draw of his pistol.

Ultra grew still as he took aim.

"The weapon is out of ammunition," the swordsman forewarned.

Jedd snorted in disbelief. There was no way he should have known.

"Lucky call. And you can bet your mother's sweet ass that's not a bluff I'm about to all-in on," Jedd conceded as he lowered the gun.

Ultra remained silent, then continued his advance.

Meanwhile, Sky maneuvered between the metallic spikes as he made slow gains on the central staircase.

As Ultra stepped before Jedd, he put the blade to him.

"Shoulda *damn* knew it," the madman snarled.

"Disaster approaches, and we don't have much time. Tell me where your commander is," the swordsman ordered.

Jedd glanced left and right, then looked upon the swordsman in lax defiance. "Look, you think there's like, one supreme leader of this planet, space man? And what makes you think I'd make a dog bowl traitor of myself and tell you?"

"I don't have to be diplomatic. I'm choosing to be. Answer the question."

"Oh, piss off—"

"Jedd, stop. We owe this man our lives," said Sky.

Ultra glanced at the sergeant, who stood propped up by the second spike that had sprung from the ground. He pushed off of it and walked over to join at Jedd's side.

"I don't owe him diddly," Jedd resisted as he took to his feet, then brushed himself off before the eyes of the swordsman.

"Enough," Sky ordered. "It's clear we have a common enemy. If we can link up with General Myres, maybe we still have a chance to turn back the enemy—to save the city—"

Ultra's head sank. "A common . . . enemy."

He sheathed his blade as his thoughts circled for a moment. A feeling concluded his thoughts. It brought faint discomfort, but was truth, nonetheless.

"Much more is at stake than the fate of this city. This world's existence is to be judged. What will come after lies beyond imagination, but you must be willing to face it in every form that it will take. This task force, which has destroyed your city, is a mere test of your capabilities. I have no intention of misleading you. Even with my help, no victory can be assured," Ultra warned.

The two soldiers lingered in silence, troubled by that grim assessment from a man more capable than any they had ever seen.

"I don't like him . . . but I wouldn't call him dishonest. Don't like him one bit," Jedd stressed.

Sky reached down and retrieved his rifle off the ground. "We'll get you to the general. He'll know what to do, and even if you can't win us any battles, he will," Sky assured. "Let's go, Jedd. We'll have to find ammo as we go."

The resolute sergeant turned from them, clearly overcome with frustration as he made for the decimated capitol building. How could this incredible warrior from another world fight so fiercely, but have no hope to win? This was their city, their home, a symbolic beacon of freedom, and surely they could not allow it to be surrendered. But the emptied halls answered otherwise—more invaders, surely on the advance.

Jedd and Ultra followed behind, with a fair distance maintained between each other. As Sky continued into the great hall, a feeling began to invade his mind. He sensed a presence nearby. At first it brought him unusual comfort, but the longer it remained with him, the more unsettled he began to feel. The haunt was right there behind them, and all he needed to do was turn to behold an uncanny truth. But he resisted and led them straight to the breach at the end of the west hall, guiding them through without ever looking back.

I am here for you.

Inheritance

Little Eddie Bowitz had eyed the movements of the swordsman ever since his arrival at the makeshift camp, which had been haphazardly assembled in the middle of an ample metropolitan park. He had taken perch atop the rubble of the collapsed brick face of an apartment on the outskirts and watched on as the distant invader inspected the ruins with an empty gaze.

It was no wonder why the once-faithful admirer of the fantastic had taken such an interest with him. Finally, there was something—a shining affirmation of the vast possibilities that lay beyond the reality to which he had long been chained.

The terror was nearly welcome, and the feeling of awe left him in euphoric buoyancy against even the heaviest guilt. A brief acknowledgement of that guilt, however, redirected his attention to the camp upon the blasted earth. His resilient eyes of innocence watched a distant, unceremonious scramble in which dutiful soldiers hauled the lifeless victims of the passionless slaughter to mass graves dug along the perimeter grounds of the park.

He had never felt more filled with hope that there was something that could be done to remedy their cruel fate. Though the world was under siege by that which had lurked beyond the reality, its mere presence gave credence that old promises may yet be fulfilled, and not just for him, but for all as one.

"You there," bellowed a voice from below.

Eddie stumbled as he turned, caught off guard by the assertive roar.

Across the street at the camp's head stood General Myres. Along with him was Second Lieutenant Schneider, who was engaged in an exchange with General Henson. Their once proud uniforms had faced the rough touch of war, a look that befit the defiled dignity of the ruined city that they were sworn to protect.

"Yeah, you there, soldier. Get your ass down here and make yourself useful, why don't ya?" Myres barked with the beckon of his hand.

Schneider and Henson were severed from discourse as their superior's attention was seized by the abrupt intrusion of a distressed officer, who had his ill-fated beloved slung across his arms. The officer yelled, but Eddie couldn't catch exactly what it was he said, though his wet and reddened face offered a vivid glimpse into absolute dismay.

The boy descended the jagged rubble with long strides, and hustled along until he was with them.

General Myres grimaced as the flustered officer shoved the corpse into his arms.

"She said the boys are trapped in a pileup near Skylar's Square. The bastards dropped right on top of them, but our troops forced her out! We gotta go back in. We gotta send help, sir. You got to do *something*. This is murder!"

"Pull yourself together, soldier. We're doing everything we can," Myres gently stressed as he passed the woman back in genuine lament for his loss.

Schneider, troubled by the officer's brash conduct, waved over two soldiers, who stood guard not far from a burned-out sedan.

"I can't lose them—can't afford to lose it all," the man echoed with darkened vacancy.

Eddie gazed at him and felt each fragment of that very sorrow within himself—once smashed in defiant anger but set aglow in the revealing light of empathy. Anyone, the boy thought, could understand the heaviness of that grief, though mere comprehension of strife, he knew, could offer little aid. If he could do it, he would go, but ever since the fateful end of a more sacred childhood, something had left him undeniably restrained, though he refused to assume it was hopelessness. Instead, he turned to the miracle in the heavens above. It was surely that, which offered so much more promise, that impelled him to forgo reckless bravery.

The soldiers had nearly made their way over when Eddie's wandering eyes found Schneider, who seized him with a glare, then waved him over, to which the boy wasted no time complying.

"Where's your weapon, junior?" Schneider inquired with a cold lift of his brow.

"I lost it on the way, sir," Eddie replied, much to the lieutenant's displeasure.

Overwhelmed by duty, General Myres wiped the sweat from his brow, then dragged his hand down his wrinkled forehead and bony cheek.

"Listen to me, sir," the crestfallen officer began.

"Help this man to a medic," Schneider ordered the soldiers upon their hasty arrival.

They stepped over to the officer, who had broken down into tears upon hearing that poignant command. One of them laid a hand on his shoulder in a silent offer of condolence, though it did little to ease him in the face of a lifetime of certain loneliness. It was a judgement he could only understand as iniquitous in nature, especially in his deteriorated state.

"Cadet, take care of the body," Schneider ordered.

Eddie nodded. "Yes, sir," he replied, then went over to fulfill the task. He reached for the woman. "I'm sorry about—"

A bundled fist whipped across Eddie's face and sent him to the ground across large chunks of rock.

"Get your hands off her," the man yelled. "You sons of bitches do something. My boys are out there, and all you cowards care about is yourselves," the man erupted.

The soldiers seized his arm as he flailed and lashed out at them with tremendous force. Eddie stayed on the ground as they struggled, still dazed from the hit.

"Get him under control," ordered Schneider, without a reasonable semblance of pity.

General Henson held his hand out to Schneider in gentle confrontation against Schneider's heavy-handedness.

"We'll handle this," he said in a tone laden with disappointment.

The soldiers ripped the man away from the corpse, and down she fell from his enduring grasp to the tormented earth. They were promptly brought to collective stillness as they each caught a glimpse of cloudy eyes that gazed deep into some inevitable oblivion. The struggle against truth was over, however, and the officer collapsed to his knees, General Henson beside him as he consoled his stricken compatriot with snappy, expressive gestures of the hand.

"Soldiers, let him be," Myres instructed. "Got one hell of a mess here. Along with the proverbial iceberg stuck up our ass, we just got our heads knocked right off, and while we're busy trying to screw 'em back on, we haven't got a clue who we're fighting or why."

"Aliens, sir. Never thought I'd say it," claimed one of the soldiers.

At the wayside, the solemn exchange abated as a few nurses arrived to aid the despondent officer back to the camp, joined at the side by General Henson at his vehement request. In wake of their civil departure, a lone medic arrived to retrieve the body of the soldier's dearly beloved, and once he took her up into his arms, he headed for the mass graves to lay her to a half-dignified rest.

"Hard to argue with nonsense when it's dropping pods on you. Just when you think the Union has gotten the hang of fighting off giant megalomaniacs, these guys show up . . . We can find out the why when we regain some semblance of control. In the meantime . . . getting the city secured is our top priority," the general remarked as he broke from a hopeless brood.

He turned to his soldiers, save the boy.

"You two, I need you to support the med teams in Midtown. I've already dispatched a reinforcement platoon, but you oughta be able to catch up with them. Take the route we've established through Eleventh and be ready for a fight. We've struggled to hold onto that intersection between Main and Thirty-Seventh, and judging by the . . . unusual reports coming out of there in the last hour . . . they're gonna need all the help they can get."

Oblivious to such reports, Schneider raised his brow. "What's more distinctly unusual than what we've already faced?"

"Let's just say they're being watched by . . . something. And I think we'll leave it at that until I get my next update, which, by the grace of heaven, shouldn't be too long now," the general assured. "Soldiers, you know what to do. Move out."

Though unsettled by that murky revelation, the soldiers mustered courage with a resolute salute, then departed in a determined flight across the perimeter sidewalk and into the blasted avenue beyond. It was a grim, desolate path, lit by raging fires that reached out from the windows of cooked-out apartments as far as the eye could see and as far as reasonable imagination might take one thereafter.

The wild embers had lain claim to spring's hapless blossoms, and their pampered young mothers. A few of those charred corpses were found in crackling furniture-fed bonfires, whose crimson guidance led both the brave and the wavering to the horrors of the front lines, where the reaping thing surely lurked.

Eddie watched as the soldiers shrank into that hellish portal, then climbed back to his feet, steady, yet still shaken within.

"Sorry, General," he said, with the rub of his bruised cheek.

"Not your fault, son. Welcome to war and the first effort to end it," Myres said.

"Why not send him along to Chennington where his aid might be most effective? I'm sure the medics there could use help moving supplies from the hospital back to the camp," Schneider suggested.

"No," Myres rejected without giving the idea much thought. "We still haven't received any communication with the teams there. We're blind and can barely keep a foothold beyond this *pigpen* we all have the displeasure of calling a camp," the general bellowed with the accusatory cast of his thumb to the haphazard tent city.

"So, your suggestion?" Schneider pressed.

"Baby steps. We've got enough to worry about with this swordsman in our midst . . . the entire high command is right here, along with the prime minister."

Schneider nodded, withholding any further suggestions to his superior, though glaringly vexed by the cadet's massaging of such a benign injury. Myres turned to Eddie, who had dropped to dust off his pants. He rose to attention, however, as an instinctive sensation informed him of his superior's gaze.

"Cadet, bring me the fellas who brought in the swordsman," Myres ordered.

Eddie saluted. "Yes, sir," he said, then turned and departed with haste for the camp of tents and military trucks, which had come to occupy the ravaged city park.

Eddie disappeared into one of the modular temper tents, which was busy with the traffic of officers. It was only a moment later that the remnants of Saber Squad had emerged with the boy behind them, his eyes glued to the marshy earth with his fists clenched, imbued with the fulfilling boon of being utilized for the cause.

Sky and Jedd, now well equipped with helmets, concealed ballistic vests, and replenished ammunitions in both their rifles' and bandoliers' pouches, planted their feet and threw up their hands in salute upon arrival before the commanders.

"I want to commend you boys on your actions at the capitol building. The prime minister is safe thanks to you, the able task force, and a great many valorous patriots that didn't make it out of there," Myres addressed.

Neither soldier spoke a word, united in solemn show of their condolence for the Union's loss.

"Sir," Sky led after a pause, "without him—the swordsman—we probably wouldn't have made it out ourselves."

Myres turned to the distant staircase, which led to the city skywalk—an innovation designed to reduce traffic in the grand capital and offer breathtaking views to both visitor and metropolitan. There, upon one of two imposing stone pedestals, sat the swordsman, his head turned to the darkened peak, which began a passage between twin stygian towers.

All had turned to see him, except for Jedd, who stared just above the caps of his commanders, unwilling to budge nor wander. Myres realigned himself with his soldiers and took immediate notice of Jedd's unconcerned disposition.

"So I've heard. That true, son?" Myres asked with the raise of his brow.

The madman shed the act of defiance with a nonchalant nod, certifying the truth rather shamelessly. "Saw things I wouldn't believe were possible outside of a really bad fever dream. Maybe one that you wouldn't quite wake up from. Agreed to take him here in the hopes he wouldn't do to us what he did to the enemy."

Myres's inquisitive eye sharpened. "What kind of things are you referring to, soldier?"

Jedd bared his teeth and gave a slow nod. "There are some things that a man shouldn't say but should see for himself. Wouldn't want everything I say to just become a buncha noise."

Myres eyed each of them, keen now that the answer lay both in truth and absurdity. "Well, you both saw it, didn't you?" Myres asked.

They both nodded. "Yes, sir."

A dead silence captivated their commanders. Myres looked to the swordsman on the stone, then back to his soldiers. "Wonder what the hell he could have done to put the tail between your legs," the old general mused.

"We need answers, now," Schneider interjected.

"No," Myres asserted. "We don't have time to sit around and do a research paper on the enemy that's already through the gates. Our only hope to win this war is to drive them out. At the very least, Salamandra has to survive."

"The whole world has gone dark, General. It's hard to know precisely what we can do here," said the returning General Henson.

Over his shoulder, the bereaved officer stood at the distant burial site, accompanied by two empathetic medics, who lingered at his side for a moment reserved for humanity before they departed together to attend those pressing matters of war.

"Maybe a lot more than what we thought was possible," Eddie chimed in.

It was a remark that brought upon him crooked glares and baffled gapes, all of which aided to silence him. Then came two firm steps in the ground behind them, effectively rescuing the shrunken cadet as their attention was stolen by the sudden intruder.

"You will not be able to drive them out, and each moment we waste only adds to the burden that awaits us. You must escape this city and leave everything behind if you have any desire to survive," warned the swordsman, who had journeyed over from the distant steps.

They were iced in pensive stillness by those bold declarations. The steadiness of his voice offered grave reassurance that what he said lay only in truth, one that those proud commanders were hesitant to accept, even as the mere forewarning stole away any confidence in their humble stronghold.

"Those are some interesting armaments there, son," said Myres as he looked the tatter-cloaked invader up and down, trying to make some sense out of him.

The swordsman gave no response.

"So, let me just get this out of the way so we can continue in earnest. Are you here to help?" Myres asked.

"I've abandoned the path forged for me. So, if you have the will to push onward, I'll forge a new one alongside yours, but we can do nothing but struggle here," the swordsman replied.

Myres stared at him a moment. At first, he saw nothing but emptiness in his eyes, yet found there was undeniably something in him worth trusting. The general nodded at that quiet conclusion, then looked over his fledgling squad.

"Then you're on the front line with Sergeant Sky. Welcome to the Union Armed Force. Get him a real weapon, why don't you?" he ordered in a turn to Schneider, who had fallen to a tenebrous stew in regard to the hasty decision.

"Are you serious about this, General? There were reports of similarly dressed swordsmen among the invader ranks," Schneider advised.

Myres raised his brow, taking mild offense to his mistrust. "Now, Schneider, wielding a keen judgement of character is something I take a lot of pride in. Do you want to refute that . . ." he started to inquire, prying for honesty with his inquisitive gaze.

"No, sir," Schneider surrendered.

The dissent squashed, Myres turned back to Sergeant Sky, ready to put a plan into action. "You said this man did the unbelievable? Then it's time to show me the magic, because right now, we're in need of a miracle, and nothing short of one. The enemy has had us encircled from the start, and every hour, we lose a few more blocks. If we don't find a way to beat them back, we're all gonna die. So, share with our new friend the pride of the Union. We got no time to waste."

"Yes, sir," Sky replied. "Jedd, arm him."

The madman turned in abrupt astonishment. "You kidding me? What's an abomination like him gonna need from a rifle? Something to pass along to a buddy and play *catch the bullets between your teeth?*"

"Those are orders, Jedd," Sky reinforced, without the patience for the madman's colorful defiance in the face of their superiors.

Jedd yielded and threw out his frustrations with the fling of his hand. "Alright! I'll get him the damn gun," he fumed.

"Now, there's the good spirit, Jedd," General Henson endorsed, sneaking a grain of pleasure from the tempestuous breach in his perceived reservation.

"Guess war always has a savage, huh, General?" Myres teased.

"I've never understood why they decided to conflate a hearty defensive with savagery . . . but oh well. The name stuck," Henson lamented.

"And not every corporal was charging into camps with MG-mounted jeeps to raid supplies for his buddies," Myres added.

General Henson shrugged. "They eventually learned to shut the back door."

Eddie, aglow with anticipation, rushed to the side of the resolute sergeant and his flustered corporal.

"And where do you think you're going, son?" General Myres asked.

"To the front lines to fight with the heroes!"

"Not a chance, son. We need you right here—to be a hero helping survivors and keeping civilians safe. You'll be much better off staying at the camp."

Promptly stripped of his enthusiasm, Eddie's head fell as he nodded against the will of his heart. "Yes, sir," he recited from the constraints of order.

Myres turned around to the swordsman, who yet lingered in gifted patience. "Miracle man! I'd like to have a word with you when there's time. Of course, not right away, but . . . there will come a time."

The swordsman remained silent.

"Sky, you take lead down to the defensive line in Midtown. We have to hold it until we can get air support in there. Lieutenant Reines is your shot-caller up north. We're not alone in this. The Beilkans are in this mess with us. Reports say they're hunkered down at the treaty base, but if we manage to keep that post secure, we have a shot at linking up with them sooner rather than later."

"Understood, sir. You can count on us," Sky assured.

"I have no doubts, Sergeant. Exercise great caution and use every skill at your disposal. Learn the enemy, expose their weaknesses when you find them, and make us proud," Myres ordered at a calm pace. "Hereafter, I'd like you to report as Nova Squad. If at all possible, you report directly to me."

"Understood. It'll be a high priority, General," replied Sky.

"You'll find a makeshift armory a short ways up Eleventh Street. You can pick up a rifle there," General Henson advised.

With an affirmative salute between Myres and his able new fireteam, save the swordsman, the general tapped Eddie's shoulder to guide him away, and together, the boy and his commanders departed for the encampment.

Ultra eyed the boy as he shrunk toward the distant tents, where a nervous congregation of officers awaited their commander's return. It was a gaze that lingered long enough for Jedd to take notice.

"What? You missing your fan club already?" the madman razzed.

The swordsman quietly broke his gaze and set it upon Jedd, who awaited rebuttal with a gaping smirk.

"Knock it off. A lot of people are counting on us to take this serious, you know?" Sky said in an effort to refocus them on the mission ahead.

"Time's running out. End is set in motion, and we tempt a cruel fate in this pitiful effort to guard old stone and brick. This is an overwhelming event, and our departure is all but inevitable . . . but if your command wishes to dally here . . . then I will serve," the swordsman said.

The grim declarations did little to faze either Sky or Jedd, now. General Myres was their supreme commander, and his orders had been clear. So, without further hesitation, they departed together for the road to Midtown to first seek out the armory.

Further along the way, Ultra's eyes meandered to the burned-out windows in the street-side apartments, some of which had been utilized as machine gun nests in the wake of the inferno's reaping. Below, weary refugees lined the streets in small packs near the bonfires, and subtle whispers teemed as the invader's uncanny presence became recognized.

"I ain't no damn savage," Jedd battled.

"You still thinking about that?" The sergeant smirked.

"Me and that word got bad history."

"Well, here's something to do to take your mind off it. Armory's straight ahead," Sky notified. "Go grab him a rifle."

"With all the pleasure, sir," Jedd replied, then stepped off toward the guarded, cloth-draped shanty.

Sky guided the swordsman away from prying eyes to a shady backstreet further along, which they found blocked off by a mountain of charred armchairs, couches, and amassed household items of good size. Without a doubt, it was an act purposefully executed by the armed forces in an effort to secure the area. Though they could not enter, the corner gave them a glint of privacy while they awaited Jedd's return.

"I can understand your pride," said the swordsman. "But if you are truly determined to seize back your destiny, you must come to understand that this foe is unlike any your world has ever faced before. It is an enemy that will strive to learn you in intimate ways—give back to you what you've lost, yet keep it just out of reach, beyond the veil of Eternia . . . Perhaps I don't have to tell you, as you've possibly encountered its unusual presence since we've begun."

"No," the sergeant lied, shaken by the invader's peculiar insight. "I don't know what you're referring to, actually . . . but listen, if there's something you know, then speak up. How do you imagine we win this fight?" Sky asked in a gradual bloom of frustration.

"With none of the weapons we have at our disposal. Though they may aid in your defense, defense alone will never ward off the determined conqueror. To achieve any kind of victory, we must be willing to chase opportunity, as opportunity alone can bring about salvation."

"But *this* will aid in *your* defense, invader, and give me another reason to worry about you," said Jedd as he returned with a submachine gun set against his shoulder.

"What's this?" Sky scrutinized. "Standard issue is an AM88 rifle," he asserted with a firm pat to the top of his rifle.

Jedd shrugged. "Out of stock, boss. I was told last stock went to the front lines two hours ago."

Sky snatched the gun from Jedd.

"Alright—alright. Don't shoot the delivery boy," Jedd pleaded.

Sky put the weapon right into the hands of the swordsman, who, after a brief inspection of the gun, clipped off the safety.

Jedd raised his brow.

"You any idea of how to use that thing?" he questioned in unease.

"You'll be fine," the swordsman replied as he snapped the safety back on.

Sky acknowledged his word with a nod, thankful there was no apparent need to train him. "Good, then we're done chatting. Let's move out. We're going back into the fray. We need eyes everywhere. No mistakes. Stay in close together. Don't get separated."

"Supply captain reported that the Iblis District's south end got completely glassed. Said it's a pretty nice landing zone if you don't mind melted wheels, and we'll be cutting in pretty damn close," Jedd informed. "You think the general knew about that?"

"I'm not sure . . . But it'll be the whole city if everyone doesn't do their part. We all have a job to do, so let's do ours so we can take back our city. If there's an opportunity to be had, I can think of a thousand reasons as to why we need to keep this city intact. If evacuation becomes necessary, I have no doubt General Myres will make that call."

In accord with that belief, the Union-devout set out toward the billowing black smoke that swept away the horizon. The swordsman followed closely behind as the fledgling—but capable—Nova Squad advanced upon the unknown. He took the gifted weapon and set it beside a strip of thick, magnetized straps integrated into the inner lining of his cloak. An obscure technology beneath the fabric detected the killing machine, and the straps pulled across, securing it in place. Within the cloak lay four other empty straps, each weathered to a varying degree from extensive use.

With sights set on the burning war zone ahead, Ultra went prepared to cut down whatever chose to impede their path. A terrible machine of war loomed somewhere out in the city, its great eye watching from behind the darkened mass of skyscrapers. Though it could evade the mortal's limited perception, its ominous presence was unmistakable to the rogue swordsman, who knew disaster's harbinger merely lay in wait for their master's dread command.

***

Back at the camp, Little Eddie Bowitz pondered the movements of the swordsman as he stood guard in front of the field hospital. The sounds of the raging battle throughout the city offered a grand ambience to the fantasies in his head. Upon imagination's versatile stage, the swordsman cut through unworthy foes across the cityscape and, with splendid ability, triumphed over those who had breached oblivion's veil.

The remnant Union high command had congregated around a war table nearby, which lay partially obscured by a shoddy old tent, which had surely been salvaged from the marketplace. On the table was a map of the city, upon which they traced their fingertips up and down between fits of frustration and vehement bouts of disagreement.

Tranquilized by his fascinations, Eddie relaxed from right shoulder arms as he pondered the topic of their intense deliberation, though he knew it was no business of a mere cadet. His form compromised, the icy barrel fell against his neck and sent a sharp chill through his skin. The boy shivered and pulled it away, then slipped quietly back into his fantasies.

Within the tent, Schneider and Brigadier General Rhodes were approached by the prime minister. That tall sovereign, an imposing monolith in his black trench coat, wiped a few bloodied wounds on his face with a rag.

Eddie became distracted with them once again. He tried to listen in, but he couldn't make out a word from their careful exchange. Though disconnected with the plans of their nation, the cadet remained certain that those revered figures had the mettle to confront their woes, in the same way the swordsman could. All he needed to do was wait, yet something about that rather unspectacular truth left him undeniably bothered.

In an escape from growing insecurity, his mind began to drift until he found himself transfixed by the majesty of the swordsman. The boy recalled the brilliant blade as it struck down the fearsome invader titans. Those perfect cuts, executed like movements through wind, without any resistance at all. He wished he, too, could be so capable, and thus reliable.

Wandering deeper into the abyss, the visions sharpened until it was no longer the swordsman he saw, but instead, the eyes of the nameless invader. A forbidden memory seeped back into subconscious, and the indigo eyes split and multiplied into thousands among the dark ruins. Once he had seen them, there was no other option but to escape.

He emerged from the dream out of the scrutiny of the watchers, but no sooner did he find himself in the gaze of another. Though they were not the eyes of any invader, those innocent reflections were no less enchanting and foreign. Young, lively, and expressive; wide and round in familiar curiosity, Eddie found himself spellbound by that natural twinkle between the tents just ahead of him.

She was a civilian girl by the looks of it, with shapely soft lips, ageless skin, and finely rounded cheeks. Black-as-the-midnight hair lay tossed over slender shoulders, a luxuriant flow that focused the eyes in on her piercing watch and could leave one forever imprisoned by her mystique. She sat with folded legs upon one of several supply crates in a cache, which lay just beyond the hospital's supplementary tents.

Though young, he was no fool. There was a subtle ominous presence about her. She seemed a little too free from the world as she laid upon him that pleasant, carefree beam. It was an uncanny serenity falsely bound to a reality that simply didn't exist, or perhaps an invitation to a distinct alternative. She was present in the nightmare in that she offered thoughtless glances to the passing soldier and escorted wounded civilian, yet melted into the scene, unnoticed, as if she were merely a moonlight-drenched hallucination.

Unbelievable, yet there she was, like a treasure in the forgotten cranny—a mystery lying in wait with an allure that couldn't easily be resisted. Not at all by Eddie, and deep down, he knew it. He even thought of going to her right then and there, but the orders of his superiors kept lead in his boot.

"Bowitz! Bowitz, look alive," a gruff voice commanded.

Eddie snapped to mental sharpness. It was General Myres, flanked by both Schneider and Brigadier Rhodes.

"Yes, General," said Eddie as he gave a salute.

Myres rubbed his stubble-covered chin. "You said you regard this swordsman as a hero. I was curious . . . what kind of things are you sure he's able to do?"

General Myres scrutinized Eddie's immediate reaction, analyzing the boy as he gathered his thoughts.

"Well—he's fast. Faster than you could ever imagine, unless you had seen it for yourself."

Rhodes glanced at Schneider, who stayed fixated on the dizzied cadet as he marveled at the memories of the fleeting encounter.

"How fast are we talking, son?" Myres inquired.

"It was as if he wasn't moving at all! It was like he was already there, in the next place he wanted to be. I'd suppose he has to be pretty strong to do all that, too . . ."

Myres set his eyes upon Eddie, then raised them up to the invader's incredible warships, and then lastly, to the ruin they had wrought. "My . . . what has changed in just a few days," the old general lamented. "But you really believe in him, don't you, son?"

"Yes. I know he can fight for you. He saved me when I was all alone . . . And I'm sure he didn't have to. But I would have been dead otherwise," Eddie testified.

Brigadier Rhodes looked to Schneider with a face of unexpected satisfaction.

"You hear that, Lieutenant? The accolades are growing on this guy. Seems like an asset to me," she assessed.

Schneider maintained a suspicious glare, however. He was adamant they'd see no benefit in following the advice of Eddie, who surely had no better idea of the swordsman's true nature than any other child might.

"But there's still a problem, Rhodes. He's an invader, and that being the truth, there's no telling what he's really capable of or what his intentions are," Schneider said.

"Schneider, we've got scores of soldiers falling to those damned troopers. Civilian survivors are piling up at the camp, and we've got nowhere to offer them shelter. Enlighten me. Our weapons have little effect, and we don't even have a grasp on what we're fighting against. Do you have a better plan?"

Schneider scoffed; he found it ludicrous that anyone would assume the boy had any depth aside from the ardent surrender of absolute trust. "I don't have answers yet, but I know time is best not wasted on the back of an enemy. A uniform has a deeper meaning than simple garb. Regardless of how much the new world is shaped, we must be grounded in the reality of the old one."

General Myres looked at him, and looked at him hard, all in the hope that he might derive a semblance of understanding. "We'll do everything in our power to hold the city. That is my intention, but if it comes down to it, we'll have to consider all options," the general concluded, then turned back to the cadet. "Thank you for the insight, son. Now, if you'll excuse us. Schneider, Rhodes, pronto." He directed them with the swing of his finger toward the command tent.

And so, with nothing more to gain beyond his testimony, and much business to attend to, Myres and Schneider departed. Rhodes looked at Eddie once more before she followed and found that his attention had been seized. She followed his eye to seek out what had bewitched him. Her eye, too, lingered there for a moment, before she turned and made for the tent without a word.

He had caught sight of her again. The whimsical prowler peered up the staircase to the skywalk from the very first step. She lingered with calm composure, a demeanor that was distinctly soothing in contrast with the frantic platoon that descended the steps in a dramatic rout.

She took a step, and then, on a sudden whim, turned back to Eddie. In an instant, all the noise around him became muffled as her silent beacon became the only vibrance in the world.

But what would be there waiting if he went? Surely only apocalypse across the horizon, shrouded by dark smog. It would be teeming with those invaders on the advance, their eyes peering out like sapphires in the night.

For too long, he had chased the mesmeric enigma to the brink of the unknown, only for it to vanish before he could prove it real. A rainbow's end lay beyond the horizon line, alongside a fallen star, just as his grandfather had told him long ago. All he needed to do was chase it, and it would be there waiting for him, as it had always been.

As the girl's smile came to fullest bloom, he was set into a drift that would eventually bring him there. Across the blasted earth and alongside the fires of annihilation, he passed, on a collision course with an awakening destiny in which the storybook would never close, and the summertime would never end.

His muddied daydream bridged the gap between child's and High Fantasy's siren, and he found himself before her with wetness in his eyes, which he hoped had gone unnoticed. There was an undeniable relief in being there beside her.

She was all the more beautiful right there before his eyes, though it was not a beauty found upon the face, but instead in the essence of what he believed her to be. Some fantastic illusion, at last, proven to be something much more real than ever before.

In their brief time together, she didn't say a word, but neither did he. It was she who took the first step toward the tenebrous landing of the grand staircase, a careful step unto tomorrow. Eddie followed, his senses reduced to merely those footsteps to the shadowy summit.

There, at the top, they ventured through the dark passage and, at its end, found the ruins of civilization in panoramic grandeur beyond the parapet. Beaming glimmers and rays of death streaked here and there, all throughout the dense veil of ash. That sweeping gloom had risen high and left the horizon shrouded, as surely as the invasion had relinquished their future to similar impenetrable obscurity.

But there upon the world, all throughout the city, were stars, those he had come to fear in his flight from the barracks. Something else lurked among the darkness, however. A goliath watched them from behind a distant, darkened skyscraper, in hover high above the city streets. She had brought him before the oculus of the otherworld, an entity he could not distinguish as beast, machine, or mere illusion.

"He's seen us," said the girl with eyes widened in wonder.

Eddie looked at her, into those starstruck eyes. It was an expression that, when directed at him, rendered him but a child, there at the world's end. It was a spectacular resurgence, one which brought upon the breathtaking revitalization of old sensations that had long been numb.

Electrified, the boy looked deep into that mystic mirror as he fought to decipher the magic behind it, but alas, he could not. And perhaps, he pondered, that was more brilliant an answer than any he might ever find.

Invader soldiers approached from the unknown beyond, but he found himself so woven in their moment that he couldn't see the danger. Not even when the shouts of the soldiers over his shoulder pierced his ear, or even as they seized him in their vicious grasp and whisked him away.

Away from the gunfire of war. Away from the eye—out from its sight.

Through The Stars

Oh, how I've watched you!

Wandering through the ever plain with that look in your eye.

Scouring in and through the nook and forgotten bend.

And looking for what?

Looking for the unbelievable.

Your spirit is a great messenger, shining brighter than the elder star's death.

Never let it fade, or those who follow may never find their way.

I give to you, the prophecy of fire.

So, go and breach the gates of resistance and release the gears of restraint.

End is at hand, but end is not all.

At the Crossroads of Fate

The old SUV sat parked across faded white lines in the lot of a decrepit gas station. Raised high above the countryside, it overlooked a vast rolling green whose hills went bounding across the emerald horizon.

Having braved uncertainty, the young adventurers had ended up there at sunset in a bubble of respite, before the hills which hid a great tragedy behind their supreme majesty.

The lonely stalk of plantain and huddled crabgrass swayed deep as the breath from the world's end swept them through, there along the asphalt's jagged end where the decayed lot ended and the verdant cliffs began.

Young, daring spirits had lain a fleeting claim to the forgotten backroad, a place where they could be alone among themselves and put distance between the new world that surely awaited them upon their eventual return.

The night was the apex of excitement, so like many of those young to the world, they had lingered deep into it. Though much of their dwindling time was spent on the float of lighthearted banter, it slipped every now and again into elusive existentialism in the form of a clever joke or sharp rebuttal, with some greater meaning smuggled within.

The roads of their destinies were bound to split, and so it was their solemn desire to make the absolute most of their time. From those cherished moments, they could forge unforgettable gems that would someday serve as the basis for nostalgia's pleasant gleaming. There, at the brink of the next chapter of their lives, lay so much possibility, so much time, that the road ahead, like the road through the valley, seemed as if it might have no end.

There was time to make mistakes. There was time to wander.

Time is forever running out.

What was there to gain, however, from this thoughtless meander through old backroads, out of society's gaze and free from the burden of imminent responsibility? For more reasons than one, this is what they had gone in search of; a land unbeknownst to them, found on a pleasant whim upon a fleeting journey. Like life ahead of them, the next step of their aimless adventure remained a mystery beyond a promising horizon.

From a crevice in the asphalt, a lonely stalk bounced in the cool night's breeze and grazed the wall of dusty tires. Within, Ashe slept in the passenger seat, with only a slight bend in consideration for Mitz, who sat just behind her. With hands folded in his lap like a monk in a deep meditation, his chest rose and fell with each breath.

Across from him, Setz shifted in his sleep. By the strings of his subconscious, his hand rose and scratched at his head until he had found the source of the sudden tingle. Then, it fell again, and he returned to gentle stillness.

Kaiser lay sprawled out atop the third row seats, which had been folded away to accommodate his slumber. Plagued by a constant fumble, he found himself unable to find quite the right comfort upon the centralized latches on the backs of the seats.

The driver's seat sat empty, the door mindfully shut without the force to engage the latch, ensuring the others wouldn't be woken their slumber.

Just beyond the door was the laborious descent that led to the grassy expanse. The steep hillside was dotted by patches of gravel and dry dirt between boundless, wild greenery. Hefty boulders, both sharp and dull, lined the emerald dive, like bleached, abstract statues waiting for the sun to rise.

Between a small cluster of rocks was a cozy, flat bed of gravel nearly surrounded by overgrowth. There lay Miyacre and Lyal, asleep beneath the bristle and weed.

There came a wave that passed through the valley, an invisible energy that whipped through the grass and stalk before it found their slumberous faces. Lyal turned over on his side and peeked through his eyes just in time to catch a bolt of lightning as it streaked through the distant skies. A second bolt struck the top of a distant transmission tower, whose crimson-bulbed lull remained constant—a somnolent flash in the impenetrable darkness.

He rose, stretched out his arms, then straightened up. A refreshing gale swept up the hillside and filled his nostrils as he took a deep breath that rejuvenated his entire spirit at once. Awakened to profound enlightenment, he basked in the unprecedented freedom found there on the hillside beside the conduit to anywhere. They were afloat in an ephemeral drift caused by the vacuum left in the absence of old urgencies.

With senses sharpened, he eyed the far side the grand expanse, at the end of which rose a second summit. Above, a towering dark cloud had lain an ominous claim to the horizon, revealed in the dead of night by moonlight.

Unmoved by the imminent menace, Lyal became captivated by the great distance between the peaks and thought about going there; to get up and walk until he had reached that far-flung pinnacle. He knew Miyacre would likely remain undisturbed if he chose to depart. Yet, he remained stuck in place as he lingered in that enchanting reverie, looking out from triumph to a stagnant figment of himself.

Soon, a second gust from the dark behemoth shook him from his thoughts. He shoved his hands into his pockets.

"Nearly time to go," he warned, in heed of the approaching colossus.

"You ready to go?" mumbled Miyacre.

He looked down into a pair of sleepy, hazelnut eyes. Galvanized by the gusts, she stirred, then stumbled in a sluggish ascent to her feet.

"Soon . . . but, we don't have to hurry. Not yet," he assured.

She stretched, then looked out to the valley. There was something peculiar about it to her as well—a distinct and haunting sensation to awake to the emancipation of thirteen years of academic pressure.

It was quiet there, upon that storm-rattled hillside, with the entire world left behind them. On that spontaneous journey, they had taken only their most precious gift, and that was the unique person they had become, as in their young age, they had little else to bring. Though, it was enough. A wonderful gift, in fact. One that they hoped to see flourish by the end of their short excursion.

Lyal pointed to the distance. "You see it?"

Miyacre looked on but couldn't quite figure out what it was he sought to distinguish in the lowering thunderhead and shadow-fallen hills beneath. "What do you want me to see?" she asked.

"The power lines, man."

She sighed with a roll of her eyes, an explicit expression of anguish. "Okay, first, don't call me 'man.' And second, why are you all hyped over power lines? Nerd."

Lyal reached his arm around her shoulders and brought her in close. "Because they remind me of a dream I have, baby!" he entertained.

"Okay, better," she acknowledged in a beaming glow.

"Someday, I want our electric music to reach the far corners of the world. I want it to be drama, passion . . . an experience!" he declared in a theatric crescendo that sought to grip with the emotive sweep of his hand.

Miyacre cracked a smile as she fought not to laugh, but it burst through half-hearted restraint. She would have felt guilty had he not smirked, opportunely joined in a union of humor that caused her to blossom in joy. In spite of his fierce passion, he had never been too into himself, and though she had always known that that dream of his was undoubtedly important, she had always taken a quiet fancy to his ambition. Just balanced enough in his nature that she was never quite sure if she'd get the seasoned socialite or the desperate artist.

"Alright, Mr. Way-Too-Poetic," she joked with a raised brow, then promptly broke away to the curved wall of hardened dirt behind them.

She lay into that cradled earth, curled up, and set upon him a playful gaze.

"Hey, I know what I'll do," he said, lifted by the conception of some grand scheme. He swaggered over and lay beside her, then tossed up his hair. "I'll cut all this off." He put his hands on his chest. "I'll put on my nicest suit."

"Oh, yeah? And what are you gonna do next?" she encouraged, though unsure of the direction of his fantasy.

"I'll walk into the admissions office," he said while imitating the motion with the rhythmic swing of his shoulders.

The smooth storyteller dug his elbow into the ground, then leaned in close to his mystified spectator. "My high school report card will be laminated in a pristine black folder. I'll take out the pen from the front pocket of my ironed button up," he said as he made the gesture. "I'll nuzzle open the folder with the tip . . . and inside, my name will be etched in gold lettering. Agleam, with just enough pizazz to make them second-guess the long lines of well-earned D's and C's in cold red ink.

"Then, regardless of what happens next . . . I'll be so fucked," he declared rather calmly.

Miyacre put her arm around him, then pulled him close. "You keep doing what it is you do." She then released him and laid her head against crossed arms, in a turn for the stars.

"Electric it is, then," Lyal resolved.

He set upon her a mellow smirk, charmed by her easy grace. Detecting that pleasant aura, she looked over with teeth loosely touched crown to crown and left him bewitched by the inescapable allure of her emerald-eyed elegance. "Can I be electric, too?" she asked.

They were suddenly bound by each other's gaze. Neither made a move as they lay spellbound in a moment of whimsical chemistry. In a leading maneuver to enkindle that evident chemical concoction, Lyal inched toward her lips. Her eyes fell shut in a desire to take him in, but she pulled away in sudden resistance. She was taken aback, however, as she emerged from the comfort of darkness only to discover he had stopped short of claiming her kiss.

His grin widened—a perplexing reaction which stirred her within.

"I just wanted to bring you back down to reality," she insisted.

"You should know better," he replied, then fell back against the dirt.

She eased back beside him and fidgeted with her nails, slightly shaken from embarrassment from that perceived rejection. Spurred by her subconscious, her vocal cords began to vibrate. A swift and sweeping melody fell upon them as she hummed her wordless tune with dynamic and masterful control.

"So—why haven't I gotten to hear you sing in so long?"

She stilled the wind from her throat as her fidgeting became more frantic, in a desperate attempt to ignore him.

"Come on, Miyacre. When's the last time I bugged you about it? Last year?"

She sighed as she dropped her hands. "Lyal, I don't sing."

"Okay, but you do sing. You have an incredible voice, and just because some assholes took a little songbook and exposed some of your work, doesn't mean you have to flush your dreams down the toilet."

But she had shaken her head through every word. "I'm done with it, Lyal. I know what I want to dedicate my life to . . . and music isn't it anymore."

Reluctant to press her further, he laid his head back and returned his eyes to the panorama before them. Miyacre, bedeviled by another truth, twirled her finger in the gravel as she watched his face for a moment.

"So, on that note, actually . . . I have something to tell you," she said with a slight squirm under the pressure of her anxieties.

He replied to her with the mere raise of his brow.

She put her nose between folded hands, then emerged beaming as her hands fell away, and connected fingertips drove up into her lower lip.

"What is it?" He yielded in witness to her great excitement.

"I put in my application."

Lyal looked both ways. "For what?" he inquired.

"To the college I've been telling you all about," she reminded.

In a battle for time, he nodded and snapped his finger in a desperate search for the name in the back channels of his memory.

"Oh, uh, right. Sor? Uhh. Sori?"

"Sorinne Medical. Yes, Sorinne Medical," she corrected in good spirit.

"Well, yeah that's great, but isn't it all the way in . . ."

"Salamandra City," she acknowledged. "I've worked really hard not to get too excited about this," she continued, twisted in the agony of it.

"Wow, I mean, I know you'll get in, like you religiously chose studying over, like, everything."

"Ah, except once," she corrected.

Lyal nodded in recognition of the fact. "Except once," he agreed.

"I failed one test in eight years. And whose fault was that?" she asked, her eyes searching his guiltless countenance for the honest answer.

Lyal squirmed as he fought against outright admittance. "I mean, it takes two—"

Her eyes narrowed.

"And to be completely fair, you were the one who said you needed a break from school," he dodged.

"Oh, whatever," she laughed with an accusatory side-eye. "Definitely *not* what I had in mind. Anyway . . . How long we going for? Just to the big city and back?" she asked.

"Dunno, really," he replied.

"I think it's time to face it, Lyal," she continued. "We'll all move along with life, but it doesn't mean we won't still be friends."

He became quiet for a moment as reborn urgency struck, then he leaned up. "Then, let's go. We'll hit downtown, see the school! Have some laughs . . . have a good time. Because, you know, this is about doing it one last time. I knew it wasn't going to be more than a couple days."

Miyacre nodded. "Maybe things won't be, like, super simple, but relax. Just because we go back home, doesn't mean we're going to stop living our lives. I mean, you gotta move on eventually, right?"

"Yeah," Lyal muttered, unsure if their visions were similar at all.

Miyacre put her fingers to her head in frustration, then stood.

"Hey, Miyacre," said Lyal without turning from the expanse.

Her shoulders sank as she impatiently awaited his words.

"Thanks for giving me that moment."

Those words disarmed her, and soothed all anxiety left within. Perhaps she had wanted more from him, but for now, the feeling was enough. She sank back down beside him and pulled her knees up to her chest. Right there was where she wanted to be, and perhaps needed to be, just for now, in that microscopic moment in time.

There came a shuffle of rock at the top of the peak behind them.

"You guys done getting it on out in the wild down there?" Kaiser joked as he peered down, with hands set on his waist.

"Just about," Lyal replied rather naturally.

"*Okay*, and that's how that ends," said Miyacre, once again rising up from the ground.

Kaiser leapt down to the dirt flat, and the rocks crunched beneath his shoes.

"Everybody up?" asked Miyacre.

"Yup," Kaiser replied as he looked out at the broad landscape.

"So, we're going soon?" she continued.

"Soon," Lyal promised.

Kaiser remained fixated on the menacing clouds that had rolled out from over the horizon and crept into the verdant dive. The storm winds kicked a spray of dust from the bone-dry rock below them, and the harassed companions shielded their eyes from that wild breath from the valley that left their hair ruffled and tossed.

"Looks like we'll be headed right into the storm. If we're still thinking about heading to Salamandra, that is," warned Kaiser.

"No shit. You pick anything up on the radio, yet?" asked Lyal.

"Nothing. Still can't even get a connection out here. It's like— everything went down."

"Can't look at any cringe videos, now, huh?" Miyacre razzed.

"I mean, a map would be nice, but we're only forty minutes from the outskirts of the capital of the Union. I scanned every inch of the radio dial and literally ate static the whole way across," said Kaiser.

"Could be a dead zone of some kind," said Miyacre.

Lyal shook his head. "A dead zone for the last four hours on the road? Do dead zones even exist for radio?" he asked.

"Couldn't even search the answer if you wanted to," said Kaiser.

The unworried prankster let out a long yawn, stretched out to his limits, then sank in relaxation. "But—not the weirdest thing that's happened in the last ten or twelve hours," he replied with the last wind in his lungs.

"Maybe we can add one more to the list," Miyacre uttered as she peered out at something beyond the cliffs.

The boys looked to find the subject of her troubled gaze and caught sight of the anomaly with relative ease. There, on the road from the valley, was a solitary man, who ascended the paved acclivity. He shuffled, stopped, looked over his shoulder, then advanced on again in an eerie vacancy that was detectable from his movements alone.

"Not the weirdest thing I've ever seen, to be honest," said Kaiser.

"Well, where'd he come from? I mean, did he just walk out of nowhere? Because we were watching that horizon for at least twenty minutes," said Miyacre.

"Dunno," said Kaiser, who had already diverted his attention to his phone.

Door latches thunked above, followed by footsteps and successive thuds. Kaiser returned the disconnected device to his pocket, refocused from his fruitless efforts by the sudden commotion.

"Nothing, yet . . . Lemme go grab those guys. They were pretty adamant you guys woulda chose the old, dusty-ass gas station," he relayed, much to the vexation of his suspected friends, who lingered as he maneuvered back up the cliff.

Miyacre laughed to herself with a dismissive shake of the head. "Yeah, okay. Right behind you," she surrendered. "Come on, Lyal. Let's get outta here before we get put on trial for just stepping out."

She took a few steps up the side of the hill, then stopped to address her fellow agent in escapism, who hadn't budged. He turned instead for the road where the old man walked and set off on a course to intercept him.

"Go on. I'm gonna go see just what's up with this guy," he decided.

"Why—what!? You going to give him some money or something?" she asked, then stepped back down the hillside and pursued.

"You said he came out of nowhere? How about we find out where nowhere is. This guy doesn't even look homeless," Lyal said of the man in sensible khakis and an untucked white button-up.

Miyacre filtered her stress through a sigh. "I mean, not all homeless people are in rags. I mean, I think—but whatever. I'll go with you."

"Can't assume clarity."

"I realize that," she assured him.

"Got a million reasons to wonder, and a million and a half more to get out and discover. That's why we're here. That's what I'm gonna do."

And so, they continued along the gravel flat beneath the summit. The man had neared the top, where the gas station was situated. He approached over the last bend on rickety knees as Lyal and Miyacre crossed through the untamed stalks out onto the road.

They seemed to go unnoticed at first as the disoriented wanderer scratched at his beard. Lost in himself, he stopped again to check the horizon behind him, then turned back once more.

At last, he saw them. Lyal and Miyacre stood right in front of him and held his cryptic journey hostage with their presence.

"Hello, there," the heavy-eyed man greeted with a nod.

"Must have been a long walk to get here. You come from the city?" asked Lyal.

The old man laid upon him a hollow stare. "The distance means nothing when you're not even sure where the end is and your legs never seem to grow tired," he replied.

There was a ponderous sadness in his eyes, the kind that could evoke pity, even without insight.

"There's nothing but farmland up along this road. You don't look like much of a farmer," said Lyal, still fishing for answers. "Where you headed?"

The wanderer delayed with protracted silence as he, too, sought an answer to that question.

"I'm not really sure where my destination is. When someone's lost everything, maybe it's only natural to wander. What do you think?" asked the man.

"Hey, I'll keep it real honest with you. You probably lost your job and got a lot of things going on . . . but no sense in going on any further—on this path, here. How about a ride back to the city?" Lyal offered. "You can go back and . . . get started on picking up the pieces."

"There's no going back for me this time around. We're all on this road to nowhere, whether we realize it or not," he said as he peered up to the sky as if there was evidence in the clouds.

The others had gathered on the road and came forward to regroup with their friends. The man looked out at them, then back to Lyal.

"I've come from over the horizon, and I've seen what's on the other side. There's still time for you to turn back, though I fear running can only buy you time."

"Okay, so, if that were the case, why exactly would we run away?" asked Lyal.

"To savor the time while things are still the way they are, because soon, it'll all inevitably change, and you, too, won't be able to go back again," warned the wanderer.

"Tell me, friends," he pressed. "Have you lately been acquainted with the bizarre? I'm almost certain you have—because something's knocked on that unimagined door to oblivion, and now, the miracles of its unspeakable denizens are to be found everywhere. But I cannot keep you from your curiosity, just as I couldn't keep those whom I thought I wielded greater influence—from going out to see those fallen lights."

Miyacre laid her hand on Lyal's shoulder, then rested her chin on top of it. "Lyal—" she prodded.

The others gathered around and looked upon the wanderer with a faint yet undeniable perception of the possible occurrences to which he hinted. Absurdity had gained strength in this strange new reality, which made paradox out of impossibility. And though it would settle them to deny his claim outright, their own experiences surrendered credence in his every word.

"Let's go," said Lyal, his mind made up.

He turned, and the others, with faint hesitation, followed. Setz, however, lagged behind, grimaced, then stopped altogether.

"Hey, Lyal," he called out. "Hey, where are we going? We going places we shouldn't be?"

Lyal turned and faced his friend. "Ain't nothing different than we've always done."

Setz shook his head in ardent disagreement. "Ain't the same, at all," he replied.

"We're going to see what's going on out there," said Lyal.

"What if I don't want to see what's out there? You're telling me you want to see the thing that is responsible for bringing down television broadcasting and knocking out Wi-Fi for what seems like an entire county? Lyal, I got news for you: Beilkans. I thought you wanted to start a band, dude, not go charging into a war zone."

"Come on, man," said Mitz. "You can't stand there and tell me that you see phantoms in broad daylight and come to the conclusion of Beilkans. What are you, a state sponsored newscaster?"

Setz squeezed his fingers into fists, his frustrations evolving into anger. "I'm not trying to figure anything out. I don't care about the mysteries of the suburban outback, much less the universe right about now," he stressed.

"It will come for you regardless if you care or not," the man warned.

"Yeah—screw this. Screw this," Setz shouted and pointed a finger at the cryptic wanderer. "You haven't even been clear about what it is you're warning us about. So don't sit there and pretend you have anybody's back," he said, jabbing his finger at the man with every impassioned word.

Setz turned back toward his companions and stormed through them.

Kaiser raised his hand with a wide grin. "Don't worry, I'll handle it," he assured.

He left them in pursuit of Setz as he shouted at his back with pleas.

"Take care of yourself, old man. I'm guessing you're gonna stick to the open road," Lyal said.

The man nodded. "I'll find my way. I hope you'll find yours. All of you," he replied.

"So, we're pretty clear that there is a war going on, *right?*" asked Ashe in a last plea for clarity.

"There is a conflict—and if you go, you'll find it. But make no mistake, what I have seen . . . there can be no doubt—it will eventually find us all."

"Right," Lyal replied. "So, what do you have to gain from running away? Just because you lost it all, does that really mean you'd rather turn tail and leave it all behind?"

The wanderer stirred as he made that excruciating inward turn to the vacuous void left within him and gave that question a serious pondering.

"Because as long as I walk, perhaps I can believe that there's something else waiting for me beyond these horizons," the man concluded in reemergence from momentary reflection.

"Yeah, well, I doubt that's going to help in the long run. Guys— let's go. It's time we saw what's up for ourselves," said Lyal.

Without further need of cryptic insight, Lyal broke away and made for the car just beyond the lonely road's peak. Mitz followed without a second thought while Ashe and Miyacre exchanged anxieties with a quiet glance before stepping off to depart themselves.

And the man stood there as he pondered the words further.

"May the wind of the brave give you guidance and keep you safe," he prayed in parting farewell to the young adventurer who had identified his cowardice.

Then, in commitment to his aimless belief, he followed along the road once more in renewal of his futile flight. Lyal and the others arrived at the car and reunited with a disgruntled Setz, who brooded in the silent struggle as he attempted to reestablish a cellular connection while ignoring Kaiser, who had taken up a casual lean against the car beside him.

"It's never gonna work, but it's all good, man. We'll just go up there. See what's going on and come straight home. Kick back in the seat, roll the windows down, and just live it up," Kaiser assured him.

Setz turned to Kaiser, facing off against his casual front with an aggressive snarl. "This isn't about us. It's about Lyal. I got a little sister—and so do you. If there's something really going down, you know where you should be, Kaiser."

"Come on, Setz," Lyal pleaded as the rest of the group gathered around them. "Whatever's out there is gonna put our lives on hold whether we go or hide," he argued, though Setz turned in immediate dismissal. "Let's see it. Then turn around, put it in the mirrors, and go right home. We'll tell everyone what we saw, and we'll be ready for it," Lyal continued through his blatant rejection. "How are they going to know anything if the connections are all zapped?"

Setz turned and looked at his friend with a glint of hope in his eyes. He had made a respectable point. Setz, though eager to return home, knew if they could offer solid intel, then perhaps they could deliver their home from a tragic fate, one similar to that of the legendary hero general, Rostal Schneider. He was a figure Setz held in high regard, a hero and common man alike, who had risen up against vile terrorists to protect his home. If he believed in his valiance, then he, too, should be so valiant to offer his home a brave service.

"Forty minutes to the truth . . . but, no matter what, we're not leaving you behind," Lyal conceded.

"Forty minutes? I'm gonna give you forty minutes," Setz replied as he pulled open the door and plopped into the backseat.

"Alright, now we're talking," Mitz rallied.

Kaiser, with a mischievous grin, leapt hip first into the car and nearly knocked Setz over. "Come on, scoot over, man!" Kaiser cried.

Setz swung at him. Kaiser tried to dodge but was too slow to protect his shoulder from the strike. "Kaiser . . . chill out, dude," Setz threatened.

They shoved each other until there was enough space between them that their shoulders no longer touched.

"Come on, liven up, grandpa," Kaiser teased, then put his hands behind his head and stretched out.

"You guys fuck up my seats, you're paying for the detail," Miyacre warned as she slid into the driver's seat.

"I can't believe I'm doing this with you guys," said Ashe, eyes faint with the burden of worry.

"I should warn you now that friendship with me is sort of a liability," Kaiser joked.

"A little late on that," Ashe replied with a nervous smirk as she took a seat.

"Right?" Miyacre added.

Lyal entered the passenger seat while Mitz ungrudgingly worked to raise the seats from the third row. When the job had been done, he leapt the backrest and pulled the trunk shut.

Miyacre turned the key and the engine ignited as they all silently came to terms with what they were about to do and the inherent dangers associated with such a daring venture. Gravel beneath the refurbished tires popped and snapped as they pulled away onto the main road. They each noticed that the wanderer had gone and the road to the beyond now lie barren.

"Guess he got a head start," said Ashe, with a turn to each end.

"A super head start," Kaiser articulated.

"On a road to nowhere?" asked Mitz.

"No different than us," Setz pointed out.

Miyacre scanned the roadside landscape in growing discomfort. "But, seriously guys, where did that guy go?" she stressed.

Each of them scoured the moonlit expanse through every window in search of a definitive glimpse.

"Over there," Miyacre uttered. "*Way* over there."

She directed them with her finger against the glass of the window where, down in the valley, a figure did in fact loom. It was so distant, however, that it seemed unbelievable that he would have been able to reach that place in such a short time.

"No—that guy is looking over here. Wait—" Ashe scrutinized.

Upon closer inspection, they saw that the figure seemed draped in that dreary garb, one they were eerily familiar with.

"That's—" Miyacre began.

"The guy from the photo," said Lyal. "Something's definitely not right."

"What the hell? Is this guy following us?" asked Kaiser.

They watched as the figure became nothing but a mere spec in the distance. Their first sighting was all but verified. Each of them had seen it, but none of them said a word. As the wanderer had warned, the unknown shadowed them. It had become evident, however, that they were not the only ones who were being confronted by absurdity.

Setz let out a sigh, looked up, then closed his eyes.

Miyacre laid her hand on his knee.

"We'll get back home, okay?" she comforted. "We're gonna be okay. Tomorrow will be a better day."

Setz's eyes tightened. He felt a shiver pass through him, but he said nothing of it.

Miyacre kept hold of him with a deep desire to subdue his fears and, in doing so, perhaps subdue her own.

"Let's just hope," Setz replied, at last.

A pervasive silence settled in as they began on the road toward Salamandra. It was a silence overcome only by the violent crash of thunder. The behemoth storm had soon besieged them and left the way shrouded in its torrential downpour.

This was what they had come for. The danger had found them, and they knew little of what miracles awaited them beyond the ominous precursor. Before they were consumed entirely in that hellish embrace, each of them, in their own time, passed a parting glance at the peaceful valley, which soon became eclipsed behind an impenetrable wall of water. The opportunity to turn back seemed to vanish with that eerie last sight. Those bold adventurers, now enveloped, were on a collision course with tomorrow itself.

Forward is the only way left.

Loyal Subordinate: Oculus

The swordsman peered over the jagged-toothed parapet to the ruins along the blasted road, three stories down. Through a lingering curtain of dust, he caught a glimpse of red ring craters, which smoldered with ebon plume, the land graced by the hand of the menace which lurked among calamity.

He closed his eyes and departed in search of it.

Jedd and Sky were kneeling further down, their rifles strapped on their backs as they performed a grim observation of the fallen defensive below.

"No sign of survivors," Sky observed.

"Don't like the feeling I'm getting here," Jedd muttered. The madman looked away, then stared into oblivion, his face twisted in sudden distress and his mind between worlds.

"Gotta stay calm, and keep your eyes peeled. They're counting on us to make something of this, even if it's just a damn reconnaissance report."

Jedd nodded, still lost in his cavernous brood. He wiped sweat from his brow, and no sooner did he become overwhelmed. "You know what

I've been thinking about recently—like in the last few hours?" Jedd snapped as he rose straight up from cover.

"What is it? Alcohol or women?" asked Sky.

"I couldn't even distract myself with that right now—no . . . it's that damn kid, Sky," he stressed, spiraling in an abrupt fluster.

Sky turned to the commotion and found that his comrade's face had reddened as if he were on the brink of a violent outburst. "Who are you talking about, Jedd?" asked Sky, troubled by his sudden escalation.

Jedd puffed in frustration. "The one from my old neighborhood. The one who got gunned down. He used to fuck with me all the time, but—I thought the kid had a home. Thought he was alright!" Jedd exclaimed as tenuous and unintelligible whispers filled his head.

Sky turned to confront his manipulated subordinate. "Jedd, this isn't the time—"

"You know!" he interrupted. "It's just like—you can't ever be there at the right time. That could have been me or you!" He gesticulated with the jab of his finger between them. The madman doubled down in frustration as the whispers painted vivid and insuppressible visions of misfortune deep within his psyche. "What the fuck—" Jedd growled down into his palms. "Why am I so fucked up about this!?"

Sky, enraged by his compatriot's loss of control, seized Jedd by his jacket and shook him in an effort to clear his head. "Corporal Jedd, calm the *fuck* down. Get a damn grip on it," Sky strained in a final, desperate warning.

The sergeant was suddenly shoved away.

Dumbstruck, Sky lurched back after him but was stalled fast as Jedd lifted a hand up to reassure his assaulted commander of his return to lucidity. With eyes red and watery, he sucked in the remnant moisture in his nose and nodded. "I'm good! I'm good," he insisted with forced enthusiasm; the ethereal whispers dissipated into thin air.

Stricken by embarrassment, Jedd directed a glare at the swordsman, who remained motionless beside the parapet, his eyes still closed. Sky followed his stare and took notice of the swordsman's idling.

"We oughta get moving. If we're lucky, we'll find stragglers who can explain to us what the hell happened here," said Sky. "Swordsman! Let's move. We're not getting anything else done from up here."

Sergeant Sky turned away, his sights set on the nearby stairwell. The rogue invader showed no sign of breaking at his command, however.

"Hey!" Jedd yelled to stir him but achieved no response.

Jedd lurched at him in anger.

"Hey, you! You saying a prayer, you pussy?" Jedd prodded.

To the riled corporal's exasperation, the swordsman remained deep in his trance. Sergeant Sky turned back, provoked again by his capricious subordinate's sudden outburst.

"Jedd, easy! Stand down," the sergeant ordered as he turned back to quell his rage.

"Hey, princess—" Emboldened by that unchecked rush of anger, the madman stepped over to the swordsman in meditation. "Get the *fuck up*—"

Jedd threw out his hand to seize him by the hood but, in a split moment, lost all the wind in his lungs. He had been struck at the center of his chest and was thrown back as the swordsman rose with an open palm held straight out.

Sky seized Jedd in mid-flight and stabilized him from the invader's lightning-fast retaliation.

"Sweet mother—forgot why—I wasn't supposed to raise hell with you!" Jedd gasped with awestruck, angry eyes.

The swordsman peered down at his hand and collected his fingers into a fist.

Sky put Jedd aside and charged the flash assailant. "You listen to me," he demanded as he brought a finger to the swordsman's chest. "We're not going to pull anymore stunts like that. You know your strength. Control it."

The sergeant looked at Jedd to share with him his wrath.

"We're either going to work like a team, or we're going to die as one. That's something we need to be cognizant of, every step from now, until the day the last shot is fired. Jedd, control the temper. You—control your strength," Sky threatened as his eyes darted between the both of them.

The swordsman turned to the city, its darkened skyline barely visible through the veil of dust and ashes. There, between two skyscrapers, however, was a gazing radiance, one which, in the last few hours, had shadowed them closely.

He was sure of it.

The indigo gleam pierced through darkness, but its form remained obscured. Ultra glared as the beam receded behind the brink and vanished from sight.

"You're running out of time," the swordsman warned.

"Make yourself clear. That doesn't tell us anything," Sky emphasized.

The swordsman nodded. "We've no reason to search further. The rest of your front line—they're gone now."

"What do you mean, gone?" Sky pressed.

The swordsman turned and peered down at the craters once more. "The watcher came for every one of them—stole them away from this plane and dragged them into the next . . . But, I can still feel the fear left behind. It's much like an echo, occurring . . . over and over again."

Sky and Jedd watched in alarm as they observed a change in the appearance of his eyes. His bond exposed, the faint cerulean invader's glow pierced his retina. His demon gaze rose to the heavens as the radiance achieved celestial brilliance.

"But don't be afraid," the puppet recited. "There's a place for all of them."

Jedd passed a glance between the entranced invader and his brother-in-arms. "You gonna shoot him? I'm gonna shoot him," Jedd warned.

Jedd lifted his rifle, but Sky threw his arm out to impede the barrel. "Talk to me, buddy. Who is the watcher?" Sky investigated in a resolute drive.

The invader's head fell in spiritual exhaustion, and with the surge subsiding, he withdrew two steps, then exhaled deeply as he reclaimed himself in silence.

Jedd and Sky held firm in razor focus as the swordsman's eyes crept open. The cerulean gleam had faded, and his gentle reemergence seemed to accompany a return to spiritual purity. Their wary gazes lingered, however, unsure of what that fantastic phenomenon had meant.

"Calamity approaches," the swordsman relayed to his bewildered companions. "Our great sovereign has dispatched Eternia's supreme commander, and our flight is now overdue," he warned as he raised his finger to outer space to guide them to starlight evidence.

The soldiers lifted their eyes to the besieged cosmos and caught a glimpse of a solitary cosmic streak that poured down from the celestial armada toward the ravaged metropolis.

"We lay disorganized and lack the capabilities to negotiate such a dynamic threat. We must escape if we seek even the slightest chance to prevail," Ultra said.

"What exactly are we up against?" Sky asked, sharply refocusing on the keen-sighted invader.

The swordsman sighed with a bow of his head, then stepped away from the ledge. He drew from his jacket's inner pocket a pristine-cut slate tablet. Its matte surface was covered in faint silver glyphs, which seemed to come and go from place to place in a blur of sleepy winks.

"Much more than you can imagine. The general is, without a doubt, the gravest threat, though it has become evident that several other retainers of great power already roam these streets. Even I had not expected so much focus on a single city . . ."

He pondered on something that had lingered within, ever since his arrival at the resistor's camp.

"Then, perhaps . . . no, never mind," he abandoned.

With the device gripped in hand, he crossed over to a fuse box upon the concrete wall of the stairwell, seized the main conduit, and ripped it from the surface as if it were a feeble vine. A wild whip of electricity lashed out as the swordsman wrangled the line in and mashed the severed cables against the backside of the device.

He then released the bundle, but the cables stayed bonded to the arcane material as if held by the force of magnetism, and to the surprise of the unacquainted home-worlders, a jet stream of beaming radiance flowed from the device, up through the conduit.

"First, we must send word that this plan has failed. A message by foot may be too late to be of any use to us, and I fear the passage has become more treacherous than before."

"We can hold our own here. You can deliver the message yourself," Sky offered.

Jedd passed an incredulous smirk to his zealous sergeant upon hearing that brash assertion. "We're two soldiers. We'll barely be able to hold our bladders if we come face-to-face with the abomination that turned Main Street into an open-air abstract art exhibition," he reasoned.

"Well, I hope you packed a diaper with that attitude, Jedd. Because it's a risk I'm willing to take," Sky replied, his commitment unwavering, counter to the uncertainty of the madman, who threw his arm up in the air and turned away in frustrated surrender.

"No—we're being followed by an enemy from whom you'll be unable to hide. We'll use the communicator and cast a spirit across an instant bridge. All we must do is forge the map." Ultra placed his hand upon the surface, and the device came alive in a grand birth of solid glyph and a stammering electronic screech. Jedd and Sky threw their hands over their ears to fend off that harsh shrill as it shrank them into a sharp cringe.

"Quiet that thing down! You're going to get us killed," Jedd rebuked between his teeth.

"I'm afraid our position has long been compromised," the swordsman admitted.

"Say what?" Jedd rasped.

"If anything, we may be able to save your command from the complete annihilation assured by the ravenous fires of Euphoria. His immediate foes will not be so fortunate, however, and we'll be tested to use this last gift of time wisely while he is focused on the primary objectives of the invasion."

"Boy, I tell you. I don't get half of the shit that comes out of your pipe. What objectives are you on about? And why are you bothering to try and get a signal when all the comms are down? Did you not get the memo?" Jedd lambasted.

The swordsman gripped the device tightly on both ends and closed his eyes. At the center of the device glowed a pair of eyes, afloat in a haunt of static. The once-unnoticed screen flickered with white as indecipherable illusions on ethereal planes lifted from the surface.

Their faces were lit by the intense fulguration. In an instant, the construction expanded, and a three-dimensional map of the battered city became realized but flickered quickly from existence. With the network established, the screen fuzzed over, the phantom eyes fell shut, and all became a sea of noise before the surface returned to winking textures once more.

"You gonna explain any of that?" asked Jedd, his brow raised and finger aimed at the device.

The swordsman approached Sergeant Sky. Jedd stepped away, the tablet yet alive with a gentle hum.

Ultra held the device out, and though slowed by uncertainty, the sergeant received it with both hands. With destiny at their fingertips, the swordsman turned and made for the door to the stairwell. Sky, realizing the burden bestowed, was shaken from his paralysis.

"Who was that on the screen?" he asked.

The swordsman slowed to a halt. "The one who will deliver your message."

"So, it's another one of your kind, huh?" Jedd concluded.

"Yes, one of us," he confirmed. ". . . They come. I will go to meet them. Simply open your mind and speak. When you feel your message is complete, so shall be the task."

The swordsman pushed through the door and disappeared into the darkened well.

"Hey! A tutorial would have been nice!" Jedd shouted after him. The ruffled madman pulled up his rifle and inspected it, checked the rounds, and clicked off the safety. "Jackass," he added.

Sky held the device up and checked it over for some kind of interface. "Just speak and feel the message is complete, huh? Alright, let's do this—" Sky dropped to a knee and laid the device on the floor before him. "Link—Sal Command, battle box thirteen. Reserve, Saber Squad . . . General Myres, do you copy?"

Vacant moments of silence felt like hours as the sounds of bizarre electronics hummed within. The device periodically buzzed, but there was no response.

"Guess you better tell him that this thing is busted, Sergeant," Jedd said in dismissal of its capability.

"Cool it. Let's give it time."

Jedd, having already given up on the effort, stepped away toward the parapet to await inevitable acceptance. Almost at once, however, he was left disturbed by a peculiar shift among the shadows of the ruins. An ebon shade stalked through the gloom between the darkened towers like a serpent to unwitting prey, and its sole witness crept closer, his body still as he struggled to assess the authenticity of that imminent threat.

There came the sharp movement of focused wind beyond the brink. He rushed forward in an attempt to apprehend it, but it had been too quick.

The alarmed corporal felt a vibration in his chest as the stealth menace maneuvered the night on dread twin engines. His eyes fell to the wrecked street and found it at last, the servant in black armor that had lurked deep in the ruins and supervised their cruelest annihilation with an all-seeing eye.

With a murderous jolt that nearly stopped his heart, Jedd leapt away from the ledge onto the tips of his toes as he jabbed his finger to the course of the circling reaper.

"We've got company, Sky! Down at the base of the tower! We got a fuckin' shark in the water!"

"What the hell are you talking about, Jedd? *What is it!?*" the sergeant exclaimed in elevated astonishment.

"We got a damn airship on the hunt!"

A furious scream split the air. It was a deathly cry, which, in dread unison with blaring thrusters, left the soldiers purified of courage in the spiritual havoc raised by the devil's discordance.

"Move inside!" ordered Sky as he snatched the device from off the ground.

He rose just as Jedd arrived, his rifle locked and loaded for a fight. With the sleeping demon upon them, they bolted off together for the door to the stairwell. The engines cried out from the unseen far end as the invading horror made a pass around the bottom.

"It's circling around," Jedd tracked.

"Double-time, Jedd!" Sky ordered.

Upon reaching salvation's gate, Jedd burst first through the heavy door, and with reckless abandon, the soldiers flew down the stairwell. They arrived on the ninth floor beneath the rooftop and fled through the door into its long-carpeted perimeter hall. The vibrations grew intense as a shadow passed from a lone window behind them.

In a desperate search for cover, they rushed to nearby double oak doors. Jedd slammed the brass handle down, then drove through the door with his shoulder—an audacious maneuver that caused him to stumble into the next room as Sky entered behind him.

They found themselves in an illustrious, marble-floored dining area, which featured two distinct floors, a bowl, and a plate atop a crystal staircase. With nothing to aid in their protection on the bare path, they fled for the pretentious upper level, which displayed several cloth-dressed tables.

At the top, Sky slowed to a halt, then scanned the bowed, grand panoramic window that wrapped the entire wall before them while Jedd kicked down a table and unleashed a cascade of wine glasses and plates, which shattered across the floor.

The flustered bull dropped down into cover behind it, then peered up to the towering ceiling as he listened for the ominous tremble. A suspicious silence had befallen them, however, and as they settled in that eerie void left in the absence of the invasive rumble, he took a quick look around the grandiose chamber.

"Damn—probably not the best place we could have ended up," Jedd assessed.

Sergeant Sky knelt down and set the device upon the glossy, checkered floor. "Jedd, I'm going to try communication again," he advised.

"Then do it. We got ditched by our tour guide just as the heat got turned up."

"Hold on—"

Sky stole the device from the ground, hesitated in a sudden epiphany, then closed his eyes. He settled his mind amid the turmoil as he sought to reach beyond what he believed was possible.

Jedd looked over and, upon catching sight of that unnecessary serenity, squeezed the barrel of his gun in an instant boil. "What the *hell* are you doing over there?"

Sky remained steadied, however, focused in untrained and fragmented meditation. "Maybe we gotta put a little more in than we'd like," Sky reasoned.

The lurking devil's soul-wrenching screech cried through the winds beyond the panoramic pane. Flag poles that lined the ledge outside were flung through the air as the menace rose up from the brink.

Jedd rose to catch a glimpse of the ravager in its entirety, and two blinding beams greeted his curiosity. Then, the imperiled soldiers became witnesses to the machine's thunder.

The nose of the phantom flier tipped up, and the peal of the engines amplified into a destructive bellow that unleashed a ruinous shockwave. The glass was ripped away at once, and the exposed dining area became disoriented by the heated squall that drove a few outlying tables off the upper level and into the bowl. The ebon-plated war machine roared back as it refocused its twin thrusters downward in order to maintain its hover.

"Sergeant, I'm going to need you to open your eyes and face the *bullshit* that just blew away about ten thousand square feet of glass. Drop that piece of junk. Forget it. It's not gonna work," the flustered corporal pleaded.

Sky remained unshaken, however, as he swayed in the devil's torrent. His mind wandered deeply, far deeper than he ever thought imaginable, beyond childhood's last whimsical pondering.

A new dimension had opened, and he wound through the darkened passages on a spiritual flight of unprecedented experience. By way of faith, he had been released and went with such intensity that his body was left unable to move, perhaps left in absence.

Before he could fathom that transcendent state, he was delivered right to the place he needed to be. He dove through a blurred ravine of the apartment block, past bonfires, and between amassed survivors, right up to the military camp, which teemed with the movement of the displaced.

He found there who it was he was looking for. General Myres stood in the shoddy command tent stooped over the map of their precious city in an abyssal ponder.

"General Myres! Battle box sixteen. Saber Squad. We need air support. Resistance has been wiped out. Current position is atop the Orchid Tower."

Almost immediately after his plea had been uttered, something happened that he never expected. The general turned his head toward him. It felt as though he must have looked right into a ghost, some formless sound in the middle of the trampled grass.

He said something as he approached, but all Sky could hear was a mumble. Even with only that unintelligible noise, Sky shot up in amazement.

The spirit-thrown messenger had left himself imperiled, however. The machine scanned over the communication tablet with a steady green beam, which it retracted upon completion of its analysis.

"Jedd! It worked! We got him!" Sky cried as he emerged from the realm of spirit.

"Sergeant! Look *out*—you see that!?" Jedd warned.

Just as the miracle had lit a beacon of hope, a second vicious shockwave blew the faithful sergeant and able device off the plate and down the stairs in a violent tumble.

Jedd was forced from cover as the table was thrown across the slick, polished floor. Shattered glass cascaded from the upper level like rainfall as the grim hum of the engines settled back into the room. The flushed-out corporal stumbled to a halt, and his muzzy gaze fell upon the gunship.

The ebon menace rose. Twin guns attached beneath its wings spun up into an angry blur as its ten barrels reddened with heat.

"He's spinning rounds! Hit the ground!" shouted Jedd.

The mad gunman fled for the ledge of the upper plate as the reaper prepared to unleash its hellfire. By the blessing of instinct, he dove into a slide as the guns came to life with paralyzing brilliance. As he cut across the ledge, a wall of noise deafened him as the ruinous barrage of heat glassed the surface behind him.

The storm of gunfire tore through the floor and minced every last table until the dining area was nothing but a bullet-ridden stage. A downpour of crimson sparks cascaded from above as Jedd scrambled for cover behind the central pillar that supported the plate—the only structure he was sure would hold against the brutal assault.

Sky inched up from the ground and peered up to the top of the staircase and saw nothing but silent daylight and smoke.

He crawled over to the device that lay just before him. He called out to the general once more, so as to assure their message would be heard.

However, Sky noticed that something kept him from descending to the same depth as before. Though he now wielded unblemished faith, his efforts took him nowhere, and he felt nothing. Dumbfounded, he inspected it for a moment and soon realized that the surface no longer pulsed with those strange glyphs. The device had been tampered with, its latent abilities disabled.

He threw away the device in frustration, then took up his rifle, prepared to make a stand. His comrades in arms would face a fierce enemy if they were unable to fell the phantom craft, and although he knew not the depths of its capabilities, he would answer with bravery to the call of his responsibilities.

At the top of the staircase, there was an incessant shower of sparks from the relentless assault. He would have to wait for a moment of weakness to strike back. So, he lay in wait, prepared to drop down like a wild man, ready to ambush.

His opportunity came only moments later. The scream of the guns wound down to a crawl, and an exploitable respite from the hellish cannonade allowed the sergeant the quiet to gather courage.

The craft set its high beams upon the bowl in search of the agile madman. Jedd, privy to its intent, traced the circumference of the support in order to remain contained in the cone shadow that it cast. The beast snapped to one side, and then to the other, but Jedd remained out of its sight with quick dashes.

Sky lurched up, then inched for the stairs with his finger light on the trigger. He rose up the glass-ridden steps, then lifted from his crouch with gun raised and opened fire on the distracted craft.

With hell in his heart, he held down the trigger and clasped his teeth tight as the bullets struck a strange, watery surface—a protective veil, which seemed independent of its armored plate.

As the magazine ran dry, Sky realized his attack had failed. The invader menace had been left unfazed and lifted its beams to him in a swift yaw. He gazed into those white lights and felt himself become paralyzed for a moment, a brief splinter that parted life from death.

Like a man awaiting judgement, he remained.

The barrels ramped up into a blistering spin once more, its target in sight. Just before the guns exploded to life, however, the ship cut to the right as it unleashed its rapid-fire assault. The misdirected barrage cleaved through decorative stone columns and essential steel supports.

Awoken with his life, Sky turned and dove from the top step to the ground below. The stricken beast let out a variety of distressed screeches and whines as it made erratic movements in search of stability.

"Hey, big boss. You still alive up there?"

Sky rose on trembling arms. "Jedd?" he answered.

The shaken sergeant scanned the area, but his cornered companion remained out of sight against the support beneath the stairs. His dazed eyes soon fell upon the discarded invader device. He stumbled over and retrieved it with a faint hope that, with repair, its proven abilities might be able aid them again.

A distressed howl seized his attention, and as he listened in closely, he was able to determine that the craft was in a tailspin.

"You gonna have a look at this? They're putting on a hell of a show!" Jedd shouted between the steps.

Sky, stirred by the craft's erratic maneuvers, crept back up the staircase, and peeked over the top step. Beyond the shattered maw to the darkened city in crisis, he found the ship in full spin, the swordsman atop the windowless cockpit, delivering sharp punishments via precision slashes with his blade.

Each impressive cut shaved the tyrant's hulking armor, a staggering spectacle that left the sergeant astounded by a mere blade's extraordinary capability. He flinched from his gawk as a hand fell to his shoulder, and turned to find Jedd, his red face aglow with a wild grin.

"Isn't that something? Now, we're gonna skin that big metal pig," he salivated, roused by the sudden shift in fortunes.

He took up his rifle and, to the surprise of his comrade, rushed up the steps.

"Jedd! Hold on," the sergeant protested in pursuit.

The moment his boot hit the top step, Jedd raised arms and set the whirling menace in his sights. "Suck on this—"

The nose of the ship pitched upward. A blazing silver glyph carved itself through ebon armor, and the machine unleashed a defensive shockwave that sent Jedd and a storm of glass into full flight toward Sky, who leapt away just in time to avoid dicey repercussions.

The sergeant rolled across the ground, then raised his arms over his head to shield himself from the imminent shower of sharpened shards. The walloped madman slammed down onto the path beside him, and as the flung glass pelted the ground all around, he let out a long groan, his attempt for triumphant retribution an express failure.

Sky lifted his head up and crawled over to his fallen compatriot. "Jedd—what the hell were you thinking?"

The madman lifted his own head in a starry daze, and his eyes wandered in search of his commander, who merely sat beside him. "Well! I wanted to shoot him . . . but he wasn't having any of that," the mad gunman replied as he swept the glass off his uniform.

"Let's play it smart. You're going to get yourself killed."

"They haven't got me yet. I'm feeling lucky."

Sky took Jedd's hand and heaved him up. "Easy—"

With only a few imbalances to walk off, Jedd found himself stabilized on his feet once again.

". . . Hey, look," Sky uttered with uncanny vacancy.

He had turned to the top of the staircase, the epicenter of their battle. It had become doused in a cerulean glow, and a single shadow lay stretched down the steps.

Jedd squinted in suspicion as he struck his gun to knock the frame of remnant glass while the unwavering sergeant slipped the invader tablet into a pouch in his jacket, then reloaded his rifle with a fresh magazine.

Prepared to face the nightmare, they took to the steps once more and, at the top, found the swordsman at the center of the smoked arena, his blade drawn on the gazing beam. Before him was the menace, and it had begun a transformation into something entirely different.

The ship's nose folded inward, and the entire ebon case shattered. A thousand diamond-shaped particles shifted and filed away as its form opened like a blooming cybernetic flower.

As that dark armor retracted, a gradually exposed beacon within swelled to extraordinary intensity. The stage was set alight by the luminescent burst stream, and soon had become so overwhelming that neither soldier could bear to look right into it. As the building blocks of absurdity came into perfect formation, the glare diminished, and the machine reemerged in its truer form. The transformation was complete, and the obscure craft they had once gazed upon in awe now gazed back unto them.

"So, this is the new normal, huh?" said Jedd, his defiant spirit subjugated, at last, by the glory of Eternia.

"You thinking about giving up?" Sky tested.

"Wouldn't dream of it," Jedd assured.

The swordsman dropped down into a predatory stance, ready to strike. "Get off this floor," he ordered, then leapt back in a tremendous flip to the corner of the room behind them, where a severed steel support listed from the weight of gravity.

"Let's move," Sky complied.

They leapt down the staircase and made a dash for the door. The abomination's liquid retina became engorged, appearing twice as large as before. Swelled in its astonishment, it suddenly focused in on the swordsman with razor-sharp fury.

Ultra drew his blade high and swung into the resilient steel, which freed the beam from its foundation—a pristine cut. The liberated support tipped forward, struck the ground, and the destabilized structure let out a cavernous groan. He then sheathed the blade and seized the beam from the sliced bottom. Then, with extraordinary command of its immense weight, flung it forward toward the central plate.

The twenty-foot beam walked, end to end, across the ravaged arena until it came to an upright rest before the glaring eye.

With a razor focus of his own, Ultra dove down, ready to pounce, his enemy's demise prepared.

The invader super soldier erupted into a shadowy dart across the air. As he approached the top of the beam, he reached down, secured it with both hands, then rolled forward, which put the beam behind his head.

With all the gathered momentum from his flight, the swordsman unleashed the magnified weight of the bar right down into the exposed nether eye.

Sergeant Sky, who had nearly reached the door, turned just in time to witness the terrible flash, a gut-wrenching, thunderous burst that reduced all other noise to complete silence in its wake. The eye shattered like a mirror, and a fiery cascade of crimson beacons fell into the night.

Ultra retained control of the beam. As it swung back, he transferred its weight across his chest and delivered a second, bone-splitting crack against the dazed invader craft.

The bar came all the way across as the menace cut into a spiral under the sheer force of the strike and left the gathered momentum for the swordsman to utilize one last time.

Relentless in his decisive assault, he stepped off to center out the weight, then dug his heel into the ground as the bar continued to spin. He built the energy into a monstrous hurricane, then, with merciless resolve, unleashed whirling steel annihilation upon the battered invader agent.

The watery veil was bypassed once more as the steel bar met the eye with a resounding and conclusive burst; the delicate inner eye was left in pieces. A thousand mourning sparks rained through the darkness beyond the maw as the whopped reaper descended into a howling spiral.

The swordsman landed with the finesse of a wildcat, his blade drawn behind his back, the other hand planted upon the ground.

Sky stumbled into the doorframe in a struggle to break free from the paralyzing awe inflicted upon him by that remarkable onslaught. Their once-dreaded foe tumbled out of sight, surely helpless to rescue itself in the aftermath of such brutality.

The panoramic portal stood clear, and only the victor remained within the arena. The struggle was over, and ease set in as the treacherous battlefield became a little quieter.

"Jedd, he did it! He got him!" cried Sky, his spirit emboldened by the thrill of victory.

But the moment was extinguished all too soon by the vengeful screech of the revenant's amplified power core.

The enraged devil machine rose from the blasted brink. Its bluish, miasmic core pulsed and arched as remnant tears poured from the shattered impact points. The swordsman rose and turned to greet it with a grim scowl. Dark armor took shape along the perimeter as the transformation was reversed to conceal the eye from further harm.

Reborn engines let out a wicked blare as the airship cut away to the right. Sky snapped from his trance in delayed reaction to the resurgent threat.

Its wrath came swiftly. Twin pods deployed from the ebon wings and fired off a gleaming barrage of rockets. Sergeant Sky cut back into the hallway and found Jedd in a cold sweat of anxious fury at the distant doorway to the stairwell.

"Come on! I thought we were supposed to get off the floor!" he bellowed.

Sky stumbled down the hall as the tower was rocked by the devil's lethal fury. The black blur passed repeatedly beyond the window as it fired without a target, pounding the structure in blind, raging vengeance.

An explosion ripped through the end of the hall, and Jedd pulled the door shut to protect himself from the heated shrapnel. Sergeant Sky arrived upon the shards before the smoking breach, and Jedd shoved the door open to accommodate his entry, then took off down the steps.

"Get the hell away from the door!" the madman shouted in impatient flight.

Sky slammed it shut as the hiss of a rocket pierced his eardrum. Hellfire's judgement was upon him, and so he made a desperate leap for the staircase.

The missile made an impact with a heart-stopping quake. The door exploded off its hinges, and the flaming steel carcass cast a wide shadow over the imperiled sergeant. At the fingertips of death, he cut the corner at the next flight, just as the door slammed down behind his foot.

The structure rumbled. Sky flipped around and stumbled back to the wall, once again escaping death's ever-dynamic grasp. He held still for a moment, feeling the entire structure rock a few more times before it maintained an eerie stillness.

"Jedd?" he called down the next flight.

There was no reply.

He hurried into descent but stumbled on shaking legs.

As he neared the door to the next floor, he overheard the chopping of gunfire and took cover behind the wall. He raised his rifle and double-checked his magazine. When he was ready, he pulled the door handle back and peeked the barrel through to the other side.

Across the hall from the stairwell door was a large room, which had been utilized for storage space. It was packed wall to wall with tables, chairs, and other optional decorations for the restaurant, which included two stone fountains and a few pleasant marble maidens.

On the far side of the room, he caught sight of Jedd, who fired off several rounds from a shattered window. With due caution, Sky pushed through the door and entered the storage room to lend his aid.

"Jedd! Don't bother with it! Those rounds are not gonna work—" Sky advised as he made his way through a maze of stacked chairs, both standing and toppled.

Before he could arrive at his side, however, the berserk reaper dove down in front of the window. The sudden burst of air from the thrusters threw Jedd off his feet and slammed him into a row of folded tables.

Sky froze.

There was a flash. A ball of light split through the room, and everything went quiet.

All became darkness.

Sky felt himself go airborne and remain there, swallowed up in oblivion's embrace, lifted by the explosion and set adrift across the unfound horizon. Obscure waves passed through him, which invoked a surreal sensation that he hadn't ever felt before. They were peaceful and tranquilizing, providing those blessings with greater depth with each and every steady pass.

The spirit-snatched sergeant felt himself leaving something behind and entering something else entirely, and the further he journeyed, the more intense those bizarre light waves became.

He had vanished to a place where he lacked physical form—transformed into something of the purest energy—and lingered there until the white waves no longer passed, and all before him was darkened architecture.

By the passage of a few moments, he could make out parallel sidewalks, trees, and houses on both sides of a lonely street. It was a neighborhood bewitched by silence and lifelessness, even as the soundless wind blew leafy branches and a lone sedan sped down the street, leaving a ghostly trail in its wake.

Sky recognized all of it, even that particular car. He felt no surprise nor wonder, however, and was only able to drift through that unperfected alternative.

There was suddenly a young girl before him, standing on the sidewalk just a few impossible paces ahead. He didn't know where she had come from as his eyes had never wandered, though she was made an undeniable truth by the odd workings of Eternia.

She had appeared with slender arms pulled behind her back, in a gentle swing from side to side.

The ethereal vision smiled. He knew her, too.

She ran to him and stole his hand. Captivated at once by that quaint interaction, he looked upon her with an innocence lost to the erosion of time. Her mouth moved, eyes so full of excitement, yet he couldn't hear a word of what she had said.

The familiar frolicker pulled him along, and the world moved with them. Across the sidewalk and beneath the bustling branch, they went— past a few houses with fenced yards and up to the intimate house with the young but ample beech, well-rooted in the open front yard.

The girl's long tail of hair lashed his face as they moved through that land of reminiscent reality, and when they had arrived upon the welcome mat to old sanctuary, she turned to him with that lovely beam that now burdened his spirit with a sudden but ever-dwelling weight.

The door crept open behind her, but all that lay within was the white land of unconsciousness. She turned back to that memoryless expanse, then around to her lone companion in oblivion.

There was sadness in her eyes now, but he couldn't quite understand why.

Something about that place began to change. The empyrean glow faded and unveiled an obscure truth. An industrial indigo-plated hall had become bonded with Eternia's intimate realm of stillness. A bizarre bridge that evoked emotional destitution, it was an impossibly long corridor to somewhere very far away, or, perhaps, nowhere at all.

The girl lowered her head, then released his hand. Though it pained him, he could say nothing, nor do anything. He was merely an observer here.

Then, he felt someone seize his arm. He was sure of it. The world began to distort as determined interference disturbed the fragile bond. The spirit-flung sergeant felt himself moving backward. The girl, the house, the hall; all started to become distant as he was pulled up into the sky.

The disheartened guide hung her head, there in her sadness; yet now, he had remembered her name. He called out to her but couldn't make a sound.

Vivid sensations coursed through him—frustration, panic, and grief—all at once upon a mind heavily taxed by the hysteria evoked by the miracles of that surreal encounter. A fragmented fever dream, it had offered an alternative to a long-established actuality, in the grim aftermath of an unreconciled tragedy.

The heavenly waves passed back through him, retreating up and out through oblivion's fleeting manifestation. He called out to her once more with desperate vigor but still couldn't force a sound. Through the waves, however, he saw her head raise up, and in a last miracle to part them, she looked upon him with eyes full of wonder.

Oblivion tore open, and the cruel beyond greeted him first with the repulsive smell of fire and ashes, which struck with such vile intensity that it left him dizzied with gut-wrenching nausea. His eyes burst open, which released the heat that had been trapped behind his eyelids and had left his retinas baked.

His vision focused through the gush of tears as he looked up into Jedd's angry eyes, his face caked with soot. Perilously disoriented, Sky took in a gasp of smoke, choked, then grasped at his throat, yet managed to force out a name from strained lungs.

"Everyn—"

"Come on, Sergeant! We've got to get the hell out of here!" Jedd cried.

He tried to heave his comrade up, but the overwhelmed commander sprang up and drove Jedd back with a defensive push.

Taken by surprise, the madman fell back and struck a wooden podium, which fell back into the embers and exploded into flames. Jedd, enraged and without patience for such distress, forced his way out of the weakened wood and left it in pieces.

"Everyn—I'm here!" Sky cried out as he rose up into the dense smog and was no sooner choked back to the floor.

Jedd caught the wisp of flames squirming on his sleeve. With his teeth clenched in anger, he stopped a moment to beat the flames out with his fist.

"Everyn! We're going to be alright!" he cried out in agony.

The relentless sergeant rose again and searched the smoke for a glimmer of the dream. The heat wafted against his face, so blisteringly fierce that he had to throw his arms up to defend against it. Suffocated almost immediately, he retreated in short steps until he had struck the back wall of the room whose center had been transformed into a burning pit by the rocket strike.

"Where are you, Everyn . . . ?" he called out to the departed void.

I'm right here.

Jedd caught sight of the restless sergeant through the smoke and grimaced. With the flames along his sleeve extinguished, he made for his tormented commander to take a more aggressive approach.

The wall rattled against Sky's back, but he was too dizzied to heed the warning. Their hellish interlude ended as an armored gauntlet burst forth from the scorched wall, its fingers curling with an intent to seize. Then came another further down, and one more after that.

"Get off the wall, Sky!" Jedd cried as he came to life in a vivid frenzy.

Sky turned in horror as he came face-to-face with the cold gaze of the armored titan that peered in through the cracking breach. The wall was ripped open as the invader reached for Sky, who became subjected to acute paralysis as it took a cavernous breath behind its mask, a wretched sound that seemed to echo through the corridors of his burdened mind.

Jedd, with few options left, pulled up his rifle and opened fire on the soldier who had emerged from the enfeebled wall. The invader stalled its advance as it came under pressure from his fierce offensive.

"Sky, get down, you idiot!" Jedd shouted, nearly foaming at the mouth in the face of their obscure enemy.

The sergeant dropped down as a second invader forced its way through, sending fragments of plaster through the air. Pressed by their numbers, Jedd sprayed the open wall with the remainder of his magazine, the discharge of the rifle rattling his chest.

The formidable abominations refocused their attention on the defiant gunman. The soldier closest to Sky ripped his massive rifle through the remainder of the wall and hoisted it up into its armor-encased hand.

Jedd patted down his uniform in search of another magazine. As his hand dragged along empty pockets, his gaze raised back up to a cerulean-lit barrel now aimed between his eyes.

He went still as a faint whine whispered in his ear, the weapon primed to deliver unwelcome liberation. In that same moment, however, the ceiling in front of Jedd ruptured, then collapsed into a rain of debris.

The swordsman dove in from above, the submachine gun ready in his hand. He took aim for invader helmets as he opened fire in a forward dash, making sure each bullet hit its mark.

Jedd dropped to the floor as the swordsman pushed forward toward Sky, who yet remained mentally incapacitated. The bullets popped and sparked as they struck the helmet, and although they appeared to have little effect, the swordsman drove forward until the barrel touched the scarred helm.

The gun clicked. He flipped it up and grabbed it by the hot barrel and released it at the second soldier, who had nearly put him in its sights. The butt of the gun struck with terrifying force and sent the invader's colossal gun back into the breached wall.

He drew his blade through the soldier before him, flash charged into a downward slash through the chest plate of the second, then snapped away with an explosive flip as his torpid foes toppled over.

From a tabletop, he reached his arm across his chest and released the blade like a knife through the air. The flawless point punctured the staggered trooper, and the diamond edge behind it drove right to the hilt.

Ultra leapt for the protruding grip as the walloped invader stumbled back toward the ground. In an instant, his boot met the armor-clad trooper with thunderous impact. He pulled the immaculate blade from its target, flipped back through the air, landed upon the ground, and left the slain giant to complete its descent into the ravenous flames.

Jedd scurried over to Sky and pulled him from the ground, then guided him through the smoky furnace. In a desperate drive for the exit, he cupped his hand over his nose and mouth and, with determination, soon found relief back out in the darkened hall.

They crossed the hall back into the stairwell in hopes of continuing their descent. However, the staircase now spiraled down to a treacherous brink. A vast gorge had been left in the wall, and a stunning view of the sweeping ruin was all that remained in sight.

"Well, would you believe it?" said Jedd as he retreated back and set the dazed sergeant on the floor.

He knelt down beside his exhausted comrade, took a small canteen from his jacket, and unscrewed the top.

"Open up wide. You aren't about to leave me with Twinkletoes the Eviscerator after surviving that," he mocked as he held the opening to Sky's lips.

"Damnit, I didn't find your rifle . . ." the madman lamented. "Damn missile nearly sent you straight to the flower field. After I fix you up, I'm gonna get me a piece of that airship, and make a little chew toy for the dogs."

Sky looked on with eyes that yet sought out the netherworld. His mind had remained loosely bonded to it. The memories of that place had begun to blur, but the true memories of which it attempted to mimic remained. Soon, most of what he remembered of that idyllic parallel was but a car disappearing over the road.

The dryness in his throat. The uncomfortable pressure in his chest. The searing burns on his skin. They were all relevant again. These sensations each served to sever him from the vacant touch of the otherworld and did so with excruciating intensity.

Refocused in a truer nightmare, he took the canteen from Jedd and drank from it, then stopped to steady his breath as the remnant phantom memories slipped quietly to oblivion.

"Come on, no time to be sitting around," Jedd urged.

From the hallway beyond the door above came the thundering of heavy steps. Jedd sprang up with teeth gritted, then took aim up the flight with his emptied rifle.

"Madman—heads up," said Sky as he threw him a magazine from his ammo belt.

The able soldier caught it, snapped out the old, and loaded the fresh with exceptional speed.

"Come on," ordered Sky as he rose to his feet. "The stairs—let's see if there's any way we can cross, or this'll end up one hell of a firefight, and I think it's fair to say those guys can take a few more bullets than we can."

Jedd growled, then pulled his sights from the door. They moved ahead, cut left, and arrived before the two steps into the open abyss.

"Got any bright ideas?" asked Jedd.

With due caution, Sky edged forward on shaky legs, his body enfeebled from their hellish encounter with the revenant flier.

Beyond the gap, a sliver of stairs remained on the next flight, but a misplaced step would put them over a sheer drop four stories down to a ramp of fallen concrete and the street side beyond it.

Sky secured himself on the handrail and inched himself along the narrow, jagged cut of ledge until he reached the lip below. Though the rail creaked and rattled, it held his weight all the way across. Jedd, faintly enthused, followed behind as the ominous steps echoed through the stairwell.

In front of them lay a new obstacle, a second plummet between the flight that parted them from the door to the eighth floor. The winds from the city swept across their faces as the rumble of the footsteps found their hearts, though they were confident the invader troopers couldn't afford the previous maneuver.

"Jump for it," Sky ordered.

"Just don't slip, right?" Jedd replied.

Together, they stepped back to the edge, then, with necessary courage, dashed toward the deathly brink. They leapt, landed, and stumbled into a hectic descent down the remainder of steps beyond until they struck the safety of the wall.

"Remind me never to take the stairs again," pleaded Jedd as he limped off a sharp pain in his ankle.

The eerie din of stressed steel haunted the halls of the stairwell. The soldiers felt their balance shift beneath their feet and exchanged a solemn glance as all became still again.

"That didn't feel good," said Jedd.

"I don't think this thing is gonna handle much more," Sky acknowledged. "Look—" he continued, with a tap on a gilded plaque screwed to the wall beside the door.

It read "North Merik Tower Crossing."

"Looks like the skyway is on this floor. Let's see if we can sneak across without attracting any unwanted attention. Get help from air support and maybe take this thing out of the sky before the sun comes up."

"Alright . . . right behind you," said Jedd, grounded in skepticism as he lifted his rifle in preparation for the worst.

Sky limped ahead and pushed open the door, and they were greeted with the ash-scented gale of the night. Directly ahead of them was the skyway, battered and with a path covered in fallen glass from the shattered ceiling portal.

"There's no sneaking over to that. Let's just book it," Jedd advised, the hairs on the back of his neck standing straight as he patrolled the open brink with nervous eyes.

"Alright, come on!" the sergeant approved.

The soldiers picked up onto the tips of their toes for the final stretch to reach the presumed safety of the other side. They heard the ferocious cry of the airship in the distance but retained hope that the swordsman would keep its wrath at bay.

Their boots soon fell upon the broken stone tile of the bridge. The structure seemed stable, but they dared not linger. A gale whipped their faces as they made their crossing. Jedd looked all around for hints of danger, but there was nothing but a burning expanse and the night.

Just as they had cleared the bridge and arrived upon the narrow path to a rooftop garden court, they heard the roar of the tyrant's engines. The entire bridge went up in pieces with a cacophonous clangor. Jedd and Sky leapt through the air and fell across the ground like rag dolls, the madman losing his rifle in the flight.

The invader airship rose as the remnants of the pulverized passage crumbled over its battered exterior. It began to transform before their eyes once more. With irreverence for their capabilities, it assumed its true form to execute duty and exact vengeance at once.

Jedd stumbled back up to his feet and drew his pistol on the relentless scourge of the sky. "Alright, you son of a bitch—"

He fired the entire clip into the watery miasma that guarded the cracked nether orb, but only viscous rings resulted from the bullets' impact.

Their faces were stricken in awe as the watcher's glow bathed the area in vibrant blue.

"We're just a damn joke," said Jedd as he threw the pistol away.

The eye's pupil became a hypnotic spiral of color. They swirled together until the neon chromas had become a single point. Then, that pinpoint beacon became a devil's crimson, the machine ready to deliver them thoroughly to the realm of Ends.

A window from the balcony of the Orchid Building burst through, and an invader trooper fell out and plummeted to the ground. The swordsman came to the ledge of the window, his blade in sheath.

He caught sight of his adversary across the way, primed to deliver the gift of transcendent fire. Spurred to action, he leapt from the window, bolted toward the divide, then shot from a severed support of the collapsed bridge as the red core gazed upon its helpless victims.

Judgement was nigh.

The swordsman fell between them as a spectacular beam of unfathomable energy was unleashed with a deafening peal. The swordsman crossed his gauntlets, and a barrier of mystic iridescence rose from the ground. It encapsulated them with a hum just as the watcher's glare split the air and all in front of them went red.

Both Sky and Jedd dove to the ground in a last effort of pure instinct.

The blast ray struck the surface of the barrier with tremendous force. Though their hearts rumbled within, it held strong and caused the beam to split away into a deathly starburst. The ground and the flowerbeds around them were wiped away by the glorious eraser, which purified its path of all content.

As the beam washed over the barrier, faint glimmers of light settled within the bubble and were gathered from the air to Ultra's gauntlets, which grew radiant.

The resilient defender, whose arms struggled in the fearsome force of the purifying burst stream, seized the grip of his blade. The unrelenting machine amplified the beam beyond limitation to achieve the power to break through. There came a luminous spark of white that broke the red torrent, however.

The swordsman had drawn.

Empowered, he brought back his glowing blade to full extension, then struck forth with such force that a vicious wave of energy split the incoming flare. That crescent moon strike diced the red glare straight through and ripped into the brick wall of the Orchid Building beyond.

The beam faltered. Something had happened, a judgement of the traitor's blade. The wicked scream waned as it withered into a strident whine.

Sky opened his eyes to find the ground beyond his nose erased by pure heat, his hands just meters from the smoldering edge. The red beam had gone but left a curtain of black smoke, which billowed all around them. The sergeant sprang up and put his hand on his face to assure himself that he was indeed still alive.

Miraculously with his life, he looked through the smoke in front of him and caught first glimpse of the stricken machine. The glass-like dome was shattered, its eye lined with red cracks, which made its appearance all the more monstrous. But the sound, the whine, was something of such sadness that it nearly evoked something within him.

Ultra, with one gauntlet still aglow, threw it forward and unleashed the final burst, which ripped through the vulnerable glass, pulverized the sensitive hardware within, and put the great eye to rest.

The victor drew the razor point to the bloodshot menace as it listed to one side, then slipped quietly into a vacant descent as the shockwave unleashed and raced throughout the ravaged city.

Sergeant Sky scanned the abstract devastation around him in disbelief, then turned to the swordsman who, after a conclusive explosion ripped through the air, sheathed the blade.

"Damn, that thing was more pissed off than me," Jedd admired as he struggled up from the ground.

Sky hustled over and pulled him to his feet. "That bother you?" he joked, with raised spirits in wake of their success.

"Makes me uncomfortable," Jedd admitted.

The swordsman watched the edge of the cliff with a solemn stare. Something seemed to haunt him. "It is done . . . but I warn you now. There may come some enemies that I will be unable to rescue you from."

"That makes me uncomfortable, too," Jedd added.

There was a sudden burst of air, and the roar of engines. The swordsman turned calmly to search out the source beyond the brink.

"Hold on! Is that—" Sky hesitated, as he assessed the sound of the craft.

"One of ours, baby!" Jedd assured.

An armored Union plane rose up beyond the severed bridge, its side door open. Grasped to a handle beyond was General Myres, who greeted them with a rifle in hand.

"Saw someone took down that flying pain in the ass, and boy, was it a hell of a show! Thought you might want a complementary lift," General Myres shouted.

The general motioned to the pilot to move in, and the airship glided toward the ledge. The swordsman stepped onto the ship while both Jedd and Sky made their way over. As they stepped across the remnant skyway, the sound of crumbling concrete rippled through the air, and the ground beneath them began to dip.

"Something just went," warned Jedd.

"Book it," Sky barked.

They both picked up into full sprints as the remnants of the bridge collapsed in and the city opened up before them. General Myres handed off the rifle to Ultra and turned toward the cockpit.

"Hey, pilot, time for some fancy maneuvers! Keep that lineup tight," he ordered.

The transport craft rolled up on its side as the shelf cracked. Jedd and Sky stumbled forward as they careened toward the brink. Myres stepped behind one side of the door while Ultra took to the other.

The descent of the broken ground accelerated and nearly left Jedd and Sky suspended. The ground vanished beneath them as they slipped over the edge of the eight-story drop. They threw their hands out in a desperate plea for salvation. Ready to answer, Myres stole the arm of Jedd as he passed into the bay while Ultra plucked Sky by the jacket, whipped him inside, and pinned him against the wall.

The ship pulled off, the deck nearly ninety degrees to the ground four stories below as the rock plate almost struck the fuselage.

Myres wrapped his arm around the metal bar as the weight of the well-equipped soldier taxed his arm. The airship leveled quick, however, and the aged general dropped Jedd as the floor connected with the madman's cheek. Jedd cursed the sharp pain as he pushed with his arms to pull his face off the cold metal plate.

The daredevil pilot leveled the craft just in time for them to witness the heavy fragment strike the street below, which unleashed a spectacular eruption of dust. It was a seismic event of enough strength that it caused the battered Orchid Tower to collapse, at last, with a vicious tumult.

"Pilot, get us out of here!" ordered Myres as he struggled to his feet.

A barrage of bolts screamed through the sky and struck the ship, which caused them to break into a desperate yaw. Myres stormed into the cockpit and dropped into the first officer's seat beside the pilot. With the strike of a few buttons and the throw of a knob, the doors slid shut.

"That's a hell of an entrance, sir," Sky hollered. "You been practicing?"

"Strap in, soldier. We're leaving the city."

Sky fell still, dumbstruck by that sudden revelation. "Sir, are those orders?"

Myres turned back to Sky, who remained in frustrating paralysis at the entryway of the cockpit. "You think I didn't put much time into that decision?" Myres inquired with his brow raised.

The plane jolted. Sky stumbled back. Jedd seized him and pulled him back into the chair beside him.

They roared off as invader fire peppered their wake.

"The lines are caving in. We aren't able to hold them off. Anywhere. We'll head back to regroup, then blow a hole in their brainless advance to make way for the retreat."

The plane jolted once more. The right-hand engine let out a whine as the plane slowed back. A second string of direct hits battered the hull just beyond the door.

"Sir, looks like one of the engines took a hit. It's holding, but wouldn't put my money on it for long," the pilot advised.

"Give it all she's got. Bring her down outside of the camp. We'll have to ditch it and walk the rest of the way."

"Yes, sir. Lighting it up," the pilot replied, then pulled a handle, which punched the jet into a final throttle.

"So, Sky!" cried General Myres.

"Yes, sir?"

"Mind telling me how you managed to get ahold of me, son? The connection isn't so good out here, these days."

Trouble

And so it was that Little Eddie Bowitz would not go to the front lines. Although, in truth, he had no wish to fight in combat. He feared the goliaths of the enemy force, and his flight from the barracks had opened old scars, which lay heavy on his mind.

The boy yet held fast to his faith in the swordsman to deliver them from the unforgivable hand of tragedy. He had seen his capability with his own eyes, that valiant soldier of miracles who had saved him, just as he had saved others. A hero from the page, reel, or cartridge would do no less.

Eddie had been confined to a small tent for hours after the incident. He sat upon a salvaged wooden stool as a young nurse knelt before him and tended to a mild burn on his arm, which had thankfully only left his skin inflicted with manageable swelling and swept clean of hair. They rarely traded interactions—she, steadied in concentration, and he, lost in an aimless scan of the perimeter in search of nothing at all.

He looked down at her but once, and the purse of her lips, along with the sharpening of her gaze, was enough to dissuade him from a second glance. After conditioning the wound and wrapping it in gauze, her task was complete.

She rose, stuffed the rest of the supplies into a medical bag atop an adjacent table, then fled him without a word. Eddie remained there in silent vacancy, and soon, his mind wandered. From the invaders to the swordsman to the girl he had failed to rescue from misfortune; all of them had become stuck inside his head. The boy reached into his pocket and felt the chain of the cherished charm between his fingers.

"You're never left behind. I won't forget you. None of you," he swore aloud, his eyes closed and adrift in a fantasy in which none were lost.

There was an old sadness that swelled beneath his burgeoning aura of hope. Though that familiar sensation had certainly abated with the passage of time, it, too, seemed to undergo a resurgence in the aftermath of the invader's arrival and the possibilities he had derived from their miracles.

There came a shuffle of canvas that stirred Eddie from his reflection.

"Why'd you bother joining the military, kid?"

Eddie opened his eyes to greet his sudden guest. It was Schneider. He stood in the entrance to the tent with a hand in his pocket and a cigarette drooped in his mouth, scowling, as he awaited an answer.

"I—just wanted to help people," Eddie replied with a shaky footing on his own principle.

Schneider huffed.

Though it was the only answer Eddie knew, he searched for a more suitable motivation, one that might please his grim-faced commander.

"I wanted to serve, sir."

Schneider offered his spiritless efforts no reply, however. He took a drag, then choked the smoke back out, and once he had regained his composure, he set his glass gaze upon Eddie's pocket, on which his hand yet lingered.

"What've you got in your pocket?" his inquisitive superior scrutinized.

Eddie froze for a moment, unsure of how to explain himself. He nevertheless drew upon the golden strand and revealed it to Schneider, who moved in closer.

"Whose is that?" Schneider asked as he reached out to receive the trinket from Eddie.

The boy hesitated at first, but then reluctantly laid the lovely chain into the blemished glove, dirtied by vile war.

"It belongs to someone—a girl I saw near the marketplace," Eddie admitted.

Schneider lifted it to his unexpressive eyes, and flipped the avian pendant between his fingers, then let it dangle by the chain.

"Where's she now?" he asked.

"I—She's—" Eddie stuttered.

"She's dead, isn't she?" Schneider concluded. "Well, you can't return it to her if she's dead, can you?"

Eddie searched for an excuse, embattled by the reality of the matter. Schneider, without patience and certain of the truth, threw the necklace away to the ground.

"I wish I could," Eddie spat out, heated by that blatant act of disrespect.

The lieutenant gauged his reaction closely, pulled the gifted cigarette, then released another puff of smoke between his lips.

"Well, that doesn't really matter now, does it? You said it yourself. She's dead. Don't you think for a second that just because of what's going on out there, that now, somehow your wishes have some value. Take my advice and leave them behind. This is war. It's misery, and do you know when it ends? It ends when you're empty inside and you feel like a ghost of the person you used to be. That's how you'll know it's over."

Schneider came down onto a knee there before the transfixed cadet and looked at him with all the disappointment of a father to a failure of a son.

"The only miracle we can perform is surviving this war. Because I won't lie to you. It's bad out there. Much worse than you could ever imagine. So, you pick up that rifle sitting over there on the table, collecting dust"—he directed with a slack finger to the weapon that lay in wait of him—"and fight for all the good people in the world."

Eddie said nothing. He held his pain inside, just as he had learned to, just as he had been told to do.

"But whatever it is you choose to do, don't you endanger any of my soldiers again in service to your childish stupidity," he concluded with a foreboding vacancy.

Schneider, feeling his point made, lifted back up and departed for the exit with a hack on his smoke. As soon as the bewitched lieutenant had gone, Eddie rose and went right for the necklace, which lay partially buried beneath the dirt.

He seized it from the defiled earth and rubbed the filth away with his fingers, then stopped as the words of his commander sunk into his frail mind. *Was it foolish*, he thought, *to hold onto this memento when he had surely seen the girl dead?*

A far more compelling thought arose inside him, however, one that caused him to grasp the chain tight in hand. The swordsman, the invaders, and the past he once knew all furthered him to believe in something he had nearly given up on.

As he sat there upon his knees with head bowed and eyes closed, Little Eddie Bowitz made a vow within. It was a decisive oath that he would keep secret from the world and bear the weight of its burden all on his own if that was what was necessary.

For him, the choice was easy, given the circumstances. It was instinctive, almost. An innate desire to chase after the elusive had been truly reborn, and no naysayer would steer him from his course.

With spirit rekindled, the boy returned the necklace to his pocket, and when he was sure of his path, and could see it even with his eyes closed, he opened his eyes.

Little Eddie reopened his eyes to the world, and there in front of him was the girl with her twinkling eyes, peeking out from under the nylon curtain. Certain she had been noticed, her lips parted into a toothy smile, agleam in her mischief.

***

Outside at the tent, the commanding officers were alive with movement, all in the works of vaguely organized chaos. Schneider came down the road with sluggish steps, took the cigarette from his mouth, and smashed it against the charred door of a burned-out car. Before he could arrive at the command tent, two officers bounded over to him with haste.

"Lieutenant Schneider, we've been given the order to abandon Salamandra City. General Myres has requested your presence at the tent immediately," a colonel reported.

Schneider scowled, then shook his head in frustration. "That can't be right. I told him!"

He refocused.

"We've got nowhere left to go. Do they expect us to swim to Fortuna City on the other side of the world?"

"With due respect, sir, we're not entirely sure why this course of action was taken so suddenly. There was a claim the general received contact from—"

"Contact?" Schneider interrupted. "No one informed me of that—"

Schneider pushed through the officers and marched into the command tent.

"Gather what we can. Med teams will be divided among the companies and civilian groups. General Henson is on the way to beat their offensive down and clear the way. He'll direct the forward, and once we've got the civilians situated in a caravan, you and your force will move up and support. We need those routes through the old district clear at all costs, but don't expect much support from the sky. I got most of what's left moving survivors," Myres briefed the officers who had been gathered.

"This is pure mayhem, General. What do you hope to accomplish by ordering a retreat INTO enemy lines?" Schneider bellowed upon his entry.

General Myres turned, his brow raised in irritation with this brash contest of his command. "Second Lieutenant, would you prefer the swim?"

"Has it already been discussed how and from whom you acquired contact from? Just what kind of intel slipped through the cracks and caused you to believe a full-blown retreat into enemy lines was the best course of action?"

General Myres denied him a direct response and instead turned to the crumbling city beyond the tent.

"There's a new threat in our midst, Schneider. When I got the communication and took that transport to Midtown . . . and saw what was left of it, I realized that all of our plans since this thing began have ended in *undeniable failure*. Quite frankly, we're holding on by strings. So—I took the advice of someone who might know what they were talking about."

"And who would that be?" Schneider pressed. "Or do you prefer I guess? The invader, isn't it?"

"I trust him," Myres declared. "I learned something a long time ago . . . that you can tell a lot about someone who has the capability to do a lot but chooses, out of principle, to value restraint and do what's right. Sky and Jedd seem like they got their heads on straight, and if what they're saying is true, we may have one hell of an ally in this shit show."

"Or he'll be the death of us."

Myres grunted in dismissal of his pessimism.

"Only one way to find out. We don't have much time for pedal picking, as you might have been able to tell with my entire city going up in flames. We're in no shortage of problems, but there's one that I could use assistance with right now . . . planning a strategic way into the crossfire."

Schneider glared at the general as he fought to put his pride aside. Somewhere in the back of his heart, past the wall of his ego, he knew that Myres was right in his assessment. Their defensive had shrunken from the very moment it had been established. The enemy roamed between the lines, and in any natural scenario of war, it would have been fair to assume they had no position at all. So, in reluctant concession to the new reality, Schneider went to the table, and together with the remnant high command, they forged their desperate plan for departure.

Salamandra City had been lost.

***

Back in the tent, Eddie sat on the stool, his arms dangling as he gazed down into starry, glossed eyes unlike anything he had ever seen before. She was on her knees before him with her arms crossed over his lap, her smile a mystic crescent moon that beckoned him to return to himself.

"Come on! I know a place," said the girl.

Eddie closed his eyes tightly and lowered his head as he struggled against her will. "I'm a soldier. I have to stay . . . I can't go with you."

His frail defiance only proved to widen her smile. She tilted her head with playful charm.

"I know you want to go with me. I can see it in your eyes—something searching," she said as she scrutinized his face for an inevitable sign of intrigue. "This is your dream."

He surrendered his eyes and gave her what she wanted, and as he peered deep into those odd mirrors, he became nothing but a breathless witness to that crystalline exhibition of intimate yet foreign wonder. Her presence was unprecedented to him; dreamy yet real, a whimsical entity that enjoyed an existence at the brink of fantasy itself, and any other witness to that delightfully arcane aura certainly would be unable to describe her as anything different.

"My dream?" he repeated to her.

Her mouth fell agape, and she nodded with enthusiasm.

"Don't you know that? The world is more unbelievable than you know . . . Or perhaps you did so once . . . a long time ago," the dreamy trespasser teased as she softly took the gauze between her fingertips.

With a gentle pull, she maneuvered it down his arm, until it slipped over his wrist, and fell to the ground. To his surprise, they found together that the wound had already healed.

She slid back and pointed through a crack at the back of the tent.

"I know a place, you know?" she said as she redirected to him. "A place where we can find something incredible, but you can't tell anyone, okay?"

Eddie felt an old feeling creeping up from within. He couldn't stop it now, even if he wanted to. It invaded his consciousness, his thoughts, and laid a vast claim to his fertile imagination. What incredible power she wielded over him. An immediate empress, she spoke not to a cadet but to the one that was lost long ago. Perhaps that was all she saw in him.

"But it's dangerous out there. You just can't run—"

"*I* can do what I want!" she interrupted. "You don't have to worry about me. Because I know where I'm going. I know where it is I wanna be."

She cocked her head, her expression faintly sobered.

"Do you?"

The question sent him back into the depths in search of answers, but he could not find it fast enough for her.

The girl stood. Distress had taken hold of her.

Rushed to his true feelings, Eddie straightened up on the stool, unable to hold the question in any longer. "Hey! Are you . . . real?" the boy asked the starry-eyed enchantress doused in moonlight.

She peered down upon him with her brow raised in the spirit of her mischief. A smile crept across her face, and a sharp snicker escaped her. She composed herself, however. She did not flee nor play coy. She looked down at the wonderer with resolute conviction.

"I'm real. I'm here."

Her eyes shot to the entrance of the tent where the sound of footsteps grew near. Without another word, she scurried for the split at the back of the tent, passed through, then fled down the grassy lot beneath the glimmering stars on a course for the ruins on the smoking horizon.

"Wait!" Eddie snapped as he leapt from the chair.

He took a step after her but drew back in restraint. The conflicted soldier released a deep breath to calm himself, then listened in close. The footsteps had faded to silence, and all that remained was distant chatter and the incessant ambience of war.

As he calmed himself, Eddie pondered over all the things that had happened on that fateful day. Surely, there had to be some kind of magic out there. Maybe this was just the beginning, but he would never know unless he went. That was the ultimate truth, and not even the invasion launched by High Fantasy could change it.

Yet there was still a struggle within, one between the indoctrinated intelligence and the determined connate spirit.

"I know where I want to be . . . ?" he recited.

The words haunted him. Where was it that she wanted to be?

Something about that whimsical trespasser had left him irreversibly altered. None of what she had said had seemed so far-fetched, especially now in the wake of the new reality they all faced, and though the intentions of her fascinations were but another mystery to him, it was true.

There was nothing more he wanted than to go with her and chase down the miracles that lay beyond the reality, to where the swordsman fought at lightning-fast speed against terrible foes who wielded terrible weapons. To go and be alongside the heroes and not be pushed away to the side. No longer a spectator to the incredible but a pursuer of those wonders that had remained locked away in dreams for far too long.

And so Little Eddie Bowitz stood.

With a resolute breath, he wiped his mind of uncertainty, and with clarity secured within, he looked out the back of the tent through which the enchantress had fled. She had made it far into the distance, however. Like an opportunity about to slip him by, she became something of a speck in the distance.

A star fading from existence.

Electrified, he sprang up and shot through the tent as he fell apart inside. In a flight of desperation, he felt a sensation he never wished to let go of again—the feeling of being in pursuit of the unbelievable.

He was on the tail of the mythic beast. Giving chase to the seer from beyond the veil. He could finally see it. This was the only life for him. The only one that should have been.

The boy passed others in a blur but refused to see their faces in fear that they might obstruct him. Once he had cleared the marsh, he crossed the blasted road and entered through the alleyway that he was sure she had fled through. Following it all the way down to a blockage of cars, the AWOL cadet was left between two desolate alleys.

Little Eddie looked all over, but the daring siren was nowhere to be found, and panic set in fast as the thought of losing her threatened his determination. There was still time to turn back, but he knew he would be unable to do it. He couldn't bear to face that reality again and all but give up on his chance to experience the teased alternative.

This was all he had ever wanted—a real chance—and now, he had it. Here, the journey would begin, or sadly, the journey would end.

Suddenly, a shadow swept across him. Eddie turned, wide-eyed with a spirit impelled by the offering of hope. It had come from the alleyway to his left, which glowed in a somnolent fire that lay hidden around a corner.

He took off, heedless of danger as the shadows closed in around him. Once around the corner, he found an abandoned bonfire at the corner of a recessed wall, which was comprised of old clothes and a few mattresses.

He felt a presence watching him in that eerily intimate place. In the immediate clearing, he could find nothing at all. Upon a concentrated inspection of the narrowed pass ahead, however, he spotted something peculiar among a row of dumpsters. The subtle wave of ebon cloak whispered ahead. Discovered, the man beneath the hood stepped out but remained facing the wall ahead of him.

Unlike that of the swordsman, this stranger's garb was not worn by battle, nor did it bear any sign of reinforcement. Just as Eddie had become captivated by an oddly familiar sensation, the man turned on him, and his blood was chilled by the sight of piercing golden eyes.

A demon lurked within.

Eddie fled the alleyway through an open passage to his right, unsure as to where it might bring him. There was certainly no turning back now as hope slipped fast into dread.

He emerged from the demon's den and came upon a crater in the road, pulverized by an invader pod, which now lay opened and empty. Eddie approached the impact site as he searched out the surrounding area for signs of the girl, desperate to expel a deepening loneliness that had been exacerbated by bitter terror.

The boy caught the sound of shuffling rubble from somewhere behind the pod. He stumbled away in surprise as the runaway enchantress emerged with her arm cocked back, prepared to lob a stone fragment at the unsuspecting prowler. As their eyes locked, however, she wilted until her arm dropped, and the rock fell from her fingers.

He had never felt such relief, and she looked at him with starry amazement as he fled the world for her.

"I thought I—I thought I lost you," Eddie panted upon his arrival.

"Wow—it's really you," she replied with her head cocked and a hand pressed firmly against her upper chest.

"Hey! Why'd you go running off all of a sudden?" he asked.

"I thought you didn't want to go with me . . . You were too busy with your war and all," she said as she turned away from him, stuck in remnant bitterness, but only for show.

"Well . . . I'm here. I want to see what it is you see," Eddie conceded, then pressed his back against the pod and slid to the ground to catch his breath.

"Then, trust me now . . . What we're searching for is just beyond the city. We can make it there together," she explained as she fell down next to him.

As they sat there together, the release of fear forged a bond between them for young Eddie. This girl, the one with all the answers, gave him comfort. A comfort that felt rather magical. How wonderful it is to have someone to pursue the same dream with, he thought.

"This is the night of possibility, Eddie Bowitz. We're going to do it, but I'll need your help," she said, her eyes searching him for reassurance.

Eddie, who wondered at first how he could ever help that fearless spirit who seemed to carry such confidence through the turmoil, saw a rifle laying on the ground. He leaned forward and took it from the stock, dragging it over and pulling it up onto his lap.

This was how he would help them accomplish their goal. He would do it by doing exactly what he had been trained to do. Their audacious undertaking called on him to take action, and he would answer that call with a valorous heart. No longer in duty to a country but in duty to them—in duty to the dream they chased.

Eddie's mind wandered to that hooded man he had encountered in the alley, still not far away. He knew not what the intentions of this man were, nor why he had stood alone in some obscure place. Had he waited for him there, or was it mere coincidence? And why had that dark presence seemed so oddly familiar?

Now that he was with her, perhaps it didn't matter. She laid her head on his shoulder, his heart teased by magic and stolen by the dream.

N o w   t h a t   I   h a v e   y o u .

Waiting Here for You

And I have seen the wonder in your eyes, limitless like beyond the stars!

So, I'll take you there, to the edge of creation

While there's still a moment to apprehend it

Call upon the wishing star

Spur the forerunning to action!

For there is no better time than now.

Tomorrow is surely crumbling.

Be Alright

The SUV rushed through the silent residential streets of the metropolitan suburbia. Through the backroads, across the darkened blocks, beyond the crescent moon, and out into the main street, there was nothing but the abyssal shadow of apocalypse in the wake of the torrential storm.

Lost in the oppressive, tenebrous embrace, the car wandered alone through the empty three-lane road. Inside, Lyal and the others were locked in a pact of silence. They dared not break it lest the shadows of the netherworld leap out at them from beyond the window.

Petrified eyes drifted across the blur of dark houses and huddled complexes, a sight that evoked a distinct familiarity with the vacant destitution of Fable.

At the approaching intersection was the sign they had been waiting for.

Salamandra City, twenty miles.

The boulevard rose with the land on a gentle slope, and upon the ghostly peak of suburbia was the journey's end.

"Guess the storm knocked the power out, huh?" Kaiser proposed.

"Still think this is a good idea?" asked Mitz.

Setz turned and engaged him in a sharp snap of anger. "Oh, so now you don't want to do it?"

"I'm just saying, man . . . it's weird," Mitz clarified.

"Guys, chill out. You're all worked up over people taking shelter? Like, it's just common sense," Lyal assured them.

"I don't know, man. It just seems a little bit odd that there aren't even . . . police cruisers out here. You know, warning people to go home . . . But, maybe there isn't a war after all! Maybe that guy was just an empty jar of nuts," Mitz reasoned.

Miyacre let out a long sigh as her eyes jumped around the unrelenting gloom.

"Uh—hey, anyone else seeing what I'm seeing? Look up there," Kaiser directed with a finger out to the sky beyond the front windshield.

"Yeah—I see it," Miyacre replied as she fought to stay composed, the world falling apart piece by piece.

The skies above teemed as a great billow rose across the moonlight and eclipsed the stars.

"Is that smoke? Man, there really *is* something going on out here," Kaiser escalated.

The direful view was swept behind the summit as they came before the hillside's base.

"Holy shit—guys, we can't do this. We need to turn around," Ashe pleaded in release of pent-up anxiety. "This isn't what I signed up for."

"Yeah—you're right. I think you're right," Miyacre conceded.

"Miyacre—just hold on a second," Lyal protested.

His words found no consideration in her head, however. She cut the wheel and swung the car around to the other side of the street, which slung the others off to the right.

"Watch it—damn!" complained Kaiser as he pushed himself off of Setz's shoulder.

"There's nobody on the street, so deal with it," Ashe snapped.

Miyacre hit the gas just as her headlights struck someone out in the road.

In that split second, they saw him, the shadowy entity that had stalked them throughout the land of tomorrow. They let out a collective and horrified yelp as he vanished before the car could settle to a halt.

"Get us out of here, *now*," Ashe cried, to which Miyacre responded with her foot to the gas.

The transmission slipped, and the car crawled.

Miyacre looked down at the pedal and stepped on it again. The engine remained unresponsive, however. She stomped it until her leg grew tired.

"Oh, fuck, no—no—" said Ashe in a spiral of hysteria.

"Ashe—calm down," Miyacre urged as she placed her hand upon her knee. "I need you to calm down, okay?"

Ashe shook her head in frantic dismissal of that gentle request, and as the car came to a stop, she unbuckled her seatbelt and fumbled with the door handle until it opened.

"Ashe—wait up a second," protested Lyal as he stepped out after her.

The rest of the group followed as they abandoned the disabled vehicle.

"I told you this was a bad idea. What the hell were you guys thinking?" Setz blamed. "What were *we* thinking?" he quickly admitted as responsibility laid its weight upon him.

"Dude, did you honestly believe there was a *war* here? They had like, a billion motherfuckers with loaded guns at the speech yesterday morning," Kaiser argued.

Setz stepped up into Kaiser's face. "Well, guess what? *Idiot*," Setz snapped.

Kaiser shoved him back. Setz came at him again, but was caught by Lyal, who forced himself between them.

"Guys, will you stop it? This isn't the time to be acting like children," Miyacre berated.

"Hey!" Lyal said as he shoved them away from each other. "Have either of you actually seen *anything* yet? Yeah, didn't think so. There's literally nothing going on here. So, let's find someone, get a phone, maybe even a ride, and everyone will be alright," he assured.

"Oh—oh, you want a phone?" Setz shouted as he took out his cellphone. "You want a phone!? Then, take mine," he bellowed as he smashed it upon the asphalt. "You selfish son of bitch."

Lyal stepped over the cracked phone and went nose to nose with him, his eyes swelling with anger.

"That what you think? I'm selfish? Then, how about this. I'll go see what's really going on, and I'll come back and let you know. Whatever's happening over there, yeah? It's bigger than beef between you, me, or any other one of your friends."

Lyal turned away from Setz as he broke for the hilltop.

"Friends—right," Setz mocked.

Lyal, turning a deaf ear to Setz, turned back to the others, his face alight in unease. "Where's Ashe? Ashe!" he called.

Their eyes all found her at once. She marched away in frantic urgency down the road and beneath the streetlights, which hung in dark stasis.

"Go take care of her," Lyal asked of Kaiser. "I'm gonna go see what's up there so we can get the hell out of here."

Kaiser leapt into departure with a nod. "Come on, Mitz. Wingman me on this," Kaiser rallied as he took off into a sprint after her while Mitz trailed behind at his best speed.

Miyacre, who had taken a few paces to join them in flight, hesitated and turned back to Lyal. He had already started up the hillside, and after a brief moment of indecisiveness, she gave chase to him. Setz, left alone with the car, turned and unleashed pent-up rage with a ferocious kick to the back tire.

"Lyal—stop—just wait," she called out to him.

In heed of her desperate call, he slowed to a halt upon the slope.

"Miyacre—just go with them for just two seconds," he threatened as he pressed his fingers into his head in frustration.

She swung her head in adamant defiance, then pursed her lips as she searched for the best words.

"I promised your mom I'd look after you."

"Okay, you can look after me from the bottom of the hill—"

"I'm going with you, Lyal. So, just—get over it, okay!?"

Overcome by her assertive persistence and annoyed with it all the same, he turned from her and returned to the climb with his forceful companion fast at his side.

There came a sudden and steady din that tore long through the air before it settled into an eerie quiet.

"What was that?" asked Miyacre as she slowed pace.

"Just keep climbing," Lyal urged, reinforced in his agitation.

Then came the long, cacophonous drone of monumental collapse, which left them electrified in anxiety.

"Something just fell," Miyacre cautioned.

"Just keep climbing," Lyal repeated, rattled yet unwilling to turn back.

They soon were upon the peak. Anxiety gripped their hearts tight as the soft ambience of warfare settled into their young ears. They knew it was looking grim, now. Whatever lay beyond the crest would undoubtedly leave them forever changed, yet to go back now would be to deny themselves the horrible truth.

And so, they continued in their ascension to behold that truth for themselves.

Upon that peak, the delusional invincibility derived from the shroud of youth dissipated in its entirety as the world fell out from beneath their feet and a new one opened up before them in a breathtaking panoramic view of sheer desolation.

Their hearts twitched at the sight of the cataclysm. The distant highway guided young, awestruck eyes to the capital in flames, the once bold skyline battered, ravaged, and spared only ruinous humiliation. Though gruesome detail was left inconspicuous by sheer distance, the visions in their heads haunted them with the missing images of misfortune.

Most terrifying of all, however, was the colossal invader warship that loomed above in the stars. A final anomaly to lay the old world to rest.

Miyacre crumbled away from the brink as she sought to escape the vision of change before them. She could feel the future she had promised herself slip between her fingers like the ashes of the historic capital into the winds of calamity. It was leaving, and she knew she wouldn't be able to get it back. That hard-forged destiny had been denied to her, and she wasn't able to hold back the tears.

"Lyal!? What is that thing!?"

"Miyacre!" She stumbled back, and Lyal caught her, then pulled her close. "Miyacre—you're going to be alright, okay? Okay!?"

She trembled so badly that she couldn't find the stability to speak. Lyal held her by the cheek so that he could see her eyes. "We're going to be alright, remember?"

But she had become blank, something within corrupted and totally erased. "I want to go home, Lyal. Can we just go home?" she asked with vacant eyes, her spirit lost in free fall.

"We're going home," he assured in hopes to quell fast her restless heart. "We have to warn everyone of what we saw today. That's what we came here to do. So, let's go."

She nodded, only able to grasp his concession, the thought of being home again the last string to hold her from the darkest oblivion. With his arm wrapped around her shoulder, he guided her toward the bottom.

"Let's go," he repeated.

As they shuffled, he turned one last time to the starship and caught glimpse of a particle in descent from outer space. His eyes lingered on it as it became still.

Lyal focused on the glimmer, and then his eyes grew wide.

The object had not come to a halt but instead shot right for them.

He turned and hurried Miyacre down the road.

"What's going on?"

"You'll be alright," he reassured her, even as the thunderous roar grew behind them.

"What's happening, Lyal? Lyal!?"

"Just listen—"

A burst stream of displaced air sent them stumbling for balance as a cylindrical craft shot overhead, agleam in a bizarre whirling illumination as it darted off into the night.

Miyacre fell to the ground with her hands cupped over her face, desperate to shield her eyes from madness. Lyal fought to lift her back to her feet.

"You can't give up. Just trust me and stand up. We'll get through this, just like I promised."

"I need your help, Lyal. I just want you to help me, right now," she sobbed.

"And I need you to help me. Get up so you can help me warn everyone to get to safety. That's what you want to do, right? You want to help people. I need you to stand up so we can go do that."

She took in a few breaths, then inched to her feet. "Okay—okay."

"You can do this—we're doing it together."

"Okay—"

With gathered stability, they began down the road once more with renewed vitality. There was no sign of the craft, but they remained wary.

"Lyal!"

"Lyal, Miyacre! Did you guys see that thing?"

They searched the road and found Kaiser behind a parked pickup truck with both arms flailing in an attempt to gain their attention. The others crouched behind him, a reluctant Ashe noticeably distant from the pack.

"Get your hands down, man," Lyal shouted back. "Didn't you see that thing!?"

"Dude, it's gone. It *took off* straight off back the way we came," he informed with the jab of his finger. "That thing was like, doing sonic speed or something."

"Might be a good idea to just start knocking on doors," cried Mitz.

"For what? Isn't there a *war* right over that hill? What do you think will happen if we stay?" Setz reasoned.

Just as Lyal opened his mouth to deliver news of the unimaginable invasion, the wind was taken from him. From the dark sky, the crude, geometric craft reappeared in a meteoric plummet and slowed to an instant crawl above the road, which left Lyal and Miyacre parted from the others.

A gale swept through and knocked Miyacre into Lyal's arms as the anomalous craft descended and graced the dreary landscape, with the somnolent glow of its ten-thousand-glyph scripture. Malleable Destiny.

The hectic whirl of those sapphire, carved glyphs relaxed into a gentle glide. They floated just beyond the surface of the craft's smooth, obsidian body, cut into seven slabs that gyrated in independence.

Miyacre and Lyal stood paralyzed in the starlight aura of that arcane flier, she with her head on his shoulder and he with a steady glare set upon the star-born monolith.

A hundred tiny, crimson rays beamed out from apertures in the miracle matter. The plates snapped back into a whirlwind, and the ethereal rays hunted the area. With each pass, they adjusted their angle until they found the dumbfounded faces of its paralyzed spectators.

Each of them was identified by the craft, but as the plates crawled back to a halt, every beam fell solely upon Miyacre and Lyal.

The thousand laser points crawled across their entireties and left them unsure as to what it might do. Lyal glared at the machine that threatened them, sure he wouldn't fall without a fight no matter what it was that stood before them.

"Whoa, Lyal—get outta there, man! That thing has it out for you guys," Kaiser shouted.

The craft lifted before they could make a move, however, and just as it seemed likely that it might simply depart, the monolith slammed into the ground with the thunderous peal of cracked asphalt.

Lyal and Miyacre stumbled from the impact as the craft raised back up. Without remorse, the invader hammer slammed back into the earth again, and unleashed vibrations deep throughout the otherworld.

Lyal hesitated to act, impaired by the arcane summoning that occurred before his eyes.

"Now would be a great time to run, guys!" cried Mitz.

Lyal's eyes grew as he was spurred by the words of his frantic friend. He seized Miyacre by the arm and guided her around as the craft rose once more and delivered abyssal resonance into the ground.

Setz met them on the other side, his eyes alight with the fire to survive. Together with Lyal, he guided Miyacre away, toward the truck where the others awaited.

"Come on, you guys! Let's get the hell out of here!" cried Kaiser as he came out from behind the pickup to meet them.

The three friends stepped off into full flight but were abruptly taken off their feet by a colossal gut punch in the earth. It deafened them as they were thrown forward onto the ground and left to scramble away. Mitz and Kaiser rushed to their aid while Ashe remained rooted behind the pickup, left in complete disbelief by what she saw half-emerged from the ground.

The whirling plates of the monolith slammed to a stop, one after another. When the obscure process had concluded, the craft crept upwards, then shot up into the clouds as the lights exploded into celestial brilliance.

Mitz and Kaiser aided their friends to their feet just as the ground ruptured. At once, they turned to greet the monstrosity that had risen from the darkest of all depths. The discordant symphony of hydraulics sent chills up their spines as they peered at the moonlike apertures beneath the hood of the exposed observation deck.

The invoked tower forced itself out from the ground and into a slow ascension, just beneath its cryptic summoner.

"What in the . . . hell is *that?*" Kaiser shuddered.

Setz and Mitz stood in silence, their mouths agape in unflinching terror. With Miyacre cradled in his arms, Lyal held strong. He fought to keep that image of courage so that he might instill his friends with the same apparent caliber of strength, even if it was a lie.

What fate awaited them beyond that day, he didn't know, and perhaps not a soul in the world did.

Lyal turned over his shoulder and found Ashe in a preemptive rout down the sidewalk, his last glimpse of her a fading flicker of blonde into the deep curtain of the night. Confident that it was best for her to escape to safety, he kept her departure to himself, then turned back to face the rising terror, knowing he had to act if he hoped for the others to do the same.

"You're going to be alright," he swore as he moved Miyacre's trembling hand from his thumping chest.

Lyal stepped out with one foot, and then the other. With a forced courage, he parted with her to stand alone before the machine from the otherworld as it rose high against the majesty of outer space and the imperial fleet from beyond the stars.

"Lyal!" she cried as he pulled away from her grasp.

The boy looked up into the eyes of the machine that gazed back down unto him. He felt a shiver deep within but couldn't stop his feet. As he stood there out in front of his friends, the tower released a sharp whine that escalated into a deafening roar—a terrible sound that ripped through his enfeebled spirit. Though he tried to stand resolute for his friends, his hands began to tremble, and as the dread siren unleashed the peak of its terror spectacle, he felt a tear roll down his cheek. Before that dread machine, he could only be a child.

There came a spirit-raising interjection to the grim dirge. Jet engines broke the menacing chord, and a glorious spark carved into the night. It exploded into the neck of the tower, and the resulting shockwave flung the imperiled back across the asphalt.

They scrambled to their feet as shards of superheated metal broke away from the monstrosity and burst into sparks upon the ground. Lyal felt himself yanked up by the jacket and pulled away just as a second missile struck the observation deck.

The machine's right eye flickered to darkness as its siren wound down in blaring system failure. From above, two fighter jets shot along the hillside and disappeared over the darkened suburbia, their first striking pass a crucial success. Under new threat, the strange monolith raised high, then shot back into outer space as the tower jolted repeatedly, unable to reach its peak—effectively disabled.

"That's gotta be our guys," Kaiser rallied as he aided Setz in steadying their disoriented friend back on his feet, Miyacre beside him.

"No doubt about it," Setz reassured.

The inspirited band looked up to the one-eyed oppressor one last time before a third missile struck and severed the neck. The second eye went dark as the weight of gravity took hold of the liberated structure. It tipped forward with an eerie groan, and at once, their hearts were injected with instant adrenaline.

They fled the burning carcass as its last support succumbed with a snap. There, at the edge of the shadow of death, they dove forward just as the odd colossus slammed into the road and unleashed shards of metal and fragments of forbidden technology all across the road. With that thunderous finale, their encounter with madness was over, though none of them believed it would be their last.

Lyal leapt to his feet and came aglow in the spectacular aftermath. "We're okay—you see that, Miyacre? What'd I tell you?" Lyal said with a heart reconquered by hope.

Miyacre kept her head down, however. She said nothing.

Lyal knelt down to her and shook her by the shoulders. "Miyacre, it's gone. We gotta move now. Come on."

She nodded frantically and, in compliance with his determined request, rose to her feet. Setz, Kaiser, and Mitz had all gathered at the tower's impact zone and scrutinized the outlandish wreckage with solemn stares.

"Man, that was one weird tower thing . . ." Kaiser remarked.

". . . That's definitely not Beilkan," Setz added.

"Then, what is it?" asked Mitz.

Before they could speculate, there came another military jet, which screamed over the street and descended in hover.

Miyacre recoiled in fear, but Lyal pulled her back toward him. He tried to comfort her, but she could no longer hear him. She kept her eyes closed so she couldn't see it. Whatever machine of war it was, she hated it.

She couldn't bear the sound, and the only thing that drove her toward it was the guidance of his hands. She laid all the trust she had in them, even as every fiber of her spirit sought to crumble.

Setz and the others fled for the jet, which drove them back in its downward draft. They flailed their arms at the aircraft in a desperate effort to gain the pilot's attention.

The jet turned away, however, and rose into the darkness. They gazed upon their sole savior as a white light gleamed from the underbelly and pierced the darkness in quick flashes. After that moment of silent communication, the plane yawed toward the north and took off beyond the hilltop.

"They're not gonna just leave us, right?" Kaiser worried.

"Just have a little patience," Setz replied with a confident deduction from the communication that had just been performed.

Not long after the jet had departed, another Union craft arrived. The bulky armored transport descended to the ground on a slight wobble. Its wide bay doors opened, and the soldiers inside beckoned to them with urgency.

"Come on, guys. Let's go," Setz urged as he led Mitz and Kaiser to the ship.

The boys boarded with the help of the troops as Lyal and Miyacre followed close behind. The soldiers reached out to receive her and pulled her aboard. Lyal was hoisted up behind her, with Kaiser pulling at his jacket to assist.

Setz screamed something, but Lyal couldn't quite hear it. He looked all around the chaotic scene as the craft lifted back into the air. The boys were being put into seats, and Miyacre was being tended to by a medic.

Perhaps it was the shock. Time began to skip as his mind melted into a blur of a broken reality, and instant images of the past became all that he could see. So, he closed his eyes, somehow at peace now, and imagined flying through the air, spiraling in the darkness. It was a feeling of weightlessness, like something of feathers in the wind. Lyal felt himself forced into a chair, and in the next moment, his consciousness slipped entirely into the darkness.

Breaking Point

At the makeshift camp, the remaining soldiers of the crumbled republic were gathered along the blasted road in file. The officers gave those battered battalions the order to march, and the camp soon bustled with their advance.

Schneider and Rhodes, headed by General Henson, stood in salute at the intersection of the northbound road atop a pedestal built of stacked supply crates. The ghastly look of uncertainty was visible among each and every one of them, the outcome of their endeavor far from the reach of vision.

From the emptied command tent appeared Prime Minister Roland escorted by two stone-faced and well-equipped guards. He trod on careful steps through the trampled ground on a path toward General Myres, who stood watch over the assembly of amassed civilians at the far end of the park. It was a staggering congregation, one whose numbers reached deep into the streets and alleys and left the seasoned general quite overwhelmed with worries, much more of them than he'd ever wished to admit.

"How goes the retreat, General?" the prime minister asked, then settled into a faint smile—gentle, but radiant.

Myres grimaced. "Absolute hell," he promptly admitted, unwilling to compromise his honesty. "But nearly set to move. We're getting civilians on the same page as us—it's just taking more time than promised. It's gotta be done soon. Shoulda been done a lot earlier."

Myres's gaze deepened. He rubbed his chin as recent tragedies weighed heavy on his conscience, and his imagination struggled to build reasonable scenarios from which he could derive sense.

"We bounced from building to building in an attempt to set up resistance headquarters, but—those soldiers—they come out of nowhere. We set up safe houses—but, in not just a few instances, the people we put behind guarded doors, they weren't there when we opened those doors back up. Lost a handful of senators from that alone . . . So, we just stood outside in this park like we got evicted from our own city . . . Our best bet is to get out as soon as possible. We've got to regroup and get a grasp on what's happening here."

"We also can't afford to rush, General. I know you and I both understand the weight we carry here tonight and into the very near and, heaven forbid, the distant future."

"I think it's safe to say these scars won't ever heal. The capitol of the Union is in shambles. Over five hundred years of stability laid to ruin in one night," Myres lamented as he shook his head.

"Have faith, Myres. The government we serve is nothing more than ideals—ideals that we cultivate within ourselves and others. Cities are monuments to our success and our prosperity. The Union, however, is never gone as long as we continue to stand for what it represents. Every sacrifice made before our time in the name of this nation was in the hope that when it was our turn to serve, we would rise to the occasion; so, when the invaders came from another world and the stars fell, we would stand in resistance.

"And just look here—" he continued with the cast of his finger to the road where a soldier raised the Union banner high over the army's courageous forward march. "The brightest beacon of this nation isn't in flags or monuments. It's in the hearts of the people who stand together beneath them."

Myres nodded in reverence to those shared beliefs, then turned his eyes to the invader warship high above. "Absolutely. I couldn't agree more—but that still leaves a very big question as to how we're supposed to fight back."

Silence settled upon the general. His eyes fell from the starry heavens to find that the prime minister had stepped away. The guards departed behind him as he made his way from the park grounds toward the street side where the dispirited masses were gathered.

There upon the sidewalk was a shaken young mother and a little boy, wrapped in the safety of her arms. She heaved back in fear as her grip on the child strengthened, leery of his presence.

The prime minister offered a bow before he engaged with the woman in lighthearted banter. Myres stepped off, lured by his mystique and a desire to hear what it was he had to say.

"Don't worry. We're going to take care of all this, ma'am—isn't that right, General?" he asked without even having seen him.

Myres stumbled to an attentive halt. "Yes ma'am—we'll get it under control. Trust me, we're doing everything possible . . . There's a light at the end of the tunnel—and we're all gonna find it, together."

The Union leader fell down to his knee and looked at the child, who nestled against his mother's breast to hide from his eyes.

"You be strong for your momma, okay? And whatever you do, don't lose the hope inside your heart," he inspired with a jab toward the boy's chest.

The boy returned to him a silent glare.

"How about that? Can you do it, champ?"

And the boy nodded and took up the responsibility bestowed upon him. His mother relinquished a gentle smile, then thanked him. The prime minister rose and turned to his guards. "Why don't you two find someone who might be able to fill these good people in on what's going on here? Myres—let's go and have a quick chat," he said with the beckon of his finger before stepping off in a return course for the tent.

"Yes, sir," Myres blurted, as he fumbled over rubble to catch up. "You seem—oddly full of optimism, sir," the general remarked upon arrival at his side.

"Now is the time to pave a steady way forward, Myres. It would be all too easy to be crumbled together in fear and hopelessness. Just as in the times of The Great Beilkan War, or our own Titan War, we should be keen to keep up our collective spirit and face the darkness ahead with nurtured confidence."

"Aren't you looking at all this around you? We must not be seeing the same things," Myres replied.

"I am. I see a night of heroes, General . . . and if you look hard, I know you will see it, too. Without a doubt, it is a moment in which our mettle and vision will be tested. Nothing more and nothing less in the grandest scheme of it all."

They arrived back at the command tent with Myres entrenched in thought. A distressed officer fled for them as soon as he found them; behind him in the hospital tent, a crumple-faced soldier sat upon the ground as a medic tended to a sprained ankle.

"General Myres, there's been a development on the front line."

"What is it, soldier?" he inquired.

"The invader commander has driven into Uptown. The eastern defensive line took a hell of a beating, and they've been pushed back. They're requesting orders, sir. If the line breaks apart . . ."

There came a hellish, gut-wrenching discordance from the skies to the east that commanded their collective attention and all but verified the danger that encroached upon them. The wild screech of a thousand rockets and their calamitous impact upon their sacred city left an ominous air of unease among the resistors.

"Then our escape route will be lost," the general acknowledged. "Son of a bitch—I'll go meet with the other high command. Prime Minister, you coming along for this?"

The prime minister, however, had stepped away to the injured soldier now held on his feet by the medic and a staff sergeant.

"Go—have your meeting, Myres. I will stand aside this time. Please, act as my surrogate and report to me your plans when you have finished," the prime minister ordered as he laid his hand upon the soldier's shoulder.

Myres watched as the prime minister bowed his head in prayer, and then, in acceptance of his request, turned to the officer who awaited his command. "Alright—let's get down to business. Go and retrieve my high command from the podium. I need everyone for this."

"Yes, sir," the officer responded.

Propelled by the winds of urgency, in a mere matter of minutes, the high command was assembled. Within the tent, Myres stood at the head of the table, which now lay barren. Schneider, Rhodes, and three other officers of stature stood around and digested his expeditiously constructed plan.

"So, we just ditch 'em then?" asked Schneider, who leaned against the table and folded his arms.

"I don't see much of an alternative. Moving the route throws us into an even worse predicament . . . an indefinite amount of energy expended to clear a new path . . . that's a recipe for a recurring nightmare."

"You think they have the firepower to bring down those buildings?" asked Rhodes.

"The buster rockets on those fighters should be able to pull the rug right out from under the Norman and Lockheart buildings, which are already in bad shape as it is. Pilots should be landing soon to make interval check-in. I'll give them the order to hit the buildings and ditch the planes somewhere along the route."

"Seems like a waste, General. We'll be blind in the sky if we commit to this plan," criticized one of the officers.

"Without functional comms and with Neo Cascadia one hundred and thirty-two miles away, we lack the means to maintain the aircraft, and they don't have enough fuel to make it to Bortner Airfield. That's not even mentioning the fact that we have no idea what the situation is in Neo Cascadia. For all we know, it's just as bad there as it is here at the capital."

Schneider released a long sigh as it seemed once more they were stripped of options in the matter. "Well, I suppose we're without a choice," he admitted.

"Then, let's get to it. The collapse of Norman and Lockheart will cut off the enemy advance . . . but I'm gonna guess not for long," Myres said.

The general scanned the uncertainty in each of his subordinates. "We're at the brink of a new world, ladies and gentlemen, and we've got a lot to learn about it," he said.

He took from his pocket the invader communication device, then threw it on the table to resounding silence. "But, I believe in every one of us here to do what needs to be done, even in the face of impossibility. We've got the whole country counting on us to do just that. So, let's take it on with finesse: mind, body, and soul."

"Invader tech—" One of the officers gawked.

"Controlled, from what I'm told, by a process of a much more . . . incorporeal nature than simple inputs by hand." The general sighed in his reluctance to confess the suspected truth. "If what Sergeant Sky said is true, then these invaders might be something beyond flesh and blood—or, at the very least, operate in ways that are far beyond our comprehension . . . for the time being," he assured them.

With the weight of malleable destiny heavy and their leadership beneath the gaze of endless eyes, the members of the Union high command gave a slow nod as the device struggled to life in the ghostly flicker of glyphs.

The high command was then dismissed to deliver word of the impending strike and subsequent critical drive. When they had gone, Myres retrieved the device, stepped out of the tent, then ordered the surrounding guard to pack up the remainder of the camp. As they went to work, Myres scanned around for the prime minister, who was noticeably absent from the immediate area.

On the eastern outskirts of the park, however, he caught sight of a congregated force of fourteen soldiers, who each geared up with body armor and munitions from an opened supply crate. The prime minister stood at the center of the somber squad and engaged them as one with vigorous gesticulation to ready their hearts for immortalizing valor.

Myres set off with haste to meet them, worried by their sudden assembly. "And where the hell do you think you're going, sir?"

The prime minister turned and disarmed him with a chuckle and a resilient beam. "I think it's time! Time to serve, Myres. I caught a bit of that meeting . . . and we can't continue to act as a civilization without dignity. People need leaders to lead, and there is no greater time."

Myres stepped forward to his unflinching commander in chief, dumbfounded by his words. "What in the world are you saying? What's the big plan I don't know about?"

"Don't you remember what you always used to joke about—back when I was just a young senator, and you were considering early retirement? That the government's a clumsy mess of a thousand puppeteers who can't agree on where to step? That it provided more frustration than all the years of raising two children that were bound and determined to outperform the other? But like those frustrations, it was a necessary process and, in the end, was fundamental to our sacred union. You believe in the voice we've cherished so dearly since the days our people stood resolute against Beilkan conquerors in blinding armor."

The prime minister laid his hand on the general's shoulder and smiled.

"You'll make a fine leader, Myres, I'm sure of it . . . If by chance there's a sliver of decency in these invaders, then the Union must try to force dialogue—before it's too late. I'm sure the Beilkan king would do no different, for he reveres his people more than his own holiness."

The prime minister flipped open the chamber of his revolver and loaded in the last rounds. "I'll take my personal guard, and we'll head en route to intercept the commander of these invaders."

"You're going to need an army to break through their advance. If this is what your plan is, we can provide one hell of an escort."

The prime minster shook his head in disappointment. "So, you'd rather send soldiers to protect one man rather than get as many people as you can to safety?"

The general stalled as the shame inflicted pierced true.

"Myres, the time is gone for Salamandra, but this doesn't have to be the end of us all. If I am still your prime minister, you will do as I ask." He slammed the chamber shut. "This is the time for heroes, Myres."

The general took a breath to hold back his frustrations. "You're absolutely right, sir. If this is what you feel you must do, then I won't stop you."

The prime minister nodded to his bittersweet victory. He turned and faced the misted unknown with necessary fearlessness.

"Sir . . . We have an airstrike that's going to hit the Norman and the Lockheart in Uptown. Within the hour. Plan is to bring them down on the road, so steer clear of Thirty-Eighth and Albright," the general warned.

"Understood, General . . . I'll either be remembered a fool, a brave man, or a politician very dedicated to his reelection campaign," he remarked through a smirk, humoring him.

Myres confessed his concordance with a stifled laugh, "You ain't kidding."

"Keep an eye on Schneider for me, would you? If I return, I'll be the first to take us out for a fine drink to burn up a cool night. We'll line kegs and live venues up and down Main Street, as far as the eye can see and—I think everyone will have a good time. If there is no ceasefire, however, then you should assume the absolute worst of their intentions and must proceed accordingly."

The statesman turned over his shoulder to his duty-shackled general. "So, steal me back that tomorrow, friend," he concluded with a wink.

Myres couldn't help but shake his head as their commander in chief stepped out and surrendered himself to the grasp of the unknown.

The prime minister led his brave expedition into Salamandra's miserable wastes on unfaltering steps. Within a few moments, they became silhouettes beyond the ghostly curtain, and in the next, gone; lost beyond the veil in pursuit of oblivion's fallen angel.

Schneider, no longer able to watch from afar, came down from his vantage atop the crumbled park wall and went to Myres, who remained haunted in stillness.

"It would do us a great service to keep this secret from the survivors," he said in lieu of greeting the downcast general.

"No—no, as a matter of fact, we're going to tell every last one of them what happened, seeing if we make it out of this city in some semblance of order."

"The prime minister's survival was a great asset. If people learn he's gone—"

Myres snapped to Schneider, ignited to sudden rage by his shameless surveillance and opportunistic disposition. "You are under my command and will adhere to my instruction, Lieutenant. Now, get back to your soldiers and get them to the highway."

Myres threw out his finger, done with presumptuous tactical discourse. "Dismissed."

Schneider saluted him with an undisguised glare, turned, then departed to fulfill the urgent task. Two soldiers passed him on their way over to the general. Myres noticed them right away and made quick to wipe the last sadness from his face.

"Sir, troops are in position to cross into Sherille. Planes are circling," reported one of the soldiers upon salute.

"Then the operation is a go. Inform the defenders. We're moving that caravan out," Myres ordered.

The soldiers stormed off with the message, and Myres started down the road toward Sherille, his head lowered in reflection. He tried to envision a future burdened with that void, and the man he would have to become to fill it. The task was too great, however, and he had to leave it behind to be pondered another time. With the enemy closing in, there was little time to meander in such transformative thought, though he knew eventually it would need to be confronted.

Further up the road, Schneider passed along broken rubble to assume his position, his head lowered as he brooded. On the cusp of such a dramatic event, the general, in his eyes, threatened to throw their effort into irreversible chaos. That reckless transparency was a clear disregard of the duties entrusted to his revered superior, and it was duty alone that kept him from voicing such grave concern. A bitter truth that brought the reprimanded lieutenant much discomfort.

On the wayside not far ahead, he caught sight of Gruman, huddled in the shadows with his accomplices, Lakker and Vekner, who engaged in strict whispers by a blocked alley. As Schneider approached, the former stuck to him with a toplofty stare while the latter harassed with a messy grin. The stormy lieutenant paid them no heed and continued along the road that would lead him to the rally point and his soldiers, fixated on the success of their humiliating retreat.

Gruman dismissed the hawks with a wave, pulled his ebon coat taut, then hobbled over with casual innocence.

"So, what has become of the prime minister, my friend?" the grim-faced official inquired upon arrival to his unruly subordinate.

Schneider did not slow pace. "He has gone to meet the enemy in hopes of negotiation. What a lunatic. It's the kind of mindset that could lead this broken nation to absolute ruin."

Gruman shook his head in play to his evident frustration. "What a shame. What should comfort you is that you are proactive in a change that will bring great revision to this inadequate world order."

"Soon, everyone will know of the prime minister's departure. Once that is done, there's no telling how many will desert—or worse."

Gruman reached out and took Schneider by the shoulder, then pulled him to a halt. Boiled over, Schneider turned to the forceful puppeteer with vivid rage in his eyes.

"Schneider, I am active in keeping this world's greater interests at the highest priority . . . even now. This event is a tragedy, yes—a setback, but we must continue on the path to righteousness. With that mindset, the prime minister has merely taken a step for us."

Gruman raised a finger and tapped himself on the forehead. "Don't forget."

Schneider lingered, unsure of what to say but far from pleased by these radical insinuations at such a fragile time. "My only concern right now is making sure we survive this war. I can only hope we do it the most effective way possible." He turned and left Gruman with these words, eager to return to his post, away from further talk of an unforeseeable future.

"A dire mistake, Schneider," the relentless kingpin called after him.

Schneider offered it no further attention, however, and as he walked, he sought to clear his head of Gruman's divisiveness. Further along the winding road, his incipient clarity came under pressure by a peculiar discomfort. He tried at first to shake it, but even his greatest concentration couldn't relieve him of its grasp.

In search of a culprit, he peered off to the side of the road and caught sight of a disturbing anomaly that forced him to slow pace. It was the lone swordsman, who glared back at him from further up the bend. The reticent invader held in a discomforting stillness, his hand upon the hilt of his blade, as if ready to strike from over fifty feet away.

Schneider turned to face the silent observer, then took the grip of his pistol. His grimace deepened as he prepared to draw on the invader, surely no different than the rest: spiritless murderers.

"Stand down. Take your hand off the blade," ordered Schneider, to no avail.

The swordsman remained motionless.

The marching soldiers stopped to watch the confrontation. Some drew up their weapons and set their sights on the lieutenant's defiant foe, and the movement of troops soon came to a standstill.

"I said off it. You want to stay here—on this world!? Then, you're going to learn to follow commands." Having lost his patience, Schneider pulled the pistol from the holster, prepared to open fire. "I'm going to blow that blue hair right off your head, you son of a bitch," he hollered.

"Schneider, lower that weapon," barked a voice from afar.

It was Myres. He surged over with terrible force, drove the gun down, and got right into the flustered lieutenant's red face.

"I'm asking you not to screw everything up for just a second, Schneider. Can you do that?" Myres bellowed.

"You have an invader with his hand on his blade. What happens when he snaps and decides to go back to what's natural for him, and one of us has to pay for your decisions?"

Myres released him. "Then you can go."

"What—"

"I said you can either go, or you can fulfill the duty you swore to uphold. The choice is yours."

Schneider raised his chin and scowled.

"Do not let your ego get in the way of this operation, or you will no longer be a part of it." Myres stepped forward to drive the barbs deeper. "This is the last time we're having this conversation," the general vowed, then departed down the street with a commanding shout to his soldiers to continue their vital march.

Schneider turned back to where the swordsman had stood, but he had gone. In a brief search, he encountered Gruman nearby, who shook his head in a glaze of disappointment, then turned to regroup with his accomplices, who shared a silent smirk.

Humiliated yet tenacious still, the lieutenant shoved the gun back into its holster, then continued after Myres. He wouldn't trust the swordsman so easily, and his act of passive aggression wouldn't be forgotten.

But why was it that the swordsman looked so long into him?

Could it be that he had overheard something from that intimate conversation with the reckless dominus? But even then, there was nothing explained in any detail. Surely not a word of it would draw suspicion when his guidance went wrapped in such elusive suggestion.

Schneider recalled the conversation over and over again, in search of a word or phrase that rang harshly. Nothing came to mind that incriminated him, and though Myres clearly had placed some sort of trust in the swordsman, there was no chance, in his mind, that the general would favor an invader over a fellow soldier in arms. His confidence grew strong, as did a resentment toward the swordsman, alongside a deepening fear of his obscure capabilities.

***

Hours passed as the Union troops carved through the escape route. The airstrike was executed sometime between, and the targeted skyscrapers were toppled with less effort than anticipated. This boon left the last squadron airborne and available for invaluable support missions, which occurred sporadically along the course of their retreat.

With light resistance from troopers from the roadside ruin, the majority of the gathered masses neared a bloat in their numbers toward the edges of downtown.

At the bridge of the burb of Sherille, there was a fierce firefight that needed to be resolved. The invader troopers laid down a stream of fire from across the road that blocked all access to the highway.

Far behind the lines, Myres approached Brigadier Rhodes as she instructed a few squads of fresh soldiers, who acknowledged her command with a salute before they broke for the front line.

"Rhodes, we need to get this caravan moving. What's the situation?"

She turned and saluted her sudden superior. "General—we hit a patch of resistance on the intersection. They had a large, armored vehicle, but it ignored us and headed right for Uptown. Guess that was a stroke of good luck."

"Uptown—that's the same district their commander's drop ship came down in," Myres recalled.

"Could be that they're grouping up on his position . . . There's other good news, sir. It seems General Gala and his Beilkan force made it. They're a few roads down, fighting through the same resistance, but if we make it through, we'll make it through together."

"He made it then, huh . . . Then, this'll be our best opportunity to blow past these stragglers. I know we wanted to save some ammunition for the journey, but blow that entire road if you have to. We aren't going to need it for a while anyway."

"Understood, General. Hang tight. I'll relay the message to General Henson that we're turning up the heat."

She parted from him to get his order through the pipeline.

"Now, where's that damn kid at?" Myres asked himself upon her hasty departure.

Myres searched the area for the swordsman, who had vanished from sight since his muted confrontation.

He heard a stomp behind him, then turned to find just who he was looking for as if the very thought alone had evoked him.

"Don't sneak up on me like that," Myres ordered with the jab of his finger. "I'll save the reprimanding for another time when we're not trading shots with the enemy. Right now, I need you to get in there and mop up whatever's left squirming after this strike."

The swordsman nodded.

"Good. Plain and simple. I like it," the general praised.

A sudden rumble took him by surprise. Myres put his hand to his heart as his body became subjected to a fierce tremble. All around, pebbles and small debris bounced in a frantic dance as the earth rattled. "Damnit, what is it, now!?"

Ultra looked up, and so followed Myres. High above, the celestial colossus, which had laid siege to the capital, had begun its grand ascension. From the thrusters came glorious fire as the cruiser's engines gained strength. The quake reached its tumultuous climax as they ignited into full power but subsided as the craft reached into outer space. With the spectacle's conclusion, a few sporadic shots from the front line returned to flurries and then endless barrages.

"Guess the day tour was enough, eh?" Myres bellowed. "We aren't getting a better shot than this. When we hit them with the big guns, get in there."

With his orders, the swordsman turned and departed for the battlefield. From the sky came a last gift from their unexpected aide. The final squadron screamed through the metropolitan ravine as they made straight for the brutal front line. As they passed, they released a final flurry of rockets that swept through the sky and ignited the far side of the road in a grand fireball.

The shockwave from the red-comet assault sent the allied force in a collective dive for cover. Rock and asphalt fragments rained down from above as the jets passed over, cut away, then disappeared behind the skyline.

Myres, electrified by the triumphant surgical strike, chased after the planes just before they vanished. "Well, hell, guess they had a lot more left in 'em than I thought . . . Another stroke of luck, eh?" he reflected aloud.

Ultra picked up into a lightning sprint, then struck forward into the cloud of dust. The Union soldiers inched up from cover to assess the fiery aftermath and found the drifting shroud alive with the blitz of gunfire and fatal cuts.

With bravery, they engaged the invaders within the curtain to carve out a path for their flight from home. Together with the Beilkan detachment, the Union Army led their desperate charge through the eroded invasion force. From the military web of communication, messages of the abandonment of the capital and loss of the prime minister were delivered on fleet foot.

A congregation the likes of which none had ever witnessed began to take shape. It was one that signified a recognition of the old world's death as the masses left ruin behind, where pride once stood tall in the clouds. Liberty's beacon had been extinguished in a single night, and forward was all that was left.

Home burned upon a horizon left behind at the rosy brink, and soon it would pass into collective memory. All those who emerged with something missing shed good-night tears to yesterday's golden lights.

Upon the next dawn, a hundred thousand footsteps would cross a land liberated from their jurisdiction. The Beilkan Supreme Commander, Gala, and the Union's political remnants would forge a pact together. All that lay beyond tomorrow they would face together as one.

The survivors would begin a pilgrimage toward fate itself, on a journey to find others. Though spared from annihilation, endless steps gave rise to insatiable wonder of the sheer vastness that had become the unknown. Just what had come from beyond the stars? Somewhere among them had lurked the legions of absurdity that came and laid siege to the principals of existence and stripped their world of reason.

The world beyond home seemed empty, like the innermost recesses of their sacred hearts. All they could yearn for lay somewhere behind them, through time and through space, while all that lay before them was the abyss.

Legend of a City in the Sky

Hours had passed since they had lost sight of Salamandra City's crushed skyline, but a vermillion halo across the dark sky served as a reminder of what had been left behind. The rural backroads had delivered them to a lonely carriageway, which bounded across the hilly suburban outskirts. It was a quiet passage, dashed through by landscaped median strips adorned with perfectly square, trimmed bushes and evenly spaced, stone-skirted trees.

Eddie followed his whimsical companion beneath the spotlights of the arched streetlights. She leapt atop the raised concrete curb and traced it until she dropped down onto a yellow line. It had brought her before an intersection where two hanging traffic signals awaited in eternal green, still as the ever-watching moon.

A road split off to the left. Flanked by a plot of tall grass, it rose on a gentle slope and disappeared over the grassy peak. On the other end, however, was rail-guarded forest and an overgrown dell in between.

The girl stopped at the intersection and waited, alert as a wild fox. There came a sound from up the road, farther than the eye could see, a muffled boom. They saw it come. The unleashed force whipped through the trees and tall grass before striking up the traffic lights. Eddie drove through the gale until he was there beside her, then glanced over at that headstrong pathfinder.

Even in the face of such a terrible force, her smile only grew. In fact, she seemed gripped in a strange state of euphoria. He didn't know what to make of her clear disconnect from the danger, though it exuded an unmistakable allure.

Perhaps it was the look in her eye, one of distinct amusement with the world, the kind that drove curiosity through his veins, into his heart, and all throughout his body. This was the way it was meant to feel. There was no better path, no greater experience, than being right there with the winds of adventure against their faces.

The gale soon diminished into a soothing waft that caused the trees to rustle in gentle whispers. Her eyes sharpened as she gazed into the dark abyss ahead that left the road swallowed in obscurity.

"The way forward is treacherous, but come with me, and I'll bring you to where we need to go."

Eddie looked, too, into the gloomy abyss. There was a dip, and beyond the distant rise was a flashing supercell. Another ferocious gale swept through and lashed the gazing wanderers, a grim reminder of its potent capability. Against its warning, however, his wayward accomplice kept on the darkened path forward. She crossed the intersection with sure steps and leapt to the subsequent median's curb, then passed beneath the next comforting glow, a midnight fantasy with hair adrift in the night.

Eddie followed behind, consumed by wonderings of where her steadfast guidance might take them and furthermore of her familiarity with nowhere's particular route. In the way she moved, it seemed as though she was without a worry, propelled without hinderance in a light-footed and graceful frolic.

In his whimsical mental tumble, he nearly passed her by. She had stopped once again, her fierce eyes fixated upon the storm. The boy slowed and took her side, then awaited some kind of direction or explanation. But she veered off to the right and made for a gap in the roadside guardrail and an opening through the tree line beyond it.

Although nearly hidden in darkness, the passage was faintly illuminated by paper lanterns of lambent cerulean and rose, which hung throughout a fanciful portal of curved branch that carved a fantastic hall through the bushy canopy of the wildwood. The only way forward was a path beaten through dirt, strewn with sticks, stones, and roots all the way to the unseen end.

"Are you coming?" she asked with cheerful allure.

Eddie nodded, then proceeded into nature's garnished arch. He felt the need to finally confront her with questions that had begun to plague him. He wasn't sure where they were going nor why they were going there and had merely followed in her footsteps as she pulled him along like a toy on unseen ethereal strings. A truth that came to badger him.

They began down the long dirt path until the breach behind them had nearly disappeared and the perilous winds were stifled by the mystic forest's impenetrable grasp. The nagging questions inside his head were quieted, too, as he caught sight of tiny glints of silver up in the trees. It was a phenomenon that he had never been witness to before, and as his gaze lingered upon those false stars, he nearly passed her by again.

With a jolt back to lucidity, his eyes fell to find her aglow in a pleasant beam. They had arrived in a small clearing, half circled by brush and riddled with sticks and pebbles.

"A-are we stopping here?" asked Eddie.

The girl nodded. "Just for a moment—to rest!" she assured.

Without need of being further convinced, Eddie sat upon the ground. He was taken aback when she sat down right in front of him, though he tried hard not to show it. She folded her legs and looked right into his eyes, the same way she had always done. He had hoped he would have gotten used to that piercing gaze by then, but he had not.

As if he were some kind of relic or a memory from the past, she became fixated on him with explicit fascination. Her glossy eyes never seemed to lose their dreaminess, those eyes that could never wake from unspoken fantasy.

They instilled in him a certain confidence that, although he knew not where their destination lay, he would follow with anticipation in his heart. Anticipation for the moment that the curtain would be pulled back and all the wondrous things that she saw beyond the reality might be there for all to behold. For perhaps, eyes that were forever lost in a dream could see with clarity all the things that had gone missing and all the time that had been lost.

"So—I should ask your name. Who are you? I don't think I've ever met someone like you," she crooned.

"Really? You haven't . . . ? My name's—Ed," he spat out. "And yourself?"

"Ed . . . Eddie!" she said with joyous glee.

He was thrown by this sudden adaptation and couldn't understand why she would prefer it.

"Yeah—Eddie. I'm Eddie," he conceded. "But—didn't you say my name before? At the city," he clarified.

She looked at him, blank and smiling. "No, I don't remember that. Do you?"

Eddie rubbed his head as he tried to recall it, but the more he tried, the hazier his memory became until it seemed easier to simply forget. "Yeah—I guess it was just a hard night. I don't even know how I managed to survive it, to be honest."

She leaned forward and captivated him again with her starstruck gaze. "You don't need to remember it. All we need is ahead of us, now," she insisted in soft celebration.

He nodded, taking what comfort he could from those spirited words. "What about you? What's your name?"

She snapped up straight, seemingly at a loss for words. "What do you think? How about you give me one? A special name, just between us."

Eddie cocked his head in bewilderment. "You want me to give you a name?"

"Uh-huh," she replied with excitement.

"That's just weird. Why don't you just tell me your real name?"

She froze for a moment. She seemed to ponder it over but arrived at concession. "It's Mirika—my friends call me Miri—you can, too," she replied.

Eddie nodded, aglow in that she considered him so. "Okay, Miri," he said. "But what about your friends? Where are they?"

"My friends are always here with me. I can see them when I close my eyes," she said in demonstration, with fingertips pressed against her temples.

His curiosity deepened. "What do you mean by that?" he inquired.

Somewhere within, however, he believed he understood what she meant, though he'd dare not say it in fear of what it might release. From the moment he had met her, there was something rather familiar about the innocent enchantress.

Yes, how dreamlike she was, those oddly glossed eyes, ethereal-like strands flung over shoulder, and her aura, perpetuated with fanciful remarks. Yet, something about her made perfect sense, though she seemed apt to speak through the filter of obscurity.

There was an internal struggle against a voice that called on the stability of reason, though the boy was compelled to disobedience. Perhaps it was because she numbed him, stole the need for reason, and left his enamored mind trapped within a realm without consequence.

"They're in my memories because they can't be here with me anymore. So, sometimes before—I would just close my eyes until I was sleeping." She reemerged to Eddie, aglow in a warm beam. "But, now—you're my friend, Little Eddie Bowitz. There's no need to dream all the time, now—right?"

"But don't you miss your friends? I mean—I'm happy to be your friend, but don't you miss them?"

She scrunched her face up as she took in the thought. "Well, I have one other friend with me!"

"Really? Where?" the boy asked.

Her hands came together before him with a piercing clap. His eyes focused on her fingers as he awaited the trick.

She parted her hands, and a silver gleam split between her fingers.

"Whoa!" the boy yelped as a ball of light whirled up into the air between them.

His whimsical companion rolled in a burst of laughter as she inspected the shock on his face. "Ha! You've never seen a fairy before, have you?"

"N-no, I haven't," said Eddie as he inched away from the excited silver sprite, who had taken an immediate interest in him.

Mirika folded her arms as she looked upon the boy's fading fear with a bold grin. "Sh'shami's like a little nightlight . . . and a friend since as long as I can remember! She can watch over us while we rest and help us find the way if need be."

Eddie settled into fascination with the girl's mythical pet, which all but verified her ties to the beyond. "Wow . . . Shashami . . . she's beautiful," the boy complimented as he inspected tenuous beams of light from its celestial body that seemed to expand and contract in a somewhat organic fashion.

"Not, *Sha-sha*-mi. Sh'shami. Shh-shami—got it?"

Eddie shrunk, embarrassed by his failure to pronounce the curious creature's name. "Uh—yeah. Sorry about that," he apologized to the lively fae, who bobbed once in acceptance, then zipped up into the trees, chasing away the darkness as she went.

Mirika sighed a breath of endearment, then beamed. "Just another star in the sky, isn't she?"

Eddie nodded to that fanciful sentiment. "Yeah . . . so—Mirika? Where are we going? Why did we come so far out here . . . to this forest?"

She glowed at his curiosity. "There's a great master, don't you know . . . who watches on high, from a moving star. It's a place far beyond the clouds. I know you'll find what you're looking for there, and I'll find what I'm looking for, too."

The boy grew still inside. He didn't know what to make of that bold answer. Was he so transparent to her that simply nothing could hide? Could it be that she somehow knew the content of his deepest prayers?

Those old, desperate pleas once cast up to the night sky, back in what seemed like forever ago.

"You do have a wish, don't you?" she pressed in a vie to break through.

And Eddie knew there was one, and the thought of fulfilling that singular wish sprung him into a cascading fantasy. One wish became many until a grand convergence transformed them into alternate realities. Potential gateways that offered idyllic redemptions for Jamal, the girl from the city, and perhaps a million others.

"What can he do? Can he do . . . anything?" the boy asked, baited by her whimsical tease.

"Life, death, time, and space." She lifted her finger in front of his nose. "Don't forget, okay?"

Eddie, a little shaken by this sudden request, nodded. "Okay, okay—I won't forget," he swore, without truly knowing what it was she meant, but because this was often the case, he simply did as she asked in trust that these words held vital importance.

A grin crept across her face as Eddie recounted the four elements on his fingers then made a fist to express his comprehension. "So, how can we find this—great master? And how do we get to a moving star?"

She put her finger to her lip and thought a moment. Her eyes opened wide as if a solution dawned upon her but then closed them back to scour the pilfered cosmos.

The boy observed her with mouth agape, heavy with anxiety, as he awaited a discovery. His curiosity flared up within. He wanted desperately to know what it was she was doing but couldn't spit out the words in time.

"I see it!" she yelped.

"What is it?" Eddie replied as he sprang up to his knees.

"A city in the sky," she revealed with fingers spread wide.

"A city? In the sky?" he echoed.

She nodded, ecstatic in her cosmic revelation.

Eddie fell back as he envisioned that extraordinary place somewhere among the clouds. "Are you really serious?"

"Of course I am!" she assured. "There's a city that can take us to the stars above, to the great master himself!"

The boy peered up to the glittery night sky, his mind wrapped in sheer amazement with the mere prospect of reaching through to some cosmic palace. Galvanized, he focused back on her with evoked energy. "Well . . . where do we find it?"

"Up to the north. It's hard to see right now, but I know I've seen it. I think it's hidden," she informed with an enthused nod.

"Why would it be hidden?" he asked.

"Because of your war, *of course*. So, we need to go and find it." She stood without waiting for her baffled companion's response. Eddie rose after her as she took to the path once again.

"There's a town ahead. Don't you know it?" she quizzed.

But Eddie knew of no such place. They were already far from anywhere he had ever journeyed to. He noticed a wooden sign by the wayside which read in bold, black lettering "The Jaava Path." Beneath was a map of the local area with a few lines that cut through here and there. There was no town marked anywhere upon it, however, and the nameless lines fanned out to the far corners of the map.

"Sorry, I don't. Are you from around here—or from that town?"

"I know it's the best way we can get there. You believe me, right . . . ?"

The enchantress set down the path at full speed without waiting for an answer, a relentless guide to the fabled metropolis. She reached down and snatched a sturdy stick, then burst forward. Ahead was a small boulder that offered itself as the sole step to a three-foot wall of raised earth.

"Through the forest," she declared as she took aim.

Eddie hurried after her but struggled to keep pace.

She jabbed the end of the stick into the boulder and sprang over the dirt step. "Off the rock!"

The nimble daredevil planted, spun around, then threw her arms out to the sides; the energy matched with a booming smile in hopes to soak in the glorious reception of her stunt.

"Nothing but adventure," she finished.

Her tunnel-visioned companion was concentrated in his step-by-step pursuit, so she threw the stick to aid his imagination. Eddie threw up his hands and managed to snatch it from the air. It slipped twice from his grasp, but he finally secured it to his chest.

The boy slowed as he came to the ledge, sure of the failure that would meet any attempt at the stunt. "Hey—why did you say you hadn't met someone like me before? Am I that weird?" he asked.

She smirked at his blatant insecurity, clearly derived from some deep inhibition. Though, the finer details yet eluded her. A truth that would require changing. "Not everyone goes out to chase the wishing star, Eddie," the girl replied. "You care about me for some reason, right? But you don't know why. Yeah—I know why," she declared with sudden calmness.

Eddie, however, did not quite know why with the precise words, though he knew that bold proclamation reflected an undeniable truth.

"C'mon, the journey is just beginning, and you won't make it far if you don't learn to take a chance."

"You're right," the boy admitted. "Okay! I'll try."

Emboldened, he slung the rifle across his back, stepped away from the ledge, then sank down to prepare his charge. With the hope that he might seize success on the first shot, he took off. The boy aimed for the same point to assure he could mimic her achievement and struck with vigor.

As the force carried him forward, he felt his body begin to rise, and the feeling of flight raised his spirits. But a sudden snap stripped him down to the animal instinct of survival as the entire world turned upside down. He slammed into the dirt wall and slid down the slope until he settled into a seated position at the bottom.

Mirika peered over the ledge, completely unfazed by his comical failure. Eddie turned himself over, stood up, and shook the dirt off in a frantic attempt to regain his composure.

"Well! How did it feel?" she asked with glowing anticipation.

"What? I didn't do it."

"No, I mean the feeling when you thought you were about to."

His anxiety began to settle as he realized what she meant. She closed her eyes and turned away.

"It's a wonderful feeling, isn't it?" she cooed as she continued along.

Eddie climbed over the ledge and took off after her, and soon they were on a path much sparser than before with a clear view of the spectacular night above.

She put her arms up toward the starry sky and soaked in the moonlight as her celestial companion wove through the branches high above.

"Yeah—I guess it was," Eddie replied. "I never really thought of it like that before."

Her arms remained high in the air as she took in a long breath of nature. "It's a pure sensation; the spirited pursuit of the thrill."

She lowered her arms as they continued onward. He felt perhaps he knew what it was she meant as those words stirred up distant memories of childhood, the hillside, and the adventures that had once cultivated his young spirit. Her legs began to pick up into long strides. Eddie gave chase once more without a clue as to why they were running.

The daredevil leapt from a fallen log over a shallow ravine, caught the other side with a foot, then planted the other in a thrilling conclusion. She made an about face, still aglow with the hopeful expectation of the boy to join at her side.

Invigorated by her enthusiasm, Eddie jumped after her but was snatched in midair by a lone branch, which had snagged his pants. It snapped, but not before it robbed him of his forward momentum. The boy fell to the ground and tumbled along a bed of protruded root, down to the dirt of humiliation below.

Her mouth fell agape, but her smile lingered. Eddie rolled across the ground as he pushed his arms into the dirt to regain control. The warped earth of the ravine rescued him in its cradle and rolled him back to stillness.

His agile companion dropped to the ground beside him, as he picked himself up.

"Wow—didn't see that. What was that? Something on that log?" he sputtered.

She grinned and nodded, regardless of the truth.

"You know, we should be careful. There's really no telling what we could run into out here all by ourselves," Eddie advised as he cleaned himself of dirt once more.

She released a gale of frustration, then went to the slope, which was crawling with tree roots. With limber agility, she climbed to the top of the ridge. Eddie, who realized he had been left behind, hurried to the path taken and mimicked his way up.

The nimble thrill seeker raced across the dirt until she reached a clearing. She cut to a halt, faced the forest, then cupped her hands around her mouth. With a single breath, she transmitted a somnolent note, throughout the forest.

She rose a step in her voice then fell three in a graceful portamento glide to the last note. That hypnotic call transcended into a pulsating dream pad and fell three times over as it swept through her captive audience of trees.

Like something from the angel's lips, it sliced through silence like petals through the wind, and each echo lingered in expressive resonance. By the birth of the final reverberation, the notes had fluctuated into a chillingly serene chord, which haunted the forest with its enduring grace.

Eddie slowed to a crawl as that bewildering sound found his ears. It soothed him into a deep paralysis as he attempted to tune to the million vibrations that tickled his spine and brought even the faintest rustle to pleasing clarity.

The progression of noise was of such ethereal characteristic that it took on inhuman distinction, a sound of the astral or electronic imitation. Though he stood just beside her, the sound came at him from everywhere at once. Eddie looked all around as he tried to find balance, but before he could do anything at all, it seemed to evaporate into silence, and he was freed from its dynamic grasp.

She held still with eyes closed in deep assessment of that complex system of noise, her hands still cupped at the mouth as she diagnosed distinct vibrations that her confounded companion could no longer hear as they now wandered the depths of the forest.

Her eyes opened, and she recaptured the boy's attention with a nonchalant turn. "Okay—let's move on."

"What did you just do?" asked Eddie, dumbfounded by the obscure performance.

"Checking what lies ahead . . . Didn't you say you were scared?"

"I didn't say that—" Eddie resisted, in quick rescue of his pride. "I just thought we should be careful. I don't want anyone else getting hurt."

She cocked her head and smiled in appreciation of his concern.

From beyond her eyes, Eddie caught a glimpse of a growing light through the dark. She took notice of his distraction and turned her head upwards. Through the dense canopy, the rays of the moon pierced the leaves and branches. From those heavenly breaches fell ether-tailed glimmers in a sleepy glide through the delicate planes of focused moonlight.

Eddie became fixated with them, yet stepped away as a few neared his face. Mirika retained her gaze, however, and with the daredevil's grin, spectated the sudden downpour as the cascading bulbs curled off over her body.

"Are these—fairies, too?" Eddie asked.

"Uh-uh," she replied.

The showering orbs settled upon the forest, on the ground, brush, and trees. Eddie gave chase to them and watched as they melted upon gentle impact, absorbed into the land with a golden flash.

Mirika, unfazed by the bizarre phenomena, turned to Eddie, who had stuck out his hand in a half-hearted attempt to catch one.

"We've already made great strides today, doncha think?" she asked. "Let's go ahead a little ways more and find a place to stop tonight."

Eddie yanked his hand away, then nodded, though strangely enough, he had endured no discomfort throughout the course of their journey. Even the humiliating tumble had seemed to cause him no lasting pain, although he knew it probably should have.

Of course, it had been Mirika who had led the way with the use of her special abilities, he reasoned. Thus, perhaps, it had caused her to grow weary. The shroud of obscurity surrounding her had been peeled back, and something truly of the beyond shined true and left him little reason to believe it wasn't something of a possibility.

And so, the whimsical outlander led the way once more without protest, the silver sprite meandering the branches above. He followed in her dedicated steps with trust in her apparent familiarity with the mystic wilderness.

With due vigor, they negotiated its woodland path, over moss-covered stones, up steep dirt shelves, and across fallen trees, until they had stumbled upon splintered darkness, a silver spell that cast a moonlit circle upon a distant rise of land.

The tranquil burble of running water wafted to their ears almost as soon as they had found it.

Mirika threw her finger to the glistening peak. "There's a place," she cried, then shot off with impressive agility.

Eddie trailed behind as she kicked from rock to rock, dropped to the soggy dirt, then stormed up the ramp of earth. She scraped to a halt as her companion rose behind her, then lingered, with her gaze lifted to the moonlight.

He joined her there at the top and found that their respite lay right beneath the stars. Left speechless by that hidden splendor, his eyes scanned the dreamy heavens as memories swelled up within. It had been so long since he had looked upon the night sky without overwhelming emptiness inside. Now, there was something to be chased, and an opportunity to fill that relentless void.

That glimmer of truth was magic enough.

"This spot will do," she said in a delighted glow.

Eddie nodded, then laid the unneeded rifle against the gnarled trunk of a stocky elder tree. "It's really beautiful, huh?"

Mirika meandered over to a flat-topped bolder near the cliff's edge, slung herself across the top, then crossed her legs. Her fae companion raced down beside her and circled her a few times.

"Rest, now. The city in the sky awaits us, so let's make energy for the road ahead."

Eddie wandered to the end of the rise, his head still held high. Finally, there was a way. From that spectacular pinnacle, he stood, too, upon the deathless hillside of Somairsville, one foot into tomorrow and one foot in the past.

Soon, however, those realities would be one. In that moment, far away, yet closer than ever.

"I'll never stop until I find you again," the boy vowed.

And he took from his pocket the star pendent, then looked back to the glimmering heavens above. He raised that shining oath high and put it there, among the stars, a mission reborn at last.

"These pieces of a life that was left smashed . . . I'll put them all back together again."

Mirika pulled her legs to her chest and wrapped her arms around them, then beamed up at the boy, who turned to her with an eager glow and all the wonder in his eyes.

Set Adrift in His World of Eroding Reality

In the weeks that followed the flight from Salamandra City, the disorganized masses were graced with a respite from the invader force. The sky eventually cleared as the evicted denizens of the city made their way north along the empty highway. The invader siege had dealt unfathomable damage in every manner. The saddest days were suffered in that desperate first march, a time marked by despair, disappearance, and death.

A gathering of the remnant political leadership saw temporary authority handed over to General Myres, imbued with the sacred duty to reinstall the Union government over the seized lands.

Joined by the Beilkan detachment, they made their way toward the nearest metropolis, Neo Cascadia. There, they hoped to find survivors, more information on the bizarre invader force, and unified forward momentum.

The swordsman departed them soon after the battle. Though he meandered along in the distance for a few days, sightings of him became sparse until on the fourth day, he vanished altogether.

Even in the absence of the invaders, there was much for them to worry over. Food, drink, and rest were an initial concern, but the survivors were quickly confronted by further absurdity. Supply parties were dispatched to ghost towns and returned with fresh rations, which were swiftly handed out. After two weeks' time, however, the rations had built up, and very few had been used. Their natural hunger and thirst had mysteriously vanished, and it unleashed worry and panic among the masses. The desperate resorted to force-feeding in fear that deceptive invader magics would cause them to perish quietly from dehydration or starvation. Most waited, and until there was reason to believe there was danger otherwise, simply kept a modest share of rations on their person.

The army ordered the newly formed civilian caravan to maintain those rations in case the need did return and took on a stance that it was a temporary sensation due to shock. As the days turned into weeks, however, there soon became a quiet acceptance that this simply wasn't the case. Something very serious had transpired, and there was not a single one of them who could offer the public a sensible explanation. And so, it was made truth with silence.

At the end of two arduous weeks of organization and travel, the caravan neared their destination. Generals Myres and Gala assembled at the front of the advance and departed ahead to scout the area from a vantage.

"We can take the freeway around the Plains of Amarand to Veromoor. From there, we'll be within a short march to where your buddies are, heaven permitting, still holding out," said General Myres as they ascended a rocky steppe. "Just tell me again that you're confident it's worth our time."

General Gala heaved his way up as his guard followed behind. "The best thing to do in this time of peril is to gather as many allies as possible. The wars fought between the Beilkan Houses taught us that securing an adequate force is of paramount importance to any armed conflict. Regardless of the foe, there can be no mistaking our position of glaring weakness. A push north to the Reotundra base in the honorable land of Veromoor is by far our best option beyond this confounded city. It is the storage place of many assets useful to our cause, and the people there will surely open their doors to Beilkan soldiers."

"Well, that's good to know," the other general replied with palpable sarcasm.

Distracted by meandering thoughts of the puppet state's corruption, Myres stepped to the final stone plate on an unstable foot, but stole back his balance with a swing of the arm from the grassy top.

"And, now—I give you, a scenic view of Neo Cascadia," the Union general introduced as he regained his breath.

Neo Cascadia marked the geological split where the rolling green ended and the flatland began. A few large hills and rock towers stood watch on the city's southern outskirts, but beyond the northern suburbs, there was nothing but forest and an endless green expanse beneath vermilion skies.

Known for the glittery pomp of its nightlife hub, it was a popular host to lavish festivals of wine, art, music, and cultivated bustling community events. Dubbed "The City of the Smile," it was once ravaged sixty years prior during the horrific Titan War, ignited when Beilkan government entities successfully engineered the secession of two southwest Union provinces, Neberke and Trulosa. The result saw a rapid Beilkan deployment into the region to defend their fledgling allies, with Cascadia and its air force base their premier targets. The Union, meanwhile, was so weakened by political turmoil that they were left to a humiliating scramble to defend their manipulated territory, a historically shameful three days after the armored divisions rolled across the border.

In contemporary times, however, it stood as a modern metropolis, which boasted a respectable skyline, and while the scars of a brutal occupation and relentless resistance had faded, they went immortalized in oxidized copper plaques bolted to marble memorials in peaceful, manicured gardens.

Gala scanned the distant city with a steady eye. "Seems to lack activity—no signs of battle, but no movement on the roads at all." The Beilkan general grumbled in concern, "Something's not right."

Myres scrutinized the scene alongside him.

"Maybe the local government has everything situated and they've got everyone hunkered down. Look at this—" Myres said as he pointed up the empty skies. "Nothing. Invaders must not have hit every major

city, and with comms being down, nobody knew what was going on
. . . Maybe they caught a glimpse of one of those ships and locked it
down. I mean, this isn't a small town we're talking about . . . this is Neo
Cascadia. Somebody's got to be down there for heaven's sake."

General Gala maintained his apprehensiveness with a cold stare.

"Alright, alright—let's get the caravan situated for the night. We'll
rest 'em here, take a battalion downtown, and see if we can't find
anyone—again, there's not a smoking gun over there, and it didn't
appear the invaders had any administrative goals in mind when they
blew Salamandra to pieces. Should be alright to go poke around a bit . .
. if for nothing more than to get some closure," Myres concluded.

Gala nodded in agreement with his plan. "Very well. We should
have our best accompany us. When oddities are abundant, we would do
well not to give our trust to the shroud of normality."

With the plan in place, the generals dispatched their able teams
to scour the city. They would go in search of survivors, for clues, for
anything at all, but what they would find was unsettling silence and
cavernous emptiness.

***

The civilian caravan was moved to the outskirts of the city and split
into several suburban towns, each completely devoid of life.

Lyal Abra and his companions were guided by the flow of the
despondent masses as they were shepherded into the vacant burb. Each
of them was drooped in a crestfallen glaze, plagued by a misery that
was rampant among the survivors. Upon arrival at the checkpoint, the
fortune-favored friends were set adrift through a hushed sea of grim
whispers as they were filtered into an area abundant with poverty-
rescued strip malls and drab commercial shells left neglected in varied
stages of decay, though none of them were touched by the fires of war.

The glass doors of those street-side shops were broken through
to convenience their scavenge for supplies. The racks were cleared to
make pallets of clothes, rationed out by the volunteers and officials
alike. The floors were then cleared to accommodate the vulnerable
orphans, pregnant mothers, and disabled survivors in those makeshift
sanctuaries of thin carpet and bare drywall, summoned forth from the
crowds by the soldiers' commands.

As the somber band stepped to the crowded sidewalk of the strip, Setz broke away from the group in apparent urgency to escape.

"I'm going to help," he said, without concern for any particular response.

"Yo, Setz—"

"Kaiser—let him go," Lyal interrupted before Kaiser could take the first step in pursuit.

Miyacre turned and sat down on the edge of the sidewalk and put her face into her hands. Lyal peered down at her but knew there was nothing he could say to ease that insufferable pain. It was something that had to heal with time.

Kaiser shook his head in disbelief. "This is surreal. I just . . . can't get over the fact that this is all really happening," he said as he scanned across the refugee camp.

"We'll get through it. We just gotta stick together and stay cool. Other than that—that's all we can really do," Lyal said.

Mitz nodded. "That's right. Can't turn back time and make any other decisions . . . This is the way it is."

They heard the sharp sniffle that comes from sobbing and peered down at Miyacre, whose head bobbed as she fought to suppress sheer despair.

"It's going to be fine, Miyacre," said Lyal. "I wouldn't say that if I didn't—"

Her head shot up, and she swept a finger beneath swollen eyes. "No—I'll be okay. I'm just—feeling a little overwhelmed right now. I'll be fine," she insisted.

Then, she stood and turned to them. The boys sank at the mere sight of their ruined friend. Her face had melted into gruesome misery, an embarrassingly unacceptable portrait that she tried in vain to conceal behind a cupped hand.

"Hey—I'm just gonna go walk around a little bit—you'll be right here, right? You'll be here?" she asked hurriedly, on the verge of a mental burst.

"Okay—we'll be right here," Lyal assured. "Just don't go far, alright?"

She nodded mid-turn and stormed away into the crowds.

Lyal watched her until all that he could see were strangers. As his eyes lingered upon those downcast countenances, he suddenly saw them all at once, along with the very essence of the time. It was truly the bleakest moment he had ever witnessed in his life, a visceral anguish that was infectious like a calamitous pandemic.

He could hear the harrowing stories exchanged between complete strangers, of treacherous journeys through the razed capital. Those tales told on fragile tremble ached for the comfort of empathy, if not, too, a mere rudimentary bond to fill the cavernous void left by those who had gone missing.

All across the parking lot and all throughout the road were the remnants of a society; a puzzle trying to put itself back together in any way that its pieces could seem to fit.

"You think anyone else back home made it out?" asked Mitz as he kicked a few stone fragments around on the ground.

"Man, I really hope they did. And Ashe, too . . . hope she's alright," Kaiser lamented.

Lyal's eyes searched the distance, beyond the crowd and through time and space, in search of plausible answers. Yet, there were none to be found, nor were there any clues to guide his troubled conscience, and as he returned from the depths of thought, he came to the only logical conclusion. "I don't know."

***

Not far from where the boys awaited their friend's return, Gruman and his associates oversaw the distribution of supplies from the baked asphalt.

Gruman took a handkerchief to his reddened forehead as the afternoon sun glared down upon his polished scalp. Larus, a Union officer of Beilkan stature who championed their old warrior tradition with his long, silken black hair, scanned the masses with arms folded in front of him. An entity of sheer intimidation, his hands were encased in thick black gloves, lovingly preserved in mint condition despite the unprecedented war effort.

At the nearby storefront of a home goods retailer, Lakker directed the steady flow of traffic to receive a ration of bedding for the night.

Further down the sidewalk, Vekner engaged in a furious exchange with a man who had secured three pillows beneath his arm.

Larus smirked at his comrade's tempestuous predicament, then returned to his observations without much concern. "How long do they expect us to wait here?" he asked his sun-withered superior.

"It's beyond me. Let these people have their way with this—poorly maintained mini mall. This is no way for a chief operating officer of the governor of Salamandra to spend his time, to be bluntly honest. At the end of the day, most of them will have to walk away empty-handed, anyhow."

"Luckily, we have the two 'star protégés' to listen in our stead for now," Larus replied as he maintained his defensive scan for any who would move too close.

Gruman, however, didn't share his dry enthusiasm. He scratched his chin as he pondered the happenings within Neo Cascadia. "Rhodes I'd trust in a quiet place with a loaded gun. She has long proven her loyalty to our cause, but Schneider still requires—guidance."

Larus's eyes crept over to Gruman. "What makes you say that? He seems alright. Can't imagine he'd want to backstab the ones who showed up to finish his fight eleven years ago."

Gruman chuckled. "Yes—yes. Our 'hero general' . . . Those sacrifices must pay off in the end, and all of this happening now presents a unique opportunity. His closeness with Myres, however, is problematic. We've invested too much. This organization would be unable to sustain such a loss, especially now that we've made certain— commitments."

Larus fleered at the thought of interference. "What's your call, then?"

"Make ready to leave, Grand Marshal. We'll get things situated here, then head downtown. There's some . . . other things that need taking care of—out of the sight of the public eye, of course. With how disorganized this mess is, I doubt we'll be missed."

"Can do, Lord Dominus. It's a little stale around here, anyway."

Gruman turned his attention to Vekner, whose heated bout had escalated into a hurl of insults as he attempted repeatedly to seize back the pilfered rations. "Corporal! Enough! Get over here!" Gruman hollered.

Seething, Vekner forced his attention from the man and looked to Gruman, who beckoned to him with the wave of his hand. In obedience to his superior, he cast aside his feud and stormed across the pavement to hear him. "How are we supposed to control this situation when there's no sense of law and order!?" Vekner vented, his face red with fury.

"That will come in due time. You waste your energy on such pitiful things. Set aside your anger for more important matters. We're leaving for Neo Cascadia," Gruman said.

In reverence of his wisdom, Vekner nodded his head as he worked to subdue his vengeful temper.

"Go and inform Lakker—and for heaven's sake, where is the doctor at?" Gruman asked as he swept around in search of him.

With a quick glance, Vekner picked him out from the crowd. "I believe he's over there, sir."

"Ah—perfect," said Gruman as he followed Vekner's line of sight straight to the man in question. "Now, what buffoonery is he up to? There really isn't the time—Larus, go and retrieve him, see what he's hunted now."

***

Through the crowd, Miyacre carved an aimless path, on a journey within to rein in wayward emotion which yet left her overwhelmed. Her eyes dodged the faces of others, those windows into their pain, surely a host to some faint reflection of herself.

She raised her head to contain a drip from her nose and caught sight of a figure just ahead who, unlike the organic movement of the masses, stood eerily still. She passed it off as nothing at first, but upon second glance, it became clear that the stranger's eyes had followed her.

He was a taller man who rose above many on long scrawny legs. Though he was distant, she became privy to a longing in his gaze, a murderous focus that left her deeply unsettled.

She redirected her path, grounded in the reasoning that perhaps she simply bore resemblance to someone who was now gone from his life. As she settled in that revised aimlessness, however, she snuck another glance. Her hopes that he had abandoned his intrigue were dashed as she found him fixed on her with a scarecrow-ish gaze.

The odd observer was joined by Larus, who followed his laser-focused eyes right to the prey. The ominous duo engaged in a brief exchange, though at no point did the man in the tattered white button-up take his eyes off her. Miyacre was swept up in anxiety as the crooked officer sneered her way, and she realized quickly that she needed to put distance between herself and those noxious harassers.

The hunted breakaway-turned and hurried back the way she had come, but without warning, she was chased down by Larus. She let out a yelp as she stuttered to a halt.

"Hold on there, young lady—" he called with affable and charismatic articulation.

She stepped away, wise to the act. "No, thanks."

"Hey, listen—" he pressured. "You just seemed like you were in a big rush to nowhere. Didn't mean to frighten you . . . but if you're alone, why not come travel with some folks who can look after you? They're good people . . . and that's a soldier's promise," he lied through a grin.

She shook her head in swift rejection of that death-laced proposal. "But I'm not alone. So, leave me alone—and tell your friend to stop staring at me."

Larus dropped the facade and sneered at the lost catch as she hurried off through the crowd. "And there goes that little fish."

He turned and returned to the scientist, whose expression had drooped in disappointment with his failure. "She wanted me to tell you to fuck off. Now, let's go. You'll have plenty of time to find another one from the walking buffet," Larus said as he blew past the scientist, who persisted in pensive obsession.

Miyacre, freed from their aggression, returned to the relief of Lyal and the others but did so without a word as to what had transpired. Setz, too, eventually returned as night fell upon the camp, but maintained a certain distance with Lyal, their feud unresolved by that short passage of time. With hope it could all be forgotten, and with a mind more cleared of despair, Miyacre refocused herself on the journey ahead of them. To be overcome by anguish was just as dangerous as any invader. This she knew for certain, just as she was certain depression was the enemy of mankind.

Silent Heaven

In the night, Eddie had lain upon the lush grass in the moonlit circle to rest. At first, he felt it too ridged to pass easily into slumber. Unable to settle, his mind ran wild with the thousand possibilities that might be achieved from the great master's extraordinary powers.

Gradually, however, a calm serenity came about him. Occasional glances up to the stars became a progressive blur until he settled peacefully into the darkness behind his eyes. Within the realm of sleep, he became privy to subtle sensitivities in a strange consciousness that he had never experienced before.

In that unusual state, he became aware of an entity without form or luminance. It was distant at first, but as unquantifiable time passed, it jumped closer and closer until, at last, it had arrived right there beside him.

He could feel the piercing gaze of the invasive entity as it lingered in his dream state. With a tap to his forehead, it entered through his mind, and he could suddenly see it pass through every memory that raced by as if it flipped the pages of his subconscious picture book.

Those images flashed in rapid acceleration until a distinctly hellish drone grew within. The boy trembled as it intensified. An impenetrable darkness swept over all else, and just as he regained the willpower to break out, his lingering consciousness collapsed into the nothingness of deep sleep.

The rest of the night was stolen, a leap from the depths of unconsciousness to daybreak, until nature's delicate prod gradually stirred him.

The brook's gentle babble and sunlight's warmth permeated the boy's slumber. His eyes cracked to the power of morning's golden glow, and he pulled himself up from the ground. From a drowsy survey of their respite, he found himself alone on the rise.

Eddie set his hand upon his brow to fend off the dawn's rays, which cut through the forest as far as the eye could see. The latent memories of those mid-dream sensations escaped his mind just as he sought to grasp them.

Then, there came a shuffle of leaves from above that hastened the expiration of his interest with the faded evidence. He turned up toward the canopy, from which the piercing light of dawn gleamed. High above, he saw movement from a branch. Two black shadows swung to and fro.

The boy rose, and the movement ceased. As his eyes focused, he could make out the silhouette of hair caught by a sudden breath of wind. She peered down at him from her perch.

There was a sharp snap of wood as the shadow kicked off of the branch. The form plummeted down and, in the next moment, slammed into the dirt before him.

Eddie leapt back a step as Mirika rose up with a grin.

He took in a breath of relief. "How'd you get up there?"

She laughed. "With my hands and feet," she razzed. "I rose to catch the dawn!"

"Really? You can climb that high?" Eddie remarked as he peered back up to the broken perch near the crown. "Must have been a great view from up there."

"Ha! Someday, I'll take you to the mountaintop where you can find the sharpest view of the sun . . . but we should go now. There will be plenty of time once we find what we are looking for."

He looked back at her with a wide beam. "That sounds awesome! Maybe when the war is over, we can go to all kinds of places—I haven't been far from the city since I was a kid."

"Believe in my promise," Mirika said.

Her eyes narrowed.

"So much lies beyond the forest," she teased with a subtle side-to-side shake of her head as if playfully privy to whatever lay on the other side. "Not all that goes missing is gone."

Eddie, half sure of what that meant, nodded with a fading smile.

The boy retrieved his rifle, and the adventurous duo set off. They descended the rise and cut across the brook via a meandering line of rocks that broke the surface. With a leap and a pass through a narrow dell, they were soon back on nowhere's path again with a city in the sky in their sights.

"Hey, where's—Sh'shami?" Eddie asked with attention to past errors.

"Resting."

"Oh—okay," he replied.

"Don't worry. You'll have a chance to see her again. But—tell me more about your dream, Little Eddie Bowitz. Why exactly will you seek out the great master?" she asked.

"Well—" he began.

He hesitated. Eddie had never revealed such intimate desires with anyone. He had come to find its truth embarrassing. From the unforgiven promises made to the blind faith he had laid in their precious star; for once, however, he wanted to expose it all. As one who closed her eyes in search of lost friends, she would surely understand.

"A long time ago . . . I had a very good friend, and his father got sick. We found this . . . wishing star, and we thought—maybe . . . it might be special enough to save his life. Well, it wasn't, and—a lot of things changed after that night. A lot of things were lost."

Mirika listened in closely, her glossed eyes gone completely still and her mouth agape.

"But it's okay now. If what you say is true, then it doesn't matter what happened. Maybe it can all be changed."

A breeze swept through the trees as the boy's resolute eyes stayed fixated upon whimsy's siren, who had become rapt in glassy curiosity.

"The great master's powers are vast. No doubt he will be able to aid you in this request," she replied.

Resolved in their path, they continued onward for a moment in silence, though it wasn't long before curiosity got the better of her again. "Why does their death bring you such sadness?"

Eddie was taken aback by her tactless exploration, still haunted by the voices of those who had impelled him to move on. "We were just kids. No one should ever have to suffer that kind of loss."

She cocked her head. "Ever?"

Eddie tightened his fist in bitter frustration but found himself without words.

Mirika nodded in sympathy, cognizant of the deep chord struck. "I see . . . So, returning this person to life will make you happy. This is your dream?"

"Well, yeah—part of it . . . I guess."

She pondered something further. "You'll find that with a lot of magic, desire is certainly the first part of the trick. This wishing star of yours . . . you had it last night, didn't you?"

Eddie nodded, then produced the precious relic from his jacket's inner pocket.

"It's very special to you, isn't it?"

Eddie nodded with a beam of pride. "I would never let it go. It's my promise . . . to JJ, to myself . . . and everyone else. If there's a chance someone can really help me, I'll take it."

"Aren't you afraid of death, too?"

Fierce determination left the boy's chest, but something made quick to stabilize him. "I—don't feel so, when I have this star," he said as crestfallen eyes fell upon the timeless framed rock. "Maybe it's silly, but—it's more than true."

She chuckled. "Is there such a thing?"

Eddie blossomed at the sight of her cocky smile. "Well, it's true. We'll leave it at that," he leveled.

Mirika beamed together with him. "You know, you're pretty brave. I'm going to help you find your way, because—well—I believe in you! So, worry not, Little Eddie, I'll protect you and help you make these wishes come true," she vowed in a spirited glow.

Her words struck him with wonder. Until that moment, he had felt as though it was he that served in her protection. The more he thought about it, however, the more he felt it was truly the opposite. It was her spirit that had rescued him with its whimsical enthusiasm for possibility, along with a new opportunity to go bravely in pursuit of old dreams. She had become the sacred heart that pumped vigor to a drained existence and, perhaps in more ways than one, emancipated his life from war, from shadowy emptiness, and from a much darker, unresolved entity within.

What a joy it was to travel on the high road in pursuit of beyond the reality. How liberating it was to dream so freely, and how wondrous it was that there was hope; hope that one day, all those old promises might come true after all.

They took up a determined and energetic stride for tomorrow's lands. Two adventurers, both on the path to paradise, both lost in the dream.

In their drive through the last leg of nature's embrace, they soon reached a break in the trees. The nimble fire blossom shot forth in a straight cut for the foot of the town, marked by a distant line of yellow painted posts.

Like a frolicking fox, she leapt from the tree stumps and dove beneath the low hanging branch. Following in her wake once again, Eddie felt a childish comfort knowing that the way forward was at the tips of their toes and all he had to do was follow.

The forest's end arrived abruptly behind the line of yellow concrete posts, beyond which a narrow, weathered road began. They crossed through, and Mirika busied herself in leaps across the cracks in the asphalt. Eddie trailed behind as he peered out at the morning sun, which lingered above the horizon of houses before them.

Their journeying had brought them to the outskirts of a suburban town that had flourished in the bubble of an old world. Along the road, they encountered resplendent flower fields, dismally realized in meticulously measured rectangular plots, which seemed to contradict the organic beauty of their contents. From vibrant, heart-petaled goldies and parted, swirling luna-blue mollies to breathtaking pink raleighies. Together, they swayed on long stems in the gentle breeze, a subtle invitation into their lovingly nurtured prisons.

The floral captives clumsily adorned the roadside as it wound to the top of the town, where they eventually became imprisoned twice over between stark white apartment complexes whose ugliness sapped the town of the beauty the flowers were meant to achieve.

There was little greenery there beyond them, however, and their existence seemed like a desperate grasp for levity in a land of rigid constitutions.

With eager steps upon the unmaintained asphalt, they pushed deeper into the town. Seemingly of arbitrary design, quaint, single-family homes were dispersed throughout the neighborhood, sometimes found along entire streets but often splintered by commercial shops that sprang up out of nothing at all as if each plot of land was sold off individually.

These humble homes were easier on the eye with a design that harkened back to an old heritage, sometimes adorned with white fences but often left open, guarded only by stone gardens.

Adjacent to the main road, a small stone waterway, overgrown with creepers, cut through the residential area but wrapped away just before it reached the city center, where five moderate-sized buildings rose high above all else.

The town itself was barren, quiet, and empty, but that thick eeriness hadn't hindered Mirika's enthusiasm in the least. She leapt upon the stone wall that guarded the sheer descent into the river and traced the narrowed top with masterful balance.

Eddie continued on the main road, mesmerized in his observations of the hollowed village. Though there was an undeniable mystique to it, something was clearly amiss. In the yards of a few homes beyond the waterway, he noticed freshly air-dried clothes still clipped to old lines, and on the ground beneath one was the wicker laundry basket that they were meant to fill. The haunt of absolute stillness permeated all that there was to see; from the humble family-owned restaurant to the bakery and even the corner side market, not a soul wandered but theirs.

The road drooped downward then began almost immediately into a second ascent. Off to the side of the road was a cradled convenience store, which lay at the far end of a fenced-in parking lot.

The lot lay empty, but strangely enough, there were two bicycles parked out front at a dark green rack.

Eddie looked back at Mirika, who had also taken interest in the shop.

"Two bikes," said Eddie. "You think anyone's there?"

She held in her silence for a moment, as if to steal the time to mull it over. "Only one way to find out," she encouraged.

"Can't you do the thing where you close your eyes?" Eddie asked.

She put her hands on her hips and grimaced at him. "Don't you like surprises? C'mon, we'll take a quick pitstop."

So, with guts for guidance, they went together across the parking lot, whose condition was far worse than that of the main road. Though the war hadn't seen these streets, age alone had done enough.

Eddie stepped over a yellow wheel stop in front of a curbside parking space, then stepped up to the door. As his foot fell, the door promptly slid open, which turned his attention to the overhead sensor that had mysteriously remained in operation.

"Weird," Eddie remarked. "Is everything still working?"

Mirika passed through without a word. Eddie, with the assumption that all was well, followed behind her.

Inside, they were greeted with the cheerful ambience of jazzy nonchalance played through the ceiling speakers across the aisles. Mirika stepped slowly over the door mat, passed a wire-metal display of stacked postcards, then checked everything over with a curious eye. It was as if she had taken interest with it all: the brightly colored candy bars, the bubbly characters upon bags of chips, and the neatly stocked lunch bar, which hosted plastic-wrapped sandwiches, yogurts, and other on-the-go delights.

Eddie started down the front of the aisles, hoping to locate the owners of the bikes that stood baking out in the morning sun. He took notice of how neatly the store was kept. It was almost as if nobody had thought to buy a thing when the war broke out.

Wouldn't they have wanted to stock up on supplies, even if they left the town behind? It was all very odd to him. At the back of the store, he gave each bathroom stall a knock, and both times, he received no reply.

"Guess nobody's here," Eddie concluded.

"Uh-huh," Mirika replied rather naturally.

Eddie stepped away to the nearest aisle, having only succeeded in stoking his anxiety. "It's weird . . . I actually haven't eaten a thing since . . . they came," said Eddie as he peered down a row of chocolate bars and other sweets with unusual indifference.

In the first row, Mirika browsed the magazine display with a casual stride, stopping periodically to flip through the pages of a thoughtless selection before setting it back and moving on to the next.

"You can eat if you want," she advised.

Eddie continued along the back, passing an aisle of chips, pretzels, and other bagged snacks before stepping out into the final aisle, which hosted refrigerated deli meats, dairy, and cold drinks. From there, he found absolute certainty that there was nobody else within. "I'm not hungry at all, though—and I don't have any money."

"Then, don't eat," she concluded for him, then started flipping through a military magazine with a smirk.

"But it's like, I don't even go to the bathroom—am I alive?"

"If the invaders catch you, you'll die," she assured him.

"Yeah, well—guess more has changed than I thought. I wonder if anyone else is feeling the same . . . wherever they are."

He sighed as the humiliation of his flight found him there. "I hope they made it out," he continued, his thoughts now fixated on that fateful night.

"There's no need to worry. This journey can make everything right," she encouraged.

With interest evaporated, she dropped the magazine back into the slit, and the bottom struck with a loud bang. Eddie came back around to the front and noticed a small bar area that looked out to the baked parking lot. Across the road and beyond the waterway was another modest field of tall, golden flowers, which stood radiant in the beams of the dawn.

He ambled over, took a seat at one of the stools, then set aside the rifle and laid his head into the padding of his open palm. There, he soaked in the sunlight that doused the roadside sanctuary in a comforting glow and transformed it into a truly pleasant respite, far from the war and far from familiarity.

Mirika wandered over to the postcard display and scrutinized the idyllic destinations and baked-in proclamations with muted fascination. They featured a variety of beautiful, stone-clad castles, bounding gardens splashed with all the vibrant colors of spring, the snowy peaks of a mighty range, and emerald glades that had been set aglitter in the sunset. Alongside those distant places, however, were cards that featured the metropolitan glitz of the local downtown district with its smooth, elegant architecture that charmed in jarring contrast with the surrounding town's old-world makeup.

She spun the display and watched the world go round. "Soon, there'll be no place we can't be, you know?" she teased.

"I've heard—there are some incredible places out there," the boy replied as he gazed out to that foreign world just beyond the window.

The coy enchantress turned to him and cocked her head in playful curiosity. "You haven't ventured much, huh?"

He shook his head. "No—but I want to go all over. I mean—what we're doing now—I've enjoyed it a lot."

Eddie had almost thought of lying to her, telling her of the amazing places he had never been, perhaps some of the ones he had dreamt of as a child. Doing so, however, would defy the new reality he hoped to realize. Now was not the time to live in lies but instead to bring about a greater truth.

Mirika caught the spinning rack, pulled a card from the stack, then wandered on back through the second aisle.

"You know, we could use those bikes," she called from there, beyond.

Eddie raised his head and looked upon the two abandoned bikes at the rack. The thought of a pitiless snag evoked an introspective sadness in the boy, who safeguarded cherished memories of days when he, too, would ride out alongside his friend. It was a sentiment that would be too heavy to bear if ever betrayed. Two friends somewhere out there surely needed them to forge those memories for themselves, and he simply couldn't just take them away.

"I'm actually enjoying the walk," he reasoned with a nervous scratch behind the ear, hoping she wouldn't press the matter any further. "This place is . . . pretty peaceful."

Mirika reemerged from the aisle with a marker in one hand and the postcard in the other. She walked straight up to the counter and slapped the card down on the table, popped off the cap of the marker, and began writing something on the blank back.

Eddie's eyes wandered over to catch a glimpse of the place she had favored, but she shooed him away with the sweep of her hand.

"Hey! Don't look. It's meant for later," she insisted.

He complied without protest and turned back to the window, though his curiosity remained in silent defiance. The boy pondered those confidential words just as deeply as the hidden image on the other side. Was it a sprawling beach, besieged by the crystalline waves of the South Sea, perhaps? Or maybe a charming, forested hillside with old temples nestled in the dense trees. The possibilities were certainly endless.

With a keen ear on the elegant sweeps of the pen, he looked out at the floral dance performed in the energetic winds of a new summer. The city, dazzling in the radiance of imminent noon, and the bikes ahead of him awaiting their absent owners' returns. An adventure waiting somewhere across the land.

When her rigorous scribble was complete, she slipped the card into his pants pocket. "There you go. You can read that when you're ready . . . Preferably when I'm not around," she said, glowing. "Because I'd be embarrassed, you know?"

"Okay," he replied. "I'll wait."

"You promise?"

"If it means that much to you, I'll wait. You think I'm going to forget or something?" he asked.

She raised her shoulders in innocent ignorance and, with a brightened beam, stole a seat next to him and spun around on the rotating chair.

"So, you said you like it here, huh? But there's nobody here! Just you and me . . . Are these the kind of places you enjoy, Little Eddie Bowitz?" she asked as she came to a halt and rested her elbow upon the bar top.

"No—I just meant it was . . . quiet. Maybe it's a nice escape from the war . . . from reality," he admitted.

She smirked. "What about your friend?"

He knew she was right; they couldn't remain here forever. It was a burden he had to carry with vigorous resilience. Nobody else could do it for him. The great master was the indefinite answer to the riddle of his salvation, and he would need to depart this gentle respite for whatever lay ahead, regardless of the danger tomorrow held.

"Don't be afraid. There will be time for so much more," crooned the enchantress, her eyes in a sleepy gaze; that peculiar look that always seemed to set his mind adrift with wonder.

But he liked it when he felt this way. Longing, yet nearly fulfilled. Not a hostage to the dreams of the past but instead liberated in a pursuit of a new promise; a feeling no nostalgic sensation could ever match. Walking through those moments that he knew might compose the best days of his life.

"It's time we left, Eddie. You wanna take anything at all? Last chance!" she declared with shining enthusiasm.

"No," he replied as he retrieved his rifle. "I'll be fine."

A bell chimed as they made their exit through the front door and resonated as they crossed the lot. They continued along the sidewalk up into the town and were soon compressed onto intimate roads made all the more lonely by the bizarre absence of the untraceable townsfolk.

Eddie glanced around at the immediate anomalies, from the ghostly bus stops along a public transit–exclusive roundabout to a deserted park just beyond it and a porch-swept boutique further up the way that had been left with its doors wide open.

"Where is everyone?" he asked as he peered down the empty roads to the distant outskirts.

"Missing, I'm afraid," she responded with relative indifference.

"Missing?" he repeated, coming to realize an unsettling alternate meaning in her peculiar use of that word.

She replied casually, "Mhmm." In sudden reverie, she continued, "You know . . . this town, it reminds me a lot of home."

The boy's mouth fell agape in immediate intrigue. Her words revealed something of a vulnerability, an unusual departure from the enigmatic shroud. In her eyes, too, were the subtle hints of a distinct sadness suppressed behind a faint smile; a reflection so familiar that the boy picked up on it as soon as it was revealed.

She turned to him. "What reminds you of home, Eddie Bowitz?" she asked with soft sincerity.

"Uhh . . . home?" he repeated, refocusing on the question.

Instinctively, he drew from his pocket the cherished wishing star and peered down at it for a moment to channel his innermost thoughts. With sweet memories in mind, Eddie cast his eyes to the sky where the golden sun beamed. He set his hand over his brow to fend off the rays.

"I guess, the sun. That's what reminds me most of home."

Mirika lifted her head, then smiled up at the radiant ball in the open blue. "The sun . . . what a special gift. Because no matter where you go, or how far away you are, it'll always come to find you."

Eddie nodded with a smile, delighted by her whimsical interpretation. "Yeah, you're right—no matter where . . ." He snapped to mental sharpness as her eyes sank away. "Wha—what about you? What reminds you of your home, Miri?"

She snickered at the boy's tireless curiosity. "Well—I have something I carry with me, too. A special trinket that has a lot of power to me."

Eddie blossomed with intrigue at that intimate revelation. He had never had anyone share the existence of such a personal item much like the wishing star before. "Really? . . . Can I see it?" he begged.

She replied with a simple nod, then drew from her pocket the item of her hidden admiration.

Between her fingers dangled a worn but sturdy string adorned with four unique beads. Each was molded by a unique cast, those dreamy prisms agleam with vivid colored streaks that swirled in a cosmic shift as if an alternative universe were locked within.

She lifted her hand to it and ran her nails across the glossy surfaces. "They're gifts from home. Each orb from another place, another adventure in my days as a young ranger."

Eddie leaned in closer. "They're beautiful . . . You found them on an adventure?" the boy asked with brimming fascination.

"Wrong! We earned them. The kin of our village would take a pilgrimage alongside friends to different shrines on stages of our journey to respectable adulthood. There were five shrines that were to be visited before we could participate in the final ceremony."

"Five shrines . . . ? So, five beads?"

The girl's eyes widened in animated surprise of his unanticipated observation. She promptly snatched the unperfected assembly away from his intrusive gaze. "That's right—five!" she verified, with misfortune's truth clutched tight. "And they're not beads. They're spirit orbs!"

Eddie's eyes fell in embarrassment. "I'm sorry."

"Hey! It's okay," she forgave with the gentle fan of her hand. "Calm down. Let's just put it aside for now. We should stay focused on our mission."

The boy agreed with a nod, though he remained acutely dissatisfied with that misinterpreted insensitivity in regard to her cherished keepsake.

Near the heart of downtown, the resolved journeyers passed into a square-shaped tower with an open portal that went straight to the skies. The four-storied shopping center shielded them from the sun's gaze, however, and offered convenient access to the marketplace, which composed much of the first floor, while pairs of escalators ensured a quick ride to an abundance of smaller boutiques on the upper levels.

On the left-hand side, across from the market, was a donut and coffee shop, and beside that was a long, rectangular corridor to the sun-bleached end. The passage was barred off by a rope, however, and at the center of the line hung official signage that offered the brief apology:

Sorry! Harbrooke Station is closed for maintenance.

We apologize for any inconvenience.

Without time to wander, they passed through to the other side, dropped off the curb, and stepped back into the gaze of morning. The rays grew bright as they pressed into the center of the town square, where a roundabout diverted would-be traffic to the three main conduits of the humble downtown. The shadows were chased to the deep corners of the awning-covered storefronts that surrounded them on the cobblestone street.

At the center of the roundabout was a stone pedestal, upon which stood a bronze train conductor, who peered down at his open pocket watch. As they approached, Mirika loosened her grasp and looked upon the bonded charms once more, a faint smile reborn across her face.

"I—bet it's a beautiful place, wherever you journeyed . . . I've always dreamed about going out like that—to different places, collecting different things. It must have been really . . . wonderful," Eddie crooned.

The sunlight grew stronger, and those lurking shadows grew deep.

She turned to him and snickered as she returned the precious memory to the safety of her pocket. "Well, you're right. It was a beautiful place. But you and I both can agree, we can't always control where the journey ends . . . or the way it ends, either."

And to that truth, he bowed his head in profound empathy.

"At least . . . not yet," she teased with a smirk.

She turned to push on ahead, but the boy, stirred by her vague allusions, rose fast with a sudden query. "Hey, Miri—" he asked. "How do you close your eyes and see things that are far away?"

"Oh . . . so—you want me to show you how to do it? To peer through the channels of a dream?" she teased with a graceful reversal and the playful raise of her shoulder to the bottom of her lip.

"Can you!? But wait, isn't what you see real?"

With a smirk, she wilted in a deep exhale. "Oh, Eddie . . . I know you'll understand someday when the clouds are pulled back and your vision is cleared. You won't need to close your eyes at all . . . and neither will I."

Eddie blinked as his naïve mind sought, in vain, to decipher a clear meaning from those vague words. Was he truly so blinded? And by what? His curious gaze faded as he failed to find the answers within, and so he lifted his head to the sky in hopes of catching some fortuitous glimpse of inconceivable insight. All that he found there, however, were invasive gray clouds that had staked a modest claim to once-boundless blue.

"You know, for the longest time, I've watched my dreams from the other side of a glass window."

"Oh! Simple daydreams?" she chortled.

"No . . . they're much more than that," he insisted. "When I was a kid—and even more so after I left for Salamandra, I wanted nothing more than to be a part of a secret world; to walk within them and speak with those people there . . . I wanted to be a part of their story and not my own. My mind was consumed, but . . . I felt free there—" he confided as his eyes fell back to her with absolute confidence now that she would understand.

"Do you ever wonder that, if someone else could . . . visit your secret world, that they might wish to be a part of it with you?" the peeking etherealite asked, half shuttered in shyness.

Eddie mulled it over for a moment. "No—I doubt it . . . It's dangerous, you know? Going out on adventures and fighting monsters isn't something everyone wants to do." Eddie's head fell as he thought further on it and saw how those old fantasies reflected the troubles of their times. "I know a lot of people must be afraid, and in the beginning there—I was afraid, too. I just hope that maybe—we can end this without saying goodbye—" He lifted his fist and pounded his forehead. "Ah . . . that sounds stupid. I don't know."

She snickered again, forever enthralled with the boy who remained helplessly swept in confusion by the grace of High Fantasy. A flaw that was undoubtedly his, by nature alone, regardless of all the charm she might throw at him. Her lip dragged off to one side as she rolled her eyes in momentary indecisiveness.

"Okay—close your eyes, and I'll show you a faraway place."

"Really!?" Eddie cried with a spring to exuberance. "Where will we go?"

"Just close your eyes," she ordered with a confident gleam.

Eddie complied with eager haste, then fell still.

He lingered there, before the plane of darkness, with its strange, pale flashes and racing beams of light.

"Now, we draw back the veil between you and the realm of dream . . . My longing wanderer . . . Eddie!" she amended. "Do you accept my guidance as your truth?" she chanted with the cast of an open claw to her eager participant's head.

"Of course!" the boy thoughtlessly replied.

Her eyes bulged to that instant boon of impressive strength, the incipient essence of an obscure bond forged by his compliance. Stirred by the sudden discourse within, her fae companion broke from her empowered spirit and, in instant terror with the forbidden sorcery at hand, zipped away behind the bronze conductor's shoulder to await the outcome.

"Step in, and let my vision become yours!" she declared as her retinas swelled to electric madness, and she came to gaze unto the exposed constitutions of his relinquished mind.

Her eyes fell shut and sealed workable chaos within. Then, imbued with a conjured vision, she stepped closer and guided her finger to his forehead.

The awakened otherworlder found her target and struck the very center of his mind, and with the arcane ritual complete, she bowed her head in silence, and there, they both remained.

The darkness behind Eddie's eyelids was suddenly expelled. Images beyond his imagination's control emerged from a dense mist. There came congested structures along busy streets, crowded to the distant temples with strolling villagers who were adorned in dignified tribal garb, each notable variation nothing short of a foreign fascination to him.

They were well fitted in leather belts that bound crimson red and flawless white cloaks around both the men and the ladies. The mothers wore symbolic wreaths of flowers, bundled together at the front and pinned with their family crests, each forged exclusively from sanctified gold. Laced sandals covered their feet and protected their soles from the sweeping cobblestone as they went up and down pristine streets with civilized grace in every step.

"Do you see it? Do you see the people? Do you see them enjoying the last summer days, buying simple joys from the street-side vendors?" she called, an ethereal projection from nowhere.

And Eddie saw them, happy families with familiar, glossy eyes accompanied by shining cosmic companions, all afloat throughout the breezy otherworld; a splendid mystic current.

Vendors with wood-crafted carts huddled along the bumpy road selling everything from paper pinwheels and wood-carved flutes to hot pastries, skewered meat, and fluffy, berry-topped bread.

He peered down the festive streets and caught a glimpse of a little girl with luxuriant black hair pulled into twin tails who sat cradled in her mother's arms. She beamed as a pink fairy hovered unsuspectingly before her unacquainted eyes. The mischievous toddler reached her arms back and caught the fairy between her fingers. To the irresistible prod of suspense, she released the ball of light and surged to life in heartwarming laughter as it reappeared again, a quaint encounter that caused the boy to smirk.

"What about the trees? Do you see the Silver Fall, with their leaves scattered all across the streets?"

And Eddie saw them. Beautiful, lush blankets of silver teardrops beneath the foot and upon the rustic, wood-shingled rooftops of the creaking architecture led him right to the arch-trunked loungers, whose endless, long strands came adorned with a thousand lustrous beauties.

He had never seen one like it, and as he pondered, he became sure. These trees, these structures, and this culture didn't exist in his world. The undetected visitor mooned over the foreign people of the meticulously constructed parallel who went about their daily lives as the Silver Fall cried to the winds, and suddenly, he felt he could move alongside them.

And so, he went.

The boy ambled through the bustle of the town, stealing curious glances at the distant fringe where the cobblestone ended and the urban sprawl fell fast to sparse woods. The trees there stood high over any structure man had dared to raise to the sacred skies, and their bushy canopies were bravely decorated with flower bands that wrapped entirely around.

On the walls of the shops along the main road, too, were handcrafted wreaths of flowers and leaves. Each was woven with unique vines and a neatness or messiness that denoted the particular skill or preference of the creators, none of which had been purchased from the shelf of any shop. Upon the center of each wreath was a tied-down paper, which bore unique characters of an unknown language: solemn wishes for their future beyond the summertime.

"Can you see the signs of the Autumn Festival? Keep walking—go further," she encouraged through a whisper brimming with desire.

Eddie pressed onward through the streets yet unnoticed by all. Children in frolic and parents giving chase passed through him as if he were but a ghost of the ancestors. Further along, a shop owner atop a sturdy ladder proudly hung their assembled wreath at the top of his store, his small boy aglow with a cheer from below. Not far beyond, he found performers behind handled masks who danced through the streets before lively crowds to ward away bad spirits with colorful feathers, insurmountable vigor, and bulging eyes through the fierce idols of the guardians.

With due courtesy, the transmitted wanderer skirted the festive congregation. Then, after lingering a moment to enjoy their performance, he pressed on until he reached the woodland path that marked the humble town's end. At the end of a passage of bowed trees, there stood a lonely, triangular-roofed temple, its golden ornament affixed beneath the eaves, hidden behind a curtain of the silver leaves. Eddie looked on as the wind took the branches from his sights, and he caught a glimpse of an emblem, which depicted three full moons beneath a halo.

Two maidens stood on the single step before the short passage into holiness where fortunes of love, knowledge, and prospering awaited them. They waited, garlanded with fine boughed wreaths, lovingly assembled and adorned by pink and silver flora and draped down the back with streaming golden ribbon. Splendent in white cloth dresses, cut short above the knee and pulled tight at the waist by a slender rope, they were two pure spirits among the trees.

In their hands were single-beaded charms, which they lifted in a tranquilizing beam upon unblemished faces to someone nearby. He was certain that it was not for him that they smiled.

Yet, he lingered there in admiration of a first step to some wondrous journey.

All around the sanctified structure, shrine maids braided vines and leaves from the temple brackets to let them hang in the calm and only tie them down when the storms rolled in from the seaside cliffs. Meanwhile, a priestess, ravishing in an extravagant gown, spun at the center of a sand-carved glyph upon the hallowed ground. Her movements were a constant, fluttering hypnosis. The boy watched, entranced, as the endless edge of her dress sliced through the air, here and there, upon each and every pass. With eyes sealed shut, she meditated the passing of time, the changing of the season, and the comings of age in prayers that whipped through that consecrated land and all those who sought its temple's grace.

He found an uncanny reverence in all of it. The very sight of this place produced an alien nostalgia that infected his feelings, like viewing the reel of some old, forgotten footage.

"What is this place?" he asked as he reemerged with the mere blink of the eye.

He peered up at Mirika and found her deepened in sobriety. Eddie had never seen her like this before. She didn't beam or smirk. Her mouth had fallen agape, and her expression was of one who awaited some cathartic reaction.

"It's just a dream," she replied, with unusual vacancy.

Eddie stared through the half-shattered mirror, unsure of what to say. Without a decisive remark from him, she turned to the little fairy, who still cowered behind the statue.

"It's okay, Sh'Shami. That's all there was to it," she swore, which the eager fae trusted, promptly rushing to her side.

She bloomed back to the close presence of her timeless companion, though she still appeared heavier than ever before. He had sensed great sadness, even as he coursed through the idyllic realm of her dream, a pervasive melancholy that left him grounded as he pondered the truth behind those eyes that had looked so mournfully into his.

"It's a beautiful dream. It really is," he consoled.

Her eyes fell in a brief retreat but rose back in light of a new idea. "You probably want to see the flying city, don't you?" she asked.

But the boy shook his head. "No—I'm here now. I want to go and be there, you know?"

She faded once more. "I see . . . I believe someday, you won't need my help anymore. You'll be wide awake . . . and I'll have to be really happy for you."

The boy resented these words. He didn't want to fathom a world in which he lost another dear friend, and although they hadn't known each other long, to lose her would be to lose a part of himself. It would be to lose the very hope that drove him to seek out an alternative in the first place, and that was a fate he couldn't accept.

"No—I want your dreams to become reality, too. Because that's the way it should be, and it should never have changed," Eddie said. He yanked back before he felt he had gushed too far. "But for now, maybe we can learn to walk in that dream together. Maybe even when you're far away. Then, we won't ever be far apart."

She cracked a smile, as though his words were wonderfully unexpected. "I think we can try," she said, glowing. "I know that dream well, and I can show you all kinds of great hidden treasures and incredible places."

As their plan carved through the future, the sadness evaporated. The prospects of adventure returned as a light to their spirits. He smiled at her. She smiled at him. With her, there was never a shortage of surprises that left him in awe. She was a bridge that connected him to the world he so longed for. Yet, here it was, right before his eyes, and he wanted to be nowhere else but right then and there, with her. And that feeling was truly unbelievable, a gift from beyond the reality.

"If it's an adventure, then you can always count me in, Miri—and you know . . . I hope someday I can show you my dream, too."

She took in a deep breath and was suddenly overcome with emotion. "I'm done with wars, Eddie Bowitz. Together, if we can make these dreams come true, then perhaps we can be done with them forever."

Her fae companion rattled with excitement at that wonderful prospect as Mirika shook the feelings from her heart and raised her head to him with the glow of newborn trust. "Ha! Look at me—I'm sorry. We should go, Eddie! We've no time to dally in old memories," she replied, recovering.

Eddie nodded. "Okay—you're right."

"Follow me. We'll take this road to the end of town," she said as she stepped around the statue then drew her finger to the sun-gilded main street.

Eddie took to her side, then snuck in a last glimpse of the silent haven, drenched in morning's golden light.

"Sh'Shami! Pom-pom!" she called with two claps.

The electrified sprite bobbed twice then zipped straight to her open palms which snapped together as soon as it had arrived. Mirika threw her hands out and cast the remnant glitter up into the air.

"Whoa! Is she okay when you do that?" asked Eddie in concern for the creature's well-being.

"No, she dies every time I do it . . . Of course she's alright. I've been a fairy handler longer than what you could count to," she proudly boasted as she straightened in upright confidence with her hands set upon her waist.

"Now, let's find the city in the sky, and it will bring us to the place with the *highest summit*," she declared as the boy's eyes grew in excitement with those resolute endeavors.

They stepped off down the road together, more in tune with each other, the young dreamer and the siren. As Eddie took up his stride across the gleaming cobblestone, he felt his spirit rise to new strength. Like no other time before, his eyes were open. For once, after so long, there was much to look forward to. He could peer through the shroud of tomorrow, to all the possibilities that lay beyond, and that promising vision of what might be could only encourage him.

Those once-heavy steps were buoyant with the spring of younger days. Beautiful was tomorrow, and tomorrow was nigh. And all things would be corrected, rectified by a mere whim of the great master. All he needed to do was reach him. All he could do was try.

The Sacred Chains of Memories

Gruman barged through the frail screen door into the intimate hallway of a secluded back-alley home, stubbornly nestled between apartment buildings, a good-fortuned, wood-crafted survivor of the Titan War. He was followed by a line of subordinates up a rickety, narrow stoop, three of them, which included Schneider, Larus, and Rhodes. Just behind Rhodes was the lanky scientist who passed nervous glances to the barren side streets of Neo Cascadia.

At the center of their formation, two soldiers hauled a salvaged invader gun, end by end, up the stairs of the stoop. Behind them, one man lugged an invader helmet, its empty gaze aimed right ahead of him.

At the top, the corrupt lieutenant and brigadier led the rest of the devout through the door behind their impatient leader. They left a single soldier to pull the door shut and watch the alleyways from the windows for those who might disturb their clandestine assembly.

Secured inside, they creaked across the scuffed wooden floors through the hallway into a cozy living room. The walls were cluttered from inch to inch with old-world décor upon dated floral wallpaper.

Gruman took a quick look around the room, then found a sturdy-legged table along the wall beside the hallway. It was adorned with an assortment of family pictures, ranging from reunions of an old woman and her two middle-aged daughters to vacation photos taken with shy and wide-eyed grandchildren.

The restless coordinator went over, took the back of his hand, and slid the pictures across the table, onto the floor, where they shattered. He pointed to the table, and the soldiers who bore the gun hobbled over. With sharp grimaces, they set it down upon the now-vacant space, and the table creaked as the legs struggled under its impressive weight.

"Glad you all could join us. Make yourselves at home—please," said Gruman as he held his hand out to offer the space to them.

"Schneider, I wanted to take this opportunity to introduce you to Dr. Drol Novell. He's been heading the genetic research department for the last four years—dealing with projects a little bit deeper in the system than you'd ever be aware of," he explained as his shadowy company fanned out across the room.

"It's all just business, eh, Doc?" Larus razzed.

Schneider looked at the doctor, who had nestled himself in a secure corner between the back wall and a fireplace with his hands folded tightly under his armpits. Aloof in transparent disinterest, he wouldn't be bothered to make eye contact with some profitless, and thus forgettable, acquaintance. They instead exchanged a half-cordial nod, an awkward interaction that seemed to entertain Gruman, who cracked a long grin.

"What about your two associates?" the lieutenant asked in a turn to the amused presider.

Larus's head fell with a dismissive snicker as he found himself addressed by a tool. "Well, you see, I went ahead and gave them something better to do with the organization's time. For you!" Larus insisted with the extension of his hand and eyes filled with a compassion too laced with madness to be sincere.

"See, I heard a lot of pretty disrespectful things come outta those guys," he continued. "A lot of things I don't agree with . . . and since they're under the umbrella of one of my righteous contingents, I swung authority, and, uh . . . knocked them right down to lookout duty."

Larus snapped clumsily through his freshly oiled glove to resounding silence. "Like magic."

Though his eyes were wide with the anticipation of gratitude, the savvy lieutenant remained apprehensive.

"Let's be realistic. It's all a popularity contest, Schneider. You wouldn't be where you're at in life without knowing that . . . but among us, you're in a whole different school. Hero general or not. You make the right friends, and you can rely on some strong allies to have your *back*," Larus emphasized with the jab of his finger from across the room.

"It was unnecessary," Schneider asserted.

"But, hey! It's reality. So, learn to accept a gift from a fellow brother in honor with some humility. Because maybe someday you'll need the elements on the dark side of the moon to be administered. And I'll be your guy, Lieutenant. I'm always the guy," Larus insisted with daggers for eyes.

"Nothing unworthy of broad daylight interests me, but I'll keep that in mind in case rats scurry," Schneider acknowledged in good tact.

The marshal eased at Schneider's agreeable remark. "That they do," Larus testified with foaming delight. "And they never get very far."

Gruman, though unsure of the results, smirked with anticipation, satisfied with the marshal's entrusted effort.

"Let's get down to it, shall we? Given the circumstances"—Gruman refocused the group as he brought his hands down upon the backrest of a leather armchair that faced an old television set in the corner of the room—"I believe it's reasonable to bring you into the loop—the whole loop."

Gruman's eyes crept to Rhodes, and she grew nervous at what he intended to reveal. The shrewd boss chuckled as he relished having all the pieces firmly in his grasp, even in the aftermath of unthinkable ruin.

"Rhodes, tell us why it was you joined the organization—"

In obedience, she went to speak, but the wind was stolen from her lungs.

"Or better yet, Rostal, perhaps you know why!" Gruman whimsically redirected with an encouraging gesture of his hand.

The sworn brigadier and lieutenant exchanged a glance, then returned their eyes to Gruman.

"Rhodes comes from an elite political family with ties to Beilka who discovered communications between the rebels that sought the overthrow of the independence-focused government in Bevia and members of the Beilkan Royal Court . . . but before they could make those claims public, her family burned in a fire at their residence in Fortuna City. . .”

"Tied up and murdered,” the disquieted brigadier asserted. "Just like the seven perpetuators.”

"Righteous justice,” the courtly kingpin lamented to solemn echoes from the devout pack, save the reticent doctor. "And in our contemporary times, what makes the rebels of Bevia . . . rather peculiar, Schneider?” Gruman pressed in a surge of vigorous spirituality.

"They are globally recognized as the root cell that became responsible for the radicalization of nationalists across the Eastern Badlands. Pitiless marauders who spilled their unsung revolution across the border, raided uncooperative towns for supplies, enforced involuntary recruitment of adolescent boys, and expelled rightful landowners from their properties; and thus, their shameless savagery gave us the three-year sickness that was The Sorrows in the Vesterbend.”

Gruman nodded in acknowledgement of each bitter fact as they were declared by the sullen hero.

"Memories are grand devices,” Gruman concluded. Inspired, he pushed off the chair and looked at each one of them. "Most especially, the bloodiest of them. They preserve the truth in our hearts, no matter how far time drags us. They are the anchors to resilience, the fierceness of our vengeance, and the valiance in our efforts. But even more so, they are the bond that holds us together. And understanding how we all got here is the oil on the gears of our operation.”

He turned to Schneider directly once again. "But do *you* know why any of these others have joined us, Schneider?”

Schneider looked around at each gruff, dirty-faced stranger, who then peered back at him, then turned back to Gruman. "No, sir. I’m afraid I don’t.”

Gruman cocked his head and bit down on his lip as if his response was incorrect or invalidated. "You see. We’re in the business of a more righteous reform. We’re all vital constituents of this organization. Though you do wield great admiration because of your exceptional heroism years ago, if you wish to retain that respect here, you must be willing to educate yourself on the many aspects that cause the valiant to flock. That clarity will help to make you a more dynamic leader—and aid to baffle you when those you've invested precious time and resources in heedlessly turn their backs on their sacred oaths."

Gruman brought his hands together with a piercing clap, and then a smile swept across his face as if he had cleared his conscience of that evident resentment with apathetic ease. "But more on that later. To preface the primary function of our congregation, I'd like to present you with a gift, Schneider. Captain?" he summoned with a rather lordly gesture to a Union sergeant who stood guard in the passage to the front door.

The stone-faced subordinate approached Schneider and, as per the aforementioned instruction, removed from his belt a holstered, black-framed revolver of colossal size. He handed it over to the lieutenant, who wasted little time unholstering it and inspecting with amazement at its remarkable proportions.

"A new gift from our friends at the Beilkan arms company, Junnel. The Shashtrakka, or Black Widow. It's light, it's big, and it'll put a hole through almost anything you point it at," Gruman gloated. "And do forgive the presentation. We had to test-fire it a few times breaking through in Salamandra, but I can assure you it works rather well on our resilient invader foes."

"That's impressive," Rhodes complimented.

"You're gonna need a thicker belt for that son of a bitch," Larus joked as Schneider holstered the weapon once more, slipped the clip onto his belt, and adjusted the cant to his liking.

"Alright, now. Let's get to the substance of why we've gathered here today," their leader reoriented.

Gruman turned to the invader gun on the table and began to trace intricate lines of cerulean illumination across the barrel with his finger. "You see, during this long lull in the aftermath of Salamandra, we've been attempting some research into the invader force. Something our friend Myres has arrogantly overlooked."

The smug puppeteer beckoned to the soldier who bore the soul-piercing helmet. In heed of the command, the sworn carrier went to a dusty side table whose ample surface area accommodated a solitary lamp. He knocked it right off and slammed the helmet down, its soulless eyes gazing right into them from across the room.

"The invaders, they—notice you, track you with those eyes . . . Yet, pull off the helmet, and there's no machine nor living thing . . . There's nothing," Gruman revealed as he turned to his audience with a chilling stare.

"I was there when we downed this one," he continued with a turn back to the invader technology, which he mooned over.

"We yanked the helmet off to get a good look at these odd world aggressors and, upon our obscure discovery, decided then and there that we'd have to salvage these for later if we ever hoped to learn anything about them. The truth had to be much deeper than we ever imagined, and luckily, we were able to stow them away among the *gluttonous* ration supply until needed."

The callous grand inquisitor snapped from his fevered recollection then turned back to his bewildered audience.

"But there is a function to that helmet even now! Make no mistake. Attempts at opening the shell with force . . . have proved deadly—once or twice. But one way to find out may be as simple as putting it on. A task perhaps so unsettling that it made the very thought of what we are about to do invisible to us by the deepest fears in our subconscious."

"You're not thinking of trying that on one of our own, are you?" Schneider inquired.

Gruman grimaced and waved off the very thought of it in a facetious display of hysteria. "It would be *barbaric* to jeopardize the safety of a good fellow of faith like some kind of lab rat. But, thankfully for us, when bombs drop, rats *do* scatter."

As if on cue, the front door burst open, and through the hallway came the sound of frantic steps. Two more soldiers, with another restrained in their grasp, drove toward the shadowy congregation.

The wide-eyed prisoner resisted in fits of desperate strength that sent the guards into the wall as they fought to regain control. A hodgepodge barrage of mounted trinkets fell to the floor: a collection of intricately painted spoons, framed pictures, and once-cherished glass antiquities, all of which were left unceremoniously shattered across the floor.

Larus, fed up with the captive's turbulent efforts, stepped out and struck him across the face with murderous potency. "Yeah—those snitching days are over for you, buddy," the marshal taunted as he shook out his hand.

The accused fell to his knees, was brought up once more, then was dragged to the center of the room before the devout. The man looked at Schneider in a way that seemed odd to him at first, but as his mind reached deeper into old memories, he found a familiarity in him.

Gruman saw it and gleamed.

"Recognize him, do you? One of the men who fought to protect his home from terrorists, who followed the same path as you into our ranks and served *loyally* for five years . . . or so we believed."

Schneider let out a breath of frustration, lost somewhere between pity and disappointment.

"It would seem not even time can secure loyalty from unprincipled waste. Nor can sheltering a poor, orphaned bastard and showering him with knowledge and purpose. Put the mask on. Let's have one last act of service from this perverse coward. Luckily for you, I have all the information I need, and your contacts won't live long enough to see the fruits of your betrayal," Gruman swore.

The unabashed defector attempted to flee once more as he realized the fate prepared for him but was seized by his able captors. He thrashed about as they struggled to control his energized frenzy.

Schneider had frozen over, unsure if he was desensitized to all the nudges of humanity or simply a petrified witness to the changes of time, which realized the dissolution of his once-unbreakable band of heroes. Brigadier Rhodes, meanwhile, stood with arms folded, deepened in a glaze devoid of empathy, waiting only for the results of their potentially harmless experiment.

"Damnit!" the rattled scientist yelped. "Gruman—I promise you, if anything disastrous happens, I'll be out the door!"

"And what knowledge will you attain from doing that?"

"This is beyond my field of expertise!" He cowered from his corner beneath the extruded mantle.

"Relax, my friend, I wish only to inspire that intricate mind. *Now, observe.*"

The soldier was ready with the helmet and waited in cold patience as the others reined the prisoner in. When his energy had been exhausted, he lost all will to fight them. He lifted his head to Rostal Schneider, his old champion in arms, as if they were the only two left in the room. Even as the helmet came down over his head, his gaze did not break, nor after the cold veil closed him off from the then and there and his spirit descended into sheer darkness.

The prisoner's shoulders rolled forward under the helm's weight.

"It may be a bit large, but sadness always fits, eventually," their privy dominus assured.

Once he was sure the helmet was on well enough, the soldier stepped away while the others continued their hold. The prisoner did not struggle or flinch, and after a moment, his head simply slumped forward.

Gruman grimaced and rubbed his cheek. They waited for a moment longer, but nothing of interest occurred.

"Enough of this. There's clearly nothing to it. Remove it, and we'll take care of this quietly," Gruman ordered.

The soldier went forward and grabbed ahold of the helmet, but just as he went to pull, a mechanism snapped behind the mask, an eerie sound that rang throughout the room. When it had gone, the anxious soldier tugged, but the helmet didn't budge. He tried harder, but his strained effort earned him no better result.

"What's happened? Did it attach right to his skin?" Gruman asked, boiling.

"I'm not sure, sir," the soldier replied.

Schneider, propelled by curiosity, stepped over and knelt down.

"Just yank it off, Schneider. Come on," Larus pressured as he meandered for the hallway.

The upstart tipped up the helmet to inspect underneath, and what he saw was gathered skin around the rim. Then, just as he went to speak, his eardrums were overwhelmed by a cavernous breath of arcane rebirth taken from behind the mask. With the skip of his heart's vital beat, Schneider was thrown in a terrible recoil, and as he scurried away across the floor, he turned to search the faces of the others for verification that they had heard it, too.

However, at once, they met his sudden terror with only stark bewilderment.

"What is it, Schneider?" asked Gruman through a wince of concern.

"You didn't hear it?" he asked back, gawking.

Gruman lifted a brow, but before anyone could offer further input, there came a footstep from above.

That unseen visitor's great weight caused the aged wooden floorboards to wail out in an eerie creak that lingered a little too long not to unsettle the group.

One by one, they looked at the ceiling.

And then came another gruesome step.

Gruman shot a glance at his captain, who looked back in a confused mix of shock and horror. "Did you send someone upstairs?"

"N-negative, sir. I didn't," the captain stammered.

There then came a sudden commotion from somewhere in the basement. The shatter of glass, shuffle of boxes, and scrape of metal haunted the beneath in hair-raising discordance. All around them, in the unknown beyond those walls, was the movement of anomalies that none of them wished to investigate.

An overwhelming spirit of dread trampled their courage. It was a silent acknowledgement that the boogeymen were loose to punish their trespasses, and they would be but fools to dally much longer.

"Perhaps it's a survivor," one soldier hopelessly surmised.

There was a muted creak as if whatever stood above had stopped to listen. The eerie lull elicited a match of silence from the troubled gang. Then came another step.

"Two survivors in a city that lies absolutely desolate?" mocked Gruman as sweat began to form on his forehead.

The hasty skeptic reached into his coat, and the frantic rustle stirred Schneider from his static daze and galvanized him to his feet. Gruman produced a snub-nosed revolver and, without much patience for the lieutenant's obstruction, took aim and pulled the hammer back.

"For God's sake, Schneider. Get out of the way," Gruman pleaded, to which his subordinate promptly complied, his eyes widened in astonishment.

He had only made it a third step before Gruman fired a shot into the prisoner's chest. The strike of the judge's hammer reverberated until silence fell again, and to their horror, the man hadn't flinched, nor did he cry out in pain. The bloodied traitor remained petrified in stillness until the spell wore off and he sank down onto his heels, then slumped over.

"What the hell . . ." muttered Larus.

Brigadier Rhodes monitored the eyes of the invader mask as she stepped away in sluggish unease. "We shouldn't stay here any longer," she advised.

Gruman took a concentrated breath through an ever-thickening anxiety. Finding his mind in a hopeless labyrinth for some obscure answer, he suddenly shook himself free of all curiosity, then turned and made right for the front door.

"Grab the weapon. We're leaving—now," the overwhelmed helmsman ordered, which ignited the entire group into a frantic effort to escape.

"What about the body?" asked the panicked lookout.

"The least of our worries. Let them try to put the pieces together," Gruman called back to them as he pushed through the door.

"Come on, you sons of bitches. Sheeba has her path. Back through the corridor! And the last one out gets their balls curb stomped." The marshal directed them with the sweep of his arm.

The steely doctor broke from the safety of the corner on a cautious hunch as if merely touching anything at all would reduce him to ashes. Larus, taking keen notice of his cowardly dart, chased him on with a ferocious roar, though it did little to hasten his pace.

The soldiers responsible for the weapon's transport hauled it off the table and fled in straddled steps behind Marshal Larus, who led the stragglers through the door.

Schneider lingered there, however.

Perhaps it was the ponderous burden of guilt that stemmed from his complete loss of words in a situation that could have been favorably navigated by tact. Perhaps, however, he truly had nothing to say at all and merely lamented the reality which he found himself tied to in consequence.

His inability to know for sure only made to stall him further.

There was a distinct sadness in the way that the diffused evening sunlight through the curtain laid its grace upon his turncoat companion, and although he couldn't quite explain it, the mere sight alone caused him to believe that anyone could lie behind those masks, even if their investigations could find nothing at all.

"Schneider—what are you doing?" Rhodes called out, straining.

He turned over his shoulder and found her at the foot of the hallway. Another thud from the ceiling caused her to wince.

"Come on—*let's go*," she desperately implored.

Schneider, rescued from a treacherous sinkhole of reflection, broke away and fled with her through the open front door, slowing only to pull it shut.

They left intensified commotion within.

In the distance, the others disappeared one by one into the designated alleyway. The rogue officers descended the steps of the old house then crossed the withered plot to the corridor, where the lookout stood by to guide them.

Before following any further, however, Schneider turned there at the corner, back to the besieged crypt, and caught a glimpse of invader eyes there beyond the curtain of the front door.

Without need of further evidence, Schneider broke his gaze and departed down the alleyway to escape the grasp of bewilderment. Had the soldiers been there all along, or had they been summoned? The organization had gathered there in search of answers but had left evicted, cast out and thrown into a hopeless tumble of ignorance.

Horizons

The resistance leadership rose early to orchestrate the departure from Neo Cascadia with their sights set on the Beilkan's Reotundra base in Northeastern Veromoor.

General Myres watched dawn's light cut across the metropolis beyond the window from a chair at the end of a long conference table.

The top brass had set up lodgings for the night within city hall, right at the center of downtown. Unlike all the modernized glitz of the area with its neon billboards and sleek geometric architecture of tomorrow, the city hall was something of an ancient relic. Like a castle, its walls were constructed of refurbished stone slabs of impressive size, the kind that might withstand the barbarian's bloodthirsty siege. It had survived as a monument to past glory, perseverance through suffering, and a testament to age-old craftsmanship.

Within the citadel of governance, the refurbished wood walls were lined with paintings. They depicted some of the city's most prized moments and landmarks, some of which included the exuberant festivals hosted throughout the years, the surrounding mountainside, and the city's heyday prior to its historic destruction.

Just as the light of morning crept across the rich brown grain of the wood desk, Myres's head drooped as if he had slipped into a deep slumber.

There came a knock at the door, and his head rose right back.

"Come on in," Myres called.

Brigadier Rhodes pushed open the door and presented herself with a salute. "Morning, General—"

Myres, still weighed by fatigue, rubbed his eyes.

"Looks like you didn't even try, sir," she identified.

Her superior, spurred by the perceptive comment, slapped his hands against the arms of the chair then drove himself to his feet. "Well—let's just say I had a visitor last night."

Rhodes cocked her head, unsure of what he meant.

"And let's just keep it at that," Myres insisted. "We better get going. I met with Schneider earlier and had him get things underway, but I'm ready now."

Rhodes nodded, her curiosity cut down with diligence. "Understood, sir. Let's put this ghost town behind us."

Rhodes parted with him and exited back into the hallway. Myres followed but stopped short of the door. The sound of her steps through the grand hall stole him for a solemn moment, and he turned his tired eyes back to the empty conference room where critical decisions might have been made. The old Union general pondered there as to how they had all gone missing and to where they could have gone.

Those perfectly manicured streets made to haunt him, as did those open establishments up and down the boulevard whose welcoming lights teased the prospect of normality but, upon fruitless investigations, only emphasized an obscure reality.

Just like in the suburbs found along the way, the vanishing of those people, too, lacked any indication of violence or reasonable urgency. It was as if everyone in the world had simply left them to fight the war alone.

The footsteps in his ear grew close but transformed into the click-clack of dress shoes. It took him a second to realize the bizarre transition, but when he did, he snapped back to the door. An unmistakable little girl in a Sunday dress released a sharp gasp and pushed off the doorframe to escape his sight.

Myres broke for the door as the pitter-patter of her flight echoed through the rounded halls, but as he cut out onto the marble floors, he caught only resonance, which evaporated fast into complete silence.

The plagued old man gasped for breath as his eyes remained fixated on the glaring sunlight, which shined through an arched window at the hall's end.

"Sir!? What is it? What's wrong?" asked Rhodes, who had doubled back for him.

Myres snapped up then shook his head to dissuade further questioning of his actions. "It was nothing—just saw some kind of wild animal—scamper down the hall there." He turned and brushed past her, sure to avoid her worried eyes. "Come on. Let's get back to sensible business, shall we?"

"Yes, sir," she replied with imperceptible suspicion, unconvinced by his half-baked response.

With their plan for departure in motion, Rhodes and Myres fled from the city hall, down the grand stone steps to Main Street. The units had taken formation along the street in wait of the supreme leader's command to march.

Accompanied by Rhodes, Myres performed a quick walk-around of the soldiers in the immediate area. All appeared in good shape, much to his delight.

"Excellent. Nothing like a little structure to get the spirit back in our steps," the general said, glowing.

"Permission to assume you're impressed, sir," called a buoyant grandstander.

Myres and Rhodes turned to find Schneider and a group of officers on approach. His arm was extended to the orderly legions in wait of some kind of praise from the general, who replied to that desire with a raised brow and a smirk.

"Now, hold on, don't go running off with too much credit. It's just been awhile since things were actually done right around here. What are my horizons looking like? We ready to march?"

"Understood, General. Affirmative. We have recon deployed ahead. They'll have their—"

Suddenly, they overheard the sound of frantic shouts.

"—eyes peeled," Schneider finished as he caught sight of two soldiers in full flight toward them.

Myres's gaze sharpened as he fought to identify them through the sun's glare.

"Who are those two?" asked Rhodes.

"One of the recon squads," Schneider replied rather casually as he stepped off to meet them halfway.

"That's not something you wanna see in a time like this," said Myres as he stepped off behind him.

Myres and Rhodes followed close as the two parties met further down the sidewalk. The soldiers stumbled to a halt, their faces plastered with fear.

"What is it? Why have you both abandoned your position?" Schneider inquired with invested patience.

"Sir! There's something out on the horizon, beyond the mountains! It's—it's huge!" gushed one of the soldiers.

"We thought it seemed like some kind of weird cloud—or smoke—or something like that—" spat the other.

"Alright—settle down. You have to calmly explain what it is you've seen," Rhodes counseled with her hand out to settle their turbulence.

The soldiers exchanged a nervous glance as they tried to come up with the reasonable means to explain it.

"Well? Go on! Out with it," Myres ordered.

"It's something in the distance! It peeked over the mountain, just out to the east!"

"Mountains? So, to the southeast?" Myres scrutinized.

"It reaches across the *entire horizon!*" the soldier insisted.

Those trusted senior commanders each assessed the other's reaction with a glance and found themselves assuredly unified in their bewilderment.

"Well . . ." The general sighed. "That sounds encouraging."

In a collision of messengers, a group of Beilkan soldiers appeared at the far end of the road and advanced across in an orderly step. One of them bore the Beilkan standard at the top of an elaborate gold pole, etched with the oath of their service. The lead broke from the group and negotiated his advance with a group of Union officers who had intercepted their approach.

Myres, in hopes of accelerating the process, went to meet them halfway. Rhodes and Schneider followed behind him in hopes the Beilkans, a notoriously serious people, could offer them decisive clarity.

"General Myres, Supreme Commander Gala requests a meeting with you at the Southern Spire. There've been critical developments that force us to reassess our way forward."

"What exactly are we dealing with? Does anyone have a *clear answer?*" Schneider erupted.

A pervasive silence gave him his response. The overwhelmed lieutenant shook his head as he pressed his palm against his forehead in aching frustration with their apparent incompetence.

"We're standing in the middle of a city which saw its entire populace moved . . . taken? Unless everyone calmly walked out," said Myres with the dramatic sweep of his arm. "I think it's safe to say nobody really knows what the hell we're dealing with. Get everyone ready to move. Inform General Gala that I'll be at the meeting site as soon as the ball is rolling," Myres ordered. "Schneider, Rhodes, get to the burbs and link up with General Henson. Let's get the roundup underway. By the sound of it, we're out of time."

With those orders, their departure was underway. The detachment took Main Street all the way to the southern freeway entrance. As they cut through the empty streets, Schneider scanned the faces of the skyscrapers. He came under a subtle trance as his eyes drifted from window to window, but he soon witnessed an anomaly in the mundane pattern, the faintest blue radiance from within a few of the darkened portals. The otherworld loomed beyond the glass, and as his eyes fell to the soldiers who marched beside him, he saw them cast their gaze up to those cerulean-eyed phantoms as well.

He was sure they could see them, too.

Within hours, the command had unified the caravan and delivered them to the outskirts of the suburban sprawl. All that remained was to confirm their course.

General Henson was left at the helm to oversee the finalizations of the second exodus while General Myres departed the Union camp accompanied by Schneider, Rhodes, and an able squad.

From their position in the countryside, a two-hour hike separated them from their destination. The Beilkan infantry had assembled in a winglike formation around the imposing rock spire. As the Union top brass approached, they could make out the figures of General Gala and his officers of high rank up at the peak.

Without delay, they were beckoned to the foot of the path by a detachment of royal riflemen and, together, ascended to the very top.

"Welcome, my friends," General Gala greeted upon their arrival. "A bit later than I had hoped, but thankfully for us, the situation has remained relatively unchanged."

"General!" Myres huffed from the last step to the jagged silver-stone flat. "Would you please explain to me why you've put old knees—and a really bad lower back through a second climb of these forsaken cliffs?"

The Beilkan general's eyes remained locked on something out on the horizon, and though a pair of binoculars were clasped in his hands, he had no apparent further use of them.

"A keen eye would have already noticed. You should have seen what it looked like at sunrise," he crooned, still dazed by the very sight of it. "We call it the Great Crest. Behold, a force of absolute nature that might yet withstand all the madness of mankind or take us all with it in its unimaginable demise."

As they approached the general at the cliff's brink, the Union trio became iced over by what they soon came to distinguish from the panoramic clear skies.

"Do you see that blue out there over the mountain range?" Gala directed.

Out on the horizon, there was a white streak that bounded high over the tallest peak of the distant white-capped range.

"What the hell are we looking at?" Schneider asked, mouth gaping.

"There's no time to be vague. That's not the sky—is it?" asked Rhodes, to which Gala answered with the chilling shake of his head.

"Madeline and I once hiked to the top of that mountain—Mount Mevis . . . and that's a hell of a lot higher than its summit," Myres identified.

Gala held out his binoculars to Myres. "Go on, take a closer look," he insisted.

The general, reluctant to behold any mind-bending miracle, took the binoculars and moseyed closer to the edge of the cliff. With all the courage a lifelong realist could muster, he peered through the glass to unprecedented truth, but as the monster on the horizon came to nauseating clarity, Myres dropped the binoculars and released an unsteady breath.

"Feels like—" Myres heaved.

General Gala raised his brow and held steady for a complete response.

"Feels like you should order everyone away so I can have a seat."

Gala grimaced. "Don't lose your dignity."

Myres turned from the cliffside to the paralyzed Union soldiers under his command and watched as their blank expressions became gruesomely warped by sheer terror.

A few of them even dropped their weapons as they, too, came to realize the oceanic colossus that they had become witness to.

"It's a wave?" muttered one of the soldiers.

Their emotive decay into dread proved infectious to one of the Beilkan soldiers on guard nearby. With a tremble in his legs, he, too, lost the grip on his rifle, and it struck smooth slate with an honor-tainting clap.

That strident sound of capital disgrace from among his royal legion brought General Gala to an instant boil. Roused to instinctive fury, the Beilkan supreme commander stormed over to the luckless soldier, the sound of the gun's fall still ringing in his ear.

He erupted at the mere sight of the disarmed soldier with veins bulged throughout his neck. "How dare you drop that weapon onto the *ground.*"

He drove his finger right up to the soldier's chest and jabbed him in a blind rage. The soldier threw his arm up in salute and froze, his only defense against his revered superior's wrath.

"Since when did your ancestors drop their weapons in the face of *fear* or *hardship*? You drop that weapon again, and I'll personally drag you through the victory parade, right to the king's doorstep, where you can explain to him and his people what a *goddamn coward* you are."

The soldier burst into a chant in Beilkan.

"Let the foreigners hear you say it!" Gala bawled.

"All hail the King of Beilka and the great destiny of his people!"

General Gala nodded, his lip pinched up in dissatisfied acceptance.

"Now, pick up the goddamn gun and get out of my sight. Out of all the things I've seen today . . . this will be the most memorable," he declared with the whip of his hand, to which the soldier complied in haste to make himself scarce.

Myres, Rhodes, and Schneider each passed a glance to one another, broken from the bewitchment of the distant wave and returned to humanity by the Beilkan general's irrepressible pride. The Union soldiers, guided to rekindled honor by that fiery example, reached for their weapons, too. Myres caught them in the act and gave them a silent skyward *whoosh* with his finger to hurry them as to spare them all from embarrassment in the face of such nationalistic fervor.

"So, then—we're going to need to find a new route," Myres conceded as he placed his hands upon his waist.

Gala turned to him and grunted with a nod, his face still flushed by rage. "My thoughts exactly. Is that not what my messengers told you?" he asked with refreshed sincerity.

"No—they did. Don't go chewing anyone else out," Myres insisted.

Rhodes brushed past Schneider on a course for the ledge to get a clear look at the limited routes available to them across that threatening horizon.

"Well, you aren't kidding about finding a new route," she said upon arrival to the unguarded brink.

She watched as the world-ending crest ebbed and flowed and, though staggered by High Fantasy's gut-churning monument to its own glory, remained stabilized by the heavy burden of duty.

"We all realize what that is, right?" she asked, turning to gauge their reaction. "Mount Mevis is the tallest peak of the Rasandan Range, a little over nineteen thousand feet. That wave looks to be twice the size. Twice the size of a *mountain*," she emphasized.

"It sounds just as bad as it looks," said Myres.

"Has anyone been monitoring the direction of this thing? We could be in imminent danger here," she urged.

"Hold on. Let's stay calm, Brigadier Rhodes . . . It could be an illusion," Schneider suggested.

"You could be right. Though I doubt you're going to find anyone who wants to go find out," Myres assured him.

"This would have been a great time to have someone around, who, I don't know . . . might give us some insight?" Rhodes hinted.

"Don't delude yourself in believing the swordsman was ever an ally. Even if his allegiance no longer lies with the invaders, he is an invader no less," Schneider said.

Myres rubbed his face in frustration with his subordinate's stubborn disposition. "Hopefully he turns up again," the general diverged. "I'll have to side with Rhodes on this. Anyone who puts down invaders like he did is a friend in my book. And we could use all of the friends we can get."

Rhodes lingered in a thought for a moment, then refocused on Myres with a question in mind. "Why did he leave after we made it out of the capital?" she asked.

Myres's scratched his chin as he recalled the swordsman's parting words. "He mentioned his presence among us for too long might prove dangerous. Seemed to have some kind of history with that general of theirs and decided it was best that he divert course to see if they'd set their sights on him."

"We'll be sure to keep our eye out for him," Schneider assured in blatant distrust of the invader's word.

"Regardless of his absence, we must act, now. These are your lands, General. What do you propose we do?" Gala asked, entrusting the general. "Wherever we go, we shall go together."

Myres took a breath, then stepped off into a methodical pace, fumbling with ideas to forge a new path for their unified resistance.

"Even with the Reotundra to the northeast out of the question, our next best bet would be Enedes . . . Though, that would lie due north—westerly . . . Rhodes," he designated. "What course can we take to avoid giving everyone a front row seat to this monstrosity?"

She shook her head, bypassing any and all consideration for some plausible means to do so. "Impossible. Our only hope would be to keep quiet and stick to a westward march—for the time being . . ." she clarified. "Even when they eventually catch on, we may be able to pass it off as . . ."

She motioned Schneider in regard to his position on the matter. "As just an illusion," he said.

Following through with her deduction, Rhodes moved to the west-facing brink of the flat top. "Seeing that going west alone would be a little more than fruitless, I would say northwest is our best course. Even if our goal is Enedes, moving away from the wave should take precedence. Among all other obvious benefits, doing so is just one way we can start to gauge its movement."

She took aim at a distant, verdant forest to the west, which enveloped the shrinking mountains of the southern range.

"Skirting the Tenza Rock Forest is our best option, without a doubt. It'll initially take us straight out west as we journey there but eventually connect us to a road to . It's a modest town, but if memory serves right, there's an armory there that would certainly be of use to us. Survivors aside, there won't be much other than that, but it offers a straight shot right into Enedes via the northeastern road that runs through the countryside. With luck, by the time we reach it, we'll have a better idea if travel there is prudent."

"Understood. Rhodes, I'll need your team, which you'll assemble today, monitoring that"—he clarified with the cast of his finger to the looming herald of apocalypse—"at all times. I'm gonna get everyone up to speed in regard to our new course. Schneider, I'm placing you in command of the caravan, for now. General Henson and I are going to need to work a little more closely with our Beilkan friends as we figure out how we're going to prepare for an identical situation upon reaching Enedes. Assuming word spreads about the wave—it's just an illusion, just like she said . . . Everyone clear?"

Myres looked at each of them to confirm their comprehension of their expeditiously constructed plan. They each gave an affirmative nod, his Union officers and the Beilkan supreme commander, and so, with their grave flight from Neo Cascadia set in motion, Myres dismissed his subordinates, who promptly took their leave via the cliffside path along the spire.

The Union general bid his farewell with a casual salute to his Beilkan counterpart, but before he could take the first step down, Gala rushed forward and intercepted him.

"Myres—are you sure you wouldn't rather have the more sensible one leading the people?" he questioned.

"No, no, I'm sure I'd rather have the skeptic doing that," Myres replied with conviction. "If he believes it, then I need him to be the one preaching it—and hope to high heaven he's right."

Solemn Wishes

The Union army and its civilian caravan had made great strides toward the forest beyond Neo Cascadia, all without incident from the invader army or its dreadful mega-crest.

The backroads had offered them a clean course west until they reached the outskirts of the Tenza Rock Forest. Taking the promised road, the army led the caravan north along the dense woodland that dominated the Western Tenza region. Though successful in covering a great distance, collaborating Union and Beilkan scouts soon encountered a lone invader starship, which loomed above the pass through the last hills like a deathly sentry.

In hopes to avoid a senseless engagement with the unassailable craft, General Myres, with the agreement of his top brass and the approval of General Gala, ordered the masses straight into the Tenza Rock Forest onto a covered route that fed through the mountain range.

It was no guarantee that their course would be any more secure, and the threats presented within the forest weighed heavily on all those responsible, but they had been left without an easy choice.

Rhodes's team, comprised of gathered civilian and military mathematic elites, had kept a close watch on the great wave since the moment of their inception. As they ventured through the dense curtain of the forest, however, the eternal crest disappeared behind the tree line with it being concluded that there had been little movement detected. A truth that, although minute in its evident progression, proved to be quite unsettling to those involved.

The sheer numbers of the caravan had disqualified the mountain pass itself for consideration and forced them through the dried riverbed of the ancient Aurilan River, which had once famously cut much farther north into Beilkan satellite territory. Once a conduit of trade and power, it had been reduced to a grassy bed of dried mud and the occasional puddle but carved an ample path through the lush mountainside greenery, and thus, the old Aurilan had found its importance to humanity, if only for one last time.

Across the banks on each side were grass-covered knolls that held the line against the dense forest. Soldiers patrolled their summits with the solemn duty to keep the group together as they made their way forward. The journey had not been without deserters. Disappearances plagued both the army and caravan and, outside of the siege of Salamandra, had been the only cause of losses.

At the heart of the civilian pack, Lyal and his companions slogged along the northern bank. In front of them walked a young mother who held her little girl who would periodically ask "Where's Daddy?" to which she would reply time and time again "Mommy's not sure."

Their bouts proved an annoyance to Setz, who sighed in a frustration of his own, but beside him, Miyacre looked on with eyes full of sorrow.

Lyal turned over his shoulder and noticed her anguish. "You okay?" he asked.

Those soft words broke her from the frail trance. Her eyes widened as they darted around in frantic search of her companion in misfortune who walked just beside her. He slowed pace and tapped her shoulder until she found him.

"What's wrong—"

She shook her head before he could get the words out. "It's nothing. Please—don't worry about me. I'm just—yeah," she stumbled.

"Hmm, not gonna be able to do that for you," he razzed in an attempt to lower her guard.

"Ly—come on, man," she begged as she eased him away with her hand. "I don't want to do this."

The words sank into him as he stepped away to give her that space. He hadn't meant to upset her and felt bitter inadequacy at being unable to break through, although he was mindful that her woes would not be easily remedied by thoughtless, jocular remarks.

Miyacre ripped in a stifled breath. She held it tight to prevent the echo within, then pushed onward to escape those burgeoning feelings that had lain in wait for fragility.

Her eyes wandered to the top of the bank and, in a stroke of grim misfortune, fell upon a familiar leering duo, the very sight of whom brought her to stomach-churning nausea.

The lanky scientist was once more joined by the Union officer, Larus, who looked at her and waxed into a wily grin when he was sure that she had seen him. She couldn't understand their shameless obsession to be anything more than carnal in nature and cursed their vile persistence, though only in the privacy of her mind. She knew her friends might act rashly in her stead and that their actions might jeopardize their own safety. It was best, she felt, to keep it to herself.

Lyal could see that she was deep in her thoughts, and so he let her be but made sure to keep a close watch on her. Perceptive to his friend's moping, Mitz slid up to his side to console him. "How's she holding up?" he asked in the intimate space between them.

Lyal shrugged. "Wish I knew, man. She's not letting me in right now."

"Don't sweat it, yeah? Everyone's in a hard spot right now. I mean, look around. You can't go a mile without hearing a sob story." Mitz threw out his hands to ward off any accusation of heartlessness. "Not that I'm trying to say it's unwarranted or anything."

Lyal looked at Mitz, who seemed relatively animated in countenance and in step. "So, how are you in such high spirits, then?"

"That's just the way I am when I'm nervous, I think . . . if we're being one hundred percent honest here."

Lyal nodded off to the side, hung up on a short stint of irritation with all the things in the world. "I can understand that," he said, anchoring himself.

Ahead, Miyacre had become helplessly fixated on a commotion further along the bank. There was a lone nurse who was plainly overwhelmed by eight children, each not a day over five years of age.

The flustered caretaker worked to separate two boys who had latched onto each other in a scuffle. One smaller boy stood at her side in content obedience while the rowdy rest of two boys and three girls chased each other around near some messy overgrowth, which enclosed a few large boulders further up the bank.

Miyacre took a step forward but was immediately intercepted by Lyal, who held his hand out to stop her.

"No—Miyacre. Just leave it alone."

"Lyal, move. I'm going over there. She needs *help*."

Just as she spoke the word, another nurse came to her colleague's aid and made haste to bring the children to order. Lyal held out his hand to show her. "See? They've got professionals who are here to do this."

"Some of us don't need to be professionals to lend a helping hand, *Lyal*." She searched him with eyes that hunted for the essence of his character which, to her, had clearly undergone a discouraging change. "I thought you would understand that." She stepped around and left him behind. Setz joined her in brisk separation.

"I'm with her."

"Come on, Setz. Fuck off."

But Setz shook his head and kept his eyes straight ahead. "I got nothing to say to you, man."

"Alright, alright, everyone chill out," pled Kaiser as he parted the two groups with outreached arms.

"Come on, Kaiser. Let's just go," Lyal grumbled as he pushed his arm away to proceed.

Miyacre sloshed through a pool of mud from the recent showers. Water seeped in through her shoes just as disappointment sank into her spirit. She had hoped that Lyal, more than anyone, would have understood her desire to offer aid to those in obvious need. Given her course, it was simply in her nature to do so, and she vowed, then and there, that the next opportunity that presented itself would be taken up with an unwavering heart, regardless of who stood in the way. For if she were to be forever dissuaded by the will of another, then she would undoubtedly lose her grip on the destiny that would have surely been hers, and that was a reality she could refuse with good faith and sobriety.

As she grew farther and farther from her friends, however, her mind began to wander back to the men who had been watching. A quick glimpse over to the ridge revealed them following alongside her with increased haste. Against the will of her anger toward Lyal, she slowed pace to regroup with her companions as her pursuers' presence became glaringly hostile.

Setz was the first to arrive at her side and immediately realized something was amiss. His eyes narrowed in heavy suspicion.

"Miyacre, what's up?" he asked.

The others caught up with them as they dropped back.

"Yeah, you alright, Miyacre?" asked Kaiser, her odd behavior now recognized by all.

She nodded. "Yes—it's nothing—it's . . ."

She froze. They all froze. Their ears sharpened at once to a distant roar of the likes of which none had ever heard before. So paralyzingly unprecedented that it left them iced in instinctive horror even as the grim rumble of unseen calamity grew louder.

At once, they looked all around as a commotion set in among the masses.

"What the hell . . . is that?" Miyacre whispered.

The ruckus erupted into sheer panic as a grand crash of water ripped overtop of the northern peak. The monstrous torrent cascaded over the timeless rock and unleashed sweeping ruin down through the verdant acres.

At once, chaos spread like a deadly virus as both civilian and military corps fled for the tree line beyond the southern bank.

"Look at tha—Run! Run!" Lyal shouted as he jabbed his finger to the safety of the far hills.

He grabbed Kaiser, who idly gazed at imminent death, and threw him toward the other end. Setz retrieved him from the stumble, and together, they took off for the bank.

"Miyacre! Let's go!" he cried.

She remained paralyzed for a moment, her eyes stricken with terror, but she had heard him and began to move.

"It's coming! Gotta move, *come on, move!*" shouted Mitz as the distant rock cracked from the almighty press of oceanic Armageddon.

Lyal and Mitz took off with Miyacre right behind them. They had nearly made it to the overgrown rise when suddenly, the sworn Samaritan caught the call of destiny in her ear. It was the strident cry of a child that went nearly hidden in the cacophony of mass panic. She turned over her shoulder and found him at once, that smallest boy of mannerly self-restraint. The nurses, however, were nowhere to be found.

All others fled as the demon torrent stormed toward the open graveyard. Its hellish roar drowned everything out, deafened the ears of the fleeing masses, and robbed them of every fiber of bravery as it closed in to deliver the channeled, black-eyed rage of nature.

One did, however, turn to face that relentless foaming monstrosity like a beacon into darkness, a shining star through the emptiest void.

Miyacre had taken flight for the child as her friends began their ascent of the slopes. Lyal turned over his shoulder, and his heart nearly stopped at the sight of that blatantly suicidal courage.

"Miyacre, what the f—"

He turned back without a splinter of hesitation but was seized by the arm. Under fierce resistance, he ripped back against the pull of his assailant, but the struggle proved too much. Brought to the brink of a brute force offensive, he turned and met the desperate eyes of the young soldier who had apprehended him.

"You have to get to higher ground. *Don't you see that!?*" the soldier roared, his voice trembling with terror.

"Get the hell off of me—If you're not going to help her, *I will!*" Lyal cried.

But the soldier mustered his strength and dragged him away. Lyal flailed against that formidable influence, but not even his most barbarous efforts won him any ground.

Out beyond, Miyacre reached the bawling child, who had fallen at the foot of the northern bank. She snatched his arm and yanked him up from the ground.

"Come on, we have to go!" she yelled.

The words were lost in impenetrable noise, however. The child's shrieking intensified. She dove and lifted him into her arms, but just as she had him secured in her embrace, a dark shadow was cast over them. Her eyes rose as the merciless surge blasted over the bank, and the resulting tower of deep blue lurched.

She froze as the roaring colossus bore down on them. A vicious swell punched them out just before it slammed into the earth. In an instant, they were swallowed up in mayhem's cruel torrent as it tore through the ancient cradle and brought the river back to life. Miyacre struggled to hang on to that little arm as they were lashed in the chaotic currents of reborn, raging waters. She was dragged through the mud beneath, slammed against the rocks, yanked from one side to the other, all as the monstrous flash flood slaughtered the earth beneath.

At first she had him secure. She was sure of it. But as the water filled her sinuses, she gasped, and her lungs became filled.

"Just lay the customer's prescription on the counter with a smile."

She was tossed once in a violent shift in the current and felt only his wrist, still gripped tight in her desperation even as her arm swung out to all sides and her shoulder began to throb.

"A surgeon? Well, let me be the first to tell you it isn't easy."

Though the waters had whipped them relentlessly in the depths of the unknown, miraculously, she surfaced in the angry rapids. She could still feel the little hand submerged below, but as she fought to pull him out, a second crest punched her back below the waves. The tremendous impact dazed her, and somewhere along the way, she lost her grip as it drove her deeper and deeper into the abyss.

"Don't even think about doing it unless you believe you're strong enough."

And for a moment, she lost herself completely.

There were no yesterdays or tomorrows. There was but a single moment and a singular experience.

"...unless you believe you're strong enough."

The child was gone, and gone was she. All of the world was infinite depth and blue.

And then, time skipped.

. . . believe you're strong enough."

By the breach of oblivion, she overheard the roaring torrent, though she felt an unmistakable and comforting stillness. Her cheek was planted firmly against the muddy earth, and her hand twitched as she grazed the moist ends of grass with the tips of her trembling fingers.

She let out a gasp as her head jolted up, a revival that befitted one who had just awoken from the endless passages of a nightmare. Her eyes searched the darkened landscape beneath the dense canopy of the waterlogged forest.

With no imminent threat to her life, she dug her palms into the soft mud and rose onto her knees. Her initial breaths were cut short by remnant anxiety left behind from the horror of drowning. She laid her hand against her chest but encountered no complication with any inhale. Miyacre remained there, however, incredulous to this odd state of normality, and it wasn't until her breathing had steadied that she felt ready to move.

With able strength, she rose and found herself upon an elevated platform of hanging earth. On one side was the face of the mountain over which she had come, and on the other were the cliffs to a forested and trench-like gorge that plunged to certain death.

"I'm okay . . . I'm okay," she repeated as she took feeble steps to test her balance.

As her senses gathered, she turned to the monstrous gush behind her whose waters were funneled through a gaping, rocky crevice. She heedlessly inched toward that treacherous brink and gazed down unto the hopeless cascade into the valley, which flowed with the consistency of a thousand-year-old waterfall. The torrent had torn through the forestation on an angry warpath to the bottom. Nothing that fell within would ever survive the rock and mess of uprooted trees.

The cruelest truth had met her there upon the stage of miracles. With a buckle to despair, she slid her thumb through the palm of her empty hand as she realized the boy was lost. Her grimace deepened as she fought the tears of her failure. It was only her left now, and she had to move with haste if she hoped to escape a similar fate.

Over her shoulder, the ground around the torrent gave way and was driven out with terrifying force. The gush swelled, and endless gallons began to pummel the formation upon which she had awoken.

Imperiled by the engorged jet stream, she turned and fled along the trees of the cliffside as the deluge ripped away at the ground behind her.

The path banked around the steep rock.

She followed along, and it grew to a wide shelf on the other side.

Across the belly of land she went with reckless negotiation of intertwining roots as she wove through the cliffside pines. She hadn't gone far when she hurriedly crossed out into open grass and stumbled right into the crosshairs of the underworld reaper.

It was him, the wretched officer who had troubled her with murderous persistence, accompanied by two other soldiers, surely of no greater honor. As she looked upon their drenched uniforms, Miyacre became dismayed at their survival, and even more so with her heartless misfortune that had found them back together in nauseating propinquity.

"Well—look at that! It's a little rainbow on a stormy day! I just *can't—stop—getting lucky today*!" the sworn marshal roared under the fierce influence of unrestrained madness.

She became privy to twisted desire abeam in his eyes and, finding herself nearly fixed in the vice grips of peril, took preemptive flight for the ridge, which lay just ahead.

"And you aren't the last car on the train, sweetheart . . . Whaddya say, boys? I think we got ourselves a dame to rescue," he said with evil-laced glee, and though exhausted from their chaotic ordeal, his forcefully disarmed subordinates nodded, then broke into pursuit in wordless compliance with his mischief.

In her desperate flight from the bloodthirsty rogues, she felt her feet slip within her soggy shoes, an ailment that worsened as the wet earth turned to slick rock beneath her steps. She had noticed, however, that the precarious path led to another belly of land and, possibly, an escape around the mountain, and so she kept up her pace, irreverent to any and all consequence.

The sworn agents pursued with matched audacity. So much so that when the boot of the soldier at the head of their charge met the rock, he slipped at once and nearly lost his life to the cliffs.

Larus, indifferent to his soldier's peril, raced out in front of them and took the lead of the pursuit as the second soldier fell back to assist his unnerved comrade away from the brink.

"It's too dangerous! You won't get far alone!" the mad marshal called out in hopes that his words might stumble her.

But they had no effect. The danger they posed was in her heart.

She raced up a short flight of stone steps and traced the cracked ridge around a sharp bank, then found herself on the final stretch of treachery. Dreary caves passed alongside her there, inaccessible apertures into oblivion that meandered deep into the sheer rock.

Ahead was a steady stream of water, which rushed out from a considerably larger maw in the cliffside. Miyacre could hear the faint drone of the angry torrent somewhere within the rock, but she couldn't allow herself to abandon her course. The twisted officer was right behind her now, his accomplices making up lost ground, and regardless of what horrors nature might suddenly inflict, a soul-sick scoundrel would do much worse.

She cut through the stream, but the water was deeper than expected. It caught all of her momentum at the foot, and she fell forward but sprang right back into full flight. Larus made the crossing in two seamless leaps, unhindered by the deceitful flood and now right on her tail.

There came a thunderous breach from somewhere within the cave. As Larus's sworn henchmen entered the stream, the drone crescendoed into a horrible roar. A sudden surge of water caught them on their pass and drove them straight off the cliffside down into watery mayhem.

Miyacre's blood ran cold as their hopeless shrieks grew faint, and as she reached the second suspended shelf, she found her only means of escape cut off by the cruel hand of fate. A second torrential gush and an impressive gap separated her from the hillside to possible salvation. She couldn't stop herself from going straight to the brink, however, and heard a pitiless cackle as she came to a defeated halt before the raging torrent.

"That's enough. You come with me . . . and I'll get you out of here alive. We understand each other?"

Miyacre turned back to him with terrified eyes. Not a fiber of her spirit would allow him to make her a hostage, even if it meant death.

So, she calmed herself with easy breaths as she approached the deathly torrent with timid steps, inching ever closer to a fate undeserved, but a fate decided.

"Natural selection? Is that your choice!?" he berated with a face reddened with fury.

Before she had the chance to see through that decisive self-execution, fortune found her, and a darkened, colossal mass barreled over the unrelenting gush. Miyacre stumbled away as one end of the tree dove in and tumbled across the rocky brink but rolled to a stop just short of going right over the cliff. The great barked elder, nearly stripped of branches from its ferocious journey, was of such length that it had crashed down upon both sides of the rift, and as Miyacre turned back to it, she saw the way to the other side.

"Stop! It's unstable—" Larus cried, though his reanimated prey had already turned onto the first foot into flight.

Miyacre raced right up to the waterlogged trunk, which had jammed up against the cliffside rocks while the far end lay just out of reach of the torrent's might. She took hold of the exposed root and began to climb.

"Shit—you *senseless*—" Larus hissed.

He hesitated at first with a step forward, then a step back, but then, with a tremble into total madness, committed to the chase with an explosion into full speed. Miyacre neared the top of the trunk and looked down to gauge the distance of her pursuer. Larus rocketed up in a bloodthirsty ascent after her. The seasoned killer caught a stable root with both hands, pulled his weight like it was nothing, leapt from the taproot, and snatched another, using every natural feature to assist him to the top.

Miyacre let out a gasp as she found herself frozen by his dynamic movement. The drooling leer upon the huntsman's face shook her from the daze, and she made quick to pull herself over the top of the conifer bridge. With only two steps across, however, the desperate survivor felt her weight come out from under her. She toppled forward, and her hip slammed against the wood. Haphazard momentum put her on a hair-raising slide along the soaked bark until she caught a frightful glimpse of the harrowing dive to the flooding gorge.

Gaping in terror, she dug her nails into the soggy bark as her body crept ever closer.

"You know? I see why the doctor likes you," mocked Marshal Larus as he pulled himself up onto the trunk, not far behind her. "You're a little bit athletic—bold! Lovely as a soggy peach rose, right about now . . . and albeit . . . a bit of a blunt broad, going after that kid like you did."

His fallen prey had worked herself back to the center with the fierce energy donated from desperation and hatred. She rose on shaky legs but forged ahead as carefully as she could.

Larus fleered at her tireless bravery. "You really think you're going to make it, don't you?"

He watched with a cruel glare as that nameless and near-worthless civilian girl continued across toward the other side.

"Well, then. Fuck the doctor. I think he can live with a sampler," he decided as he reached for his pistol.

He patted down the holster, but the gun had been lost. The alacritous murderer shook his head in vexation with the inconvenient circumstance.

"Guess it's the hard way, sweetheart," he vacuously lamented with the draw of a combat knife from a buttoned-down scabbard on his belt.

With careless ease, he flipped the knife and grabbed it out of the air, reverse edge in.

Miyacre had, meanwhile, neared the center of fortune's bridge when the roaring spectacle slightly ahead persuaded her to careful steps. Just as she had slowed pace, however, there came a fierce swipe barely beyond the back of her neck. She flipped around and inched away as Larus approached with the knife, reaching forward, terrorizing her with a flashy wobble, ready to kill.

"Here's to being first blood for the DNA buffet."

His foot cut forward to deliver a crippling blow, but his boot slid out, and his balance was thrown. Miyacre, stealing the moment, reversed just as he recovered.

Larus lunged out and caught her by the hair. Miyacre yelped as the sworn hunter dragged her back in. Defiant yet, she drove forward until her legs straightened and stiffened in determined resistance.

"Let's cut it out," he sneered with the raise of his knife over his shoulder.

He slashed the doctor's precious victim across the back, and she let out a gruesome shriek. Sapped by throbbing agony, Miyacre dropped to her knees, and the tickled marshal used her slaking submission to look upon the blood drawn by his blade.

"A living monument to the priestess Sheeba herself," he mused.

Miyacre refused to surrender to whatever vision he had for that blood. In a fierce revival, she kicked back at the bark beneath his feet in the fury of survival as she gripped her hair with both hands to minimize the pain. Larus stepped forward just as her foot broke the bark loose. The loose panel shot back and away, and her assailant slipped and fell forward.

He released her to catch himself from the fall, and as he struck the slick bark and fought to stabilize himself, Miyacre scrambled forward then darted away. Larus grimaced in a darkened rage then stabbed the bloodied edge into the tree and pushed against the handle as he took back to his feet.

After yanking the knife, he swept away chips of bark from his uniform as he released a sigh of deep frustration with the young girl's savage persistence. Then, with her death a personal priority, the mad marshal stepped off into a renewed pursuit of grim steadiness.

Miyacre's swift and decisive action had nearly won her enough time to reach the other end, but as she approached the mess of branches at the battered crown, she overheard the terrible thunder of a crashing titan somewhere beyond the raging torrent.

From her watery peripheral, she managed a glimpse of a huge mass as it stormed over the falls, a second colossal conifer that had been launched on a collision course for the opposite side of fortune's bridge.

Her eyes widened with horror as that monumental missile descended on the pass, its trajectory unmistakable.

Behind her, Marshal Larus had caught sight of that impending doom, and his menacing saunter had turned into an explosive flight for his life.

From the branches, Miyacre sprang for the safety of the hills. The hurled tree struck and shot the other end out over the descent to death.

The branches and trunk beneath her feet pulled away right before her eyes. The damned hunter of blood was thrown into the air and let out a terrified screech as he was left to plummet into the watery rampage, where the drowning current churned.

The ground below came fast, and her leap was made all the more harrowing by sharp rocks laid sparsely throughout the grasses. But she held her hands out to break the fall, compelled by irrepressible instinct. Both hands met the soft marsh. Her left wrist twisted and cracked as she caved in, rolled over it, then tumbled across the jagged earth.

She slammed into a boulder at the foot of the steep hill, and her breath was taken at once. Lain in acute exhaustion, she lingered long into that moment of necessary respite and, although defiled by pain, found unequivocal peace there knowing her hunter was dead.

When tranquility had subsided and the emptiness was all that was left, she sat up and leaned her shoulder against the rock. She grimaced as a deep pain sent tears rolling down her face, free yet hopelessly lost in this new tomorrow of which she could derive only sorrows.

With the injured wrist hugged tight against her stomach, she gripped her forearm as the pain resonated throughout her arm. She knew it was broken even before she saw the dislocation, the severe swelling, and the frightful purple discoloration. The damage was concerning, and she knew she needed to find help. There was nothing she could do alone.

With her body and spirit in shambles, Miyacre drove her shoulder into the rock and pushed up to her feet. The path forward was one lain by a wet blanket of leaves and reached only for the daunting unknown beyond the hilltop. She listened in close but heard only the rage of the waters, a harsh sound that offered little hope to foster in the weakened heart.

With careful steps, she scaled the slick rise, taking hold of slender trees with her uninjured hand to aid in the treacherous ascent. Through some stumbles and falls, she eventually reached the top of the ridge, but the somber survivor's heart sank further as she came to behold several other torrents beyond the summit, which unleashed an endless deluge into the gorge, all along the mountainside.

Miyacre fell to the ground at a loss for what she might do if she returned to find she had lost them all to calamity. Life had run out of blessings, and she pondered if there was anything she could have done to keep them from going that day. There was so much there for them before the war, and like all wars, the invasion had taken that promise away.

She could only pray for the survival of the others, though the outcome for many seemed undoubtedly grim. Deep down in her heart, she gathered the strength to send a message far beyond the stars. A fated wish to find the means to succeed tomorrow where she had failed today.

Only then would she find the will to go on.

That was her solemn promise, and thus became her sacred oath.

The sky rumbled. Far up in the gray shroud, turmoil brewed, the fires of the destiny forge lit by finger snap. Her eyes lifted to those warring skies, and her ears went deaf to the crack of divine thunder. Streaks of lightning struck out across the heavens as the eye of Eternia's dread sovereign peered through a breach in his storm.

The crestfallen wish caster became spellbound by an arcane experience as a million sacred tears fell from the sky. Something much different than mere rainfall, those healing droplets chased away suffering no matter its origin or manifestations, and as that cleansing downpour graced her, she became overwhelmed by an incredible lightness of spirit.

It was a sweeping release that brought her to sheer awe. The land was subjected to intense illumination as the sky detonated with bolts of light. Her vision of it became but a waxy melt of cloud and spark, and so, she closed her eyes there.

Directed by subconscious, her uninjured hand rose and slid up across her forehead as she continued to raise that wish ever higher, growing more desperate with each cast. Her fingers carved through her hair as she lifted, too, the broken wrist and pressed it against her throbbing temple. The sensation gripped her with fierce intensity as her fingers slid down the back of her neck, and as she pressed the broken wrist along her brow, it seemed to shift back into its natural state.

A decisive light from the sky invaded the darkness behind her closed eyes, and blessed euphoria beamed throughout her body all at once.

Miyacre awoke with a stumble, then lowered her arms as she searched the dreary sky and its endless rains for indisputable closure. The breach had gone, however, and nothing more occurred for a minute or two, but as she returned to her fine-tuned senses, she realized that something truly bizarre had occurred. The spectacle, she found, had been much more than a mere freak incident.

Miyacre peered down at her wrist. It was completely aligned and free of pain. Beset by bewilderment, she reached behind her back and put her fingers through the fine rip in the back of her shirt. Within it, she could feel no laceration or any tangible evidence of any injury suffered by the knife. It was as if it had all been a dream, though in the nightmare she remained.

She stepped away in disbelief as she raised her wrist up to her eyes to verify again that what she had seen was truth. After two rotations around the healed joint, however, she could no longer question what had occurred and knew then and there that she would tell no one of that miracle.

It was insanity. People would call her insane. What else could be said of such blatant madness?

The wish she had casted lingered heavily on her mind, but even in the aftermath of such a profound miracle, she found herself with doubts. But what else could have possibly caused the sky to watch her or for the bones to have realigned?

Could it have been a response?

"You there! Young lady!"

She turned around with a jolt, eyes shifting and with something to hide. Just ahead were two men in uniform, Jedd and Schneider.

"Yes? Yes! Yes, I'm here—" she said as she was swept with relief.

"You need a hand getting out of this hellhole?" Jedd hollered as they approached through the mud.

Miyacre nodded and went forward to meet them halfway.

"We have a group of stragglers just ahead. Are you alone?" asked Schneider.

He fought to make eye contact with Miyacre as she worked in evasive glances to come up with an appropriate response.

Then she nodded once more. "Yes, I'm alone—there was no one else, but one boy—"

"The boy didn't make it?" the impassive lieutenant pressed.

Miyacre shook her head as her tears for him swelled. "No—I don't believe he did."

Schneider nodded. "You did what you could. That's all we can hope for out of each other. Are you injured at all? Can you walk?"

Miyacre nodded. "Yeah, I can walk . . ."

"Then head up this way," Schneider directed, taking aim up the hillside with his finger. "Some soldiers have taken up posts that will guide you right to the survivors."

Miyacre nodded as she wiped her eyes of remnant tears. She then departed without another word in a struggle to gather her emotions for the trials ahead. Though she had rescued herself from the clutches of the twisted marshal, there still remained the chance that a dark new reality awaited. If their story together was to be hers alone from there on out, it would be so much to bear. She wasn't quite sure she could do it. So, as she cut a path to the first soldier in the distant mists, she made a second wish for their safety. Perhaps there was still some power in it yet.

Jedd turned over his shoulder to Schneider as the girl went on her way. "Ain't that the girl Gruman wanted?"

Schneider nodded as he journeyed forward to search the cliffs for himself.

"The plan change, did it?" Jedd remarked.

"We've all suffered a great tragedy today . . . She was clearly in shock . . . It's a painfully familiar look that brings me back to fighting alongside heroes that should have never been. Kids marking X's in a yearbook to keep track of the dead . . . To be quite honest with you, Jedd, I don't particularly give a shit about that frail, weak, spineless scientist and whatever nauseating experiments he's concerned with. Especially if these are his targets. The innocent. Not the guilty . . . If it were my organization . . . he'd be . . . struggling to breathe. But it's not our problem. The invaders are all that matter to me."

Jedd nodded in respect to that stance on the matter. "I hear that. Never did buy into this new wave of advancement science *bullshit* that Gruman started to push."

"Enough. It looks like there's nothing else for us here," Schneider diverted as he finished his scan of the desolate descent to the cliffside. "The storm has exacerbated our problems. Let's double back north and pick up a few more to assist with the wider search effort."

Schneider turned and headed back the way they had come.

"You got it, boss," replied Jedd as he turned and followed.

Adhering to the lieutenant's instruction, Miyacre pursued the guidance of the posted soldiers who set her on the path to the rest of the survivors. Weighed by imminent exhaustion, she slopped through the mud and over the waterlogged foliage on the upward path.

She prayed within the intimate cloister of her mind, weaving the perfect words to attain a more perfect outcome as the path began to populate with distraught others. The trees grew sparse, and soon, her eyes beheld the state of the resistance and its shattered people.

The reborn river had remained engorged with rampant waters and was fed further by flooded passages along the mountainside, which left lucky drifters divided across the northern rise. All along the southern slopes, however, was the majority of the huddled masses who moved ever further from the vicious torrent below.

Miyacre knew they could be anywhere, but she would search endlessly for them along the accessible slopes. She couldn't rest until she had tried her very best. Though what might suffice as her very best, she wasn't quite sure.

Endless worrying made her journey quick. She had arrived at the sprawling mass of survivors all huddled among the trees of the mountainside. With an anxious eye out for one last miracle, she passed through that gruesome scene of calamity, which saw all the healing done along the journey ruthlessly torn asunder. From the fragmented families to the sole survivors of short-lived friendships, the despair was so oppressive that not even those who had long wrapped themselves in the cold blanket of loneliness could hope to be spared.

She looked on with necessary emptiness as both soldiers and Samaritans pulled bodies up into rows. There were hundreds of them;

a grievous tragedy wreaked by a cruel cast, carried out to punish their cowardice at the pass.

She took glances into those mirrors of her own agony, unable to flee from their truth any longer, and as she proceeded deeper, her ears were overwhelmed by the horrible cacophony of rain, rushing water, and wails of misfortune.

Though weighed down by the grief of such a heart-wrenching display, she cut her path through the maze of misery in search of her friends. She did so for hours, going from one side of the mountainside rally point to the other until the glances of complete strangers had become familiar.

When the light of a new day had broken the miserable gray shroud, the rage of the torrent had settled to a rush. Unable to go any further, Miyacre limped to a rocky precipice at the traversable limits of the teeming mountainside from beyond which shined the morrow's golden glow upon the distant range.

Entranced by that lovely vision through the filter of fatigue's surreal melt, it drew her upon the rock, which extended over the treacherous waters below. With her eyes fixed upon that glistening dreamscape, she sat down on the moist stone with her legs stretched out toward the jagged edge.

Her head bobbed as sleep sought to steal her from consciousness, but she popped back up. With a tired glance, she noticed the sheer face of a boulder beside her and, with the nudge of reminiscence, scraped her hand across the ground. Her fingers came up with a pebble. In a subtle pass into a dream state, she threw it against the rock and heard the pop of the rubber ball against the wall of the kitchen. Satisfied with the sound, she went for another as the memories flashed behind her closed eyes.

"Where are you?"

She threw another and another, and each time, she grew a little sadder inside. Her fingers traced along the rough edges of the small rock as they drifted along a smooth curve in her hallucinations. Finding herself in a lie, she threw the pebble in anger but no sooner went to grab another.

"Where are you?" she asked again.

The fading daydreamer let out a gasp as two arms wrapped around her. She had been seized but knew immediately that there was no danger. The way he had taken her in that loving caress had only caused her to melt away in serenity.

"We're right here, Miyacre. You're alright," Lyal said.

The resonance of her fanciful reverie warped her mind in the allure of the old world's lost comforts. She had begun to slip. Those hazy delusions returned her to the kitchen before their fateful departure, and as relief swept through her subconscious, her guard fell to total exhaustion.

"H e y — M i y a c r e . C a t c h !!"

In heed of that pleasant call, she lifted against the heaviness of despair, and the red rubber ball struck her square on the forehead. Her head dropped, and she fell into the abyss.

"Miyacre!?" he called as he swung around to check on her.

Lyal examined her face closely. She still breathed and had only fallen fast asleep. So, in a relief of his own, he took her up in his arms and turned to Setz, Kaiser, and Mitz, who had all gathered behind them.

"Is she alright?" asked Kaiser as Lyal approached with their slumbering friend folded in his arms.

"Yeah—just resting," Lyal replied.

Setz shook his head in astonishment at her miraculous survival. "Honestly can't believe she made it out of that . . . and without a scratch."

"Glad that something unbelievable turned out to be genuinely good for us, though," said Mitz.

"Can't argue with that," Setz conceded.

"Right—let's go find a place to sit. Don't think we're going to be going anywhere soon," said Lyal.

And so, with their companion returned to them by the workings of determination and a miracle, they went to find a place to rest among the others.

***

The raging waters would take days to drain.

In that time, Miyacre awakened after an enduring repose and reunited with them with clear consciousness. She remained keen, however, to keep from them all that had transpired in the forest. She wanted, more than anything, to maintain a balance against the new reality and not burden them with further absurdity, even if it seemed a little hopeless of an endeavor.

As life seemed ever more fragile the further they journeyed, Miyacre decided there was something more she wanted to do. Something that Lyal had requested of her for quite some time and she had been too shy to oblige him. She would overcome that obstructive anxiety for him alone and began to craft a song in secret, and when the time was right, she would fulfill that wish, at last.

The losses suffered that day were immeasurable. The best guesses of the Union's administration teams painted a dreary picture, and as the masses were assembled once more to push on, there was noticeable loss. The wave had swept away most of their determination and left their hopes drowned in misery, but regardless of unbearable pain or the omnipresent threat of calamity, forward remained the only way left.

It always was, and until the war was over, it always would be. They chased the dreams of a better tomorrow against the tyranny of the invaders, but for some, the dream was too distant, and they surrendered themselves to the flood. The military struggled, too, as those with an enfeebled oath chose to break from command and venture out into the dense forest alone.

The triumph of their movement seemed more unlikely than ever.

Whatever lay beyond the shadows of tragedy awaited. Deeper into the unknown they pressed with only the guidance of hope in their desperate pursuit of a dream.

Shattered, but not yet broken through.

On Righteous Wings

Four days passed after the catastrophe in the Tenza Rock Forest dealt a cruel blow to the downtrodden survivors. The river had stayed engorged for two days and left them stranded upon the highland. Only by the morning of the third day were they able to resume progress through the drowned earth.

Though conditions were nightmarish, all were spared from sickness throughout the onerous slush for the forest's edge. Absent, too, were pests or creatures of any kind, which drew concern from those familiar with the area, which was well known to host numerous pollinators, parasites, and various species of larger wildlife.

This brought up the question, by those who could afford interest, as to what kept the forest thriving with the absence of these critical custodians. Even with the existential cycle of life seemingly severed, the cliffs were overrun with floral variety, each abloom with regal majesty while the trees stood with strong roots and canopies lush with green.

In fact, all seemed strangely immaculate. There existed an ominous perfection that was easily detectable if one only gave it their attention for a moment, for just beyond the washed-out gloom was lustrous beauty, seemingly disconnected from the world around it, bonded to something other than nature. For the ignorant, it was but fleeting bliss.

Their journey didn't come without further hardship, however. The treacherous landscape laid claim to hundreds more as the forest strangled their passage. They faced a harrowing journey through roots and tangles, over slippery rocks and through the waterlogged gorge, enduring such a pitiless struggle that prayer filled the night after every day.

The elderly had come to rely on the backs of Samaritans, and rescues became common as their journey threaded them along the harsh cliffs that carved the face of the last mountain, the high command unable to risk passage through the riverbed again.

By nightfall on the fourth day, they had reached a spacious relief where the forest's grasp had loosened and the mountainside had settled, which left the open horizon revealed beyond the last trees.

Relieved from the treacherous woodland at last, Myres ordered an immediate halt for the night. The caravan was brought to the Plains of Jornt, which began just beyond a dilapidated country road. The high command remained at the forest edge and set up a makeshift camp of branches, leaves, and what little supplies they had left in the wake of the tidal surge.

Near the end of the night's labor, Myres summoned both Rhodes and Schneider to the salvaged command tent, which had been erected beneath an old tree with monstrous, spiderlike roots mushroomed out from the trunk.

The dutiful brigadier stood in the wayside shadows nearby in wait of Schneider so that they could enter in tandem. As she lingered there, she scanned across the starry night sky, which she found uncorrupted by the presence of invader crafts.

Soothed to vacancy by that familiar late-night spectrum, her mind became teased by pleasant reveries of hiding and seeking with out-of-town cousins all across a moonlit campsite, the fear of the pitch darkness offset by the jovial banter between loved ones.

As she closed her eyes, she could almost smell the burning wood of the towering bonfire and hear the good, raucous bellows and shrieks of dearly missed laughter. It was a rapturous spell that filled her weary spirit with the strength to forge on, for how deeply she wished to foster such memories again.

Momentarily spellbound by those idyllic visions of girlhood, she reemerged and noticed the tranquil babble of running water over the chatter of nearby officers and was whisked away by unchecked curiosity. Near the edge of the camp, the essence-tuned explorer discovered the meandering brook, a mere corner fragment of some longer body; it fell a rocky step from the dense brush into the sweep before it disappeared again into the foliage.

Beyond the four feet of rushing crystal waters was a crumbled structure nestled there in the greenery, nearly hidden in its verdant grasp. Though gone was its ornamental spire of swirling silver and gold, and along with it every priceless gemstone embellishment that would have adorned the perimeter of the base. The surviving constitutions alone denoted a distinctly Beilkan architecture: a remnant shrine that had possibly seen over a thousand years.

Curious, she drew a small flashlight from her belt and put its potent light to work on the shadows of the forgotten sanctum. The stone staircase leading up to the portal had crumbled away, and only a jagged line was left of the first step. The gateway was left impassible by a colossal stone disc that had split in two and fallen against the curved stone arch. She realized then that it was no entrance but, in fact, the shrine's bulletin, which had collapsed long ago when the interior wood wall had finally rotted to structural failure.

Integral to all Beilkan shrines constructed across the conquered lands, the stone disc would have been replaced twice a year to introduce edicts, both new and updated, along with urgent developments from the central church located in the partitioned Beilkan capital, Torama.

An institution governed by the Order of the Agents, it was historically overseen by the high kings and queens of Beilka until the gruesome assassination of the protesting High Priestess Sheeba that saw that power eroded with support from the nobility and the four rival Beilkan kingdoms, Xerari, Mephis, Turassem, and Murelle, who each opposed the Kingdom of Larindau's dominance at the time.

Wielding an ambitious-yet-limited comprehension of the ancient Beilkan language, she scanned across the scriptures of that final bulletin.

"Xerarian—high priestess—raised to the—halls of the ancestors— by the good king's blades . . . No way . . ."

Agape in anticipation, she moved the light along the weathered stone until the circle of the beam fell upon the worn carving of a robed woman who bravely parted two sword-waving armies with her hand.

"What a find." Rhodes gawked as she moved along further to a masterful carving of the priestess's face, portrayed in a graceful turn over her right shoulder, though time had withered away every fine detail aside from those found in an ever-gazing left eye.

Beneath the ancient portrait was a single bowed line, which became of immediate interest. She bent forward and began to squint, using shadows to make sense out of the eroded lettering.

"The world—must know my—my peace," she parsed.

Nearly brought to a tear, Rhodes straightened back, that timeless message a rekindling to the radical soul.

"Lady Sheeba," the sworn brigadier hailed as she laid her hand upon her heart. "Your peace is our redemption. Your justice is our faith."

Winded by that startling discovery, she took hold of a slender tree to keep herself steady in that moment of sweeping emotion.

"Sorry to keep you waiting."

Her eyes flicked back to acuity, yanked from thoughtless awe by the toneless apology of her dreary cohort.

"Oh—not a problem, at all—" she replied with a snappy turn in hopes of not suffering the embarrassment of appearing caught off guard.

"What have you found?" he pressed with dry enthusiasm.

"Ah! I'm not sure. It's just—some old Beilkan shrine with some pretty fascinating carvings. Nothing you'd be interested in," she said as she fumbled with the flashlight until it was secured in its strap.

"You found it on a whim, huh?" he asked with a cursory inspection of the split tablet.

"Well, actually, I was inside my own thoughts, and just—happened upon it."

"You're just a wandering spirit out here, aren't you, Cheryl?" he accused with a playful glance.

She fell back against the slender trunk of the tree, her mouth agape again, now in a display of sheer guilt, overwhelmed by his steady drive. "Don't make me feel like such a child."

Schneider relieved her with a sigh, then turned up to the starry shroud that had hidden so very much from them. "Well, in the grand scheme of it all . . . perhaps we never become anything more than mere children."

She peered up alongside him but fell back with a dismissive breath. "We can't afford to think like that—"

"I know we can't afford to think like that."

"Yes!" she interrupted back with an exhausted wilt. "I know you realize that. But, maybe," she continued, "that's what makes having kids so special. You kind of get to go through that journey again, but instead, you're steering the ship and not just along for the ride."

Schneider laughed rather boldly at that exotic thought. "You're not really thinking of having kids in the time like this, are you?"

"O-of course, not!" she stammered with an abrupt shove off the tree and a subsequent charge to his face. "*You!* Just happened to catch me in a very private moment of reflection. So, use some tact, Lieutenant."

"Well, forgive me for that intrusion, ma'am," he apologized with soft sincerity.

She turned away from him and decompressed with a deep breath but lingered there in silence, still needing to reign in wayward emotions. With a lack of time for such regulating meditations, however, and a nagging regret to clear from her conscience, she stepped back around to his side.

"Hey . . . I'm sorry I tried to convince you to stick around longer than you felt was right. I was wrong to do that. Not that I don't find solace that we're in this together. At least, one last time, right . . . ?"

Without words for that gentle confession, he turned to look upon the solemn face of his most revered ally in arms.

Feeling the heat of his gaze upon her cheek, Rhodes shook the intensity with a sharp breath and the shake of her head.

"Come on. We better hurry—he's waiting," she diverted with a turn away to flee him.

"Right . . . Let's get this over with," Schneider grumbled as he stepped off in pursuit.

Once at the tent, they entered one by one through the flap. The drab interior was lit by a single LED lantern, which was tied to a corner support. Myres, broken from thought there at the center of the empty tent, turned to greet them. He folded his arms, the reason for their assembly dire to their mission's overall success.

"Thank you for joining me here tonight. I'm going to be working to get everyone on the same page, starting with you two. Now that we're clear of the Tenza Rock, it's imperative that we refocus our efforts . . . in lieu of the latest—tragic occurrence."

Both officers nodded in silent acknowledgement of their losses.

"So, before we abandoned the riverside, I did a little inspection of the water from that unholy kick in the groin. No doubt, it was saltwater."

"From the ocean, then?" Schneider clarified.

"Where else would saltwater come from?" asked Myres.

"We were thousands of miles away from the closest ocean," the skeptical lieutenant retaliated.

"And I wish what I was saying made more sense. Anything else you want to point out?"

"Just the possibility that the entirety of Neo Cascadia lies in ruin— once again, it would seem."

"Well, at least nobody was there, huh?" Myres jabbed back. "Listen, we need to find answers. We have none. At this point, the invaders are just throwing whatever the green earth gives them at us, and we have nothing in our goddamn imaginations to defend ourselves. It's to the point where I won't even bother asking either of you for ideas. We need someone who knows something—anything about these guys."

Schneider shook his head in blatant disagreement with his course.

Myres set a glare on his unruly subordinate. "Is that understood?" he asked, then held for an answer.

"Understood, General," Schneider reluctantly surrendered.

"I need you to help me find that swordsman."

"Sir—" Rhodes uttered. "Do you have reason to believe he's anywhere near our position? I mean—he could be anywhere—"

Myres shook his head then pushed his hands out to drive away any further skepticism from her. "Listen—" he interrupted. "At this point, he is our *only shot*. When we come up with a better idea, then by all means, we can try it. But we cannot afford to waste time," the general asserted.

"Understood, sir. Forgive me if I seemed to lack trust."

He nodded in acceptance of her swift apology, then refocused on the both of them at once. "We're only going to be able to get so far with overwhelming suffering before people stop believing in us. When that happens . . . all of this is over." He followed with silence to allow for due resonance.

"We'll continue northeast for Eredes, as planned. Once we hit , we prioritize that armory. Stockpile as many supplies as we can. From gun to uniform, you name it, I want it, and if at any point you catch sight of him, you bring him right to me. If what I felt is true, he wasn't going to stay gone for long."

"Then we'll get that search in motion right away, sir," Rhodes complied.

"Excellent. Brigadier, Second Lieutenant, let's keep our eyes on that big, beautiful prize. Freedom. Don't let anything stand in the way of your duty to that goal. Dismissed."

"Understood, sir," Schneider replied, seeing no use of further protest.

The sworn duo lifted their hands in salute, and when the gesture of respectful order was satisfied, the chary lieutenant turned and took his leave. Rhodes stepped off behind him but was reeled back at once by the abrupt call of her superior, to whom she turned in reflexive obedience.

"Rhodes, I'm gonna need you on top of getting the results here. Between us—and only *us*, General Henson has gone missing within the last few hours. I need *you* to figure something out before we depart, or I fear the truth might be lost forever."

She presented to him a gentle smile of confidence. "Don't worry, sir. You can lay that trust in me."

With that private request committed to urgency, Rhodes departed the tent and went to regroup with Schneider, who brooded over something not far ahead.

"I'm going to get some soldiers together and go look in the immediate area. Should be our only real shot," she presumed.

"Don't you think it's a bit unbelievable that we're being asked to seek out an invader to lead this war effort?"

Rhodes paused on him with narrowed eyes and a raised lip in subtle disbelief of his nonnegotiable animosity. "Did you listen at all? There's sound reasoning," she argued.

Schneider scanned the dark woodland in silent refusal to give it further thought. His aimless gaze happened upon a grinning Lakker, who loomed in the distance, leaning against a tree with his hawkish gaze set upon them.

With the flick of his wrist, the crooked observer beckoned.

"Looks like the ghoul wants a word," Schneider relayed.

Rhodes sought him out herself. "I've got to get some headway on this sweep. Think you can report it back to me?"

Schneider shrugged. "He might be pissed, but I'll pass the word along."

"There's a lot to do, and I'd rather start sooner than later."

"Go—I'll take care of it."

"Thanks, Schneider. Give it some thought. We're just here to do what's necessary. We won't allow anyone to misguide our vision for the reclaimed world. Invader or otherwise," she assured him.

With that sobering guidance, she stepped away to attend to the mission that had been laid in her trusted hands with a theory already in mind as to what fate might have befallen their valorous general and little intention to interfere. Schneider turned back just in time to see her go. With nothing left to say in the face of her untarnished faith, he redirected to the midnight's phantom and stepped off to answer his call.

"Gruman wants to meet with you, Schneider," he greeted upon Schneider's arrival to the gloomy thicket. "Things are picking up. A lot's about to happen tonight, so we gotta move fast . . . Can you do that, buddy?"

"What's going on, Lakker? If I need to know something, just cut straight to it."

Lakker smirked at his posturing for authority, then let out a contemptuous sigh when he had finished. "Well, if you're eager, then pick up your feet. We're short on time. The night won't last forever."

And so, with their grim sovereign in wait of them, the organization hounds slipped through the shadows into the wilderness and took the unbeaten path through the night until Lakker's guidance brought them before a rundown wooden shed nestled in somber oblivion.

The area was guarded by ten armed others, all dressed in civilian garb, their faces veiled to obscurity by the rampant dark. They kept a steady watch on those overdue attendees as if the traitorous heart could take its first beat at any time.

The gleeful henchmen pushed open the door to the tenebrous interior in which Gruman sat in wait on the workman's bench, his boot upon the slanted backrest of a rickety wood chair. Against the wall leaned Vekner, who rubbed the top of a downturned pistol with his knuckles, slack-jawed as if waiting for an exploitable slip of the tongue. Unblinking, Schneider stepped through and passed between two armed soldiers as Lakker shut the door behind him.

Schneider grew still. In a chair purposefully faced to the corner was General Henson, beaten, bloodied, murdered, his shattered spectacles upon the table beside Gruman. The upstart broke his gaze with haste. Without a doubt, the maestro of righteous mayhem intended to test him.

"Good of you to join us, Schneider . . . Where's Rhodes?"

"She wished to proceed with new directives from Myres rather than attend the meeting but assured she would offer us an ear at a later time."

Gruman scoffed. "Did she, now? Always the diligent one, that elusive girl. She has her heart set on it, then. We may exclude her for now."

Gruman kicked the chair to his pivotal assembly's last attendant, who seized it before it struck him.

"Have a seat, Schneider."

The lieutenant turned the chair around, sat in a wide stance, then dug elbow into knee with his chin held by folded fingers.

"It comes as no surprise to any of us that the civilian caravan is in a complete uproar. The passage through Tenza was an utter disaster. General Myres sits in a tent of lofty superiority while the people sleep out in fields. All the while, he doesn't do the due diligence of even reporting to the political representatives of our government to whom he is sworn to serve."

Schneider snickered at that blatant ignorance of their circumstance. "It hasn't been particularly easy to keep everyone organized to any standard after the invasion," he casually defended with a confident rise to good posture.

Gruman sighed in disappointment. "Let's look at the bigger picture, Schneider. Keep focused on it . . . We observed an incredible wall of water and were mindlessly ordered to march through a dried-up river."

The energized leader threw his arms up in hopes of stoking cunning, righteous outrage.

"And wouldn't you believe it . . ." he continued, even as his arms fell to no fanfare, "attempts were made to keep the civilian caravan in the dark about the existence of that ungodly wall of water. It was not merely a disaster of roaring tides, it was a disastrous betrayal of trust, a breakdown of integrity, and a decisive failure of leadership," he raved with the jab of his finger to Schneider's unexpressive eyes. "*Each* were lacking that day we set out, and the people deserve better. Since the days of sword and shield, it has been the organization's duty to persecute the enemy of the people. Tonight—we fulfilled that duty," Gruman declared as he gestured to the murdered Union general.

"Why did you kill him?" Schneider rasped in a sharp snap of anger.

"Vengeance for those *who were lost*, Schneider. What can't you understand . . . ?" The murderous mastermind's eyes narrowed on him. "It was a grave error . . . and just think what the people would say if this truth were to find its way out. Good social business. *Justice*," he concluded with emphasis on that righteous resolution.

"The ol' Desert Savage didn't put up much of a fight in his old age," Vekner bragged, his gloves guilty with stained blood.

Schneider shook his head in defiance of their misguided wrath. "It was a collective call, Rhodes and I included. We decided the riverbed was the *only passage* large enough to support a march of that scale," he stressed.

Gruman glared at his subordinate's words of ineptitude. "You seem to be missing the point, Schneider. Remember what I've always told you about opportunity. If Rhodes is willing to accept responsibility, she will suffer the same fate."

Schneider rose in sharp disgust with that morbid suggestion. "How could you sink to *killing* one of your most loyal retainers?"

"Because she would die for the cause, Schneider!" Gruman exploded. "Now, *sit—down!*" he roared with the slam of his fist upon the enfeebled bench.

The flustered tyrant scaled back his rage as Schneider returned to his seat as instructed.

"Yes—she's kept much about her life secret. Even from you," Gruman enlightened. "You simply don't know my lucky little reaper the way I've come to. If she wouldn't die for it, then how would she enable the new world that she has long envisioned? You see, Rostal, the world is built on sacrifice. Wars, transitions, ebbs and flows, they are the very foundation of society, and if we lack the strength to guide it, our vision will remain but a fanciful dream."

Schneider sat overwhelmed, disarmed by the sheer scale of his madness.

"So—our plan is to host a small meeting with Myres. During this meeting, a group of unruly civilians will rise to action to dethrone a power-hungry general and restore the rule *of the people.*" Gruman peered deeply into his wayward subordinate in wait of detectable comprehension. "Do you understand?"

Schneider looked all around the room as the truth of what was about to occur sank in and brought him to ponder the ominous void left in the general's absence.

"Do you really believe we can afford to lose him now? Myres and Henson were the last generals of revered experience who survived Salamandra."

Gruman shooed his concern with the flip of his wrist. "Worry not, Schneider. I wish to elevate your image to the best of my ability. You won't need to do a thing—just keep away from the camp for the next hour while we take care of business," Gruman pleaded. "A transition of power. One leaves . . . another takes his place. Soon, the hero general himself will lead the people to victory . . . and our victory will be cemented. Am I understood, Schneider?"

With an enormous burden saddled upon him at the organization's will, Schneider replied with a nod tainted by hesitation.

"Excellent," praised Gruman as he rose to his feet. "We will go and inform Myres of our grievances immediately. Feel free to depart at your convenience, in adherence to the guidelines . . . Yes, and with that, gentlemen—Grand Marshal, we're off."

The restless prime mover stepped past Schneider and led the armed men out of the putrid shack. Vekner shoved off the wall and stepped in line behind the grim procession. As he passed Schneider, he bent forward and spat beside his foot.

"Oh—sorry about that," he razzed. "Didn't see you sitting there, bub."

Schneider lingered in the silent embrace of darkness as the steps of his committed allies grew distant. His fist was clenched in anger as he found himself bound in the web that he had long ago thrown himself to. He sat conflicted and unable to fathom the world that the others had set out to actualize, yet unable to stand in defiance of it.

Was it because he was afraid? Was he too weak, or did he simply welcome their vision, which had designs to see him empowered? Fragmented within, he fixated upon the spectacles on the table whose empty gaze sent a silent plea for cathartic reflection. Those shattered gateways epitomized a brave step forward, and their heinous truth made the more daring subsequent step explicitly inevitable.

Gruman had been a man of his word, and his reach, in that moment, seemed nearly without limitation.

A World in Change

General Myres stood outside of the command tent with a line of officers at attention before him.

"And so, just to summarize, the plan remains to march to Eredes. That armory in remains essential, however. Your salvage teams will be responsible for getting any vehicles we can into operation. ATVs, tanks, jeeps—hell, anything sitting on wheels and in Union colors, I want up and running. With any luck, we'll run into other survivors and proceed expeditiously with integrating them within the armed forces or caravan respectively . . . That about covers it. Get those teams assembled and ready, and remember, ladies and gentlemen . . . guns ready, eyes peeled. Feelings of safety or comfort are not your friend, so dole out those short sticks for the first shift of night watch, and rest well."

Myres adjourned the assembly with a salute, then dismissed them to deliver his message to the lower ranks. With a sleepless night ahead of him, he returned to the tent, which was now outfitted with a makeshift desk crafted from bound sticks and topped with a shaved-up stump. Laid across the top was an air-dried map of Eredes and the region's outlying towns. The road to the city was sparsely spotted with an assortment of rocks that acted as placeholders for the army's plans going forward.

Myres went over and peered down for a moment with his finger pressed up into his lower lip. He dove into concentration as he mulled over the next best move against their unimaginable foe. His fingers fell upon a rock that stood beside Eredes and moved it due north, all while avoiding rivers and large lakes.

He dotted a serpentine path that would add weeks to an already arduous journey to the next city. In a sudden swell of emotion, he raised his hand and slapped the map clean of every rock.

The outburst had left him vulnerable to the influence of the bizarre, and the general suddenly became aware of a peculiar grasp upon his taxed psyche, one that had grown undeniably stronger ever since they had left Neo Cascadia behind. Myres shot a glance to where it beckoned and saw the lifted curtain fall. His chest rose and fell as he watched the phantom's dark body line move across the tan cover. This time, he didn't pursue her. Instead, the dutiful general took the ends of the severed stump in front of him as he hung above the trenches of a treacherous anxiety.

The absence of his peer, General Henson, lay deeply in his enfeebled grip. A hero of his time, he had been a man who had offered a reprieve from the full responsibilities of their brave endeavor, which had been all too daunting at each and every turn. There was respite, too, in his simplistic, peaceful disposition; quick to humor but never unfastened from reality. An honorable man through and through and a man who, Myres was certain, would never abandon his duty to the country he loved.

That sole surviving general of the Union banner feared the worst, and the burden left to him was great.

"Guess we're gonna need a prayer, little Elysia."

That cruel hallucination tipped forward in cock-headed curiosity of his gentle request.

"You remember how to do that? Just like you did for Grandma?" Myres asked as he turned to gauge the ghost's reaction for authenticity.

The attentive silhouette perked up, and although his vision of her was restricted to mere movements upon the veil, he detected an enthusiastic nod. With the clap of little hands, the general's dismay was lifted away into sheer amazement as his request had found the ear of something if not authentic to form, then undoubtedly sentient.

"This can't be real . . . Can it . . . ? You can't be real . . ."

There then came a rustle from the branches. The little well-wisher shook in astonishment as something dropped to the grass beyond the veil and, with a gasp, took off running. Ignited to her defense, Myres sprang forward and rushed to the back of the tent.

The canvas there was cut aside, and the swordsman stepped through with eyes agleam with a cerulean radiance, which settled quickly to a lambent aurora.

Myres, taken by surprise with the invader's bold entry, stumbled to a halt. "You! You're—You came. How . . . ? How did you get here?"

"Am I unwelcome?"

"No! Not at all . . . You're very welcome here, as a matter of fact."

"Then, here I am," the swordsman replied with determination alight in his eyes.

Myres released a sigh of sweeping relief, then turned to his world's imperative ally with a shake of his head. "We got some things to talk about . . ."

Setting aside questions of the phantom visitant, Myres dove into detail with the invader defector about their encounter with the Great Crest and the tragic event's occurrences that had befallen them in the Tenza Rock Forest. Though the swordsman could offer little advice on how to defend against such cruel forces, he assured him that the way forward was the way to victory.

"Master detests cowardice, and this was likely his wrath . . . We must press on without fear, however. There is much left to do, and stillness is death. If you hope to grasp a chance at victory, we must continue north at all costs," the swordsman insisted.

Myres narrowed his eyes in apprehension. "But why north? To where, exactly?"

"To a place that lies at the edge of existence. There is a weapon of sorts being constructed to achieve a certain set of goals. Goals which, if left unhindered, will be the demise of all you hope to save."

Myres put his hands upon his waist as he took it all in. "Well, you really do have it all figured out, don't you?"

"There is much to understand but little time to explain it. I expect you understand that."

Myres nodded with a raised brow. "As a matter of fact, I do. We have a course set north, as it stands. Come with us. We need your help and can't afford to go it alone. Especially if it's the edge of existence we're headed to," Myres stated with a nervous laugh, pondering.

The swordsman looked away in distant thought for a moment then returned to him with a decisive nod. "Then, I will go. What would you have me do?" he inquired.

"What I need from you is to do what's right to help us win this war—nothing less than that."

The swordsman nodded.

"Whatever you feel is fit," Myres insisted. "If you acquire any knowledge about a threat, act on it. I won't object to you acting of your own volition. Just don't wander far. Above all, I need you to be here to help me understand how I can navigate this war. Because we can't do it alone, as much as we might hate to admit it."

There came the sound of footsteps from beyond. Shadows approached.

The swordsman nodded, in full comprehension of those orders. "Then, I go. I will go see what threatens your resistance."

An apex predator unleashed, the swordsman emerged from the tent and stepped out into a gathering of men. Gruman, who had arrived to act on his treachery, choked at the very sight of him but came to leer from the comforts of his cohorts who surrounded him.

"It was an avoidable tragedy, Myres," Gruman barked with all the authenticity he could muster in face of that lightning executioner.

"General! Come out! We would like you to answer for the decisions you made prior to this tragic loss of life. The political body of the Union deserves an explanation, as do our citizens, who have suffered—*unimaginable loss.*"

Unthreatened by the mob's pertinacious dissidence, the swordsman stepped forward on a path that eventually put them side by side.

The sworn soldiers split fast to make way for his passage.

Gruman grimaced as he found himself unable to look steadily upon the passing reaper who had suddenly taken on a keen interest in him. Pushed to the cowardice of peripheral, he became a reluctant witness to a swell of cerulean beaming as the adamantine hunter peered into a thousand tomorrows.

The focused schemer's eye shifted as he began to realize that he was unable to hide those intimate intentions, his great plans laid out in plain sight. His grin sank until his mouth had fallen agape, for the longer he gazed into those eyes, the more attuned he became to the invasive ethereal force coursing through his mind.

Even in the face of imminent ruin, the seasoned deceiver found himself unable to cloak his exposed consciousness with anything righteous at all. All that shined true within was ambitious evil that had long taken root and infected all virtue. It would never conceal itself, not even to save its devoted host, and only in that critical moment of vulnerability did the ruthless architect of the new world realize his tragic subjugation to it.

"What are you doing just standing there? Step along," Vekner ordered, his temper close to a flare.

The swordsman stepped over his planted foot to face the paralyzed conspirator. Vekner stepped in to intercept him, but it was too late.

The blade was drawn from the sheath, and the empowered executioner struck to the cries of havoc. Gruman fell to his knees with bulging eyes and his blood spilling from the fatal cut.

Vekner pulled his pistol but, in sheer astonishment, found himself unable to fire it. The reaper's blade swept up and sank into the staggered subordinate's neck as he yanked the trigger by death-touched reflex. The barrel exploded and raised a single shot to the sky.

The last of the guilty had drawn his pistol. Ultra swung forward and discarded the limp husk from the blade. As Lakker reached out to take aim, the swordsman seized his arm. The barrel exploded with gunfire just as Ultra snapped his wrist. Lakker let out a wail of agony as the weapon fell from his hand into his enemy's, who, without hesitation, unloaded four rounds into his head.

Gruman's last able protégé slumped to the ground. The civilian-dressed assassins had already taken off into the tree line, their plan in shambles, their supreme visionary cut down. The swordsman did not pursue any one of those vile enablers and instead tossed the gun to the blood-soaked grass and returned the blade to the sheath, the course of destiny forever changed.

The soldiers of the Union, both sworn and ignorant, had erupted into a wild frenzy. Through the chaotic yells and barks of orders from superior to subordinate, the swordsman was soon all but surrounded by carefully aimed firearms.

General Myres had emerged from the tent, his eyes moonlike in alarm as they hunted for the source of sudden chaos. They fell fast upon the swordsman, whose somber gaze lingered upon a dying Gruman.

From the crowd of soldiers emerged Schneider, who looked upon his butchered comrades in vivid disbelief.

"Look at what you've done," Schneider growled as he ripped his colossal pistol from its holster and took aim at the murderous invader whose eyes remained fixated upon the victims of his judgement.

"Why! Why did you insist on bringing him back to the camp!?" the hysterical lieutenant thundered.

Myres, at a loss for words, could offer no defense for those drastic actions. Gruman had set his bulging eyes upon the enraged lieutenant. He reached his trembling finger forward and pointed right to him as his chest convulsed at death's silent beckoning. With that last execution of authority, his arm fell, and his gaze became endless.

His debut objective fulfilled, Ultra took a step away and became aware of all those startled spectators. A distressed General Myres fled right for him, distraught by that swift breach of trust, gone with it all hopes of seeing the journey and its trials through together.

"What's going on here? Why!? Why'd you kill him? *Tell us!*" he pled, on the brink of hellish fury.

The swordsman looked at the lifeless conspirators, then back to the targeted general.

"Is it so unclear?" their reaper replied rather casually, a nonchalant response that caused Myres to be momentarily taken aback.

Somehow, he had known.

"Now, the choice lies with you what will happen next. I will depart for now. You know the path to victory. Take it . . . or all will be lost."

Schneider rushed forward with his finger firm on the trigger, foaming for justice. "You aren't going anywhere, you son of a bitch," he snarled.

The swordsman scoffed, then dipped low and shot into the air with a superhuman flip. Schneider followed him with his gun as the shadow cut across the night sky.

"Don't shoot! Don't shoot! Are you insane!?" Myres barked as he sank low in reflex of that sudden departure.

Schneider struggled against the very essence of himself to keep his finger from pulling, and in the short time that he had stalled, the swordsman was gone in the night.

"Fuck! *Fuck!* How could you let this happen, Myres!?"

"Don't you raise your voice to me, Lieutenant—"

Schneider stepped off to confront the general, and a swarm of soldiers, both loyal and traitorous, rushed forward to seize him, and the upstart lieutenant surrendered in a fluster as he found himself totally restrained.

Myres took a deep breath as he looked down at the three slain aggravators.

"*Shit!* What in the hell have we gotten ourselves into?" he lamented as he wiped the sweat from his brow. "Alright," Myres announced. "We all know what we just witnessed here. In wake of this attack, the swordsman is to be identified as foe . . . but, no one—and I mean no one is to engage him to any capacity. We will bury the dead and continue north. There is no time to mourn this tragedy. We have a job to do, people—and no matter what happens, we are sworn by oath to fulfill it . . . no matter who our enemies are . . . or who our enemies become."

And so, with a weapon looming on the horizon, they proceeded with the burial of the three men with haste. Rhodes would eventually return to the news of Gruman's passing, which she would receive with a long departure alone into silence. The man who moved the world for them was gone, but his vision flourished in all of them. Now more powerful than ever.

With the swordsman gone and the blood of the politician and servicemen forever stained upon his hand, the Union remnants had lost a critical ally all too soon. Along with the unsolved disappearance of the revered General Henson, the resistance seemed all the more weak, their vision for success as inconceivable as the invaders they faced.

The division grew deeper that night, an outcome which General Myres had long feared. With the departure of Norris Gruman, the organization would seek direction from the new dominus, one which had been crowned the same night as his death with the mere point of a finger. There would be many who would abandon due to his lack of accolades, Schneider himself more of an outsider with stature than a recognized member with standing. A considerable number of loyalists would remain, however, and the organization would retain a looming presence. By bloodshed, a new era had been born. Schneider would make quick to shift their priorities to winning the war against the invaders.

Regardless of allegiance, the survivors would take the northbound road to nowhere as one where greater trials surely awaited. The resistance departed the Tenza region shattered, like spirits in the face of the all-powerful invader force whose weapons and capabilities redefined radical imagination as they assembled unfathomed monstrosities in the shadows of obscurity. Divine terrors designed to bring about the end.

The Current of Change

On the journey into the town of Brekka, Miyacre relegated herself to deep silence, lost in the trenches of the soul. Though the others tried to resuscitate her spirits with hopeful meditations, more and more often, she would relapse into unseen torment.

The thunder of the tide woke her in cold sweat each and every time her eyes fell shut, and total exhaustion only sought to put her down when the caravan's advance was in full swing. So, she dragged onward, unable to rest and, with a mind devoid of hope and vacant of consciousness, soon came to accept the recurring nightmare as inescapable. The torment of her failure had dragged her deep into the abyss, and she knew not where the bottom lay.

Miyacre took solace, however, in that she drifted alongside friends, the remnants of the old world who aided her limping spirit through the subspace of tomorrow. They propped her up when she could go no further and livened her mood with the banter of old stories and dear memories. Ones which seemed like so long ago.

She took solace, too, in that she suffered no further encounters from the men of Officer Larus's stock and hoped only that the rest had drowned with him in the wrathful waters, for anyone who could serve such a contemptible man was better left flushed.

The army marched the caravan from daybreak to sunset until ranches and barns turned into suburban developments on the outskirts of . Though hopes were never deficient upon reaching a potential holdout of survivors, the familiar quietude that stalked them through the streets spoke definitively of the fate that had befallen the residents of the town.

Like Neo Cascadia before it, all those who had once resided there had come up missing without a trace. The modest town, too, had been left fully intact, untouched by war, a disturbing revelation that left many to surmise that everywhere beyond Salamandra City was simply vacant outland.

General Myres, reduced to Schneider, Rhodes, and a few officers of rank among his remnant high command, sent an order to seek out "the missing." Small squads were dispatched to search nearby houses, apartments, and designated places of shelter to verify the obscure reality in each part of town. Among those who went were some that returned with eerie tales of phantom gazers who monitored their efforts from a distance, only to step away and vanish when attempts were made to approach them.

Those stories, once numerous enough to garner attention from the top brass, initially inspired hope that others may have, in fact, survived.

However, disturbing details of these "individuals" arose from more aggressive pursuits, claims that glimpses caught of their faces revealed something undeniably inhuman about them. They would assert an unusual blurriness that not only veiled blank visages but worked to distort their entire appearance during any movement.

Eventually, Union leadership issued a command to steer clear of the odd observers, coming to the conclusion that they were somehow related to the invader force. By sunset's approach, however, those vacant plane shifters had disappeared altogether and left the search parties to walk the quiet suburban streets alone.

Faced with another fruitless search, the top brass and its unusually patient Beilkan counterparts concluded that the best course of action was to rest for the night, then press on to Eredes. By the end of the day, they could almost reliably claim that not a soul remained.

The military fragmented the caravan once more and assigned them to areas with structures that could offer ample refuge. It was a task made no less easy by General Henson's vacuous absence, which left coordination efforts increasingly cumbersome.

Without sounder options, General Myres left the duty to Schneider and Rhodes while he turned his attention to the armory, where he was sure they would find critical supplements to their resistance. It wasn't but a thirty-minute march from the humble downtown, which was situated around three four-story buildings that stood huddled along the town's commercial strip.

The supply party arrived to a familiar vacancy. An investigation into the guard station's computer system offered them few answers as to the events leading up to the town's abandonment. The last log entry would have occurred thirty-four minutes after the initial invasion of the capital, a scheduled sweep of the facility without incident. No security protocol had been initiated.

Bewildered soldiers swept through the command center with the expectation of coming upon some sign of a struggle. Rather, each chair was pressed right to the desk. Headsets of those who would have been responsible for the institution's operation were set to the side. To Myres and his officers, it was as if they had simply laid them down and walked away.

They would find, too, that the armory itself was left untouched by disorder. Rifles lined the heavy gray storage cases, their perfect symmetry left unbroken. Not one APC or ordnance within the garage had been mobilized. This left them to theorize that whatever had caused their disappearance had occurred suddenly and with chilling effectiveness.

It must have been so. Surely those under siege would not have gone willingly into oblivion.

Lost for the rationale behind the mass exodus, they could only pray that there had been an orderly evacuation, though they were left with few signs to support such a restful theory.

As the army rolled out the salvaged APCs along the street, Lyal and his companions were guided by the flow of the masses as they were funneled into the accommodating structures of a high school compound. They glazed over the red-bricked buildings as memories of home swept them into momentary saudade. Their final descent of their school's entry staircase seemed like a sprint into the arms of freedom, but here, they trudged in as refugees of a war-torn world.

They each took the black-painted handrail as they rose to the breached, steel-rimmed glass doors of the gymnasium. Along the wall, beyond that forced portal, was the name Hudson High School, displayed in proud silver lettering.

Lyal looked across the front lawn as they filed in. A second line had formed from another entrance at the other end of the building. Further along the way and across the busy road, a group of military personnel had gathered at the middle school which, unlike the high school, was comprised of only a solitary structure. One of the soldiers kicked through the glass door, which drew the attention from others in the line.

His eyes lingered there, then lifted to the dark clouds in the distant skies that had chased them down once again, the rains of the new world relentless, as were its sorrows. A brisk wind struck them through every now and then as they made gains on the extruded entrance.

"Jeez, kicking up at a school. I really hope we're not sleeping on the gym floor," Kaiser moaned.

"Yeah . . . If we're lucky, maybe they have some of those blue mats," Lyal replied in a turn back to the others.

"Probably some in the weight room, for sure," Mitz surmised. "Lucky for me, I'm going to sleep, like, anywhere. Especially if we're getting some rain."

"Miyacre—you going to be alright?" asked Lyal with chief concern for the wellbeing of their bedeviled friend.

"Yeah. I'm fine." The girl, who had shoe-gazed for most of the way, had popped her head up in an eerie reaction to her name, but an invisible weight had strained her, and thus, their eyes never met. "It's okay—it's—" She faded.

Crestfallen friends watched her, each keen on her inner struggle, though none of them could quite find the words to ever relieve her of that doubtless guilt. Silence settled in between them, and before long, they found themselves before the breached gates.

The suburban band stepped in and crossed from shattered glass to the glossy checkered floor of the main hall. On the white-painted wall, they could make out light scribbles of teen graffiti: heads with Mohawks, poorly erased expletives, and inappropriate delineations of the human body conjured from the juvenile mind.

Along the way, they encountered the assembled would-be mothers whose bellies had tragically fallen flat, their unborn children stolen from the womb. They cried to flustered nurses, who checked them three to four times over, the doctors tasked with their care nearby at a loss for words as they paced helplessly in pensive strides.

The friends filtered through the heart-wrenching halls of misery until they had come to the gymnasium, where polished wooden floors had already been packed from wall to wall. In a careful meander, they scouted out a place to sit and found a feasible location near center court.

"Oooo, oh yeah—that's as bad as I thought it would be," said Kaiser as he dropped slowly upon the cool wood grain.

"You've slept on desks in class since *freshman year* but can't sleep on the floor? Come on now, son," said Mitz as he curled up over the ground like a house cat.

Kaiser threw himself back onto the ground and spread out his limbs. "I'm about to be up all night."

Miyacre dropped to her knees and released a long sigh as her head swayed in fatigue. Lyal took to her side and laid his hand upon her shoulder.

There came a sudden sensation in his palm, an acute zap, which shot right up through the veins of his arm. The electrified consoler flinched away and rattled his hand to rid it of all resonance.

Her eyes crawled over to his. "You feel it, too?" she whispered.

Thunder rumbled over the chatter of the masses.

"Right on time. And that's my cue—" Mitz doubled back and turned to Kaiser. "Hey, why don't you—"

He fell silent upon discovery that the adamant complainer had slipped right into the deepest slumber.

"Well, then—" he said with a swift glance to the others to flaunt his cheeky grin. "Goodnight, everyone. Remember—they said we leave pretty early. So, enjoy the roof while it lasts."

Mitz lay back down and assumed his position of comfort. Setz, who had taken a spot furthest from Lyal, lay down without a word.

Yet fixated on Miyacre's obscure aura, Lyal reached out once more. This time, however, his hand began to tremble even before his fingers had made contact with her. "What is that?"

"I'm not sure," she replied, ". . . there's a place I go to when I close my eyes, Lyal."

Overwhelmed, he yanked his hand away once again and shook off its bizarre grasp. "You know what? Let's just forget about it. There's a whole lot of freaky stuff going on, but—I'm sure they're going to figure it out," he said with waning confidence. "They have to, right?"

Miyacre bounced her head in a half-hearted nod, then eased herself down onto the floor. Within, she was glad that he had avoided further investigation into her condition. She, too, couldn't understand it, even as she cast a hundred different wishes within the depths of that place.

Lyal huddled close to her as she lay motionless. Her stillness lasted a mere second or two. She shot up with her arm thrown out for the fated rescue, trapped in perpetual torment. Lyal stole her back in his arms, desperate to calm her.

"Hey—stop. It's alright. You're alright."

Her head fell upon his shoulder as he wrapped her up in his arms. Lyal held on tight as her rapid heartbeat thumped his chest, and her pain became his, too.

"Tomorrow will be a better day."

Tomorrow will be a better day.

Her Sanctum of Ascension

A vibration tickled Lyal's heart.

His eyes widened, but it was too late to pull away. Lyal stiffened with a jolt as the arcane force swept through his entire body at once. Severed from control, he fell with her into instant slumber with only a fading fragment of consciousness left behind.

In that fleeting darkness, his mind wandered alongside whispers until they came to reverberate throughout unseen chambers, a sound soon accompanied by the tranquil drop of water into the shallow puddle. Lyal glided through the endless void but soon came to feel sure steps upon stable ground. His footsteps resonated as came the visions of depth and the walls of a passage.

Lyal felt his senses sharpen as he left the darkness behind and found himself at the center of an ancient hall whose stone surfaces were soaked in the somber tint of indigo. Upon the side walls ran mythic symbols of such homogeneous obscurity with the rest of the temple that they simply faded into the background to Lyal, who passed them by without a thought.

Something else did catch his eye, however: a mere puddle of water, pooled just slightly off the center of the path. He crept up to it, unsure of every step, and looked upon what it wished to show him.

Though there was familiarity, his eyes were full of an innocence long lost. Gone was the masculine definition, replaced now by softness and gentle curve.

"Whoa!" he yelped, somehow just a boy again.

Almost immediately upon becoming witness to that truth, an invasive sensation overwhelmed him. He pressed his palm against his head as it recessed deep into his mind. By the workings of the temple's soundless spell weave, the boy's memories became compressed, some preserved, and others driven to oblivion's edge.

He dropped his hand as the spell released him then, without much further thought on it, he stepped through the sacred waters, and his reflection vanished in the waves of the disturbance. There was a doorway not far ahead, but conscious of the danger, Lyal looked over his shoulder to where he had come from, though he found only sheer darkness.

"Huh . . . no going back. Where the heck am I?" the boy mused, his voice trapped between the walls of oblivion's temple.

Young Lyal refocused himself on the doorway, beyond which he could hear the gush of a mighty torrent. On thoughtless steps, he passed beneath the invader crest, carved in the timeless stone of the arch.

The hallway took him around a slight bank, and as the curve fell away from in front of him, he discovered another child there by the wayside. It was a little girl with suspicious almond hair, and just beyond her, the blue stone path narrowed into a sturdy bridge across the pitiless void.

Beyond those dark depths on either side were four recessions in the wall, each adorned at the head by a stone arch. From apertures hidden within came jets of water, whose sweeping reach fell so close to the bridge that their spray alone had left the passage drenched.

Lyal watched her for a moment. Though his mind was left in a haze of manipulation, he knew just who she was, this girl who appeared rooted in an endless trance.

Upon his first few steps forward, she became aware of his presence and turned over her shoulder with mouth agape in astonishment.

"Who are you!?" young Miyacre asked. Her eyes softened. "Lyal . . . ?" She stepped around to him. "How . . . How are you here?" she asked with eyes half fallen in a sleepy glaze.

The boy shrugged with a nonchalant demeanor, a buoyancy that quickly offset the gravity of their situation. "I don't really know!" His eyes wandered the cavernous, icy-blue passage. "Where are we, Miya? This place is really weird!"

She turned and looked around in mirrored unfamiliarity with its ancient pillars, winking glyphs, and gazing statues. "I'm—not sure, but . . . I've come here a lot, but I don't want to anymore. I *hate* this place," she decried.

Her eyes fell back to the bridge between the treacherous gushing and found that the intrusive boy had foolishly wandered upon it. He gazed at the ground where his steps fell upon intricate channels cut through the rock to accommodate the flow of water. His head rose as he followed them clear across to the other side.

"Hey! Be careful! It's really dangerous over there!" the girl cried with fists clenched in distress of his heedless meander.

"The door is on the other side! C'mon, I'll be right here with you," he stressed with enthusiasm for reaching the far end.

"This is my problem. I have to do it myself!"

The boy slowed to a stop. "Well . . . we're both here now. So, it's our problem. Are you coming or not?"

The girl's mouth fell agape, and she forced a nod, her eyes widened with terror at that endeavor.

The boy grinned as he relished her commitment to the adventure, then sprang into an onward press. Her vow cast discomfort in the distance between them, so she sped off to his side.

Just as they had reached halfway across, the gush empowered with a roar. The girl let out a yelp as reflexive hesitation caused her feet to slip out from beneath her.

"Lyal! Help!" she cried.

"Don't stop!" the boy called as he cut back and seized her by the arm.

He pulled her back to her feet, and together, they fled to the far end as the torrent engulfed the bridge at their heels.

Hundreds of gallons of sanctified water rocked the ground as they neared the hall to sanctuary. Lyal turned to the aqueduct's mouth beyond the endless pitfall. From within, he heard the vicious growl of angry waters forced through a constricted neck.

In the crosshairs of the last torrent, he took her hand tight and dove in through the doorway as the white wall exploded from the aperture. Miyacre was yanked off her feet, and together, they slid across the damp ground as the entire passage behind them was cut off by the endless wrath of the blessed waters.

Lyal sat up as he fought to catch his breath. He looked back at the monstrous wall behind them, then to the young girl, who quivered upon the ground.

"Jeez . . . we are way too little to be in a place like this," he mused.

Met with no reply from his rescued companion, he zeroed on her fierce convulsions as she lifted herself up from the ground and rested upon her knees.

"Hey—calm down. It's okay," the boy said as he stood and went to her side.

Miyacre's head shot up, and she searched his face with a bulging gaze. Young Lyal, yet entertained with her excessive trepidations, reached down with a grin and pulled her up by the arm.

Back on her feet, Miyacre grew still as the rush of their harrowing flight left her and, with a sharp sigh of frustration, stamped her foot in sudden fury.

"Why did you do that!? This place is really dangerous! If you don't stop being stupid, you're going to get *hurt*!" she erupted.

Lyal's brow raised in amused bewilderment. "Relax. We made it okay, didn't we?" he gloated.

The wily adventurer bounded away as his cautious companion seethed in a flustered bake.

"Can't go back, now!" he rallied against her sizzle.

Almost immediately was the boy's frolic brought to a halt, stricken with fascination by what they had stumbled upon in the next chamber. On the wall at the far end was a black plane cut through the ancient stone. Within the void loitered an ever-still hologram of an open hand, the bodiless Samaritan's eternal offering of aid.

Lyal, seeping mesmerization, stepped closer.

The chamber was darkened by indigo gloom. Four pillars stood in each corner, and there was a central recess in every wall. A wishing stone maiden under veil stood at the back of each shrine with the only noticeable difference being the state of an iridescent flower at her foot. One flourished. One wilted. One transformed from soul's seed to breathtaking bloom before returning to its cosmic dust while the last vanished and reappeared here and there upon the face of a levitating slate.

As Lyal approached, he noticed something across the wall near the ceiling. Wrapped along the top was a frieze adorned with the obscure carving of the Samaritan's hand, reached out to the right, an image that repeated all the way across the room in a complete band.

In his peripheral, Miyacre stepped out in front of him and threw her arms out to block his path. The boy flinched as he was shaken from his thoughtless meander.

"I said, stop. You don't know this place better than me, so if you're going to go any further, you're going to follow me."

"How do you know anything at all if you've never been past the bridge?"

She threw her head up with a moan of frustration. "Just trust me, alright? I told you . . . I've been here a lot."

Lyal put his finger to his lip as if to inject suspense to his resolved ponder of her solemn request. "Hmm . . . okay," he conceded. "Then, what's your plan to get out of here, ya bossy Beilkan?"

Her eyes wondered from his, as she sought the answers from muddled memories. "I just have to make it to the end. I think if I can do that, everything will be okay."

Her overzealous companion cocked his head. "Why do you think that?"

"A voice told me—" She hesitated, knowing the answer would only leave more questions.

"Sounds weird . . . but we got nothing else to do. You have any idea of where to go now?" The trickle of water caught his ear before any reply could satisfy his voracious curiosity. A nudging tranquility, it brought his attention to the eyes of the maidens, which, upon further examination, he found to mourn together some unspoken tragedy. Those streaming tears cascaded down flowing robes to the tarnished stone of the ground where they passed into swirling channels that carved throughout the ancient chamber.

Lyal traced its elegant sweeps until they delivered his eyes to a suspicious pool at the center of the chamber where the intricate design appeared to centralize.

Heedless of trickery, he headed right for it.

"Hey—" she called after him. "Don't get too close. You might—" But before she could finish, the young boy dropped his foot into the mystic waters. The bottom of his shoe hit the ground beneath.

"*Relax!*" he exclaimed as he stepped all the way in with both feet. "It's just a—"

Before he could get the words out, he plunged right through. The boy let out a yelp as he was swallowed by the silver pool of sorrows. Miyacre darted forward in panic as he disappeared into the breach.

Lyal broke through the water on the other side, fell from the ceiling, and struck the ground below.

"Ouch . . . Great idea, *huh*, Lyal? *Sheesh*," the boy scolded himself as he rose up to new surroundings.

He found himself spat out at the back of a short hall, accompanied still by the omnipresent white noise of rushing waters. A brick path of luminescent turquoise cut through the center, and on each side wall were three sets of waterfalls. The waters emerged from narrow splits in the ceiling and cascaded through crisscrossed steel grates upon the floor.

Just as he made to stand, the puddle on the ceiling burst forth with a violent spray as the girl emerged from the watery gateway with a yelp. Lyal dove to evade an imminent squashing, but her weight caught him in the act and struck him back to the ground.

They wrestled away from each other until they had comfortably separated.

"Told you not to do it," she grumbled.

Lyal shrugged. "Can't go back now."

"Are you going to keep saying that until we're lost?"

"You don't know. Maybe we'll find what you're looking for," he encouraged.

She released a long sigh of frustration with the boy then stood up.

"Follow me. I'm leading the way now," she said with her spirit burning with new strength stoked by exasperation.

Finally in control of his bumbling, she turned and crossed the turquoise brick, which took expressive breaths of radiance. Lyal rose and gave chase to her through the spray of the falls along that path compressed by the water grates.

They passed one after another beneath the invader crest, which lay centered on the doorway's arch, and beyond it, they beheld in awe a colossal chamber from a high balcony.

At the center of the balcony was an indigo pedestal that cradled in its ancient stone cup a cloudy gem with all the spectacular beauty of the sun-touched crystalline seas.

The two wanderers scampered past the pedestal to the sheer brink. Beneath, the walls of the trench faded to a lifeless green until all became sheer dark.

"Whoa—look at that." Lyal gawked as he gazed out across the chasm.

Beyond the harrowing dive were two hands of pristine stone reaching toward each other, close, yet left in tragic separation. Suspended by beams, those fated two were bonded to an enigmatic mechanism operated by wheel, chute, and cog.

Just beyond those stones' grasp was a glossy semisphere lodged into the wall, transparent in its dormancy. From the sphere pocket, five narrow channels descended the wall to a door upon a landing below with no discernible means to reach it as it lay completely surrounded by the endless plunge.

"We have to get in there . . . but how?" the boy pondered aloud.

A steady drip from a hidden brink high above caught young Miyacre's eye. She traced the fine trickle down to the wooden chute of one of the wheels and seized, at once, the answer.

"Look!" she cried with the charge of her finger. "That's it!"

Lyal's eyes darted to the designated brink. "What? I don't see anything," he replied.

"The water, you goof."

"Oh . . . how's that going to help us?"

"Haven't you ever seen a watermill before? I bet if we can get up there, we could find something to get the water running—and it'll fall on those big wheels," she theorized.

Lyal nodded as her idea took root inside his imagination. "Okay, okay . . . I see what you mean. But how are we going to do that? We're trapped on this island," he observed with a scan of the brink that surrounded them.

Young Miyacre turned to examine the area alongside him, and at once, their eyes fell upon the orb in the cradle. In a scamper for a solution, they went before the pedestal and gazed upon its gleaming treasure. Without a word, Miyacre reached out and stole the orb from its cradle and cupped it in the palms of her hands.

"I feel . . . I feel like we can do something with this," she stated, divining with wistful eyes mirrored in those enchanted crystal waters.

Lyal turned to her and cocked his head, unsure of what it was she meant. There was a jolt beneath their feet. The temple was set into a fierce quake.

Their eyes darted all around as a series of scrapes pierced their perked ears.

"Over there!" cried Miyacre with a turn to the right side of the platform.

From the wall, a staircase of stone slabs grazed the walls of their recesses as they extended out over the abyss and offered them passage to a hidden landing further below.

With due caution, they crept up to the very edge and peered over to the teased avenue to new progress. Each slab was separated by a respectable gap that would need to be negotiated with a modest leap. The cost of a single misstep, an eternal plummet.

"Well—are we going, or what?" asked Lyal with a fire in his eyes.

"Of course! You think I'm afraid of heights, too?" Miyacre leapt in sudden bravery and went bounding across the steps.

"Hey! Wait up!" Lyal cried out as he raced down after her.

At the bottom, the sudden daredevil fumbled across the landing while her companion came crashing down. On a lost step, young Lyal toppled to the ground behind her as she fought to control her momentum in her flight for the brink.

She skipped along in a haphazard stumble for death until the tip of her shoe snagged the edge of a crooked stone block in the ancient masonry. By fortune's grace, she was flung forward. Miyacre clasped the orb with both hands as she planted upon her knees and slid all the way to a halt before the open arms of oblivion.

Her eyes sank to greet the depths. Thanking her lucky stars, she gritted her teeth in anxious relief, then rose quick to her feet, the fabric of her pants torn and her knees covered with scrapes. The pain was quick to subside, however, and with the orb still secured, she hurried back over to Lyal with ample motivation.

Her steadfast companion inched up from the old, jagged stonework, shaking off a pain of his own. Upon her arrival at his side, she reached down, took him by the arm, and assisted him in his wobbly ascent.

"Okay, we need to be more smart from now on," she advised.

"Yeah . . . smart. So, how's that gonna work?" the boy asked as he brushed himself of ancient dusts.

The girl seized her hips and peacocked in over-the-top vexation. "Just leave it to me, goof. Come on!" she cheered in a turn of tides and a break for the doorway, which loomed nearby.

"Hey! I'm not a goof!" the boy protested as he gave chase to that shooting star once again.

With spirit in their steps, the daring duo sped through the promising doorway that had been spotted from above, and entered the next passage, which greeted lively young eyes with sweeping exuberance of turquoise stonework in both the walls and smooth-cut slabs beneath their feet.

Those electrified pathfinders passed under the blank gazes of petrified maidens beneath veils who poured liquid graces from shoulder mounted urns in recessed shrines along the walls. Separated from the grated catwalk by a gap to oblivion, their blessed waters filled intricate channels within those individual chambers before finding the abyss at the labyrinth's end.

Out through the other side, they found themselves in the throat of a curved cavern, an odd, organic departure of flowing metamorphic rock of the same turquoise makeup as the prior passage's craftwork.

Further along the slippery meander, three shallow streams coursed across the passage, each born from a crevice beneath the bulged bank. Though their flow appeared fierce, a lack of depth made them of little threat and did nothing to stall the explorers' pursuit of the upper levels of the main antechamber.

"So—you really don't know how you got here?" asked young Miyacre as they splashed through the first stream.

Young Lyal lowered his head in an earnest effort to recall any distant memory of his arcane transmission, but alas, it had become lost to him.

He shook his head as he resolved his fruitless recollections. "I dunno. I just remember walking in the dark . . . and I remember you! Somehow . . ."

Miyacre nodded at that shared perception. "I know you, too. I feel like . . . I've been here a bunch of times. But, I'm sure this is the first time I've been here with you." She lifted the orb to her eyes. "And—I know what my dream is. I remember that here, too . . . Why did these memories stay with us, huh?"

The boy shrugged again to come up with an answer as he kicked through the divine water. "I dunno! Maybe, because they're always in your heart—so, they're always close with you, no matter where you are or where you go," he guessed rather naturally.

The girl surrendered a gentle beam as his effortless words sank into her vulnerable heart, then nodded in overwhelming delight.

"I think you're right! No matter where we go, we take our dreams with us. It's part of who we are. Yeah . . . so, I'll never let this dream go." She looked at her companion with an unusual energy. "You, too, Lyal! Never let go of your dream, either," she encouraged.

"Huh?" he said, distracted by the glimmer of gemstones beneath the mythic waters as he kicked his way through. "My dream? Yeah, I won't. Sometimes I feel like nobody believes in me and I can't do it. But I won't give up, don't worry—I wouldn't do that."

Her beam faded as those inner meditations came to surface. "I believe you can do it."

"You mean it?" the boy asked his spirits lifted by her beaming warmth.

"I always have. So, maybe your dream is in my heart, too. I guess I can carry it with me . . . Wherever I go!"

"Thanks, Miyacre. . ." the boy replied. "I want to make these more than dreams, though. Both yours and mine. We'll do it together, okay? Promise."

His dear companion nodded with a euphoric glow, their bond nearing bloom once more.

The time-warped adventurers sloshed through the final stream and arrived at the end of the bend where a sloped passage to the next chamber awaited. They shared a moment of hesitation before beginning their ascension into the deeper clutches of the temple.

As they approached the top, the roar of turbulent waters threatened their bravery. Miyacre's enthusiastic press withered, stricken with sudden imbalance as the warning struck its mark. Her foot rose, then drifted backward as if she wobbled on the verge of retreat.

"I can go first—"

"No," she interrupted. "I'll be fine."

With mustered courage, she drove through fear to the next step, then led him straight to the top. A wall of sheer noise assaulted them upon the last step as they came to face down the roaring hall to the next chamber.

"You okay?" the boy asked, seeing distress reborn in her eyes.

She snapped from the anxious stew with a nod. "Yeah—I can't let it stop me this time—Because next time, I might not have you here with me," she said resolvedly, then stepped off with renewed determination.

The boy's eyes lingered on that warring spirit as she pressed on ahead, but he scampered along without much pause, keen not to be left behind. He retook her side as they emerged into the imposing chamber whose cavernous ceiling of gray rock stalactite cupped to a central shaft to the temple's heart.

Drawn in by an alluring aurora of a celestial grace, hanging there, beyond a distant parapet, the eager explorers raced by a staircase to a raised landing on their left.

"This has gotta be it," Miyacre assured as they dashed for the decrepit stone barrier.

Upon their arrival to the parapet, they caught their first glimpse of the raging waters beyond. A maw-like whirlpool agitated the body of water and made any hope of traversal impossible.

A whirling reservoir comprised much of the chamber. On each side of the grand plaza built alongside it were broad staircases that guided the faithful to hexagonal platforms, which offered spacious ground to colossal stone maidens of those sacred waters. Each of those enraptured keepers of the sorrows bore an urn over shoulder and, unlike any others, raised a free arm to the towering portal, out from which fell the shimmering stardust curtain.

Lyal scanned the cove's far bank, which lay spotted with emerald stalagmites: grim, rocky jaws that only grew longer as the waters recessed in the ferocious current. Centralized along that craggy coast was a pathless altar that hosted a monumental golden basin of articulated significance.

"Looks like a dead end," he determined. "How are we supposed to go up from here?"

Miyacre had fixated upon the lustrous basin of offerings. "That bowl might do something," she surmised.

"Yeah . . ." Lyal said fadingly, seeing little to be gained from that remote shrine of presumed embellishment.

Then, something of more promise caught the boy's eye: a severe crack in the base of the statue upon the left-hand rise.

"Hey—maybe we could knock that statue over!" he cried with the cast of his finger to guide Miyacre's eye.

She turned to him, perplexed by that outlandish suggestion given their comparative size.

"You know," he continued, "to maybe put a plug in that whirlpool."

"Ahh—I see . . . but how are we gonna knock that thing over?"

Lyal shrugged. "Worth a shot, right?"

". . . I guess you're right. Let's go."

Riding momentum, the tireless duo doubled back to the stairs they had passed in hopes to topple the ancient monument in vigil at the top. Upon the last step, Lyal peered up into the hollow tower in the ceiling. From there, he could make out intricate glyph work inscribed upon perimeter stones of the peculiar portal. Without a doubt, it had to be of some importance, he suspected.

"Lyal—over here," called Miyacre, who had already secured both hands upon the cracked surface.

The boy dashed to her side and laid his hands upon the cool rock. Together, with their strength delivered at once, they drove into the structure.

But it was no use.

Even in its damaged state, their efforts did little to cause any significant change. Not even a loose fragment dropped.

"Ugh! We can't do this," the girl exclaimed as she broke away from it.

"We'll have to try something else," the boy concurred with a turn from the statue.

Almost at once, he discovered that alternate avenue, which had gone hidden in plain sight.

"Hey—what about over there!" he bleated with the draw of his finger to the distant staircase.

Miyacre focused in as she examined the platform's solutions. Her eyes were crossed a thousand times over by the fiery golden beams of a spectacular glyph sunburst emblazoned upon the wall at the top of the steps.

Just to the right of that dazzling fixture was a door sealed by an impenetrable slate, and to the right of it, the bronze nozzle of an ancient pipe.

"Let's check it out," Miyacre agreed, enthusiastic about the offerings.

They descended from the maiden's summit, crossed back over the plaza, and rose up to the obscure sigil. As they grew close, they could distinguish a faint ethereal plane that existed just beyond the surface of the extruded rock. As it fluxed and phased in and out from existence, playful glimmers shined in one place, then zipped around to another.

"Look at this," said Miyacre as she leaned in closer.

At the very center of that triumphant obscurity was a half-circle insert central to the design. The clever girl lifted the orb to the cup. It was a perfect fit.

"What do you think it'll do?" she asked Lyal, who chased a glimmer with his eye.

"Hopefully not be a self-destruct button."

She sighed at his tactless musing. "Right. Here goes."

She reached the orb toward the socket. Like a magnet, it was plucked from her hand and fixed into place upon the wall. The fledgling adventurers flinched as an illusionary shockwave of the ghostly sigil echoed forth through them. The fiery rays of gold stretched past their carved limitations, then settled into gentle radiance, the glyph's inner capabilities roused from a millennium of slumber.

They exchanged a glance with widened eyes, neither of them able to produce the words to follow in wake of that arcane awakening.

Miyacre's eyes drifted to the doorway and found that the featureless slate had dissipated in its entirety, which left the passage accessible to their explorations. She tapped Lyal on the shoulder and turned his attention to the waiting portal. With steady eyes, they crept over to the open crypt and peered beyond the glimmering frame.

The chamber beyond lay draped with the thousand-year-old mists. A man-sized serpentine run of dingy gray pipe wrapped across the turquoise stone, an old mechanical carcass left to soak in the mists of Eternia, prone to unpleasant discoloration yet resilient to the rust.

At the far reaches of the chamber was a caliginous recess in the wall sealed off by dripping chain links. Within that forbidden abscess loomed a bizarre machine of a sort. Its indigo casing was rounded along the top, and its face glared with six angry eyes, each agleam with a cerulean glow from the energized core.

A gentle hum and subtle rumble were enough to prove its operational state, though neither of them were sure to what end that functionality might serve.

Protruded through the fence was the severed mouth of the mechanical menace, which gushed endless gallons of wasted water. Without a place to go, the waters flooded extensive narrow corridors found below the steel grate that served as the chamber's floor.

As they waded into the mists, they came to notice that the pipeline was fragmented multiple times on its journey to the wall. The dislodged segments were rolled off to one side or the other, and at each splice was an increasingly familiar engraved hand that reached toward the empty space.

Lyal, spurred to curiosity, went to the nearest segment and inspected the hand, finally cognizant of its reoccurring presence. "These hands . . . they're everywhere here."

He looked over to the pipe's main body just beyond. It appeared to be a clean fit if they could just roll it into place. More fascinating was the second hand he discovered upon the side of the main pipeline.

"Look!" Lyal exclaimed as he moved over to it. "Looks like we have to connect the pipes together. Like—connecting the hands. I think that has something to do with everything here," he surmised.

Confident with that deduction, he rose up and passed a glance over the coiled layout.

"Over here, here . . . here . . . and over there," the boy identified as he pointed out to each the four disconnected pieces.

But Miyacre had oddly fallen silent. He turned over his shoulder. "Miyacre?"

She lingered there, in the somnolent mists, her eyes closed in a subconscious trance. "Hm?"

"Are you okay? What, are you sleeping?"

Her eyes crawled open and unveiled a sleepy glaze. "No—no. Sorry, I just felt a little weird."

"What? What do you mean?" he asked.

"Uh—just felt like my thoughts were flying away or something—I'm not sure." She perked up in a sudden swell of energy. "But I heard you! Let's connect those pieces and see what it does."

Together, with the plan in mind, they went to work at different ends of the room, going backward to the first severed segment. With one foot dug back into the ground, they shoved the old pipes to set them into a roll. After an initial determined drive, each of them went easily across dampened stone.

As the sheared edges aligned, they were bonded in a flash. The magical reconstruction energized the young duo and spirited their departure for each subsequent segment.

With a push, a roll, and a seal, three pieces of puzzle had been set in place.

"There's one left," said Miyacre as they regrouped before the barrier of the roaring machine.

Lyal nodded. "Let's go."

Swiftly at the side of the last segment, they planted their hands and, with a final drive, rolled it back into alignment. With a flash, it was sealed to the main pipeline, the flow to the nozzle restored. The enraged goliath let out a thundering growl as the sacred waters were unleashed through the main conduit with potent force.

A blast from beyond the door informed them of their success, and the consequent roar of high-pressured rage against the rock motivated them into an all-out sprint for the other side. Upon arrival at the entrance, however, their hearts sank as they found the jet's misguided ferocity inflicted upon the back of the cove.

"Well, what are we going to do, now?" asked Lyal.

Miyacre scanned the rocks where the water collided but came up with no immediate solution to their dilemma. Hopeful still, she turned and made for the glyph, which yet lay empowered by the temple's orb. Her eyes darted all over in search of meaning, but she could gather nothing from the bizarre icons and radiant sweeps.

"I don't understand any of this," she bleated.

In a release of frustration, she took a rightward swipe at the mystic plane. The haphazard explorers jolted at a flare of sparks that spilled out from the mere pass of her hand.

Miyacre lifted her arm high and stepped all the way back until the stairs were at her heels.

"What the heck was that!?" Lyal roared.

"I—I don't know," she assured him with anxious inspection of her hand.

The grinding of rock snatched their attentions and turned them to the great nozzle upon the rock, which had been set in motion. They dipped their heads and descended the steps as the mighty spray swept across the chamber.

Just as they reached the last step, the jet stream made contact with a stone maiden. The structure shattered at the weak point just above the base, and the surge drove the idol of the divine keeper down into the grasp of the whirlpool.

Those fortuitous companions lifted their heads. Only severed rock remained upon the altar.

They had done it.

Young Lyal took off toward the parapet to gauge their success. Miyacre took a step after him, then doubled back. She rose up to the top and opened her hands before the orb, though hesitated to boldly reach forward given its fierce reaction to her reckless swipe. That thoughtless pause was rewarded as a wave of luminance pulsed through the glyph, and the orb was released into her palm.

With the mystic source missing from the gilded pocket, the ethereal bloom began to dissipate. Miyacre, with that vital relic secured, turned and descended the steps.

"Miyacre, look! The whirlpool!" Lyal called from the parapet.

She rushed to his side with such intensity that she nearly threw herself from the balcony. Below them, the waters had grown calm, yet remained stimulated by some unseen force.

"What now?" asked Miyacre.

Lyal shrugged. "Maybe we can swim somewhere—hey! Look!" The boy pointed down at the water levels below the parapet, which had begun to rise at a fearsome rate. "It's coming up!"

Before Miyacre could get the last word out, the waters began to pour from overtop the reservoir wall. She turned back to the nozzle, which persisted in its relentless burst stream. With the statue cleared of its path, the focused water blasted the back wall and created an endless cascade that further fed the flood.

Water surged through the lower beams of the parapet, and their shoes became submerged.

"We've got to get out of here, Lyal," Miyacre urged as her heart began to race.

Lyal, however, had zeroed in on the towering ascent. Miyacre seized his hand and tried to pull him into retreat for the doorway. Doubtful of means of salvation behind them, he pulled away in resistance to that confused guidance.

"No—wait," he cried. "Miyacre! Look, there's a way up if we swim," he illuminated with the cast of his finger.

She looked up and found it, too, though failed to find the same enthusiasm in taking up such a harrowing venture. As the waters crept up from their shins to their knees, the door to the way back was sealed by sheer slate. For her, the temple had resolved her wavering, but the courage of the decisive heart could go missing no longer.

"We have to go now. If we stay, we'll be trapped!" the boy cried as he sloshed through the water.

Miyacre, with all her trust in him, gripped the orb tight as she fought her way forward.

They floated over the submerged parapet and began to swim through the dark waters. As the levels continued to rise, they grew ever closer to the jet stream, which yet punched through the surface.

"Swim away from it!" Miyacre cried.

The temple's young captives of destructive ingenuity swam with tireless vigor as death swarmed them on every side, the deadly jet just ahead, and the jagged jaws of stone above.

The waterline met the top of the gilded bowl, and the blessed waters dove into its heaven-tuned reservoir. Upon being filled to the top, the gilded frame burst to life in a spectacular activation, a calamitous blessing that only served to exacerbate the treacherous flooding.

With fierce maneuvers against the watery chaos, they managed to put distance between themselves and the jet, whose power became muffled as the water level continued to climb.

The current beneath intensified, however, and the imperiled adventurers fought helplessly as it drove them further into the center of the chamber.

Lyal cast his head up to the temple's sacred vault, which awaited them beyond the portal's reach. Swept within the twilight shaft, they had become surrounded by those smooth, sculpted stones of radiant turquoise. Encircled by recessed shrines, those maidens of the sorrows offered silent prayers for their struggle until they, too, became submerged as the chamber was engorged by the rampaging sacred waters.

"We're almost there, Lyal! Hang on," Miyacre cried as the surface broke in endless turbulence.

The angry rapids slammed the walls of the well, then returned in a mighty sweep. The consequential waves repeatedly submerged the two in their ferocious rage until they were left to gasp for the next breath.

Miyacre flailed beneath the surface as the rapids tossed her toward the wall in their merciless strength. Lyal, however, remained trapped near the center as he fought to keep afloat in the ruthless battery.

Suddenly, the currents of chaos ripped him away. He flipped beneath the water and found himself turned upside down and face-to-face with a demon from the abyss.

The smooth turquoise wall turned to jagged, sharp rock just before the shaft ended in a band of scripture–infused gold plate at the peak. Miyacre found a tangible surface with her desperate grasp and latched hold of it. She scanned across the stormy waters but caught no sight of her dear companion. The water in front of her dove. A wave thundered forth. With one hand free, she clung to the rock, then took the full force of the impact.

Her body jabbed into the rock and left her disoriented. The waters rose relentlessly and forced her to climb. On shaky footing, she ascended the slick gray slope of the wall but shuttered to a subaqueous thunder. Young Miyacre felt her heart race as the waters grew eerily still.

Just further around the bend, Lyal burst from the surface with a rejuvenating gasp.

"Lyal!" she cried. "S-something happened!"

Those words of warning were lost to the boy, however, as he appeared engaged in a grueling struggle, fighting to yank one of his legs from beneath the settling waves. Miyacre stumbled as she locked up in visceral unease.

"Lyal!? What's wrong—"

Before she could get out the last word, he had secured his arm around a stubby spire and heaved his foot from the raging beneath. To her horror, a black-gloved hand came up latched to his ankle, a spine-chilling sight that returned her to gut-wrenching nausea she had felt during her encounter with the sworn savage.

The nightmare had stalked her into the otherworld, a wretched fiend she had no intention of ever being victim to again. In spite of good wisdom, she had hidden that trouble to safeguard them from the burden and would surely be dead before she allowed it to reap a moment more of torment.

With eyes widened in madness, she cocked back in her hand all she had left to unleash her fury with: the mystic temple orb. To bury the beast was her only path to joy.

"Don't do it!" the boy protested, one arm raised to stall her righteous wrath. "You need it to get to the end of this place. We can't give it up!"

"But, Lyal!" she pled to the fool.

"Miyacre. Don't—do it," he stressed, sworn to keep his promise that someday their dreams might be ushered in together to some glorious new reality.

But against his will, her eyes sharpened on that despised revenant as she prepared to make the sacrifice. There came a second thunder from the forbidden beneath. Before she could make the fated cast, the water level plummeted. Lyal kicked off the hand as it went, and the plunge took demon back to the depths along with all the temple's rage.

"Lyal!" she yelped as she watched it drop before her eyes.

The boy squeezed the rock with all his might as a chasm of open air opened up beneath them.

"Hang on, Lyal!" the girl cried.

She looked up toward the ledge and threw the orb up to the top. It cleared the brink and bounced somewhere beyond her sight, and in that moment, it didn't matter where.

With bravery in her heart and her eternal soul bound to a wondrous dream, she went from rock to rock with the iron grip of a hero. As she neared the golden band, she found a cupped rock to deliver an energized drive off the toe.

Her palms found the stone-tiled surface beyond, and she pushed away from the clutches of death. Without a moment wasted to relish in her safety, she spirited around the edge to where Lyal hung from fortune's spire.

Miyacre dove to the ground just above him and reached out her arm. "Take my hand, Lyal! I'll pull you up," she cried.

He looked up to her, then down into the deep dive.

She stretched out her fingers. "Lyal!"

The boy refocused on her desperate salvation and, against the duress of death, reached forth. A miracle in distance, she seized her dear friend by the hand and locked hold of him. Statues of the temple maidens in prayer gazed upon them from shrines along the summit's perimeter, their pedestals each adorned with the same two hands, carved in sacred stone.

Secured by her weight, the boy kicked off the spire to catch the edge. The first kick cracked the formation, and a second broke it lose. Lyal turned over his shoulder and watched as his last anchor of security tumbled into the abyss. Now, there was only her and explicit death.

She held on with an adamantine grip, as if her own life depended on it, but could do nothing more from the floor. Lyal raced to conjure up a means out as fatigue began to strain him. In a last-ditch effort, he kicked against the wall in an attempt to rid his outsoles of tragic moisture. Miyacre buried her hips into the ground as the boy shifted below.

His foot connected with the rock wall, and his legs stiffened. His determined savior slid toward the brink.

"Miyacre, get ready to pull—I'm gonna run for it," he called out to her.

She replied with a nod through a tight wince.

"Alright—ready . . . and go!"

Lyal scaled the wall as Miyacre crossed one leg over the other and twisted into full force. With two firm steps and the momentum of her swing, he caught the ledge with his elbow. Relieved of his weight, she scrambled to her knees, took him by the shirt, and pulled him over the golden band and straight down to the floor with her.

The gasping duo lay there at the summit as the rumble of the thunderous torrent grew faint. They had done it. Lyal heaved off the ground, and Miyacre rose after him. She threw her arms around her dear friend; he, fighting to catch his breath, and she, no less depleted, yet simply unable to allow her overwhelming joy to suffer any hinderance.

"Wow—that was—really something of you," he complimented between sharp breaths of fading anxiety.

"I'm so glad you're safe, Lyal. I don't know what I would do if I lost you," she gushed.

"Probably be a lot safer."

She shook her head in adamant defiance of that critical presumption. "Don't say that!" she cried. "Can't you see how much you've helped?"

She searched him for faith but found only insecurity as her waterlogged companion scratched at the back of his head, his pride cut down by embarrassment following his precarious encounter with her devil from the depths.

Exasperated with the boy's needless diffidence, she surrendered with a sigh, then took his arm and pulled him from the washed stone. He settled to steady composure there in the comforting presence of his benevolent priestess of selfless charities. There, at the peak of that odd temple of subconscious, he came to recognize the true strength of her character: a courageousness that he found himself able to take from and utilize for any trial that might lay ahead of them and, at the heart of that vivid sensation, faith in himself. A faith that could transcend dreams and manifest in whatever reality awaited them on the other side.

And though he struggled to produce the words to express that truth deep in the heart, they blossomed in smile together in quiet reverence, and that alone seemed to suffice.

The gleam of divine radiance and dynamic shimmering caught Lyal's attention from over her shoulder.

"Whoa—check it out. There's another one," he informed with face fallen in astonishment of empyrean grace.

Miyacre turned and was brought to the euphoric brim by the mere sight of the temple's grand crown. A bounding altar of timeless serenity awaited their resolve, beckoning with the ravishing grace of a sprawling flare, whose staircase rays cut across the walls and down throughout the floors like the open wings of some unseen seraph.

"That must be it!" she cried in blissful triumph.

She broke from his side into an exhilarating dash and ascended the flight in a mere few leaps with Lyal in spirited pursuit. Upon the summit's sacred apse, she found the ground gilded with the glorious image of a maiden and a whirling orb of water wrapped together in the intimate embrace of self-reconciliation.

Lyal became distracted before reaching the steps, however, when his wandering eye happened upon a lone window to infinite sky along the outer wall where a patch of vibrant green creeper grew over the crumbled sill. The fine strands of curling emerald stalk blossomed out into a voluminous nest of fluffy white bristles, atop which crawled a blue winged flier, lambent with exquisite ethereal wings that came to an end in long, black tails.

His eye became fixated on that otherworldly butterfly as it took flight across the room with a gentle bat.

"Hey—look at this," he whispered as it neared.

Miyacre, however, had prepared herself for action, the orb already cupped in her hands. She lifted it to the arcane activated module, her eyes set alight by the restrained energy that glittered through the lines of the glyph like blood through veins.

Lyal, who had wandered off the elevated path to investigate, lifted a finger to the butterfly as it arrived just above his head.

The orb was seized from her cradle and locked into the socket with a mighty jab. The glyph exploded to life with extreme brilliance, its power unleashed.

There was a quake, the grind of enormous rock, then, the roar of water. A wide section of the wall on each side of the room crawled upward and unleashed a raging surge.

Lyal froze as he watched the white rapids reach forward and carve along the ends of the sweeping staircase. The tide caught him fast, taking him by the ankles and sweeping him off his feet.

The boy was struck at the shoulder and became submerged beneath a thunderous gush for the brink.

Miyacre turned to a startling yelp just in time to see his hand vanish beneath the waterline. Her mouth fell agape in horror, and she leapt from the summit into a full stride across the central path that split around the harrowing pit.

Hugging the left path, she chased a rolling disturbance further downstream, but in a near-effortless roll, the boy burst out from the shallow rush and flopped back onto the path.

Miyacre fell to his side with a heart unfit for such incessant distress. "Lyal! Are you alright!?"

He peered up into her worried eyes, and through fading terror of some would-be catastrophe, he cracked, then burst into laughter.

"What? Why are you laughing!?" she said, as she rose back to her feet.

Still immersed in his joy, he lifted to his knees before her.

"It's not funny, Lyal! I'm serious!" She stamped her foot.

But the laughter continued until she couldn't quite take it anymore. That aching chaperone raised her hand and slapped him right across the cheek; a resounding whip that brought him straight to silence.

Her chest rose and fell in deep breaths of release, her hand still frozen out to the side.

"Hey . . ." the boy muttered as he raised his hand to that spanked cheek, dazed by her sudden strike.

Overwhelmed inside, she fell to her knees before him, with a heavy head bowed in sorrow. "I'm sorry."

"Miyacre, why are you so worried about me?"

She stiffened in bewilderment. "I'm . . . sad that you wouldn't know why, Lyal," she lamented. "But, I wouldn't want anyone to get hurt because of me."

"Relax. Who got hurt?" He shrugged it off with a casual breeziness. "We made it, just like we promised. Miya . . . how are you supposed to lighten up if you worry all the time? Believe in the promise! It's not hard," he bragged.

She met his smug audacity with a tender beam. "Yeah! You're right," she concurred. "Thanks, Lyal . . ."

With a breath of release, there, at reconciliation's summit, she raised a steady head, focused on the fulfillment of those promises. "Come on, let's see where the water—"

The answer sparked in the girl's mind. She looked to the fated hands that lay carved upon each maiden's shrine. With that epiphany, she rose and departed alone to the brink where the summoned falls thundered.

Below, the crank of wooden wheels creaked. The cascade drove them round and put the cogs to work. To their clamorous churn, the colossal stone hands of the main antechamber were reunited as one, and the temple's silent task was fulfilled.

The lonely gemstone emitted a coursing blue radiance, which split through the stone channels as it fell. That blessed light of the ancients draped the sealed door in celestial brilliance, and as its luminescent grace faded away, the barrier was gone with the glow.

The light from the beyond shined through the opened breach, waiting for them to come.

"We did it," Miyacre cheered as she turned from the brink and found him still there upon the ground.

He looked at her with an invigorating beam. "You don't have to be afraid anymore. Look!" said the boy as he passed his fingers through a ghostly drift that rushed for the dive.

She took in a stifled breath as her eyes swept the ethereal flow that had come to take the place of those raging waters. Lyal lifted his hand, but only the cool mists came cupped in his palm.

"See? We can leave this place behind. It's over now," he declared just as the butterfly returned and landed upon his shoulder.

Her face fell in gaping curiosity as the effortless creature took flight for the brink, fluttered over her head, then dove out of sight.

Their eyes lingered there for a moment, and from beyond darkness, a hexagonal platform crafted of ancient stone rose in perfect silence. At once, they caught sight of that nonchalant beauty as it climbed the emerald vines of a midnight's posy of neon blues whose overgrowth had bound a central stone pillar.

"I guess that's our way down," said Lyal as he joined at her side.

"Yeah—this must be it. Let's go, Lyal . . . let's get out of here."

Beyond the brink, a short gap divided them from the platform's edge. In a short burst, they leapt over and found stable footing upon the cracking stone. With fate's passengers aboard, the platform descended the chamber, and they passed in front of the stone hands, their cold fingers nearly intertwined.

"Lyal—I—"

The boy turned to her in patience as she fought to get the right words out.

"I'm—never mind. It's nothing." She folded, unable to produce articulated truth.

The platform arrived before a doorway that lay draped in the phantasmal curtains of glimmering arcane particles. With a short leap, they stepped before the shrouded gateway to the temple's final hall but turned to each other in the face of resolution.

"Well, here we are. That wasn't too bad, was it?" Lyal encouraged.

Encumbered by her thoughts and unable to muster a response, she merely looked back at him and smiled. Their eyes wandered back to the doorway ahead. Beyond the mystic cascade was cerulean stonework majesty whose grounds were split by narrow rows of grated flooring. Installed above the flooded abyss, they vanished into five waterfalls, which gushed from linear-lipped mouths along the top of the chamber's back wall.

"What were you looking for in here, anyway?" Lyal inquired.

"Walk with me, Lyal. When we get there—I'll explain the best I can."

Though unsure of what to expect from her sudden cryptic disposition, Lyal nodded, and with a promise to keep, they set out through the door and passed into the chamber of the misty falls. Across the walls, the cerulean stone was cut through by the sinuous lines of the gemstone's starlight. Those guiding streaks gathered upon the ceiling halfway, then shot right into the central cascade.

"Looks like that's the way forward. You ready?" Lyal asked as they approached.

Miyacre turned to him and nodded.

With lingering anxiety, she stepped up to the wall of water, lowered her head, then passed through. The gushing waters fell as a cool mist against her skin and left her blinded in its dense embrace until she had emerged on the other side.

Lyal stepped out behind her, and they found themselves in a second chamber, which presented them with five more passages through water, the meandering light to guide them through to the decided destination.

Her fear overcome at last, she stepped alongside the boy as they passed through the falls, chamber after chamber, deepening into tranquility.

"Lyal—thank you for being here with me," she spilled, unable to hold back any longer what needed to be said.

"Don't mention it. That's what friends do. There's nothing more to it, is there?"

"But there is," she interjected. "There's so much more. You and the rest of the guys always helped me, especially when we were younger—and I was the new girl in town. I know we ended up with different friends, but . . . you guys are one of the reasons I wanted to help others. My dream wouldn't be the same without each of you . . . and these special memories."

Though she had mustered the strength to look him eye to eye, she shrank away as a more tender truth came forth from within.

"That's why I'm so afraid to lose you—to lose part of myself. Especially when we've already lost so much—without you guys, there would be nothing for me but—"

She shook her head, desperate to restrain her gush which she presumed to paralyze. "I'm sorry—I don't mean to burden you with all that."

But he laughed at her incessant worrying. "You don't have to say sorry for being honest with how you feel. Me and the guys will always be there to have your back," he swore just as they passed through the final misty falls and entered out into the dark abyss; beyond the veil, children no longer.

Her head fell in a guilty laugh, privy to some tragic truth.

Their steps across that vague realm of shadows fell upon the dusky element of colorless, abstract block. A plane at the end of consciousness before the elemental cycler's conduit to the forbidden realm; an imperceptible finger firmly set upon the workable third eye.

At the perceived center of the boundless end of Eternia's tenebrous dock, a hexagonal platform awaited, agleam with the fiery stained glass of the nameless seraphic champion, his staff of transformations raised to a starlight breach in the cosmos.

Beyond the unfathomable abyss was an enormous structure that cradled the invader's crest in its bulwark of a thousand twinkling towers, a fortress of a cathedral made nearly nondescript behind the odd world's eternal ebon shade.

She went to the edge where the ambient dusk and seraph's perimeter stone met, there upon the bridge between destinies. With a subconscious release of the world, she stepped onto the blazing glass and accepted the destination to which she would be delivered.

Lyal moved to join at her side, just as he had promised: to be there together, wherever the journey brought them. She turned, however, and took him by the wrists in gentle restraint.

"Lyal . . . I have to do this one on my own," she confessed.

His face fell in bewilderment, blindsided by her sudden resistance. "Miyacre, what are you doing . . . ?"

She sighed as her head fell to the fated heartache of that inevitable moment. "I knew exactly where I would go if I could make it, Lyal. I wasn't able to make a difference last time, but I'm . . . I'm going to change that," she swore, with fierce resolve burning in her eyes. "The truth that's waiting for me doesn't matter anymore."

Prepared for the dawning of destiny, she turned over her shoulder to the shadowy monolith that loomed out in the vanishing realm.

"When I go there—all will make sense . . . That was what I was promised."

"Promised to who!?" Lyal cried.

She turned back to him, heavy headed, as discomfort battled mental fortitude upon her face. "I don't know," she admitted.

Though she was unable to find the answer in any corridor of the mind, the memory, it lay somewhere within, she was sure of it.

"Tomorrow will be a better day. I'm sure of it now, and I hope you continue to believe that, too," she declared, with a smile.

Those last words lingered within him as the platform pulled away from the ground and her fingers slipped away. The young dreamer looked on as High Fantasy stole from him that cherished friend.

She drifted across the dark chasm toward the slumberous temple, within which a greater destiny had been prepared.

As Lyal watched in agonizing helplessness, his mind became overwhelmed with voices from the past, the ones that forged the foundations of their friendship.

"Is this a 'goodbye'?" he asked.

The tenacious oath keeper sprang forward in a twitch from his aching heart in hopes of reaching her, though it was far too late. She peered back at him from the edge of the shadow of oblivion with a faint glimmer of fear and hope, then turned her head to the place where fate had brought her. Lyal caught himself at the very edge and swung his arms to force his balance.

The otherworld's clock was brought to a crawl as he faced down the abyss.

A monotone sorcerer from around the ether's bend droned between the progressive intensity of those instant visions.

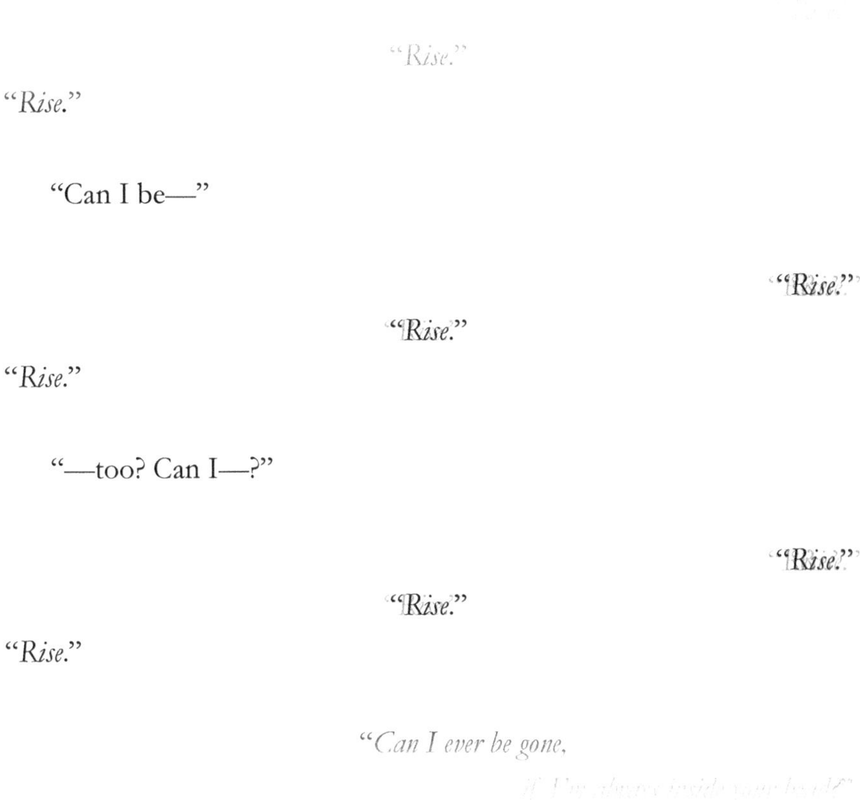

And each time the voice spoke, a luminescence grew into a shining blaze. A circle of empyrean orbs descended in a sleepy spiral there in the oblivion above Eternia's shrouded temple, the journey concluded to the otherworld's fanfare. The farplaner ascendent's sacred ritual began.

A lightning streak. A flash. Thunder!

The odd world was struck into a blur, and the darkness, and all that had lain in the unknown behind it, vanished by empyrean light.

Awakening

Lyal stirred from deep slumber but squeezed his eyes, lacking motivation to wake. Another wicked lash cracked the sky beyond the gymnasium's roof, then another in thrilling succession. In surrender to nature's strident prod, he rose to suffer the daze.

He searched the dark room in a lethargic sweep and detected nervousness teeming throughout the darkness. Others had risen to their feet and were oddly still, as if they were listening for something, and so he began to listen, too.

"What's going on?" asked Kaiser as he swiped his wrist across his sunken eyes.

A ferocious bolt split the air, causing the shadows to jump, and as the rumble of thunder settled, the sounds of a commotion became evident. Lyal leaned up straight, alert to the disturbance.

His heart jumped. Widespread terror erupted behind him, but before he could turn his head, the ceiling above the home bleachers burst into flames. At once, the imperiled survivors were lifted into a frantic tumult as burning ashes descended across the stormy court. As if targeted for annihilation, a second, then a third bolt struck from the angry heavens, unleashing havoc and burgeoning the fires of ruin.

Setz scrambled to his feet "We all here!? Hey—we gotta ditch this place," he urged.

Kaiser seized Mitz by the shirt and pulled him up from the ground. Miraculously still between dreams, he rubbed his eyes as he gradually came to.

But there was one missing. Lyal looked all over the ground upon which they had slept, but she was gone. He sprang up to his feet without a second thought, driven by hazy memories of calm acceptance in the realm of dreams but without a clue as to where that sleepless deep dreamer might have wandered.

"Lyal! What the hell is wrong with you, man?" Setz cried.

"You alright!?" asked Kaiser.

Lost in the grim vacancy of determination, he broke away into a desperate sprint through the chaos as loose clothes, blankets, and bags sprouted up fires. Against the wail of protest from his friends, he maneuvered to the overwhelmed gymnasium door and drove through the crowd.

A defender eternal, he flew through the halls and hit the bar of the door with all force. It resisted his brutish effort, however. Unwavering, he leaned back, then drove his shoulder against it until the darkened landscape beyond was revealed to him.

The sheer winds snatched the door away and slammed it wide open against the wall.

He stumbled out onto the sidewalk as a silver glow lit the area in its majesty. A blinding bolt snapped a lamppost a mere few yards up the path, and it exploded into a bloom of sparks, followed by a near-instantaneous crash from the warring heavens.

Lyal dove for the grass and buried his head, too startled to guard his ears from the heart-rattling wall of noise.

When it had settled, he lifted his ringing head from the marsh and looked upon the melted javelin. That sparking beacon proved to be unexpected guidance as it aligned his terrified eyes with the double doors of the middle school that swung free in the hellish winds of the lurking supercell.

Without another lead, he scrambled back to his feet and took off for the vague promise that the unguarded gateway extended.

A spark in the skies beyond the middle school revealed the nightmarish tower of clouds. From that churning colossus, a jagged bolt struck the roof and brought the dormant structure to life in a grand flicker, its circuitry possessed by the electric specter.

He cut through the grass for the roadside as the sky ignited in the spectacle of heaven's rage. Its scorching barrage lashed the shelters of the displaced as if to expel them and make witnesses to its wrath.

By the blessing of darkness, he wove through the chaos in the streets and reached the other side, the military in a frantic scramble to get their requisitioned APCs up and rolling.

As Lyal neared the double doors, an odd illumination in the skies above caught his eye. In the churning clouds was a bizarre breach in the dark heavens; a portal in the cell.

Imperiled by his distraction with that surreal majesty, Lyal's foot caught the edge of a protruding segment in the sidewalk. He was flung forward and found himself in a frantic stumble for the doors, bounding from foot to foot until his stride became too long and he tumbled across the cement.

Relentless yet, Lyal rose back on a limp, the doors just a few feet ahead of him. As he came just beyond the ruinous reach of swinging mayhem, he lunged and seized in the frame from its wild pass. Securing it from flight, he drove through and heaved it shut behind him.

In the darkened central hall, the unwitting trespasser stalled a moment in the ambience of relentless thunder. At the passage's end were three imposing white walls, over the tops of which the upper portion of a red, rippled stage curtain was visible. A short pass into the center of the triangular formation split both left and right before the central wall, and on either side, the ghostly dance of flames could be seen.

Lyal crept onward and raised his head as he approached the intersection. There were breaches in the ceiling, out from which endless ashes poured.

"Why the hell are you doing this?" a wrathful authoritarian berated. "Absolute insanity!"

Cautious now, the infiltrator crept forward, but as he neared the main hall's end, he froze at another discharge of virulent rage.

With care in every step, Lyal treaded out into the intersection that bonded the central hall to both wings of the building. He looked first to his left. It lay in complete darkness, and he could make out no signs of activity. He turned then to the right and saw a lambent walker turn the corner of the distant row of lockers, an apparition of unmistakable ragged-chic attire and ebon locks.

He nearly cried her name, but a gunshot stole his voice. Undeterred by death's rattle, he stepped forward into the hallway on a route to pass by an opening to the cafeteria that had been beset by the fires of judgment.

He had only taken a few steps when a startling blast ripped out from somewhere beyond the wall.

The cafeteria went up in a blare of gunfire and havoc that galvanized Lyal into a spirited blitz for the end. Between the discordant shouts and high-caliber gunfire was the ominous gleam of invader weaponry. He knew he had to find her fast lest he lose her to the grasp of the unknown forever.

At the hall's end, he cut the corner in hard pursuit. His shoe kicked out, and he slid down to his knee, recovered, then made a quick inspection of the area.

The still serenity in the halls was haunted by the frantic rattle of steel from somewhere within. Directly ahead was a central staircase that wrapped down to the lower floor while the halls on either side were closed doors and gray lockers.

Confident that he hadn't been compromised, Lyal took the left and continued his pursuit. He looked at each door as he traced the phantom's steps and, one after another, found them closed. The rattle escalated into an incessant slam. From there, he could identify where it was the raucous clash came from—somewhere around the corner of an opening ahead.

After an inspection through the window of the last closed door, he continued forward and came upon the top of a staircase to his right. The only means of continuing onward, those old steps dressed in worn brown casings fell to a midway landing that then connected to an adjacent flight to the very bottom.

Upon the midway was a steel-framed glass door that offered a view of the brewing chaos in the night. The panic bar rattled as the entire frame shook in the ferocious winds of the storm, a strident movement of discordance accompanied by the dramatic bustle of leaves that swarmed the barred doors like souls begging for sanctuary.

He descended with haste and felt an unusual coldness as he neared the portal to the twisting nether. From beyond, he stood face-to-face with six glimmers afloat in the void.

Spellbound by their sleepless gaze, he stumbled to a halt upon the landing and watched them. By strike of lightning, the titans in armor were revealed, but more terrifying than those sudden strikers was the whirling goliath of dust and debris that was cut out from the horizon.

Lyal stumbled back and struck the handrail that wrapped down to the bottom.

The facility's PA system came to life with a fragile pad that built its confidence in a crescendo, yet fell away, was reborn, and fought its way to strength again.

Like a lovely bud so desperately trying to bloom.

"...W-who are you talking t-to?"

"Never mind—I don't w-want to know."

That aural misfortune arrested Lyal as it spoke. The pad strained in an impassioned crescendo to crest but, at last, failed again. The tragic resolution served to quicken his heartbeat as its vague message spoke clear anguish to that seasoned apprentice of the keys.

He spun around and leapt the last short flight to the bottom as the struggle began again over the old wooden box speakers. He cut left as soon as his shoe touched the ground, and he came face-to-face once more with the gleam of eyes at the end of the hall.

The invader soldier barred the far exit with its sheer mass. The doors had been burst through, the steel frame left bent and mangled and its glass scattered all across the floor.

Conditions outside were fierce. Debris of the battered town swept across the ruined portal and left all that was beyond the short canopy gone by the dark gale's claim. The intrusive winds swept through and ripped the walls of miscellaneous school notices and laminated posters.

The invader took in a cosmic breath, that cavernous sound engulfing the hall, and stole the breath from Lyal's chest. Ahead, however, he caught sight of a passage blessed by light. Through deep, subconscious terror, he took flight toward the invader menace at the gates.

The ominous bending of steel echoed through the corridor. The building rattled under the force of the devil upon them. Tiles from the ceiling fell and struck Lyal over his shoulder and head as he neared the passage.

He cut into a short hallway and shot right for the end, passing by four booths that were each populated with two to three cheery, orange chairs aside from the last, which was entirely filled with music stands.

Out from the hall, he fell to stillness on the first step of a humble amphitheater, upon whose raggedy carpet was tolerable disorderliness, a few stands around the steps and forgotten sheets in the racks.

It was there that he found her.

She stood at the very bottom, faced toward the whiteboard with head bowed, her body bathed in the eerie glow of starlight goddesses.

With her hands planted upon a music stand, she stood in a stillness of purest tranquility, one only a mind bonded with higher conscious could achieve.

"Miyacre—what . . . Why!?"

His old friend turned her head, and between the strands of ebon hair, he saw that painfully undeniable glint of blue radiance in her eyes, too.

And it caused him to take a step back. It couldn't be true.

The glow faded to her lovely emerald, however, and as those eyes wearied, so, too, did her posture sink.

Her right hand slung off the stand and a pen fell across the floor. The other ripped a lone sheet as she turned around, a staggered movement that caused the stand to tip over and slam against the ground.

A lost spirit fighting for resolution, she lifted those scribbled verses in wordless bequeathal through a comatose step.

To him, it was but a nugatory sheet of paper, and he found himself unable to understand why she had bothered with it.

Incapable of letting her remain out of reach any longer, he shot forward with the only hope being that if he took hold of her, all other tribulations could be handled thereafter.

But fate wouldn't allow it. Though he had come so close.

The sky rippled with deafening ferocity as a grand bolt of divine concentration split the room and struck her through. All became a white glow. It was as if heaven itself had opened up and encapsulated them. Yet, somehow or another, even within that blinding white realm of divinity, he could see her with crystal clarity.

She was there, right in front of him.

Something of pure energy now; however, her eyes fell shut as she lifted her head to that obscure portal to ascendancy. Although it had struck before her last work was complete, she felt unable to hold on any longer. So, she lifted herself to the impatient overseer and surrendered herself to celestial grace.

To the embracing of her solemn oath, the pads from the speakers ripped from limping fragility up into the ether sphere of true life, a sound that sharpened to such acute frequency that it became inaudible in its transcendence.

As she rose, the light became truly blinding, and he lost sight of her in the empyrean screen, which left him in awestruck paralysis. Just as his courage returned, however, the light wall snapped away, and a sudden shockwave threw him off his feet. He tumbled across the floor as the speakers exploded across the school, the sound trapped within released to the world at last.

He soon struck his balance from his new destiny's decisive swat and rose back to find scarlet ashes fluttering where she had once stood, the only remnants of that finely tuned sheet of enlightenment. Lines of vague insecurities with perhaps one last strikeout and ruminated articulation, feathered by intimate reflections with a few vital words written twice over and ended with hopeful resolutions proclaimed with confident strokes, free of confusion or hesitancy. Her truth gone with the celestial snap.

His heart began to pound as a harsher reality set in. She was gone. Somehow or another, she was gone.

Stricken by disbelief, he rushed back to the steps and searched the enkindled strike zone only to confirm her vanishing in the lone discovery of the reddish embers in the ghostly pall.

Lightheadedness dizzied his buzzing consciousness as he struggled to cope in the face of that despicable tragedy. A failure to their friendship, he put a hand to his head as he suffered a senseless barrage of self-butchery—virulent inner loathing that echoed into the corridors of Eternia.

And he cursed the fruitless promises once so effortlessly cast to those disconsolate hearts as he deepened recklessly into sorrows. Evocative anguish that did not go unheeded, nor would it go unanswered.

There came an ominous rumble beneath his feet, and all mental vitriol went silent. The abyssal eavesdropper beat on the door to reality with a mission to deliver the odd world's therapy—Eternia's defiant blessing.

The ground erupted and raised a spew of shattered cement as a steel fin breached. In bone-chilling familiarity and with a sudden dread symphony, Lyal inched away from the expanding rupture until he had frozen over at the foot of the hall.

With the whine of hydraulics and the piercing screech of pressurized air, the armored tyrant unleashed mechanical mayhem as it drove up from the beneath. Through dirt and rubble came the turret-mounted observation deck and its moonlike eyes, which gazed upon his anguish and defeat and into those hopeless visions of the new world. Under the influence of its deep analysis, Lyal found himself unable to move, afflicted by a potent paralysis.

Nightmare's construct screeched onward in its hellish climb with one goal left to achieve before its reaping could commence. The fin punched through to the second floor, and the eyes of the netherworlder lifted beyond the crumbling breach as its shaft of mangled hoses, twisting circuitry, and smudged cylinders rose from below.

An alloy ring with four fixtures emerged beneath the gazing deck, each mechanism outfitted with a hulking gun. Between those twin-barreled repeaters were enormous plated arms locked in a lowered position, the tower equipped much differently than the first monstrosity he had encountered on the outskirts of Salamandra. A terror of dreamy uncanniness, lines of multicolored bulbs fell through the middles of each arm and flashed in the somnolent celebration of Eternia's triumph.

That herald of eternal rest drove forward.

Chunks of ceiling began to collapse all around as did the ground split beneath the boy's feet. Spurred by sudden peril, he snapped from the trance of the blinking bulbs and fled for safety as the rest of the amphitheater's floor gave away.

The tower unleashed its oppressive cry as it crashed its way upward. Lyal flew through the short corridor toward the hallway, where he overheard the blaring discord of a fierce firefight. In quick vigilance, he dropped fast to a crouching stalk, noticing only then the heated exchange in the hall ahead.

"Drive them out!" ordered a soldier from the right end. "Another one's coming from the door."

The building shook once more as the tower continued to breach the facility.

"Tower's going up fast, sir," called another voice just as the gunfire subsided.

"We need to bring it down right! Now!"

Lyal drew closer to the corner but dared not step out. "Hey—can you hear me!? I'm stuck over here," he called out, hoping to reach them before they departed.

"Who's there? A civilian?" asked one of the men.

"Yes—I'm from the caravan. I came here looking for somebody—but they aren't here anymore," he replied.

"What's your name? Are you armed?"

"My name is Lyal Abra. I got nothing, man. It's just me."

He leapt as a second exchange of gunfire erupted.

The wild rampage gradually decayed into solitary shots until the fragile hush had effectively returned. An enormous crash thundered in the halls to the muffled fanfare of extravagant cursing, followed by sharp orders from the relentless commander.

"Hey, kid!" the unvanquished soldier called. "I need you to do something to prove you're not one of them. Can you do that?"

Lyal's patience reached a breaking point. "I am not a fucking invader. I came here trying to be a hero for someone else, and now, I could really use some help here." The despondent lionheart sank down against the wall, having lost half the will to continue.

He perked up quickly, however, to the blazing cry of the charging wild man and turned to the doorway just as Jedd barreled his way through. With teeth gritted in a ferocious frenzy, he bore a half-body ballistic shield that he had lifted toward the opposite end of the hall.

Two other soldiers dashed into the hallway behind him, chased by gunfire from the invaders' advance.

As Lyal made way for their dramatic entry, he looked at one of the men and identified him immediately as the hero general, Rostal Schneider. The other soldier, a medic whose half-exhausted utilities were evident in emptied pouches, knelt down and checked Lyal over for injuries.

"Guess it's my lucky day, huh? A civi really did come poking around in here!" the madman cried.

"He seems fine. Just a little dirt," the medic assessed from his rapid examination.

"You had orders not to be here," Schneider scolded. "What the hell were you thinking?"

"I know! And if I were a different kind of person, I wouldn't be here," Lyal defended.

Jedd nodded in respect to his apparent bravery. "Never minded a man who wears his virtue in face of adversity, eh, boss? And this is the kind of stuff that *really* brings the cowards out," he swore.

Schneider struck his boisterous comrade on the shoulder and, with the point of his finger, refocused him on the hall, where the invaders surely drew nearer. "Hit them again," he ordered. "We can't allow ourselves to get boxed in."

With an affirmative grunt, Jedd readied his SMG, then crouched down before going shield first for a precarious peek into the hall. With half a target, he unleashed a suppressive barrage upon their foes.

Lyal drove his fingers into his ears as the gun ripped through the magazine.

By the click after the last shot, the madman's barrier suffered a strike of such vicious severity that it caused his legs to buckle. Eyes bulging in fury, he popped back out from behind the frame but was met by three more direct hits that drove him back behind cover for good.

Gasping for breath, Jedd put his back against the wall, then looked through the drooping holes put through his shield. "Shit, they're really not having any of it," the bested brute remarked as he tossed the blasted barrier aside.

"We need to get out of here before the tower peaks out and those weapon systems go live," Schneider warned.

"What are you talking about? You can attack it right now. It's exposed—there! See it?" Lyal pressed as he directed their attention with a finger to the rising shaft.

Jedd looked over at the wailing tyrant through the vista. "Think we could punch through that?" he mused.

The sworn medic looked to Schneider, who nodded. "Go, hit it with the charges," the resolute lieutenant ordered.

With a nod, Jedd scrambled up into a determined sprint and, in his flight, drew the compact, square package from his utility vest.

"Once the explosives are set, we'll drive them back—but just enough to make our escape," Schneider clarified.

"Hope we don't plan on running right out into that storm," Jedd replied.

"You got a better idea, Jedd?" he fired back.

Upon reaching the treacherous breach, the soldier pulled his arm back to deliver the decisive explosives, but just as he did, the tower let out a wicked cry of mechanical chaos. The bulbs on the dormant arms came to life at once with dazing brilliance. The hulking arms lunged outward with pneumatic fury, bursting free from the ground as if it was all the frail bark of a dying tree.

One of the whirling sweeps caught the ordnance-armed soldier in the waist with bone-breaking force, then pulverized the ceiling as it lifted upwards toward the sky. The murderous monstrosity let out a blaring wail as the four arms spiraled through the dark winds. The soldier, nowhere to be seen.

Schneider, ignited to righteous fury, struck the wall with his fist. "Damnit! Take the kid and relink with the others in the main hall, Jedd," he ordered.

"While you do what?" the madman replied, with a raised brow.

Schneider turned to the crawling mess of wire and hose. A weakness, now exposed. "Take down the tower. Give me your charges."

Jedd complied with due haste and rummaged through his coat until he had produced the desired device. Schneider seized it and turned to the hallway now littered with heavy debris.

"Alright, kid," said Jedd as he slid the next magazine into his gun. "We got at least one more to take out before we can make a break. Do not move from here until I give you the okay. We clear?"

Lyal nodded as Jedd eyed him for reassurance. "You got it," he promised.

At the edge of the hallway, Schneider had taken a knee to observe the movements of the tower arms above, which remained lifted in steady gyration.

Seeing no deviation in their movement, he took the risk, leapt up onto his feet, and threw the package right into the tangle.

His pitch was successful, and the device became nested in the wires. Even a fleeting moment of satisfaction was denied as the invader sentinel's blare caused the bold lieutenant to wince in place. His eyes shot up. The arms fell toward him in a heart-stopping descent. He retreated through the hall and dove onto sharp rock and glass as the arms of havoc reentered the room.

Schneider turned and watched as the last remnants of the music room were ripped to pieces. He suffered a second wince, however, as he was seized by the arm but raised only to find Lyal, who fought to pull him to his feet.

Humbled by that civilian boy's brotherly aid, he drove off the ground to assist in his effort. When the lieutenant had found his footing again, he nodded in thanks to Lyal, who thought nothing of it, and returned to him an easy thumbs up.

"Let's go," said Schneider, keen on a hasty regroup with the others. "Jedd, the detonator. Hand it over."

Jedd, who had stood guard at the doorway, threw his head with the roll of his eyes but produced the device from his jacket as ordered.

"You want all the fun for yourself, don't ya?" the denied demolitionist complained as he passed along the small cylindrical device to his uncompromising commander.

"Alright, let's clear the area. We link up in the main hall, but if worse comes to worst, an exit's an exit."

"Out from the inferno and into the deepest pits of hell. Just another day at the beach," Jedd mused.

The thud of footsteps stole their attention. The invader was near.

"Jedd, for fuck's sake, lay down some fire on those husks," Schneider ordered as he stormed to the wall and drew his pistol.

"It's not like it stops them from walking right down the center of the damn hallway," Jedd barked, then hit the corner once more, then put another full magazine into the advancing colossus.

The rabid defender snapped away from the doorway as four bolts of return fire ripped through the ground and kicked up a geyser of chipped granite and concrete.

"He's close. He's real close." Jedd lowered his weapon, then tore a grenade off his vest, his teeth gritted in manic excitement. "Alright! It's time we got a little crazy with these giant assholes." Ready for chaos, he pulled the pin and closed his eyes, abeam as if casting a solemn wish for carnage.

Lyal watched in humored nonchalance as the soldier, of whom he was quickly beginning to deduce by intuition the unspoken moniker of "madman," cooked the grenade in his hand.

"You gonna throw it?" Lyal prompted.

Schneider grabbed the smirking teen by the shoulder and dragged him further from Jedd as the fuse of his mania raced a fuse within the explosive.

"Stand back," Schneider ordered.

Lyal, motivated to staggering incredulity, stumbled to his forceful guidance just as Jedd's eyes reopened with kindled fury.

"Walk into this—bitch," Jedd rumbled.

He snapped his arm forward in a blind pitch for the encroached titan.

With imminent hellfire in flight, Jedd turned and leapt from the doorway. Lyal dropped and threw his arms over his head. Schneider sank to a knee.

The grenade flew over the shoulder of the beaming-eyed colossus, bounced off the wall, and exploded into a scorching ball of blazing vengeance. A potent shockwave swept through the hall and burst out of the shattered entryway with a draconic roar.

The heart-shaking eruption concluded with a decisive thud, a sound that evoked the wrath of the ravenous grenadier.

In a joyous sweat, he loaded a fresh magazine, pushed back onto his feet, and turned the corner without any semblance of caution or tact. With great luck, he found the invader trooper knocked to its knees, its rifle's barrel having struck the center of a webbed crater.

An eager opportunist, he lined the sights of his SMG right to its padded neckline and, with the purse of his lips, unleashed the entire magazine into that vulnerable segment.

By the strike of the last two shots, the cerulean glints went out. Severed from its bond, the dormant armor fell forward and struck the ground in quaking defeat.

Jedd released a sigh, his reckless gambit a satiating success. "Fuck you," he spat in piercing resolve of his fury.

Schneider and Lyal emerged from the side hall, and Jedd turned to greet them with the grinning charm of the guiltless champion. The lieutenant and specialist exchanged looks, one of pellucid solicitude and the other, striking indifference.

"Make sure you know what you're running out into next time before you end up full of holes, madman," warned the sober lieutenant.

Jedd snickered. "Don't you worry, sweetheart. I won't go dying on you. Not yet."

"Uh, hey—hey guys, there's another one," warned Lyal, his anxious eyes locked on something beyond Jedd's shoulder.

The soldiers fixed their attention on the shattered entryway where yet another armored trooper had emerged from windswept oblivion.

"We use the central stairs and regroup at the main hall. Move it," Schneider ordered as he broke first to lead them.

Focused on retreat, Schneider holstered the Beilkan cannon as he led both subordinate and the boy back through the blasted hallway and up the winding stairs, the detonator still clutched tightly in his hand.

Schneider turned his head for only a moment as he reached the top step with the intention of giving them further direction. A sharp blow to his stomach stole the wind from his lungs, however, and his weight was transferred to one foot just before he was lifted from the ground.

The sucker-punched soldier managed only a glimpse of the invader trooper as it retracted its goliath fist before the sound of breaking glass prompted his eyes to shut.

He burst into a classroom on the other side of the wall and struck the top of one of the scattered desks. The legs gave out under his weight, and the whopped lieutenant rolled out across the floor as it collapsed.

Through the clamor of the tower's gradual ascension, he overheard the hysterical shouts of Jedd out in the hall between piercing bouts of gunfire.

Dazed, but not undone, Schneider flopped his hand out on the ground. He could feel the broken shapes of the shattered pane against his palm but, in a daze, pushed himself up from the floor. It was only then that he came to the heart-jolting realization that the vital detonator had been lost.

The dizzied lieutenant sprang up and found himself in yet another harrowing predicament. At the treacherous outskirts of the bottomless chasm again, he had been struck back in range of the tower, which had driven right through two classrooms. Sensing its gaze, he raised his head and came face-to-face with the spellbinding eyes of the climbing tyrant. It had breached the roof, and all that was left above were the black winds of untamable chaos.

In resistance to its bewitchment, he broke fast and, by a stroke of luck, caught the subtle gleam of chrome trim. He froze over as he identified the device as the detonator, there across the room, stopped near the brink by a small pile of debris.

Then, there came a breach. The remnant floor gave way to the arms, which came parallel to the ground and laid a challenge against the lieutenant's bravery. The detonator rolled toward the infinite abyss as the machine's cosmic motor began to whine and shriek.

"Lieutenant! Come on, we have to get the hell out of here!" cried an officer from beyond the shattered window.

The shell-shocked lieutenant turned to find his loyalists and the flustered Jedd in wait of his return. Schneider knew the tower could not be left to reach its peak, however, for the fleeing civilian caravan and newly formed mechanized division would become the tragic victims of a ruthless free-fire zone.

Resolved in his course, the audacious commander faced down the risen arms and charged for the detonator.

"What the *hell* are you doing!?" shouted Jedd, with a furious lunge through the open frame, though he stopped short of going through.

The soldiers raised their guns to fire on the tower, but Jedd's forthwith arm brought the barrels back to the ground.

"Whoa! Don't even think about it," he protested.

The first arm came in low and slow. Schneider focused in, then leapt clear over it, his goal already close within reach. The second arm rose up to meet him. The unbreakable lieutenant dropped into a slide and felt the bottom plate brush across his hair.

Focused still, he picked back up into a spirited blitz around the pit's crumbling verge all while the treacherous rotation continued to gain momentum.

The gamble had nearly paid off, but the next arm approached, and at its speed, Schneider knew he would have to evade it. It came right at him, not high nor low. In a nimble maneuver, he leapt to one of the desks just beyond the arm's reach, and as it ripped past, he shot off toward the device, which rocked against the rubble at the brink of fate.

He swept up the detonator along with a handful of mystery debris without breaking his stride. With respite nowhere in reach, he leapt the incoming arm like a wildcat, fell into a roll, then sprang back into an invigorated sprint.

Just ahead, Jedd smashed through a window at the far side of the room with the butt of a newly acquired assault rifle.

"Come on and jump for it! You gotta jump before that thing takes you up to high heaven!" the beet-red soldier bleated.

Another armored sweep came around for Schneider, and at its speed, the next wouldn't be far behind. He dove for the window with all the strength he had to muster, but the arm caught him by the foot and stole his momentum just beyond the sill.

In the dire juncture of fates, Jedd reached out and managed to catch him by the jacket. The energized cohort then pivoted off his foot and, with the full strength of his back, pulled the airborne commander out of the room and threw him to the ground as if it were personal.

The breathtaking impact sent excruciating pain throughout his body, but he held tight to the prize of his drastic efforts, unwilling to let it escape him again.

Without time for a comfortable recovery, he sat up, keen to walk it off. Jedd caught his arm and assisted him to his feet.

"Couldn't have been a little more gentle, could you?" Schneider hassled.

"You're starting to talk like a gal I used to know, Lieutenant."

"Keep me out of your private life, Jedd."

"Sorry, the filter never quite grew in right . . . Your righteous men and ladies got the main hall secured, but the east wing got swarmed, and they're moving in."

Schneider straightened up.Let's move forward with the evacuation and put a hole in this tower," he rallied.

Anxious to fulfill that critical objective, he shook the debris from his hand to get a better grasp on the device but felt something else, a pain that had gone unnoticed. The lieutenant opened his hand and found an impressive shard of glass stuck in his palm.

"Damn . . . that's gonna need a looking at," Jedd grumbled.

Schneider took the detonator with his other hand and, with finger and thumb, pulled the glass from his flesh, then threw the bloodied edge to the floor.

"We'll worry about it later," the sworn lieutenant insisted with only a brief inspection of the gushing wound, unwilling to deal with it when his goals were unmet and his organization was in disarray. "Where's the civilian boy gone to?"

Jedd nodded toward the main hall. "Escorted up front . . ."

"Let's go."

The upstart dominus led the sworn band as they made their push back to the main hall. A stalwart congregation of soldiers had taken up a defensive position there as they fought to hold off the two-pronged invader assault; a steady trickle from the infested oblivion of the east wing and another from a fresh breach in the cafeteria.

Upon his arrival, the lieutenant let out a commanding shout, which brought his righteous to heed him. "Everyone out. There's a det charge on the tower," he ordered, with the directing sweep of his finger.

"Let's get gone, boys. Thunderin' Navies are pouring in. Tower's coming down," Jedd amplified.

"Mesh back with your units. If you get any trouble, you know who your contacts are," Schneider reminded in safeguard of his sworn.

Among the routing troops was the displaced Lyal Abra, who was rushed to the door by two stony-eyed soldiers. The lieutenant caught sight of him and stepped off quickly to intercept them.

"You! Abra!" he called out with compelling vigor.

The drooping interloper answered the call with a raise of his brow and faux wince of astonishment, bewildered by the sudden excitement.

"I'm going to be keeping a mental note of that name, and I want you to make it your top priority to make me forget it. Don't let me hear about you snooping around outside of designated civilian zones again."

"Yeah, don't even have to sweat that," the boy mumbled, certain he would have no further reason to do so.

The soldiers moved to carry on with their duties, but a sudden recollection spurred the lieutenant to stop them once more. "And what about the doctor? Where's he gone to?"

"Gone, sir. Took off alone when they breached the walls," one of the men informed.

"The coward . . ." Schneider mocked as his head fell in a pensive stew.

"He'll slither back eventually, sir," the soldier assured.

"Always does," the other added.

Resolving to set aside his wrath for a later time, Schneider waved them off. "Go, then. And Mr. Abra . . . Remember my patience."

The boy, divining no future in which he would need to do so, nodded away. "Will do," he replied.

One of the soldiers gave him a nudge, and together, they stepped off to face the storm.

Jedd watched on as the soldiers broke from their positions with understandable ardency in their flight for the door, and though far from some incriminating evidence of any wrongdoing, something about the sight of those fleeing comrades caused his mind to become beleaguered by prodding suspicions. "You know, I wouldn't be surprised if we're already compromised. Especially given the number of breakaways we incurred after Gruman and his boys got hacked and popped up. It ain't unlikely that at least one snitch scurried over to the main camp—twinklin' in every step."

"In my experience, the organization, in several facets of its existence, was never a well-kept secret. All that matters to me is what they'll choose to do with any new intel. As of right now, the mission, regardless of the oath, remains the same: ridding the world of this grotesque plague. I only hope Myres has truly come to his senses in regard to that lordless lunatic of an invader . . . lest he prove Gruman a man of exceptional foresight." Schneider, keen on a swift refocus on pressing matters, turned his attention to the cafeteria, where a fierce firefight raged on. "Jedd, go alert them to fall back. We're out of time."

"On it, boss," Jedd replied as he broke away with due haste.

The lieutenant ordered a resilient few in the main hall to abandon courage and flee as the last attacker from the carcass-congested east hall toppled to their focused assault. The stragglers could only enjoy fleeting respite from that neutralized threat of imminence, however, for the cerulean death glimmer pierced fast from the invisible contour of the distant corner.

The remaining troops from the cafeteria flooded out in full retreat to the chase of invader gunfire. Among them was a grim-faced young soldier who fled straight for Schneider upon reaching the safety of the hall.

"Sir! I'm sorry, I . . . let the doctor escape. He asked to get some air, but just took off on me—I wasn't sure if I should shoot him or—"

The unperturbed dominus raised his hand to silence his hysteric gush. "Enough. It's done now. Your service to us was much appreciated, but we can't hope to contain a devout coward for an entire trial, now can we?" He shrugged it off, much to the boy's relief. "That uniform suits you," Schneider complimented with faith even in wake of his failure.

The eager recruit straightened up with great pride in his fledgling membership. "Thank you for the opportunity to serve, sir."

Schneider nodded with profound reverence in his adamance to service, which painted for him the most vivid reflections of crucial valiance in those unforgettable struggles of yesteryear. "There will be a great future for you alongside us. Be safe, and we'll speak again about your place among us."

"For the glory of the Vesterbend," the boy professed.

And to that brotherly commitment to a common homeland, the general of heroes replied with bold transparency, "Sounds about righteous to me."

The sudden cry of the tower shook them from their moment of solidarity.

"Sir, we have to move. A tornado's on the approach, and the invaders are marching right through it!" stressed a passing soldier.

"Understood," the lieutenant replied. He struck the boy on the back to send him along. "Go. Follow the others. They'll get to you to where you need to be," he assured.

As the last of his sworn fled into wild havoc, the sinister cry of the tower returned him to urgency. There came the sudden blare of gunfire in the cafeteria and from the corner emerged Jedd, firing at some unseen enemy.

"Madman, it's time," Schneider yelled. "Drop it. Let's go."

Jedd, taking a final few shots, angrily turned from his sturdy opponents and picked up onto his toes in spirited retreat.

The screeching shriek of the tower dug into their eardrums as it neared its dreaded peak. Schneider took off for the door with Jedd right behind him. They flew through the open breach into the turbulence in the night and were assaulted fast by the vicious gale of the superstorm.

The whisper of lost spirits in the all-consuming maw chased them as the whirling devil crept through the shadows, revealed only by the teeming movement of debris and the snap of lightning in the clouds.

Nature's thrashing savage produced a treacherous downpour of all that had been swallowed from the hollow suburbia. A thick, framed picture slammed into the ground just beside Jedd followed by a handsome desk whose oaken body shattered like glass upon the brutal impact.

The madman let out a gruesome yell and leapt into a hopping stumble. "Damnit! Something got me in the leg," he cried as he began to trail Schneider on a limp. "We're clear. Knock out the damn tower!"

"We need cover—"

"Just light it up!" Jedd cried.

In swift surrender to his reckless will, Schneider hit the trigger. An enormous fireball ripped up through the school and sent a rising crown of smoke high into the air. The tower's screech spiraled into a dying whine, and with flickering eyes, it started to tip forward.

Against good judgement, Schneider slowed near the end of the lawn to allow his hobbling companion the time to catch up. An ominous din drew his eyes back to the severed monstrosity. Its descent had slowed to a crawl, but then, it began to rise. The howling vortex lifted it higher and higher, back into the shroud of obscurity where the sparking eyes illuminated pitch darkness until they died somewhere deep within.

"We've got to get to cover, Jedd. Hurry it up," Schneider yelled.

With a more formidable threat upon them, the lieutenant hunted the area for a suitable option. His desperate eyes found one of the armored personnel carriers, which had been abandoned just down the road.

Jedd arrived alongside him at last and appeared to have regained stable footing. Suddenly, the land was subjected to a fierce bombardment of disassembled metal panels and bars that impaled and pulverized the sidewalk, earth, and road with fatal ease.

"Head for the APC," Schneider cried, his only offer of guidance in the course of his frantic flight.

A promising shelter in sight, they fled raining destruction across the bombarded earth, each step a new miracle as death struck at random.

Though the lightning had ceased to strike upon the town, their ruinous marks were left in a widespread inferno whose initial embers had been engorged by the unrelenting winds of the rainless storm. Save for the smallest hall, every structure that composed the high school compound had been engulfed by that spectacular conflagration, and evident of a surgical judgement by lightning, numerous other shelters across had become subjected to the celestial designator's hellfire.

As the sworn stragglers arrived at the APC, Schneider noticed the frenzied wave of flashlights further down the road. He was quick to his confidence, however, that they would stand no chance of making it before the storm struck its luck.

Unsure of what fate they would suffer, he pulled open the door to the APC and let it slam to the ground.

From the tempest's ferocious swing came a heavy metal rebar that struck the sidewalk behind them at a forty-degree angle and snapped into a vicious whirl. The aero-javelin came right at them, but the first impact had given away the skulking hand of death.

Schneider and Jedd fled into the safe confines of the reinforced APC bay.

The rebar made contact with an earsplitting bang.

It struck the armored vehicle with such incredible force that it was displaced in a screeching three-wheel slide across the pavement before it dropped back down with a thunderous crash.

Schneider, dizzied by a pounding headache, stumbled forward from the back of the bay and took hold of the handle. He strained into a desperate heave, joined fast by Jedd, and together they brought up the armored door and sealed themselves off from the storm's wrath.

And they remained there as the storm bitterly struck the APC a final few times before it seemed to give up.

They wondered if the invader troopers would come to find them, but they never did.

In an hour's time, the drone of the tempest would dwindle into eerie silence, and when they emerged from their battered bunker, it would only be them.

A journey across town to regroup with the caravan and shattered divisions would prove to be a nauseating tour of extensive ruin. Throughout the streets, they would discover the charred remains of the luckless judged whose foul smell was as unmistakable as was it unforgettable.

And despair stalked them like a monster through the shadow of death while the element of fire crackled all around with laughter.

Eternal Saga

Motivated steps had taken Eddie and Mirika far from the eerie comforts of the vacant town, back through the tree line and into the depths. In their venture from the remnant hollows of civilization to High Fantasy's shrouded flier, a deepening shade had found them alone in a forest touched by dark magics.

The ground had grown tormented, the verdant splendor of the land browned by incurable decay. A progressive sickness of arresting pervasiveness, it left Little Eddie aptly stirred but seemed to go completely undetected by breezy Mirika, who carried on across the wastes with careless exuberance.

The roll of the land had long settled into a gentle earthen carpet, populated throughout by towering conifers whose mighty roots had earned them an ample cut of the terrain. A pathless network of mirrored confusion, the broad gaps allowed one to gaze deeply into the abyss that awaited the wishful wanderers everywhere at once.

To Eddie, it was a harrowing quality. One which stripped the woodland of the intimacy felt during their maiden passage just days before. Here, there was nowhere to hide.

"We'll find our way out. Promise," his buoyant guide vowed with resilient, whimsical delight. "You trust me, don't you, Eddie?" she asked in an effort to steer his attention from the swelling of shadows.

"Yeah! Of course," he said in a snap from his cautious survey. "But don't you notice everything's . . . changed?"

She stopped along the crusted heap of dead leaves, and the boy drew to a halt beside her.

Though yet bound in her whimsy, the intrepid trailblazer took a solemn moment to scan the decayed landscape as if she truly hadn't noticed at all.

"Hm . . . keep focused on the road ahead. A great light can cast a mighty shadow . . . It fears the new dawn we can bring, no doubt."

She moseyed forward with carelessness to the brush. Its leaves fell in a surreal succession of death as if the plant had succumbed in a mere instant. She swept the back of her fingers against a few which lingered, and they fluttered down onto the poisoned earth. "But we can't let fear stop us, can we?"

"No . . ." he acquiesced. "But—it's getting really dark. We won't be able to see a thing—"

Though stricken by trenchant hesitation, she drew her arms back, then clapped in a sudden summoning whose energy whipped the decayed foliage nearby.

Eddie winced as it struck him, too, then opened his mouth in gaping astonishment.

She remained still as the frantic rustle calmed.

"What? Are you sure?" he asked, worried for the fairy's safety.

Without acknowledging his doubt, her hands parted, and the fairy's light was unleashed upon the dark disease. That energetic luminance hovered in a playful bounce between her palms, a joy that she opened to with a vivacious grin.

"Awaken to me, Sh'shami."

The ball zapped back and forth, ready to be put to the task.

"Go! Light the way!"

Her faithful spark bounced twice in affirmation of her command, then went streaking through the shadows.

Eddie looked on with unease in his gut as she wove the titanic trees, her heartening gleam a gradual victim of caliginous envelopment.

"Will she be okay?"

Mirika's arm struck out in front of the jittering boy and put him quickly to silence. With all distraction laid to rest, her eyes narrowed as a distant anomaly transpired.

Eddie, startled by her sudden departure from whimsy, looked to the forest where she did, to where their light of guidance suddenly flickered from existence.

Electrified by that portentous occurrence, he snapped to her in pale-faced panic. "Mirika!? What's going on?" he pled.

She turned to him with a countenance recast in delicately maintained serenity. How greatly did it burden his anxious mind with further frustration, now, when trouble had surely found them.

"I need you to follow me on a different route. We mustn't cross here—and need to make time."

Eddie stepped to her and engaged those eyes of enchantment to level a protest. "Mirika, please tell me what's going on—"

In a swift denial of that solemnest reaching, she turned over shoulder and stole his hand. Latched firm to her sacred prize, she steered the boy through the plagued forest on some alternate route, though all that lay around them was oppressive gloom.

"Miri!?" he cried as she dragged him across curling death and decay.

"Run for me, and I promise I will make things clearer when we're through."

So, the boy laid his trust in her once more. She released his hand, and they picked up into full sprints through the storm of embrittled pedals and leaves.

The lambent aura of the cursed night's odd eye settled through the forest's bone-clawed silhouettes and offered silvery guidance through open terrain as they flew in pursuit of a luminescent breach.

They broke away in frantic vigor through the rotted foliage and slipped out into a sleepy glade. On their way, Eddie detected movement on the outskirts from his peripherals. Two nebulous jets billowed around in a race against them to the far side.

The hunted wanderers penetrated a deep haze as they reentered the gloom with a leap across leafless shrubbery and found the afflicted lands doused in an ominous veil of gray. Stygian silhouettes of the colossal tree husks loomed throughout the menacing dark shroud. Still, they ran, unhindered by the bone-chilling presence that pursued, and soon, the mists fell away and became a mere shifting, thin sheet upon the tormented earth.

"My, my, what two lost souls wander the night alone?"

Eddie's trot slowed as his eyes zipped in search of the mellifluously voiced stranger who had spoken out to them.

Suddenly, his arms were flung forward as he was yanked by the back of his collar.

Mirika stepped out in front of the boy as he recovered from the fling, her eyes sharpened on a phantom in cloak who blocked their way. Gone was the whimsical glimmer in her eyes. Here, they were serious, stern; dangerous.

"M'lady? Is that you here? Why have you ventured so far, alone? Surely, the mission hasn't lost meaning to your *troubled* soul." The servant from the accursed shadows grew still to relish in the aura of their grave encounter with a malicious grin to prove his ill intent.

"Yet, here you are with this trinket of yours . . . Boy—can't you feel the cold wind? It's best to go and seek shelter . . . so very far from here," he said with a menacing tremble.

And no sooner did Eddie feel an eerie chill creep up his back. "Who are you!?" he asked.

There came a piercing gleam that caused the boy to flinch, snapped from the shadow's grasp as his ever-mystic companion performed a final miracle of revelation. She drove her fist into her open palm as she fell into an intensive incantation. With desperate grasp so very deep within, she took hold of the mystic essence of herself.

Her eyes then reopened, ablaze with the white of the moon as she lifted an open hand in a plea for celestial strength. Eddie's eyes raised, too, and watched as its lunar beams intensified in heed of her worthy plea. Sacred moonlight swept through the darkness and turned the shadows long and thin as it laid grace upon the death-struck land.

The shining radiance of obscure evolution blossomed from the transcendental chamber of her hexed soul. It swept through and dissolved that deceptive civilian garb into a silky dream flush that sailed like effortless reverie in the winds of misfortune.

Then, from evoked ripples through time space came a rapid swarm that coursed up her legs and waist. Those ethereal wisps of diaphanous cyan blue assembled behind her, one thousand divine tails that opened wide to the half-moon sweep of her arm.

Adorned now in elegant imperial robes of damning indigo, they gleamed with faint glyph work, though the gossamer tails crawled with endlessly changing script of graceful curve and organic strikes, a spell chain of characters foreign even to invader designs.

The lively tails sparked to glorious fulguration and flickered to the most hopeless oblivion. One thousand false dreams tuning to vulnerable subconsciousness in her surroundings.

Her eyes sharpened like a wild cat's, her left hand encased in a blood-ready ancestral iron claw. She drew, too, from her jacket a wooden baton and held it parallel to the ground. With a ferocious grin, she snapped the baton, and out shot the pristine silver blade of her wrath.

She stood ready with feet dug into the drained soil, and her thousand tails honed in rage at her leering opponent, ready to strike at any opportune moment.

"Yes, come out, now. There's no need to hide any longer," the shadow stalker goaded.

"Mirika!" Eddie pled.

But in a sudden reversal, the tails flipped back and encased the boy within a hollow dream's sphere.

Inside, Eddie's eyes grew in disbelief at the sudden idyllic vision to which he had been confined. The gloomy forest had been swallowed, and he had been left abandoned in rolling fields of golden stalks, a land of endless falsities. A fabrication of peace, warmth, and sedative calls of birds out somewhere in a heaven for all and a heaven for none.

"Leave us, Erepethiel," she warned in a tone steadied for confrontation.

The golden-eyed haunt listed in the shroud of his nocuous plague, aloof to her rage with his gentle grin.

"I thought I sensed a special bond between you. Tell me, by what means did you lure the boy's naïve heart? With false worlds . . . empty promises? I'm sure it was just as entertaining as all the others . . ."

Within the prison of the thousand tail's dream, Eddie cut through the perpetual stalks in search of an escape, but no matter how far he went, the edges of the realm remained forever out of reach. "Mirika!? Mirika, let me out! You don't have to do this alone," he called out from that most pleasant nowhere.

Beyond the illusion, the dark messenger stepped forth, his immovable opponent prepared for fate to strike an absolute.

"Go on . . . *do it!* He's right there, in your grasp! You could have devoured the boy's will from the very first night, and you know it. At what point did he ever resist!?"

The manifested viper entertained none of his crude manipulations.

"Spend him now, Lady Seora . . . you know you can . . . look how much trust he's placed in you to go so endlessly into your lies!" he hissed with his fingers curled in his madness.

As the winds settled across the tortured lands, her defiance came in steadfast silence. Winning no ground, the umbral agent's arms fell away as bloodthirsty fervor faded to a solemn chill.

"But, then what husk would you have to make reality of your rogue ambitions? Bring a lost dreamer to make the fated cast with a mind warped *helplessly* in your twisted visions . . . Then, at last, you would be free. A dream eater, liberated from the same misery you gifted hapless, naïve others."

The servile shadow's smile widened as he revealed his cognizance of her intimate plans.

"Surely you must have known the truth would come out. Your actions speak so plainly that it's saddening, my lady. You have forsaken your duty in pursuit of a selfish endeavor . . . and no traitor may go unpunished."

She held firm even under threat of the reaper's judgement, and all that made a sound was the unintelligible whisper of the wind.

"You have made your choice . . . and we will discover the consequences together."

Erepethiel threw out his arm, and three spiraling portals into the accursed void rippled open. From those darkest depths came cloaked huntsmen, born from the miasmic chaos of the unfathomable nether. They twisted, twitched, and distorted to the fluctuations of dark energies, their faces veiled by curtains of black fabric, armed with serpentine blades.

"He was just easy prey, that boy. It pains me. It truly does, but I must give to him the gift of liberation from this fate," the executioner vacuously lamented before he flipped his finger forward and put them to the attack.

They flew with terrifying speed, and the lone Mirika, in her awakened form, stood in wait of them.

Eddie stumbled to a halt in the ever fields as the heavenly vault parted all around him. Suddenly, the tails ripped away at once, and through enfeebled darkness ahead, he caught sight of the shadow assailants in full flight. The young soldier overcame hesitation and drew his rifle from his back, then took aim at those who threatened their dream.

"Get back—" Just as the words left his mouth, a shockwave struck him off his feet.

The viper had snapped forward with her ready fang at a speed to match the attackers. She drew that shining blade over her shoulder and slashed the foremost assailant; a precision cut that pierced with a dazzling moonlight flash.

The first victim of her lightning onslaught dropped in abrupt lifelessness and was left behind in a vicious spiral across the barren earth.

Undone, she faded to a ghostly illusion in a dart to the subsequent two and became true again only when her blade had been nestled into the neck of the first.

The second swung fiercely with his crooked blade. An able half dozen of the thousand tails swarmed his arm, however, and fixed him right in place. With an anchored yank and a weightless flip, she was right behind him, her blade in striking position above a helpless foe.

She cut, swung through into a midair roll, dropped her knee into the neck of the stricken assailant, and buried him in the poisoned dirt

The lethal defender's keen ears detected distinct disturbances through the chanting dark winds. There were two more. She was sure of it.

Eddie flinched from the paralysis induced by that deathly performance and promptly beheld the wicked daemons in flight to lay an impermissible claim to his companion's life. Though chilled to the marrow by the sight of those soulless wraiths, he somehow struck courage deep within, and with the flip of the safety, he raised his rifle with trembling hands and took aim down the sights.

For now was the time to fight for the visions they had sworn to lift to the stars.

The rogues were nearly upon their patient prey. She cut around to greet them with a low sweep; one leg cut out wide to her side. Her arm ripped forward as she stepped into a thunderous pitch, then struck once more in a mere flash.

The deadeye assassin reappeared with her blade-clenched fist dug into the dirt, abeam with bloodthirsty radiance as she awaited the outcome of her strike. A silvery shard struck the first of the attackers with such force that he stopped dead in midair; the hellish umbral crawl of his corrupted form electrified by a lively cerulean current.

The second was struck into a wild flail as the pinpoint razor shard snapped him from flight and put him through the air in an erratic tumble. Together, the assailants struck and fumbled across the decayed earth, nearly defeated at once.

Then came a sole disturbance through the mournful whispers of the tormented forest as a lone stealth slayer sought to flank her. The awakened elite reached for a charged knife with her nimble fingers as she tracked the wicked flier with a steadied mind.

Just as the chilling aura of death touched upon her lustrous skin, she turned to face the putrid entity. The thousand tails whipped forth and stole the reaper from his flight. A decisive snatch, which offered doubtless impunity, as she cocked her arm and laid the electro shard right between the squeezed daemon's veiled eyes.

With her electrified attacker still in restraint, she cocked back again and swung into its face with the ancestral claw. The tails released as her fatal strike landed true, and the assailant was flung through the air before punching cold into the ground before its insouciant master, executed with graceful brutality.

There was no time to rest, however. Two more assailants rushed her with swords raised to cleave away at flesh or formidable spirit.

A warrior of inexhaustible vigor, however, she engaged them in a fearsome flurry, meeting them blade to blade without a clip, slip, or fumble.

Eddie, meanwhile, scoped down two others that moved in to join the fray. He closed his eyes tight to gather confidence, then reopened to the choke of the trigger. The resultant bullet storm shredded their ebon cloaks and brought them down to the young soldier's fiery amazement.

That small achievement delivered a potent rush to his morale.

He could do it, at long last: protect that which was cherished from the miserable clutches of tragedy.

Emboldened, Eddie refocused and turned his sights on the fierce battle between Mirika and the twin grim servants. He found her fixed in the lock of blades with one of the cloaked assailants. A masterful foe, she drove back the hissing hunter from hell, then laid her armored fist into the chest of the striking second, which unleashed a web of paralyzing electric arcs.

Unrelenting, she slashed off its impaired hand and left one of her opponents disarmed of its crooked blade. A cloud of dark smog burst forth from the remnant stub. The assailant stumbled in excruciating pain inflicted by her divine silver, yet produced no shriek to certify its suffering.

A sudden burst of fire struck the soundless wailer through the head and put him fast to the ground. Mirika turned to her activated companion as the shoved assailant found its footing and moved back in.

The inexperienced marksman saw the danger and pulled the trigger without looking down his sights. The shifting barrel erupted, and an unfocused bullet storm was set upon the messenger's ghoul. Mirika turned back and drew up her blade as the bullets whipped past her. That fatal spray ripped through the assailant's face, chest, and shoulder and felled it before she could strike.

The abyssal hunter toppled over. Just as Mirika seemed to turn to her comrade in surprise, she snapped suddenly to a gruesome strain, her back stretched to full extension and her eyes pressed shut in a piercing anguish that left her vulnerable there in the golden-eyed gaze of death.

Eddie's jaw fell as he realized the horror he had inflicted upon his dear friend. Down her exposed leg fell a vibrant cascade of tragic crimson, an ample flow that was unmistakably dire. She grabbed her thigh and dug her nails in deep to curb the pain from those stinging wounds all while her thousand tails twitched at the agonizing needle.

The boy sprang up in desperation, but she fired her hand toward him, and a ferocious shockwave took him off his feet. Eddie tumbled through the depleted soil, the rifle broken from his grasp and left behind in the oppressive shadows.

The dark messenger held in gracious patience as his enduring opponent battled her crippling affliction.

"Don't worry," Mirika consoled through sharp breaths as her guilt-stricken ally limped up from the ground, distraught by the sudden reality he had inflicted upon them.

She inspected the wound, then turned to her adversary, who calmly awaited her next move all while a vigorous new legion of cloaked fiends stepped from dark portals all around him. "And so the boy has done what the servants of the abyss could not. Wouldn't you rather put to rest this suffering?"

She lifted the blade once more to the ready parallel and sank into striking stance. A defiant force to the death, whether in eternal service or solemn treachery.

"Come, now. Let revelation be the essence of our grave convergence . . . This! Judicious sacrament! It was evident in his eyes alone that you hid your accursed actuality from him. The least you could offer from the alter of End is the inherence of truth to this misguided pawn of ours . . . before the time for such grace is gone," the leering executioner taunted.

Mirika's eye twitched, but her wild grin only grew. She wouldn't be manipulated by his hollow consolation, for she enjoyed absolute confidence that any reconciliation between herself and the boy was of no genuine interest to the pitiless persecutor.

"Lady Seora . . . eons before our paths crossed beneath our dread sovereign's crest, I lent unequivocal trust to those who were keen on tactful misinterpretations . . . and for reasons lost and better left . . . forgotten . . . they would each find themselves loosened of their will with a ravenous hungering that could only be satiated by absolute servitude to the void. So, tell us, me and the boy . . . whose dream did you intend to serve?"

The steadying dissident yet again refused to humor his provocations, however. As no words could ever change their fate, only by the blade could they negotiate.

"You could have had armies of mindless puppets by now with the world so ripe with despair! But you chose only one." The inclement menace cocked his head as if some elusive catharsis had struck him. "Ah . . . I feel I know this story all too well. What a shame," he said with such a genuine tone of sorrow that it almost seemed real.

Without order, the tenebrous force snapped into a renewed assault. Mirika's celestial form ignited to grand illumination. In defiance of her grievous wound, she sprang to the sky and became a ball of purest lightning, a storming beacon that bathed the cascading canopies in its banishing glow.

The devout aggressors stormed after her and so, too, chased Eddie's wonderstruck eyes as that dazzling spark raced across the view of the ever-haunting full moon.

The sentient bolt dashed from branch to branch as bodies of the outmatched hunters rained down from above. A slain slump slammed into the dirt beside the gazing soldier and snapped him from his acute transfixion.

Eddie remembered first his weapon as he came to there at the center of the fierce engagement. Determined to rectify his grave mistake, he scoured the shadows until he found it, then took off through the oppressive shade to make a swift retrieval.

Before he could reach the fallen weapon, he sharpened to the crunch of earth just over his shoulder, a sound that caused him to seize up in fear. With the vital rifle just ahead of him, Eddie hurried forward and snatched it from off the ground.

Eddie the gripped the handguard tight and turned to face his bum-footed pursuer. In front of him was the expected lone assailant with its crooked blade down at its side. It came hunched over with a wicked hiss, though it threatened the boy with no sudden strike.

Eddie fumbled with his rifle and set his sights upon the imminent threat. With the pull of the trigger, there came nothing, however; the glorious fire burst of his salvation was replaced by an unnoticed click. Set fast into a frantic recollection of those days at the range, his addled mind raced to figure out what he had done wrong while his hand went right for the safety. Just as he had started into flipping it on and off without effect, a silver knife pierced the chest of the ebon-cloaked fiend.

With a lurch, the last of the attackers fell to its knees, and when the cerulean arc web had subsided, it struck the barren earth in resounding defeat.

Mirika leapt from tree to tree until she found the ground between the boy and dark messenger once again. She hit the land with a stumble but stabilized fast with anticipation to fend off an unprincipled strike, though found unexpected respite in a gifted lull in the executioner's murderous blitz.

Exhausted, she looked to her unscathed adversary, who loomed in the shadows with the same gaze of deathly serenity as when they had begun. He would never be done.

"Forgive me, my lady. I must end your selfishness here," the grim reaper lamented.

Peering into all the last possibilities tomorrow could spare, Mirika sighed, then looked back to her dear companion, who had fallen spellbound again by her staggering proclivity for breathtaking miracles and boundless majesty.

"How can you do that? Are you just like him—the swordsman?" the boy asked, marveling.

She forced out a grin and tried to nod with the same glee as she always had before, though the pain in her eyes made the old act impossible. "Uh-huh ! I'm part of him, too—the great master, and his power flows through me—alongside the power of my ancient gift."

She jolted at a shooting agony, then situated again on her uninjured leg.

"Hey—are you okay? I'm sorry—I—"

She shook her head to dispel his worry. "It's okay. Everything's! Going to be fine," she insisted with frail enthusiasm, her voice atremble from the coursing spurts of pain. "You know, before recently, I had forgotten myself," she continued. "But something about us made me remember, and I started to believe—in all the things I used to."

Eddie found himself paralyzed in dread, so achingly keen on the suggestive truth hidden in that sorrowful reflection.

He couldn't believe it. Here prevailed the nauseating aura of tragic capitulation, a sensation of gut-wrenching familiarity that whispered to his tormented subconscious, the words of cruel sobriety before they could be spoken.

"Eddie, you know, not all dreams come true—but it doesn't mean you should give up on yours. There is a city in the sky—a gift from the stars—waiting for dreams. It can take you to the highest summit, where you can cast your wish upon the Missing Star. All you'll need is—"

She suffered a cathartic jolt as a revelation befell her. Without the time to waste, she stumbled to him and forced something into his hand, then immediately retreated away before her heart could stick.

The boy opened his fingers and revealed, to crestfallen eyes, the unfinished charm she had carried with her throughout her journey.

He shook his head in defiance. It could never end like this ever again.

"Take it. It is all of me that is left. I'm sorry for the truths I kept from you. I thought I could take someone away with me. Away from wars. Away from this world . . . and make something more than practiced deceptions. To live for more than this curse I suffered and the oath I vengefully swore."

"Don't say that. I'm here for you—don't you know that!? We can still make this dream real, together."

Those words of naïve resilience caused her to smirk, though she felt something undeniably special when she heard them, and for only a moment, all the ancient torment in her soul was lifted in suspension .

And that unexpected alleviation alone was beyond the reality to her, and she hoped he would never take them back. "Your words are like knives to me, boy. And yet here, I stand . . . I'm glad—and I'm right here for you, too. But, no matter what happens, you must find your way. Nothing will come of darkness but sorrow! I turn my blade against the tyranny of Endsborough," she declared in a resolute turn to the reaper.

She doubled down in pain but rose back up, ready for resolve. "Tomorrow could have been ours!" she proclaimed with a bite of malice. ". . . But I really hope you fulfill your dream. I really do. Don't be afraid—don't be afraid of whatever comes after." She took a sharp breath as she readied to face her fate. "Eddie—are you ready!?" she cried to rally his spirit for tomorrow.

"Miri! Mirika! No! I won't let you do this! You're my friend, and your dream is mine, too!" he shouted to her with a fierce grip on the relinquished trinket of a stolen childhood, wishing that his words alone held some kind of power.

Wishing faith might bear the force to ward off the tragedy. Wishing the hand of fate might intervene to its heaven-piercing cry.

Her eyes fell shut as she took in those words with a single breath. Then, with a steadied spirit, she awoke with blazing willpower, her smirk replaced by a calm grimace as she achieved absolute inner unity.

Mind, body, and soul.

"And now your dream is mine, too," she whispered.

"Please, don't forget."

On the breath of the last word, she shot for her damned enemy, her eyes lost in a blinding glaze of desperation and fury. She banked around to come at him from the flank, leapt forward, and drew sacred silver over her shoulder.

Erepethiel reached out his hands as if to embrace her hopeless strike. The hellbent viper came in close, her divine edge just moments from a decisive bite. The dark messenger's arms went out, however, and the fabric of space itself ripped open into a purplish world of sheer nightmare. From within that twisted, warped world came a horrid abomination of rotten flesh and rampant disease.

A hodgepodge terror of gut-wrenching mutations, the excreted reject of creation appeared as a titanic humanoid head, conjoined by two undeveloped stillborn others.

The misfortunate duo's running red eyes rolled lifelessly in the monster's voracious movements, and to the irresistible scent of luscious flesh through snorting nostrils, the starving corpse of unholy genetic confusion focused with a murderous tremble.

Hunger's hysteric head burst open with an earsplitting shriek that revealed its ravenous maw of endless crude shredders, a dripping membrane of viscous toxin and struggling veins that spiraled into an abyss of ineffable misery.

The rampaging jaw's twitching eyes darted all around, rolled in and out, and spat up vile fluid as if its excoriated suffering had spared it no peace to master even the most rudimentary control.

As soon as that hellish monstrosity appeared, Mirika's energy began to fade to its indefensible aura of mind-melting disgust.

Young Eddie's heart skipped at the sight of that wailing, odd world horror. As his face fell pale, the rifle slipped fast from his limp fingers and to the gut punch of instant nausea; the sapped soldier dropped to his knees and lodged his fingers into the cursed earth.

From the heaving maw came four tumor-ridden tongues, fimbriated to the balled tips across the countless black and purple lumps of eternal sickness.

They darted out and swung in a frantic search until one found her in her weakened state. It struck the unconscious glider once and put her to the ground, then swiped through to yank her closer while the others beat her into a mangled mess.

Frenzied at the scent of death, the ravenous rampager tore through the bloodied earth and devoured whatever remained. Then, almost as soon as it had appeared was the insatiable man-eater forced back into the fissure to unfathomable madness, gone together with the valiant betrayer of Eternia.

And it was done.

Eddie trembled so fiercely beyond his control that the sensation in and of itself terrified him.

He keeled over and began to choke. The appalling stench of death had seeped into his lungs and forced him to gasp for a new breath. Thusly subjected to the putrid funk of a millennium's rot, he sucked in the rancid taste of a thousand atrophying bodies, festered into a gruesome mold from laying slain in a bloody stew and overgrown inside and out with fetid infestation and disease.

He exhaled to expel the toxic curse but couldn't take anything back in. Desperate hands took to his throat as his eyes bulged at the pungent taste of decay on this tongue.

The plague introduced a deathly dryness that engulfed his mouth and spread fast into his throat, all as he fought to drag himself away from the calm murderer, who yet lurked in the dark.

Eddie gagged helplessly on tainted air, strangled and unable to free himself of the miasmic clench.

"This is not the first time your heart as ached so deeply. And yet you continue to squirm. Do you cling merely out of instinct? Or has a greater prospect truly called . . . to your troubled young soul . . ."

Erepethiel sauntered closer, yet Eddie couldn't find him. His hostile presence lingered, however, like a predator, waiting for the blood to run dry. "Was it hope that guided your pitiful hearts, or was it hopelessness that bonded you?"

The boy collapsed, unable to go any further.

"The pain that you were feeling is gone now, isn't it? The sorrow of loss, stifled by each and every inch you take closer to death. Because survival is of capital importance for all that lives. Instinct, too, has you pulled by the strings, desperately fighting to preserve your life, but you must see . . . nothing thrives were I go. I find that truth rather unfortunate . . . my liege."

Eddie trembled as he began to slip from consciousness. In a vision of the realm between worlds, he encountered arcane flashes, odd phantasmic movements, and evolving silhouettes that took to shapes of faint familiarity yet remained too abstract to bring an absolute to memory.

"Remember this; in the beginning, there was only death," the reaper preached with a tremble, his gaze upon something in the heavens above, pondering the boy's true fate with two fingers pressed to his lip.

The agony Eddie felt became numbed, replaced by the feeling of floating . His ejected consciousness wandered through simple reveries of the starry-eyed wanderer, Mirika, of his grandfather, and of his childhood companion, Jamal, whose departure seemed like forever long ago. The boy who sought magics in the valley, the girl who saw a city in the sky, and old sage who cultivated a mind to believe in something more.

How dearly did he miss them.

An ineffable sadness passed through him in waves, but they calmed him and coaxed his weary spirit to fall deep into endless serenity.

Yet, something caused him to linger.

In a sudden release from the chokehold, the afterlife traveler snapped back to life with a spectacular tremor that heralded his miraculous restitution. He turned onto his back and laid his hand upon his chest as he gasped for breaths of fresh air.

Staring wide into the night sky beyond the bare clutches of the cursed forest, he watched as his vision of the glittering stars came in and out of focus.

There came a step in the dead foliage nearby, but the boy found himself in no condition to flee.

"But today you live, young Eddie Bowitz. I leave you with this warning to guide you on your way. The shadows of men and monsters are not so easily distinguished, but take faith in those who are earnestly twisted by the nether, for we have no truth to hide. This world engages in a fiasco of hopelessness, and you're between destinies. Trust in me, young well-wisher. Nature is eternal conquest while the dream is eternal peace. So dream for me a world in which your people survive! How many countless souls would be born into the shadows of apocalypse only to suffer a fate far more miserable than yours? Can you live with that truth? Can you stomach it? Once you have seen the horrid face of reality . . . I wonder which side you will stand on."

Eddie looked up into those sinister golden pupils that gazed so piercingly into him.

"There is still a way to fulfill your dream, my liege. Your true dream," he clarified. "And not one of any dream eater. You have lost your guide, yes, but master has seen something in you. He will surely lead you to fate." The dark messenger grew still as he came to a bewildering conclusion of his pondering. "Yes—I believe you will make it there, as well. All that remains is to see what you'll become."

Resolved in himself, Erepethiel turned from Eddie and threw out his hand. A frantic prismatic bolt drew out an obscure glyph, and once complete, it ripped open into the creeping nether.

The golden-eyed haunt turned from his petrified victim and vanished through the ripple into chaos. Left alone on the decimated earth, Eddie lay there with only his memories and one solemn conception to give him solace.

And he envisioned it again and again: a flying city to take him to the throne of High Fantasy where, before the great master, he could plead his wish for divine reversals and resurrections. He embraced its truth until it numbed him, until that horrific tragedy seemed like just another distant memory, until he was too tired to think at all, when all, at last, became nothing.

The Moon Doesn't Shine

It seems I've found you again, crying at the wayside

Let not sadness strain your every step

For all across the stars, I have been watching . . .

And I have seen strength in you yet.

The moment is nearly upon us.

The bonds that restrain you are bent to their limits,

And soon . . .

You shall be unleashed!

So, set aside your despair and seek the road again

For those who go missing are never truly gone

The Wanderer

A dense and foreboding fog had stalked the Union displaced in their march for the city of Eredes. It eventually caught them and swept throughout the flax-sprouted plains, laid its vast horizon to obscurity, and enveloped a distant deciduous copse.

The crispness of the night kept the watchmen's eyes sharp, and as they wandered the shroud of Eternia, they became privy to beady radiances that glared out at them from within that creeping oblivion. Those starlight twinklings would linger, even as wary soldiers put them in crosshairs, but then evanesce into naught without an eventful occurrence.

Though the odd encounters became unexceptional, there soon appeared a far more astounding anomaly, one that drew a gathering of outriders as they sought to collectively verify the remarkable sighting.

The soldiers looked on in amazement. They were all sure they saw it: a boy, adrift through the veil of unconscionable content. Bewildered, the sentries dispatched word immediately of their discovery, and in a short time, the Union high commanders had gathered to investigate.

"Sir, those are Union garments!" cried one of the soldiers, who had trained his rifle on the manifest wanderer.

Myres squinted hard at the approaching figure, but it was clear this was no invader. "Guns down, ladies and gentlemen," the resolved general ordered.

The AWOL adventurer continued forward, oblivious to the imminent danger that might have befallen his blind rove, and as he broke from the dense belly of the nebulous creeper, his identity became apparent to those who were privy.

Little Eddie Bowitz drove the unknown through as he searched the endless gray abyss for glimmers of hope. With rifle strapped to his back, he clutched in his hand what appeared to be salvaged notebooks.

"Isn't that just the damndest thing," Myres pondered aloud with the scratch of his chin.

Schneider's eyes sharpened to the sight of him, that boy of irrational ambitions, who in his mind had doubtlessly fled duty for self-preservation.

"Can't be you," he cursed as the seeds of a dark resentment took root.

Rhodes's eyes crept up to his. "You recognize him, too?" she asked.

Schneider remained perplexed and couldn't come up with a response to her muffled nudge.

"Never heard of anyone coming out alone. What do you make of that?" asked Myres.

"I would be gravely concerned. That rifle on his back has been a mere decoration. There's no reason why he should have survived out by himself," the upstart bitterly mocked.

Myres, with a pinch more faith than his lieutenant, shook his head. "I think that's a little too harsh . . . but now that you mention it, that *is* the kid that took a knock to the jaw in Salamandra. The swordsman's little gospeler. So, he's made up of the stuff that can get you to the other side, eh?"

Schneider scoffed. "Absolutely impossible."

"One thing's crystal clear, folks. We have some *very extensive* discussions to have with him. Because if we lost track of him in the capital, then he's made quite the trek on foot."

"And don't think for a moment he did that alone," Schneider assured.

They looked on as the distant figure stopped. He noticed them gathered there, at last, and seemed to ponder his next move.

"We need to apprehend him now, before he gets it in his head to escape—"

Myres waved off Schneider's concern. "*Escape?* There's no telling what he's been through. If he managed to survive out there and come back in one piece, then that's nothing less than a blessing to us, who've lost something over five-hundred in the last two days. And if you think this caravan is going to operate on paranoia rather than hope, then you're in need of an adjustment in mindset, Schneider."

With that, Myres took the first step to retrieve the wanderer. "Let's get to it," he rallied.

Rhodes looked to Schneider, who could only grimace.

"Very well, let's find out how he survived," Schneider acquiesced.

Rhodes nodded, then stepped off in pursuit behind the troops of the security detail. Those hurried soldiers arrived first to the anomalous stray, who had remained anchored in crestfallen petrification. They encountered an odd vacancy in those miserable eyes, a look so very pitiful that his emptiness seemed eerily radiant.

The sympathetic brigadier went right over without a ponderous step of caution and laid her hand upon his back.

"Hey, it's okay. You're back with us, soldier," she consoled, then bent forward to assess his affliction.

She took quick notice of a piercing gaze, which informed her of indefinite inner torment. Confident the boy's experiences were extraordinary, her eyes went next to the notebooks gripped tight in his hand. With a gentle pluck, she confiscated them from the listless wanderer's hand, which remained hauntingly still, even in wake of the precious paper's swift removal. "Here, let me take those for you."

Myres, realizing the severity of his condition, went up, took him by the shoulder, then gave him a rattle to stir his battered spirit. "Hey, son . . . how does help sound? We're going to get you help."

Without the words for his profound relief, Eddie laid his head against Myres's shoulder. Though at first discomfited by that sudden act of tenderness, the benevolent general set his hand atop the boy's helmet and, in that most solemn moment of humanity, felt as if he stood in a memory with his dearly missed granddaughter.

For the first time in two arduous weeks, Eddie was freed from the drive of survival and restless instinct, and in the moment that followed that emphatic release, he fell into a chasmic slumber.

The comatose revenant was promptly moved to an allocated personal tent at the field hospital and lain upon a dented and tattered foldable cot to recover for the night. In the meantime, the eager high command flipped the pages of his intimate notes in hopes of painting a picture of his journey, but the bizarre drawings and half-conscious scribbles only proved to further bewilder them. Though ripe with questions, they would let him rest, for the next day there would be a great deal to discuss.

To some, he was a miracle, one who had returned from the foreboding beyond, but to others, he was the subject of grave suspicion, and while the divide was unpronounced, whispers throughout the night proved that news of his return had spread like wildfire.

***

Late in the night, Eddie stirred to the grumbling of an incoherent argument outside his tent. He lifted in sluggish vigilance to investigate the disturbance. Blessed by the lantern light from beyond, he was able to distinguish two shadows in the cloth veil: one who stood tall and broad shouldered while the other appeared a bit slender.

The boy inched up, and the cot let out a tiny squeak.

The midnight prowlers were quick to choke their negligent bickering and hunted the silence for a confirmatory second creak, all while Eddie held in perfect stillness. Without any knowledge of who they were or what their objective might be, he could only assume their ill intent and held fast to that instinctive intuition.

After lingering for only a moment more, they hurried away with sudden urgency.

Though perplexed by their brisk departure, Eddie relaxed in the cot, waited until his fatigue returned to him, then closed his eyes once more. Not long after, however, did the sound of footsteps stir him again.

He peered up and encountered the peculiar silhouette of a familiar cloak and hood and knew immediately who the caliginous visitor was. The polyester flap was pulled, and the fugitive swordsman stepped in, though he kept his eyes keen on the direction the men had fled.

"Who were they?" Eddie asked.

"Don't worry. You shouldn't have any trouble from them for the rest of the night," the swordsman assured.

Eddie nodded, though he couldn't help but feel anxious not having the answer.

"You should have been wary of who you threw your trust away to. You're lucky to have survived."

Sparked to impassioned fury by that presumptuous advice, a scarred Eddie lashed out against that preacher of heartless reason, no longer willing to let it go unchecked. "How would you know anything about her!? You weren't even there with us. How could you possibly understand the person *I met*?"

"I know that regret in your eyes. You put her foot in the grave, didn't you? And, I wonder . . . if the fates had been reversed, would I have seen the same in hers?"

"She was my *friend*!"

"You know what she was. Don't try to fight it . . . And regardless, what you saw in her, it doesn't change the reality—"

"But I know something that will!" Eddie shouted, lifting himself up from the cot. "It didn't have to be this way. The wonderful things I let slip through my fingers because I was"—the boy lowered his head—"I was afraid. I'm going to change. I'm going to find a way to bring them back. Then, it won't be in the past. It'll be right now."

The swordsman looked down on the innocent dreamer with an empty gaze. "And so, who is this effort for? For them, or for you?"

"It's for *us*," Eddie pressed. "Why don't you understand? You're not supposed to be like the others."

Ultra drew his blade and flipped the hilt to his fervent critic. "Then, what would you be willing to do, Eddie Bowitz? Would you take time by the neck and rip open the beyond to bring her back? Only action can shift the universe."

Eddie looked upon the blade of innumerable executions and experienced an icy shiver as the damned whispered dread sorrows to naïve ears. The invader's words were potent, however, and if it only meant seizing the handle of the blade to fulfill his dreams, he would do it.

"Take it," the swordsman ordered.

Daring, Eddie reached out to the withered hilt and took hold of it. Staggered at once by the weapon's weight, he pulled it to his stomach, then became overwhelmed by a sudden tremble in his head.

An anomalous alternate world had been born in the depths of his subconscious, a void that opened up into a dominant vision, a teleportation of whimsical sorts.

The boy froze over as an image of nightmares began to take shape. From the deep shroud appeared two distant figures beneath the hood, one with eyes of indigo gleam and another of furious crimson.

Who were they, and what did they want with him?

The otherworld blade wielder looked down to the shining edge and noticed his feet trapped in heavy boots. A warrior reborn, he stood upon a barren flat of dust and rock, which overlooked a war zone shrouded by the impenetrable ashes of complete annihilation.

Beyond the watchers were two grand silhouettes in the calamitous panorama: an ignited city and starless starship.

The boy's heart froze to a muffled explosion that rippled long throughout the cursed land as if the detonation had occurred deep beneath the waves.

He gasped just as the shockwave struck and broke him into a stumble. A bubble rose up in the distant metropolis, and the blazing structures tumbled to dust.

Violent flashes of light dazed his eyes. Between the fingers of his unexpected gauntlet, he peeked, but another explosion ripped out and left him blinded him once more.

Again, the skyline of the city was consumed by a rising sun. A second shockwave slammed into his chest, lifted him from the ground, and flung him across the wastes, like a fragile toy.

But the sword did not leave his hand, and as he fought his way back to his feet, he realized he couldn't drop it.

In a panic, he intensified his grip in hopes that perhaps it could somehow deliver him from the hellish dimension.

He looked at the half-leveled city with reddened eyes and a heart pumped hard by the primal drive of survival. The warrior's furious spirit terrified him and had nearly overwhelmed him when a white garb whipped the air and stole those burdened eyes. His mad gaze fell upon a woman who stood suddenly before him, her hands clasped and eyes closed in perfect calm at the brink of the chaos.

Another explosion ripped out through the air, and the piercing light lashed his eye once more. Eddie knew the shockwave would follow, and so he dashed toward her in a hopeless effort to lend some kind of aid.

He seemed to move at an incredible speed, but it was still wasn't enough. The shockwave tore over the side of the cliff, ripped through the immaculate robes, and abandoned them to whip in the tempest left in its wake.

Eddie didn't stop and struck the shockwave head on. His leg lifted to take another step, but his body went backward and caused him to land on awkward footing and tumble across the ground.

He raised his head and found that the woman remained, unmoved and unfazed by catastrophe.

There were no answers to be had here, he surmised, only perpetual torment, and as he looked down upon his shaking hands, he found himself without the faith for triumph.

"What do I do?" Eddie asked, trembling, unable to command his way in the nightmare.

The wishing maiden did not respond to that vulnerable plea, however. She remained gone in her prayer, even as a ferocious rumble shook the ground beneath their feet.

Eddie watched from his knees, defeated and without direction, but the longer he looked upon the windswept goddess of the grace, the privier he became to an obscure serenity that came to wash completely over him.

The way her diaphanous sheets rolled in the heated breath of war sedated his troubled mind. The ruffle from the fabric stole his ear from the ruin's heart-rattling tumult, and somehow, he found peace there in the midst of total chaos.

No smile, no frown, no hatred, no pain. She was there, and yet absent; gone but undoubtedly there.

And I am not alone.

The boy's eyes began to close. His grip on the blade loosened as the mayhem of warfare became ever distant until at some point, there was only tranquility and white.

The swordsman saw Eddie settle, then put his hand against the wanderer's forehead. There came a lambent blossom as a glyph appeared beneath his palm. Bonded to the dimensional visitor's vulnerable subconscious, the invader defector closed his eyes and peered into sacrosanct memories in search of clarity.

He held in perfect stillness as he sifted through the weeks, both cherished and despised, then nodded to himself when he found the necessary answers. Ultra released Eddie from his arcane grasp, and the boy subsequently collapsed back onto the cot as the forbidden blade fell from his hands.

The true wielder of that haunting misery took the blade off the bed, closed his eyes, and sheathed it.

"This was an answer for me, just as much as it was for you." He paused, as the truth left him momentarily perplexed. "So, rampant Seora wouldn't go on without you. Even one of The Dream's most effective elite, who seemed forever spellbound in such hopeless intoxication with her own malice, seemed to have changed. And perhaps what she saw in you was remarkable. A diamond among the stars. One who shared in her fascinations . . . and believed . . . and in the orphan's faith . . . empathized."

Ultra, resolved his search, went to the tent flap but, over his shoulder to the boy who had seen more than him, said, "Thank you, young soul seeker. Forgive us for this terrible loss." He knew the words would go unheard and, in the end, be utterly meaningless.

There was only one thing that mattered now, however. Time, as he knew, would not wait for sentiment.

The swordsman left the tent and departed Little Eddie Bowitz, who lay sound asleep again.

***

The dawn came fast for the graced sweet dreamer. From visionless oblivion, he woke to the frantic shuffling of a rosy, round-cheeked nurse who, after preparing some supplies on an unfolded chair, performed some checks to assess his vitals. Working with few supplies from a scraped-up canvas bag, she bobbed back and forth like a doting mother in a way that made him feel like he was but a child again.

"You'll be going to meet with General Myres and his commanders now, dear," she informed with chipper enthusiasm. "I've got you all checked out, and you're about as healthy as a young man should be."

Eddie thanked her, and she helped him out of the cot and onto his feet. As she returned to the chair to collect her things, the boy fixed on two dread silhouettes in the polyester veil.

The nurse, who had taken to the door with bag in hand, turned back to her unsettled patient. "Well—come on, now. Wouldn't want to keep them waiting now, would we?"

Though wary, he followed behind the tireless nurse as she led the way out. Two stern-faced soldiers awaited him outside. When the boy emerged, they stepped up to him with a grim iciness in their eyes that caused him to feel immediate discomfort with their presence.

Something was amiss.

"You're coming with us, Bowitz," directed a weather-beaten corporal.

Eddie inched closer, unsure whether it was too late to trust instinct and refuse outright. The soldier seized him by the arm and yanked him over. Just as Eddie realized his mistake, two other soldiers intervened.

"Whose order is that on?" shouted a snub-nosed soldier from the other group.

The rogue corporal refused him a reply. They made to pull Eddie away when the other soldiers engaged the assailants. A scuffle broke out between them. Eddie pulled his arm from his evident attacker and broke away.

The sworn scoundrel stole back Eddie's arm and pulled him to the ground, all while receiving a barrage of bundled fists to his head.

From afar, the scuffle caught the attention of Sergeant Sky and Jedd, who had been standing guard near at the central tents of the field hospital.

He motioned to Jedd, who lagged behind as his commanding officer rushed over to assess the situation.

"Cease and desist, soldiers," the good sergeant cried. "You're all in violation of the code of conduct."

The scuffle seemed to intensify until a strident burst of rifle fire put them all to the ground with their hands over their heads.

Sky turned back and grimaced at Jedd, whose gun smoked at the barrel.

He shrugged. "Worked all the time at the bar near granddad's farm."

"Safety on, Jedd."

Disgusted with the brazen display of humiliating disorder, Sky turned his attention to the pacified men on the ground. "What's going on here? Someone start talking," Sky ordered.

"We were sent to retrieve the boy and bring him to General Myres, but these unauthorized soldiers tried to cuff him," shouted the snub-nosed chaperon.

"Our sergeant can verify our orders, sir," verified the soldier's comrade in honest oath.

The other two remained eerily silent, each with smirks of treachery bold upon their faces. Behind Sky, a group of soldiers had gathered to assist in the correction of the situation.

"You two got something stuck in your throat?" Sky pressed without the patience.

They rose up without a word, however, in a daring test of the sergeant's willpower. "You can have him today, junior," the weather-beaten corporal defied.

Without care of consequence, they turned from Sky and made their way out as if nothing had happened.

The provoked sergeant stepped after them in a firm answer of strength to their test. "Hey—no. I don't know where you guys got it in your head that you can just leave this behind without answering for it," he warned.

The two men, however, did not stop. Sky turned to Jedd. "Hey, am I dreaming here, madman? I think these guys are in need of some old school persuasion."

Jedd shrugged. "I mean, he did desert," said Jedd. "And that *is* a crime some might share some . . . hard feelings about."

Sky was left baffled by his blatant reach for understanding, then turned back to the men in hopes to stop them himself. "Hold it! You guys aren't going anywhere!"

The rogues, however, had been greeted by a group of armed others who swallowed those devout brothers and sisters into their masses. They looked at Sky with a stern gaze to offer him a glimpse of the consequences of his further interference in their failure.

"Well, they oughta get the boy where he needs to go, huh?" asked Jedd.

Sky looked at Eddie, who had gotten to his feet and taken refuge alongside the risen soldiers of official responsibilities.

"This isn't the end of this. This is just the beginning," Sky warned his impassive compatriot.

With the incident resolved but a new divide exposed, the dutiful escort led the boy away. Sky remained focused on the rogue assembly, which promptly dispersed in all directions in rest of their shameless intimidations.

As one, those soldiers had fought alongside each other, lost so very much together, and had so very much to reclaim. Yet, there was something that had unified them against their brothers in arms. It was a truth that left the good sergeant deeply unsettled; a feeling that the greatest threat had yet to be revealed.

The feeling of being splintered in those hardest of times, to him, was to watch death creep up on the vulnerable. Though Jedd urged him that it was all but an unruly fit of emotion, Sky would report the incident as soon as a more direct line to trusted authority was feasible. With that dutiful promise sown in heart, the sergeant expelled his anger and, together with the vexed onlookers, returned to his post.

At the command tent, Myres and Rhodes sat at the rickety white top while a brooding Schneider had taken a place against the post near the door. A few other officers of high rank were gathered on foot around the table, upon which a salvaged transceiver chirped.

They looked on, stifled by a grim silence, which turned a static haunt as Myres's gentle turn of the tuner caused the speaker to stir with interference. He settled on a frequency, then leaned up to the silvery tabletop microphone.

"This is Doomsday, Union Shield. Does anyone copy, over."

Through the dense sea of noise came no response.

"This is Doomsday, Union Shield . . . Anyone copy?" he repeated to no greater avail.

The steady general looked at Rhodes, who gazed back without a word.

"Welp," Myres grumbled with a turn back to the chirping box. "Let's try another frequency. If a kid can survive that kind of journey, then there's gotta be others left out there."

He placed his fingertips on the tuner knob and gave it a calculated spin. The interference crackled back to consistency.

Myres sat back and pulled the microphone up. "This is Doomsday. Union Shield. Does anyone copy, over."

A sudden wave of harsh noise flooded the speakers. Myres lurched forward and spun down the RF gain until the blare was restrained to gentle burr.

Then, from the unfathomed terminus of the lost parallel, there came an utterance from the cryptic entity, hushed as if desperate to stay hidden from something that lurked just around the unseen bend.

"..."

"..."

"*. . . Is anyone out there?*"

"No.."

The hairs on the backs of their necks stood straight. The interference choked, then steadied back out, as if whatever had been there was forced to make a swift departure.

Myres crept forward to the microphone, his brow raised in bewilderment. "This is Doomsday, Union Shield. We copy you. What's your location? Over."

The sea of interference went undisturbed. Myres waited for a moment longer as discomfort set in throughout the potent gathering.

The general pushed the microphone away. "Better not burn out the battery browsing around," he said as he reached out to the box and flipped the power switch.

"What do you think's going on out there, General?" asked Rhodes.

Myres ran his hand across his forehead as his brow raised a plain confession of ignorance. "Our perception of the outside world is limited to what our eyes can see, I'm afraid . . . but, that boy—he might be able to give us insight. Especially now, when we can't count on conventional means to paint that . . . undoubtedly grave picture of the world."

With their effort to reach into the beyond a conclusive failure, the radio was removed from the tent in preparation for the boy's arrival. When it was done, Myres stood before his tireless navigators of the bravest tomorrow.

"Listen up, people. I'll be holding a follow-up briefing with all of you to fill you in on the relevant details. To keep the kid from being totally overwhelmed, I'll have Second Lieutenant Schneider and Brigadier General Rhodes alone with me for the debriefing. Be on standby to reconvene, because this information could alter the course of our journey, and we've no time to dally. In the meantime, let's get the ball rolling in preparation to march. Those are your orders. Step to it."

In heed of his command, the tent was promptly cleared of personnel until only the designated three remained. The escort arrived not long after and passed Eddie on to the officer of the guard, who delivered him through the entry flap then returned to be confronted with news of the incident of brazen obstruction.

Within, Eddie approached the table, where General Myres sat, his notebooks laid beside the poised Rhodes, whose effortless confiscation had slipped his mind.

The cadet offered up an obligatory salute, then took a seat in the lone chair across from them and bowed his head in silence. He didn't know what he was going to do or say and only hoped that answers deep-seated in fantastic truths would suffice.

"You've come a long way, son," said Myres. "A hell of a long way." The general put out his hands to his two counterparts to imply their solidarity. "We all are glad to see you're alright, but." He veered as he took on a look of bewilderment. "How the hell did you make it out of Salamandra City . . . and end up here?"

"More importantly, why did you find it an acceptable action to break away from a combat scenario?" Schneider chastised.

Eddie looked up at his acquisitive superiors with an anxious heart. He didn't know where or how to start. Fumbling with the fragments of memory, he found himself without the certitude to put them together. He wanted to lie, to make it all more believable, but he didn't know how.

"I—left with a girl," said Eddie, spitting out the simplest truth.

"A girl . . . ? I can't imagine what compelled you two to leave together," Rhodes said.

Eddie shook his head, feeling the answer too intimate to reveal to her.

"Is she the girl in these?" Rhodes continued as she lifted the revelatory notebooks and dropped them right in front of him.

And he looked upon those crumple-cornered keepers of odd visions with a great deal of sadness, a look that proved to certify the suspect truth without the need to tempt the tears. Eddie had wished to keep those scribbled chronicles from the eyes of others, keen that those extraordinary scenes of actualized surrealist grandeur would become defiled by innocent misinterpretations. The cherished journey was not one he had the heart to expound on in great detail, and so he wavered in reluctance.

"What happened to her?" Rhodes inquired with employed tenderness.

Eddie's incessant hesitancy broke the restless lieutenant, and he slammed his fist upon the tabletop, which caused both general and brigadier to flinch at the unleashed strident rattle. "You'd best get snappy with the answers to her questions, because she fought real hard to make sure I wasn't the one asking them," Schneider threatened.

"Second Lieutenant . . . why don't you take a step out?" Myres sighed in exasperation with his subordinate's needless hostility. "Call me crazy, but I've got a feeling he isn't the great enemy of the Union, so you don't need to brandish your malice. You take one look at this kid— he just isn't it. A little foolish, but no enemy. I'm sure of it."

The overheated upstart took a deep breath and vented his pent- up frustration in favor of prudence. "Any information on how he managed to survive is too precious to our objectives. So, go on," Schneider acquiesced.

Eddie stood up, pulled the top notebook over, and opened it. The first page was a pencil sketch of the star-bound enchantress, the scorched city, and the ominous cerulean beacon in ruinous shroud.

"It was the girl I met in the capital. When I got myself in trouble, she was there with me, and when I went back to the tent, she followed me and told me—there was a way for us to escape." He swallowed. "So—I went with her."

"Escape the city? How'd you manage that? From what we assessed, there were no safe avenues out until we blew one out ourselves, for heaven's sake," said Myres.

Eddie pondered hard but could produce no sound reasoning for their survival, or even recall the exact direction they had taken in their flight from the city. It had all become something of a blur; a breathless rush of excitement, passion, and terror.

But something, a name, returned to him: the abandoned suburb they had traversed just before taking the country road to the forest's obscure portal.

"Harbrooke," Eddie recalled. It was the only relevant fragment that seemed to return to clarity.

"Harbrooke? You went out east?" asked Rhodes.

"Yeah, at first . . . I guess. I wasn't even really paying attention," he stated with a pensive bow of his head, yet astounded by the spirit of bravery that had possessed him in that movement between fates.

"I would assume you kids weaseled your way out of the city, then took up a northbound route toward Eredes . . . something inconspicuous like the Harcur Rail's north line, or maybe something a little less so, like the I-9. Obviously you didn't follow either the whole way through, but perhaps got a little lost once you hit the mists," Myres offered in a desperate effort to lace together the fragments of the boy's journey with cogency.

"No, we didn't follow any train line or any road. We cut right through a forest just outside of Auspeux—stayed the night there, then ended up in a little town. It was just us, though . . . Everybody else was gone, but I don't know why," Eddie recalled to his keen audience.

"A little town, huh? Might've been ol' Yuvine that you ended up in. But that would still put you quite aways from here."

"We cut through downtown and entered the forest again at the northern outskirts," Eddie recounted with a hollow glaze in his eyes as he struggled to fend off vile visions of the brutal slaughtering thereafter.

"So, what transpired between Yuvine and here that caused you to separate?" asked Rhodes in hopes of training his focus on the critical juncture of his journey.

Eddie suffered the twisting nausea as he was put to the task of peering into those forbidden memories again. The mere thought of some grotesque dissection of the horrors they had suffered was nearly too much to bear, but he knew he had to do it lest the messenger's wickedness come as a deathly jolt to the hearts of the naïve.

"We were attacked by a man . . . in a black cloak . . . with golden eyes. She fought him, and just like the swordsman—she was incredible, but—"

Rhodes looked at Myres with worry in her eyes.

"Not incredible enough, it would seem," Schneider replied. "So, suffice to say, he survived merely due to another rogue agent of the invaders. I've heard enough, then—he should be stripped of all rank in this military. He is a deserter, and that's all there's left to see in him."

Unable to bear his disgust any longer, Schneider stood and stormed out of the tent. Myres looked up after him and grimaced in disappointment at his lieutenant's indecorous lack of restraint.

"Don't lend that a bit of worry, son. War's been eating him up, as it has with many of us, but any information you have on these uncanny individuals is vital to this liberation effort, so I want to hear everything you've got," Myres asserted.

"General, he said the girl was capable of similar feats as the swordsman. You think they could have been working together?" Rhodes suggested.

Myres's frown deepened as he mulled over the possibility. "Hard to say without putting the question straight to him. Granted, I'm not sure why some invader hellion would go out of her way to string along some kid only to put him on path right back home," Myres replied. "I'm assuming that's not the case, and he struck the stride of fortune."

"How did you come out of it alive? Was there any interaction between you and this man that might . . . inform you of his objectives?" Rhodes inquired.

"He came for her, alone," Eddie replied. "She said—she had wanted to change . . . to chase a different dream, and when she resisted, we were attacked by his agents—different than any invader. They came from the shadows . . . strange, twitching swordsmen in black cloaks, with crooked swords . . . but even ten of them couldn't beat her."

"So, what did?" Rhodes pressed in swift bypass of his eulogy.

Eddie's vacant eyes lifted to the focused brigadier, his torment too striking to be conscientiously overlooked. "A monster that I've tried to forget. It came from . . . nowhere. Out from a place that shouldn't exist—a dimension where all the misery of the universe coalesces. The last thing I remember was choking on the smell of it, then looking up into *his* eyes, but when I woke up, I was fine. I could stand, so I walked . . . through empty towns and quiet pastures, until I found you all here."

Myres and Rhodes nodded, each with a unique manifestation of that gruesome encounter in mind.

"Wonder how we're going to deal with that if it ever comes down to it," Myres mused with a flippant glance to Rhodes.

"I'm not sure, sir," the staid brigadier replied.

Alone in his drollery, the general sighed to the bleak imagery of absurdity that he had dreaded. "That about leaves us with one question, son. What was the end goal of your northbound quest? She was one of them, right? Bettin' she had more in mind than just grabbing an ice-cream cone together in Eredes."

Eddie's chest grew tight as he teetered between the bold truth and frantic lies. "A city, sir," he said, caving. "A city in the sky."

Myres fell still as he found himself outright unable to contest that spectacular revelation. He eyed the boy with steady patience, in perhaps a last-ditch hope that he might blurt out that it was only a dream, but the boy remained resolute in silence.

"A city in the sky, huh?" he echoed, unfit to believe the words from his own mouth. "Son, do you have any idea why an invader might to ask you to tag along to find some city in the sky?"

"No . . ." Eddie lied, with a shameful bow of his head.

"Alright . . . And how confident are you that this city actually exists?" Myres probed.

The boy lifted his head back up with starry-eyed faith. "Very much so, sir. She saw it herself—in visions. When she closed her eyes, she was able see things, no matter how far away they were," he said.

Myres tipped his head back and rubbed the back his neck as he worked to balance in the unrest that their new reality continued to afflict. With the exile of the renegade, he knew he would have no choice but to lay his absolute trust in the boy's word and the vision of his fallen comrade.

"She was an invader just like the swordsman . . . and became a friend. I believe what she saw was real," Eddie proclaimed.

Myres, though hindered by his keen disposition for pragmatic sensibilities, surrendered a nod in solidarity with the boy's brave sentiment. "I don't doubt it for a second, son," the general openly concurred, then leaned back in his chair as he rubbed his chin in a pensive stir.

"Sir, have a look at this," Rhodes prompted.

She had opened the first few pages of the other notebooks which revealed sketch after sketch of a city among the dense, nimbose scribble. Presented with an image of evident obsession, the sober officials grew certain that those manic expressions could be produced only by the heart of the faithful or the fevered mind of a lunatic.

"How bad could a flying city be?" Myres mused as he looked from drawing to eerie drawing of arcane interpretations. "Be damned if I didn't know just the person I would have liked to ask. . ."

Myres paused as a passing thought captivated him. ". . . Did this girl—did she ever mention to you where this city is?" he asked.

After a brief sift through the hazy spiral that was their journey, Eddie returned with a shake of his head. "No, sir. She said somewhere north. I just followed her, and when she was gone, I followed the stars until I ended up here."

"North, huh? I'm gonna assume that's no coincidence," the general said, beginning to believe.Confident that he would be unable to extract any further information of necessary clarity, and with much to accomplish before the march, Myres slammed his hand on the table. "Guess we'll just chalk it up to 'you got lucky,' " he concluded. "Son, that'll about do it. We're going to have somebody escort you to the civilian caravan. You're free to march with them, then rest at their camp for tonight—gives you a little time off duty while I get some things figure out. Tomorrow morning, when we continue north toward Eredes, you'll rejoin under my direct command."

Rhodes gathered the notebooks together, then slid them over to Eddie who thanked her with a sheepish nod.

The commanders rose from the table to see their fortune-favored informant out, no surer of the future than when he had stepped through.

"We still got a long march ahead of us yet. Try to stay put this time, understood?" said Myres.

"Yes, sir," the cadet replied.

He rose and saluted them, then gathered his belongings and departed the tent with detectable urgency in his steps.

"Shall we order the briefing to update the command of these conditions?" asked Rhodes.

Myres held in silence, and when he was sure the boy had achieved sufficient distance from the tent, he nodded. "But, first, I'm gonna need to see both you and Schneider for a quick huddle."

Within twenty minutes' time, the flustered lieutenant was reined back into the command tent, his patience still as thin as the ice he had left on. Myres stepped before those dual-oath associates and put them to attention. "Alright you two—" he began in a breathless huff.

Schneider's eyes crept over to Rhodes, who stood poised for whatever was to be discussed, a bulwark that offered no hint of weakness. Schneider's mind, however, delved into suspicion as he fought to hide his festered anxiety. He drew from her confidence, however. The aura of her mettle was like an impregnable barrier around the both of them against which any accusation was plainly extravagant.

"I'll make this quick. The Union leadership has been in shambles since the day Salamandra fell. With the loss of most of the high command, I've been long overdue to make some changes in our ragtag resistance. Sorry there won't be any fanfare or fireworks, but I've decided to promote you both to the rank of general. What that means is you'll be working close alongside me in a much more effective sense, which roughly translates to a lot more responsibility and virtually no sleep. Nothing you shouldn't already be used to."

Schneider and Rhodes became aglow in nonplussed astonishment. Never had they expected such radical empowerment from the man who had retained the backbone of Union military order and tradition, even in the face of supreme annihilation.

"Sir, this is . . . greatly unexpected," Rhodes stressed.

"But absolutely necessary. You've proven your capability over the years, so here's your chance to make a difference in a time when we need the most." The general's eyes narrowed. "Can I count on you?"

They nodded.

"Absolutely, sir," Schneider swore.

"We won't let you down, sir," Rhodes said.

The underworld successor grew reticent in his exuberance with the opportunities laid before him. Secured at the prestigious rank of general, Gruman's wicked gift had come to bear its fruit. With diligence and wit, he could utilize unprecedented power to surpass the organization's contemporary architect and perhaps even his revered network in the shadows.

Myres nodded in satisfaction with his course. "General Rhodes. General Schneider. Generals of the Resistance."

In a spurious concord, they saluted their seasoned superior who had bestowed upon them such great responsibility. Entangled between two irreconcilable institutions, effective execution of their roles could soon come at odds with the cravings of the obscure syndicate. Surely in time their loyalties and characters would be tested in the trials that lay ahead on the arduous roads of war.

"Let's get started, shall we? There's much to do, and little time to be had. You've got the world on your backs . . . Yeah, now it's time to get conditioned for the struggle," Myres stated.

***

Across the camp, a despondent Eddie ventured alone through the masses of the civilian caravan, his cherished notebooks held tight to his chest. It seemed like such a long time since the stars fell at Salamandra, where he had walked alongside so many others.

It was a scene of muted tension, but without a doubt more comforting than being a stray in the mists. Their sorrow was infectious, however, and couldn't be readily shaken from the depleted spirit. There was no magic here, no wonderful feeling of freedom or the excitement of possibility. This was the reality he had so selfishly left behind on his spontaneous adventure with the whimsical wanderer.

And how he missed her, that smile, her words, and those inimitable sensations he achieved when he merely stood in her presence. This was reality in all her mundane glory, where he needed to be to defend the innocent, but somewhere deep inside, he felt displaced from the road toward truest salvation.

He hated himself for feeling the way he did, but the truth was undeniable and all powerful.

The boy turned up to the horizon beyond the camp, hoping to see a girl with the spirit of adventure ablaze in her eyes, a wild horse ready to take on the prairie and charge forth into the unknown. But alas, there was nothing to behold in the hopeless obscurity of the night but a pitiful reflection of an insufferable tomorrow.

Never before had he felt so close to the child he had been. Their time had been something of a renaissance when compared to the days he had first trained at the Union Junior Academy, as stark a difference to those somber nights of an unsung city life, to the golden dawns upon the emerald hills.

But he felt that childhood's entity had vanished.

Then, beyond the reality had lain yet before his eyes, but now, in the absence of her, it almost seemed that going alone was too painful. He knew eventually he would see the front line again, and that perhaps the battlefield would stake a tragic claim. In the end, there might be nothing more to that advent of opportunity than the stars they had chased, and that perhaps the chance for something greater had slipped him by.

Anxiety put him in a spiral of regret, which made to drown his spirit in its unrelenting torment, and as the caravan stopped to make camp for the night, Eddie could no longer depend on his hurried pace to subdue the despair.

His mind slipped to the conclusion that his return was a mistake. He couldn't protect anyone if he couldn't even protect his dearest friend and should have avoided the camp, disappeared in the mist, and then perhaps he would have found her again, somewhere beyond the veil between life and death.

Routed by grief, Eddie collapsed to the dirt as tears swelled at the corners of his eyes. Ashamed of the outburst, he guarded the mess with a hand as his arm tightened around the notebooks. Profoundly breached, he sobbed there in an unrestrained release of all the pent-up emotions he had kept sealed within since the moment of her death. He remained there in the darkness behind his eyes, its solitude offering the sole comfort to ward off his anguish.

"Hey—" a cozy-voiced stranger called. "Hey, man. You alright?"

Coaxed by the empath's outreach, Eddie emerged from his vacuous respite to find a burly stranger stooping down by his side. With kind eyes and a benign smile, the bristle-bearded consoler laid a gentle hand upon the boy's shoulder in hopes to supplement strength to his spirit, which suffered clear deficiency.

"Hang in there, bud. Got a hell of a road still ahead of us, but none of us are on that road alone," he said, comforting him.

The boy, caught off guard by the stranger's compassion, nodded with the wipe of his eyes.

"Hey, babe—" the clement altruist called in a turn to his weary companion, a solemn-faced woman who sat cross-legged upon an unsightly wool blanket. "Can you throw me a water?"

Though strained to answer his request, she straightened up and reached for a stuffed navy backpack, which lay propped against a shadowy lump. With two snaps of twin buckles, she lifted the wrapped flap and produced the requested ration.

In maintained taciturnity, she made a languid toss. The man caught it, then handed it off to Eddie, who fought through his sobs to receive the favor with some dignity.

"We're all in this together. Stay strong, alright?"

"Thanks . . ." Eddie replied.

"No, thank you for your service, sir. Don't be afraid to reach out when you're stuck in the fields of hope."

Faith's good patron stood and gave Eddie a parting slap on the shoulder before returning to his dolorous missus, who stared off into the vast emptiness of a thousand forlorn tomorrows.

Eddie, with greater gratitude than thirst, twisted off the cap and drank until there was nothing left. Although thankful, he knew inside that he didn't deserve it. He hadn't fought alongside the others who had bravely risked their lives to deliver the people from the besieged capital. Ashamed of that unpublished truth, the castaway cadet lowered his head in an effort to veil his insecurities, though he surely felt their eyes on him, a soldier in their midst who clearly lacked poise to serve.

In a search for strength, he reached into his pocket and drew the postcard given to him for safekeeping. He held it by its preserved crisp corners, but hesitated to look down.

Was it the time?

At the brink of depressive relapse, he felt himself too weak to withstand another moment in absence of her whimsical intimacy. He broke, and crestfallen eyes fell upon the voiceless whisper, left stricken across the printed lines.

Let's Just Pretend.

He stared at those immortalized words for he couldn't say how long. Gobsmacked by her provident tease, he plummeted into a spiral of thought as his teary eye was strung along the carefree script, which left him adrift at the whooshed tail off the last letter.

In his pursuit of hidden meanings, his mind became a quick addict to the old chase. Her echo had resuscitated his curiosity and given life to the promise still somewhere within. So, he went to seek her out in memory, the girl who saw possibility through wild kaleidoscopes: a city in the sky and the most incredible tomorrow sadly beyond her reach. She would surely have never lied about such cherished possibilities, and if he could only put together the missing pieces, he was sure he would find nothing short of miracles.

"What's that?" asked a tender-voiced intruder.

Snapped from his delusion, Eddie lowered the postcard to find a younger boy standing before him, his eyes aglow with curiosity.

"Can I see it?" the boy asked with his head cocked to the side.

Eddie, taken aback by his interest, nodded and passed over the memento. The boy took it in his small hands and inspected the other side.

"What's this place?" he asked to Eddie's bewilderment.

The child turned the card around and presented his obscure findings.

And Eddie couldn't believe what he had found.

On the other side was the sought image that had evaded him for so long, the thing the clairvoyant had seen when she had closed her eyes, an enigmatic metropolis shrouded by clouds, situated in its entirety atop a conical platform, with searchlights that beamed true through an otherwise impenetrable gray abyss.

"It's like a city on a big top," the boy remarked as he passed the card back to Eddie. "What's that place called?"

Though at first unsure as to how he might answer to that curiosity, a whim compelled Eddie to search. From a spiritual rush of divined inner expression, he reemerged enlightened, and spat out, "Infinity Land."

"Infinity Land? Is it real?" the little boy said, goggling.

Eddie lifted his eyes to meet that wonderstruck reflection, and a smile swept across his face as he found himself able, at last, to answer that old question with wondrous certainty.

"Yes, I believe it is," he warmly confided.

Frantic footsteps of an agitated other approached. "Noa, don't you bother him. Come here. I told you to stay put on the blanket," called a hysteric mother in a mad rush to her wayward son.

The boy turned in blasé nonchalance to his flustered supervisor. "But mom, I'm bored," he protested. "I don't wanna be out here anymore!"

"Noa!" she snapped, though managed to arrest her ferocity before the worst of her fury went unleashed.

Courteously sedated, she directed forced placidity to the serviceman, whose fixation on the cardstock had proven resilient.

"I'm so sorry, sir," she apologized in deep release.

"No—it's alright. It's no trouble," Eddie assured, in a brain-skip break from his entrancement.

The woman grimaced, then took the boy's hand and led him away.

As the discordant duo was swallowed into the resting crowds, Eddie became fixed on the note once again. He examined the monolithic towers, whose lambent cerulean beacons dotted the gray realm of obscurity like an abstract constellation.

Though there wasn't much more he could derive from that odd image, it was there, a testament to extraordinary truth. Somewhere out there was a soaring starlight metropolis that could lift one to the stars: the great master upon the throne of dreams with the power to bend reality at his whim.

"Hey! You're the kid that came out from the mist, aren't ya?"

Eddie snapped again from his reverie. It was that same scruffy-bearded man of prompt generosity that had comforted him.

"Yeah!" he replied. "I came back. I don't know how I did, but I did."

His enervated companion had fallen asleep in his lap, and he soothed her in sleep with the pass of his compassionate hand over her frayed locks.

"You know, I went out alone, too. I've seen a bit. If it isn't too personal, I was curious to see how your experience compares."

Eddie turned toward him and nodded with genuine interest. "Really? What did you see?" he asked.

The stranger wiped his mouth then gave his beard a stroke as he conjured back the memories. "It was way back in Neo Cascadia. We arrived at the outskirts of town; it was completely abandoned. Not a man, bird, bug in sight—nothing. We got word that everyone was to stop and make camp while the military went downtown to go bust down doors."

"It was abandoned? The places I've visited were abandoned, too, but—an entire city? That's . . . scary," Eddie pondered aloud.

The man nodded to that sentiment. "Absolute ghost town—and the darnedest thing was . . . there wasn't a stone out of place. No cars in the middle of the street or ransacked storefronts, bullet holes, or smoking craters." He dismissed it altogether with a wave of his hand. "It was as if everyone fell asleep at once and never woke up. I've been to that city about a *hundred* times . . . Never thought I'd see it that way."

"Whoa . . . You went downtown alone? Why?"

"Well, something happened that night. I used to visit Neo Cas all the time back in my early twenties. Me and some really good guys used to hit the music venues when summer rolled around. Back then there were so many of 'em that you could hop around until the break of dawn if you knew the map. And, I tell you, those nights never got old."

A few families away, their conversation stirred the restless Lyal Abra, who lifted himself off the ground to listen; his friends were already gone in their slumber.

"My wife, daughter, and I were put up in a little house with two other families. Spent some time talking, got the rooms ready, and lay down for the night. I don't know exactly what time it was, but I woke up. Felt really anxious, full of energy, and just really wanted to walk. So, I did. I got out of bed, opened the front door, and took to the streets . . . and somewhere along the way, I got a glimpse of Neo Cascadia, all alight on the horizon. And without really thinking about what I was doing, I went there."

Lyal eyed the spellbound soldier, who listened intently, like a child to a storybook of timeless enchantment read aloud. He felt bitter distaste for the boy who took on such puerile fascination with the tale, though, irksomely, he couldn't help but feel something a little similar. A tale with roots in the whimsical abandonment of those loved, he was certain, had no good end.

"I don't really know how long I walked, but I had reached the towers of *downtown*. Needless to say, I was a long way from where I was supposed to be—all alone. Then, I received some unexpected guidance: music, the song of a siren. It was a tune straight out of an old playlist, whose name I had long forgotten. I followed, and it led me through streets, most familiar, some not. Pretty soon, though, it all started looking *real* familiar. I had ended up at my favorite place."

Arcane fascinations gripped the apprehensive eavesdropper, and Lyal couldn't resist listening even more intently.

"Bar signs, broken brick road, and neon glory. First time I had ever walked down that tiny road without being shoulder to shoulder the whole way through."

"What did you find there?" Eddie asked.

"Well . . . I went right to where it was calling. It was a spot we always used to hit first on the way in and last before the journey back home. Fahrenheit Bar. I've probably had more memories in that two hundred feet of seedy good vibes than anywhere else in my entire hometown."

There was a name Lyal remembered. From recounted memories of his mother's teenage misadventures, he recognized that iconic hotspot from days in which she had little more to give than merry company and hot passion burned to a disc. It was a temple of wild soundscapes that he had once dreamed of making a pilgrimage to, yet if his memory served him, the Fahrenheit Bar had closed ages ago, transformed into a docile coffee shop.

"I went up to the graffiti-covered door and saw shadows moving behind the diamond of stained glass . . . And I felt in that moment that, if I turned the handle and stepped inside, I would live it all over again, and that everything would be just alright."

"What did you do? Did you open it? What happened?" Eddie pressed in eager impatience.

"What happened was, the little one had followed me out. She only had to say a couple words to put me back on the right track," he said.

Eddie stiffened in bewilderment, as there was no child to be seen, but the man inched aside, and there, at his side, was the ruffled hair of a young girl fast asleep upon the ground.

"Bringing her back through that city was more terrifying than anything I've ever been through since the night of the invasion. I think she broke me out of it—that trance. There's no telling what was waiting for me beyond that door, but I'm in the mindset now to believe it wouldn't have been any old friends or a step back through time. I'm not the same young man I used to be, and the allure to be there again was something to be feared, because it was as if nothing else in the world mattered at all. I'm lucky I had someone looking after me, which is why it's a miracle you made it back all by yourself."

By the conclusive assertion of that fantastic excursion, Eddie found himself swept in wonder, as did the unnoticed Lyal Abra, who put to serious questioning what he might find in that forbidden outland of phantasms and lost sirens. But while one boy took fascination in the purported strength of a little girl's words, the other found it instead in the obscure revival of a golden age.

With a mind abuzz with mystic conceptions, young Abra lay back down. He closed his eyes and slipped fast to a thick manifestation of that hectic street, side by side with the good-time disciples, dipped deep in the euphoric aura of unrestrained energy.

He worked with broken figments derived from the spoken story in an attempt to capture the bustle and glitz of the neon night, and through the induced furor of festivity emanated a familiar tune. The dream-bound producer tinkered with that mental track until he became pleased with it, yet something about its ephemeral completion left him thoroughly unsatisfied.

In a swift return to sobriety, Lyal emerged from the starry reverie only to behold sheer darkness above. With this as their new reality, he knew a thousand nights would produce nothing more special, nor anything more wonderful than what that bleak vault of Infinity provided.

Unless he went and sought the miracles out himself . . .

Lyal sat up, but the boy was already gone. The man, asleep with his family. But he would find him, and ask him of this land of illusion. If wonders lay beyond the mists, Lyal knew only the brave would find them.

And so, he closed his eyes again and set aside those brave endeavors for another day.

No sooner did he find himself thinking of her again, however, the way he always did at night.

Perhaps they would return as specters someday, he worried. Ashe and Miyacre both; what would he say to them, if he could do so again? What would they say in return, or had he failed them so greatly that they wouldn't bother to reach through Eternia's mystic shroud? Was he capable enough to prevent the rest of his friends from suffering the same cruel fate?

Frantic thoughts swarmed his mind until it grew silent, and he lay there in that discomforting silence, haunted by his failure. A resilient glint was born deep in the vacuum, however. Alive! And unable to be readily snubbed out by misfortune's most dynamic press.

It was a temptation he knew shouldn't chase, but the lure of possibility had taken hold, and against all sense, it reeled him ever deeper into the mental shroud of High Fantasy.

A dreamer's soul, eternal.

Together With You, on the Road Toward Destiny

Late in the night, Eddie stirred, unable to sleep. He had taken a place among the civilian caravan ground and lay surrounded on all sides by strangers. The boy had grown fixated on the dark wind's howl, which served to remind his enfeebled consciousness of unbearable misfortune at the hand of the dark messenger.

There came footsteps and rustling somewhere out in the camp, but he wouldn't lift himself to see exactly where they came from.

Perhaps it was out of fear or exhaustion, but whatever the cause was, it had melted down into a single feeling of heaviness, discomforting enough to stay him from slumber or activity.

His mind drifted between dreams, from that vision-traveled town to some life where things were normal, from a stroll through the streets of the otherworld's festival night to the grassy corridor through the starlight carnival, joyous faces aglow in either by the grace of the immortal sunset.

But it could all only ever be a distraction from the twisted reality: the war, the invaders, and the undeniable void left by the cruel hand of death.

As he lay captivated by imaginary ventures, a more vivid shuffle of footsteps jogged his heart. He pushed himself up on his elbow and searched all over, still keeping as low as possible. They were close.

There was subtle movement out in the abyss, but he could not make out who they were or what it was they were doing. He lay back down and closed his eyes in hopes of utilizing the darkness as cover to hide from whomever troubled the peace.

Soft crimson broke the ebon veil. He opened his eyes and raised halfway to find the source.

Three soldiers stood illuminated by the crackling torch's light just a few yards down, on a designated path between the resting masses. He wasn't sure if he had been seen. However, they appeared to face him rather directly.

They engaged in a muffled, yet rough exchange.

Eddie lowered his head, though he felt as if he had already been caught. A boot fell to the dirt beside him. The boy shuddered, lifted his gaze, and came eye to eye with lambent cerulean beneath the tattered hood.

He breathed a sigh of relief, comforted by the swordsman's presence. "What are you doing here?"

"Stand—come with me," Ultra replied, with invader gaze set on the shadowy prowlers.

They had frozen over, no doubt in reaction to the swordsman's sudden appearance. With trust in his heart, Eddie stood as directed, and together they began the journey out from the caravan and into the darkened plains.

Upon the first time Eddie looked back, the men appeared huddled together in apparent conversation. After a few minutes longer, a second glance would reveal that they had gone, and gone with them the last threat to keep them from the path of solitude.

The swordsman guided him through the sleeping masses, past curious glances and between sharp whispers from one to another as the returned wanderer and the wondrous blade's man cut a path right to the distant hills.

They shared no further words between each other, opting to avoid greater attention, and as they pressed on, the minutes of silence accumulated within Eddie's subconscious until he realized the sheer size of the displaced.

The boy gazed out at the huddled masses, the once proud people of the Union's capital expelled to the dirt of the world. It was jarring to him, a dark fantasy and hopeless reality made nearly indistinguishable by war.

Although they had not gone unnoticed by authority, fear of a lightning confrontation kept the perimeter guard's protest at bay. The odd duo slipped from the grasp of misfortune's congregation and broke free at the sparsely defended outskirts.

They journeyed out for a forested hillside to the north, which lay far enough removed from the camp that any who ventured close would be easily detected.

The rugged land accommodated their ascent with a series of recessed rocks in the slope. Eddie leapt and pulled himself over each dusted ledge as the swordsman shot from edge to edge. Nature's ancient staircase delivered them to a small clearing near the top, which offered sufficient space to camp for the remainder of the night.

Ultra stepped to the edge of a long shelf and peered out to the military camp, which yet bustled with movement, their work never done. Satisfied with their vantage, he informed the boy that it was where they would remain for the night.

After a brief meander around the hilltop, Eddie tried to relax on the grass, but his vigorous curiosity nagged him, and he was unable to be still for long. The restless fidgeter lifted himself from the ground and peered up to the swordsman, who had his gaze set on the horizon.

"You know, she never really talked about you."

The swordsman turned away from the expanse and took a seat upon a boulder near the cliff. "Your companion?" he asked, knowing exactly who he spoke of.

"Yeah, and she could do incredible things—just like you . . . You knew her, didn't you?"

"I knew only a ruthless warrior, a mad manipulator of the weak and seeker of powers far beyond her reach. Instructed, no doubt, to plant herself within the resistant force, but instead opting to stay her wrath and leave alone with you. Perhaps you had come to know someone much different, as you said."

He nodded with ready confidence. "She showed me how to see a place far beyond this world, but I haven't been able to do it since," the boy admitted as he shrank in a hopeless search to understand why.

"You have to ask yourself if that is really what you want to dedicate your time to."

Eddie snapped up. That advice, of holistic absurdity. "Of course I do! I could only dream of doing any of that a long time ago . . . Like jumping between the walls like you did when I first saw you in Salamandra. Boy, what I would do if I could do *that*."

"The feat in itself isn't magic. You can do it, too, if you put yourself to the task."

The eager aspirer turned to the nearby landscape and discovered a narrow rock ravine further along the cliffs, which fell only a few feet deep.

"What about over there!?" he cried.

"Go there and get a running start, and be ready to analyze your mistakes."

So, the boy went without hesitation. With tireless determination, he tried and slipped, then tried and fell, each time rising back to perform the task with a little more grace. He remained dedicated for nearly an hour, stopping only to catch his breath at the peak, all while the swordsman kept a keen eye on the shadowy camp from the cliffside.

"Seek out why it is you failed. Don't do it mindlessly. The rock surface is a chaotic element. You'll have to feel out every step if you wish to make the pass," the swordsman advised as his eager student fell once more.

The boy stood up, covered in dust, ascended the dive once more, then bent over in exhaustion. "I almost got it—I just—"

"Once you feel you've got a grip on the movement, all you have left to do is believe in each step. Without confidence, you will always fall further."

Eddie nodded with spirited attentiveness. "Okay, yeah—I will," he swore as he straightened up. "Is that how you do it? Just believe?"

"Perhaps I did—a long time ago."

"You don't anymore?" asked Eddie in a push for clarity.

But the question had struck a truth too deep, and the swordsman turned his head away to escape his intrusion. "It's not important."

Eddie shook his head in steadfast opposition to that dispassionate sentiment. "Lost faith is never something to call unimportant," he argued.

"If only it were all so simple, Eddie Bowitz. While instinct has come to suffice for me, you do not possess such vast time to cultivate those abilities."

Eddie opened his mouth to preemptively dispute the apathetic fatalist, but caught the meaning of his words and recognized them to be of genuine truth.

"When you've caught your breath, you should lie down and rest. Morning will come quick, and we will need to do our best to stay ahead," the swordsman said.

But the boy shook his head, keen on returning to the rock he wished to conquer. "I'm gonna keep trying. I'll aim for two—maybe three steps, and then I'll be done. Promise."

Ultra nodded in silent accord, unwilling to press him further. "Action—is the sword," the disgraced farplaner recited, then closed his eyes as he returned to the winds in hunt of disturbances in its natural rhythm.

By the sole blessing of repeated failure, Eddie accomplished his goal of two successive leaps after his foot found divots along the rock a few times over. Thereafter, his grasp on the technique was loosely attained, and his stubborn energy evaporated, at last, as he settled with his humble accomplishment.

He could finally rest.

With a full moon shining above, he limped from the stone crevasse back to the swordsman, then dropped to the grass to catch his breath.

"There—I did it," the boy huffed, without wind to put into his words.

The swordsman raised his head in a show of respect to his willpower. "Put yourself to the challenge, and you will become great."

Eddie lay back into the lush spread as he set to task of memorizing what he had learned. He did so until he began to lose interest in it, and his mind began to wonder.

The boy tossed and turned, then passed a curious glance to the swordsman, who maintained an ever-watching eye on the distant camp.

"What are you looking at out there?" he asked, yet unable to put his mind to rest.

"Nothing in particular," the swordsman replied.

"Are you thinking of going back for something?"

"Neither of us can go back. There are those who will come looking for you and me, to use us for their justice."

"Is it really all that special that I came back alone?" the boy asked, troubled that the threat yet prevailed.

The swordsman lowered his head as he pondered that truth with genuine intrigue.

"Now is not the time to wonder too deeply about it," he broke. "Be thankful you are here tonight. Those who seek you out, on the other hand—I feel their curiosity will not be easily satiated, and their fascinations may come to ruin them."

"Why don't we tell someone about them? If those guys are— trouble or something—shouldn't we say something as soon as possible?"

"I have mingled enough in your society. When the war is finished— if we are victorious— then your hands alone will guide this world's destiny. Keeping the interloper's goals at bay will suffice here."

Eddie laid his head into his palm, unable to quell the storm within. "But what about that world after? You know—after—"

"It's too soon to ponder such a future," the swordsman interjected. "Rest. The days ahead only grow longer, and you will need your strength."

"If you won't say anything about it, I will. Because it is my world, and I believe it's the right thing to do."

The swordsman closed his eyes, in disappointment with his tactless approach.

"The right way is not always clear, and even a sun-soaked path is riddled with danger. Exposing them aggressively may cause unintended side effects, but that choice rests with you. I will not stop you if you must go."

"But, if I did go, would you go with me?" the boy asked, baiting him.

The swordsman peered down at him without a word, his intelligible reticence satisfied. On a fruitful offensive, Eddie sat up with a wish to put another mystery to rest.

"Tell me. Why do you fight each other? What happened before you all came here? I want to believe that you're helping us because it's right, but I know it's something more than that. I understand you don't like to talk about these things, but if we're going to travel together, I want to know why you're doing this."

The swordsman mulled over the request with uncertainty in his eyes, but closed them as he resolved all objections.

"Little Eddie Bowitz, I have journeyed a very long time, through the collapse of greatness, the hollows of perfection, and the battlefields of the millenniums, bringing calamity to the kingdoms of the unconquered, for the sake of a single dream. Lady Seora and I . . . we served at this capacity without a question to our merciless exterminations. At one point, we were no different, she and I, and in the end, I suppose we became quite similar again."

"What made you change?" the boy asked.

The swordsman emerged from those malefic visions to meet the boy's persistence.

"Though I cannot speak for her entirely, there was another . . . a defector before me. A fearsome retainer who remembered who he once was, when a clever foe broke the bond and lured him into his realm of prisms, during the twilight of the Warring Heavens Period. Though we were able to put down the Reclaimer Seraph, our cohort's mind could not be relieved of his grim epiphany. What he had found in those revelations had turned his blade. Something had to be done about it, and it was carried out with haste. What remained was an orphan memory, a cruel inheritance. Yet, a necessary burden. With that glimmer of wisdom, I went searching for answers myself . . ."

The swordsman fell silent and left Eddie's imagination to run wild.

"Well . . . you must have found what it was you were looking for," the boy presumed. "What was it?"

"A long time ago, before I was an incredible warrior, I was an incredible fool. When it was I who first took the cursed blade, I was sure I had the answers," Ultra confessed as he drew that sullied blade from the ancient sheath.

Eddie grew quiet as they peered together upon the gleaming silver.

"Back when the thunder of the elder cruisers stilled my heart, and the very sight of their starlight cascade drowned my spirit with fear . . . but unlike you, I was not lost in my place, nor did I falter when it came to the task. I remain Ultra, the Unforgiven."

That admission of guilt caused Eddie to search the face of his hero for deeper explanation of those forbidden memories. The swordsman sheathed the blade, however, in hopes to escape them.

"Lately, I've struggled with the phantoms. They come to walk with me wherever I go, and so I cannot rest until we have found the road's end . . . where I will go pleasantly across the divide . . . wherever it may lead."

"You have something you wish you could change, too. Haven't you found a way to do something? It must have been easy for you to try—to ask," Eddie pressed.

The swordsman lifted his eyes to the stars, where Eternia's sovereign stood waiting at the imperial helm. "The passages of time are closely watched. One may not go easily whenever they please, for upsetting the balance of the realms causes great upset throughout the cosmos. Endsborough is his . . . temporary solution."

Eddie suffered chilling intrigue with that name of grim familiarity. "Mirika mentioned that place, too. What is Endsborough?"

"It is an accursed place of dream and memory, an endless realm of his consciousness, a place of reflections of all reality. Of what was . . . what is . . . or what could be. At times, genuine, but without a doubt malleable to an ambitious whim, though I've no evidence to convict him of such manipulation." He lowered his hand and brushed along the tips of the lush bed beneath them. "Even every blade, every leaf, and every creature."

"All life?"

The swordsman nodded. "Like some unheard-of machine, its will works at an unbelievable task. Stripping away and rebuilding for the lost ones. But for what? Because of some unspoken conviction or simple emotion? I've never been sure."

"It seems like there's a lot you don't know about your master, too," Eddie said.

"Like a path over the rolling hills, you always think you're beginning to understand until you reach the next summit and realize the great vastness the world around you. It's to be lost in life, let alone among the stars. But our goal is simple. We needn't worry about the mystery behind his mayhem. Just as in my service to him, my service to you is all but the blade. I'll leave my mistakes in the past and follow the path we have forged together."

He turned to Eddie, with aim to challenge him. "But what will you do, Eddie Bowitz?"

The boy lowered his head, for he knew he could not do the same. "Yeah, I have some things I regret, too—but I hope I find the answer soon."

"We both have mistakes behind us in the past, but what will we do today, and what will we do tomorrow? That is something worth pondering . . . before a time comes when you will need to know the answer."

"I will," said the boy. "I'll figure it out. I promise."

"Yes . . . You may find yourself," the swordsman said in rest. "If you do, then never let it go."

Those solemn words rang within the boy as he lay there, looking up, dreaming of what was beyond Infinity's curtain of obscurity. With a heart full of ambition and a spirit fueled by the thrill of achievement, he would fulfill the task, even if it meant his life. Somewhere, over the horizon and beyond the clouds, it would be there, just as she had promised, and the righteous sovereign from the stars would make everything alright.

An unseen, ever-watching eye observed from somewhere out in the cosmos, prepared to test his will. A gathering of dreamers was nigh. A dawn of destiny, at the intersection of fates.

The Winter City

The caravan was mobilized before dawn. A dense, gray haze had swept through and thickened all around them. It denied the pure grace of the sun and left them to meander between the occasional beam that pierced the murky underworld to which they had been sentenced.

The officials gathered people into their respective groups and delivered them the daily briefing.

They would be pushing forward toward the city of Eredes, which lay half a day's march ahead.

A long way away was the sound of gunfire from the south. The Eternal Army was reported to be on the approach, which meant their immediate departure was of utmost importance.

Lyal Abra and his friends stood around listening with half an ear. Kaiser kept his eyes toward the sky where the guns blared. The official made quick to double-check her notes.

"Last, but certainly not least, we'll be taking a position rear of the caravan . . . Not to worry, though, the generals have assured that we'll be nowhere near the skirmish occurring . . . From what I've been told, it's a relatively small group."

Lyal grimaced at the news, then looked to a rock on the ground. He kicked it.

"What's going on with you?" asked Mitz.

But he had no intention of giving him transparency. "We're moving to the front of the pack today," Lyal informed them.

Kaiser returned his attention back to the earth. "They said we can't break from our assigned group, though," he said.

"You actually think they're going to assign people in groups and enforce it? How? Put us in jail?" Lyal argued.

Kaiser shook his head with a shrug. "I actually highly doubt it. Worth a mention?"

***

When the assembly had concluded, Lyal and his friends went ahead as planned while the officials gathered for one final meeting.

"See? Nobody is going to care where we go," said Lyal.

"Why are we going to the front anyway?" asked Mitz.

Lyal remained conflicted on whether he should stay honest about his intentions. His silence lingered too long not to create some suspicion, especially in Setz, who glared at him.

"Well, Lyal? You going to say anything? I mean, you're only stringing your friends along just like you did before, right? No big deal, I guess."

Lyal lowered his head for a moment, then rose up with resolve. "You all heard about the boy who came back, didn't you?"

The others exchanged glances. "Yeah—he came back yesterday after disappearing in Salamandra. Heard it from the crazy loony with the faux-hawk and star tattoos down the side of his face a little ways down from us," said Kaiser.

"Guess what? That same kid was right next to our spot last night talking to some other guy who also happened to leave camp and come back," said Lyal.

The boys, at first, had a rather muted response to hearing this.

"Really . . . ? Is he like, some kind of war celebrity, now?" asked Mitz.

"Right? Who cares if he came back. It's got nothing to do with us," Setz argued.

552

Lyal stopped and stepped up to Setz. "Oh yeah? And what about our friends who disappeared and haven't come back yet?" Lyal asked.

"They're dead," Setz replied, unfazed and cold.

"You're dead."

Kaiser came between them and eased them back. "Cool down, you guys. Don't want to cause a scene now that we're out here breaking the rules," he joked.

"Lyal, dude, it's hard for everyone here, but you gotta let it go. It'd be a miracle if we survived this crazy shit *without* trying to jump into . . . whatever's out there," said Mitz.

Lyal wouldn't break his gaze with Setz, who stared back at him, stone-faced and empty. "I'm not giving up. Not if someone came back—then anyone could come back, right?!" he said with his hands held wide, desperate to make a point.

But the others looked at him with sad or stony eyes, unable to share in his enthusiasm for the possibility of their friends' return.

Lyal, seeing this disheartening response, turned from them and continued forward alone without another word.

Kaiser looked to both Setz and Mitz with his cheeks full of air. He released the wind, shrugged, then went after Lyal. "Hey, Lyal, you aren't going to, like, walk—right—into—that mist are you?" Kaiser called out to him.

Setz and Mitz remained behind. "If he's going to get himself killed, he's going to have to do it alone. Why should we have to die for his dumb decisions?" asked Setz.

"I don't think he planned on dragging us in if we didn't want to. Him and Miyacre were pretty tight. When that tower attacked us, he was the one who tried to save her. He's the one who braved the storm to try and find her . . . It's just commitment. Can't hate him for that." Mitz sighed. "I don't think this is good for him. I honestly don't. But, I've known this dude for too long. These are the times you can really believe in him. Setz, if I were you, I'd go where my heart is, because then at least I'd know I tried. But if it were you who was lost, you already know this fool would be thinking up ways to come get you out."

Mitz took his first steps to Lyal and Kaiser, who exchanged playful jabs ahead.

"You really feel that way, don't you?" he asked Setz, whose stone gaze sank.

Mitz nodded.

"Yeah . . . I know," Setz admitted.

Persuaded by his reflections, he followed behind Mitz as they moved in to regroup ahead. Together, Lyal and his companions reached the group nearest the military escort without incident. Among the front pack, they traveled for what seemed like hours through the mist, one direction looking no different than any other.

Soon, however, they stopped to find something very peculiar in the gray shroud above. From unseen heavens fell white particles through the crawling gray. Those icy fragments meandered the skies in a harmless float until they reached grass below.

As one, all others had stopped to inspect the event as well.

"Is that snow?" asked Mitz.

Lyal lifted up his finger to the nearest one he could find. It disappeared as soon as it touched his skin.

"That can't be snow. It's like eighty-one degrees out here," said Setz as he passed his hand over his forehead so that sweat could verify his assessment.

"Look, dude," said Kaiser.

Lyal rubbed his fingers together. They were wet.

"And look over there—look at this shit," said Kaiser as he leapt forward.

They looked in awe at the sight of a white glaze that covered the ground ahead where the soldiers walked. Some had knelt down and passed their hand through the white powder to inspect it themselves.

An inspirited Kaiser rushed ahead and brashly scooped a handful of it and crafted it into a messy ball.

The others ran over to regroup with him.

"Man, don't touch that. We have no idea what it is," said Setz.

"It's snow, but it's—not cold," said Kaiser. "At all."

Mitz kicked at the substance, and it splattered forward. Baffled, each boy put their bare hands down into the slush.

"I can't even comprehend what's going on right now," said Mitz as he brought up a handful.

"The key is not to think too hard about it," replied Kaiser.

There was a near childish joy that came over each of them as they all descended into it. The soldiers looked on without action as people all around from the civilian caravan went through their own inspections.

"Must not be dangerous. The military isn't doing anything. Not that they have all the answers or anything," said Mitz.

Relieved, but still a little unsure, they got down and began to craft in false winter's powder.

"Well, there's one thing left to do," said Kaiser, with a mischievous grin.

He was suddenly pelted with a barrage of snow from his friends, who were prepared to deal with him.

"What the hell—you guys are getting smarter every day, I swear," said Kaiser as he returned fire at Setz.

The melt slapped him across the face. "Damn, it's like . . . room temperature," Setz said as he wiped the watery slush from his cheek.

Kaiser took his shirt and pull it off his head.

"You crazy?" asked Lyal.

"Thought you guys knew by now," he replied, then dove through the snow. The others recoiled, unable to fathom anything but an unpleasant icy touch.

He popped up from the snow and shook himself of the white powder.

He had been left completely drenched.

"Damn, that's like jumping into a pool," he said as he retrieved his shirt and wrung it out.

"Of course, you idiot. What did you think it was going to be?" asked Setz.

"Cold," Kaiser replied.

"Obviously not," Setz concluded.

A period of carefree indulgence ensued as the forward guard continued a slow and cautious advance. The farther they went, the heavier the snow fell, and the larger the drifts became. Soon, it was all but a rolling winter wonder. The forest and fields were unified by a blanket of white, surreal in the baking embrace of absolute summer.

For the first time in so long, there was the vibrance of happiness among the displaced. It seemed as though they had stumbled upon a peaceful respite from the fight, a quaint opportunity to bury their troubles beneath the snow, a welcomed placebo to steal despair away for a few nights, or however long the sensation of awe endured.

Though the invader army never lay far behind, and to some, the winter retreat was merely a cunning distraction from whatever lay ahead, here, it was evident that High Fantasy reigned supreme. The old world and its workings were crumbling, subjected to the will of the one at the empire's throne.

Lyal became conflicted with his fascination, however. Perhaps there should be greater concern over the nature of this surreal phenomena, but what harm could snow at eighty degrees bring to them? Whatever the answer was, the question in and of itself reined in further enjoyment he could seize from it.

An odd radiance pierced the winter's shroud. It brightened into a glittering sunburst of such brilliance that it appeared like a sunrise beyond the gloom. The spectacle drew the attention of many, though whatever lay beyond remained lost behind the dense shroud of gray.

The boys pressed ahead and eventually found themselves alone beside a solitary cave sealed by a bizarre circular plate. Inscribed upon its dull golden surface was an unintelligible glyph. It depicted seraphic splendor of a sort: a long, winged creature formed from deeply carved lines while the invader emblem stood on high.

"Wonder what's caused all this," asked Lyal, as they inspected the alien engraving.

Mitz shrugged. "You mean this as a whole, or just this one episode of pure madness we've experienced thus far?" he asked.

"Nah, I just want to know who or what's behind it. That kid—you know the one—" Lyal said as he wiped his face down, shaking off the swarm of theories. "I don't know. I got a feeling he knows something."

"Why are you so obsessed with him?" asked Setz.

Lyal stepped away from the group. He knew what he had to do. "Forget it," he said. "Hey, listen. I'm going on ahead, but I'll come back. There's got to be a way to find answers to all this. And if we don't go searching, we'll probably never know."

Kaiser, with eyes blank in arresting consternation, stepped forward to confront his dedication. "Well, hold on now. You wouldn't go without us, would you?" he asked.

"I don't want to pull you guys deeper than I already have. Let this be my thing. If it turns out to be alright, then I'll come back."

"But why would you want to go ahead of the pack?" asked Mitz.

"Because I saw that kid leave with the swordsman last night, and I bet they know exactly where they're going."

The others held in their silence, knowing there was nothing they could do to stop him.

"Well . . . alright, man," Kaiser surrendered. Suddenly, he perked up as an idea came to him. "Here. Take this. You're missing something, right? Catch it. Pull it back," said the young trickster as he presented the magnet hooked on the retractable lanyard.

Lyal eyed him in disbelief.

"Never know when you're going to need it," Kaiser insisted.

"Probably never. But, hey. Never hurts to have a way to piss someone off, right?" Setz concluded.

Against his own judgement, Lyal took the lanyard and stuffed it into his pocket. Appeased, Kaiser stepped away with a nod and a beam.

"Be careful out there, dude," said Mitz.

Lyal nodded as he took another step away, then turned in pursuit of the wanderer and his miracle.

"Hope you find whatever it is you're looking for, Lyal," Setz muttered, then took a parting glance at the closed gateway before he set off to return to the caravan.

Mitz and Kaiser, not without a moment of hesitation, turned, too, and followed under the weight of pent-up contention with their unforeseen separation.

They could only be unsure of his deep dive into the heart of the unknown, to which so many others had been lost.

Left to his ambition, Lyal sloshed through the snow in a hard drive, though sure to keep distance from the perimeter guard, who he believed lurked somewhere ahead.

His lonesome advance through the arcane blizzard offered him time to contemplate his precipitous undertaking. He had it in his head that he would find the boy and consult his forbidden knowledge of the realm beyond. Though even he was skeptical, there was only one way left to find the answers now, and it wouldn't be found behind the army in the civilian caravan. Regardless of what others or even he himself believed was possible, he would tear down any barrier in search of clarity, a spectator never again.

Each step forward, his shoe fell deeper into the warm fluff. Soon, however, he crossed the mound's frosty summit, and the drift began to fall in a sparkling slope. Through the flow of thought as dense as the shroud, he heard the sound of chatter from those around. He lifted his head, and his eyes grew wide at the sight of a dynamic glimmer out far beyond, which weakened the depressive gray curtain with its splendor.

A dreamy line stood all across the horizon. Like a vision through sleepy eyes, he beheld a murky starlit city, beyond a far-spanning river. He looked all around in search of those who could share in his awe, but there were none. Invigorated still, Lyal pressed onward, broke from the snowdrifts, and stumbled into the powdered grass.

There, he stole a closer look at the deep dream vision that lay across mystic waters. Shooting stars raced along the street while long silver beams rocketed parallel above the ground on high rails. Nestled between the skyscrapers were billboards that struck out against the veil in flashes of brilliance. The neon-infused paradise teased with its vibrant bustle, a sole survivor in a ruined world, and the first such dreamscape Lyal had ever laid eyes on.

The sheer excitement of that distant metropolis ignited his spirit with limitless energy.

Could it be that this was a place untouched by war?

The thought alone encouraged him to accept any and all risk. There had to be a way across.

A brief search of the area for the means to cross was brought to an abrupt halt by something in the distance. It was a figure, something like a ghost, aglow in a halo of golden light.

Lyla stopped to identify exactly what it was, and as his eyes focused, he captured her in vivid form. A coat flapped in a wind he did not feel, and her hand pulled at the collar in guard from a cold he did not suffer.

She pulled the strap of a purse over her shoulder. He saw now that her eyes watched him. Her face was stern and serious, unsure of him while he was unsure of her.

Lyal turned behind him. There was no one else but them, alone in the storm before the starlight metropolis.

"Who are you, and why are you wearing your sleeves up?" asked the woman in a strangely phased tone.

Lyal jerked in surprise. She had spoken to him. "Why am I dressed like this? Why are you dressed like that?" he asked rather naturally.

She eyed him as her assessment progressed of this strange visitor. "Is that a joke?" she finally asked.

But Lyal shook his head with his lip driven up in confident denial. "Sure isn't. What are you doing way out here?" he asked the young woman.

"I live here . . . in the city across the river," she replied.

Lyal looked once more to where the phantom liveliness beaconed. Seeing this ghostly illusion, however, caused him to lose hope of any escape from madness. This was madness, too, just another product of it.

"I've seen many visitors come here, all so different, all so curious. But they're not here. They come, and they go, and never come back again."

"That's probably because our worlds are different or something. Does it matter?" Lyal asked, his patience lost.

The girl cocked her head, not understanding his frustration. "Matter? I suppose not. But I came here every night until someone else appeared so maybe I could ask and understand."

Something about her response caused him to regret his words, but as he searched for the words to patch the feeling, she turned from him and began to fade.

"Hey, you want to learn something, right?" he asked.

She stopped and turned in temptation to the modest lure.

"I'll give you a chance," he said with a grin and the fold of his arms to assure her of the confidence natural in his commitment.

She watched him for a moment as she determined her choice. "Come with me. There's a place we can go," she said in acceptance.

The fantastical specter turned and continued toward a distant structure, which loomed on the far-off riverside. Lyal followed in an energized stride until he caught up with her. When he found himself at her side, he inspected her unusual aura. She wasn't transparent like any phantom he had ever envisioned. She was chromatic, like a movement of mist, yet when still, completely there.

He turned over his shoulder. There was yet nothing but the shroud and endless crystal white. He hoped the others were well, but found comfort knowing they had stayed behind at the caravan.

"Are more of them coming?" she asked.

"There's a whole lot of us . . . trying to win this war—or running from it."

She turned to him. "You're fighting a war? A shame."

Being this close allowed him to detect her tender, soft voice, which proved soothing. Their journey to the river took them along a path, detectable only by the gentle slopes on each side, which vanished at the outskirts of a small park, a haunt in its emptiness among the snowfall.

The flower beds lay barren in each square-shaped plot and left only the evergreens to populate the area. The humble inner court was centered around a stone statue of a metro car upon a pedestal, which was set to a slow rotation. They strolled through the falling white flakes to the court and cut around the edges of the statue's base. It was a journey made quaint by the subtle accompaniment of choppy, bass-fueled dance music from speakers on the corner lampposts, an acute juxtaposition from the snowy ambience that captivated the area.

Upon reaching the far side of the park, they arrived upon the corner of the impending metro station, whose smooth, stone-slab walls stretched far into the distance.

She led him farther along the path until they came to the leg of a stone-crafted arch, comprised of two crowned towers joined just below the peak by a thin sweep, which bore the inscription, METRO CITY.

Carved into the bevel-divided sections in the thick, cylindrical post were illustrations of empyrean, seraphic, and icy elemental design. In all, it seemed more a gateway to a temple rather than that of some ultra-modern rail station.

Lyal passed his hand over a series of snowflakes as they entered between the twin monarchs. Beyond them was a long and narrow corridor between the two elevated tracks. At the very end of it was a wireframe arch adorned with a mess of yellow fairy lights.

The ramp lay ahead at the center of the compressed plaza, the entry to the left and the exit to the right. Lyal looked at the woman from the corner of his eye as she proceeded. He smirked, knowing no matter what questions he asked, she would relinquish no direct answer nor bring him any closer to understanding any of it. It had all become something of a cruel machine to him, an infinite cycle of bizarre mechanisms and happenings with no explanation.

In this thought, he suddenly experienced an epiphany in that he became content in his ignorance. Until he found the boy, he would seek no answers from this world. Instead, he would take it for all it was worth, a fleeting joyride through the otherworld wielding impunity. In doing so, he would steal back the time of his youth stolen from him by the invader's war.

"So, what about this place? Is it even real?" he asked, humored.

She turned around slowly, then looked inquisitively to the city she claimed to know, as if she didn't really know it at all.

Lyal turned around and leaned against the silver railing along the wall, intrigued by her confusion.

She approached the railing and took it with both hands, and her bag swung down around her arm.

"I often wondered the same about you. Most people turn away from . . . things like you. It's easy understand wanting to avoid what's strange."

Lyal's brow rose, and his grin widened. "Strange? Why am I strange?"

"Tell me," she continued with predicted disregard for his question. "What do you see in me? Am I not real to you?"

Lyal looked long at her, the ethereal skin, eyes lost in gaze, and coat slipping in and out of existence. "No," he replied honestly. "You don't seem real."

"But you're talking to me, and what you're thinking—I understand you. So, that's real enough . . . Not to mention, I've seen a lot of weird things lately, so I think today, I'm going to let everything slide."

She didn't move her gaze from the city, so her reaction to his comment remained ambiguous.But he was okay with that.

"I want to bring you there. Bring a dream within a dream, right?" she said as she turned to Lyal. Her smile was radiant with elegance. Perhaps it was due to her phantasmic form. He didn't know, but there was something about it that was undeniably appealing; a welcome trait, though merely a cherry on top of the cake.

"So, how we going to get to your city?" he asked once more, driving his phantasmic wanderer further and further to action.

"Really? I'm happy," she said. Her eyes closed as she retreated into a recollection. "Hm, yes, happy—I think I'll bring you to the square." She turned to Lyal with politely restrained glee. "We'll take the bridge. I don't—it'll be easier to not bother anyone that way . . . Not many people take the bridge anymore."

The illusion turned, leaving a baffled Lyal behind as she started along a path toward the sparkling end.

"That's odd reasoning," he replied, but followed nonetheless. His adventure awaited. "Hey—totally forgot to get your name," said Lyal.

"My name? Oh—I was hoping you wouldn't ask," she replied with the nervous rubbing of the back of her hand. "Don't take it personal. I don't really know you."

Lyal shrugged. "No big deal. I'll just give you a nickname."

She turned to him, intrigued. "A nickname? Like what?"

A good name evaded him, but he toyed with the ideas. "I don't know. I'll let you know when I got a good one."

"Okay—I look forward to hearing it," she said to him with a look as though she were truly excited about it.

There was something odd about the girl, much more deeply bizarre than he imagined at first. He saw himself move with this girl so casually. Into the hands of what? It didn't matter to him anymore. This was the road he chose, the road closest to the beyond, where the ones in his heart possibly rode on. Absent of the fear of death, he followed her to the bridge, marked as proclaimed by a metro entrance on both sides. In a glance, he found it led right to the city, but it appeared to stretch on for miles.

"So, how we getting over that?" asked Lyal, both humored and bewildered.

She stopped and turned to answer him. "We'll walk across it. This is the only way for me—"

"The only way?" Lyal interrupted with a haughty chuckle.

Her companion was unleashed and took off for the ramp to the metro line, which sent such a shock through the phantom that she reached her hand out, desperate to stop him. Lyal jolted back to her, his brow raised in excitement of his release.

"You coming or not?" he asked.

"I can't! It's not possible for me right now to—"

Lyal let out a roar of a laugh to minimize those unspoken inhibitions. "Impossible? Impossible!? Look at where I'm at," he said with his arms wide out to introduce the otherworld.

Her expression remained stern. "You won't be able to go without a ticket," she warned.

Lyal dropped his arms and let his shoulders droop. "Aw—guess I'll just have to wish for one." He threw up his fingers, pinched together as if there were something there. "Oop—got one. Beat you there," he said to her bewilderment.

Lyal flipped around and shot up the ramp.

"Stop—don't!" she cried in one final protest before he vanished and she was forced into pursuit.

The wayward rogue rose to the top, then leapt the entire first flight of steps into the belly of the facility. He kicked up a spray of sleet as his feet left the ground in a blitz for the far end.

The hallway was dull and gray, but thin slivers of incandescent light lit the way forward. As he neared the corridor's end, he heard the squeal of wet shoes on the ground. He turned over his shoulder and found the girl had stumbled to the bottom step and clutched to the handrail for dear life.

Lyal laughed in the glory of the chaos then cut hard down the second hallway and leapt down a second flight.

Uninhibited by force of law or feeling, he ran and ran, the girl desperate to keep pace, and young Lyal desperate to find hope.

There was one last gap to close until the main platform. Three hallways cut the way forward. One to the lockers and ticket machines, another to the next platform, and the last to the gates, a waist-high barrier at the ticket tables dividing them from entry.

The girl landed on the bottom step, her hair bursting forward in the power of the halt. A sign that depicted a metro car in motion flashed to a monotonous beep. Lyal turned and greeted her with the beacon of his hand. "C'mon, slowpoke! We'll miss our train!"

He bolted for the gate, to her astonishment, and, before she could get a word out, had latched onto the railing and jumped the silver bar. He went right past the ticket master's box and landed on the other side.

An alarm blared. Red lights spun into a flurry all around. Lyal laughed as the halls swelled with crimson anger, then smirked as if it brought him only ecstasy. Unthreatened, he shot down the remainder of the hall and leapt a short flight to the bottom, where a flickering illustration of a train above guided the way.

The metropolitan otherworlder stumbled and made right for the ticket machine on first instinct, then cut back toward the blocked gate.

Her distress-plagued eyes rose to the flashing warning above. Against her purest judgement, she grabbed ahold of the bar and, with great uncertainty, pulled herself over and returned to her desperate pursuit.

Not far away, a camera on the wall zoomed in on her as she fled down the hallway.

Lyal sprinted down the remaining stretch of gray hall and was first to reach the platform. The tram sat on the rails just to the left, the white gates still pulled open for passengers.

The electronic bell rang through the terminal, and the lights above the doors flashed to signal an imminent departure.

Lyal took off for the doors and leapt in before they had budged. Still lacking his fantasy-bound companion, he stood right at the line between the car and the yellow-painted concrete.

The door panels slid in on each side to close, but Lyal threw his back against one panel, and drove his foot up against the rubber guard of the other. The force of the closing panels drove his knee nearly up to his chin, but the system, detecting an obstruction, gave up, and every door reopened.

Lyal kept his foot up against the guard, prepared for the system to reinitiate the process. The departure bell rang once more. From the crimson-bathed tunnel of the platform's entrance appeared his coerced accomplice. She noticed Lyal almost immediately and dashed for the opening.

The troublemaker grinned as the doors came in for the second attempt to close, this time forcing him to enlist all of his might to keep it at bay. She arrived right in front of him just as the strength in his leg was about to give way. She dove beneath his leg just as the pressure became too much. He released his hold and was sent back onto one leg. His balance left him, and he fell right to the ground alongside his troubled companion. The train tugged, slid forward, then took off down the terminal.

Lyal lifted to a knee, then stood straight. He reached out his hand to offer her aid, but the girl stared at him.

She scoffed then dug her palm into the ground, lifting herself.

"Honestly didn't think I could even touch you, anyway," he said as he glided his hand away with a wild grin.

The girl, less enthused, got to her feet and brandished her teeth, lost between bewilderment and astonishment in his actions and her own.

"That wasn't so bad, was it?" he asked without the expectation of approval.

He laughed in fantasy's face in a rebirth of himself.

She scoffed between gritted teeth. That laughter went undeterred, however, and instead grew heartier. She couldn't help but be captivated by this spirit of play and surrendered the faintest grin, but forced herself not to smile.

"I promise I won't do it again unless we have to walk over some other ten-mile bridge."

"Did you forget? We still have to get off," she reminded him.

He waved off her concern, then took hold of a strap handle that had beaten him over the head a few times as the train raced across the track. "Relax. Leave the worries behind. I'm here to have a good time."

"Selfish, aren't you?"

"Actually—you know, I'm looking for some friends of mine. This place seems like somewhere they might be."

The girl became disarmed as she took a moment to consider the possibility. "Why do you think that?" she inquired.

"Because it's, you know, magical—or whatever," he replied. "Some other friends of mine don't think there's a chance. But I'm not into giving up so easily."

"It's been a long time since I've heard of others coming here."

"Isn't there anyone who came here before me? Or maybe there's another place they could be that's, like, connected to this place? I don't know how it works. It's all basically fake anyway, right? This city, these rules, the whole train thing—"

The girl turned to him, these words in infliction of unmistakable sorrow. "And me, too, right? That's what I am to you."

Lyal sank back into the seats and sprawled out in an attempt to maintain his carefree demeanor, but her challenge to his mindset had caught him off guard. "No. You know what I think? I think I'm a figment of *your* imagination," Lyal leveled with her.

"My imagination?"

"Answer me this. Why would you hop on a train with a guy who just broke into the station and risk your own well-being for—someone you don't even know!? A reasonable person would say that's pretty weird . . . right?" he pressed.

The girl dropped her head as his dissection of the incident saddled her with shame. "But, you're my guest. So you're my responsibility."

Lyal gave a slow nod to that logic. It was either truly foreign or the deceptive fabric of a false realm. "That right? Well . . . guess that makes sense," he said, keen to not upset the entity any further, regardless of what he believed to be the truth of the matter.

Lyal let out a sigh in frustration.

"You're so obsessed with what's fake and real. I'm fake, you're fake. Maybe we're all fake. We're all pretending to be real," he ranted.

The phantom was buried in her thoughts, however, and didn't react as she sifted through memories. Suddenly, she had a breakthrough. "Ah—ah. You know—there was someone—"

"A girl. Long, almond-colored hair and on the tall side, right?" he interrupted as he took to his feet.

"I don't know. But it was a woman. But—"

"Where's she at, then?"

"In a place you shouldn't go. The area is restricted."

"Restricted like this train? I'll take my chances."

"No, this woman isn't what you think she is—"

"You gotta take me there."

"She's not like you," she said, getting up to his face to show the seriousness of it.

"I. Don't. Care." He turned his head with each word, then smirked at her, watching her disgruntled face through sharpened eyes.

Her head swayed as she processed his indifference to her warnings. "But it's on the other side of town—they'll be leaving soon. We won't make it in time," she said, giving it one last chance.

The dark fled the train car. They had burst from the underground through a tunnel in the river and were in full flight toward the city, which shimmered like an ethereal illusion in a spell of night. Lyal leapt onto the bench and peered out to it with excitement in his eyes, never realizing the daylight fading as the tram grew ever further from the odd threshold the boy had unknowingly crossed.

"Then, good thing we took the train. No time to waste. We're about to hit this place like a shooting star," he said, held fast to his belief of what might lay beyond.

She nodded in realization and acceptance of his persistence. "Okay, I'll take you there."

The car raced toward the next station in a weave between the towers that rose on all sides. Surrounded by the glitz of the phantasmal city, the cabin was filled by an evolving melt of celestial blues, flourishing pinks, and hypnotic purples from the million-bulb billboards that fired their instant transmissions into eyes in the night.

The train started into a turn that threw Lyal across the seats while the girl remained steady with her hand grasped tight to a dangling handle. He pulled his face up to the window once more and was greeted by faux joy on billboards that crowded the skyscraper's walls. He squinted and raised a hand to shield himself from the engineered luminosity behind the thousand promises of a journey toward a life of perfection.

The car passed above street after street, each doused in the mystic mists, alight in the sparkle of metropolitan magic.

"Alright, this is a little awesome," said Lyal.

"We'll be arriving soon. Try not to fall."

The train completed its bank and entered between two towers that fed them into the station just beyond. The facility was held high by an array of metal beams from the towers, giving it an explosive appearance. The ironclad scaffolds crisscrossed all around as if its construction remained incomplete, yet was so consuming that it appeared simply left to become one with the final design.

Lyal grabbed ahold of the support rail beside him as the train screeched to a halt at the station.

Lyal sprang right to the door. There was movement beyond the window. Other ethereal figures just like her all waited in their hats, scarfs, and earmuffs, with eyes gazing toward the ground in patience.

The bell rang upon their arrival, and the doors opened. Lyal burst right through the gathered phantoms and made for the handrail at the station's edge, leaving the girl to struggle through the incoming crowd to get off.

The city grew as he neared the handrail. Below was a magnificent square with an overabundance of shops, bars, and other entertainment facilities for the hedonistic society. In comparison to his suburban roots, here was a place where he could burn his entire youth and still feel a great deal was missed.

Centered around a golden sphere half submerged in a pool were circular parks all across the square, each of varied size, which together gave the panoramic view a sort of bionic expression. The parks were covered by transparent arbors, which appeared to safeguard the oddly blossomed pink- and blue-flowered trees from the endless winter flurry.

Lined around the perimeter of nature's refuge were bands of light, which transformed in a sleepy fade from one color to the next.

Most spectacular of all, however, was a central great tower at the far end of the square. Two noble curved spires met at an enormous golden star high above. That pseudo-sacred relic appeared to emit gentle multicolored rays down upon the streets below. No doubt to Lyal, it was some kind of government institution, an imposing town hall of the otherworld city.

All around, railcars raced through the night, over, in, and between spectacular structures as dazzling lights chased them beneath the track. Lyal stepped back to take it all in with one glance. The golden sphere half emerged from the waters of the fountain set the area aglow in its grace, and he then realized the image it sought to create.

"Oh man, the parks are the solar system? This place is nuts."

He wished he could share the sensation that pulsed through him and made him feel so very alive. Reinvigoration: a transfer of electric sensation from the realm of midnight lights. Nothing else was so surreal.

For a moment, he wished that his friends had joined him on his journey through the winter's grasp. What a wonder it would be if they were there, all of them, together again. The thought of what experiences might have awaited in this place without consequence nearly caused him to want to turn back for their retrieval. It seemed he had truly found a paradise in the madness.

His beam faded, however, as he noticed someone who stood out from the illusionary mystique of the city as he did. Upon closer inspection, he saw just who it was.

It was impossible. It was him, Little Eddie Bowitz, standing in the courtyard, there before the enormous star-peaked tower, surely with the same curiosity as he had. At once, he realized they had become one and seemed to bear the otherworld with the same eyes.

But how did he reach the city before he had? Perhaps the swordsman guided him through another way, though as far as he could see, the boy stood alone.

No good answer came to him, and the sound of hurried steps caused him to break from thought and turn. It was his new companion, with hair cast to the air. She arrived by his side and bent forward to catch a breath.

"Are you ready? We have to keep going if you want to make it in time," she said, noticeably flushed.

She pushed past him without waiting for a reply.

"I'm just waiting for you," he replied in nonchalant ease.

He followed her to cylindrical tower in the middle of the facility. As they approached, there was an audible rumble that ceased as the doors slid open and allowed access to a circular platform. They stepped in together. Lyal proceeded farther in and reexamined the view of the city from the far side window in hopes to find the boy, but as far as he could see, he had gone.

"We'll take this to the bottom and—"

She turned to the control panel, but froze. Lyal turned and took notice of her strange behavior. Before he could ask, he noticed movement at the corner of his eye.

He looked over.

There came two phantom officers in full sprint toward them.

The girl, with eyes filled with fear, hit a button on the wall, and the door came around and shut. Lyal chuckled as he approached his imperiled guide.

"Damn, what a rush, huh?" said Lyal in facetious delight.

"We have to get there fast. If we can reach the forbidden zone, they won't follow us."

"Let's hope not," Lyal remarked.

He then got a feathery sensation in the pit of his stomach as the platform dropped toward the city streets. He turned and peered from the window unto the otherworld, which stretched high above as every light became a streaming blur to his wonder shrouded eye.

The ground leveled out before them as the platform crawled into its cradle, and then the door flew open.

Under the heat of pursuit, the fugitives bolted into the crowd toward the snowy square beyond the central station's entry corridor. Down a starlit path they went, him through the mystic mists and illusions, and her, in and between them.

Dormant capsules along the walls ignited into frantic crimson fury as a sharp horn cried out in a repeated blare. Lyal closed in on the corridor's end where the silver bar which separated them resided. The area was full of movement, however, so much so that Lyal was unable to tell each person apart. He knew the pursuers would lay in ambush somewhere, but he remained undeterred.

The miscreant foreigner cut away from the gates, in favor of a bare double-bar fence that guarded the far ends. He leapt clear over it, then drove for the snowy square, a brazen insult to their lax defense against his simple roguish behavior.

The security team bolted out from around the corner behind them; a second team closed in from a terminal to the left. Lyal was far gone beyond the station, but the girl stumbled, vulnerable to apprehension.

He took noticed of her predicament and dropped into a slide. He reached out and collected a handful of snow, then cut back to her as she tried to pull herself over the rail as he had.

The guards closed in. Lyal drew back and launched the mashed ice ball right at the ground beneath their feet.

"Hey, boys! Snatch this up instead!" he cried.

Their steps turned hectic as the moisture robbed them of their grip on the slippery floor. One fall turned into two more as hands went out to rescue their balance. Eventually, nearly every member of the team had hit the floor, with those fortunate in their recovery left to assist the others up.

Relieved from the pressure of pursuit, the girl crossed over the bar. Lyal ran to meet her, and together they fled the scene of their mischief, the guards still busied with picking themselves off the ground.

They had left the central station erupted in pandemonium. Lyal laughed at the uproar of hysteria as they hurried through the nearest park, then emerged back among the trampled slush along the path.

Lyal turned around into a back trot. All around, passersby had stopped to observe the commotion at the metro station, though there were none left in pursuit of them. He looked to the girl, who was clearly exasperated with their antics, but it couldn't subdue his jubilation.

"You alright?" he asked.

"Yes, I'm okay! You'll need to follow me. We need to hurry," she said between gasps for breath.

Lyal dropped back behind her.

"It's your lead, then. Show me to the magic."

Somewhat relieved by his submission, she led the way without further comment, hoping the impulse for mischief was out of his system.

"Hey—you know—" Lyal broke in recollection of whom he had seen from the station's summit. "There's another guy here—just like me, I guess? Do you have, like, a 'phone' to check the news or something . . . in case anybody's noticed him?"

Her eyes crept over to him in a blank stare. "I'm afraid that's not how it works," she replied.

Lyal stopped.

"What does that even mean?" he asked, throwing both hands in the air before jabbing his finger at her back. "Hey, you know what? I've never respected straight answers more in my eighteen years of life."

She offered no clarity, however, which further reinforced Lyal's belief that no matter his demeanor, serious or otherwise, his search for answers would hit a dead end. The cross-dimensional duo passed through the bustle of phantoms on their journey to the outer path of the enchanted square. With the distance put between them, and the hectic scene at the station, he discovered a moment of tranquility in their movements through the mystic sheet of mist in the streets.

"Can they see me? A simple 'yes' or 'no' will do," Lyal asked.

"They know you're there, but they don't want to look at you."

He laughed. "Okay. Then, maybe if you stand real close, they won't look at you either."

The girl passed through the crowd with great care to those around her. "It's like I said before. You're different—you're trouble."

"Yeah, I know," Lyal replied as he carelessly meandered through the flow of phantasms, taking a moment to examine that winter-cursed metropolis.

A faint line cut down in front of his eye, and he raised his head. The star relic in the tower's grasp cast down hundreds of starlight beams. They scanned all across the square, like the sensors of a machine performing analyses.

"You know, this place is pretty incredible. It would be a real shame to not see it all," Lyal said.

She turned to him, surprised with his sudden change in decision. "Well, we have to go to the other side of town."

"Great. You got a car or something?" he asked.

"We could hail one around here—hold on—"

She turned to search the area for vehicle in the immediate area, but their moment of peace was cut short. From each side of the square emerged police cruisers in hover across the alloy street. They burst out onto the square and banked into a full stop that left the chassis wobbling.

"Looks like we're out of time. We gotta split, stranger," Lyal warned, then greeted trouble with an arrogant grin.

He tried to grab her hand, but it passed right through.

"Oh, right—" Lyal chuckled. He shrugged, turned, and took off for the spire-peaked goliath past the garden ahead of them. She stepped after but, but hesitated, wide-eyed in shock.

"Come on! Don't just stand around," he teased.

She did a double take, first to the cruisers, which reared up as they sped forward, then to Lyal, who had already cut into a nearby garden.

There, large pinwheels spun atop small man-made mounds. Spread throughout were brushes and greenery, the landscape carved through by a cobblestone road. Lyal bounded across the plain and slapped one of the silvery wheels with his hand, which sent it into a wild spiral.

He arrived at the road's end and came face-to-face with the spire in all its striking glory. The grand entrance of the city center rose fifteen feet to massive double doors, proceeded by rounded stairs much too bold and conspicuous to be of any aid to them in their escape.

The rogue visitant searched with excited eyes and found a promising destination only a few yards down. Suddenly, a haunt cut past his focus.

It was her.

Lyal pointed out their possible salvation as she arrived at his side then; together, they sprinted crossed the main road. From every road into the square, the police cruisers swarmed. They cut to the left and shot across the sidewalk until their destination was just within reach.

He had discovered an open grave, a staircase down to what he believed was a dive bar that lay nestled between two neon-traced nightclubs, each of them a blur behind the mists. At the head of the covered descent was a hanging brass plate that bore the image of a beaming star: to Lyal, a symbol that made him sure that he had found the way.

The patrol cars hit the corner on all sides of the road. The phantom fugitive turned to the troublemaker with worry in her eyes, uncertain of where his guidance would take them. Lyal looked back at her, completely apathetic. He gave a nod toward the pit with a wily grin and led the charge toward the unknown beneath.

***

Arriving at the stairs, Lyal cut around and leapt on the rail. He rode into the descent as his clumsy companion stumbled down the steps behind him, the police strobe shredding the darkness all around them.

A black iron door wrapped by a pulsating strip of violet neon awaited them at the bottom, a portal into an obscure place. Lyal struck the ground at the bottom, turned the handle, then burst through the door with his shoulder. His companion entered behind him, and they fled through a dark corridor, together. In a bizarre twist, they found themselves on a meandering path into a forming reality.

They drove through door

after door

after door

after door

. . . which seemed to take them ever deeper into dreary catacombs that refused to end.

"Whoa, where does this place even go?" asked Lyal, entertained by the arcane experience.

They breached a final doorway and were met by a breath of wind that kicked of their hair, of both the boy and the illusion. They crawled to a halt, having finally reached a place undisturbed by the sounds of police sirens.

Above them swung an iron-framed lantern, whose haunting grace revealed odd guidance upon the red bricked wall, the words FORGET EVERYTHING sprawled across in black spray paint.

Lyal examined the words, admiring the fragments of a foreign culture in that seedy crypt. It was vastly different from the pristine, winter-cloaked city they had left behind, and standing there left him unsure if they were in the same place at all.

The corridor was like that of a grungy back alley, a weathered brick road, and dilapidated brick walls, all contained inside a starless void, as evidenced by the darkness that hung above them, that place, a channel of another realm linked to that winter city in a pocket of time and space.

"What is this place? Some kind of underground?" Lyal asked his troubled guide, so enthralled with the odd realm that he had forgotten his expectations of her.

"I don't know . . . I never come down this way, but we can't go back now," she stressed.

Lyal waved her off yet again, however, still unthreatened by the hazards of fantasy.

"Relax. We're just taking it slow a moment," he said.

"They're not going to stop chasing us. You don't understand what will happen if we keep causing trouble."

"I—think—I—do—it'll be another unexplained thing. Then, another something more out of the ordinary," he said as he circled the phantom. "What else is there to expect?" Her unruly guest bent forward and slapped the back of his hand with each point to drive home the message.

"It'll be one more reason to ask another question. One more moment to get caught up in confusion. It'll be one more metaphysical road to nowhere . . . and look where I am, now," he said as he opened his arms to the obscure world around them.

Feeling his understanding was made clear, he turned away from her and started down the hallway in a nonchalant stride.

"I'm gonna call you Tory," he said in conclusion. "Because you *worry* too damn much."

She shook her head to the visitant's brazen ignorance, but followed as he proceeded through the corridor. They eventually went around a bend and encountered a sparking crimson that illuminated the corridor from across a short bridge.

It was a flicker born from a finely traced neon glyph, a sprawling scribble that, although unintelligible in meaning, appeared thrilling in its design.

The fugitives traversed the bridge, over what appeared to be an endless abyss. Across the way, the foreign signage beaconed while neon eyes blinked in the wayside shadows, sharpened in curiosity, like glances across a bar. To Lyal, it was a choice passage that might proceed to some otherworldly pub.

"This place is restricted. We really shouldn't be here. It's reacting to you," the phantom warned as she hid her face from the hypnotic gazes in the dark.

"Great! All the more reason to be right here. Besides, isn't it just a bar?"

Through the timeless corridor came a dance of celestial keys and the rhythmic tap against the symbol's edge. His ears perked up, graced by a sound more familiar to him than anyone else. Accompanied by dreamy pad and driving bass, a danceable track was molded by the collision of sounds that drifted in softly, then climbed in anxious focus. As it played, he followed in his head an identical composition.

"Speaking of which, you hear that? That's a real familiar one," Lyal said.

She looked at him in silence, her head cocked in bewilderment.

"Yeah, this place is just what I'm feeling right now. Where's that at?" he asked, as he looked around in search of a source. "Where's that coming from?"

Lyal noticed a dingy metal door just below the flickering neon scribble from behind which the music seemed to originate. He found it rusted and plastered with the graffiti of love and countless stickers, layered so many times over in each corner that it was difficult to distinguish them, an alluring divide.

The clearance beneath the doorway was a multicolored fuse that skimmed to a brilliant light show within. Lured by the thrill, Lyal went right for it.

The electronic track came to pummel his eardrums as he approached the entrance of that lively place, but just as Lyal went to take the handle, the phantom stepped out to block his way.

"What are you doing, *Tory?*" he asked with faux bewilderment. His smirk returned. "Oh, yeah." He then stepped right through her. "Never a bad time to have a good time," he advised from over his shoulder.

Lyal pulled open the door, and blinding lights and thunderous aural energy were unleashed upon them. The outsider threw up his hand to shield his eyes but continued through, eager to take in every experience the otherworld's haunt had to offer.

He had never heard that particular track played for an audience, and even in that cranny of nowhere, hearing it played over the sound system felt incredible to him. He relished in the punch of the kick that laid into his chest and rattled his beating heart. It filled him with drive and made the long nights spent to craft it worth the headache, the doubt, and anguish.

Was this real? It couldn't be.

But that was okay.

It didn't have to be to be enjoyed.

As Lyal meandered through the dark room, he drew the sunglasses from his pocket and slipped them over his eyes.

The music moved him and returned him to a place of familiarity. The track picked up momentum, and he smirked. It energized, relaxed to a starry cascade, then picked up again to ethereal chords, all while riding on waves of an endless ocean toward destiny. An evocative storm approached on a cerebral dark horizon, and each time an arpeggio peaked, something moved to the rhythm in the shadows before him, a phantom being, just like his companion, though adorned in something that shrugged off the touch of winter.

The phantom dancer was adorned with ribbons in her luxuriant hair and around both arms, and wore a stack of bracelets along her forearms. Lyal watched in curiosity as she twirled in an opening in the crowd, just ahead of him, but she vanished when a couple passed in the space between them. He pondered to himself for a moment. There had been something undeniably familiar about her.

The electronic track faded to simmering static and a dramatic chord, and somewhere in the void left behind, a lost maiden sang. Lyal recognized those words of yearning at once but couldn't grasp the songwriter's name from a strange fog that had come to envelop his mind.

Although lulled into a trance by the tender-voiced siren, Lyal realized something was missing in that odd fantasy, the ones he had been searching for. He searched for the dancing spirit, but she was nowhere to be found.

From above came the glow of a sparkling disco ball, and its silver beams glided across the glossy checkered floor. The otherworld, it seemed, wouldn't let the celebration end so easily.

Lyal, realizing he was adrift, began to make his way politely through the illusions, forgetting that he could simply pass through. His eyes began to hunt the chaos like that of a lost child, finding himself abandoned in his own dream.

From an arcane flash, the revelers became encased in nightmarish blue armor, soldiers looming on the dance floor. Lyal blinked as he shuttered to that vision, but reopened his eyes to find them as phantom folk again.

In that moment, he realized the danger that was present. That city, this realm, whatever it was, had to be more closely connected to the invaders than he hoped.

He had to find the ones he had come looking for, and they had to escape.

Upon reaching the outskirts of the dance floor, something caught Lyal's eye: the peculiar dancer sitting at a high-top at the distant bar, glowing with a smile as she conversed with some phantom stranger.

Spellbound, he approached her like a mindless puppet, and as he stepped onto the rise off the dance floor, he became sure it was her.

"Miyac—"

Before he could get the name out, a trio of young ladies rushed by with arms linked, and when they had passed, she had gone. Frantic now, Lyal hurried to catch another glimpse of her but found no trace, so he turned to the crowd.

He thought he caught something just at the corner of his eye, a wisp of almond hair aloft in her wake. She vanished into a vibrant bustle almost as soon as he had noticed her, so he turned around, then noticed her against at the far side of the dance floor.

Lyal pursued the phantom as she pulled him all over the room, offering only a glimpse each and every time.

"What the hell!" he said, frustrated with the chase.

But it was Miyacre. There was no doubt in his heart, and he wouldn't give up now when his suspicions had been all but confirmed.

"Stop, that isn't who you think it is," called his phantom accomplice. "I'm trying to help you."

Lyal turned and yanked off the glasses to expose his frustration.

"Are you joking?" he cried. "You said there was a strange girl who came here, or whatever, and I literally just found her."

The girl shook her head, barely visible in the strobe lights all around. "She's—oh no," the phantom said, her eyes wide in terror as the music went silent.

Fed up with her interference, Lyal turned to confront the disturbance himself and was stricken at once with awe. He inched forward, mouth agape as he returned his sunglasses to his pocket.

It was Miyacre, standing in perfect stillness, her back turned to them.

As he looked upon her for the first time in months, he noticed the silver crest of the invaders molded on the bracelets around her arms. As he did so, she turned over her shoulder and began to watch him.

"Miyacre . . . why are you wearing those bracelets?" Lyal asked, though she only continued to look on in silence. "Miyacre, say something! I came all this way to find you."

Lyal stepped forward to take her away from that corridor of illusions, but his companion gasped as he took the step, and reached out to try and take his hand. Lyal's heart skipped a beat as the lights of the venue came on, then yanked his arm back.

The revelers had all stopped and now stood with their attention turned to Lyal with an eerie vacancy in their gaze. Miyacre closed her eyes, and her entire form became enveloped in light, which was transformed into a fierce bolt of lightning that lashed up to a balcony at the far side of the venue.

"Whoa! Wait!" Lyal cried as the streak became a luminous glint between the fingers of an ominous figure.

The fugitives froze in the heavy presence of an imposing authority, who glowered in an imperial uniform of sleek indigo. It was a woman with bleach-blonde hair whose ponytail ran down to the tops of armored boots, and bangs hung over her eyes, so lush that they were left completely hidden. She flicked the light back over her shoulder, and it spiraled into nothingness. Then, from a dark corridor behind her emerged two jet-black drones with sinister, red-eyed sensors.

With a mere glance at the woman, Lyal became certain she was of invader allegiance. She was rather unique from other invaders, however. She wore no hood and was outfitted with a snug electronic device around her forearm.

The invader lifted her finger and struck a button on the controller.

Lyal's companion stepped back in a preemptive retreat.

"That's the overseer. I told you we shouldn't have come here," she said.

"Don't worry. Just back away, slowly. We just came here to party," Lyal said as he followed her lead.

An ominous rising hum of energy sang through the room.

The drones ascended as the invader leader raised her finger.

"No—no, it's time to get the hell out of here," Lyal said as he stumbled into brazen retreat.

The fugitives fled the checkered dance floor at full speed for the door behind them.

With the flick of her pinky and index finger, she signaled the drones to pursue the intruders.

The servants shot forward on fierce thrusters and fired twin beams from hornlike emitters at the bottom position of disc-shaped mechanisms. The beams met midair and merged into a deadly band of purifying heat between the machines.

Lyal looked over his shoulder and caught sight of the attack formation.

"Look at that bullshit. They're trying to fry us over a little trespassing?" he remarked.

"They're coming too fast. We've got to jump," the phantom warned.

"You think those beams can touch me, too? Never mind—not trying to find out."

The searing rays were upon them fast.

"Ready?" the girl asked. "Jump, now!" she shouted.

They leapt through the air, and the rays passed beneath their feet.

Lyal laughed nervously as the drones shot ahead. "Aye, I could do this all day," he bragged.

The invader leader reached out her arm and pulled her fingers back.

"They're coming back. Watch out!" The girl warned.

Lyal snapped from his swagger. The disc mechanisms had rotated. The beams were now locked into the top position, and death came right for their throats.

With a heartbeat to spare, the phantom ducked under and Lyal dropped to his knees, slid across the ground, then jumped back up when the beams had passed.

The gambler laughed again as his confidence swelled.

"We're almost at the door!" the girl said.

The overseer, refusing to let them escape her sport, jabbed the air with tremendous energy, and the fugitives watched as the room, and the door in front, extended farther into the distance.

"What the *hell* was *that*? Can she just keep doing that!?" Lyal cried.

"Stay with it. They're coming back!" the phantom warned.

Lyal looked over his shoulder and saw the drones approaching in a new pattern. The hornlike mechanisms had engaged in a swift rotation, bringing a newly formed oval cage around in a treacherous whirl.

Lyal's mind raced as he struggled to come up with a way to handle the predicament. It was too late. Something had to be done.

He felt the vibration of the beam in his ear and the heat at his back.

"Screw it—take a chance!" he said aloud, then sprang into a backflip as the cage of beams swept through.

The second pair of rays came around and missed, and Lyal slammed onto his back as the beams came around again and passed just beyond his nose, missing again.

He lay still a moment, realizing his fortune.

"Whew… been awhile since I pulled one of those off," Lyal said as he raised his back off the ground.

Rubbing the back of his sore head, he searched for his companion and, to his astonishment, spotted her at the wayside near the wall, just beyond danger's reach.

"Really!? Are you always gonna take the easy way out?" he complained.

She offered no reply but returned to his side upon noticing the hunters on approach.

"Look, here they come again," she warned.

"These guys don't take a break," Lyal remarked as he rose to his feet. "We can't keep this shit up forever."

The drones fired forward with a strident cry, their crossbeams offline but with pinpoint sensors crawling across his shirt. The gambler moved, and they moved with him, like a fight between wild cats.

The machines split away and ended up on each side of the fugitives, then threw up a semi-circular cage of beams around them, so tightly packed that there was no escape.

The machines' captives would need to participate in the overseer's deathly game.

In a sudden shift, the scorching cage was split down the middle by a wall of beams with the only means of passing through being two circular openings on each side.

The inner wall rotated, and Lyal and the girl leapt through the circle on opposite sides of each other.

He looked at her, slightly entertained; the phantom, not so much.

The wall rotated back. They leapt back through again. Suddenly the circles formed into a lone diamond at the center, putting them at opposite ends. Their eyes grew wide as the wall came around, scorching the ground with soot. As it made its treacherous pass, they leapt through the middle, passed right through each other, and landed on the other side. But it wasn't enough.

Lyal and his companion rose to the deathly glare of red. The beams came around once more, but before they could lay into the trespassers with searing heat, a wild bolt of lightning exploded out from an overhead light. It struck one of the sentinels with such strength that it was sent spiraling out of control.

The gate of death dissipated at once, and Lyal and the girl dropped to the floor just as the drone exploded against the brick wall.

The overseer turned her icy gaze on the source of the arcane attack, but another bolt had already left. The lightning lashed the second sentinel with even greater force as the unseen spirit's imbued ability awakened.

The second sentinel exploded in a ball of fire, which forced Lyal and the girl to cover their heads from a shower of red sparks.

"It's getting wild in here. We better split!" Lyal called out to his companion.

The gambler stumbled to his feet through the cloud of smoke and went to the girl, who still lay petrified with both hands over her head.

"Hey, shell bug, this is our chance! Come on, let's roll!" he cried.

She rose as quickly as her nerves would allow, and together they fled for the door again. Noticing their brazen retreat, the invader leader drew back her fist to expand the room again, but another bolt targeted her, and she was forced to reach for it instead. When the lightning of the rogue reached her, it was absorbed straight into her device, effectively neutralized.

The fugitives burst through the door and left the overseer fuming, but undeterred. In grim serenity, she hit a button on her device, and by her command, a hovering platform rushed out from a corridor behind her. It fell before the balcony, and she stepped onto the parapet and dropped down onto it. Then, with her targets far beyond the reach of salvation, the cybernetic disc lifted her and whisked her back into the corridor, where the walls were dotted with cerulean glints. The trouble had only just begun.

The Overseer

Lyal and his accomplice fled through the hall of the dark hollow. The brick walls gradually gave way to alloy plating, as did the cobblestone path, and the unmistakable crest of the invaders eventually appeared in the architecture of the arcane beneath.

They passed through an open steel-framed doorway, which was topped with a familiar element: the imprint of a shining star.

Their frantic footsteps echoed in the darkened chamber, which housed a massive computer console whose screen displayed the schematic outline of a sprawling city perched atop a top-like platform. Numbers on the side panel raced as countless unknown mechanisms ran diagnostics on the construct.

Subtle vibrations began to rattle the hunted as they dashed for the far end of the chamber.

Lyal tried at first to pay it no heed, knowing the source couldn't be anything short of a problem. Within a matter of moments, however, those vibrations strengthened to powerful tremors that began to throw them off their balance.

A distant siren wailed deep the abyss, and a warning beacon on the ceiling flared in tandem, bathing the area in crimson light. The fugitives slipped through another open frame at the opposite end of the chamber and raced across a canvassed overpass that cut across an immense drop into apparent oblivion.

"What do you think that was all about?" Lyal asked his winded companion, whose eyes darted around the vast assembly chamber.

"I'm not sure . . ."

A potent quake shook them and left them struggling for sure footing. Whatever it had been, it was closer.

"Let's not find out. Come on. There's only one way we're going now," Lyal said, hoping to encourage her.

They began again for the distant end, where a door etched with the invader's crest awaited beneath a balcony draped with long, indigo banners.

Before they had even reached halfway across, there came the terrible cacophony of grinding metal, machine joints, and pistons compressing.

The overseer's titan had come for them.

Lyal turned and watched in horror as a colossal shoulder of sheer super-reinforced alloy rose up from the abyss. It bore the inscription MVG.

The fugitives' flight came to an abrupt halt when a fierce tremor knocked them against the railing, and they latched onto the cold bar as the wicked blare of the titan's mechanized ascension left them deafened.

The cerulean radiance of its eyes seared the hope of the guilty as its armored cranium rose high above. Lyal turned from the blinding brilliance, his heart racing out of control.

The titan's joints screeched to stillness as it came fully upright, but the fugitives remained frozen, like prey before the jaws of the apex predator.

"You think it noticed us?" Lyal whispered to the girl, who was crouched just ahead.

The machine brought its hand back, then smacked the covering off from over them.

Terrified eyes rose to the gazing giant as the mangled steel soared across the chamber and crashed somewhere in the depths.

The titan, realizing its objective, brought its arms into an X formation, then drew them all the way back, its chest protruding as a brilliant light erupted from a tunneling clock with a thousand hands—installed within its luminous core and guarded by a translucent material.

Blessed with a surge of instant energy, the trespassers sprinted across the exposed walkway. Even at their most spirited, they could not outrun the giant, which needed only a few strides to match their pace. It stepped into the walkway behind them and smashed right through it, sending the entire structure sinking into collapse.

Lyal and the phantom were flung against the rail as the overpass swung out to one side, then rushed upward as the bridge began to sag, its structural integrity failing fast.

Behind the armored enforcer descended the platinum-haired invader on her flying disc. She opened her arms, and machinery began to assemble around her hands, encasing them piece by piece.

The giant plowed through the walkway as the fugitives fell across the ground before the open doorway. With the target in sight, the overseer reached out her hand, and her servant mirrored the motion, reaching for him as well.

"You shouldn't have ever come here," the phantom said, panting.

Lyal, seeing there was no escape, stepped up to the front of the path, which crumbled beneath the titan's advance.

"Don't worry. I wouldn't cause you all this trouble just to have you suffer the same consequences as me," he said. "Besides, I'm the one who broke all the rules. I'll deal with it."

"Are you crazy!? Just come on—"

"Run. If we're lucky, it's only gotta be one of us."

The ground quaked as the machine took another step forward, but Lyal smirked at the reaper's gaze.

"Hey, Clock-Blocker Unit 9-9-9! How about we chalk this up as a misdemeanor, first offense, huh?" the gambler teased.

The machine, unrelenting, went straight for him.

"Archangel!!"

The thunder of the word jolted Lyal from his moment of heroism, but he couldn't peel his eyes away from the enormous steel palm headed straight for him.

Something flashed before his eyes. It struck the colossus in the clock heart with such tremendous force that it sent the titan barreling backward, unable to regain control until it slammed against the wall at the far end of the chamber.

The last groan of the drooped bridge broke Lyal from his daze. He turned just as the swordsman planted firmly on the ground behind him, a vicious rage burning in his eyes as he prepared for a confrontation with the dread overseer.

The platinum-haired invader descended on her disc with icy glare set upon an old ally. She lifted her hand and brushed away her bangs from her right eye, and a glimmer of crimson beamed out from the dark, a machine eye much like those of her sentinel guard.

The sword split the ground before the swordsman and caused Lyal and the phantom to share a flinch in terror. Ultra pulled it from the ground and swiped it toward the invader leader, a sharp promise of what might come next.

The overseer let her bangs fall back, concealing that sinister red glow. Accepting that silent challenge, the disc pulled away from the path of the titan, which struggled to keep steady as stomped away from the crumbling wall.

Lyal fled the severed bridge and stopped just behind Ultra, who remained ready for his opponent's next move.

"Dude, you really got him good—"

There came a rapid click from the far end of the room that silenced the gambler at once. The giant took a step back. Then, the noise stopped.

"Get out. Now," the swordsman warned.

"I don't think he's getting up from . . . that . . ."

The odd clicking from the machine's clock heart sounded off again, identical as the first.

The giant took another step back, and the noise cut off again.

"Get out! *Go!*" Ultra shouted with desperation ablaze in his eyes.

Lyal exchanged a glance with the phantom, who had already fallen back in heed of the stranger's warning. Then he, too, began to inch toward the doorway, slowly realizing that the machine was possibly capable of something he wasn't prepared for.

The clicking rang out again, but this time it plunged into an ominous deceleration, dragging itself down into a deep crawl.

TICK

TOCK

TICK

TOCK

The colossus took a step forward, then another, until the hulking powerhouse was picking up speed at an alarming rate. The click accelerated as the thousand hands of its tunneling clock whirled round and round, the ticking merging into a single, piercing note, and the titan becoming a blur through time and space, its arms swinging in a ferocious assault.

Thrown in horror, Lyal and his accomplice turned and fled for the door to escape imminent annihilation. The swordsman stared down the time-shifted mega bullet until they had cleared the doorway, then turned and ran in after them.

The fugitives dashed to the center of the shadowy laboratory, and found five passages within, every wall crawling with the mechanisms of madness. Enormous glass capsules of neon-green fluid hung in clamped claw fixtures, each one alive with the heartbeat of test reactors sealed behind hyper-tempered glass, like a row of ovens built into the walls.

Their eyes suddenly crossed with twin glares of crimson. Two sentinels had awaited them there.

The swordsman stormed through the chamber, prepared to make it a battlefield, and leapt for the nearest drone and cut through it in a flip. It exploded as he planted back on his feet and then leapt over the second. He pierced the drone through the top, planted his feet, then launched the impaled machine at the wall, where it met a fiery demise.

"Go. We'll meet again," Ultra said as he threw out his hand to send them away.

The phantom spun around to seek direction from Lyal, who was dizzied by their options.

"For f—! Just pick the one farthest away!" he cried before breaking away.

As they fled the lab, five more drones stormed in and attempted to surround the defector.

The lead unit fired a scorching beam at once, but the swordsman raised his blade and caught it with enchanted alloy. The searing ray was deflected straight to the ceiling, where it reduced the metal along its path to a dripping melt. Ultra swept the blade around, guiding that scorching flow to cut down every other drone as they raced to fall into formation around him. He then turned to the lead unit, sidestepped its beam, and unleashed a wind slash with the swipe of his blade—a decisive strike through its armored shell.

In a moment, all his foes had all been dispatched.

The fugitives meanwhile sprinted through a supply bay whose stack crates were rocked by the footsteps of the colossus. Upon their arrival to a hallway at the far side, they heard the enraged titan rip through the last of the walkway just before the heart-stopping impact of absolute ruin knocked them off their feet and left them deafened.

The lead sentinel ignited into a fireball just as the colossal hand of the titan tore through the doorframe and wall, and its great padded shoulder finished off the rest. The swordsman had leapt fast from the ground and landed upon its arm.

The titan barreled through the chambers of the subterranean facility, attempting to seize him and failing time after time as Ultra raced along a treacherous landscape of vibrating plates, glowing cerulean fissures, and cooling vents—all while hunting for a way to neutralize the overseer's devil machine.

Even in its state of temporal overdrive, the swordsman proved too agile for the colossus. He leapt to its chest piece and slashed away at the glass-like material that guarded its whirling clock. It snapped away on its shoulder blade thrusters, retreating into the ruinous chasm, and the blast of its departure flung the kill-switch hunter onto collapsing ground below.

The swordsman reengaged the titan in a full-powered leap as the floor crumbled away, but in mid-flight, he was intercepted by a fierce uppercut delivered by the great war machine.

He tore upward through eight floors before bursting from the ground beneath the star-bearing megatower, across the streets of downtown.

The ground shattered under his impact, but without hesitation, he lifted himself back up—injured, yet resolute. Ultra glanced down, sensing the enormous energy of the titan on approach from beneath. He tightened his fist and realized he was without his blade. The disarmed duelist turned and found the instrument of his judgement pierced in the dirt before an arch that welcomed guests into a little park between the boulevards.

Ultra shot for it as the rumble from subterranean annihilation grew fierce. In a near instant, his desperate hand found the grip. He yanked the blade from the dirt, then leapt with his full strength. Just as he cleared the way, the arms of the titan tore through the frosty park plaza, its hands widened to apprehend him.

Concrete, mangled metal, and stray debris erupted into the air as the titan surfaced—nothing had hindered its advance.

Ultra had landed atop a skyway a few blocks away and watched with sharpened eyes as his mechanized foe began its approach from the shattered outskirts of the pit of ruin, its clock core, now silent.

From the cavernous abyss came a second swarm of sentinels from the subterranean nest. They stormed his position in angry fury, a last attempt at overwhelming him.

Gleams of crimson flickered through the night as they battled him between the parapets. They fired in short bursts, trying to deny him any opportunity to manipulate their weapons again, but their revised tactics couldn't match the elite warrior. Ultra carved through his foes' feeble armor as they struggled to surround him until the last of them tumbled lifelessly to the ground below.

Though the sentinels were unable to outmaneuver him, they had bought time for the colossus, which now stood just a few yards beyond the skyway. The devil machine set its cerulean gaze upon the swordsman. The swordsman raised his blade.

Over its shoulder, the platinum-haired invader rose on the hovering disc. She reached her arms forward, and the machine followed her movement on cue. Ultra watched closely and identified her ability to take control of the construct.

Flames erupted from the machine's wrists, and its colossal fists detached, then rocketed straight for him.

They reached out.

Just as they came within range, Ultra cut away to evade them, and they blew straight through the skyway—missing him both times but leaving the architecture severed and crumbling.

He glanced over his shoulder to see them circling back. As one punched through, he leapt onto it, letting it carry him high into the sky before he sprang onto a low rise. There, before the sleepy majesty of the winter-blessed Metro City, Ultra engaged the machine's fists in a dance of masterful evasion.

Lyal and the phantom woman sprinted out along a skyway on the far side of the plaza—a pathway linking megatower to skyscraper across the road, its façade bearing a gilded emblem of a crescent moon.

"See? I told you the elevator was a good idea," Lyal said. "Now let's find that future scrap metal."

They dashed to the smooth, lipped stone edge that was lined by a single rail. Eyes wide with the sparkle of awe, they watched the spectacle of battle as it played out below.

"I take it you've seen this guy, too?" Lyal asked.

She shook her head. "Just another invader, isn't he?"

"No, I think he's something a little more than that—" Lyal replied as she tried to keep up with the swordsman as he bolted around the plaza.

He turned away in a fit of frustration and slammed his fist into his palm.

"I'm tired of sitting on the sidelines. There's gotta be a way we can help," he said.

The phantom remained fixated on the colossus. "Look," she said. "Its arms."

Lyal turned his attention to whatever it was she saw. From the giant's severed wrists, twin silver barrels emerged from the empty sockets.

"That's not good . . . That thing's about to put holes in this city. We gotta do something," Lyal said.

The gambler sprinted toward the center of the skyway to get as close as possible to earshot.

"Hey! Hey! Watch out! That thing's packing some serious heat over here!" Lyal shouted.

The battle seemed to continue seamlessly.

"Okay, that was just a bad idea. I'm an idiot," Lyal admitted to himself.

The woman ran over to him, her eyes still fixed on something below.

"It heard you!" she said, panting.

"What?" Lyal asked.

He turned, still buoyed by excitement and not yet grasping what had transpired. But his smile wilted fast as starlit, blue eyes met his own.

The machine had fixed its gaze upon them.

"Bad idea is causing other bad things to happen," Lyal remarked.

"Well put," the woman replied. "Run."

Together they fled the railing in search of cover, just as the titan lifted its arm to put their refuge in its sights.

Amid his bout with the raging fists, Ultra cast a glance to the machine and noticed it was preoccupied. He gritted his teeth, and the immaculate blade shined bright. When the machine's left hand swept in to strike him, the swordsman leapt and sliced clean through its armor plate.

The hand went limp midair. Ultra caught hold of it as he landed, grimacing as he dragged the severed weight by the split plate. Spinning twice to build momentum, he launched himself into a vicious spiral. Then, with every ounce of strength he could muster, the airborne swordsman hurled the massive, weaponized fist straight at the distracted titan.

The mechanized missile struck the side of its head with a thunderous clap, which sent a sonic boom rippling across the city. The giant staggered through the park, tearing up the grounds with each unbalanced step. It finally steadied itself by slamming an arm into a nearby skyscraper, producing a terrible cacophony as it tore through the structure's interior.

The titan righted itself, then redirected its focus toward Ultra, who was in a low stance, ready to evade. Putting its foe to the test, the machine took aim with its right arm and fired without hesitation. A great red bolt erupted from the cannon, accompanied by a strident thunder.

Ultra leapt to an adjacent rooftop, then went from antenna to antenna to escape, just before the bolt met its mark. The roof of the low-rise blew away in a fiery explosion that lifted a thick column of debris and smoke through the air, and as the echo of the blast rolled across the sky, the smoldering shell began to fall into a slow collapse.

The temporal click of the tunneling clock rang out again as the titan trained its cannons on Ultra, tracking him even at his incredible speed. It fired off a merciless barrage, ripping through the buildings across the park-side block with the fury of an apocalypse.

Distant explosions made the skyway to rattle and shudder beneath Lyal and his phantom companion's feet. They dropped to the ground as they reached a suspended landing just before the double doors to the upper levels of the great star spire, then threw their hands over their ears as the mechanized menace unleashed hellfire upon a nearby block.

The skyway's supports released a spine-tingling din.

"It'll be alright. Just gotta believe everything's gonna be okay, right?" Lyal said, half-humorously.

Then, they lifted their heads to the ominous crawl of a deep crack. The girl lurched forward, yanked open the door, and rushed inside.

"Come inside, quick!" she cried, but misfortune had come for him.

Lyal turned to the door just as a cascade of falling stone filled his ears. The landing tipped backward, pulling his body with it, and plunged toward the street.

He swung upward and leapt out with a desperate grasp. Miraculously, his fingers closed around a firm metal door stopper, gripping it in a red-ballooned vise of strain. The door swung open over the newborn abyss to heaven, leaving Lyal suspended by a single, trembling hand.

The phantom rushed to the edge, her eyes widened with horror. She dropped to her knees, reached out, hesitated—then forced herself to commit.

Lyal shook his head in frantic refusal.

"Don't worry—I know you can't help—I'll figure it out," he said. "But man, I hope these are some—Beilkan-quality door stoppers."

The phantom's eyes flashed with the spark of an idea. She drew a deep breath, stood, and reached out toward the silver handle beyond the brink. It jiggled beneath the tips of her nails but stayed just out of reach.

She retreated to catch her breath. Lyal meanwhile took the side of the door with his free hand but slipped again, unable to catch the centimeter-long metal lip. The eternal snowfall fell around him as he watched the phantom with terrified eyes, his fate teetering on the mercy of her resolve.

Once more, she pushed herself past the edge of safety and into the grasp of death. She flicked her fingers down at the handle and, with persistence, managed to hook them around it.

She felt her weight creep forward as the door swung open to its limit, forcing her onto her toes to stay grounded. She dared a glance past Lyal, into the plummet to the sliver of road below. Her abdomen stretched and stretched from the strain until she could bear no more, and her toes began to drag toward the brink.

"You're doing great, shell bug! You're doing great! Just don't keep looking down—because I will instinctively reach out to catch you if you fall, and I can't promise we'll bounce— just sayin'!" Lyal called up to her.

In a stroke of fortune, her foot slipped into a crack in the ground, anchoring her in place. With newfound leverage, she drove her weight into the divot with all her strength.

Her efforts brought the door back toward the edge. At the brink, Lyal slapped his free hand onto the jagged ledge, released the sturdy stopper, and pulled himself over the severed stone until he was folded over the edge.

The phantom pushed the open door wide to give him plenty of room.

A vicious barrage from the battle below shook the structure once more, rattled the door off its hinges, snapped the fixture free, and it tumbled toward the street.

"That was a hell of a door," Lyal remarked.

"Grab here—right here," the phantom said, panicking as she tapped her foot against the divot she had anchored herself in.

Following her lead, Lyal dug his fingers into the jagged groove, mustered his strength, and pulled himself up over the ledge.

He crawled along the ground until he was certain he'd put enough distance between himself and the edge, then fell onto his back.

The girl scrambled over with frantic haste to see if he was alright, and to her surprise, she found him with a bright smile. This boy, always chasing a thrill.

Together, they had bested the cruel hand of tragedy, and as he lay there—alive with heart racing—he couldn't help but laugh.

"Get up," she snapped. "Don't sit there and laugh."

He continued, however, until there was something he wanted to say.

"You know—before, I really thought you were just some kind of illusion or whatever, but now I see that you're really somebody . . . somebody from another world. Hope that doesn't come off as offensive or anything."

"No," she said, shaking her head. "I get it. I didn't really understand you either. To me—to us—you're the phantom, but—"

She put her fingers to her temple as she tried to gather her feelings into something she could actually say.

"Somehow—before we met—I felt like I wasn't all here, like I was as fake as you thought I was. My life had already been decided, and no matter what I did, nothing was ever going to change. It's been that way for longer than you can imagine," she said. "And it's not just me. It's everything in this city, you know? It's like everything is all just—moving on rails to nowhere."

"Can't say I don't get it," Lyal replied. "So, it was an escape for you, too, huh?"

"Maybe I really was running for my life, running with you because it woke me up from the monotony. And now I'm running because it's what makes me feel real again."

Lyal laughed, humored by that reflection, and yet it spoke loudly to him, and he found something quite special in that woman from beyond his reality.

"Real, huh? Well, lucky you, running into a troublemaker, huh?" he joked. "We oughta do it again sometime. My world, maybe?"

Lyal rolled up, then got to his feet.

"Well, anyway, thank you—?" He rolled his hand, urging her to offer her name.

"Surelia."

"Surelia! Okay. Lyal. Lyal Abra. Glad we're on a first-name basis. Now, how about we find a way to make a change?"

He hurried back to the brink and peered out. The giant was advancing through the fiery havoc that now consumed the park below. The graceful sheet of winter had been erased—flames sweeping across the land and leaving only charred ruin in their wake.

The colossus closed in on a fierce clash between the swordsman and its flying fists, the right hand restored from system failure to fight once again.

One after the other, they lunged at the defector with relentless fury, bursting through ruin and ripping across the flames in an attempt to seize him.

For a moment, Surelia and Lyal found themselves entranced by that spectacular bout—but the giant's trajectory snapped Lyal from his daze and gave him an idea.

"Look," he said as he threw out his finger.

The titan approached a suspended metro rail line as it took aim at the embattled swordsman with its cannon.

"He's about to hit that line!" Lyal said.

He looked out at the multitude of cars in motion across the city's complex system, then turned back to Surelia.

"Tell me, is it possible to call a car to this area—like, fast?" Lyal asked with hands open in urgency as he awaited an answer.

She nodded nervously, aware of some consequence the visitor could not yet see.

"Yes, but—never mind. For me, though, it might be locked down—because of what we've done."

"Damnit!" Lyal said as he threw his hands down in defeat.

"But I know a way we can override it."

He sprang back to her, reenergized. "How!? What do we need to do?"

She pulled a slim silver phone from her pocket and swiped through a few screens while Lyal watched from over her shoulder.

She then tapped an icon that bore the image of a metro car, and after two quick flips through the application, she reached a barren menu with a strikingly large red button at its center.

The glow of mischief flickered across Lyal's face. "Nice."

"We have to use the emergency call, but—"

"But what?" he pressed.

"If we call it from here, then the car will arrive—"

She leaned out over the brink and pointed downward. Lyal bent forward and followed her gesture. Below them lay the blasted remnants of a small station for the star spire. Now it was buried in debris, the rails smashed and twisted from the collapse.

"Down there."

Surelia looked up and noticed a troubling scene in the distance.

"Look . . . your friend," she said.

Before a looming clock tower near the far reaches of the ravaged park, the swordsman found himself worn down by the titan's hands. His movements had slowed, every lightning dash met with near-instant repositioning from the pair of relentless pursuers beneath that towering monument of quiet divinity until escape seemed impossible.

One of the mechanized assailants rose into a fist and, with a rapid click from the titan's arcane clock, came down in a near instant to crush him. Ultra summoned the sphere barrier and defended himself against the impact, though he struggled to keep it steady as the fist hammered into the liquid surface with barbaric fury.

All the while, the titan advanced—still on a collision course with the metro line.

Lyal turned away and paced back and forth in search of an idea. Too much was on the line for them not to prove—not only to the swordsman, but to himself—that the victims of the war could have a hand in their fate, even against the dread force of fantasy.

The gambler stopped as a thought dawned on him.

"The tracker," he said with the snap of his finger.

"What? What do you mean?"

"That application probably tracks location, right?"

She nodded.

"Not our location. The phone's location," Lyal clarified.

She grew still as she realized his intention.

"But how would we get it all the way over there?"

Lyal walked back to the half-vacant frame and looked up at the spire that rose into the shroud of snow, far beyond its ornate cornice.

"We go to the top and take a chance," he said as he turned to her and reached his hand to claim the device.

Surelia nodded, then placed the phone in his palm, laying her trust in the foreigner from beyond her world once more.

"Wait, there'll be medical staff on an emergency car, right?" Lyal asked, squeezing his temple in frustration.

"Just medic drones," Surelia replied.

"Oh! Okay, great!" Lyal remarked with a shrug of instant relief.

Wasting no time, he hurried into a grand hall where a lambent cerulean starburst hung above a junction of paths, its glow washing the marble floors in its shimmering light.

"Come on! We're going up—all the way up," he declared, and she followed with faith swelling within.

***

Out on the battlefield, the flurry of the fists had greatly weakened Ultra's barrier. It sparked and splintered, a complete shatter all but imminent. Then the scarred hand, breaking its rhythm, suddenly snatched him.

The flickering barrier held as the hand rocketed high into the sky. Presented with an easy target, the titan raised up its right arm and allowed the cannon to charge to full strength, then unleashed a single bolt upon its immobilized foe.

The raging blue bolt intercepted the hand with a hellish explosion that unleashed a dreary cascade of ash and debris, which rained down with blazing fragments that scattered across the battlefield. The colossus watched the downpour with its lifeless gaze.

There seemed to be nothing left.

It lowered its arm around a hundred yards from the metro line and, with is objective seemingly complete, retracted its guns back into the chambers in its arms—just before the last hand returned and reattached itself.

Lyal and Surelia emerged from a door to the snow-covered summit of the tower, a ravine between the horned spires. High above, the tranquil star at the city's sacred peak shined through the nether's shroud.

The gambler hurried toward a distant cornice at the far end of the ravine, a vantage where he was certain he would find the swordsman engaged in battle.

A sparkle in the sky drew Lyal's attention, however, and he noticed the remnant cloud of ruin.

It was eerily quiet atop the lonely summit. All the sounds of combat had ceased. Unsure why, he pushed onward until the burning park came into view.

There, he found no sign of the swordsman, and the machine had ceased its advance. The moment for triumph, it seemed, had passed— and the heavy weight of failure and disappointment settled over Lyal's consciousness.

Although it seemed so clear that all was lost, something inside wouldn't allow young Lyal to believe it was over. It was an odd sensation—one that made him think of someone else, the boy who had returned from the shroud. He felt it now, too, and could not deny the strength of that unbreakable faith.

With a sharp clank of metal, the process of reattachment completed; the titan's hand locked back into place. The colossal body turned to make its departure from the battlefield.

But then, there came another glint from high above; the shining rebirth of hope.

The gleam fell like a shooting star and struck the back of the titan's head with such tremendous force that a piercing shockwave rippled through the skies.

The invader monstrosity lurched off one foot, nearly toppling, but stabilized itself with a swing of its arms and a burst from its thrusters.

Lyal became frozen in awe. This battle was not yet lost.

A smoke-drenched fragment fell from the ruinous plume. Prismatic beams pierced the wispy cloak, and the barrier-encased swordsman plummeted toward the city. Urgency rekindled by that vengeful strike, Lyal turned for the sharp precipice of the metropolitan temple.

The swordsman dropped the barrier, threw out his arms to right himself, then slammed onto the roof of the clock tower's extruded entry hall. The clock face loomed just above him. Like the colossus's heart, it was a gutted portal, and within were a thousand hands, turning in an eternal spiral—every point, every moment, all at once.

The battle-scarred soldier stepped forward, small flames flickering across his tattered cloak. Ultra raised his hand, and from the sky the falling blade dropped into his grasp by the handle. Ready for battle again, he drew it over his shoulder and awaited the titan's move.

The titan slammed its foot to the ground in thunderous rage, its creator fed up with the defector's persistence. A rapid burst of the titan's clock tick split the air. In a near-instant movement, the machine lunged through the suspended metro track and seized the defiant swordsman, who managed to throw up the barrier just in time.

The section of rail that once stood between them had crumbled in the wake of the arcane blitz; the severed steel track now jutted toward the giant's back like the tip of an ever-still blade.

Lyal vaulted a short stone barrier and dropped into a dangerous dash toward end of the precipice. Two wings unfurled on each side beneath the way—an ornate stone seraph carved into the architecture, her palms cupped around a lambent snowflake.

He slid to a halt on the snow-covered plane, then patted down his pockets. In a desperate pinch, he pulled out his own phone—only then realizing he'd mistaken it for hers.

Stuck to the back of it was the Velcro ring and magnet-equipped lanyard.

He peeled the jokester's contraption from the smudged screen, then looked to Surelia, who hurried over with the key device in hand. Without thinking, Lyal dropped the useless items from his grasp. The magnet sank into the snow while the phone struck the stone through a footprint, which shattered its screen.

He clapped his hands together and then threw them up to encourage Surelia to throw the device over. But in her reckless hurry, her foot came down on a patch of covered ice.

Surelia's body pitched forward as her leg shot out from behind her. The phone flew from her hand, arching through the air—and soaring right over Lyal's head.

Their hearts went still.

In that moment, all Lyal could think of was the joker, the phone, and the trick, instant images in rapid flow.

As the Surelia lifted herself up from the snow, her hopeless gasp startled him into action.

The phone was in midair above him, coming down toward the edge like hope's sunset over the horizon. Happy neon faces along the walls of the surviving structures nodded in two framed laughter. Endsborough was the only answer, after all.

The machine pushed its capabilities to the limit, unleashing its full might, and put the crumbling barrier to a final test.

Lyal snatched the Velcro ring from the powder, turned, then took off for the pointed ledge. Guided by hope, the gambler cast the line. The magnet whipped out over the abyss, streaking toward the tumbling phone.

With a marvelous metallic snap, the magnet locked onto the back of the device, and Lyal felt his heart begin to pump again. The cord dropped over the edge, and Lyal dove after it. The weight of the phone gave a faint tug on his wrist as he slid across the snow toward the precipice—coming to hard stop just as the edge scraped across his chest.

Half-dangling over the abyss, his spirit filled with the fervor of triumph.

The phone swayed on the magnetic-tipped line—hope hanging by a thread, but saved.

Lyal let out a whoop of joy.

"Kaiser, you're the man—*the man!*" he cried in celebration as he carefully reeled in the line until the phone was safely back from the plummet.

He retreated from the edge, pried the magnet from the back of the phone, and flipped the device over. The emergency button remained.

"Here's to having one more chance," Lyal said, ready to act.

The battle wouldn't be stalled for their revelry. The giant had pulled the swordsman in close. The pistons in its arms cranked and thundered as the barrier cracked and splintered under the raw force of its grip. It watched with void-like eyes while Ultra strained to keep the shield intact.

On the star spire's precipice, Lyal closed his eyes to steady himself for the final pitch. He pinched the phone between finger and thumb, then tapped the emergency button.

With the critical function engaged, his left foot came back as his arm swept across his waist. Then, with all the strength he could muster, he unwound into a full-bodied swing and hurled the device across the sky.

An incessant screech rang out as the twinkling red star arced through the night.

In moments, the blare of the alert grew faint as their wish sailed long and far.

Ultra faltered beneath the gaze of the giant. Kill driven, it crushed down with relentless force, driving it's might against the failing barrier as cracks split across its surface and the etheric sparks flew.

Silence remained at the tranquil summit, and Lyal turned to Surelia to take in her reaction. Her expression remained blank—uncertain of the outcome and suspended between hope and dread.

Then, a strident siren pierced the airwaves. Lyal spun toward the sound, and there it was—the fruit of their efforts, blazing into view.

On the high rails shot the speeding missile, its emergency bar burning with crimson fury. The giant turned, but fate's gavel had already struck. The emergency car flew off the severed rail and slammed into the alloy hull, erupting into a fiery explosion born of pressure and raw energy.

The titan released the captive swordsman as it staggered forward, then barreled into the neon-covered building across the road— silencing the midnight mockery.

Lyal threw his arms into the air in celebration as the sparks of ruin lit up across the park like a festival of lights. The metropolitan wanderer rushed out onto the spire, her face alight with excitement and hands clasped.

"You really did it!"

"Yeah, we did."

He smirked at her.

She smiled at him.

Overjoyed, Lyal turned back to the battlefield and lifted his arms to the shrouded skies in the realm beyond his reality, then whooped at the top of his lungs in defiance of Eternia's glorious reign.

The swordsman collapsed to the ground, crippled but saved. He passed a glance to the distant summit where Lyal and the Surelia celebrated. A subtle shame tugged at the invader elite—knowing he had been delivered from defeat by their interference—yet gratitude followed close behind,

But he knew the titan would not fall so easily, and with a fight still ahead of him, he dismissed further thought of it altogether.

Ultra glanced to the staggered machine, then shot to a nearby light post. With a charged sweep of his blade, he carved through the top to sharpen it into a spear, then cut through the bottom to liberate it from the base.

Ultra sheathed the blade, seized the crafted spear with both hands, and leapt onto the concrete stump.

The swordsman knelt, then burst forward toward another light post across the path.

He snatched the pole with his free hand and whirled around into a fierce spiral. The titan crept up from the debris as the invader observer saw his plan unfold before her eyes. He wouldn't allow her to intervene.

With the momentum he had gathered, Ultra released the sharpened kinetic thunderbolt at the giant's clock heart.

The tick of the clock revved, then choked to a stop as the energized javelin impaled the protective barrier. The hands of the clock stalled to the obstruction but tore soon through the feeble metal, freed once more.

The titan grabbed the javelin and tore what remained from its temporal heart, then returned the makeshift weapon with deadly force. Ultra leapt clear to the far side of the park as the fragment ripped through the ground and vanished somewhere beneath.

The machine lifted itself from the ground and slammed its foot down onto the debris, channeling the overseer's rage. Then, from deep within its core came a sound, one so very ominous that it seized the attention of the three heroes at once. Lyal and Surelia looked on, oblivious to the catastrophe that was about to unfold.

The giant limped toward the center of the decimated park, then faced the clock tower. It brought its arms together in an X formation once more, then drew them back—and before its temporal core, a bizarre and sinister dark energy began to form in a wicked spiral.

Lyal felt his foot slide toward the edge of the precipice and instinctively yanked it back.

"We need to get back inside," he warned, realizing that something menacing was being formed.

"What is that!?" Surelia asked.

Something struck Lyal's foot before he could make a guess. He looked down and noticed his phone pinned against his shoe. In a swoop, he retrieved it, then returned it to his pocket.

"Yo—come on, you seeing this!? We have to get off this roof," he said to Surelia as he retreated from the treacherous ledge.

The forming void sphere before the clock whipped, lashed, and spiraled ever more violently as it continued to swell.

"Hey—time to wake up! *Go!*" Lyal cried, waving his hand through her phantasmal form to try and grab her attention.

Snapped from her fixation by his frantic movement, Surelia nodded and bolted for the door, Lyal following closely behind. Loose rubble began to rumble and shake—an omen of impending destruction.

The giant's arms drew back to their limit as a zipper of time and space ripped open inside the dark sphere and roared into a cosmic inhale that swallowed dust and debris from several blocks away.

The flames across the park vanished at once, and the swordsman bolted away as the pull of the gravity well intensified.

In his desperate flight for safety, the swordsman searched his mind for a way to vanquish the titan. His gaze rose, and he spotted twin forked spires at the top of the clock tower, spaced only a few feet apart.

The force seized him, dragging him backward, but he resisted and leapt away, then fought his way to the back wall of the clock tower.

Ultra drove his fingers into the bricks and clawed along the side wall of the building as fragments of stone, metal, and earth ripped past him toward the monstrous singularity.

His foot slipped, and the phantom hand of gravity jerked him loose. In full exertion of his power, Ultra blasted forward in two lightning dashes that put him within reach of the tower's corner.

A wall of sound slammed into him as he pulled himself around the edge—yet even there, he found himself pinned to the wall under the well's influence.

At the summit, Surelia burst through the door, and Lyal followed close behind. He turned and swung the door shut, but the instant it met the frame, it warped, buckled—and then, just moments later, was ripped into the air. They gathered behind a wall inside as the star spire rumbled and groaned to the singularity's ever-growing strength.

The swordsman vaulted up toward the forked spires and was yanked back to the wall.

Eyes wide with desperation, he planted his boots and forced himself upward with all his might.

With his entire being poured into each agonizing step, Ultra climbed the left-hand tine. Near the peak, he swung his right leg out onto the opposing prong, then drew his sword.

The battered warrior steadied himself and took himself through the narrow gap—dead on target.

The sound of the all-consuming gravity well alone sent shocks through him as he fought against its impossible grasp. His teeth clenched under the strain, the pressure intensifying by the second. The invader's ethereal spirit seemed to wane as the clock tower splintered in cracks and suffered breakaway fragments.

The singularity let out a wicked growl, and the swordsman's boots punched into the concrete.

Within the star spire, Lyal and Surelia jolted as a section of wall farther down the walkway tore out through the sky, prompting them to inch toward a safer position to escape the newly formed vacuum.

Meanwhile, Ultra—driven to his limit—closed his eyes to steady his mind and spirit. Given no other option, he tapped into the forbidden bond to secure the strength necessary to finish the fight. His eyes snapped open in a burst of cerulean light. Rejuvenated in an instant, the invader arched his back, ready to give the blade to gravity's pull.

Below, the thousand hands of the clock crawled through their rotation as the well expanded, stretching the fabrics of time and space. The monstrous void bellowed a guttural howl as debris from across the land spiraled into the dark and winked out of existence.

The swordsman's eyes blazed as buildings around the park lurched toward the gravity well, and the titan's armor began to rip away, piece by hulking piece.

Then, came the fatal opening Ultra had waited for.

Unable to supply enough power to sustain the singularity, the colossus began drawing its arms back together, and in the very instant the well's strength faltered, the swordsman let the blade fly—releasing at the final moment of maximum force.

It was over. The guillotine's edge flew at near light speed.

The hungry abyss beyond the temporal nexus vanished, and the titan's arms flung forward as the sword's impact against its heart hurled its massive frame into the air, sending it crashing through the arch at the head of the park.

The forks of the clock tower snapped in unison, and the swordsman flew forward to the closing force of the vanquished singularity.

The clock tower's prongs slammed into the ground and exploded into rubble, and the swordsman was driven face-first into the charred earth, his legs lifting skyward as his momentum carved a trench through the dirt.

Far above, atop the megatower, the great star was snatched from its cradle, too, and the sacred relic plummeted and shattered across the street below. The city's ruin was complete.

The death-fated titan staggered as it stood from the violent recoil. The blade had found the deepest chambers of its precious mechanism. Across the battlefield, the swordsman's legs finally struck the ground— bringing his savage trek through the dirt to an end.

It was a direct hit. The colossus staggered back to regain its balance, but its legs malfunctioned beneath it, trembling with erratic jitters. It lifted a finger to its shattered core, but didn't touch—hesitant, as if it stood in disbelief.

The titan's head lifted to find the swordsman stumbling from the trench. One eye still gleamed, but the other hung heavy with exhaustion. He stood on shaking legs, weaponless, awaiting the outcome of his strike—no longer possessing the energy to move.

The ticking of the temporal heart surged—then stopped. Then surged again, only to fall silent once more.

Up in the spire, Lyal raised his head and looked to Surelia, staring in disbelief.

"No way."

He jumped up and dashed down the hallway to the breach; she lifted herself up and followed behind. Lyal and his companion arrived at the breach and beheld, with awestruck eyes, the giant—its finger still raised to its stricken core.

The device's tick surged again, then plunged into the dreaded crawl. Terror gripped them as they prepared to witness yet another all-out assault from the titan.

But then, with a loud, metallic click—a final, gentle release—the mechanical tyrant toppled back into the abyss from which it had risen and vanished into darkness.

The impact from below shook the city, causing loose bricks and fractured architecture to tumble away.

The swordsman, victorious against the mechanical monstrosity, leaned up against a nearby mound of displaced dirt. As the cerulean glow in his eye dimmed back to clarity, he pushed forward, stepping slowly through the absolute devastation left behind.

It was all the remained—destruction, just as it always had. Perhaps he had achieved victory, but the outcome was all the same. As he gazed out over the ruin and unseen death behind it, a familiar misery nestled up to his spirit.

The overseer peered out with her hand beyond her chest just as the giant had. In a sudden fit of rage, her fingers curled like claws. Wild scarlet electricity crackled between her fingers, which blasted away the mechanisms that had encased her hands.

The invader leader's crimson eye glared upon Ultra, who staggered forward, held together by sheer will alone through his severe injuries. The machinist turned away, however, and retreated into the mist, leaving her wounded opponent to a moment of respite.

Up at the breach in the spire, the fortunate companions from across time and space erupted in a victorious cheer. Lyal threw his fist into the air, his triumph reflected in the bright, breathless smile of his phantasmal friend.

"Oh—sh—hey, we better get down there and see if he's alright," Lyal urged.

With fresh urgency, he turned back to the edge and scanned the ruin below, searching for any sign of the battered warrior. Surelia stepped beside Lyal and noticed the swordsman almost at once.

"Look—there. Near the middle of the park . . . what's left of it," she said as she guided Lyal's eye with her finger.

There, a lone figure limped toward the great maw beyond the shattered arch.

"Damn . . . he looks hurt. But, hey—maybe he can, I don't know, put himself back together with some of that magic or whatever," Lyal said.

"I'm not sure," Surelia replied.

"Let's get down there before the flying psychopath decides to show back up with more machines and other bullshit," Lyal said.

They beat a hasty retreat back to the stairs to begin their descent to the ground level, where ash and ruin awaited them.

Ultra limped past a crumbled base where a leg of the arch had once stood. He went step by careful step through the remnants and stopped when he reached a severed segment of wall not far from the ruinous pit. Exhausted, he set his hand against the slanted plane and collapsed against it.

The Consequence of Faith

Surelia and Lyal eventually emerged from the rear entrance of the megatower, beneath a crumbling portico of polished stone. He faltered a few steps after they reached the shattered street, bending over his knees to catch his breath as shards periodically sprinkled from the ruin behind them.

"Now, I'm really feeling like I was a part of the battle. Whew . . . those stairs kind of became a mind fuck after the twentieth flight . . . You good?" he asked, turning to his phantasmal companion, who appeared relatively rested.

She offered no reply, however—only a gentle, reassuring glance.

"We're good . . . Okay, let's get there," he said.

Together they left the road and crossed onto barren earth to reach the wounded swordsman, who remained braced against the torn masonry.

"My man—you alright? It's kind of insane what you just pulled off," Lyal said.

"It was what needed to be done," the traitor replied. Ultra rose and steadied himself against the wall. "I thank you . . . you both did well," he said.

Lyal grinned, pleased to hear him lower his guard. "Yeah, man," Lyal replied. "But, hey—you heal yourself or something, right? You're in bad shape."

"If my bond with Eternia were not tarnished, these wounds would be nothing; torn asunder in one battle and restored by the next. Without that blessing, however, I'm afraid they will not go easily . . . Still, this bond remains. Master, it seems, has an enduring vision for me," Ultra said, then pushed himself off the wall with what little strength he had left.

"So you plan to carry on like this?" Surelia asked.

"It'll all simply take . . . time," the swordsman replied, as he stumbled forward in a renewed advance on the pit. "But, I will continue forward. Eternia's retainers.

(As long as the Eternia's remains, I cannot fall. Because—if he comes to face your army and I am gone, you will all certainly perish.")

Lyal, confused and frustrated with his response, threw his arms into the air. "So, where the hell are you going?"

"To retrieve the blade. Go, I will return to you when time and opportunity provides. Archangel has gone, so you should be safe, for now."

Lyal turned to his companion. "Gotta love the guy. He just does his own thing."

Lyal returned his gaze to the swordsman, who continued through the fiery remains en route to the dark maw ahead.

"Whatever, he'll be alright."

"You think so?"

"I highly doubt we could help anyway—let's get out of here," said Lyal.

He turned around and faced her. Her head sank, but popped up again. Her mouth fell agape as if she went to say something, but failed to let it out. She nodded without looking at him.

"Right—it's not far now—follow me, okay?"

She turned and started into a shaky ascent toward the fallen arch. Lyal saw through the faulty facade, but decided against further comment until they had come upon the final destination.

He followed her and sunk both hands into his pockets.

They crossed the entire park without a word, maneuvered around the severed clock tower and through the leaning city toward a distant staircase that was enormous in size, reaching twice the width of the entire boulevard. The city seemed to end at a wall and continued against at the manmade second level.

There was no movement on the streets there, no phantasms, no bustle of the city; it was devoid of the mystic life he had first encountered there. It was no surprise, given what had occurred. Though he could see no bodies, he wondered if there were those who had perished in the battle between the invader elite. There was discomfort in the thought of asking his companion, especially now when she had confined herself to silence.

Perhaps, he thought, *she knew there was someone she had lost.* And Lyal Abra shared in that feeling in regard to his mother, whom he had kept at the back of his mind in fear of the emotions her absence might produce. But as he looked upon the girl, he noticed that she had lost much since he had first encountered her there outside of the city. Gone were her purse, scarf, and now, her phone.

This otherworldly stranger had given more for him than any other before her, and for that, he felt a desire to keep this stumbled-upon friendship forever. Such a kind soul, he felt, deserved a friendship and existence that was so much more real than this.

Silence yet infected their journey, however. They came to the base of the barren staircase, lit by cerulean bars beneath each step. Anxiety grew with each step, and the closer they got to the peak without speaking the more it bothered him.

As she set her foot upon the top, he stepped out in front of her.

"Hey, I'm not blind. What's wrong with you?" he asked.

Her eyes dove, her head already shaking in dissent. "No—nothing."

She sidestepped him up the last step but kept herself from breaking eye contact. They stood face-to-face, locked in each other's gazes as she fought to prove her innocence of conscience.

"Sometimes you only get one chance to say what you want to. Not trying to tell you how to live your life or anything. Just something that's been on my mind."

He turned from her and started on through the tunnel of the arch. She took a step forward, hesitated in frustration, but then pushed onward.

Far away from them, near the abyss where the machine was lain to rest, a figure appeared from around the alleyway.

With hand reached around the corner, out peered Little Eddie Bowitz, who searched the ruined plaza with that old glint of wonder, completely unnoticed by the world.

Lyal and the phantom had come to a long path with a shrouded end. The city lay darkened on both sides of them and left them abandoned beneath the hazy glow of the street lights.

Surelia looked at the ground beneath her steps with her lower lip pushed up in a thoughtful twist. Since she would not speak, he decided to push no further, a decision he knew he would regret.

He turned back to the road ahead of him. It was a somber one, dark and lonely into the mists of the unknown. What a dreary path it would be to take alone, unbearable, perhaps. What lay beyond the mist was lost in that veil.

Lyal lingered in his struggle, unsure, but took nonchalant steps toward end, trapped in the rhythm of forward.

"Lyal Abra . . . Show me what your hometown looks like, now that you've seen mine. I'd like to see what's outside this world—just as you have. Maybe I won't get the chance."

Delightfully surprised by her breach of silent reservation, he turned to her and nodded, calm and collected, as not to make curiosity anything more than normal.

"Yeah, sure—let me check that out for you," he replied, only hearing half her words.

He rummaged through his pocket, found the shattered phone between his fingers, then drew it out.

"Can't promise it'll hold a candle to this place," Lyal replied, his eyes down on his phone, going through motions to get to the photos.

Her head shook in a gentle fit of frustration with his assumption. "You're fine. I just want to see it," she assured with narrowed eyes.

Lyal handed her the device to reveal a world across the stars. She slid a finger over images of blue sky, backyard gatherings, and quiet suburbia; contemporary dreams behind a cracked window. Wonderstruck eyes beheld a gathering of friends at a forgotten temple with a striking portrait across the wall.

Intrigued, he watched her flip from photo to carelessly snapped photo, somehow enthralled with the transparent beauty of a normality now sadly out of reach.

Suddenly, he realized the sheer distance between these two realities, and he felt her; the heart in the phantom. It was undeniably human. That twin cerulean twinkle could hide nothing now that he understood.

Surely as the invaders had lain a terrible siege to their world, they had taken others. Was this a city that was or one that merely used to be?

"So, is that real to you?" he asked in a search of clarity himself.

She turned to face him, at the brink of spiritual fortitude. "Real to me . . . ? It's so much more than that."

"You know—I think that after all we've been through, you're more than real to me, too . . . Real doesn't have to end tonight."

She looked deeply into him as teary sparkles fell from her eyes, the heartstring snapped, in a free fall through a flurry of unleashed emotion.

He reached out his hand and placed it on her shoulder. He could feel it. The fabrics of the coat were nothing but true, and as he brought his hand up to her cheek, he could feel the tears.

Something greater than themselves became bonded, their spirits made one in the hot forge of destiny, leveled by great Infinity's hammer.

"This is real to me—thank you! I want to help you find what's real to you. You have only a little further to go—let's go."

Surelia pulled away from the gifted embrace and erased all that could tell truth from her face. She knew there was another whom he sought, and she wouldn't allow herself to desire more.

"Let's go," she repeated as she pushed on ahead, which left him to question her feelings.

Lyal pursued, but fell short. He hadn't meant to cause harm, but his mind remained entangled with itself. Perhaps, the explanation lay in plain sight, but he wouldn't meander any longer to find it.

"Hey—Surelia," he called.

She stopped almost immediately but refused to turn.

"Don't look so blue," he said as he went to her with a swing in his step.

As he arrived as her side, she struggled to come up with the words. "Sometimes, I wish I wasn't so confident in the things that I am."

He took her by the ear and pinched it. She flinched and jumped away.

"Ouch—don't do that," she complained.

"Yeah? You gonna do something about it?" he said as he continued after her.

"I will," she said with a brightened grin. "I'll kick you right in your face, asshole."

"Ooo, don't do that—I kind of want to get a date."

His confidence was swiftly countered by a scoff.

"Yeah right. I'd feel a little bad for anyone who'd date you," she toyed.

"Well, I mean—you already have a head start on feeling bad for yourself. So . . ."

"Oh, shut—up," she begged.

They went along together into the mists, locked in playful banter, the sadness swept away in the passage of time. She mocked him. He said something in return—a playful quip. She pushed him, and he pushed back, then fled. She pursued and soon they were completely gone among the electronic haunt of the billboards along the empty boulevard.

The Approach

Little Eddie Bowitz crept out from the alleyway and began navigating the ruin in the street. The air was heavy with gloom in the aftermath. Debris fell and tumbled somewhere in the distance.

The boy hurried across shattered ground, slipping once as brittle shards of concrete shifted beneath his weight. He picked back up on his stride and slowed as he neared treacherous outskirts of the gaping abyss.

Loose rock shook free from the shaft and tumbled into the depths. As he inched closer to peek in, he heard the crack of disturbed earth somewhere below. A gauntlet came up from the dark and snatched the edge with incredible force.

Eddie jolted, startled by its sudden emergence, and retreated a few steps before he realized it was only his hero of cloak and blade.

The swordsman pulled himself over the edge, then stood to his feet with a tremble.

"It's you—" Eddie said.

Before the boy could finish, the swordsman buckled in agony. He pushed himself against the face of a boulder that lay cratered nearby, though he knew he couldn't rest long.

Stillness was death. If fate grew impatient, time would surely strike him through the back.

"Are you alright . . . ? What happened to you?" the boy asked.

The swordsman looked to Eddie with a grim expression.

"You needn't worry about me. Look around. No outsider should have come here, but because another was able to slip through with us, the consequences are now immeasurable."

Even surrounded by the devastation, Eddie felt no inclination to derive from the path to find what he and Mirika had gone searching for. He could never leave it behind, not when it beaconed to him on tangible card stock and appeared to him when he closed his eyes.

"Why do you seek out a city in the sky? And what is it you hope to find there?"

Eddie looked up to Ultra with a confidence rarely felt. The answer was clear.

"Because that's how I can get to the great master. I'm going to go there and see him—and he'll make everything the way it needs to be—"

"Or the way you want it to be, Eddie Bowitz?"

Eddie fell silent at once. The swordsman, ready to press on, pushed himself off the rock.

The boy stepped up to him, compelled to contest his assertion.

"I don't want to hurt anyone," he said.

"But what would you do if you went opposed? What if the world refused the miracles you offered? What if a dream only became another reality full of suffering?"

He didn't know how to respond. How could his friend, Jamal, not desire a second chance? How could Mirika not want to find her home again? Who couldn't be convinced? Any defense the swordsman's assertions seemed ever more absurd and misplaced.

"Perhaps life, death, time, and space should not be tampered with. Maybe you will not understand until you've seen a million worlds burned in his vision. But, if you can look at all this around you and be unmoved, then how much misery will you be willing watch before your mind changes—or are you already numb?"

Eddie turned his eyes from the wounded hero but couldn't escape the ruination all around him. He looked across the smoldered park, then to the shattered star, and lastly the crumbling buildings, where surely there were many unseen who had perished.

As sadness weighed on the boy's spirit, the swordsman took up renewed stride toward the crumbling clock tower.

"I will take you to the city so you may see it. And maybe soon . . . you will find yourself. Let us complete this journey, together."

Those words stole Eddie from deepening grief and threw him into confusion. If the swordsman was willing to take him to the city in the sky, however, he would follow without a second thought. For in trying to reach a better world alone, he would find peace.

Although injured and limping, Eddie kept his faith in the swordsman, believing he couldn't fail in doing what he set out to do. Once they had found the great master, all that was wrong would be made right. If Mirika believed that were possible, so, too, would he.

"Whatever it takes—I'll see this through to the end," he swore to himself.

So Eddie trailed the swordsman through the park and onto the same road Lyal and Surelia had taken.

The boy went in silence in hopes of repelling further questioning of his faith. If only the swordsman knew it was all he had left.

Clutched tight to the vision in his head, he manifested that realm of promise, so that when—or if—that time came, he would be able to cast a wish that would let none of them down.

Those grand imaginings made short of their journey up the grand staircase and down the roadway on the second level. From there, it wasn't long before they encountered Lyal and Surelia, who were both leaned against the rail of an empty bike rack along the sidewalk—her hand raking his hair, his thumb passing her lip.

Lyal noticed them as they drew near and took immediate interest in the boy beside the swordsman—without a doubt the one of whom he had gone in search of.

"That's him! The kid I told you about," said Lyal to the phantom's bewilderment.

"Why did you want to find him so bad?" she asked.

"He made it out of the mists alive—all by himself," replied Lyal without further explanation.

He jumped down from the railing and made for the duo at the middle of the road.

"So! I took a high-speed train into the city, and you beat me in somehow. Care to explain that?" Lyal asked.

The gambler beamed with interest, but Eddie shrank, finding himself unable to comfortably match energy with this new character who had greeted him with questions.

"I—I'm not sure. We just walked until somehow . . . we were on a street," the boy replied.

"We went ahead of the pack long before you, but no one way into this place is the same . . . It is concerning, however, that you managed to reach this place at all," the swordsman said.

Lyal laid a hand on his waist, then released a deep sigh in acknowledgement of that exhaustive misadventure they had endured.

"Well! Here I am. Lyal Abra. Pleasure to meet you . . ."

He refocused on the boy of fortune again.

"You're him, right? You made it out of Salamandra all the way here? How'd you do it?"

Eddie was unsure how to answer, knowing the entire story would be too cumbersome for their urgent journey and, perhaps, too unbelievable. But Lyal disarmed him with his vigorous, bright-eyed interest in the beyond.

Perhaps they weren't so different.

"Yes, I did—but nothing I did was special. I just—walked, and didn't stop until I reached the camp."

"Well . . . what was out there? Did the invaders just let you just waltz on by?"

"When we left the capital, I never saw any invaders—except one . . . I guess," said Eddie.

And he suddenly didn't want to speak anymore. The memory of Mirika infected him profoundly, like a plague of despair. And so, in that silence, a noticeable oddity to Lyal, Eddie drove the thoughts of her to the back of consciousness with the other ghosts of the past that awaited his resolution.

"You were with someone else?" Lyal asked.

"It's irrelevant now," Ultra intervened. "We should push ahead before trouble comes our way. From here, our destination isn't far."

Lyal turned toward the swordsman, agitated now.

"Irrelevant? I finally meet this guy, and now I can't even ask questions? What the hell is up with that, my man? Why do you seem so opposed to the question-and-answer system?"

The swordsman continued down the road, leaving his questions unanswered.

Lyal dismissed him with a wave of his hand, then turned back to Eddie, who had taken interest in the phantasmic Surelia, who now approached.

"Who's she?" he asked with wonder-lit eyes. "You made friends with one of them?"

Lyal turned to her as she arrived next to him, then back to Eddie, taking notice of his curiosity.

"Yeah, you could say that. Why? You didn't talk to anyone while you were down there?"

"Well—no," Eddie admitted.

The sudden wail of police sirens seized their attention. The fugitives and the boy each turned to the road behind them but saw nothing.

"And that's where this conversation ends, because I totally thought they gave up," said Lyal, stirred by the sudden reemergence of authority.

The gambler turned and started down the road just fast enough so that his companions could join in.

"Come on! You guys trying to end up in the back of a cruiser?" he called back to them.

Eddie nodded and went second while the girl lingered for a moment, lost in a private thought.

But she, too, turned and fled with them toward the end.

"Guess they couldn't give us a break," said Lyal as Eddie and Surelia caught up. "Hopefully our man with the sword can."

They passed through a crawling fog and soon emerged to find their capable guardian, who had remained relentless in his onward press toward a final destination. The swordsman came to a sudden halt, however, and Lyal and the others stopped behind him.

Ultra's eyes fell shut.

"Hey—sorry to put this all on you at once, but we brought some— baggage. Nothing big . . . maybe like, one, two, or a hundred guys," Lyal said.

The swordsman lingered in stillness as he verified what lay before them.

". . . You alright?" asked Lyal, half expecting him to pronounce some cosmic awareness of their grave situation.

Ultra's eyes opened to the shroud that could no longer contain the great master's monument.

"It rises."

The rush of excitement sent Eddie tearing down the road. He stopped before he had gone too far alone, his eyes alight as he searched the dense cloud of gray that shrouded the distant skyline, though the miracle eluded him.

Lyal took a casual glance over his shoulder, noticing their pursuers had stopped behind them.

"Did we, like, step over the county line or something?" he asked.

There came a faint yet penetrating whistle from the distance beyond, one of which the phantom and mortal intruders had never heard. The ominous signal came first as something delicate, like the voice of an angel, but grew into a divine ring.

"There! It's there!" Eddie cried.

The boy raised a finger to the expanse where a rising glimmer pierced the dark. The glint sparked before it became a brilliant dazzle, and the noise grew to a guttural roar from the construct's mighty engine, a melt of harmonious sound that could only inspire awe from the most intimate depths of imagination.

As it's roar crescendoed to a screaming peak, a second skyline lifted across the horizon. Complete with ferris wheels that flickered in celebratory illumination, the construct flooded the foggy oblivion with vivid color while an enormous medallion on its face illuminated the invader crest in its sovereign glory.

The radiant awakening struck its limit, then settled into a lambent glow. Twin beams of light struck out into the dark skies and eased into a slow back-and-forth, the fabled city searching the vast reaches of the unknown.

And there it was, the city of legend before their eyes, liberated from obscurity, freed from the story of legend. Glorious fantasy, triumphant over a crumbling reality.

Eddie yanked the postcard from his pocket and raised it to the distant glitz, though he already knew that this was it. The boy felt happiness rush through every fiber of his spirit, and that feeling seemed so far beyond his reality that he realized it as something unparalleled by all that life had ever offered before.

"What the hell is that?" Lyal asked, turning to Eddie. "Is that what you went looking for?"

The boy inched forward, keen that he should hurry before anything tragic could separate him from fate. The transport had been summoned, and he couldn't be weak in his resolve, for the throne of Eternia was surely in reach, a mighty wish ready to be cast.

"I've got to go—I've got to go!" Little Eddie Bowitz cried.

"What!? You're honestly thinking of just going to that—whatever that is?" Lyal asked the boy with starstruck eyes.

Without a word, Eddie took off down the road, headed straight for it.

Lyal reached out to grab the boy but came up short of his shoulder, then sighed in frustration as he deliberated his next move. Growing ever more certain that this could be his only chance to find answers, he decided to proceed the only way he knew how: to leap with faith.

"What am I thinking?" Lyal asked himself as he began for the mists to absurdity.

 "Coming along?" he called back to his companion and the swordsman, who seemed rather unfazed by all the fanfare.

Feeling no presence at his side, he turned back around.

Surelia remained there before the lingering veil of mist, which was aglow with flashes of blue and red now, the hand of authority not far behind.

Lyal doubled back to her, and she looked away, knowing the time had come.

"Didn't you say you wanted to see other places? This is a good time to start—"

"Lyal—I can't go with you," she snapped, then let a smile slip through as she looked at that which was unattainable.

His eyes searched hers hopelessly for reason, and sadness took hold inside his chest.

"Why's that? Just come on! You'll be alright—I mean, I hope we will—"

The phantom wanderer remained quiet, as if she only wished to linger at that crossroad a little longer as time slipped away from them.

"We live in different worlds, but exist right now, in this moment, together. But in your world, I won't be able to go on forever," she said as she laid her hand against his cheek. "Nor would you in mine. Eventually, one of us would slip away . . . Until the day our worlds are sadly one in a dream. Against my selfishness, I pray that never happens."

She had made up her mind. He could feel it—and inside of him, a familiar ache returned as his thoughts wandered to the moments he had failed Ashe and Miyacre.

His sadness turned quick to anger, and he shook his head in disappointment in her decision. To him, she had chosen to cast a chance at escape aside.

Surelia's head fell in embarrassment but rose back with a spark of joy.

"I want to be like you, free of consequence. I want to feel the warmth like you do, too. But I think I've finally figured it out," she said. "This isn't my story, Lyal."

"What does that even mean?" he snapped at her.

"It means you have to go alone. The place you are seeking—it's right ahead."

"If there was going to be so much trouble for you—why even do all this? Why didn't you tell me? Why didn't you just leave me to do it alone?"

He was angry. Angry at her, and at the world. The fact that he had failed so many times to rescue a friend enraged him. Why did she have to disappear, too? He had never felt so powerless.

Beyond the swordsman, Little Eddie Bowitz had returned to them with the same excitement in his eyes; the city of dreams rising behind him. The boy sobered, however, as he realized the solemn farewell unfolding before them.

"Do you even know?" Lyal asked.

"Because you gave me what I wanted. A chance to see what was out there and to know more about the ones who come here from far away from time to time—and I know you. But if we could have run away—for who knows how long. Maybe—I would have," she said, her head tilted to the side as she humored the thought.

She turned her back to him but took one last look over her shoulder.

"Just maybe," she concluded with a raised brow.

Without waiting for a response, Surelia entered into the flashing mist and was swallowed in the gloomy embrace. Eddie, crestfallen now, looked to Ultra, who watched like a silent sentinel, then turned back to Lyal, who remained stricken with confusion.

"Hey, don't worry . . . I know of a way—" Before Eddie could finish, Lyal took off after her. Eddie, astonished by his break, shot forward in pursuit of him.

Leaving his mission of finding Miyacre and Ashe behind, Lyal searched the lonely veil for Surelia, chasing the red and blue lights that led him to empty patrol cars, seemingly abandoned all over the road.

"Where the hell did everyone go?" he shouted, then went to the next one. "Surelia!?"

One after the other, he was met with the same hollow result. His frustration grew as the gap between them surely grew wider.

"Hey, stop, don't go too far!" Eddie called out from somewhere behind.

His words were dismissed by Lyal, who had found the last empty patrol car. He turned and noticed the shimmering lights of the Metro City's lower level ahead, then took off down the road with every hope of finding his way back there.

Before he could make it through the breach, however, a gloved hand came through the thickened veil. Lyal slid to a halt as an oblivion walker reached out to him. He peered into the shifting gray and saw two invader eyes pierce the shroud.

They were not the cerulean gleams found in helmets of the invader troopers. Its possessed eyes were wide, as if lost at the brink of insanity; something oddly more human, though undeniably alien.

From behind him came two more. Those invaders, dressed in navy imperial side-fastened jackets and pants, had hair that drifted through the air like the mane of the wild beast, free from the discipline of a hood. They all approached with hands raised, their fingers curled with intent to apprehend him.

Eddie raced out from a sheet of mist behind Lyal and immediately caught sight of those odd invaders.

"Run!" Eddie shouted. "Don't just stand there! Move back!"

But Lyal was petrified in their gazes. They looked not at him but at the emptiness carved out within, and the aura of their presence filled him with unspeakable terror.

Lyal stumbled away as they approached in a soulless lumber. He jolted at a hand on his shoulder and broke away in full sprint away from the gazing invaders, running until he had escaped from the crawling mist once more and collapsed to his knees in front of the swordsman in exhaustion.

As he sat there and caught his breath, the flashing lights faded until all that was left was gray. Little Eddie Bowitz appeared there not long after, his eyes still filled with worry.

"Hey—are you alright?" the boy asked.

Lyal unleashed his fury upon the plate with the fierce jab of his fist.

"You should have done something about it," Lyal shouted, directing his rage to the idle swordsman, who stood in watch of the distant crest upon the medallion.

Ultra turned over his shoulder and grimaced at that bold assertion.

"She has gone to take responsibility for your actions and her own. You should be grateful for this lesson."

"Fuck the lesson bullshit. When you have power, you should use it to help people on your side," Lyal replied, snapping back him.

Ultra, enraged, swung his arm out in a turn to the reckless interloper.

"How long will it be until you take responsibility for what you've done? With bloodstained hands, you've abandoned both shame and self-awareness, you narrow-minded child."

"If I even had half the power you had, this war would already be over."

"How many would you kill, then!?"

"What?" Lyal asked, his face twisted in confusion.

"How many of them would you kill in order to get her back? And what would she say to a murderer? Do you think Eternia's sovereign to be some unworthy foe?"

He stepped menacingly toward Lyal, who shrank just a moment before straightening in defiance.

"If you think I am so powerful, could you ever fathom the one who presides as my master? Your daydreams betray you." Ultra turned to the cityscape beside them and eyed it with destructive rage. His pupils began to burn as radiant sapphires as he took the handle of the blade and drew it out inch by inch as growling electric bolts struck out from the illuminated edge.

"Let me show you what we executioners of the Dream are capable of."

Lyal jumped out in front of him. "Great! Show us how big of a joke you are!"

The swordsman flipped the rage-imbued blade around and presented the grip, his eyes shining with invader madness.

"Reach for the answer . . . Suffer the truth."

Lyal's eyes flickered in uncertainty but, driven by sheer anger and unwilling to be proven wrong, he reached for the handle.

Before calamity could be unleashed, Eddie stepped out between them, just a boy between the city and the destroyer.

"Stop! You have to stop," the boy cried. "You can't keep getting so angry. You're a hero now, remember? You've changed."

"There's nothing that has changed. Just the direction of the blade. Step aside. Let this fool have his way."

"Yeah! Let's do it. You're not going to intimidate anyone, buddy," Lyal said, antagonizing him.

Eddie shook his head. "I know you wouldn't allow it . . . I'm not afraid. There's something stronger than that sword . . . inside us all."

And those words disarmed the swordsman at once. The burning gleam faded from his eyes, the sword faded back to silver. Hollowed once more, he returned the sword back to its place.

"I know that you know a lot of things, but that means you have to be a little more—understanding. Because nobody here is perfect and you aren't either. Not him, not me, or even your master—or anyone else. We've all got something we don't know, and a lot of us are trying to learn."

". . . Yes, you're right. Forgive me," Ultra said, realizing his error. The swordsman turned away from the city and looked into the mist with a vacant gaze. "There's only one way left to go. So let us move quickly."

With that, the swordsman departed in reflection of the words of a child, one who had lived a mere fraction of his life. Those words brought him to reminisce of another who had sought to change his ideals. Change, no matter how difficult, could never be impossible. Too much depended upon realizations, and without them all would surely be lost.

Eddie went over to Lyal, who glared at the swordsman, though he shook his head as he laid their feud to rest.

"I'm sorry for what happened to you back there," Eddie said.

Lyal rolled his eyes, wanting none of his sympathy. "What do you care?"

Eddie looked at him, knowing he knew that same exact same pain he felt. "No, I've lost dear friends of mine, too," the boy said, ready to make his pitch. "I think I know a way to get them back."

But Lyal silenced the boy's appeal with a dismissive toss of his hand. "Don't talk to me about that raising-the-dead-type stuff. After I find who I'm looking for, I'm out of this place."

"Who are you looking for? Why are they here?" Eddie asked to the spark of curiosity.

"Surelia said there's a girl who came to this city—but she's somewhere ahead, in another place . . . I'm guessing that's it."

"A girl?" Eddie repeated.

"And you don't need to worry about it. I'll handle that myself. I know you got your own thing going on, too."

With nothing left to say, Lyal pushed onward in the footsteps of the swordsman, and the boy watched him as he went.

That stranger's evident willpower caused Eddie to ponder the strength of his own resolve. The boy knew he had to be just as strong for those he had made promises to—and so he would do his very best.

Invigorated, Eddie hurried down the road with a spirit buoyed by hope. As he went, all his worries were washed away, and he came alight in the thrill again. Deep inside his head he could feel Mirika and feel her smile.

He flew past Lyal and the swordsman and didn't stop until he reached the boulevards, which tapered to a glittery staircase. Free of hesitation, Eddie climbed the flight in long strides and emerged through a low-hanging mist at the top before a bridge that passed between a network of black comm towers and other obscure devices. It was a distinct departure from metropolitan splendor, shaped instead by the austerity of a military base.

From there, Eddie beheld a panoramic view of Infinity Land and hurried straight for it. For once, the stories were not just stories; for once, the legends were true.

The city's climb continued, steady and slow, and as it separated ever further from the Metro City, it began to exert dominance over the land. Around the perimeter of the construct was an alloy belt, which periodically came to life with a hypnotic sweep of vibrant colors, instant glyphs that left ghostly echoes behind as they whirled around the band.

The rumble from the unseen engines shook Eddie's throbbing heart as he arrived to the end of the bridge. It had delivered the wanderer to a half-moon dais forged of navy plate, the invader crest emblazoned at its heart.

The boy eyes filled with awe as he gazed up at the hallucinatory display, dizzied by that chromatic spectacle which illuminated him in the dark. The celestial city continued to rise away, and Eddie found no obvious way to reach its salvation, and so he began to hunt for one.

He hurried to the end of the dais but came to a sheer drop to infinite oblivion, stopped, then followed the rounded perimeter with his eye. He followed it all the way around and found only the brink, then all the way around the other side, but found only the same. Everything there was barren, and he could find no landmark that hinted of anything useful.

So, Eddie returned to the middle, somehow still full of hope as the city continued to rise before him. He reached into his pockets and produced the postcard, then held it up to the miracle that Mirika had seen from very far away.

"Please, don't leave me here. I need you—more than anything in my entire life. Don't leave me," he plead. "We don't have to pretend anymore."

And from above, as if in answer to his solemn plea, a shimmering ramp of starlight silver flew down for the platform and struck the edge right before him with a triumphant thunder. Four colossal beams of light exploded up from below in the abyss, and the gloom all around him was banished at once. Little Eddie's face came aglow to the glory of High Fantasy, and his heart went wild in an excitement recaptured from a lost childhood.

High above, the city settled in full bloom, multi-colored lasers racing all along the city's conical base.

Its majesty shined in his awestruck eyes and made every star-chased dream seem right within his grasp. For the first time in so long, all that hurt was gone . . . and all was right with the world.

The boy went to the ramp and took his first step upon the starlight that shimmered up and down the metallic ramp. It was a special movement, a departure that he would never forget no matter how far the journey took him—and there was no going back.

Eddie took another step, then his pace quickened until he was running, headed straight for the shining gates, where everything beyond the reality lay waiting for him; a miracle, a great master, and a righteous dream waiting to be realized.

A festival of rebirth awaited him, and in the boy's heart, there was only faith—and it overflowed as the cold wind rushed against his face. Perhaps he would find himself after all.

Acknowledgments

INFINITY first came to me when I was a child, when mysterious things made sense in the most wonderful of ways. My Sparking Moon—this second realm—took shape in scribbles and daydreams that often stole me away from the life I was living to record its struggles, yet also gave me purpose and the chance to witness something uniquely incredible, I believe.

Even as adulthood ushered in a world stripped of innocence, INFINITY evolved, though it was never stripped of its principle.

My resilient beacon of the last twenty years, its light never once dimmed on the road to actuality—and in a miracle, the dream prevails at last, crossing the boundary between fantasy and something indefinitely real. It is an honor to join other creatives from all across the stars in fulfilling that grand undertaking. It is truly something surreal.

This would not have been possible without the help of many others who offered their time, effort, kindness, and faith over the years.

First, I thank God and Jesus Christ on High for assuring success in this often grueling trial that has spanned from Orlando, Florida, to Tokyo, Japan, and for continuing to oversee and guide my spiritual walk. When I was at my lowest, You gave me strength, put me to the keyboard to take action, and promised that action was worth taking.

I also thank Him for His work in assembling the individuals who have come to walk with me through thick and thin, through hardship and celebration alike. With you, I toast to this triumph—the First Order of the Stars:

To Kelli Davis, I thank you for carving a path through all that seemed impossible, and for shining a guiding light when the path forward grew a little too dark to navigate alone.

To Leon Doiley Jr., thank you for always believing in a positive outcome to every hardship, and for offering words of encouragement at every juncture.

I also extend a special thank you to LaMark Davis for always reminding me to believe in the higher plan of God, to seek Him out for knowledge, and to trust that all things happen in His time.

To Melanie and Bernie Schneider, I am forever blessed to have had your guidance throughout my childhood. Thank you for giving me the opportunity to travel the world and for helping me become defined as myself.

To Betty and Leon Doiley, Sr., thank you for always reminding me to stay grounded and to keep one foot in reality, but also for never hesitating to give your love freely to make a difference in the lives of our family whenever it is needed.

To Ruby and Dave Hughes—and Poncho and Fiona—a massive thank you for offering your support when life grew difficult and for opening your doors to me. You are among the most understanding and down-to-earth people I have ever known, period, and I am truly blessed to have you in my life. I owe much of this success to your tireless patience.

I also thank Peyton Jolly for being a voice of encouragement and positivity, for offering to dedicate her time to make art, and for being a beta reader, all while raising children. Thank you to Beth Fogle for offering your time to look over key documents as I put together the final pieces and for providing valued insight into the business.

I thank Daulton Rife—my childhood best friend—and his family for always treating me like a brother or a son, and for making me feel as though I had a second home. Sorry for sneaking in through the window when no adults were home. To be fair, Daulton said it would be cool.

To Owen Henderson, I cannot thank you enough for offering a spare room in Florida for me to edit throughout 2022. It was a once-in-a-lifetime opportunity that I will never forget. You are one of the kindest people I have ever met as a complete stranger, and I am forever grateful to have been your roommate and to call you a friend.

I also extend a very special thank you to A.E. Williams for working alongside me from the very beginning of my editing journey and for offering me the opportunity to bring this dream to life as the first new author with CrazedNovelist Books. It is an absolute honor.

To Madison Eigel, I thank you for your tireless efforts in editing the manuscript from front to back. You have truly come to know this story in a way I once thought nobody else ever would. Madison's critical eye resolved countless bumps along the road, and I cannot thank her enough for helping bring this vision to life in its truest form.

I also thank the other members of A.E. Williams Editorial whom I have had the pleasure of working with along the way. I thank Emily Williams for lending her expertise to help market the book, and Danielle Treherne for being the steady force behind the scenes—organizing every moving piece and ensuring progress never stalled.

A special thanks as well to Wes Locher for connecting me with A.E. Williams Editorial when I went searching for help, as well as to Full Sail University for all the assistance provided.

I would also like to extend a massive thanks to Shiba for creating a wonderful cover and back cover art design, and for bringing these characters and scenes to life in such vivid detail for the first time ever. Watching it go from a sketch to completion was an experience I'll never forget.

I was also fortunate enough to connect with a talented map designer and thank Ian Durneen for crafting a beautiful map of Worltu, and for investing the time to make sure every detail was in place and well crafted.

I'm also grateful to have worked alongside Yoko Matsuoka, who made two stunning illustrations that have brought the story to life beyond the pages. There are certainly others who have had an impact in INFINITY arriving here at the end, and to you all, I say thank you.

And lastly . . . here's to you—journeyer through the pages, wanderer in the unknown, and dreamer somewhere far beyond these stars.